THE UNLIKEABLE DEMON

HUNTER COLLECTION:

BOOKS 1-3

DEBORAH WILDE

te da media
vancouver

Book Layout ©2015 BookDesignTemplates.com

Cover design by Damonza

The Unlikeable Demon Hunter Collection: Books 1-3

ISBN: 978-1-988681-09-2 (paperback)

ISBN: 978-1-988681-08-5 (epub)

ISBN: 978-1-988681-07-8 (Kindle)

Praise for the Nava Katz series:

THE UNLIKEABLE DEMON

HUNTER

(Nava Katz, #1)

DEBORAH WILDE

te da media vancouver

Publisher's Note: This is a work of fiction. Names, characters, places, and incidents are a product of the author's imagination. Locales and public names are sometimes used for atmospheric purposes. Any resemblance to actual people, living or dead, or to businesses, companies, events, institutions, or locales is completely coincidental.

Book Layout ©2015 BookDesignTemplates.com

Cover design by Damonza

Library and Archives Canada Cataloguing in Publication

Wilde, Deborah, 1970-, author
    The unlikeable demon hunter / Deborah Wilde.

(Nava Katz ; 1)
Issued in print and electronic formats.
ISBN 978-0-9920709-8-4 (softcover).--ISBN 978-0-9920709-9-1 (EPUB).--ISBN 978-1-988681-00-9 (Kindle)

    I. Title.

PS8645.I4137U55 2017   C813'.6   C2016-907805-1
                                                C2016-907806-X

1

Mornings after sucked.

Walks of shame were a necessary evil, but that didn't mean I enjoyed shimmying back into the same trollop togs twice. I picked glitter out of my hair, then straightened my sequined top. I was officially decommissioning it. Multiple washings never quite managed to remove the lingering aura of bad decisions I made while wearing party clothes. My philosophy? Cross my fingers and hope for the most bang for the bucks spent later on new outfits.

The surly cabbie evil-eyed me to hurry up.

I complied, rooting around in my clutch for some crumpled bills before handing them over and stumbling out of the taxi onto the sidewalk.

Fresh air was a godsend after the stale bitter coffee smell I'd been trapped with during the ride. I pressed a finger to my temple, a persistent dull throb stabbing me behind my eyeballs. My residual feel good haze clashed big-time with the glaring sun screaming at me to wake up, and the buzz of a neighbor's lawnmower cutting through the Sunday morning quiet didn't help matters. Best get inside.

Smoothing out my mini skirt, I readied myself for my tame-my-happy-slut-self-to-boring-PG-rating body check when a wave of dizziness crashed through me. Whoa. I brought my gaze back to horizon level, swallowing hard. That sea-sickness technique was doing dick-all so I rummaged in my bag for my ginger chews.

No puking in the bushes, I chided myself, letting the spicy smooth and sweet candy fight my nausea. My mother would toss my bubble ass out if I defiled her precious rhodos.

Again.

The rise and fall of my chest as I took a few deep breaths spotlit a slight problem. My spangly blouse was missing two buttons. And I was missing a bra. Hook-up Dude had been worth the loss of a pair of socks, maybe a bargain bin thong. But the latest in purple push-up technology? No. I allowed myself a second to mourn. It had been a good and loyal bra.

The sex, on the other hand? Total crap. The girls, who were normally perky C cups, seemed a bit subdued. I couldn't blame them. What's-his-name had started out with all the promise of a wild stallion gallop, but he'd ended up more of a gentle trot. I didn't know if the fault lay with the jockey or the ride, but it had been a long time since I'd seen a finish line.

Since I couldn't keep examining my tits on the front walk with Mrs. Jepson side-eyeing me from behind her living room curtains, I thrust my chin up and clacked a staccato rhythm toward my front door on those mini torture chambers that had seemed *such* a good idea yesterday.

Every step made our precisely manicured lawn undulate. I clamped my lips shut, willing the ginger chews to kick in while fumbling my key into the lock. Dad had screwed up the measurements on our striking cedar and stained glass front door and, being a touch too big for the frame, it needed to be shouldered open.

I crashed into the door like a linebacker. Once I'd extricated myself and my keys from the lock, I brushed myself off, and stepped inside. Our house itself was comfortably upper middle class but not huge, since my parents preferred to spend money on trips and books instead of the overpriced real estate found here in Vancouver. A quick glance to my left showed that the TV room was empty. I crossed my fingers that Mom and Dad were out at their squash game, my main reason for picking this specific time to sneak back in.

Really, a twenty-year-old shouldn't have had to sneak. But then again, a twenty-year-old probably should have kept her last menial job for longer than two weeks, so I wasn't in a position to argue rights.

I kicked off my shoes, sighing in delight at the feel of cool tile under my bare feet as I padded through the house to our homey kitchen. No one was in there either. Someone, probably Mom, had tacked the envelope with my final—and only—pay stub from the call center that I'd left lying around onto our small "miscellaneous" cork board. The gleaming quartz counters were now free of their usual clutter of papers, books, and latest gourmet food find. That meant company. Come to think of it, I did hear someone in the living room.

A study in tasteful shades of white, the large formal room was off-limits unless we had special guests. Mom had set that rule when my twin brother Ari and I were little tornados running around the place and while there was no longer a baby gate barring our way, conditioning and several memorable scoldings kept us out.

Hmmm. Could Ari be entertaining an actual human boy? Le gasp.

I beelined for the back of the house, past the row of identically framed family photos hanging in a neat grid, my head cocked. Listening for more voices, but all was quiet. Maybe I'd been wrong? I hoped not. Both finding my brother with a crush—blackmail dirt—and helping myself to the liquor cabinet were positive prospects. What better way to lose that hangover headache than get drunk again? Oh, the joys of being Canadian with socialized health care and legal drinking age of nineteen. After a year (officially) honing that skill, I imbibed at an Olympic level.

The red wine on the modular coffee table gleamed in a shaft of sunlight like its position had been ordained by the gods. I snatched up the crystal decanter, sloshing the liquid into the glass conveniently placed next to it. Once in a while, a girl could actually catch a break.

I fanned myself with one hand. The myriad of lit candles seemed a bit much for Ari's romantic encounter, but wine drinking trumped curiosity so I chugged the booze back. My entire body cheered as the cloyingly-sweet alcohol hit my system, though I hoped it wasn't Manischewitz because hangovers on that were a bitch. I'd slugged back half the contents when I saw my mom on the far side of the room clutch her throat, eyes wide with horror. Not her usual, "you need an intervention" horror. No, her expression indicated I'd reached a whole new level of fuck-up.

"Nava Liron Katz," she gasped in full name outrage.

My cheeks still bulging with wine, I properly scoped out the room. Mom? Check. Dad? Check. Ari? Check. Rabbi Abrams, here to perform the ceremony to induct my brother as the latest member in the Brotherhood of David, the chosen demon hunters?

Check.

I spit the wine back into what I now realized was a silver chalice and handed it to the elderly bearded rabbi. "Carry on," I told him. Then I threw up on his shoes.

Forty-five minutes later, I huddled on top of the closed toilet seat in my ensuite bathroom sucking the cheesy coating off Doritos while replaying my actions in grisly Technicolor. Even with all the lights off, the room was as bright and insistent as Martha Stewart's smile. A dusty Costco-sized sanitary pad box lay open on the counter–the hiding place for my secret stash of arterial clogging happiness.

Now, though, the chips were less illicit joy and more bite-sized snacks of self-loathing.

I stuck my hand into the bag for another nacho, careful not to crinkle it and give myself away. Hard to say what had been the highlight of that little disaster: drinking the ceremonial wine, vomiting, or the wardrobe malfunction that had released my left boob into the world and caused my dad to strain his back jumping in front of me to block the view.

Go me.

Someone rapped on the door. Chip in mouth like a pacifier, I froze, listening to the raised voices from downstairs–the rabbi yelling, my mother cajoling, and my father reasoning. That left Ari, and right now I was too chickenshit to face him. How could saying sorry cover wrecking the most important moment of his life?

"I know you're eating Doritos," he called from outside the door. "Let me in."

"Nope." I swallowed down the now-mushy chip and gave a lusty groan. "I'm making a hate crime."

"If that were true, you'd be running the water because you're paranoid people will learn you have an anus." He jiggled the knob. "Let me in."

I glared at the tap, assigning blame to the inanimate object for failing to carry out its part of my brilliant plan. Dumping the bag down on the counter with a sigh, I washed orange nacho residue off my hands before I tightened the belt on the fuzzy housecoat now wrapped around me, and unlocked the door.

"I'm so, so sorry, Ari," I said, hanging my head. My fraternal twin deserved all the success and more. Ari never treated me like I was "less than" in any way, not even once. "I know you have no reason to believe me but–"

"Shut up," he said, brushing past me in his navy fitted suit. Very bespoke, except for the tired slump of his shoulders.

He lowered himself down on to the edge of the bathtub, knocking one of the many bottles of citrusy shampoo into the tub. With one hand braced on the mosaic shower tiles for support, he removed his kippah, tossing it onto the counter where its embroidered, gold Star of David winked among the chaos of make-up and hair pins.

"Damn, that itches." He scratched his blond head with a relieved sigh, then jerked his chin at the Doritos bag still in my hand. "You gonna share?"

I locked the door, returned to my throne seat, and held the chips out between us.

We sat there in companionable silence, munching through the party-sized bag.

"These are so disgusting," Ari said, stuffing about ten of them in his mouth.

I reached over and brushed orange crumbs off his suit. "Careful, bubeleh. Wouldn't want you to get dirty. Oh, if the elders knew that their healthy-eating chosen one was up here taking years off his life."

"Eh," he said, spraying chips. "I'd just blame you, o defiler of innocents."

"Useful having an evil twin, isn't it?" My tone was light; my stomach twisted.

He wiped his mouth. "Don't give yourself that much credit. You're not evil. Just misguided."

I drew myself up to my full height. "That's a terrible thing to say."

We finished the bag, then elbowed each other for first rights of tap water. A quick sip later and I slid onto the brown cork floor, bloated and happy. Well, as happy as I could be.

"I don't know how you're not puking given you were still drunk an hour ago," Ari said.

"These chips have magic properties. Plus, I got it all out of my system on the carpet."

He shuddered. "Don't remind me. I think Mom is angrier about that than your spectacular entrance. She was a fairly impressive mottled red when I left her."

"Merlot or tomato?"

"Nava Red," my brother replied. "A special shade named in honor of you."

"Why were you doing the ritual anyway?" I snapped. "The induction is tomorrow. The sixth."

"Or, today, the sixth."

Shit! I hugged my knees into my chest. "Ari–"

He stood up, one hand raised to cut me off. "No. You really want to apologize? Take a shower and get dressed so that I have one person who wants to be at this ceremony for me. Not for status or whatever the hell I am to those people down there."

"Ace," I gasped, "isn't this what you want?"

He affixed the kippah back on his head, staring at his reflection in the mirror above the sink for a long moment. "I've never had a chance to decide whether I wanted it or not. We were five days old when they determined I was an initiate. I didn't get a vote."

We'd both seen the photo of our parents' stunned faces when a somewhat younger, yet still astonishingly ancient Rabbi Abrams had visited my mother–a descendent of King David–to check Ari out. Since the Brotherhood is top secret, my parents weren't clued in to the true nature of the rabbi's visit until after he'd determined Ari as an initiate: a chosen demon hunter. The photo in question had been taken after a lot of explanations and convincing that yes, this was all real, and yes, their son had a hell of an important destiny.

I went into my bedroom to grab some clean clothes to put on after my shower.

Back in the day, and by day I'm talking Old Testament, this shepherd called David took out the giant Goliath for King Saul. While that landed David his place in history, there was more to him than his crazy rock-slinging skills.

I don't know if David was an adrenaline junkie or a major do-gooder but when King Saul was later possessed by a demon, David was all "leave it to me," and cast the hell spawn out. Guess David figured demon removal was a good public service to keep up, because once *he* became king around 1010 B.C.E., he gathered up his buddies to continue the work. Kick-ass Jews. Awesome.

Though it had never made sense why he called his hunters Rasha—the Hebrew word for "wicked."

I tossed my clothes over the hook affixed to the back of the bathroom door. "Talk to me."

My brother had spent his entire life studying and training in preparation for the day he was formally inducted into the Brotherhood. I cocked an eyebrow at Ari, annoyed when he shrugged off my question. "Don't pretend you aren't excited to see what magic power you'll end up with."

His eyes lit up for a second. "Telekinesis or light bender. Those would be cool." He jerked a thumb at the shower and I obediently ran the tap, waiting for the water to hit blistering temperature.

"Slime generator or asphyxiation via lethal ass gas, more like."

"Ha. Ha." Ari gnawed on his bottom lip.

"You want out?" I cracked my knuckles. "You could totally take all three of them downstairs. I'll help."

He shrugged, the motion bunching the dark fabric around his muscles. "I don't know what else I'd do. What else I'm good for."

I poked his bicep. "Kill the pity party, Mr. Perfect GPA. I'm sure between your chem major and biology minor some giant pharmaceutical company somewhere will have a small fortune and loads of interesting problems for you." I wasn't jealous. He and I didn't roll that way. He may have been chosen and wicked smart but the only thing that bugged me about him was that he had prettier lashes than me. It was always the boys with those camel eyes. So unfair.

I tested the water temperature, shaking droplets off my hand until, satisfied with its magma levels of hot, I pulled the knob up to send the water cascading full blast through the shower head.

Ari mussed my hair. "You're gonna do something great some day too," he said. I smacked his hand off of my head. "You just need to find your thing." He rushed that second sentence as if hoping I wouldn't remember that I'd found my thing a long time ago and the chances of finding something else I loved as much were pretty slim.

"Yeah, yeah, whatever." I pushed him toward the door. "Go keep them from cutting me out of the will. I'll be there in ten. The picture of respectability."

Ari snorted. "Don't strain yourself. I'll settle for clean." He sniffed me, fanning in front of his face with a grimace. "Screwing hobos again?"

"College boys. Same, same." I reached for the belt of my housecoat.

He unlocked the door, half-twisting back to me. "Would you care? If I didn't do it?"

I paused, belt still tied. "God, no. The few Rasha I ever met were dick-swinging balls of testosterone. Though I'd hoped for your sake some of them were also dick-sucking. Like that smexy Brazilian they brought in last year to train you in Capoeira."

He failed to appreciate my eyebrow waggle. "Why do I bother?"

King David had realized pretty early on that even if he rid Israel of demons, there was a reason they were part of every culture's mythology. Demons were an international problem. Since Jerusalem was close to this trade route called the King's Highway, David sent his band far and wide to find all the best specimens of manhood from various races and religions including Muslims, Egyptians, Phoenicians, Celts, and Thracians to fight the good fight. The Brotherhood was formed.

It was kind of cool to see how far ranging those original bloodlines had traveled into present day. But what wasn't cool was how serious and stressed my brother was, so I smacked my lips, hell-bent on getting a smile. "Mmm. High quality Brazilian meat."

Ari made a sound of disgust and whipped my loofah glove at me. I ducked, laughing, and it sailed into my shower. "What? You don't want a boyfriend? All those butchy men?" I leered at him. "Odds are good there'd be some friends of Dorothy in that crew."

His lips quirked, despite his best efforts to look stern. "I have no time for dating."

"Me neither. But *I* have a whole bunch of sex instead. Something you, my dear older brother, could use. Regular doing of the nasty might loosen you up."

"I'm loose," he said, tightening his tie.

"Yeah." I shoved him out the door. "A regular whore of Babylon. Now get outta here. I've got to pretty up."

One thing I'd say in my favor, I was not one of those girls who took forever to get ready. I was showered and dressed in something practically Amish in the allotted ten minutes. I twisted my hair into a sleek chignon, and fresh faced, headed downstairs.

Time for my close up, Mr. Demille. Bowing my head, I shuffled into the living room.

"Forgive me, Rabbi." I prostrated myself like a wedding guest begging the Godfather for a favor. "I was involved in a car accident on my way home," I lied. I stood up again. "It's why I needed a drink. I was so rattled." I infused as much pathos into my voice as possible while blinking up at him. Tricky, since I was four inches taller, but not impossible. "I'm sure you've never had that problem."

Men, whether straight, gay, holy, or otherwise, could be such suckers. The rabbi patted my hand in forgiveness, his touch papery dry. "You need to show more respect, Navela," he said, using the Yiddish diminutive of my name.

I nodded, side-stepping around the wet-yet-once-more-spotlessly-clean former puke site on the white, short-velvet-pile carpet. "You're so right. I should come to schul. Isn't your son the Cantor at Park West Synagogue? Such a beautiful voice when he prays."

A look of abject horror contorted the rabbi's features at the terrifying prospect of me getting my hands on his precious son. Trust me, the guy was a middle-aged balding chub. I had zero designs on his person.

"Start small," Rabbi Abrams said.

While the rabbi had mentored Ari his entire life, having served as a head demon-hunter coach, my contact with him had been limited. In addition to coordinating training and fight instructors, he also taught my brother everything from demon types to creating wards and learning the various aspects of the Brotherhood itself. Ari tended to get pretty vague on those details.

"Shana," the rabbi called out to my mother. "Now that the entire family is here, we can start the ceremony again."

My mother handed him the newly washed chalice. "Of course, Rabbi." Mom watched him shuffle off to prepare something, trailing a faint smell of mothballs in his wake, then, patting her sleek honey-colored bob, stepped past me with a murmured, "Carnage *and* lies? A busy morning."

Mom was a lot harder to fool. A whip-smart, tenured history professor at the University of British Columbia with an annoying tendency to recall events best forgotten, she was also a best-selling author of, big surprise, a tome on King David.

My dad, Dov, dark-haired like me, was a prof, too. Law. Oy vey. Everything was fact-gathering to build a case with him. Case in point, he walked stiffly into the room, courtesy of his recent back injury, all pleated pants and sweater vest, the usual mug of coffee welded to his hand.

I gagged at the smell.

"What's this about a car accident? Was this in the taxi? Did you get the information from him and the other driver?" His questions were gunfire fast. "You'll need it for the claim."

Shit. I hadn't prepared for questioning.

Ace to the rescue. My brother tugged on Dad's sleeve, leading him to his recliner. "Sit. Rabbi wants to start the ceremony." Out of the corner of his mouth he muttered, "You owe me big time."

I gave him a sheepish grin and sat in the brushed twill armchair at the far end like a good little girl, stuffing my hands under my butt.

Rabbi Abrams motioned for Ari to come stand beside him. While the rabbi was the picture of reverence as he lit the first candle, my brother's hand jiggled madly in his pocket.

I threw him a thumbs up. Ari was going to be great.

The rabbi lit the last of the dozen or so large pillar candles on thick glass bases placed in a circle around the living room. The soulless space with its white carpet, white furniture and, wait for it, black and white brocade wallpaper was softened by their glow.

The ceremony involved a lot of singing prayer or chanting or something in Hebrew. I'd pretty much spent my Hebrew school classes reading *Sweet Valley High* so I didn't understand it, but I'd been to synagogue enough that the singing and ritualistic gestures were familiar. The rhythms and cadence of the language lulled me, even soothing my grating headache a bit.

The old guy didn't have a bad voice, probably where his son got his talent, and the ceremony itself was kind of lovely. Even my cold, dead heart couldn't fail to be moved by the reverence and history of this ceremony.

All male descendants of King David—or of any hunter—were tracked as potentials. The first ritual, performed when they were a baby, determined if they could be bumped up to initiate—one who carried the Rasha make-up, versus the regular Muggle descendants. It weeded out about 98% of the potentials. If level two status was unlocked, they were labeled initiates and slated for training. Their second and final ceremony, the official induction to the Brotherhood where they became Rasha, happened at age twenty.

There were a couple of reasons for the wait. First off, it took initiates their entire childhood and adolescence to master the training and studying necessary to take on the gig. And, for more practical reasons, they needed to be inducted once they'd physically stopped growing and were in the prime of health for their body to accept the magic powers that this final ceremony would confer on them. After much trial, error, and loss of life, twenty had been hit on as the magic age.

Rabbi Abrams blessed the wine then handed the chalice to Ari. Once my brother had taken a sip, he dipped his finger in the wine and dripped three fat red drops back into the chalice. A reminder of the precious human blood that would be spilled if they lost their fight against evil.

I discreetly waved off some smudgy smoke, suppressing a tiny smile at my mom doing the exact same thing. If it had been up to my parents, they'd have rented a ballroom and invited every person they'd ever known to watch their little boy become a badass mensch. Let's face it, a demon hunter induction had way more bragging rights than a Bar Mitzvah. But alas, the general populace was not to know the Brotherhood existed, so my parents had to keep quiet about Ari's abilities and his big day today.

I'd always wished Ari's induction would happen in a stone cavern with chanting, hooded members, but old David had mandated humility into Demon Club's mission statement. The chosen one was supposed to selflessly devote his life to demon hunting for the greater good, not personal glory. So it was always just a small ceremony with immediate family, if that, performed in the home.

The rabbi wrapped a small handkerchief around Ari's wrist—white to symbolize piety. Yeah, right. Based on the very few Rasha I'd met, it would take more than a hankie to tamp down their enormous arrogance. Try a textile factory's yearly output.

Rabbi Abrams held fast to the other end of the cloth as he lay his free hand on my brother's head. More Hebrew.

I snuck a look at my parents. To their credit, they didn't look disappointed. In fact, seated there, watching the ceremony with rapt looks, they pretty much glowed with delight.

My own chest warmed in tight mushiness and a tear leaked from my eye, streaking its way down my cheek.

Ouch.

I blinked against the sudden stinging. Everything took on a drugged, underwater quality as the room swam around me. I clasped my hands together, pressing them between my knees. Breathing through my nose. Determined not to mess up the ceremony.

Again.

Ari repeated some Hebrew phrases the rabbi gave him. Aww, look at that twin of mine, embracing his destiny. I focused on my excitement to be here with him as he stepped into his future.

Better him than me.

The edges of my vision flickered. The rabbi's voice, harsh and far too loud, scraped over my skin. Clapping my hands over my ears didn't help. My flesh broke out in goosebumps as whispers sounded around me. A million voices, a million Rasha spirits brought together to welcome the newly chosen.

Carpet fibers pricked the soles of my feet as I stood up. The room spun. Sweat dotted my brow, slid between my shoulder blades.

The rabbi had his back to me but Ari glanced over, a flash of concern rippling through his serious expression.

Did I have delayed alcohol poisoning? I pulled at the neck of my shirt, fighting for air. Was that even a thing?

Rabbi Abrams opened a small, intricately carved box, revealing the fat gold ring that would mark Ari as one of the chosen. Gold from the ancient Judaic symbol for divine or celestial light, a holy blessing sought since David's time.

Propelled by a force beyond my control, I opened my hand, reaching for the ring. Every atom inside me screamed out for that band.

"Sheli." Huh? How did I suddenly know the Hebrew word for "mine?"

The ring floated free to hover in mid-air.

Every head in the room whipped my way. Mom tensed, her body straining forward to look at me. Dad's eyes widened, his coffee mug falling to the floor, brown liquid pooling in a sludge.

Ari and Rabbi Abrams gaped slack-jawed at me.

"Sheli," I repeated, trance-like. My voice was a deep, rich, resonating command. Even though I was freaking out at my total lack of ability to control my actions, I also felt a deep sense of rightness in my gut as I spoke.

That freaked me out more.

The ring launched across the room to fit itself on my right index finger with the mother of all electric shocks. My hair blew back off my face. I snapped out of the trance, once more in full-control of my faculties.

"Fucking hell!" I cursed, shaking out my hand while jumping up and down.

The candles snuffed out, leaving everyone in stunned silence.

Ari was the first to move. He reached over and snapped the ring box in Rabbi Abrams' hand shut with a thud that cracked like gunfire. "It appears you had the wrong twin," he said. He hefted the silver chalice. "L'chaim," he toasted and slugged the whole thing back.

2

"I don't want it," I protested for about the hundredth time, yanking on the ring.

"It won't come off." Rabbi Abrams' face was so wrinkled up in horrified anxiety that he resembled a Shar Pei with a Dumbledore beard.

"It's water weight. Bloating." I ran for the kitchen, dumping half a bottle of dish soap over both my finger and the stainless steel sink. "Move, you motherfucker," I muttered, pulling on it with all my might.

The ring spun round and round in the thick yellow goo, but wouldn't move even a millimeter closer to my knuckle. A hamsa, a palm-shaped design with two symmetrical thumbs meant to ward off the evil eye, was engraved in the center of the band. The single open eye etched into the middle of the palm stared up at me with its tiny blue sapphire iris.

I swear it smirked.

Ari swaggered in. He'd abandoned the chalice and was now swigging directly from the bottle.

"Take it," I hissed, grabbing his wrist.

"Fingers keepers." He flicked my hand away with a painful snap. Soap splattered on to my shirt.

"That is enough of that." My mother marched into the kitchen and snatched the bottle out of his hand, slamming it down on the counter with such force that a chip of white quartz flew off. "You, stop drinking. And you," she whirled on me, finger wagging, "take that ring off right now."

"Have at it." I thrust out my hand at her.

Mom couldn't get the ring off either. "Dov." She smacked her hand on the dented countertop to get Dad's attention. He hovered in the doorway with his mouth half open, in full brain short-circuit mode. Even my boob flying free hadn't upset him this much.

Her second smack shook him out of his Medusa-victim impression.

"Right." Dad hurried over and reached for the ring, but hesitated, his hand hovering just over mine.

I shoved my hand into his. "Get it off me, Daddy," I said in a voice two-octaves too high.

He tried. God knows he tried.

As did Rabbi Abrams, who insisted on running the ceremony again. Of course, he had to do it with Ari sprawled in the recliner because he was now hammered. My brother, the light-weight.

I spent the ceremony holding my breath, my gut knotted into a pretzel as I awaited the outcome.

The rabbi got to the end and tugged on the ring. Nada.

"How could you?" Mom asked, back in the kitchen where we'd reconvened in a glum silence. She twisted her hands together so forcefully, I worried she might break something.

"What part of 'chosen' implies I had any say in the matter?" I bit down on the band, trying to budge it with my teeth.

It was cold and tasted of metal and imprisonment.

Ari belched. "Told you, you'd find your thing." Having reclaimed the wine bottle, he now shook the last few drops into his mouth. "'Course, I didn't expect it to be my thing."

That hurt. I hadn't done this deliberately and I certainly didn't want to be part of a *Brotherhood*. I scrubbed a hand over my face, way too sober to handle taking the blame for this. "You didn't even know if you wanted it, asshole."

My brother wasn't fazed. "Too true. But," he said, looking off thoughtfully, "I think that was pre-wedding jitters." He met my eyes;

those distinct blue-gray twins of my own that always let me know what he was thinking. Right now the sorrow in them broke my heart. "I think that in fact, I did. Want it," he said.

I dropped my head on the counter.

"Fix this," Mom demanded of the rabbi. "Nava isn't a boy. She can't be Rasha."

My head jerked up. Ari's sorrow and my parents' incredulity were understandable. It just would have been nice if for one second, any of them had stopped to ask me how *I* was doing with all this. Because I wanted to run. Hide away until Demon Club proclaimed that this terrible joke had gone on long enough and we could all return to our regularly scheduled programming, where Ari was the bright shiny twin with a destiny and I most decidedly was not.

"Way to set women's rights back two hundred years, Mom," I snapped. For once, I was innocent of any wrong-doing, but no one could see that. No one cared.

"She didn't mean all women. Just you, honey," Dad said to me in his infuriating, even-handed way. He extended an arm to the rabbi, leading him to the heavily-nicked kitchen table. Twins were a bitch on furniture.

"Let's be logical here," my father said. "Does it matter if some ritual picked Nava? Ari is the one who is trained and competent. He's devoted his life toward this goal. What if we simply ignored this as an odd blip and proceeded with the plan as is?"

Most of me cheered this sentiment. Was completely on-board. A tiny part of me desperately wished that one person had my back.

"Nava is the chosen," Rabbi Abrams said. "She can do this." Wow. Of all the people to champion me. The rabbi stroked his beard. "If Ari takes on demons without a Rasha's power, he will die. Better to let Nava handle them, trained or not."

That sounded suspiciously like "send out the expendable." I snatched the dish towel off its hook and savagely dried my saliva off of my hand.

The rabbi was right. It was the magic that killed demons. Pumping one full of lead might slow it down, but then again, it might simply piss it off enough to rip your head off faster.

Obviously, Ari couldn't go after a demon without having magic power. That was tantamount to a suicide mission, but I refused to believe that he was definitely out of the picture. This destiny fit him with a snug certainty.

"There has to be a loophole," I said.

Dad touched his index finger to his nose then pointed at me like I'd brought up a valid idea. "You can't expect the fate of the world to be in my daughter's hands," he said. "Might as well invite Satan to move on in and throw him a housewarming party."

"Really?" I asked, tossing the towel on the counter.

Dad shrugged. "Do you think you're capable of battling demons?"

I refused to confirm or deny, leaning forward to address Rabbi Abrams directly. "Do I have a say in this?"

The rabbi struggled up out of the chair, came over to me, and laid a gnarled arthritic hand on my shoulder. His knuckles were old-people-XL sized. I tried not to flinch—or think of demon claws. Good luck. A mélange of weirdo animal parts and other unholy bits fused into demony shape assaulted me in image form, courtesy of every nightmare bedtime story Ari had ever foisted on me. I shuddered.

"This situation is…" Rabbi Abrams frowned.

"Unfortunate? Unfair?" I supplied.

"A tragedy," he said.

"Excuse me?!"

He dropped his hand, giving a sharp tug to his black suit jacket. "I need to inform the Executive. We must figure out how best to proceed." He sounded like I'd murdered his favorite puppy and was asking him to shake my blood-drenched hand. Symbolically, that may have been true.

My hands tightened on the hem of my shirt. "Again, I ask if I have a say in the matter?"

Rabbi Abrams frowned, his expression stern. "You cannot ignore your power. Your destiny."

I threw him a grim smile. Challenge accepted.

My first order of business was sneaking out of the house. Mom and Dad rehashing the impossibility of it, the *tragedy* of it, was bad enough. But Ari refusing to speak to me? He'd sent me a final look of absolute betrayal, staggered into his room, and locked the door.

He'd never locked his door against me before. Our twin connection was as necessary as oxygen. Ari had been my shoulder to cry on when my life had fallen apart, supporting me against the folks when I'd taken a time-out from university, while I'd spent my childhood making my brother laugh whenever I saw that his Rasha studies were getting to him. He protected and anchored me, while I lightened up his world. There was no place for locked doors between us.

The fact that there was now cracked my chest open for the black pain to slither in. If anything could turn me even more firmly against being a demon hunter than I already was, it was that damn door. I'd knocked until my knuckles bled. Begged and pleaded, but I was met with silence. I was dead to him.

It was worse than actually being dead.

Taking shallow breaths, I ran through one of my old exercises to get through pre-show performance jitters. Who knew being on stage and learning how to act happy would come in handy so many times in my almost-adult life?

I rummaged among the clean laundry piled on my desk chair for jeans and my favorite hoodie and got changed. Knocking aside the box in my closet filled with my most prized tap dance competition medals, I pulled my worn leather backpack out, haphazardly throwing in clothes and toiletries.

I allowed myself one last look around my raspberry bedroom: from the random photos of fun times hanging by now-limp tape, to the collage of speeding tickets spelling out *vroom*, to my unmade bed with exactly three pillows–two to sleep on and one to cuddle–and the clothes and books exploding over every surface.

My lucky sunglasses, the ones "liberated" from Ryan Tedder after I'd sweet-talked my way backstage at a OneRepublic concert, lay on my dresser, under my black and white poster of Gregory Hines. He wore an expression of sheer delight as the camera caught him mid-tap step. Somewhere deep inside me still lived the ghost of a memory where no matter what was wrong in my life, I could dance my troubles away. *A one, a two, you know what to do.* My mantra for dance and life.

Yeah, well. That was then.

I grabbed the glasses, stuffing them on my head. Then I hefted my backpack over one shoulder, and pushed up the window. Tap had been the one place I'd shone. My realm. Yeah, I'd readjusted my life around the void when the dream was taken from me, but why should Ari have to experience crushing disappointment and heartache? At my hands? Fuck that.

Maybe if I ran away, did something selfish, or acted unworthy of the power, the ring would decide I wasn't the right twin after all and Ari could resume his path to destiny. The Brotherhood had invested twenty years in him, after all. Hopefully they'd work a little harder to bring him back into the fold.

Taking a deep breath, I swung my leg over the sill and reached for the gnarled tree branch outside my window. My stomach surged in that split second before my fingers connected with the rough bark but once they did, it was an easy climb down. I dropped the final few feet to the ground in a hard crouch, then commenced running away from home, trotting past well-kept family homes toward the main street.

Much as I hated to admit it, my dad was right. Demon Club and I were a terrible fit. First off, it had always been kept secret through the centuries, both to preserve its existence under the official "no demons here" stance of organized Judaism, and, since very few knew that demons existed, to keep mass panic from breaking out.

Sure, I'd kept mum about all of it, but let's be serious. If magic powers could score me free clothes or booze, #MoveOverBuffy would be trending by dinner.

I slowed down when I hit the corner house two blocks over, just long enough to stop inches from the fence and do a little dance for the old Golden Retriever, sending her into a yappy frenzy of joy. Still barking, she jumped onto her hind legs, resting her front paws on the fence so I could scratch her between the ears.

The uptight gay couple that owned her twitched their curtain aside to move me along with a dismissive point of their fingers. I wiggled my ass one last time, snickering at their twin expressions of thin-lipped displeasure. Knowing Goldie would keep barking for another twenty minutes was just an added bonus.

Then I took off.

It might seem amazing that in this age of CCTV and camera phones, where every little transgression was posted to social media, that the Brotherhood and demons managed to remain a secret from both the Jewish community and wider world. As Ari had taught me, the explanation was simple: never underestimate humans' desire to stay within our comfort zones.

Case in point, the yoga-clad mommy mafia clogging up the tree-lined sidewalk, venti lattes in hand. I swerved to avoid their race car pricey strollers and the judgmental stank wafting off them as they eyed me. We all sought affirmation. That's why, as a species, we were such hypercritical assholes. We wanted proof we'd picked the right career or married the right person, even if said proof was of the *at least we're not them variety*. We wanted our lives to tally in the positives column.

Only the whackjob paranormal bloggers sometimes got closer to the truth than everyone gave them credit for. Ari and I had spent a bunch of late nights being highly entertained by their theories.

While membership had grown since David's time, the formal structure of the Brotherhood wasn't put into place until October 10, 1871 with the great fire of Chicago. With the city destroyed, hundreds dead, and the entire thing being blamed on a *cow*, the Brotherhood had stepped up and gotten globally organized to make, well, order of the chaos. No more pockets of hunters fighting demons under a loosely affiliated umbrella. They were now ruthlessly efficient in the war on evil with chapters all over the world.

Which was the second reason I wanted no part of this. "Ruthless" and "efficient" were not words to describe me. If humanity was depending on me to be part of some protector squad, they were screwed. I'd be dead within minutes of my first demon encounter, destiny notwithstanding.

A horn blared at me, jarring me out of my reverie.

I scrambled across the busy retail street, narrowly avoiding getting pancaked, and stepped onto the far curb in front of the dry cleaners, my heart pounding. "A little respect for the jay-walker here!"

Where was this magic I was supposed to have received? Had there been a glitch because I was female? Because *I* was glitch? If I really had some cool new superpower, wouldn't I have sped after the Mazda and flipped it on its side, mashing it to a pulp with angry pounds of my fists instead of standing here shaking? And if my magic did show up, would I have some stupid or embarrassing power like I'd teased Ari about?

I made my way to the bank machine, opening my wallet to sort through my credit cards. The Visa was bunk. I was scared to even stick it in an ATM for fear some collection agency bruiser would appear to hustle me off. But the AMEX? I tapped it against my chin. This baby was my emergency card, paid in full each month by Daddy Dearest.

Sliding the card into the cash machine, I punched in the ten thousand dollar limit. It made a beeping noise that sounded suspiciously like laughter, informing me in neat print that my cash advance limit was $500. Bah.

The money got tucked deep in an inside pocket in the backpack. Then I boarded the downtown bus, unsure of my destination. What I needed right now was a best friend I could crash with. What I had were tons of fellow partygoers and acquaintances.

The bus driver slammed on his brakes. I stumbled forward, whacking my head on the guitar case of the dude next to me. I'd had an awesome best friend in high school. Leonie Hendricks. It wasn't as if we'd had a fight or anything after grad. We'd still hung out. But Leo had jumped headlong into university while I'd bounced around for a few semesters before withdrawing.

My hand went for my phone. Maybe I could call Leo. I snorted. Yeah, right. We could catch up. Leo could tell me about her criminology classes and I could tell her that in an impossible twist, I was the first lady Rasha and newest member of Demon Club. Oh yeah, and that demons existed. Then she'd roll her eyes sadly at me making a joke of everything, finish our social call with polite small talk, and that would be that.

Well, that decided where I should go. A drink was in order. I headed over to my favorite business district pub for their pint and burger lunch special. A girl had to have a decent last meal, and the football-sized patties this place served would keep me full for a good twenty-four hours. Plus, the barkeep was adorable and amenable to flirting for free refills.

I sailed into the dimly lit interior with its multiple screens offering various sports replays set to classic rock blasting from the speakers, and seated myself at the scarred wood bar.

Josh, my barboy, grinned his hello. "Hey, beautiful," he said, all white teeth, platinum hair, and that unnatural level of pretty attained by certain actors. It was enough to give a girl an inferiority complex. "Haven't seen you around in a while. What can I get you and whatcha been up to?"

"Burger special and becoming the chosen one," I replied with a breezy flip of my curls.

"Sweet."

His attention reaffirmed my determination to stay far away from all things demon and huntery. I was young. I had my looks. Why would I want to mess that up fighting nasty creatures from the bowels of Hell? Or wherever they came from, since they didn't exactly leave a home address and weren't just a Christian concept.

I know Buffy looked good killing vamps, but come on, even I could separate fiction from fact enough to know that a team of hair, make-up, and wardrobe experts were not going to be a perk of my gig. Besides, hunting would cut in to my important to-dos like be adored and get free refills.

I waggled my pint glass at Josh as he placed my burger in front of me, noticing he hadn't skimped on the fries. Salt and grease good. "Thanks, barkeep. What's new with you?"

Turns out he'd landed a small but pivotal role in *Hard Knock Strife*, some big-budget picture shooting here in Vancouver. Something about childhood buddies caught up in the lure of easy money. "That's worth celebrating," I said, raising my new full glass in cheers.

"Stick around till I get off?" He nodded at my backpack, stuffed on the seat beside me, which was ringing for the umpteenth time. "Or do you have plans?"

"Nope." I pulled out my phone and turned it off. But not before glancing at the screen. Seventeen messages all from my home number. My parents, not Ari. With a sigh, I shoved it into my hoodie pocket and threw him a coy look from under my lashes. "I'm all yours."

"I'm counting on it," he replied with a wicked grin.

Ladytown flooded like it was time to start collecting two of every animal. Whoa, baby. Praying that Josh was my golden O ticket, I found myself back at his place hours later, half-drunk, partially naked, and totally giving him the hand job of his life. Doing it for him, in hopes that he'd be able to do it for me. Honestly though, my thoughts pre-occupied me more than his cock. That I could work on autopilot.

"Maybe they chose me because of my attitude issues." I lay on my side facing Josh, my head propped in my free hand. "Though technically, the choosing happened when I was born so they didn't have any way of knowing how I'd turn out." I kept the details vague since there was no knowing if Demon Club would kill Josh for hearing top secret intel.

"Mmmm, yeah," Josh moaned, kicking his jeans off. His movement made the thin mattress bounce. His sculpted abs jiggled not at all.

"But what if that's why I'm such a dick? Such an epic failure. Because I was destined for something amazing and denied it." *You talking dance or demon hunting, Nava?* "You think I could sue them for existential pain and suffering?"

"Full-on." Josh thrust his hips in a rhythmic motion.

I rolled onto my back, my hand still working away. I'd always been a good multitasker. "I didn't ask for it. It's not fair for my brother to be so pissed off."

"Uh, babe?" Josh poked me in my side. "Discussions of brothers while your hand's on my junk? Kinda killing the buzz."

"Sorry."

He leaned over me, his eyes glazed with lust. "Think you could…?" He motioned for me to go down on him.

"Yeah, sure." My hand was getting tired anyway. I slid down his body. "Thing is," I began. With my mouth full, the words came out garbled and I guess I caught some skin because Josh flinched.

"Go back to the hand job," he sighed.

Geez, make up your mind. I shimmied back to my starting position. "I don't even want this. It isn't some lady-doth-protest-too-much shit either. The pressure would be insane. Everyone would be watching me, waiting for me to screw up. Plus the possible death of it all. I'm not big on that either."

A niggle of guilt prodded at me for dumping my problems on Josh, so I gave him a flirty smile. He shot me a heated look in response. Lust tumbled hot and furious down from my now-dry throat to much, much lower. I crossed my legs, squirming, as I stole another glance at him.

His face seemed to… *flicker?* for a second. The line of his jaw blurring, his skin suddenly much furrier than his five o'clock shadow warranted.

I blinked and the room snapped into a sharp clarity. Just me and a gorgeous guy. But his serious sex appeal had me so lightheaded that all the color in the room bleached out briefly. In fact, I felt like I'd bleached out briefly.

"As I was saying… ouch!" My hand seized up. I shook it out and switched to my right.

My fingertips tingled. I amped up the speed, hoping he'd finish already. More than ready for my turn. I'd give up a kidney for an orgasm after the day I'd had.

Josh's eyes were closed, his breathing ragged. All positive signs for his happy ending.

Thank God, because my hand hurt. Had I pinched a nerve? I grit my teeth. Cramp or no cramp, I wasn't about to break my personal record of every man left satisfied. A girl had to have some skill she could be proud of, even if she couldn't put it on a résumé.

Josh let out a guttural moan.

Being well-versed in the nuances of guttural, I translated this one as "gold star, Nava." But my smugness fell away at the tugging pull starting low in my gut. Not a virulent food poisoning, all-out cramping, but more like my soul was being manhandled. I slowed down my strokes, rubbing my belly with my free hand.

Josh's eyes sparked like he was getting off more on my discomfort than on my expert dexterity. A prickle of unease danced across the back of my neck.

"Let yourself go, baby," he growled.

Please. He was hot but coming by osmosis wasn't a thing. I was overreacting. Josh wasn't a threat, just a douche.

Sweat trickled down my scalp and a sharp pressure rose through the fingers of my right hand, now cramped tight around his knob. I hadn't been jerking him off long enough to be this tired. Pain pulsed outward from the middle of my palm as if my synapses had starting shooting electric bullets.

"Almost there," he mumbled. His hips were practically levitating they were lifting off the bed so high.

My belly twisted and I drew my knees into my chest for some relief, yet I couldn't stop touching Josh. The more I tugged, the more he moaned lustily, and the more I grit my teeth. My abdomen felt like it was a leaking tire, but I wasn't injured. More like with each stroke I was losing something essential, growing wearier, and I wasn't able to explain why.

Sparks flew off my hand.

Holy. Shit.

Josh's body flickered like a stuttering screen, revealing a ram's head.

Oh, hell no!

I spasmed, engulfed by a snapping blue electrical arc that traveled through my hand to envelop Josh's dick, momentarily gluing us together with a disturbing sizzle and a whiff of burning flesh.

His eyes snapped open in alarm.

Given how every blink caused sparks to dance in front of me, I figured I was lit up from head to foot, but before I could check, Josh convulsed with a hot spurt. Then his body exploded into gold dust.

Both the pain in my hand and the pyrotechnics immediately ceased.

I wiped my fingers off on the rumpled sheet with a grimace. The downside was that I'd just met my first demon. The upside? Not only was he not naturally better-looking than me, my record was intact. Another satisfied guy. Dispatched to oblivion, but not every date was a winner.

3

The shock kicked in about thirty seconds later. I clutched Josh's pillow, rocking back and forth emitting weird "guh" noises until I got my throat working again. Sure, I could step on a very small spider like the manliest of men, but that smattering of gold powder on the sheets had been Josh. My intermittent flirt buddy for the past six months.

An icy slither ran up my core as I stared at my right hand, its tremors Richter scale violent. Was this my demon-killing ability? Destined to be some supernatural whore luring hell spawn into back alleys for deadly rub and tugs?

Leaping from the bed, a hand clapped over my mouth, I sprinted over the cheap beige carpet to the bathroom. I barely made it to the toilet, throwing up all the contents of my stomach until the dry heaves kicked in. Beer and grease did not taste better coming back up.

I cleaned up as best I could, blowing my nose and using an entire travel bottle of mouthwash that I found in Josh's cluttered medicine cabinet to rinse out my mouth. I considered using his toothbrush but that seemed too intimate for a guy I hardly knew.

I hiccuped in a half-sob, half-laugh. Orgasming to death okay, shared oral hygiene a line too far.

I gripped the sink so hard my fingertips turned white, forcing myself to take deep, calming breaths. Getting myself down to the functioning side of hysterical. I ran my fingers through my sweat-matted hair, taking in my reflection in the mirror of his bathroom cabinet.

Pale, crazed, I couldn't stare too long at myself so I yanked on the tap, washing my hands vigorously enough to rub them raw.

Taking a layer or six of epidermis off myself helped. The color had returned to my cheeks. Somewhat. But with my shocky adrenaline high wearing off came the painful realization that my boobs burned like crazy.

With the utmost care, I peeled my shirt and bra off to find a scorched, puckered burn line matching the now-melted underwire. As a natural disaster show connoisseur, I knew that metal conducted electricity but, come on! My girls demanded underwire.

I pressed a fingertip to the red angry skin with a hiss. Seems right now they demanded burn lotion. I rummaged through Josh's cupboard but he was light on first aid products, so I tossed the bra in the trash and eased back into my shirt, flinching as the soft material made contact.

It was too much.

Wobbly from a cocktail of exhaustion and pain, I pressed my head to the cool glass of the mirror. Giving myself a moment to get my jumpy pulse under control and let the throbbing in my tits subside enough to be able to walk because that basic motor function seemed an impossible dream.

I had no idea how much time passed before I was able to move, though moonlight now streamed in through Josh's bedroom window as I dressed. No drunken ramblings were heard from homeward-bound revelers, the city deep in slumber.

I shrugged on my jeans, unable to shake my sense of unease. Sidling over to the window, I peered outside through the slats of the bent plastic blinds.

Some guy stood in the alley framed in a pool of light cast by a poster-plastered streetlamp. Hands in the pockets of his leather jacket, he seemed every bit a relaxed bystander, but I wasn't deceived.

The question was, was he here hunting Josh? Or me?

I widened the blinds a touch.

Startlingly gold eyes bored straight into my soul, rooting me to the spot. His hair, several shades darker than his light brown skin, was kind of shaggy, curling thick and sexy around his ear lobes. He had to be a demon. My hand didn't tingle or anything in recognition but ordinary mortals were not created this ridiculously gorgeous. I'd know. I trolled the internet plenty looking at hot dude Pinterest boards.

Plus, perched above him on the telephone wire was a white crow, albeit a weirdly stocky one. Contrary to popular opinion, white crows were not an albino rarity but demons who, once fixated on their prey like this one was on me, dive-bombed a person feeding off their blood and flesh. I had never been so glad for a pane of glass. And when Alley Dude trained his sights on the bird, the white crow exploded off the line with a panicked "caw," flying away so fast that it trailed feathers.

Some primal survival sense screamed at me that whoever or whatever this guy was, he was a million times more dangerous than Josh. But it also kicked me into gear.

I jerked away from the window, pressing myself flat against the wall. My heart threatened to explode out of my chest. Had Josh's death set some demon phone tree into motion and now they were all after me? Keeping low so the guy couldn't see me, I gathered up my backpack, smelling the lingering scent of Josh's cologne from when he'd carried it home for me.

He'd never carry anything again.

I pressed my fist to my mouth. I'd killed a man. Demon. Barkeep. Panic flared hot and bright. I jammed my feet into my shoes then raced for the front door. Fleeing the scene of the crime while cradling one arm against my chest to keep my poor burned babies from jiggling.

As I reached for the lock, my hip bumped the small white plastic table next to the door. The green sides from yesterday's shoot–the small, color-coded script pages for that day–fell to the ground and I bent to pick them up, not wanting to leave his place in worse shape than I found it. Other than its loss of occupant.

Josh had been cast as the happy-go-lucky playboy of the group. In this scene at least, no woman could resist his charm. That was one word for it. I shivered, remembering the unsettling tugging right before Josh had orgasmed. In retrospect, his "let go" was probably a command, not a suggestion. Had I not been Rasha, they would have been last words I ever heard.

I dropped the paper like it was a hot coal, fumbling in my pocket for my phone and punching in Ari's speed dial number. The call went straight to voice mail.

"Ari," I mewled. I slid down the wall, hugging my arms to my chest, paralyzed between fright and flight.

Shortly after, there was a frantic pounding on the door. "Nava!" The cavalry had come. I scrambled to my feet, unlocked the bolt, and flung open the door, launching myself into my brother's arms.

He patted me awkwardly. "Nee, what's wrong?"

The story poured out of me. Ari let me ramble, leading me to the sofa in Josh's cramped IKEA-themed living room and listening in silence as I described killing my hook-up.

"Say something," I begged, clutching the leg of his blue plaid pajama pants.

Ari hadn't even gotten dressed. Just stuffed his feet into slippers and thrown on a sweatshirt in his haste to save me.

"You washed your hands, right?" he asked.

I punched him in the arm. "That's the sum total of what you have to say?"

He punched me back. His was harder than mine and I pouted as I rubbed the sore spot. "You," he mimed giving a hand job, "a demon to death. I think I need therapy." He shuddered.

"You think you need therapy?" I screeched. "How do you think I feel? You know what my big plan for today was? A nap! Instead I've made you hate me and my hand is a red light district instrument of destruction."

I paused for him to interject that of course he didn't hate me, but he didn't. So I babbled the rest of my story, punctuating my words with flailing gestures. That just sent a fresh shaft of pain through my boobs.

"I mean, what happens when I meet a nice guy that I like and things start to get intimate?" I said. "Will my hand know the difference? Because I'm not sure there is an appropriate greeting card to apologize for penile third degree burns!"

"I'd say it with flowers," he pronounced.

The clock on the wall ticked once. Twice.

We burst out laughing. A brittle manic laughter that morphed into way-over-the-top snorting guffaws complete with shaking body and streaming tears. Cathartically spent, I sagged back against the couch.

Ari stood up, rolling out his shoulders. "You ready to quit running away from home now and go deal with this?"

I scrunched up my face. "How'd you know I'd run away?"

"I always know."

A wistful pang hit me square in the chest. I rubbed my hand over the back of my neck. "Right."

"Dumbass." He boffed me across the head. "I don't hate you."

My relief swam clear down to my toes. "That's because I'm Twin Amazing and I brighten up your life," I said.

He shot me a look of fond exasperation.

I could have kissed him in a sister-appropriate way for it–e.g. raspberried his cheek. "Think you can help me not get killed?" I asked.

"Up to a point. But we're going to have to call Rabbi Abrams."

"And get our heavily edited stories straight," I added.

Ari pulled me up. "That's your area of expertise."

My right hand gave an aftershocky jerk. I placed my other one on top of it to stop the shaking. "You may need to carry me."

"You need electrolytes." Ari went into the kitchen, opening and closing cupboards. "He doesn't have any salt," he said, coming back and finding me slumped over the top of the sofa. "Come on, I'll buy you a Gatorade."

I threw my arm over my brother's shoulder, letting him support me. He grabbed my backpack and helped me out the door. Any comfort I took in having Ari's forgiveness disappeared when we hit the front sidewalk outside Josh's three-story stucco apartment building and saw the hot platinum blonde leaning against the glass front door, all long limbs and porn star mouth in this slinky gold halter dress I coveted.

"Hey, lover," she said to Ari, ignoring my existence.

I was so not in the mood to deal with some west side chick on the pointless make for my brother.

He gave her a polite smile, maneuvering us past both her and the broken furniture someone had left out for garbage pick up.

"You think you could help me?" she asked, catching up to us and waving her cell. "My friend stood me up and my phone is dead."

I stopped, forcing Ari to stop with me. I couldn't in good conscience leave this woman stranded in the middle of the night. Especially outside this dump with its sketchy lighting. I dug out my phone, shuffled a few steps closer, and handed it to her. "Here. Use mine."

"Thanks," she said, latching onto my wrist with a talon. My phone tumbled to the concrete as her mouth elongated into a distorted sneer. "Have fun with my brother tonight?"

I tried to scramble back, terrified her jaw was about to unhinge and swallow me whole, but she held me fast. Good thing because I still hadn't recharged and lack of energy plus fear equaled my knees buckling.

I batted at her with my right hand, which was totally failing to shock her.

"Bitch," she snarled, her stilettos morphing to crow's feet, "I liked him. He was the only one of my siblings I hadn't eaten."

Ew. Phrasing.

A surge of adrenaline raced through me and I snapped my knee up into her crotch.

She gasped, doubling over.

That's when I head-butted her, a technique learned while hanging with this hockey player I'd wanted to bang. The demon's nose made a satisfying crunch as the cartilage shattered. I snatched my arm loose with a laugh. "Booyah, mother–"

With a roar she puffed up into an ogre. A solid muscle demon ogre with a now-tattered dress hanging off her body. Her shiny mane of hair erupted into white feathers and her nose transformed into a pointed beak. The crow/ogre hybrid grabbed me by the throat.

My powers were still in absentia and all thoughts of *electrocute the bitch*, were supplanted by *get air to brain* as she continued to squeeze. Spots danced in front of my watering eyes, my vision tunneling down to the narrow pinprick of her bumpy chin. I flailed my limbs.

"Get your own sibling," Ari said, "I spent years training this one."

SPLOOSH! Murky goo splattered all over my face.

She dropped me like a hot potato.

I stood there wheezing, staring in incredulity at my brother. Not only had he jammed a standing lamp through the demon's neck, he'd taken advantage of her clawing at the thing to whip out a knife from an ankle sheath, firing it into her just below her navel.

A scream ripped from the demon's throat, her skin blistering in a way that made me think of crackling. I might never eat bacon again. Yeah, who was I kidding? Tendrils of smoke wafted off her bubbling flesh. She screeched a high-pitched, inhuman cry of pain and rage.

"Nee, finish her!"

I stared at him blankly. Ari grabbed my hand and, hauling me over to the demon, placed my fingers around the knife so they touched her rubbery skin.

A tingle deep inside me rippled into a concentrated bolt of lightning, firing straight into the demon.

She exploded. The lamp and the knife clattered to the ground.

Shimmery gold dust floated down from the star-filled night sky. It coated Ari, turning him into a sparkling hero.

"How?" It was all I managed to stutter out.

He shrugged and picked up his knife. "Training."

"But…" I pointed at the weapon.

"Iron blade coated in salt. Two things demons hate."

"And…" I made a thrusting motion with my hand.

Ari stared at me for a second before he clued in. "Ohhh. The lamp. Again, training." He ran his fingers through his hair, shaking out the dust as he walked along the sidewalk. His slippers made soft padding sounds with each step.

Avoiding the trail of demon dust on the sidewalk, I scooped up my phone with my thumb and index finger, not touching any more of it than I had to, then hurried after him. I punched his shoulder. "Don't fight demons without magic."

"I didn't. You were right there."

I growled at him. "Your own magic."

Ari turned the corner, pulled his key fob out, and beeped it at our father's blue Prius parked at the curb.

"I know you, Ace. Magic or no, you come across someone in need of saving from a demon, you'll rush in. You can't."

He shrugged as he opened the passenger door and helped me inside.

"Unlike me," I said, "you possess that stupid selfless gene that Rasha are supposed to have. Tonight proves there's been a colossal mistake."

"You killed the demon," he said. "No mistake."

"*You* killed that demon. I was merely a tool." I forgave him the small smirk at my word choice as he shut my door. Didn't lessen my desire to throttle him, though.

Ari got in the driver's side, tossing the blade into the pocket on the door.

Pushing him about staying safe would only spur him in the other direction. "Why are you not more excited about this? Or upset about it? Or something resembling anything?" I asked.

My brother placed the key in the ignition and started the engine with the press of the power button. He pulled out into the street to the strains of shitty soft rock. Dad must have been the last one to drive the car. "Big deal. Another assist. Not like I got to score on goal directly."

I rested my feet on the dashboard, slouched in my seat. "Not enough excitement for you, brother dear?"

He shrugged. "Eh."

I stuffed my fists under my butt, the sight of my hands still troubling. "That disturbs me about you." As did the fact that the idiot was *going to get himself killed.*

"Sucks a bit less since it was only a PD." He flicked on his blinker, pissing off the chick behind us who honked multiple times.

I lowered my window to shoot her the finger. The cool night air streaming over me was invigorating enough to keep me upright so I kept it unrolled. "What kind of a demon is a PD?"

"Old Rasha joke. What do you call a half-demon?"

I shook my head.

"Practice. Practice demon."

"PD. Ooh, bitchy. But she was a hybrid."

"Yeah. Probably some genetic throwback on the demon side. Still just half-demonic. Half-human."

"How do you know?"

"Dust 'em and you're gold. Literally. PDs explode into gold dust. Josh was a halfie as well." Ari made a sharp left, pulling into a convenience store parking lot. "Back in a sec," he said, leaving me in the car with the motor running.

I fiddled with the stereo knob, unable to take any more musical torture.

Moments later he was back with a plastic bag. He pulled out a blue sports drink, cracked the cap, and handed it to me. "Drink. You need the electrolytes."

I wasn't a fan of these things so my first sip was tentative, but the liquid hit my system like a rush of cocaine. I chugged the rest down in one go. "More," I breathed.

He handed me the other drink that he'd purchased, this one a yummy orange-esque flavor. Once I'd downed that too, I sighed in satisfaction. "That was amazing."

Ari backed out of the spot, shaking his head. "Don't ever make that sound in my presence again."

I twisted the cap shut, jamming it back into the bag with the other empty bottle. "If I could give the power back, I would. It should be you joining Demon Club."

My brother merged back into the light traffic, homeward bound. "I know." He ran a hand through his bedhead, spiking his blond tufts. "But it doesn't seem like either of us are going to get what we want."

There was nothing I could say to that, so I channel-surfed, looking for a song to reflect my mood. The only thing that came close was "Bound," an angsty charged hit from a few years ago by Fugue State Five. I sang along to the last verse.

"You know the words?" Ari didn't sound impressed.

I shrugged, betting he did too since we would have had to have been living in a cave during our teen years not to know the emo boy band that had taken the world by storm. Also, Leonie had been obsessed with them, playing their music incessantly.

The next song was some crap rock ballad so I punched the radio button off. The silence was deafening.

Ari shot me a sideways glance. "Gotta say I'm surprised you're not celebrating. Finally having a tangible way of keeping people at bay and all."

I slapped my feet onto the car mat. "I don't do that."

My brother snorted. "Right. You welcome them in with open arms." He pursed his lips. "These last few years? It's like you decided to make yourself this prickly ball of chaos."

"The PC among us call it 'hot mess,'" I quipped.

"Kinda ironic that your power is a physical manifestation of that."

The vein at my temple throbbed. "You're wrong. My sucky superpower is just that. Sucky. Not some kind of subconscious desire made real."

One hand on the wheel, he waved the other around, speaking in a mock scary voice. "Whooo, don't get too close to me, I might shock you." He dropped his voice an octave into horror movie voice over. "And this time, it's deadly."

"I'm not the only deadly one," I said waspishly. "Got any other weapons strapped to your body?"

"Nah. The knives were something I started playing around with a while ago. Doctoring up the best high salt concentration, finding the most effective method of coating the blade." He flashed me the thick silver ring on his middle finger with a ruby or red garnet in the middle. "See this? Iron poison ring. Literally." He spared another glance at the ring before his hands tightened on the wheel. "I was playing around with stuff for when I took my rightful place and all that."

My anger deflated at the reminder of what he'd lost. "You, Ari Katz, are my hero."

My brother took his eyes off the road long enough to give me a crooked grin. "And you, Nava Katz, are a really shitty demon hunter."

4

The lights were blazing in every room in our house when we pulled into the car port out back. It kind of kiboshed my plan to sneak in and then hide out in my room until my parents cooled down. Ari, the keener, bounded off ahead of me. My walk had more of a "headed to the guillotine" vibe to it.

I veered into the backyard to snap a few stalks off Mom's aloe plant to apply to my still-throbbing chest. It was a gorgeous night, made more so by the fact that I was still alive. I raised my face up to the stars, calmed by their distant pulsing. All was peaceful and still until my shoulder blades tensed like someone was behind me.

The maybe-demon from Josh's alleyway was back, having stopped about five feet away, triggering the motion sensor. What with Josh's sister trying to kill me and all, he'd fallen off my radar.

Aloe gooped over my fingers, having clutched the frond hard enough to break it, and my terror and an intense curiosity resurfaced. There was no denying his compelling presence. Plus, he had those long lashes that were my Kryptonite. I opened my mouth to scream. Or drool.

He held a finger up to his delectable lips to keep me quiet, circling me with lazy strides, checking me out.

I'd have been offended by the blatant appraisal except under his intense scrutiny, my clit, Cuntessa de Spluge lit up with an electric zing. I found myself stroking the aloe stalks in an obscene manner. Even knowing he couldn't see my blush since I was in the shadows didn't kill my utter mortification at jerking off plant life in not-so-subtextual yearning.

He stalked toward me, his leather jacket rustling with each step.

I held up a hand to stop him, the faintest electric crackle pulsing off my skin.

He didn't stop, didn't slow. In fact, he kept up his steady approach until his hand covered mine. My magic shocked us both at his touch. I gasped and shivered as pleasure, not pain, rumbled through me.

Hand still clasped in his, he stared at me suspiciously, instead of in fear, but had I wanted, I could have broken his hold. Not a demon, then? He fingered the thin silver necklace I wore with surprising gentleness, toying with the cute floral pendant dangling off it that read "I will kick you in the balls if I have to."

"Should I be scared?" Given how he sounded like sex, sin, and salaciousness–the true definition of a triple threat–I decided that yes, he was most definitely a demon.

I met his mocking gaze, my rooted stance and beating heart placing me somewhere between morbid fascination and noping the fuck out at warp speed.

"Nava," Ari called from the top of the stairs.

I jerked toward his voice. "Here."

My intruder backed away, melting into the night. I might have followed had Ari not called for me again. Instead, I hurried into the kitchen to find Mom, Dad, Rabbi Abrams, and a tree trunk of a man, about ten years older than me, with shoulder-length black hair and sharp blue eyes sitting at the kitchen table. His hair, combined with the hemp bracelets around his wrist, made him look like a Special Ops surfer dude. The floral yellow espresso cup that my parents had picked up at some overpriced ceramics studio in Italy was like a toy in his huge hand.

A platter of mostly untouched Danish pastry sat in the middle of the table, though given the three on his plate, Rabbi Abrams was doing his best to plough through them. I sent the dessert a longing glance, but before I could reach for a pastry, Tree Trunk rose to his almost six and a half feet, cracked his neck that was bigger than my thigh, and lumbered toward me.

"Baruch Ya'ari," Ari said in the most awestruck voice I'd ever heard him use.

I didn't care if this Baruch guy was the second coming, I hid behind my brother. Ari tugged me out to face the scary stranger, pushing me forward into his path.

"Baruch is usually based at HQ in Jerusalem," Rabbi Abrams piped up, chewing. "He–"

"Invented the Stinger," Ari said. Wow. Fanboy a little more, bro.

"Ari is the chemistry student I told you about," the rabbi said to Baruch.

My unflappable brother actually squeaked when he said that.

"But due to the... situation," Rabbi Abrams continued, "it is Nava you will be training in fighting and weapons skills."

How about showing some tact, old man? Couldn't he see Ari's shoulders slump? Though I perked up at hearing there were weapons. I looked down at the aloe in my hand. I could do weapons.

Baruch let his gaze roam slowly up my body like he was cataloging my every weakness and maybe taking my blood pressure.

I jutted my chin out.

Mom tapped her finger against her cup, her wedding ring clinking against the ceramic.

"No," Tree Trunk barked when he'd finished his inspection. He spoke with that gravelly abruptness of many Israeli men.

I dropped the aloe on the counter. "No, what?" I didn't recall hearing a question.

Baruch made a dismissive raspberry noise. "She is not Rasha material."

Mom deflated. Dad put his arm around her and she leaned into him. WTF?

I didn't have time to process them being upset on my behalf, because this was my shot. "You're right. I'm not." I shoved Ari at him. "But he is. He killed a demon tonight. Saved my life."

Tree Trunk stilled. He zeroed in on my brother who scowled at me. I nodded virtuously. There was only room for one demon hunter in our family and it was going to be Ari.

"How?" Baruch asked.

Ari launched into an explanation.

Tree Trunk's stoic demeanor loosened up enough to blink approvingly during Ari's recounting of the lamp post and ankle sheath. I took it as him being impressed with my twin.

Even the rabbi beamed with pride. My parents were certainly happy. When Ari finished, my mother prodded the still silent Baruch. "Well?"

I crossed my fingers.

Baruch gave another infuriating raspberry. "He took down some bastard of Asmodeus'."

"*The* demon of lust," Ari murmured at my questioning glance. "Major player in the demon hierarchy."

"...And the other one did the killing," Baruch said.

"Big deal. Get him a magic hand," I said through gritted teeth. "I'm alive thanks to Ari and his training. I refuse to believe he isn't supposed to be Rasha." Rabbi Abrams opened his mouth but I cut him off, knowing what he was going to say. "I don't care if you ran the ceremony again. Ari is the chosen one, not me."

Baruch swung his gaze to me.

Uh-oh. I'd put myself back on his radar. "Yes?"

"What did you do to her brother?" he asked. "What was the demon referring to?"

Picked up on that part of the story, had he? Mostly I'd done *with* her brother. Just a little bit of *to* at the end of our time together. "Nothing worth recounting." In front of my parents. "She was an evil fiend," I continued. "Talking crazy. Back to Ari."

"Nava killed him as well," Ari piped up.

I slapped my hand over his mouth. "As I was saying, back to Ari who is humble, which I believe is the first rule of Demon Club. He's so humble, in fact, that he's willing to lie like a rug to throw the spotlight off of him."

"There is no Demon Club," Baruch pronounced.

Ari yanked my hand off him at the same time that I said, "Fine. Sorry. Not Demon Club." Seems they were touchy about their nickname. "The Brotherhood of David."

"No," Baruch corrected me, "The first rule of Demon Club. It's 'there is no Demon Club.'"

I crossed my arms. "Really? You're going to get a sense of humor now?"

He mirrored my stance. "Really? You're going to keep avoiding my question?"

I mimed zipping my lips and throwing away the key.

Tree Trunk turned to Ari. "How?" Such a popular question this evening.

My brother opened his mouth, blanched at the realization that we'd neglected to create a parent-friendly version of events, then pointed at me. "Ask her."

I tugged on my lips to show they were still zipped.

The rabbi said a few words in Hebrew.

This time Baruch's blink conveyed such disapproval that everyone leaned away from him. Who was this guy? Some kind of Zen eye master?

Rabbi Abrams said a few more things. None of them the ten words of Hebrew still imprinted on my brain from summer camp.

Baruch's hand shot out and grabbed my right hand. He pulled on the ring so hard I howled in pain, attempting to jerk away. Emphasis on attempt. Vises were easier to escape. He leaned in close, his fingers tightening. "Give. It. Back." His blue eyes darkened in menace.

That was it. My limit on bullying for today. I was exhausted and I'd kill for a shower because the demon dust on my skin was starting to itch. I leaned in until our noses practically touched. "Bite. Me."

The room fell into shocked silence. Then Baruch laughed. A rusty bark of surprise. "Beseder," he said using the Hebrew word for okay. He patted my head. "Sleep. Tomorrow you start."

"Uh, no. Tomorrow you figure out how to fix this." I pointed at my brother. "He's the one you want, not me."

"True," Baruch said with a smile Ari's way that made him preen. I gagged. "But you are who we have," Baruch said to me, his smile gone. "So we will keep you alive and you will kill many demons." Before I could present any further arguments, he strode out the back door and into the night without a look back.

Rabbi Abrams gave us a kind of half bow and shuffled after him. "Baruch, wait! You drove."

Dad closed the back door after making sure the rabbi had made it down the stairs unharmed.

"I think that went very well," Mom said, rising. She grabbed a rag from the sink and started vigorously wiping down the counter.

I slumped into a chair. "In what way?" When I'd left the house this afternoon, my parents had not been onboard with this new reality.

"You made a positive impression on Baruch. Today was a bit of a shock. For all of us. But now we'll readjust. This could be the new start you've been looking for." Interesting that she was spouting all this positive affirmation crap yet hadn't once met my eyes.

Plus, I hadn't been looking for a new start. My present stagnation was warm and cozy.

My father gathered up the espresso cups. "Your mother is right."

I side-eyed Ari. He sat at the table, toying with a linen placemat. My rock of a brother looked deflated. Like sorrow was the only thing holding him together. "What about Ari?" I asked. "What's he supposed to do now?"

Mom stopped wiping. Her voice wavered as she said, "Ari will be... The world is still his for the taking."

Ari flinched.

I slid off the stool, and snatched up my aloe, bound for hot water and then bed. "I haven't agreed to this."

"You don't have a choice," Dad said. There it was again. Not, "You'll be great." Not even, "You can do this." Just, "You have no option." Everyone had made it very clear they were stuck with me. Maybe it was time for me to make it clear that I may have been chosen, but I still very much had a choice.

I shrugged. "There's not any way you can force me, is there?"

My parents froze. That fact hadn't occurred to them.

I lay my hand on Ari's shoulder. "Hey, Ace?" I murmured. "Thanks for the rescue. But the next time I run away, ignore my calls, stay out of the Find My iPhone, and let me stay gone."

Minutes later, I stood with my head bowed while scalding water pounded down the back of my neck. Hot showers might be evidence of the existence of angels and if they were, then the glowy buggers could show up any time and corral their wayward relations.

The combination of the steam and the sugar scrub smeared all over my body was softening my stiff muscles, washing away fears and tensions. All right, washing away sweat and demon goo but they tamped the fears and tensions down a tad. I washed my death hand about sixty-seven times before I pronounced it free of demon and karma.

Bad things really did come in threes. I'd been lucky tonight. No previous female Rasha meant that Josh had been unaware of the danger he'd been in from me, allowing my first show of magic to dust him. With his sister, Ari had been there. And with that last encounter in my backyard? I didn't know what to make of that whole meeting and that bothered me more than the other two combined. Loath as I was to admit it, tomorrow I was going to march myself over to the Vancouver chapter and let them take me in hand.

I shuddered, remembering Josh. Phrasing.

I dumped some argon oil shampoo in my palm, lathering up. I'd tried running away and that had gotten me nowhere. Since I didn't want to find myself in a repeat of tonight or, you know, actually dead the next time I met a demon, I'd play nice with Demon Club.

More importantly, I had to help Ari. I wasn't going to let my brother wither away. Much as Brotherhood history and tradition were screwing me hard and dry with no money on the bedside table afterwards, they worked in Ari's favor. Whenever the Brotherhood determined Rasha initiate status, they committed to that (male) person without hesitation. Right now, they thought that they'd made a mistake with Ari, so their conviction that Ari was no longer an initiate was the biggest hurdle. Get the proof to correct that and his induction would swiftly follow. He'd be back on his rightful path.

I rinsed out my hair, finger combing conditioner through it.

My plan for tomorrow had two-parts: A) master my power since it appeared demons were actively targeting me now and, B) get the Brotherhood to confirm Ari's initiate status. Me being Rasha was a weird glitch that didn't negate my brother's destiny.

Oh, and try not to be freaked by all this. Okay, three parts. But that's where I capped it.

Clean of body and soul, I shut off the tap, giving myself a small electric shock in the process. Damn faulty piece of shit hand. I stepped out of the shower, wrapping the towel around my head like a giant turban before breaking open the fronds to smear aloe on my tender boobs.

I slathered body lotion on the rest of me, slipping nice and moisturized into my pink baby doll tee reading "I know guacamole is extra" and matching pink pajama shorts with small avocados printed on them. Finally, I brushed my teeth and towel dried my hair. The normalcy of following my nighttime routine was comforting.

Dumping the damp towel on the floor, I picked up the Doritos bag to throw in to my bedroom trash, since my bathroom's was full. I opened the door with a cloud of steam, and wandered into my comparatively cooler bedroom.

Where I collided with a hard chest.

I screamed. Or tried to. A strong hand slammed down over my mouth to smother my cries. I attempted my knee smash, but was blocked before I could even finish the thought, much less execute the move. The intruder picked me up and tossed me on my bed. My memory foam mattress contoured itself around the shape of my ass.

"You telegraph way too much," a smooth voice said to me. Backyard guy was back.

Ignoring the decadent images that his voice conjured up, I shoved my hand into the Doritos bag which contained about 237% salt, crawled to the edge of the bed, and threw the crumbs in the demon's face. "Burn, fucker!"

The demon glared at me as he wiped orange dust off his cheeks and sweater. "This is cashmere," he said, frowning at the deep blue fabric.

I scrambled to my feet, holding the bag out in front of me like a cross. Which, incidentally, did nothing against demons. And since vampires didn't exist, did nothing against them either. Some demon happened to get its kicks feeding from the neck and suddenly everyone was rushing in with garlic and stakes looking to take down Count Dracula. Those who weren't romanticizing them as life partners, that is.

"There is enough salt in this bag to blister you back to your evil dimension." Smirking, I batted my lashes at him. "Feel free to be scared."

He swiped the bag out of my hands, tossing it into the trash behind him. "A, if you're gonna eat chips, at least eat decent ones. B, not a demon. And C," he said, reading my baby doll tee, "love the outfit, Nava."

I scowled at him. "You are absolutely a demon."

He pulled out my desk chair, turned it around with a snap of his wrists, and straddled it. "Why?"

"For starters, I never told you my name. Probably got it from the demon phone tree that went out about me."

He grinned at me, flashing toothpaste-ad-perfect, even, white teeth. "I'm not on the list."

I crossed my arms over my nipples which were now so hard from that grin he'd leveled at me that one good operatic scream could shatter them. I shut down all possibilities of how said scream could be achieved, locking them inside a box deep in my psyche.

"Any other proof you want to dazzle me with?" he asked.

How about the fact that his grin made Josh's seem like a neutered puppy's and Josh was a lust demon. Half-demon. Which made this guy full-evil status. "You broke into my bedroom and are holding me hostage." With your incredible looks.

Damn. Why not roll over already, idiot girl?

I hadn't been able to scope out his body in detail on our previous two encounters, but now, under proper lighting, I could tell he'd be nicely cut under that sweater that molded to him like a second skin. Underwear model nice and not the low rent, flyer-insert kind either. One of those glorious torsos caught in haunting black and white by Herb Ritts, the stark white of his briefs throwing his generous package into sharp relief.

Then there was his face. If it hadn't been for the slight bent of his nose, indicating it had been broken, his South Asian beauty would have been too painful and/or depressing to look at. Killer cheekbones, firm chin, gorgeous brown skin and lips that were created to do bad, bad, wonderful things. It was going to be a crime against humanity to kill him.

I leaned in toward the slight breeze drifting in through my open window, refusing to fan myself in front of him.

He sat there under my scrutiny, totally comfortable. A sign of excess confidence and further proof of evil. Though the more I stared at him, the more I got a niggling feeling that I knew him.

"Did we ever..." I made a fist and pumped away in a back and forth motion.

Amusement lit his amber eyes. "I was the lead singer of Fugue State Five." He smirked, saying the words as if obviously I'd heard of them. Fair enough.

Rohan Mitra had been the broody frontman whose so sensitive lyrics and rough growl singing voice induced mass hysteria at concerts world-wide. It was rumored he'd averted an oil crisis with a personal visit to a Sheik's daughter. Watching the beautiful bastard now, I believed it.

"Oh my God!" I squealed. "Your mom is Maya Mitra. I love her!"

"My mom." The smirk vanished.

The words tripped out of my mouth, I was so psyched to be one degree of separation away from this woman. "Punk rock Indian Jewish chick who blew every stereotype out of the water in her rise to hottest music producer in the biz? You get to be related to her?!" I bounced on the bed in sheer excitement, clapping a hand over my protesting boobs.

"And she to me," he said dryly.

"Whatever." I studied him. When Rohan had first gotten famous, he'd been an extremely pretty sixteen-year-old, all long limbs, smoldering doe eyes, and his trademark platinum blond hair falling into his face, but from his tightly muscled body to his five o'clock shadow, that boy was long gone. He seemed... harder. *Don't go there, honey.* Thankfully his standard issue wear of Vans, black skinny jeans, and vintage-looking weird graphic T-shirts were no longer a part of his repertoire.

Even Leo, his super fan, might have needed time to make the connection between his past and present selves.

I raked an approving glance over his vastly improved fashion sense, enjoying the view from the top of his fitted sweater, along his tailored black dress pants, and down to the tips of his Italian footwear. His leather jacket was tossed on my windowsill. "I didn't recognize you without the eyeliner and glaring dye job, Rohan."

He tipped his head. "Yeah. Thrilled that look is immortalized for all time. Now, come on."

"Come on and what?"

"Show me your power." His hand snaked out and caught my wrist, pressing his palm against mine. Holding me in a barely contained show of strength.

"Death wish, much? I showed you in the backyard."

"Barely even a tease." He drawled the words.

I meant to pull away but I got my directions mixed up and pushed back against the warmth of his skin. "I *will* fire up. I'm warning you."

Rohan leaned in. "Do it." His eyes flared and I caught my bottom lip between my teeth.

Then some last iota of common sense—and self-preservation—raised its hand. I jerked away from him. If he was a demon, I should have killed him six times over by now. What the hell was I doing? "You still haven't convinced me that you're not a demon," I said, giving the evil spawn another chance for reasons I didn't want to examine too closely. "Fame doesn't preclude that. Nor does having a super cool mom."

"That doesn't, but this does." He held up his pinky finger, showing me the same gold ring as mine, with the same engraved hamsa and blue sapphire iris, which it turns out, was standard issue. And here I'd been hoping for a succession of property-stamping jewelry as I rose through the hunter ranks.

I fell back against my headboard. "You're part of Demon Club. Fuck. Me."

Rohan ogled me. "I won't take that off the table yet." He propped his chin on his hands on the top of the chair.

I cocked an eyebrow at him. "Did you just put me on a table?"

"More invoked a proverbial table and a conditional 'yet.' The 'yet' is an important component of this potential event," he said.

You know what else was an important component? The presumptuous jerk still having attached balls for our proverbial fuck.

"I used to write fanfic about Fugue State Five," I said in a conversational tone.

Lookie lookie. Return of the amused smirk. "How was I?" he asked.

I shrugged, examining my chipped nail polish. "No clue. I wrote self-insert fanfic about the *rest* of your band. Zack, your keyboardist was astounding." I drawled that last word so he'd get the full implication.

"My keyboardist?" Rohan's smugness was R.I.P. "But he's gay."

"I assure you that didn't matter." I gave a self-satisfied sigh. "He succumbed to my fifteen-year-old self's wiles."

Rohan straightened. "Which of my much older bandmates also succumbed, Lolita?"

"Please. You guys were only three years older." I twisted a dark curl around my finger. "But pretty much all of them." I raked a pointed look over him. "The ones worth writing about." He didn't react. "Though succumbing is far more innocent than you're imagining," I admitted.

"I doubt you were ever innocent."

That was highly insulting. Did he think I'd been born this way? Please. I'd worked hard to cultivate this level of sexual awesomeness.

Totally offended here. And equally turned on because he'd said it in that low rumbly voice that made me want to roll onto my back, knees falling open. If he rubbed my belly or lower, all good.

I tossed my hair. "Excellent. Assume the worst." Straightening my legs, I crossed one over the other. Forcing them to stay closed. Then I leaned back on my elbows and gave him my best smirk. "Now, what are you doing in my bedroom?"

I prayed he couldn't hear how hard my heart was thumping.

"I'm your new CO."

"My what?"

"Commanding Officer." He picked up a porcelain Fred Astaire and Ginger Rogers dancing together in their finery, from my shelf. "That means you have to do as I say."

I leapt off the bed and snatched Fred and Ginger back. "Oh, hell no."

Rohan raised an eyebrow. I petted my dancers' ceramic heads and carefully put them back as I scrambled for a somewhat less mutinous excuse. "You're full of shit. CO's are only appointed on missions. Otherwise, Rabbi Abrams runs the local chapter."

Even though not all Rasha were Jewish, when it came to running Demon Club, tracking and training the descendants, and performing rituals, David had only trusted a select group of Sanhedrin, the highest of High Rabbis. Rabbis still performed those duties today, despite the fact that the Brotherhood wasn't technically a religious organization. Something about trade secrets and the magic involved. I suspected the Brotherhood just didn't like change.

"Your brother talks too much." Rohan's voice was a silky threat.

I stormed over to him. "Leave Ari out of this."

"Or what?" He didn't bother to hide his amusement.

I leaned in, letting my sideboob brush against his arm. "A girl can't give away all her secrets," I purred. My hair teased his shoulder blades. Bad idea. This close, I could smell him, a blend of musky cologne with an underbite of iron that had skyrocketed to being the sexiest scent I'd ever inhaled.

"That a challenge?" He tucked a strand behind my ear, his face tilted up to mine.

I refused to back down, no matter how I longed to brush my tingling skin and capture the sensation for a moment longer. This was all an act, albeit one that got results. Rohan's player ways were the stuff of well-documented legend.

Maybe that's how he killed demons. He hit them with the look and the grin and then, when they fell to their knees in a puddle of feels, ripped their hearts out.

I wasn't going to fall quite so easily. "Nope. Wouldn't want you to tax yourself, Rock Boy."

His jaw tightened. Swinging his leg off the chair, he stood up abruptly, forcing me to scramble back to avoid being clipped on the underside of my chin.

I stared up at his good six inches on my five-foot-eight self.

"Tomorrow. 9AM at the chapter house," he ordered. "Get Ari to drive you if you don't know where it is." Rohan sauntered over to the open window, all lethal elegance. "And Lolita? Don't even think about blowing me off." His smile was ruthless. "Remember, I know where you live."

With that he jumped out the window and into the night.

5

Monday morning, I slammed back two chilled Diet Cokes, my surefire technique for bright-eyed, bushytailedness after a sleepless night. I'd applied a generous smear of fresh aloe under my cloth sports bra, and popped a couple of painkillers in preparation for the day to come. I'd even prepared a demon hunter kit: water bottle, trail mix, aloe fronds, a box of salt, a pen, and an unused Moleskine journal, all thrown into my messenger bag.

Dad drove me. He'd pulled chauffeur duty since I hadn't had the heart to ask Ari. "Nervous?" he asked.

"Nope." I adjusted the A/C vent. Events of the past twenty-four hours had coalesced into a hard ball of pissed off in my chest. "I am going to kick ass and take names."

I adjusted the vent again because I couldn't find the sweet spot of cool air. A stoplight turned yellow, then red in front of us, and I kept fumbling with the A/C. Take three's the charm.

Dad reached over and stilled my hand. "Nava."

"Okay, maybe I'm a bit nervous."

"I think that's a good sign. It means this matters."

No, it means this might be my last day on earth. I gave my dad a weak smile.

The rest of the ride was silent except for his execrable musical choices. Every now and again, I wiped my sweaty palms, hoping Dad wouldn't comment.

My imagination ran riot on what our local Demon Club chapter might look like. I'd gotten as far as a stone fortress with archers on the ramparts and boiling pitch down the walls, all of which would be unleashed at the sight of my estrogen-laden fineness, before I shut that shit down. It was just a house, right?

One of three chapters in Canada, along with Toronto and Montreal, the one here in Vancouver provided training to any initiates and support to any Rasha living or working on a mission in western Canada.

All too soon, we hit Southwest Marine Drive, a street of wide-spaced mansions hidden behind tall hedges and fencing. A few more winding turns later, and Dad pulled up to a half-open, wrought-iron gate set into a high stone fence. A dense press of Evergreens swayed in the distance.

My nerves flared back up into overdrive.

Putting the car in park, he leaned over to press a kiss to my cheek. "Go get 'em, honey."

My hand stilled on the seatbelt release. "How about we grab a mocha first?" Not that I needed any more caffeine.

"Sorry, kiddo. They're waiting."

He pointed out the window at Rohan, now slouching against the fence, his hands jammed into the pockets of his worn yet no doubt expensive jeans. He probably practiced that pose in the mirror, aiming for maximum bicep bulge under his fitted charcoal gray T-shirt.

Rohan raised his eyebrows at me like I was late and needed to hurry up. That tiniest of gestures packed with maximum arrogance. My heart relaxed back down out of my throat, my hands balling into fists as I got out of the car. Bite me, rock star.

I said good-bye to Dad, waving until he'd turned the corner.

Baruch jogged down the driveway to us. His hair floated loose in black waves around his shoulders. It matched his all-black attire of board shorts and a long sleeved tee with DSI printed in small white block letters over his heart.

David Security International was the Brotherhood's public persona. Having an actual company provided a cover for everything from liaising with suppliers to allowing Rasha to answer the question of what they did for a living. Most importantly, it gave them access to high-level places and people that might provide valuable intel for their real business of demon hunting. They'd always had proxies like this. Back in the middle ages it was a knight's order–not the Templars. In Victorian times, they owned gentlemen's clubs. Nowadays, it was an elite security organization.

Eying Baruch, I totally bought him as a top level security expert. Aside from the bare feet. Nice calves, dude.

"Boker tov," I said, punctuating my good morning wishes with a salute. I glanced down at a skittering sound by my feet to find two kitten-sized, fanged spiders with glowing red eyes charging at me.

I bolted past Rohan onto the property, screaming.

Baruch caught me, turning me around. "Look." Despite throwing themselves at the open gate, the spider demons were being repelled, as if bouncing off an invisible rubber shield. "Wards," he explained. "Keeps out anything with even a drop of demon blood."

Feeling braver, but no less disturbed because *big-ass spider demons*, I inched closer. "Kind of stupid to attack Demon Club, especially when they can't get in."

"Araculum aren't known for their brains." Rohan grabbed one of the hairy leggy fuckers in mid-repel, handing it over to Baruch, who pinned it, immobile, in one hand.

I jumped back. "What happened to them not getting through?"

"Of their own accord. We can bring them in just fine." Rohan's lips curled in a small smirk. "They don't like that much."

I pressed in closer to Baruch, who despite holding a demon, seemed like the safer of the two Rasha to hang with right now.

Baruch pointed to the araculum's rows of eyes, currently trained with laser focus on me. "See that?"

"Creepy show and tell time?" I asked.

The araculum growled. A million nails raking down a chalkboard fed through a broken, scratchy windpipe filter, the noise hooked into the base of my spine.

Its friend ramped up its pointless attempt to get through the wards.

Baruch shook the fiend that he held. "Sheket!"

"Bevakasha. Hey!" I sang, finishing off Baruch's "quiet" with a "please." He shook his head at me. "What?" I said. "I went to Jewish camp."

"Araculum store images for later replaying," Baruch said. "Bottom feeders farmed out to gather intel. But what exactly?" he added in a murmur, jamming his thumb into the underside of the demon's neck.

It spasmed, keening.

Expression grim, Baruch jerked the still convulsing creature toward us. A series of images flashed across its rows of eyes as if from a stuttering projector. They were playing too fast for me to make sense of them but Rohan glared at me.

"It met with Asmodeus," he said.

"That's not my fault."

"No, but Asmodeus probably sent them here, scouting for information on who killed his children," Baruch explained.

Rohan shot me a pointed look. "That would be you."

My stomach twisted into knots worthy of any BDSM Dom. I let out a squeaky "eep."

"Ro." Baruch's chastisement was no less effective for his calm tone.

Rohan gave an annoyed sigh.

Baruch punched the demon in the left side of its head. Its eyes widened, briefly, comically, then all light and life faded as the demon disappeared with a pop and a puff of wiry hairs. Baruch brushed his hands off.

I gave him a shaky smile. "Tree Trunk, you're my hero."

Behind me, someone gave a snorting laugh. "Oh my God! I've been trying to place him for three years now. It was less celebrity, more Ent. My bad."

My mouth fell open. The voice belonged to a Japanese guy, probably in his mid-twenties, with spiky hair and a sculpted body. How could I tell? He was only clad in tight black shorts, black combat boots, and a smattering of silver dust across his bare chest. Accessorized with cool nipple rings and a giant coffee cup in one hand that he sipped at. He stepped on the remaining araculum's head without pause as he swaggered onto the property, not even bothering to confirm that he'd killed the demon. Which he had.

"Mtsots li ta-zain," Baruch replied. He pressed his hand to a scanner on the inside of the fence and the gate swung shut.

The new guy made a kissy face at him. "Promises, promises."

"What'd he say?" I asked.

In response he jammed his tongue in his cheek, miming a blow job. Then he mouthed the words "suck my cock."

Ooh. I clapped my hands. "Say it again, slowly so I can learn," I told Baruch.

"Rohan," Baruch said, "kill him and bring her to the Vault."

"That sounds suspiciously like the same thing," I said, watching with dismay as Baruch stalked up the drive.

New guy shrugged. "In your case, they'll still leave a body for the family to claim." He didn't seem particularly upset about his fate. I liked him.

Rohan took my elbow to steer me to this Vault, but I tugged free. "Don't be rude. Introduce me to my new best friend." I turned my back on Rohan in anticipation of the intro, resisting a giggle as I felt him bristle behind me.

"Nava Katz, Kane Hashimoto. Kane, Nava. Our newest Rasha."

While Rohan delivered my credentials in a disgruntled voice, Kane eyed me up and down, took another sip of coffee, and then apparently finding me worthy, held out his hand to be kissed. "Charmed, I'm sure."

I complied with the obligatory respectful pressing of lips to skin then pressed Kane's hand to my heart. "Please tell me you don't have a boyfriend."

Kane ran a hand along his body in show model form. "Like I could limit this prize to one lucky winner."

Oooh. How much would Ari adore me if I set them up? Probably not at all but Kane looked like serious fun. I grinned at him.

"You're nowhere near as uptight as the other twin," Kane said.

I flung an errant strand of hair out of my face, planting my hands on my hips. "You better not be dissing my brother."

"As if I'd waste my time."

"Ari should be the one here," I said, starting my plug to put the rightful Katz child in his chosen place.

A flash of... *guilt? agreement?* crossed Kane's face. "The power has spoken."

I let out a frustrated breath. Stonewalled again.

Rohan tugged on my arm, having reached the end of his limited patience. "Come on, Lolita."

I blew Kane a kiss and skedaddled after broody.

We headed deeper onto the property, walking–or in my case, jogging–past towering Cypress and Arbutus trees dotting a perfectly manicured lawn. I gave a low whistle at the amount of land the Brotherhood owned. "This is like a whole city block."

"Deep pockets." Rohan rounded a corner and a massive 1920's brick manor, flanked by two long, raised beds, their flowers in bud, came into view. It wasn't Windsor castle but it still qualified for mansion status.

Messenger bag pressed to my chest, I craned my neck up to take in the arched doors, beveled bay window in the turret, and multiple chimneys. Impressive, but with nary an archer or vat of boiling pitch in sight. My shoulders relaxed out of my ears. "Gatsby throw a party or two here?"

"Close." Rohan picked up the pace, forcing me to run up the front walk. "The estate was originally built with bootlegger money."

"Where's Rabbi Abrams?" The sooner I could make a strong case for getting Ari *re*-confirmed as an initiate, the better.

"Away for a couple days," Rohan said.

Hmm. Perhaps I could speak with someone at Brotherhood HQ in Jerusalem. I eyed the offices on the ground floor, sussing out if there was a lowly admin assistant I could charm contact info out of, but Rohan twirled his hand at me to move me along.

I marched up the wide front stairs, my determination to put Ari back on his rightful path the only thing keeping me from punching Rohan in the head. Though I knocked into him as I shouldered past into the cathedral ceilinged foyer. I glanced up the wide curving staircase to the second floor but no help appeared from those quarters. Fine. I'd be the perfect newbie Rasha so my new mentors would be more inclined to listen to me.

I hung my bag on the knob of the coat closet door, along with my hoodie, leaving me in my red *Good Morning, I see the assassins have failed* T-shirt.

"Nice to see you dressed for the occasion," Rohan said, tilting his head to check out my ass. "Tap," he read. The word written across my butt on my black sweats. "I don't get it. Is it some kinky promise of backdoor spirits?"

I forced my teeth to unclench. "Tap as in dance, you perv."

His face lit up in unholy glee. "Like Shirley Temple? Please tell me there's video."

There was and I was hot shit in it. I gestured to my outfit. "These are my workout clothes. Since I'm guessing there will be working out involved."

As Rohan marched me through the house, I caught glimpses of bright rooms with wide arched doorways, dazzling crown molding, and intricate inlaid wood flooring "Are all Rasha as crazy good-looking as Kane?" I asked, rubbernecking at the rooms like a tourist. From the decidedly masculine furniture, there was no doubt this was an all-male lair.

"There's a reason we're called the Fallen Angels," Rohan replied.

"Yeah, delusions of grandeur." I scooted past a massive painting of a malevolent demon hurtling toward the fires of Hell. On the table next to it was a small, painted demon statue with an exaggerated grimace and tusks who I'd guess to be of Thai or Indonesian origin. "You named yourselves."

He flashed me a grin. "If the label fits."

"Don't be cocky. It's insufferable."

"Only if you can't pull it off."

Wow.

"Question," I said, curious about how clean and clutter-free the place was. Very weird given the all-alpha atmosphere. "Who takes care of things? 'Cause I'm not doing some Snow White gig where I keep house. I am Rasha. Hear me roar." I thought about it. "Well, crackle."

"We have Ms. Clara for that." Kane had joined us, minus the coffee cup, but not plus any more clothing yet. An elaborate set of black wings was tattooed on his back, their tips licked by flame. A few feathers had fallen, scorched, to the base of his spine. Had he not been gay and already assigned in my mind to my brother, I'd have enjoyed exploring that tattoo. With my tongue.

The heavenly scent of fresh baked chocolate chip cookies broke into my lustful imaginings. "Does she make cookies on a regular basis?" I crossed my fingers behind my back.

"The best," Kane said. "Come on, I'll introduce you."

Yes please. Happy to meet the kindly housekeeper who baked. Ignoring Rohan's growled, "Downstairs in two, or else," I skipped off to the kitchen, envisioning the plump, good-natured granny wearing her white ruffled apron, a tray of cookies in hand, fresh from the oven.

I got the tray part right.

"Ms. Clara, meet Nava."

I put out my hand, my smile freezing in place as the five-foot-nothing woman at the stove faced me. Yes, with the envisioned tray of cookies but could I have been more wrong about the rest? For starters, the only plump thing about this chick were her boobs, which strained against her buttery yellow wrap dress.

She plunked the tray on top of the stove.

I dropped my hand along with the lower half of my jaw. Ms. Clara was stunning. Late-twenties, tops, she was also like a giant—*sorry*—mini ball of sunshine from her golden sun-kissed skin to her blonde curls and blue eyes.

"Another girl." She beamed at me, her voice breathy, as she tossed the oven mitt on the counter. "Finally."

"Nice to meet you, Clara," I said.

"Ms. Clara," she snapped in a voice so stern that I flinched, standing at attention.

She giggled. "Oops."

"Ms. Clara secretly moonlights as one of Vancouver's top dominatrixes," Kane informed me. He stared at her in open adoration. "She's so badass."

I was supposed to be the lone badass girl in this place. It was the one thing I had going for me here. She was supposed to be the old caretaker they adored like a nanny. "Sorry," I said, smoothing out my T-shirt. "Nice to meet you, Ms. Clara."

"Have a cookie, doll." She held out a plate of perfectly formed, perfectly warm, and perfectly melty chocolate chip cookies. Perfect seemed to be a theme with her.

"Thanks." I bit into it and moaned. "Oh. My. God."

"A sound many a man and woman has made in Ms. Clara's presence," Rohan said, coming into the kitchen. He rounded on me with a mouthed "Or else."

I took another bite.

"Rohan!" Ms. Clara was at least a foot shorter than Rohan, but when she caught him up in a hug, it was he who stumbled, her lean but toned arms pulling him down to her height. "I'd heard you were coming. How long are you back for?"

"Who knows? With this one?" He jerked his thumb at me. "You may be stuck with me forever."

"He's terrible," Ms. Clara said to me, with an affectionate shake of the head.

"With worse depths revealed every moment," I agreed, savagely taking another bite.

He shot me a wolfish grin. "Duty calls." He gripped the back of my T-shirt and gave a sharp tug to get me moving.

I stood there, finishing my cookie.

"Don't let them bully you," she said. "And make sure they let you come up for lunch. I make a great iced tea with plenty of electrolytes." She winked at me. "Plus, I'd be happy to give you some whip usage tips."

"Damn. I'm going to like you, aren't I?" I felt retroactively bad for feeling like I had to compete against her. I popped the rest of the cookie in my mouth, taking a moment to savor the joy dissolving on my tongue. "If only for more mouthgasms on a regular basis."

"Aww, smutty." She patted my cheek. "We're going to get along just fine."

Rohan groaned. "That's all we need." He led me from the room.

I tried to wriggle away from him but he kept his hand hot and steady on my coccyx. Fuck, he was turning my innocent body part into a dirty erogenous zone. "I can walk without assistance," I said. "Upright and everything."

"I'm checking to see if you go where I put you."

"First into the line of fire?"

"You're smarter than the average bear, aren't you?" He poked me in the back to steer me down two flights of narrow stairs, past the ground floor offices, and into a basement. Even though the basement walls consisted of solid concrete blocks painted a bright white, the ceilings were still a good nine feet high, with wide, well-lit hallways. It wouldn't surprise me if there were secret tunnels that they'd carted booze through back during Prohibition.

"Why'd someone choose the name the Fallen Angels? You're not something that goes bump in the night."

"We're powerful beings fighting for good in the shadows." Rohan stopped so abruptly before a thick iron door that I whacked into him. I stepped back, rubbing my nose while he placed his hand on a pad mounted beside the door to be scanned.

"Again, that's my point. Fighting for good. Not fallen."

"Everything falls eventually, Lolita, it's all just a matter of when gravity kicks in. Either way, we're the badass chosen ones wrapped in a really hot package." He tugged on one of my curls. "Time to prove you're one of us."

"One of us" as in chosen? Or did I get badass and hot status, too?

The door unlatched with a click.

"Welcome to the Vault." Rohan's eyes lit up with an evil glint, then he pushed me inside the all-consuming darkness and slammed the door.

6

I froze, straining my eyes seeking out the demons that I was positive they had stashed in here with me.

After a moment, Rohan opened the door again. "Kidding."

He flicked on the light to reveal a vast, well-lit studio. The ceilings and walls were the same concrete blocks as the hallway, but the floor was wall-to-wall blue padding. There were no windows.

"You're a dick," I told him.

He glanced down at his crotch. "It *is* legendary, but it doesn't fully define me."

"My God," I muttered. Noting Rohan's bare feet on the pads, I toed out of my shoes, stacking them beside the door. "Why is this called the Vault?" If there were valuables they were well hidden because there was nothing to see. Not even a punching bag.

"It's the most secure room."

I rolled out my shoulders. "Now what?"

"Training," Baruch said, entering.

"Shalom, Sensei Tree Trunk," I said, bowing with my hands together in Namaste position. "What's first? Weapons?" I could totally rock a weapon.

Baruch and Rohan exchanged glances. "Absolutely not," they said in unison.

Baruch's fist whipped out and bopped me on the nose.

"What the hell, dude?" I prodded for broken cartilage and blood but it had been more of a tap for shock effect than to do any damage. I was surprised, but otherwise fine.

"Demon tag. Now you're dead," Rohan said.

Baruch kicked out, swiping my legs out from underneath me.

I landed hard on my back. My hands flew up to cover my face as Baruch dove down, grabbing me lightly by the throat.

"Dead." Rohan yawned.

Baruch helped me up.

"I wasn't ready–"

Baruch mimed ripping out my heart.

Rohan smirked. "And dead. Getting the idea?"

I turned my back to him, refusing to let him taunt me. "Baruch, please tell me what I did wrong so that I do not repeat the experience. Since I refuse to give Emo Snowflake the satisfaction of dying."

The nickname earned me a sharp jab in my back.

The side of Baruch's mouth kicked up in the tiniest of grins but his voice was serious when he spoke to me. "You did not access your power. Your first instinct right now is to scream and run, like you did with the araculum." He pinned me with the weight of his shrewd blue gaze. "You'll be dead by nightfall unless you access your power at the first prickling of trouble."

"Got it. But the power seems to show up on its own."

"Your magic wants to be used," Baruch explained. "If it's not the first thing you fire up, you won't live long enough to use it. Activate it. Get in, kill, and get out with as little physical contact as possible. Run if you have to."

I shook out my arms and legs. "How do I access it?"

"How do you spit?" He waved off my grimace. "I'm serious. You spit saliva. You spit electricity. Both come from inside you. What do you do when you want to spit?"

I braced for some snarky comment from Rohan but he watched Baruch with a fascinated expression. "Okay, well." I took myself through the motions. "First, I tense up my jaw. To activate the saliva."

"Good. Then what's the power equivalent of that action? Close your eyes. Visualize. Where is your power?"

I did as I was told, eyes closed. "It's like there's a switch."

"Touch the spot." That was Rohan in a silky rumble, who now stood beside me. "Where do you envision it?"

Oh, Lordy. What I was actually envisioning right now? Very different from what Rohan intended. My eyes snapped open and I pushed him back. He didn't go anywhere so I stepped away from him. "Begone, irritant."

The look he shot me from under his eyelashes, full of wicked heat, made my mouth flood with saliva. I swallowed hard.

Baruch tsked at him. "Stop toying with her."

"I'm not toying. I'm deliberately distracting. Seeing if she can multitask." He smiled innocently at me. "I can't help it if she finds me irresistible."

"Oh, I find you something, all right," I growled, my hands out to throttle him. My fingertips sparked.

"Freeze," Rohan commanded in a steely voice.

"Anger," Baruch said. "Not fear. That's what turns you on."

Rohan barked a laugh, smoothing out his expression at Baruch's pointed stare.

I twisted my hands one way then the other, now glowing and crackling away. "So I just need to internalize you as my trigger?" I asked Rohan.

He batted his lashes at me. "Do what you need to, baby."

"Baruch?" I pleaded.

Baruch pointed to the door. "Go."

Rohan was undeterred. "You can't send me away."

Baruch quirked an eyebrow.

"Fine. I'm leaving. You're welcome," Rohan called out to me over his shoulder.

"Can you turn it off?" Baruch grasped my wrist, twisting my hand from side-to-side.

I closed my eyes, thinking about the switch inside me. I located it slightly down and to the back of my belly button, imagining it rooted there, with invisible cables snaking out to all parts of my body and the bright white switch set to on. Mentally, I flicked it the other way. Off.

I opened my eyes. My hands still crackled.

"They dimmed for a second," Baruch said. "Tell me what you know about demons."

"Nothing. Ari told me nothing." My words came out in a rush.

His expression gentled. "He won't be in trouble. I just want to know what information you already have."

I lowered my hands. "Okay, well–"

"Did I say stop your visualization?" he barked. "Do you think you'll be encountering demons with no distractions? Nothing else demanding your attention? Talk and train."

I made a snarky face–okay, imagined it–but in my head, man, did I put Tree Trunk in his place. I closed my eyes, picturing my power switch. "There are different levels of demons. Some work on a more global scale either in the shadows or more overtly to bring about civil unrest or world wars."

I tugged on my mental switch. I got the barest hold on it and it vibrated but didn't flick off. My magic continued to thrum through me. "Hey, how did Vancouver land a spot?"

"This chapter is the Canadian HQ. The fault lines along the west coast draws demons because they like the seismic activity. A naturally occurring instability."

"That's the heart of it, isn't it?" I asked, opening my eyes. "Instability. Natural, political, or emotional, demons thrive in those environments."

Baruch blinked proudly at me for making the connection. For half a second. "Again."

I threw all my mental power against the switch. "Some create more localized disasters, collapsing bridges or making sure levees fail." I had my suspicions about New Orleans. "Then they rush in to exploit an already vulnerable population. Same with areas hit by earthquakes or famine or flood. They feed off the chaos and pain."

My switch bucked to the halfway point, then crashed back to the "on" position. A sharp crack resounded through my hands. I shook them out.

"Again."

"Demons are also drawn to big cities. Tons of humans easily tempted. The New York chapter house has at least a dozen hunters stationed there at any given time."

I kept at my envisioned on/off switch. It took a while. A long while, but eventually, through sheer mind power, I made the electricity in my hands turn on and off at will.

"Mazel tov," Baruch congratulated me.

I jumped over to him like a little kid and hugged him. "That. Was. So. Cool!" It reminded me of when my balance and movement had come together and I'd done my first perfect shuffle in tap, instead of the clunky, wobbly steps up to that point. The moment when it all just clicked.

I was super proud of myself. Sweaty, metallic-smelling, and tomorrow I'd probably hurt like crazy, but proud. I'd done it. I could access my power at will. Even if this was a baby step, I'd mastered it. I wasn't sure anyone had thought I'd even get this far.

I wasn't sure I had.

Staying alive and being an asset. Yay me.

Baruch disengaged. "Now we work on firing up the rest. It might require a kick or even a head-butt to hit the kill spot and you want your power coming out of all of you."

Rohan popped back in. "How's she doing?"

I held up a fist. "The sisterhood for the win."

A paragon of blond-haired, green-eyed perfection stepped into the doorway. His loose, light brown linen pants and shirt really complimented his dark scowl. "As if a girl could become one of us," he spat in a super sexy Italian accent.

"One did, so suck it up, honey." I managed to give him the finger and waggle my Rasha ring at him, which was very talented of me, if I did say so myself.

Out in the hallway, Kane snickered.

Hot Angry Dude stalked toward me.

"Drio–" Rohan was cut off as Drio shouldered past him.

Baruch sighed and stepped into his path. Drio was a beautiful racehorse. Baruch was a bull.

"You said no one knew what to do with her. That that was why we got abruptly reassigned, with me and Ro on guard duty at the expense of our own mission. Remember?" Drio didn't back down, even with Baruch blocking his way. It was quite the commitment to hating me. "Can you say you're happy about it?" he asked Baruch.

"They reassigned people to me?"

"What did you think would happen, principessa?" he sneered. "That we wouldn't give you extra special treatment?"

I shoved myself between Tree Trunk and him. I could fight my own damn battles, thank you very much. "Newsflash, jerkwad, no one has told me jack. Believe it or not, I want to be part of your 'no girls allowed' club even less than you want me here. But you can't keep me in the dark." I whirled to Rohan. "You have to tell me important stuff."

"The Executive hasn't decided how they feel about you," Rohan answered, not bothering to soften that information. "As the first female Rasha, you're either a dream secret weapon or–"

"A walking nightmare," Drio cut in.

Rohan raised his eyebrows at him like "really?"

"With the deciding factor being what?" I asked.

Drio clicked his tongue. "Your performance. Supposedly your early death would be a bad thing."

"Wow," I said, "don't I feel precious?"

"You," Rohan said to Drio, "stop antagonizing. And you," he turned to me, "don't think I'm thrilled to babysit your ass."

"Why you?" I demanded.

"Because I'm such a people person."

"Or because you're a screw up?" I scratched my chin with the edge of my thumbnail. "Is that it? Did I get exiled to the island of misfit toys?"

Drio's hands balled into fists.

"Enough." Kane's voice cut smoothly through the tension. He pushed me back a few steps. "A little gratitude here," he said, with a tap to the end of my nose. "You've been given the best of the best. Baruch has put his brilliant military mind to use creating weapons and training Rasha to become even more effective. Rohan and Drio," Kane placed a hand on Angry's shoulder, "are two of our top intelligence officers and analysts on demon behavior. Thanks to them, we've unearthed and taken down a lot of demons living among us in positions of enormous power."

I cocked my head. "And you?"

He shrugged. "I'm just the lone Vancouver member who wasn't re-assigned."

Drio laughed. "Kane's nickname is the Kiss of the Death. He's one of the top Rasha in demon kills." His fond amusement morphed into an ugly leer. "We are the best. And you're the bright shiny trophy the entire demon world will want to bag. Be grateful or we won't keep you alive."

I rubbed my skin as if to wash his disgusting look off. "Never in a million years."

Drio shrugged, exiting with a tossed-out, "If the demons do get you, you won't be missed."

I flinched.

White spots of rage appeared on Rohan's cheeks. His eyes darkened to volcanic fire. He didn't say a word. Just sped from the room.

"Oh no," Kane said. He and Baruch raced after him, with me bringing up the rear.

We caught up in time to see Rohan leap from midway up the second flight of stairs onto Drio, tackling him. They crashed onto the main floor landing.

Drio managed to flip onto his back, but that merely allowed Rohan to pin him between his thighs.

Rohan pulled his left arm back. I tensed, waiting for his hand to curl into a fist and Drio's nose to be shattered. Instead, five short, wickedly sharp looking blades snicked out of Rohan's fingertips, with one long blade running up the entire outer edge of his arm. Like an outline. That longer blade slashed right through the center of the heart tattoo on his bicep.

Holy. Fuck.

"Finally decide to kill me?" I couldn't tell if Drio sounded anxious or hopeful.

I stared wide-eyed at the two of them. Not even daring to breathe. There was a powder keg of unspoken issues between them, and I was scared I was the fuse that could blow it all sky high. I didn't like Drio but I didn't want his death on my conscience.

Necessarily.

With a blur of motion, Rohan swiped.

Drio flinched, eyes closed, but Rohan jammed the blades into the ground beside his head.

"The demons will be after her," Rohan said, in a low rumble. "Which means we stick close and protect her. With. Our. Lives." He sounded oddly bleak about the concept. "Got it?"

Drio pushed Rohan off him. He gave a mocking salute. "Got it." With one last baleful look my way, he jumped to his feet and blazed off.

Rohan yanked his finger blades from the floor, leaving two inch gauges in the pretty planking. He shot an unreadable look after Drio before storming off in the opposite direction.

That left Baruch, Kane, and me standing there. "What was that about?" I asked.

Baruch was Mr. Impassive, which was no great surprise, but based on my short acquaintance with Kane, I was sure he'd give up the goods. Nope. He remained infuriatingly tight-lipped as well, simply saying, "I'll check on Drio."

Baruch shook his head when I glanced in the direction Rohan had taken. "Let him cool down," he said, before following Kane.

I never was any good at doing what I was told.

7

I found Rohan in the library, one of those massive floor-to-ceiling, wall-to-wall, book-filled rooms found only in Victorian mansions and Hollywood movies. It even had rolling ladders to reach high shelves, Persian carpets on the floor, and comfortable seating to curl up in. A long wood table with sturdy chairs ran along the bank of windows on the far side of the room.

I sank onto the leather club chair, a match to Rohan's that was grouped next to a large unlit fireplace, sneaking glances to gauge his mood. Tough to do since he was slumped on the sofa next to me, head bowed.

Neither of us said anything for a good long while.

I sniffed my T-shirt to make sure I didn't smell too disgusting. Not bad. Casting around for something else to do, I studied the pile of history texts left on the low mahogany coffee table, then got bored and just watched Rohan, waiting for his hands to unclench from the padded arm rest before I spoke.

"Why'd you quit singing?"

His head jerked up. "What?"

"It was around the time when you became Rasha, and maybe touring or being in the band might have been tough, but you could have kept singing. Writing music. You left the biz entirely."

"Yup," he replied in a "leave it alone" voice.

I'd only raised the topic trying to forge some kind of connection between us. I'd had my dancing, he'd had his singing, and I'd thought maybe there'd be some common ground we could bond over. After meeting Drio, having Rohan on my side was imperative. But his reticence made me actively curious.

"Was it a vocal chord thing? Did potential permanent damage end it?" In about three seconds, I wove an entire tale of the doors closing on Rohan's musical dreams, finishing up with him staring up at his doctor with impossibly sad eyes and asking à la Oliver Twist, "Please sir, may I sing another?"

Rohan glared at me.

"All right. Sheesh." I slouched back against my chair. "I'm sorry you got stuck with me," I said in a sincere voice. "I'll try not to die on your watch."

"Drio was right. You're the shiny prize. The demons are going to want bragging rights of killing the first female Rasha. And your head. They'll want that too."

"So they re-assigned you boys here to keep it attached to my body. Was this a demotion for you?"

"You'd think so."

I stopped fidgeting and met his eyes. Unimpressed. "Gee, thanks."

Rohan nudged my knee with his. "No. Until consensus among the Executive is reached on your status, they want the best around you."

I tried to ignore my queasiness at what would happen if consensus wasn't reached in my favor. Also, the tingle running up my leg from his touch.

"I appreciate it." I hoped I sounded suitably grateful. These guys were right about needing them to keep me safe and help me find my footing, especially if Asmodeus figured out it was me who'd offed his spawn. Much as I wished this would go away, I was a Rasha until death do us part.

"What happens if the Brotherhood decides they don't want a sister after all?"

Rohan took his sweet time answering. "I think if push came to shove, they'd decommission you."

My stomach squicked. "Is that a euphemism for 'bullet to the head?'"

Another long pause. Seriously? I drowned my apprehension in a tidal wave of positive sentiment but my apprehension broke free and bobbed to the surface, shooting me the finger for my efforts.

"Not murder," he finally said. "You already have too public a profile within the Brotherhood."

"Knowing I'm only going to stay alive because they might get caught is hardly reassuring." I grimaced. "What about a timely unfortunate accident? I mean, Rasha die."

"They'd try to quietly retire you. Alive," he reassured me.

"Would that be so bad?" I sat up, intrigued. "Hey, could we transfer my powers to Ari?"

Exasperation on his face, Rohan got up.

I grabbed the side of his jeans, his quad muscle tensing under my palm as I pushed him back onto the couch. "Fine. Maybe it doesn't work that way. But I refuse to believe that simply re-running the ceremony was the final proof that I'm the sole Rasha twin. Ari is still an initiate and I'm going to prove it."

"Good luck with that."

"I'll train hard. In return," I continued, "you help me petition the Executive on Ari's behalf."

"Me? No. Not interested in getting involved."

Why were all of them so block-headed about helping me with this? "You don't want to be here. The faster I get up to speed, the faster you get to go home."

"I have a mission here other than you, you know."

"Yeah, but if you're as good as Kane says you are, then I bet you'll wrap that up soon. Come on, what could it hurt to try? At best, Demon Club gets the Rasha it wanted. At worst, my training schedule is accelerated and you go on your merry way. Deal?" I held out my hand to shake.

"No deal. I wrap up the primary mission, and I'll be on my merry way regardless. There's enough other people to watch you."

I leaned back, arms crossed. "Then let's negotiate." I'd spent a lifetime listening to my lawyer father.

"You've got nothing of value to offer me," Rohan said.

"What's the mission?" What if I could help Rohan complete this mission his way?

"Look, the gig that brought me to Vancouver is..." Rohan rubbed his hand roughly through his hair, sending it into spiky disarray. "I'm getting a lot of pressure to take it in a direction I don't agree with. Got enough of my own shit to deal with as far as the Executive is concerned. You're on your own."

"Now you've got me curious. What's up?"

Rohan hesitated.

I raised my hands. "If I haven't earned need-to-know clearance yet, I get it."

"It's not that. You'll freak out."

I picked up a pen left on top of the book pile and chucked it at him.

He caught it one-handed, studying me a moment, tapping the pen against his thigh.

I tried not to stare, my fingers twitching at the memory of his steely hard muscles. Or replace the pen with my tongue.

"First off, you understand now that you're bound by all Rasha oaths of secrecy not to discuss what you've heard." He shot me a wry look. "That includes not telling your brother."

I totally met his eyes when I agreed but he stared me down until I squirmed. "All right, already," I groused. "I won't dish."

"We suspect Samson King is a demon."

Rohan winced as I smacked his arm.

"No way! He's a celeb A-lister. I mean, yeah, he's got that smug rich kid vibe, even though he's got to be pushing thirty, but I figured someone that famous was just another overcompensating," I wagged my pinky meaningfully, "asshole celeb."

Rohan leaned in, his elbows braced on his knees, and a serious expression on his face. "I'm concerned about your fetish for the peen, Lolita. Do we need to have a talk?"

"Curiosity about celebrity genitalia is hardly fetish. It's practically hardwired into Western society's DNA."

"Hence, the race to the bottom," he muttered.

"Besides, I bet you fifty bucks there's more than a few sites devoted to your particular width and girth, Mr. Mitra."

"All of which would be staggeringly wrong."

The twin desires to both smack the smug off his face and rip off his pants to see for myself should have negated each other and yet, there they were. "Seriously, his stupid reality show *Live like a King* hits douchebag territory, but a demon?"

Rohan spread his fingers three inches apart. "Our dossier on him is already that thick." His hand clenched into a fist. "Trouble is, everything is circumstantial. Rumors and speculation. We don't have the hard proof such as his name or true form that would allow me to sanction the kill."

"Yet."

His eyes crinkled at the corners. "Yet. The seven deadly sins are mother's milk to demons and that show? It's the ultimate in envy with those humiliating challenges contestants do to be part of King's entourage."

"It's almost worse that he's not around to witness most of it," I said. "He just drops in with the occasional visit, a cocky smile, and a joke, and contestants redouble their efforts to take each other out and get near him."

"He incites jealousy, even though on the surface it seems like he's inviting people along for the ride. In fact, if you deconstruct it, most of his brand is devoted to making people feel bad about themselves."

"By reminding them they're not him." I nodded. "He has that other reality show too, all about his limitless wealth and partying and he's always living large in his movies. The ultimate good-time dude and people love it. Love *him*."

"That's the problem." Rohan braced one foot on the coffee table. "His public persona is funny and charming. He's smart. Comes off as the guy most likely to buy a round, fly everyone to Vegas for a night out. No scandals, no rumors of deviant behavior. He's a huge star with a huge social media presence–a huge reach–and that makes him very dangerous." He stretched an arm out along the top of the sofa. "His brand has an adverse affect on people that's way out of line with other celebs. More than people jealous or bummed out that they don't get to live his lifestyle."

"Like what? People quitting this cruel world because they don't get to be him?" Had I known being Rasha meant getting all up in stars' dirty business, I'd have signed up years ago.

"Yeah. After *Live like a King* aired, Drio and I started tracking down everyone affiliated with the show. A lot of contestants and crew had died." He danced the pen over his knuckles as he spoke. "They all seemed like accidents: motorcycle crash, OD, that kind of thing, but given the mental state of the people, we believe they were suicides." He white-knuckled the pen. "Then there was the disaster at *Kingdom Come*."

Talk about a nightmare. Samson had invited a bunch of his rock star and hip hop friends to a concert in the desert. A couple hundred thousand people packed in all day with insufficient water and for the grand finale, when King himself took the stage for his singing debut, some scaffolding collapsed. Between that carnage and sunstroked dehydration, hundreds were left dead and wounded. And still people fell all over themselves to defend him and his shitty concert.

"Was the collapse deliberate?" I tugged the pen out of his hand because he was about to pulverize the poor thing. Had Rohan known any of the performers that had died?

He looked down in surprise, as if he'd forgotten he'd had the writing utensil in the first place. "We have questions about the mindset of the rigger in charge. He'd been tight with Samson. If King is feeding off the pain and misery he causes, he's gaining incredible power, but to what end?"

I made a *pffft* noise. "World domination. You're welcome."

He failed to look impressed. "No shit. But how? What's his final move and is there a specific trigger for it? Another disaster like *Kingdom Come* but on a bigger scale? Something else entirely? What's the timeline?" Rohan blew out his cheeks in frustration. "That's what we have yet to determine. It would help if we could figure out what type of demon he is. We need to crack someone in his inner circle, get in close to monitor him, but we've had no luck gaining entry."

"So what's causing the dissenting plans of attack?"

"Doesn't matter," Rohan said.

Nice blow off but I wasn't that easily dissuaded. "You ended up here in Vancouver why?" I asked.

"King is shooting a movie and–"

"*Hard Knock Strife!*" I bolted upright in my seat.

Rohan ducked as the pen shattered in *my* grip, sending plastic shards flying.

"Josh, the lust demon that I–" I shot Rohan a warning look as I tossed pen remnants on the table. "Anyway, he'd been cast in that movie. I didn't realize it was King's." I gnawed on my bottom lip. "How many of the other actors in the gang are demons? Samson is smart enough to cover his tracks. But what about the others? Josh didn't strike me as the sharpest tool in the shed. Has King worked with other demons before?"

Rohan studied me with a coolly assessing look. "That's a good idea."

"Yeah, I get them when the moon lines up with Uranus."

He didn't appreciate my wit. "Except we already checked that avenue out. There was one demon that King worked with on a regular basis but my buddy Eyal took him out in Boston a couple of months ago. Probably how your boy Josh got the part."

Rohan must have seen how bummed I was that I hadn't provided the golden nugget needed to get close to Samson, because he added, "You're off to a good start. Eventually, you'll become a good fighter, too."

"I have no idea how I specifically killed either Josh or his sister and I'm not thrilled about having to trial and error my way to survive every demon encounter."

"Then learn about as many demons as possible and where their weak spot is located. That will keep you alive as much as your magic." Rohan got up and walked over to one of the neatly arranged shelves where he extracted a thin, red, leather-bound book. He flipped through it. "All demons of the same type, say, all araculum, have the same weak spot," he explained. "It gets trickier with the Uniques, the one-off demons like Lady Midday. In those cases we don't have the multiple kills that have taught us where to aim for. Though if we've had a few encounters, then sometimes we've figured out the location for when we finally get close enough to make the kill."

Rohan brought the open book over to me. He nudged my elbow away to perch on the arm of my chair, shoving the book under my nose.

I read the passage he pointed to. "Okay, this weak spot can be located anywhere in a demon's body, ranging from the bottom of their foot to behind their eyes." I scanned the rest of the page. "You know, I always thought that the way to kill a demon was through its heart."

Rohan snorted. "What do you think a heart is?"

I twisted about half an inch to better face him. My arm skimmed his thigh, his muscles clenching in response. I could do this call and answer with his body part all day. "Does this weak spot have a name?" I asked.

He shifted his weight, his hip resting against my shoulder. "I told you, the heart."

The words blurred meaninglessly on the page. I felt like I was back in ninth grade at the movie theater with Adam Kim, so focused on the minutiae of movements between our bodies that the entire screen had been a giant white blob.

My chest brushed his forearm. I was more than a bit curious if all this touching was a coincidence on his part or more of some endless game we seemed to be playing. "You aren't being metaphoric, then."

"It's true on many levels."

I ran my finger over the heart tattoo on his left bicep. "What baggage-laden break up led to this visual reminder, hmmm?"

"Focus." His breath tickled the back of my neck as he leaned over me.

Dilemma. I was torn between prolonging any part of Rohan touching any part of me and giving in to being a curious kitten. I raised my eyes to his, unable to resist asking. "Come on, who was she?"

Rohan stood up abruptly, snapping the book shut.

Stupid curiosity.

"You can't be buried in a Jewish cemetery," I said, trying a different tack. "Not with tattoos."

That got me a wry smile. "What gives you the impression I think there will be anything left of me to bury?"

Wow. These dudes were grim.

"How am I supposed to know which demon has which weak spot?"

Rohan replaced the book, waving a hand around the library. "You learn."

Sure, Ari had shared some details of demons and hunting with me, but taking in the plethora of books now, I had a long way to go to even learn the basics. I sighed in resignation. "Where's my Giles?"

Rohan stared blankly at me.

"You know," I said, "the stuffy-yet-caring resident librarian mentor who provides helpful and timely info on a demon-by-demon basis?"

"There's no librarian." Rohan tapped his head. "You are your own librarian."

Great. Initiates got a lifetime of mentoring in demonology but I was told to independent study my way through. "Right."

I trolled the shelves, running my finger along the spines. Most of the books featured the same publisher's imprint on their spine: the letters BD in white against a black square background. Made sense that the Brotherhood printed their material in-house. "How about a podcast?"

"No."

"Cheat sheet?"

Rohan gave a slow, disbelieving shake of his head. "It's called reading. Your commitment to apathy is impressive."

I moved to the next bookshelf, tossing him a smile over my shoulder. "Why, Mr. Mitra, you say the sweetest things."

In the window's reflection, I caught Rohan massaging his temples. Taunting him was fun, however..."You're wrong about my impressive commitment," I said, turning to face him. "It's not to apathy. You've had your entire life to learn this stuff. I'm not against reading. I'm against the amount of time I'd need to get up to speed. Time which, if demons are gunning for me? I don't have."

"Cheat sheets." He looked glum.

"Twelve point Helvetica is fine. Start with the main bad guys, ranking from domain down through species. Or a *Demons for Dummies* book. With lots of pictures. That works too."

He brightened. "We have that." He jogged over to a far corner of the library.

I stared in amazement as he pulled out a fat primer entitled *Most Common Demons* and presented it to me. "That's a kids' book," I said, frowning at the bright cover.

"Yup." Rohan shoved it into my chest. I caught it with an unhappy thump. "None of our initiates are dummies," he said, "but I'm guessing even you can keep up with a seven-year-old's reading comprehension." He patted my head.

Did people have weak spots? Or could I just aim for the actual heart with humans? I eyed Rohan, sizing him up.

Kane strolled into the library with a pile of books, whistling when he saw what I held. Seriously, did this guy ever wear proper clothes? "*Hel-lo* nightmares for days." He dumped his books on a table, snatched mine out of my hands, and flipped through it. "This sucker frightened me out of my wits."

I peered at the illustration. "It looks like an evil Teenage Mutant Ninja Turtle."

His eyes lit up. "Exactly! It's a kappa demon from Japan. I lived in terror of it coming after me."

"Why? Some kind of connection to your heritage?"

He stared at me like I was stupid. "It sucks your entrails out through the ass. Do you know how scary that was to a chubby gay kid?" He gave an exaggerated shudder, handing the book back to me.

"I look forward to finding my own personal nightmare," I said.

Speaking of Rohan, he rolled his eyes but before he could say anything, there was an unsettling high-pitched whistle from the woods out back.

Kane peered out the window. "Demon."

I hugged the book to my chest. "Asmodeus?"

"Nope. That was the cry of the curupira." Kane shot me an odd look. "Why would you think that?"

I sank into a chair, weak-kneed in relief. "You better go kill it."

"Wrong pronoun, Lolita." Rohan tugged me to my feet. "Show time."

8

When my protests of "I've only been training for a couple of hours," and "you should never meet a demon on an empty stomach," failed to work, I went for Plan B and dug my heels into the grass in the backyard like a little kid.

Rohan hauled me over his shoulder in a fireman's carry, ignoring all my pummeling until he'd stepped through a heavy iron door set into the back fence, at which point he dumped me on the ground.

Outside the wards.

I scrambled to my feet.

Rohan whistled some bird call and a moment later Baruch jogged out of the trees, a bruise blossoming on his cheekbone. He nodded when he saw me. "Good. Now you can show us what you did with the brother."

"Huh?"

As if choreographed, he and Rohan stepped in sync to one side, right as a demon charged me with a chilling growl. Unlike the araculum, this demon was humanoid. Ish. About the height of your standard NBA player, his red eyes burned like glowing coals. Jagged fangs protruded from his fleshy lips and a matted black pelt covered his torso, but the most terrifying thing about him was his enormous cock. It jutted out erect, a non-bobbing zucchini of such knobby rigidity that I wouldn't have been surprised if he swatted Mack trucks out of his path with it.

This time when I ran screaming, hopping tree roots, and stirring up piles of damp, decomposing leaves, I shot off wild blasts of electricity. My training had really taken.

"I wouldn't," Rohan called out. "He'll just see you as prey."

"Do what you did to the brother," Baruch ordered.

I glanced over my shoulder at Penisaurus Rex. Hell, no. Having run in a wide circle back to my starting point, I beelined for Tree Trunk, determined to hide behind him. Yeah, right. As soon as I got within arm's range, Baruch pushed me back into the demon's path.

The evil spawn scooped me up from behind and squeezed. Not the boobs! I gritted my teeth against the pain flaring in my sensitive flesh and yanked my knees up to my chest, grateful for my years of tap training and core strength because no way were my parents going to identify my body while impaled on his member.

Pain quickly became my secondary concern. The pressure on my rib cage soon hurtled toward total pulverization. I couldn't access my magic, couldn't do anything except be crushed to death. At least I'd have a lovely soundtrack of gaily twittering birds to accompany my death throes.

Keeping me imprisoned with one arm, the curupira scrabbled the fingers of his other hand against my skull, as if trying to pierce the skin.

"He's going to suck your brains out like a lobster claw," Rohan said in a conversational tone.

I jerked my head sideways, trying to escape the demon's sharp fingernail now seeking the right spot to drill down into my head, and was rewarded with a sapling thwack to the cheek.

"Show me how you killed Asmodeus' bastard," Baruch said. "When it was just you and him. You've got the power. Use it."

Any second now, I'd black out and become lunch. I clawed at the demon's arms, desperate to loosen his hold so I could inhale, but there was no shaking him loose.

Assholes one and two did nothing.

My body burned. With rage. A scream tore from my throat as I fired up. The current arcing off my fingertips was a sharp agony. The air stank of burning hair. The demon's chest, my head.

Visualizing, I slammed my switch on, letting it pulsate with electricity. I imagined it racing through my veins, my very blood alight. My entire body glowed blue, a violent crackle filling my ears.

I slammed my hand onto the demon's thigh. Hang on. His thigh should have been too big for my hand to curve around.

Damnation, not again! I ripped my hand off his dick and planted it on his hip.

The demon flinched enough to drop me but he didn't die. I hit the ground in a sprawl, brushing dirt from my eyes, my shin cracking against the edge of a small boulder. "Fuck," I gasped, gulping down blessed lungfuls of air.

Sparks flew off me, one catching fire on the edge of a dry, rotting log. Out of the corner of my eye, I saw Rohan spring into action, smothering the wood with wet leaves.

I was more pre-occupied by the fact that even though the demon stood in front of me, I was looking at his heels and not his toes. I didn't have time to ponder the mystery because he grabbed my hair, yanking a good handful out in my subsequent roll away.

I jumped up. Tiny sparks crunched between the soles of my feet and the dirt, tickling in an itchy sensation.

The demon lunged for me on what I now saw were his backwards feet.

Dancing and bobbing, careful not to trip on the uneven ground, I focused on not being grabbed, because I had no clue how to fight this thing. The only thing that came to mind was Sandra Bullock's self-defense demo in one of my favorite movies *Miss Congeniality*. S.I.N.G.

I didn't think I could get in close enough to do any damage to his solar plexus but maybe his instep was a possibility. Take him down via his freaky tootsies. I dove onto the ground, rolling to grab his ankle. Once I had a firm grasp, I fired my current into him.

A furious howl tore from his throat and he kicked out, trying to buck me off, but I held strong, so he picked me up by my ankles, facing outward. The forest swung upside down with a sickening blur.

I slid my zapping hands up his sandpapery calves, trying to get a hold on him to break free. Sadly, my attack provoked more than pained him. Still holding me by my ankles, he shook me violently, his bulbous knob poking me in the small of my back. Beyond gross. Trying not to touch it, I shot my magic behind me in what I hoped was the right direction. There was a sizzling sound, like franks on a grill. Though given that his dick fell to the ground wizened and black, his wiener did not plump when you cooked it.

The demon roared, shaking me hard enough to rattle my teeth.

Using what little stamina I had left, I rocked myself backward, getting a firmer grip on his legs. I pretty much pawed him all over, and while my magic had to hurt, my situation seemed pointless until I grabbed and squeezed the demon's kneecap.

The sweet spot.

The creature was engulfed in current. He dropped me on my back with a hard *thunk*, as he exploded into red dust. White and blue spots danced before my eyes.

I lay there a moment, letting the tree canopy come into focus before sitting up, rubbing my shoulder, and spitting demony powder out of my mouth. As glad as I was to be alive, I was livid at having been pushed into that little demonstration that way. How about a gentle guiding on day one for the new girl? I glowered at Rohan and Baruch.

They stared back at me gobsmacked, all color drained from their faces. Rohan's hand snaked protectively in front of his crotch as my eyes met his.

That's what he took away from this?

I pushed to my feet. There were a million snarky remarks I could have made except I didn't trust my voice right now. I couldn't get my ribcage to unconstrict and I was shaking so hard, I'm amazed my brain didn't plop out.

Ignoring the tiny abrasions on my soles, I strode off without a look back, my breath coming in furious gasps. I entered the house via the back door in the kitchen, searching for a woman's washroom until I realized there wasn't one because *they all sucked* and then barricaded myself in the one bathroom I was able to find. For something used by all men, it was a clean enough room with the dark wood vanity/white counter combo all in vogue.

Expression stuck in a snarl, I pumped soap onto my hand, wincing as it hit my cracked bleeding skin from my demon-inspired obsessive hand washing. Kicking the vanity door didn't help. It hurt my toes and did nothing to make me feel better.

What kind of sick sadists threw a total newbie into proving herself like that? Those two would have let me die and chalked it up to *my* incompetence. I grabbed some toilet paper and blew my nose.

Forget the demons, these people were the monsters.

There was a soft rap at the door. "Nava?" It sounded like Kane but I wasn't sure so I didn't answer. "Babyslay, let me in."

I debated ignoring him some more, but I was going to need an escort to get out of this place unharmed and Kane seemed like my sole ally. I tossed the toilet paper into the bowl and unlocked the door.

The first thing I noticed was his terrible taste in shirts. A paisley pattern in lurid purples, it was a bold look. A look that slapped itself on the crotch and said, "Here I am." I respected that about it.

The second thing I noticed was the compassion in his eyes.

The third was the Gatorade he held out to me.

I chugged half the bottle in one go, before pressing it in sweet relief against my forehead. "I don't even like this shit."

"Doesn't matter. Your body craves the electrolytes to recharge after using your power. You'll learn to keep stashes handy." Kane leaned back against the closed door. "Our powers don't manifest the second they do the induction ceremony. I don't know if anyone told you that."

"I've been told very little about this process."

"It means that a lot of us find ourselves in extremely embarrassing situations when it shows up."

"Was yours bad?" I asked.

He laughed mirthlessly, his hip braced against the door. "Dad had this vintage Ferrari convertible. She was the most beautiful thing I'd ever seen in my life. He'd take me out for rides." Kane's expression grew dreamy. "We wouldn't even talk. It was all about feeling the curve of the road. The sun on our faces and the wind in our hair."

The past tense of this didn't sound good. "What happened?"

"After I became Rasha, my parents were so thrilled that Dad said I could take her for a spin. So long as I washed her first, she was mine for the rest of the day." A wistful look came over his face, as he leaned back against the door. "I think I was more excited about that then fighting demons. Picture it. This perfect summer day. This perfect specimen of a man washing this perfect car."

I gave the requisite smile.

"Do you know the effects of water and salt on iron?" he asked.

"Rust," I replied, confused at the change in topic.

He nodded and held out his arm. "Look, but don't touch." His flesh broke out in an oily sheen. An iridescent purple flecked with tiny white crystals. "It's a salt-based poison."

I would have guessed that from the smell alone. My mouth watered bitterly. I raised my eyes to his and gasped. Even his face was coated with it.

"One bad touch and the demons die," he said.

I peered at his flesh, fascinated. "What about if a person touches it?"

"Trust me. You don't want to know." The sheen disappeared from his body.

I reached out to touch him but he flinched away, shaking his head. "Wait." He turned on the tap and dispensing a good handful of liquid soap with his clean hand, washed where the poison had been. "Until I clean off, I can still burn you."

"I'm sorry." That seemed like it might be a lonely existence.

"It's always the pretty ones you have to look out for." He shrugged. "I can control it. Now. But the poor, wet car? When my powers showed up?"

"Rusted," I gasped.

"Instantly."

"What did your dad do?"

An unreadable expression flashed across his face. "That, dear girl, is a story for another day. All this to say: your. Power. Is. Fabulous!" His face brightened. "Do you know how many asshole dates I could have cut short with it?"

"I am not giving demon hand jobs."

Kane pulled the hand towel off the rack and wiped his dripping face and arm dry. "While I can't wait to hear the story of your first kill, Baruch and Rohan just did what they'd do to any new member." His eyes widened theatrically. "Oops. Phrasing."

I prodded the side of my head, wincing at the bright burst of pain. "Except I wasn't trained my whole life for this. It was horrible. A super unfair trial by fire."

He placed his hand on my shoulder with a sympathetic smile. "It's your life now, babyslay. But it doesn't mean you have to go it alone."

No, it just meant that Ari had to. Still, I smiled back. "Thanks, Kane."

"Anytime." With a wink, he took my empty sports drink bottle.

Baruch was waiting for me outside the door. "I made you a sandwich." Guilt food. Good. Those usually came with extra side dishes.

He led me into the kitchen, my stomach gurgling. On the large table by the sunny window, Baruch had laid out two plates along with big glasses of very cold iced tea from a blue glass pitcher.

There was a distinct lack of sides, but I accepted the peace offering of shaved meat, sliced bocconcini, and tomato on a crusty Portuguese bun. I sank into a chair, eager to dig in.

Baruch sat beside me. Even though his ass extended past the seat, it was so rock hard that it didn't droop over the sides. I checked twice to make sure.

"So you were in Jerusalem before now?" I asked.

"No, Cairo. They needed extra hands with all the civil unrest. But I was in Chicago when I got the heads up about you."

I bit into the pickle that Baruch had laid as garnish on the side of my plate. He'd given me the perfect segue. "If Rasha are needed," I said, "all the more reason to make sure about Ari's status. What if the ritual when we were babies determined that we were *both* initiates?"

Baruch picked up the other half of his sandwich. "And what if as your twin, Ari carried an echo of your potential, your magic, from sharing the womb, and that's what Rabbi Abrams picked up?"

"How is that possible? Ari and I are fraternal twins. We don't share DNA, we didn't share a placenta or amniotic fluid, so why would sharing the womb matter?" Mom had versed Ari and me in all sorts of twin facts.

"If your brother did not carry the magic passed down through the bloodlines to the descendants of the original Rasha, then the reason Rabbi Abrams would have thought Ari did is because he felt the residue of your power on your twin."

"Is that what the Brotherhood believes?" I squirted another dollop of spicy mustard on my sandwich.

He nodded. "If Ari was an initiate, re-running the ceremony should have worked. He would have become Rasha."

The mustard lid snapped shut with a hard click. "But I'm a complicating factor. Hasn't anyone thought of that? My existence could have screwed everything up that would normally work. You don't just give up on someone you've invested in."

Baruch bit into his roast beef, chewing slowly and methodically before swallowing. "There is a way of things."

I didn't get a chance to further refute his argument because Rohan entered the kitchen and slapped a piece of paper down on the table beside me. "Your schedule."

It was color coded to within an inch of its life. "Three entire meals a day? Wow. You really follow minimum prison standards around here." I tapped the paper. "Where are my snack breaks?"

Rohan pulled a chair out, doing his straddle backwards thing again. "What are you, five?"

"I have a very fast metabolism." I grumbled at the only eight hours of sleep he'd allotted. "You've accounted for every second of my day."

"Yeah, and?"

Baruch pushed his chair back, carrying his plate and glass to the sink. "Five minutes then back to the Vault. I want to go over what you could have done differently in the fight."

I nodded to show I'd heard. "What about free time?"

"For all your scintillating hobbies?" Rohan plucked an apple out of the fruit bowl on the table and bit into it.

"Yes. As well as the many good works I do."

He arched his eyebrow, miming giving a hand job.

"Are you ever going to let that go?"

He took another bite. "Not when there are still hours of fun to be had from it. You know you don't have to jerk the demons off to kill them, right?"

"It was one time."

He slapped the table. "Knew it! Baruch owes me twenty."

I groaned at the fact that I'd just confirmed his suspicions.

"Don't feel bad," he said with a smirk, "I puzzled it out when reaching for the curupira's dick was your first move."

"I couldn't not reach for Mount Phallus. He was hung like a horse."

He held up his hands. "If that's your kink, then hey, no judgment."

Here we go. "No judgment, huh?"

"No way, Shaft." Rohan's composure cracked, his shoulders shaking as he hummed the *Shaft* theme music. "Though I wouldn't rely on it as a kill tactic," he said, now howling with laughter.

Bastard. "How about my thanks for taking me in hand, then?" I purred, leaning over to run my fingertips up his leg. "So to speak." I was bluffing, but he'd already unsettled me so many times that I wanted to rattle him back and my arsenal of weapons was laughably small.

His hand clamped over mine, millimeters from his crotch. "Seems I didn't need to go after Drio for his gratitude crack. Since you're giving it away."

"I'm not offering it to all and sundry, asshole." I yanked my hand away. "That little tussle between you boys had nothing to do with me. And for the record, what I did to Josh was not intended as a fighting maneuver. It was grown-up time."

"I'm a grown-up."

"You're more of a growth," I said. "There's a difference. And with that thing? Trust me, his dick was the last thing I wanted to touch."

"Curupira," Rohan repeated. "From Brazil."

"It should have stayed there."

"Next objection?" Rohan took the last bite of fruit then pitched the core across the room into the trash. Nice shot.

"Do we get paid for this?" I asked.

"Yes. You start at minimum wage."

"What about danger pay?"

Rohan cocked his fingers at me like a gun. "That's a good idea. I'll talk to Ms. Clara about adding it while we're stuck with you."

I stood, snatching up my dirty dishes. "I may not want to be here any more than you want me here, but that doesn't give you the right to treat me with a lack of respect." I dumped them into the sink then whirled to face him. "Now," I continued, "we're going to set some ground rules. The first is, you're going to remember that unlike the rest of you, I didn't get to spend my entire life training and studying because Demon Club was so short-sighted, they couldn't see that a girl was the chosen one."

Rohan pushed to his feet in one fluid move. I was going to have to learn that trick. My standing up always involved weirdly jutting out body parts.

"Fine," he said, getting in my face. "Then the second has to be that you shut up and listen. Yeah, we threw you in the deep end. There's no time to pussyfoot around with you. Your magic is active. That means you need to know how to use it because I guarantee that demons are gonna be a regular part of your life now."

"You still played dirty," I said. "I get that I'm a huge target, but I thought you guys were supposed to have my back." He opened his mouth but I held up a hand, cutting him off. "How far would you have let it go with the curupira before you stepped in to help?"

His hesitation told me everything I needed to know.

I slammed on the tap to rinse off my plate, my back to him.

"We would never have let it kill you," he said in a low voice.

I blinked rapidly, my eyes hot and itchy. I gave myself to the count of five to compose myself and face him. "I'm still the special unicorn Demon Club wants protected. I can make your life very hard if I want to."

"Back at you, Lolita."

I bit back my retort for the sake of my Ari plan. "I better return to my training, then." I'd almost made it to the doorway when something pointy hit my back. I turned around to see my schedule, now in paper airplane form flutter to the ground.

Rohan smirked at me, but I gave him a sweet smile, picked up the damn schedule, and left. I saved my outburst for my bedroom later that night, flinging my bag at the wall. The thunk that the demon primer made as the bag connected wasn't nearly satisfying enough.

Ari poked his head in. "What happened?"

"They threw a demon at me."

Ari's eye bulge was gratifying. "On your first day? It took me years to get up close to one. Under major supervision."

"Yeah, well." I snatched up my bag, dumping the contents out on my bed. Perhaps a tad viciously.

Ari picked up the book, glancing at the cover with a soft laugh before turning back to me. "That was kind of shitty but they made sure it was a relatively harmless one, right? An imp or a–"

"Curupira."

Ari stilled, turning an interesting shade of red. "A what?" His voice chilled me.

I tugged the book from his hands. "Ace."

"No. You could have died."

"I killed it. In the end." He gave a choking cough like he didn't believe me. I slammed the book down on my mattress. "Thanks for the vote of confidence, bro."

Ari crossed his arms. "On your first day? You killed a curupira?"

I crossed my arms right back. "Technically, it was my second day. And my third kill." You know, put that way, I had a pretty sweet success rate.

His eyes narrowed. "No one helped you?"

"Screw you. Is it so tough to believe I did it?"

"Yeah, all right? It is." He slammed the door on the way out and I flopped down on my bed.

Even when I beat the odds and did well, somehow things overwhelmingly sucked. Thanks for nothing, universe.

9

The next few days were a blur of training, training, and more training. I'd gotten to the point where no matter how Baruch lunged at me or otherwise tried to surprise me, I could turn my power on, going all shocktastic on him. With no more screaming and running. My defense was awesome, too. I was queen of blocking and could break most holds.

The first time I earned a "tov meod" or "very good" from Baruch for my efforts, I swear, cartoon birds danced around my head. I even had a new self-anointed superhero name–Lady Shock and Awe. Ari and his pop psychology could suck it.

On this drizzly Thursday morning, or as I called it, *Nava's Origin Story, Day Five: In Which Her Last Bit of Skin Gets Pummeled by Tree Trunk,* I found my brother in the kitchen, still dressed in yesterday's clothes, asleep on his homework. Our paths had barely crossed since our fight the other night, but even our brief encounters were enough to note his descent into depression. Careful not to wake him, I moved the binder out from under his cheek, finding a scrawled "I hate my life" at the top of his chem equations page.

I bowed my head, exhausted and frustrated at being no further along with my Ari plan. Rabbi Abrams had been detained on business and Ms. Clara, though sympathetic, was unwilling to put me in touch with the Executive. The one bright spot was my brother was too bummed to go out and fight demons himself.

I couldn't let him keep spiraling downward. Dad always said to take emotion out of the equation and see what things boiled down to. The Brotherhood already owned my ass. Still, a hot start up garnered more attention and resources than a dud subsidiary. I needed a win. A big one. And the biggest potential win I could think of was already sending spider demons after me.

It was time to take my training to a new level.

Baruch showed up at my house moments later in a warded-up, reinforced Hummer. Not that you could tell from looking at it. Another benefit of the Brotherhood having a fuckton of cash.

I slumped on the leather passenger seat, stifling a yawn. "Why are you pulling chauffeur duty?"

"Asmodeus is intensifying his efforts to find out who killed his kids." He shrugged out of his sweater, tossing it into the backseat. Ragged gashes peeped above the neckline of his shirt.

I stuttered out a harsh breath. "Are you okay?"

"Yes." Baruch patted my head. Oddly, coming from him, this gesture felt sweet and did not inspire me to rip his condescending hand off. "I won't let the demon get you. You're my sister now."

Aww. My jacked-up insides went gooey. The lack of any demons waiting to ambush us when we pulled up to the gate helped too.

Rohan bounded down the stairs as I dumped my jacket and shoes in the foyer. Our few encounters had been decidedly tense since our spat in the kitchen. One look at me and he sighed. "Baruch told you."

"Yup."

He placed a hand on my shoulder. "He'll have to get through me first." Sure, because he didn't want to hear the Executive bitch about it if I died before they'd decided on my fate.

I shook him off. "Thanks. Better find Tree Trunk."

Rohan searched my face, then with a nod, stepped aside to let me go.

Ms. Clara ambushed me the moment I hit the ground floor, beckoning me over. "Well, don't just stand there."

"Better go," Baruch said from behind me. "Clara gets a hard-on for signatures."

She narrowed her baby blues on him. "I heard that, Mr. Ya'ari." She clapped her hands. "Chop. Chop." Tiny, breathy, and steel-spined. No way was I disobeying her.

I scurried down the hall past the conference room and a couple smaller meeting rooms/floating offices for Rasha or Executive in town, dragging Baruch with me. Rather, he let himself be dragged. "Since when are you given permission to call her Clara?" I asked in a low voice, as Ms. Clara turned into her office. "Are you and her...?" I was about to make a lewd motion but the look on his face had me rethink that. "Are you a thing?"

He didn't answer me. One more item to add to my list of mysteries about these guys.

Her office was meticulous. Tasteful photographic prints of the city, from towering Douglas fir in Pacific Spirit Park to neon signs in Chinatown framed her white walls. Three normal humans would have been comfortable in the small space. With Tree Trunk in there, our fit was positively snug.

Ms. Clara sat down in her black and brushed steel Aeron chair that matched her desk. She twisted the large monitor out of the way, pushing a thick file with my name typed on the tab toward me. "This covers the basics of your employment."

Like my severance pay body bag?

I flipped the file open. "Hang on. I've been here since Monday. It's Thursday and you're just getting around to having me fill out the paperwork now?" That seemed oddly lax for her. "Was the Brotherhood hoping I wouldn't last the week so they wouldn't have to bother processing me?"

Ms. Clara selected a pen from the cup on her desk with intense concentration while Baruch just sat there, arms crossed, poker faced.

"*Are you fucking kidding me?*" I didn't even apologize at Ms. Clara's admonishing glance.

"I'll need your phone and laptop," she said, handing me the pen. "Your data will be transferred over to encrypted models." Ari had been given his first encrypted phone from Demon Club when he was fifteen. I knew how this worked.

I signed about ten times, my writing furious scrawls before I was calm enough to speak. "You mean you're going to track me. Glad to know I've earned that minimal protection."

"Enough." Baruch's quiet command defused the temper tantrum I wanted to throw.

Ari. Ari. Ari. I set the mantra to loop in my head. "The phone is upstairs in my bag. I'll bring in the laptop tomorrow."

Ms. Clara leaned across the desk to tap a signature I'd missed. "Good. Our tracking program ups the odds of finding you should you run into trouble. Twenty-four hours of inactivity and the Brotherhood is alerted to its last known location. Same if it gets destroyed."

Much as I loathed the idea of Big Brotherhood keeping tabs on my every move, I wasn't about to argue with something that could save my skin.

Ms. Clara wasn't kidding about the paperwork. Forget chosen one crap. I'd joined the mother of all corporations. My hand started cramping up from the sheer number of signatures and forms to fill out, like the swearing to secrecy shit. Damn, I hadn't been bound by any oaths yet when I'd talked to Rohan in the library. "I don't get it. You're the housekeeper *and* clerical worker?"

Baruch guffawed.

Ms. Clara stilled, looking up from where she was initialing a form. "Housekeeper? Wherever did you get that idea?"

I edged back on the seat. Her tone was kind of scary and she knew how to use a whip. "I asked who cleaned the house." Leaving *who* I asked purposefully vague since I wasn't about to sell Kane out to a woman who could inflict thirty lashes. "And was told you took care of it. Plus, you made cookies."

Yeah, that sounded like reaching, even to me.

Any hope of support from Baruch was pointless. He sat there, his eye blinks conveying his hilarity.

"I take care of it because I take care of everything in this house of overgrown children," she informed me, her voice less breathy, more steely. "I'm in charge of all Brotherhood administrative business in Canada. Rasha, rabbi, or Executive member living or visiting this country, I'm their go-to."

"How does the Executive work? Do they fly out here often?" With all the training and plotting, I hadn't had a chance to learn much about them yet and every bit of intel helped.

"No. Rabbi Abrams passes on any local concerns that they need to be involved in. The six rabbis chosen to make up the Executive handle big picture organizational issues like establishing new chapter houses." Ms. Clara pointed at a couple of places where I'd missed signing.

"We have them in many major cities across the globe but as global crises change," she said, "so do locations and the number of Rasha stationed there. Hunters are reassigned all the time. The Executive has been busy with field offices in Northern Africa these past few years. And of course the head of the Executive, Rabbi Mandelbaum, also personally interacts with the intelligence department."

"Like hunter Homeland Security?" I glanced at Baruch to see if he'd weigh in but he was checking something on his phone.

Ms. Clara kept up the explanation. "Security on an international level. They monitor crimes across the globe for certain details that could be evidence of demonic activity. Social media activity as well as anything gleaned through work under DSI. All intelligence gathered goes through them before being handed over to Rasha as specific missions."

I shook out my hand. "James Bond epic."

"As for the cookies—"

"Really, really good cookies," I interjected.

Her expression softened. "Thank you, doll. I like making cookies." She picked up a stress ball from her desk, squeezing it. "With this bunch in town, I need all the stress relief I can get." She winged the ball at Baruch's head, nailing him in the temple and killing his amused eye blinks.

Baruch bent to retrieve the ball from the floor and placed it back on her desk. He tucked his hair behind his ears, sliding his phone into his pocket. "Our stress is what makes you the most in-demand dominatrix in the country. You wouldn't be half so good if we didn't push you to your breaking point."

"You wouldn't even begin to know where I break," Ms. Clara replied darkly.

"Perhaps not." Baruch shrugged and I leaned in. This was better than HBO. Oh, to have popcorn.

Sadly, Ms. Clara veered off the juicy stuff to give me a lecture about requisition forms that was so dull, my eyes glazed over. Though I did perk up a bit at the myriad of medical treatments I was entitled to. "Two massage therapy sessions a month, you say?"

"No one uses them," Baruch said with a dismissive wave.

Ms. Clara eyed him with distaste before turning back to me. "I'd be happy to provide you with a list of approved practitioners."

Twisting her monitor back into position, she pressed her palm to a small pad on her desk to be scanned. Once the light turned green, she started typing. "Better than a password," she said, noting my curiosity.

I placed the last of the signed forms in the file. The Brotherhood could proclaim Rabbi Abrams was in charge here, but it was clear to me who really ran the show.

The final item of business was to get my palm scanned so I could access the Vault and stuff on my own. Ms. Clara explained it would take twenty-four hours to process, then pronounced us done.

"Excellent. I promise to behave like a pampered princess and exploit every last thing I'm entitled to."

One side of her mouth quirked up at that. "Provided you have the correct requisition form," she said.

That's when Baruch hit his limit. He engulfed my hand in his and tugged me to my feet. "Yes, Nava will pretend the best of intentions for your forms and you will pretend you don't enjoy filling everything out on our behalf, and natural order will be maintained."

He dragged me to the door.

"Leave the pen," Ms. Clara called out.

Baruch growled.

I tossed it back at her as I cleared the door, being rewarded with a wink.

Oh yeah. Way better than cable.

Baruch warmed up on the punching bag. I watched him in amazement for a few minutes as I stretched. I'd never seen anyone's fist almost punch through the bag before. The most astounding thing of all was how calm he was. It was pretty sexy the way he pummeled the thing in a total state of Zen. The fact that he'd taken off his shirt and was working out bare-chested didn't hurt the cause any, even if he was more muscular than my tastes generally ran.

One thing Baruch had gotten into my skull was staying in the present during any fighting since letting my thoughts wander led to meat-sack tenderization. Even with my accelerated healing, I was tenderized enough. "Doesn't super strength usually come with anger issues?"

He stopped punching.

"I mean, you're pretty mellow. Which is great. I, for one, would not want my baggage infringing on Drio's. Because holy wow, two wounded angry people. That's not even counting Rohan, although Drio would win any diva-off hands down."

Baruch lifted the punching bag off the hook with one hand. "Do you say everything you think?"

"Nope. Amazingly I share merely a fraction of the brilliance in my head." I followed him over to the wall.

He touched a light on a small display panel and part of the wall slid away to reveal another good-sized room, filled top to bottom with weapons and training equipment.

"Cool," I breathed, peering in. "Did you design all these?"

"Some." He pushed me back a few steps. "You haven't unlocked entrance privileges yet," he said, heading inside.

"Nerd," I teased.

He gave me a sheepish grin as he stashed the bag up on a hook.

I eyed the weapons: knives of all shapes and sizes, throwing stars, staffs, iron-based things that I couldn't discern the purpose of but given their scary shape was certain I was better off without the visual, boxing gloves, pads, and whatever was stored in the cabinets running the length of one wall. No guns though.

The Brotherhood required a massive bottom line to run.

"Who funds the Brotherhood? Can we change the name now that I'm here?"

"It funds itself and no. Hundreds of years in investments plus, these days, the income DSI brings in." He smiled. "We don't come cheap. The Brotherhood takes care of us. If we die, our funeral expenses are handled."

My gut twisted at that last sentiment. "You're awfully matter-of-fact about death."

He spread his hands wide. "We do what we do. We try not to die but it happens. Which is why I will train you to have the best shot at walking away."

See, this was a guy who genuinely had my back. "Teach me fight moves." Defense wasn't going to be enough when I came up against Asmodeus.

He assessed me for a long moment. "Most demons will be larger than you. Stronger."

"That's a yes, then?"

"But that also means their balance and speed is compromised as a result."

I eyed him up and down. "Speaking from experience are we, Tree Trunk?"

"You're very annoying," he said.

"It's my birth power," I replied.

"Oh? That's not being delusional?"

"Ladies and gentlemen, Baruch Ya'ari," I said. "He's here all week. Try the shrimp."

He peered at me. "Is English your first language?"

"Vaudeville? The old schtick? Nothing?" I shook my head in dismay before dancing around him, throwing air punches.

He swatted me away. "Build up your side to side movement. Get inside the tip of their punches and kicks. Build an infighting and clinch game. Get comfortable striking and fighting from your back in case you're thrown down."

Baruch showed me some basic moves—a couple of punches and a few kicks—running me through them over and over again, making minute adjustments. Talking me through both my mistakes and what I was doing right.

I stripped down to my sports bra and booty shorts which was great on the heat front but left more exposed skin, and psychologically, made me feel more vulnerable. My muscles quivered as every attack became more of a grinding exertion.

The flooring pads became sticky with sweat, each footstep a pronounced slapping sound, the room turning steamy and dank. Finally, Baruch called a much-desired halt to the training but only to bring Kane down to ensure I didn't get complacent fighting just him.

Kane raised an eyebrow as he handed me a glass of Ms. Clara's electrolyte-filled iced tea. "Well?" he asked Baruch.

I'd gulped back the cold liquid by the time his question was asked.

"Help me attack her on two fronts," Baruch said.

I left the empty glass in a corner, my arms wobbly. "Awesome."

Seeing me swipe at the sweat on my neck, Kane boosted the air conditioning to blessed arctic levels and then the two of them leapt into battle against me. All right, they engaged me in slow motion combat while Baruch barked grips, counter-grips, and attack strategy, showing me how to use my weight against them.

The cool part was making connections on my own about how and where certain moves would come in handy. When my suggestions were wrong, the guys showed me why, then explained the better way of proceeding.

"For someone who hasn't spent years training, you pick things up fast," Kane said, after I'd executed a pretty sweet roundhouse kick.

"Your power isn't there yet and your technique is rough, but balance, even speed?" Baruch's approving eye blink was the sweetest compliment ever.

"I'm not a trained fighter, but I am a trained dancer. I was always good at picking up moves quickly, getting new routines faster than other people. Tap taught me balance, weight placement, being aware of my body. Those skills are transferable," I informed them.

"Those skills are a foundation," Baruch said. "Do the kick again. Don't throw your left hip out so much this time."

Neither of them held back or went easy on me because I was female. I appreciated that up until the point that I collapsed on burning legs with a plea of "Have mercy!" Not even my most rigorous dance session had drained me this much.

Kane prodded my belly with a toe. My tummy jiggled. His bare-chested, rock hard body didn't. "We better feed her. And hose her off."

I think I gave him the finger but I might have just imagined it, distracted as I was by the shiny of his nipple rings. That boy had two modes of dress–barely and horribly. I vowed to do a fashion intervention one day.

"For God's sakes, woman, get up," Kane said, holding a hand out to me.

I lay there, too tired to even reach for him. "Can I have a cookie?" I wheezed.

"Yes, Nava," Baruch said, sounding amused. "You may. They're in the cupboard upstairs."

"Will you get it for me? Pleeeeeeaaaase?"

He nodded, pulling his hair free from his elastic band. Pretty hair.

"Todah rabah," I called out in thanks as he and Kane left. I closed my eyes, my arm thrown over my face. If I played my cards right, maybe I could pull this off. Maybe Ari and I could be real live Wonder Twins soon. But you know, not lame. For the first time since I'd become Rasha, I felt like I could take a deep breath.

Footsteps neared and fabric swished as Baruch knelt down beside me. I opened my eyes, hand out to take the cookie, and then drew back. It wasn't Baruch. It was Drio, squatting down. I burst into full-body Lady Shock mode, my exhaustion trumped by adrenaline.

"Showing off or scared?" he smirked.

"Touch me and find out." I sat up as calmly as I could manage, given I was alone with a man who aggressively hated me and whose powers were a giant question mark. I didn't trust his promise to keep me safe.

Where were my guards? The ones that liked me. Or at least tolerated me.

He pursed his lips. "Just came to see the progress. Checking if you're earning your keep."

"Impressed?" My heart was hammering and I could feel the electricity rising and falling like swells within me.

"I've seen better."

"Sorry to disappoint." I scrambled to my feet, sparking so brightly that residual blue sunspots danced before my eyes.

Drio stood up as well. "Shut it down." He scowled at me.

The electricity flared, cresting off my skin in sharp bursts. I tried to visualize the off-switch but nothing happened.

"Nava." He grabbed me by the shoulders, but after one quick shake was forced to release me, flinching in the wake of my magic.

A hot tight pain speared my chest. I clutched at it, my eyes watering, sensing this was all about to go sideways.

"Porco Dio," Drio swore. "Baruch!" he yelled.

I hyperventilated. Pops and crackles jumped off my skin, a metal burning smell clogging my nostrils.

Footsteps pounded down the stairs.

I fell to my knees, feeling every charged particle in my body as the electricity wrapped around me like a snake with its coily embrace. I wheezed, desperate for air.

A heavy blanket lined with rubber enveloped me, arms holding tight around me. "You're safe," Rohan said. "Turn it off, Nava. You can do it."

My cheek pressed against the blanket resting on his chest, I latched on to the even rise and fall of his breathing like it was my lifeline. He kept murmuring to me that I was safe, cradling me in his arms, and ignoring the small sparks not contained by the blanket that were blackening his skin in tiny dots. His voice was hypnotic, soothing me enough that my magic turned off. But I still couldn't breathe for the pain lancing my chest. I shot him a panicked look.

Rohan lay me down on the floor. The last thing I heard was, "Clear!"

Not more current, I thought, and blacked out.

I came to, still on the padded floor, with four male faces showing varying degrees of concern hovering over me. Baruch crumpled the rubber blanket in one hand. Kane held a defibrillator limply. Rohan's left eyebrow was scorched.

It wasn't until I saw Drio, his hands burned from my magic, watching me like he'd missed some kind of manslaughter opportunity, that I was reassured I was okay. I struggled to sit up, Baruch assisting me.

I squinted at the electrodes placed around my sports bra, hooking me up to the bastard child of a fax and an answering machine. Ticker tape stuck out of one end of it. "What happened?"

I had to clear my throat a couple of times to get the words out.

"Not a heart attack," Ms. Clara said cheerfully. I scrunched up my face in confusion and she tapped the machine. "Portable ECG." She pulled the electrodes off of me.

"You're qualified to read it, how?"

"Two years of med school before I dropped out. Apparently I didn't have the right bedside manner."

"O-kay."

"You got... riled up," Rohan said.

I glared at Drio who bared his teeth at me. "By-product of him wanting me dead," I said.

"He doesn't want–" Kane began.

"I don't?" Drio asked.

"Drio," Rohan warned.

"I was being friendly and she freaked out." Drio cocked his thumb and forefinger like a gun, rocking them from side to side in some kind of Italian hand gesture. "Our new Rasha doesn't play well with others."

I tugged my clammy T-shirt over my head. "If you call your passive-aggressive intimidation 'being friendly' then you've got the social graces of a walnut. Pony up. You wanted my power off so you could hurt me."

"It was becoming unstable." He tapped his forefinger to his temple. "You're unstable. Are you on your period?"

Sparks literally shot from my eyes.

Baruch blocked Drio from me, saving him from being turned into a human tiki torch.

The proverbial straw had hit this camel's back. "I'm out of here."

The guys did that annoying silent communication thing. Seriously could kill the alpha brood right now.

"Home it is," Ms. Clara said, with an undecipherable look at them. I didn't know what I was missing here and frankly, I didn't care.

Ms. Clara helped me up. I didn't have it in me to make polite small talk, so I grabbed my shoes and left the room without saying goodbye. Ms. Clara accompanied me, retrieving my messenger bag, along with my hoodie.

"Thank you." I pulled out my phone as we exited onto the porch, calling home for a ride and determined to keep my shit together until someone from my family came and got me.

The second I hung up, Ms. Clara held out her hand for the phone, giving me a slip of paper from her pocket in return as my receipt. "You'll get another one when you hand in the laptop," she assured me. Because that was such a concern right now.

We sat outside on the top step, waiting. The sun provided a welcome warmth and the sound of a car driving by blasting Top 40 went a long way to making me feel normal.

"Is that going to happen to me every time?" I threaded my hands in my hair, weary beyond belief.

"The instability or the heart problem?" she asked.

"Yes."

"Magic takes a while to master, but you'll get there." Her expression grew distant. "The thing about magic powers is that there's a cost."

"How come you're a part of all this?"

She blinked back to attention. "My dad was Rasha."

Past tense noted. "Sorry."

She shrugged. "Not your fault."

Kane joined us, his footsteps creaking the weathered boards. "Rest easy tonight, babe."

"Thanks," I said, peering up at him, one hand shielding my eyes from the sun.

My dad's Prius fishtailed up the driveway. Ari threw open the driver's side, engine still running. He raced over to me in his frayed T-shirt and jeans. I'd never seen him this upset.

"What did you do to her?" he spat at Kane.

Ms. Clara squeezed my hand and went inside.

"Danger comes with the job," Kane said. He braced a hand on the top of the railing. "She knows this."

Ari led me to the car. He bundled me in, then slammed my door so hard I jumped. "You were supposed to take it easy on her," he said.

Had they discussed me before? I shamelessly eavesdropped through Ari's open door.

"Around here we do what has to be done." Kane sat down on the top step, almost insolent in his indifference. "That's how it works at the adults' table."

Bastard. I put my hand on the door handle ready to lay into Kane but Ari surprised me.

He threw Kane a cool smile. "Keep telling yourself that." On that note, he got into the car and we drove away.

10

I lasted all of ten seconds before I opened my mouth to demand an explanation but Ari cut me off. "Rest. We can talk later." I would have protested, but the next thing I knew, he was shaking me awake. "Rise and shine. We're home."

The sky flamed gold for one brief instance before relaxing into the pink and oranges of sunset. That was pretty. My mother's scream of horror at the sight of me stumbling into the house, not so much. She tried to backpedal but you know, there's no coming back from reacting to your kid like she's something out of a scary movie.

"Bath," she proclaimed and marched me upstairs to my room.

Sitting on the edge of my tub, testing the water, I caught sight of myself in the mirror. Mom's reaction was not unwarranted. My hair snarled in rat's nest fashion. Giant sweat and pit stains graced my T-shirt. All I needed was a Pig Pen cloud of dirt to complete the look. Any confidence, any pride in my accomplishments today disappeared.

First I took a fast shower, then I plugged the tub, shivering and waiting impatiently for it to fill. Finally, inching into the hot water, I slid onto my back, fully submerged except for my nose and lips.

I brushed the underside of the tap with my big toe, catching the final tiny warm drops.

The inset LEDs smudged a soft luminescence like a milky way across the ceiling. I lay there staring up at the world through my watery lens until my overwhelmed panic subsided. The same trick I'd used since I was a kid and hadn't wanted anyone to know that I wasn't tough enough to keep up with my brother, who generally took everything in stride.

Being thrown into Demon Club was like playing the world's craziest game of *Survivor*, except with no defined rules and a funeral service for a consolation prize. And now I was planning on taking on a major big bad. Was I crazy?

Submerged in doubt as much as the water, only the water grew cold before I pulled the plug. Cocooning myself in a massive towel, I gave a curt nod to my reflection then headed into my room to slip into my softest worn cotton pjs. Rehashing today was not on the table.

A while later, I was lost in the study of all the books I'd brought home, alternately fascinated and disgusted by the forms demons took, their various abilities, and the ways in which they could be killed. While none left any physical evidence once killed, some, like ghish demons, died in a whoosh of sulphuric stank so noxious it had been known to induce temporary blindness. It was all important information, but I'd gotten no closer to finding where Asmodeus' sweet spot lay. He was a Unique. Maybe no one knew.

I'd filled the book with color-coded sticky tabs and a growing pile of notes lay on my lap. While I loved technology, when it came to note taking, longhand was my preference. Something about the act of writing the information down instead of typing it helped me remember it better.

Ari poked his head in, a bowl of steaming chicken soup in one hand.

I inhaled deeply. "There better be matzoh balls in that." The fluffy Jewish dumplings were, in my opinion, the best thing to come out of my religion. Except maybe that naked photo of Adam Levine in all his tatted-up glory.

"Like you even have to ask." He placed the bowl on my bedside table.

I eyed it, noting Mom had stuffed four giant matzoh balls in it plus put in extra carrot slivers. She must really have been freaked out by my appearance to give me the deluxe soup treatment.

Not wanting my demon book or notes to get accidentally soupified, I moved everything over to one side of my bed. The pillows behind me were rearranged to optimize my eating position, then I picked up the warm bowl and dug in. I know the soup wasn't literally magic, but it was soul-soothing. I sighed happily, the hot broth filling my belly. There was an art to matzoh ball making. With some people, it was like eating cannonballs, but Mom's melted in my mouth.

"I like big balls and I cannot lie," I sang around a mouthful.

"What set you off?" Ari regarded me from his usual spot at the foot of my bed, where he sat cross legged.

"What do you know about a Rasha called Drio?"

Ari shrugged. "Don't know him. Why?"

"He has it in for me. Things were said and he got me alone and..." I shivered remembering the aggressive dislike pouring off him. I chopped my remaining balls into bits. "I freaked out. The curupira was scary too, but when you're female, a threatening human male taps into an entirely different kind of fear." I met Ari's eyes and he nodded in understanding. "My power went haywire. Then the chest pains kicked in and bam! Defibrillation."

He bunched up my comforter in his fists.

The remaining soup was gone before I knew it, my spoon hitting the bottom with a clang. I peered into the bowl, as if staring might make a second helping appear. Sadly, no. Placing it on the night table beside me, I stroked my finger over my heart. "Ms. Clara said something about the cost of magic. Is this mine? Do I run the risk of dying every time I access my power?"

"You're not going to die," he said.

"You're avoiding my question. Tell me, because I don't have time to read my way through that library."

Ari toyed with the edge of my stack of notes. "She's right about the cost. But ninety-nine percent of the time, the only thing you'll feel is tired. Craving those electrolytes."

"And the one percent?" I asked.

Ari hesitated.

"Don't sugarcoat it." I grabbed my pen, on the verge of rolling off my mattress.

He nodded reluctantly. "If you draw on the power for too long, or become agitated to the point where it controls you instead of the other way around? Yeah. It could kill you. In your case, via heart attack it seems."

I absorbed that, re-arranging my pillows to face Ari. "Then I have to control it. Now that I know it can happen and why, I won't let the situation get away from me again."

"Just like that? Sheer will power?"

"Do you doubt me?"

My brother regarded me steadily before shaking his head. "What was it like training with Baruch?" he asked.

"You looooove him." I made a kissy noise.

Ari raised his hands in tickle formation. "Keep talking, Katz. It'll end in tears and pee."

I threw a pillow at him that he caught one-handed. "He's amazing," I said. "He knows how to both motivate me and push me."

"He breaks down battles looking for ways to improve our–their– odds." Ari stumbled over the pronoun but caught himself. I kept my mouth shut. "Not to mention his inventions," he said.

"Yeah, what was that thing you mentioned the first night?"

"The Stinger." Ari's face lit up. "Baruch found a way to stabilize demon secretions in a chemical compound that worked on the neural system of most demons to temporarily paralyze them. He dipped needle tips in the liquid then he designed a wrist holder that let the wearer flick the weapon at the target."

My eyebrows rose. "Why don't all Rasha wear them then?"

"Once you take the secretion from this particular demon, it dies. Kind of like a bee with its stinger. Which would be fine since the only good demon is a dead demon, but there aren't a lot of this breed so Stingers are pretty rare."

"Wow. Tell me about Kane." My sneaky segue failed to catch him off-guard.

Ari spread his hands wide. Totally nonplussed. "What do you want to know?"

"All that delightful antagonism back there? Did you screw him?"

"He trained me for a while."

"Knowing you, that's not even a euphemism," I said.

"I don't think it's appropriate to discuss your colleagues' sex lives."

I shot him an incredulous look. "Of course it's not appropriate. Why do you think everyone does it?"

"You need new hobbies."

"You know I can sit here all night saying–" I adopted the whiniest voice I could– "did you sleep with Kane? Did you sleep with Kane? Did you–"

He flung the pillow back at me. "No. Geez. Shut up already. I didn't."

"But you wanted to."

Full credit to my brother, he nailed his poker face. The red flush on his neck, however, told a different story.

"You like him," I teased.

"I really don't. I may have at one time. Long ago in a galaxy far, far away."

I snorted.

"But he's toxic."

I gathered my notes up, tapping them into a neat pile. "That's not fair. He can't help having that poison power."

"I meant in his relationships. I wasn't kidding about your power reflecting who you are. The magic reflects an aspect of the user's personality. You shock. Kane poisons."

I sat up straight. This was fascinating. Wrong about me but amazing insight to have about everyone else. "What about Baruch? He's so Zen and strong. How does that fit?"

Ari worried at a hole in his jeans. "Baruch is a good guy."

"Relax, president of his fan club. This isn't gossip." Ari raised a single eyebrow. "Isn't just gossip," I clarified. "Pay attention. These guys are the ones sent to protect me. After today, I'm thinking that having the cheat sheet on them may help keep me alive as much as any fighting skills."

"Oh," he conceded. "Smart thinking."

"No shit."

Ari rolled onto his side, laying his head on his bent arm. He rubbed a hand over his bleary eyes. At this angle, I saw the purple bags under them.

"How you doing there?" I asked.

"Neither homicidal nor suicidal so quit looking at me like that," he said.

He lay his fist under his cheek, a lock of blond hair falling across his brow. It was so reminiscent of his little kid self, but without his even-tempered, good natured air, that it took all my will power not to hug him. He despised pity. Or sympathy, which he always took as pity. Stupid boy.

"My take on Baruch?" He scratched his jaw. "From what I've heard, he's taken some bad hits fighting."

I waited out his pause.

"He fights past the pain," Ari said. "Not always in a good way. Like he's denying its existence."

"So my guard consists of the poison prince, the man who refuses to admit he's human, angry Italian whose powers are still unknown to me, and the human blade. What do you know about him? Rohan?"

"Sorry, don't know much about him either. As an initiate I was only in contact with Rasha who stayed at the chapter house." Had Ari become Rasha that would have changed. He'd have been traveling the world, having adventures, and meeting his fellow brethren.

I sighed, motioning for my brother to hand over his phone. "You got a new one?"

"No longer an initiate. No longer worth tracking."

My hand closed tight around his phone. "Bastards." I calmed myself remembering that I was going to make this right for him. Since I couldn't do anything about that at this moment, I typed Rohan's name in to Google. Ms. Clara still had mine but hey, this way no one could track my search history on Snowflake. Millions of hits. I started scrolling.

"You're not going to find Rasha intel online," Ari pointed out. But he scooted closer to peer over my shoulder.

"Not Rasha. Break up. Dude has a fuckton of baggage. There's something going on with him and Drio. Love triangle maybe? Though I can't tell which of them was the loser in the scenario because neither strikes me as the girlfriend type." Saying the word "girlfriend" in conjunction with Rohan left a bad taste in my mouth.

I gave up after about forty pages of search results, tossing him back his phone in disgust. "Nothing."

"Maybe neither was the winner." Ari checked his email. "Demons, remember? People die."

I rubbed the back of my neck. If that were true, if they'd been in love with the same girl and somehow she died? It would explain a lot of the weirdness today. I turned bleak eyes on Ari. "If demons come after Rasha's loved ones, what does that mean for our family? I mean, what if one of them follows me home somehow?"

My brother stuffed the phone in his back pocket. "The Rasha laid wards around the house earlier. It'll keep us safe."

"That's good." Why was he staring at the corner of my wall like it fascinated him?

"Spill." I caught him in mid-rise, tumbling both of us on our asses on the bed.

"Why do I have to be the bearer of bad news?" he snapped, jumping up again. "I'm not even one of them and I have to do their dirty work? Screw that." He stormed from my room.

I pursed my lips, reviewing everything we'd said in the last couple of minutes but try as I might, I couldn't figure out what had set Ari off. I rewound further. Back to conversations at the Brotherhood's mansion.

I slipped on a pair of sneakers, threw a hoodie over my pajamas and pushed up my window. I couldn't see anyone out in the dark yard, but that didn't mean they weren't there. No way would Demon Club have left me unsupervised. It didn't account for Ari's freak out, but it did give me someone else to question.

Taking my tree escape route, I dropped onto the ground with no attempt to be stealthy, since I wanted to be seen by whoever was on guard duty.

The operative word being "seen." Not tackled to the ground, hitting it with a hard whoosh as all my breath left me. Though that may have been for another reason as my body instinctively recognized the scent of iron and musk.

"What have we here?" Rohan's voice vibrated against me.

I had to turn my head to answer or risk eating dirt. "Do you mean 'we' in the royal sense or are the voices in your head clamoring in unison?"

He stretched out on top of me, pinning me more firmly between him and the ground. "You didn't give the code word," he said, lazy amusement threading his voice.

"Eyeliner?" Grass tickled my cheek.

"Nope. Two more wrong guesses and I'll have to deal with you."

He was sick. Which made me doubly so because I shivered in pleasure at that so-called threat, my entire body yelling "throw the guesses!"

"Hamsa?" I asked.

"You Googled the engraving, huh?"

I was many things. Stupid was not one of them. I slammed my crackling left hand into him, being careful to hit his leather jacket, since frying him was not conducive to securing his assistance.

The zap was still enough to buck him off me, allowing me to roll out from under him.

"Don't mess with Lady Shock and Awe," I warned.

Rohan pulled on the jacket, examining it. "Fuck a duck, you're giving yourself superhero names already?" He rubbed the small scorch mark on his upper sleeve, then scowled.

"Your predilection for fowl aside," I flicked a spark of electricity at him. "I have a question."

"Good for you." He stood up, brushing off his ass.

Yeah, I looked. Yeah, he caught me. Yeah, I shrugged.

I pushed to my feet. "A nice butt won't get you out of answering, Emo Snowflake."

"Don't call me that."

"It's not your superhero name? Never mind." I patted his cheek. "I'll find you something."

"Lucky me." Rohan motioned for me to follow him out of the moonlight and into the shadows. "What's the question?"

I twirled a finger indicating the perimeter of my yard. "I know there are wards. You're here guarding me. So why was it weird when I asked to go home? What did Ari refuse to tell me?"

"You can stay here tonight but tomorrow you move into the chapter house." He placed his hand over my mouth to keep me from protesting. "It's the safest place for you to be. Especially if Asmodeus learns it was you."

When, not if.

I pulled his hand off, resisting the urge to suck one of his fingers into my mouth. "Okay." Was it getting hotter out here? I pushed my hoodie sleeves up.

He tensed. "That's it? No fight?"

"You have a fabulous impression of my intelligence. I'll explain this once so remember it. I'm not stupid. I'm also not endangering my family." I wound a curl around my finger, all casual. "Hey, I was just thinking. I know you checked actors on Samson's film, but what about the rest of the crew?"

Rohan rubbed the back of his hand across his chin. He hadn't shaved since yesterday, and the dark stubble along his jaw combined with the steely glint of his eyes was insanely hot, giving him a dangerous air. Correction. More dangerous.

"Drio checked producers, directors, all other above-the-line positions on King's last few films against the database maintained by intelligence," Rohan said. "No hits."

Damn. "There's a database?"

I guess I said it a little too fervently because Rohan held up his hand. "Stand down, Lolita. You don't get to troll for famous people we suspect."

Someday. When I was allowed to do more than just train and prove I should be allowed to continue breathing.

Now that I'd been out here a while in my pajamas, my skin was beginning to get goosebumps. I tugged my sleeves back down, zipping my hoodie up against the cool night air. "What about Samson's make-up artist?" I tapped my finger against my lip. "Obviously Samson is glamoured up and I get that if he is a demon, he's far more powerful than Josh, but when Josh got... excited, he flickered. Actors spend a lot of time with their make-up artists and maybe he'd want someone trustworthy around him in case he exposed himself."

Rohan was already texting a note to Drio to check it out.

"Seeing as I'm so useful–"

"Potentially," he said.

"How about a little quid pro quo?" I figured I'd work up to specific details. "I'm thinking that the downfall of a major demon would be just the thing to get the Brotherhood to listen to me."

Rohan slid his phone back into his pocket. "Don't even think of going out to look for one. You wouldn't know where to begin and you can't take one on."

"Rohan..." He waited while I debated how much of my Ari worries to share. "My brother isn't doing well. I'm scared he may not recover from this." My voice shook. "I know he's still an initiate and if I have some leverage that gets the Brotherhood to check and confirm it–"

"They'll induct him right away, and Ari will have his magic to keep him safe," Rohan finished.

"Yeah." I shot him my best beseeching look.

He sighed. "I feel for you and Ari both, but you need to be patient. It hasn't even been a week. Rushing into situations you're not yet ready for gets you dead."

And not rushing things might lose me my brother.

Shivering as much from cold as disappointment, I hooked my chin into the neck of the hoodie, folding the cuffs over my hands.

"You barely have anything on under there." Despite Rohan's contemptuous tone, when he poked at my sleeve, his hands lingered a second too long.

"Maybe the demons aren't the only ones who want bragging rights of bagging the first non-dick-swinging Rasha." I tugged away, irritated.

Rohan's nostrils flared. "Fuck you the first for thinking I kiss and tell," he said. "And fuck you the second if you think I need bragging rights when it comes to sex. You're not that much of a novelty."

The angry growl in his voice convinced me that his motives were the normal "have sex because sex with an attractive girl would be great" variety and not anything involving notches on belts.

This game I could play.

I placed my hand on my hoodie's zipper. "You want me to flash you?" My half-smile was accompanied by my best "sideways eye slide looking up through half-open lashes" maneuver.

A car's headlights swept over us.

Rohan pushed me deeper into the shadows. "Don't do me any favors."

I slid the hoodie zipper down, waiting to see if he'd stop me.

He didn't. Instead, he frowned as he inspected tonight's cotton sleepwear offering. "Yesterday's was cuter." He motioned around my cleavage. "It had that purple lace."

I glanced up at my window, realizing how far into the room I could see from here. "You perved on me last night? Some guard you are."

He didn't even have the good grace to look ashamed. "Bring more of those when you move."

"Because this is all about you."

Rohan bopped the end of my nose with his index finger. "See? Was that so hard to admit?"

Grumbling, secretly pleased, definitely annoyed with myself for figuring out how many cute, electricity-proof outfits I owned, I zipped up my sweater and headed inside.

11

What an ass.

And *what* an ass. I grasped the top of the chair in my bedroom against the full body swoon making me wonky. My body was on fire after that little encounter. Not in a Rasha way. I throbbed in a simmering coil of need, the feel of every steely inch of him imprinted on my skin.

I switched off my overhead light, pretending I was just getting ready to go to sleep, and enjoying the delicious sense of anticipation. Rohan might be infuriating in real life but he was prime source material for personal fantasy usage.

After latching my window and drawing my blinds tight, I settled myself on my bed. Letting myself get comfortable by taking a few steady inhales and exhales before I slid my hand under my shirt to skim my palms across my breasts.

Rohan's intense gold irises danced in my memory. My tits grew heavier and heavier in my hands and I tweaked my nipples, biting the inside of my cheek to keep from crying out at the zing that shot through me.

My other hand crept into my shorts, as I mentally lingered on all of Rohan's fine attributes, starting at the bottom and working my way up. The clench of his gluts as he'd jumped out the window that first night demanded multiple replayings.

I imagined what it would be like to start at his toes and lick my way up his body, lingering in the hollows behind his knees, nipping the hard muscle along his inner thigh, saving the image of taking him in my mouth–for now. My fingers met with wetness as I ran my index finger up and down along my opening. I wanted him bad, those hands holding me down. I wanted him to ask me to flash him in my backyard and I wanted to do it. My hips rolled.

Fumbling over my head with my other hand for my pillow, I stuffed it over my face to muffle the quiet moans I was beginning to make. Cuntessa de Spluge pulsed, demanding some "me time" so I obliged, ghosting my finger over my clit in the slowest of small circular motions.

I couldn't remember the last time I'd been so turned on. Or liked a guy so much. No, craved a guy. That's all it was.

Part of me yearned to tease this sensation out for as long as possible but patience was not my strong suit. I yanked my shorts all the way down and shoved the fingers of my other hand inside, pretending they were Rohan's. Praying my gasp was muted by the pillow in my mouth. Everything about him would be big and rough. His stubble against my nipples, his callused hands pushing deep within me, sending me over the edge. I bit my bottom lip, a heavy sigh shuddering through me.

Champagne bubbles danced through my body, my ab muscles tightening at the growing pull spiraling deeper and wider inside me. I rode my hand harder, not able to take it slow. My thighs shook; my breath came in irregular pants. Tipping my head back, I muffled my cries against my pillow. Tiny waves rippled out from my core, growing bigger and more intense.

Just as that final vibrating quake should have hurled me over the edge into fabulous free fall, an image of his smug grin at being my masturbatory material popped up on my internal screen.

There was a flash of blue. A burning sizzle lit Cuntessa up in high-voltage agony. I screamed into the pillow in the way one does when one has fucking electrocuted her clit, doubling over into the fetal position. I was hyperventilating, swearing in breathy gasps.

I guess no one else was upstairs to hear my shriek of pain because thankfully nobody came to check on me. Tears streamed down my cheeks. This was so unfair. My body could be literally coated in electricity and it didn't hurt but accidentally give myself one bad touch and I almost passed out. Shouldn't I be immune from myself? One more stupid detail to master.

Eventually, the pain knifing through me subsided enough for me to catch my breath. I flung the pillow covering my head across the room then probed Cuntessa gently with a gasped wince. I offered my profuse apologies to her but could practically hear her snottily informing me that this was the last straw. Mentally slapping me with a restraining order until such time as her pleasure could be guaranteed without useless dicks or lightning strikes.

Damn you, Rohan Mitra.

Damn you, Rasha.

And damn you, destiny.

With pain and sexual frustration vying for control of my body, I rolled into a tight ball. Stupid me fixating on the worst choice in men imaginable. Rohan wasn't hot stuff and he didn't have me under his sway.

On the plus side, now that he was out of my system, I was free to focus on what mattered–Ari. My mind was crystal clear, even if the occasional tear still leaked from my eyes.

A rather brilliant thought occurred to me as I lay sprawled on the covers, blinking through the hurt. Not every demon was equal on the evil hierarchy, and while lots were big bads, many more were mostly bottom feeders. Like the araculum. Still capable of doing damage, sure, but trading on intel rather than brute force and malevolence to stay alive.

If Rasha were the cops of the demon world, then there were bound to be some snitches amongst the criminals. All I had to do was find one and have him pass a message up the food chain to Asmodeus that I was the one who'd killed Josh and his sister.

I was moving into the chapter house anyway, and by the time Asmodeus showed up, I'd be living safely behind the wards and the guys could help me take him out. Even Rohan wouldn't be able to be mad at my outside-the-box thinking then, and he'd be honor-bound to help me. Of course if he wasn't, then he sucked, but with a big win like that, I'd be useful enough to force contact with the Executive, protocol be damned.

I drummed my fingers against my mattress. The good little Rasha thing to do would be to go tell my babysitter about this idea, except in this case, it was better to seek forgiveness than permission. I toyed with the primer and my stack of notes. Based on my admittedly limited understanding, curupira fell into a kind of mid-level bad zone. I'd dealt with the one I'd met quite effectively. How hard could it be to deal with a snitch?

Hmmm. Tiptoeing to the window, I cracked my blinds just enough to peer out, considering my odds. No sign of Rohan, but he still had to be prowling around. Keeping well away from the window in case my shadow gave me away, I slipped into a little all-black number–low slung jeans and a fitted, scoop neck top–perfect for cat burglary and escaping a house undetected. The final touch? Stuffing my hair under a black knit cap. Okay, perching it jauntily on my hair but it really completed the look.

Rohan was probably watching my window for signs of life, so I crept out of my room in a low crouch which wouldn't be visible from the ground. Once in the hallway, I exhaled, and strolled to Ari's bedroom.

I rapped on his door before easing it open.

Ari sat on his bed against his wooden headboard, still-dressed, his legs stretched out on his brown comforter with its graphic blocky design. Surrealist prints like Dali's *Persistence of Memory* with its melting clocks, Magritte's painting of a pipe with "Ceci, n'est pas une pipe." in script underneath it, and Gonsalves' row of ships that seemed to turn into an arched bridge, framed his walls.

"Whatcha doing?"

He looked up guiltily from texting, fumbling his phone. "Nothing."

"Or," I amended, skipping toward him, "*who* are you doing?"

He placed the phone face down on the bedside table, leaving it free for me to scoop up. "Have you no respect for personal property?" he sputtered.

I didn't bother responding to that ridiculous question, busy swiping the screen to get to the goods. I scrolled past a couple of flirty texts from whomever Ari had labeled as "Do Not Engage." Then jackpot. "Your 'nothing' has an awfully familiar nipple ring," I said, studying the well-defined naked chest in the photo that he'd been sent. "Thought you were mad at him?"

"I am. Which in his head means dial up the charm to get me to fall back in line." Ari snatched the phone away with, what was for him, a pretty good glower, stuffing it under the pillow behind his back. "What do you want?" His expression was infused with all the pain and long-suffering stemming from having a bratty younger sibling.

Younger by twelve minutes, but I did my best to be exemplary in the annoying department.

I perched on the end of his bed, suppressing my urge to rip out his hospital corners. "While I could pester you with questions that you really don't want to answer, I will skip that part because I am such a good sister."

His eyes narrowed. "You want something else."

I pointed a finger at him. "Bingo. Here's the thing." I cleared my throat trying to figure out how to ask my question while technically keeping my Rasha oath of secrecy.

"Nava." That was his impatient "talk or leave" voice.

"Know of any demon informants?"

Arms propped behind his head, he leaned back against the headboard, studying me. "What are you trying to find out that you don't want Rohan to know?"

"Just learning all aspects of this brave new world."

The gears turning in Ari's head were practically audible as he pinned me in his steady gaze. He tried to figure out what I was thinking, and I sat there pretending it didn't matter either way. It was our thing.

"Don't get mixed up in their mission. I know you and starfucking–"

"Hey!"

"Gossip," he amended.

"Don't say it like a euphemism," I muttered.

"But this is serious. They've been amassing info on Samson for ages. You charge in and you'll screw things up."

Startled, I raised my eyes to his. "Wait. You know?"

"No shit."

"Kane is such a blabbermouth."

Ari frowned. "Why do you assume I heard it from Kane?"

I spread my hands wide. "Who else would you have heard it from? How'd you get past the Mafia cone of silence?" I gasped. "Did you eavesdrop? Because only Rasha can know this stuff."

My brother flushed in what definitely was "Nava Red." He kicked my foot. "Are you fucking kidding me? You've been Rasha for the approximate life of a fruit fly and you think you're already going to know details I didn't after being around the Brotherhood my entire life?"

I bit my lip. "I don't think they live that long. The fruit–"

The mattress bounced as Ari lunged for me.

I jumped to my feet with a yelp. "I'm sorry. Jeez. I didn't know they were bandying about that information to all and–" I snapped my mouth shut at the look on his face.

"Let's try this again." I plastered on my sweetest smile.

He pointed at the door.

I straightened, wanting to present my idea with as much confidence as possible. On second thought, offering myself up as bait for Asmodeus might not secure me Ari's assistance, or worse, get my brother insisting on helping. Plan B–lie about my reasons. "Rohan and Drio have to go about this officially." I wrinkled my nose. "Somewhat officially. They have to pursue leads and all that bullshit."

"Actually investigate."

"Whatever." I picked up the cologne on his dresser and sniffed it. "Unofficial channels can make things happen so much faster. If there is a snitch, he'd be in a good position to put us on to the hard evidence we need to prove King's demon status and take this bastard down." I cracked my knuckles. "I'll make the snitch an offer he can't refuse."

"No." At least he didn't laugh. He also confirmed there was a snitch, which strengthened my resolve.

I crawled back onto the bed with my best pleading look.

Ari pulled his phone out from beneath the pillow and snuck another look at it. "Rohan had Xiaoli check that possibility out before he was reassigned to Istanbul. The redcap didn't know anything."

"Aha! Being such a devoted student, I know that a redcap is a goblin and that goblins are notorious trickster demons. Perhaps this snitch pulled one over on ol' Xiaoli. See how equipped I am to deal with him?"

A flash of amusement crossed his face. "Left off your studying at 'G,' did you?"

I pressed on. "How hard can it be to intimidate a goblin? Aren't they short old men?

"You're thinking of gnomes."

"Red hats, beards, it's all of a type."

"Goblin beards are optional. Also, gnomes don't exist and if they did, they wouldn't bathe their hats in the blood of their victims," Ari said. "Or have razor sharp teeth."

"But they share pointy ears."

His gaze drifted back to his phone. "What's your point?"

I grabbed the damn thing, trapping the phone under my leg. "Maybe Xiaoli's incentive wasn't strong enough."

"Death and torture. Pretty reliable." With a quick fake-out, he stole the phone back but didn't look at it.

"You boys," I scoffed, flapping a hand at him. "Always going for the stick. How about trying a carrot now and then?"

"Such as?"

I ran a hand along my body.

Ari's head shake was pure bafflement. "What is it with you and demon sex?"

"I'm not sleeping with him." I smacked Ari's arm. "But if he gets to be the first demon to meet the female Rasha and live...?" A nod and a wink.

Resounding silence.

"Come on," I begged. "You said it yourself. You grew up around Demon Club. You have to know who the snitch is."

Ari tugged off his socks, firing them into the corner of the room. "I don't know who he is. Just what he is."

I scooted away from his gross bare feet. "A promising start. Besides, I bet he's not all that dangerous as demons go, right? Introduce me."

"Why are you so desperate to be a part of this? Are you trying to impress Rohan?"

"No." Well, not like that. I wasn't ready to tell Ari about my plan to restore him to his rightful path because he might be angry enough to tell me to butt out and forget it. I settled for giving him a half-truth. "I want to up my stock."

Ari waited long enough before answering that I thought my idea was dead in the water. "Rohan isn't going to let you leave," he said.

I clapped my hands in delight. "Of course he isn't. Which is why you need to sneak me out. Then you can return to your regularly scheduled sexting. Or is this angry, make-up sext?"

Given the choice of helping me, the Rasha, or dishing with me, the sister, it was a no-brainer that Ari would pick the former.

The sneak out was a success. I gave a loud whoop, zipping down the street in Dad's Prius, though a cooler ride would have been nice. Hybrid electrics didn't exactly scream badass but blasting "Bad Girls" by M.I.A. went a long way to set the correct ambience.

Where would a scuzzy demon informant hang out? Or rather, the person who knew the scuzzy demon informant, since Ari could only get me to a go-between. Would I have to navigate a low-rent bar filled with sketchy clientele? A drug den at the end of a shadowy alleyway?

Or the brick bungalow I pulled up to? The front grass had been replaced with raked gravel which gleamed in the moonlight, while a giant fig tree off to one side provided the only greenery. A quick double check of the address confirmed this was the right place so I crunched my way along the dark flagstone path and up the stairs.

I rapped twice, remembering Ari's warning that this guy was human and I wasn't allowed to zap the info out of him. Still, that left a lot of leeway.

An old man with a pronounced Adam's apple, his pants and argyle sweater hanging loose off his lanky frame, answered the door. He took a long drag from the ashy cigarette in his hand, exhaling slowly with a bushy raised eyebrow.

"I'm looking for the goblin," I said.

"Stellar verbal skills, kid." He stretched an arm out to tap off some ash. Onto my shoes.

I kicked the side of my runners against the stones, trying to shake them clean while putting all my "don't mess with me 'tude" into the glower I shot his way.

"Let me guess. Bad cop?" He sucked back another hit and waved me inside.

Old Dude led me through the tiny entryway and into his living room. Every inch was covered in UFO paraphernalia. Yellowing news clippings detailing sightings papered the walls. The ceiling was plastered in UFO photos of varied graininess.

I let out a low whistle.

Years of cigarette smoke had baked into every particle of the place and was rapidly baking into me. I didn't want to spend any longer here than I had to. I lay a hand across my mouth and chin as if deep in thought, but really trying to make a filter so I wouldn't gag.

A wooden bookcase held models of different types of spaceships and figurines of alien races. I scanned them, noting the careful detail. "You made these."

"Give the girl a gold star." His sarcasm grated on my nerves but I needed the snitch's location.

"I've always wondered about alien life," I said politely.

He snorted, scratching at his stubble with a nicotine-stained finger. "Because you're stupid? They don't exist." He glanced wistfully around the room.

"Demons exist. Why can't aliens? Maybe they're just waiting to show themselves."

He exhaled a stream of smoke at me. "False hope'll kill ya."

I fanned the second-hand death out of my face. "Then why have all this?" I motioned to all his ufology stuff in confusion. "The models alone must have cost a fortune."

"African nations have smaller GDPs than I spent on these fuckers." His jaw hardened. "Two doctorates and I still got it so wrong." He ground his cigarette out in a mug with Scully and Mulder's faces on it and the phrase "I want to believe" written in blocky print underneath.

O-*kay*, bitter. "Goblin," I prompted.

The old man blinked as if he'd forgotten my presence. "You allergic to small talk? Sit down already." He dropped into a worn recliner with several burn marks on the shiny arms. "Did you bring payment?"

My face fell. "Payment?"

"A token of gratitude for my information. It's a give and take economy here, missy."

I lit up my left hand, holding its snapping crackling glory out with a cruel grin. "One zap or two?"

The unlit cigarette he'd just picked up tumbled to the carpet. "Rasha?"

"Give the man a gold star."

"How?" He reached over to pick it up, popping it in the corner of his mouth.

"Shit happens," I said. "Now, the clock is ticking. I'm not up to snuff on all the Rasha rules and regulations, plus this is an unsupervised visit, which means I have no trouble finding out firsthand how much damage I can do to you."

He lit the cigarette. "Do your worst," he rasped. "I never planned on living this long anyway."

"Figured the mothership would get you long before this, huh?"

He sucked down a lungful of death, pursing his lips and making three lopsided smoke rings. "Aren't Rasha supposed to be menacing badasses?"

I shot a couple of sparks at him. "I'm a menacing badass."

He leaned back in his recliner with a smirk. "You don't have the literal or figurative balls to hurt an old man, and since you didn't bring the appropriate bribe, we're done."

I stood there seething because he was right. I couldn't hurt him. But if I didn't, and word got out that I was soft, it'd mean a rep as easy prey.

Easier prey.

"Tell me what you want and I'll get it for you." If the Vancouver chapter dealt with this guy even semi-regularly, there had to be some kind of contingency fund for the bribe. Though I shuddered at the paperwork involved. And explaining how I'd found him. Could I bribe Ms. Clara to keep this visit from Rohan?

The old man rose out of his seat, heading for the front door at a good clip. "Out you go..." He paused, half-turning back to me. "What's your name, anyway?"

"Nava," I sighed.

He choked on his cigarette. "Nava?" He stabbed a finger at me. "What's your last name?"

"Katz," I replied, totally confused.

He burst out laughing.

"Old man, you're pissing me off."

A few more guffaws and he got himself under control. He tore a corner off a detailed sketch of an alien, grabbing a stubby pencil and scrawling something across the drawing. "The goblin should be here for another half hour."

I took the paper. "What about the cost?"

"This one's on the house."

"Why?"

He reached his knobby fingers out as if to pluck the paper away. I got the hint and fled.

I plugged the address he'd given me into the car's GPS, finding it on a two-block long street in one of the skeezier areas of town. I pulled into the tiny, weed-choked parking lot, gazing up at the sputtering neon sign for Motel Shangri-Lola, having had no idea this place existed.

Motel Shangri-Lola was a low slung building painted a faded green. More a memory of green than actual paint. Lola wasn't some former grand dame of a motel fallen on hard times, no, she'd been brought into existence a hard-livin' fungirl. An impression made more vivid by the row of outward-leaning scraggly pines extending from either side of the building, like legs drunkenly falling open.

I slammed the car door, strode up the sidewalk, flung open the lobby door, and gasped. My eyes watered at the overpowering stench of tuna fish. I threw my sleeve up over my nose until I'd climbed the worn stairs to the second floor. Sniffing and finding the air tolerable, if not fresh, I dropped my arm, searching the room numbers for 207.

It was a thick brown door like all the others in the hallway. I pressed my ear against it, but couldn't hear anything, so grasping the knob and finding it unlocked, I opened it, hoping to surprise the demon.

A dim table lamp provided the sole lighting in the room but it was strategically placed to show off the velvet painting of "Shangri-Lola" herself, a large-breasted wonder in shades of blue. On the table under it sat a digital recording device, capturing the sounds from the room adjacent to this one. Specifically the slow but steady pounding of the headboard against the wall and some man's rumbled, "Yeah, baby. Use that cat tongue."

I didn't realize he'd meant it literally until I heard his partner answer in some kind of demon language. Seems the snitch was a goblin P.I. on the case of some human/demon bow chica wow wow. Gathering evidence of a little interspecies adultery?

Speaking of the snitch... On the far side of *this* room, lay some short chick in shadow. She rested atop a garbage bag spread on top of the faded bedspread, staring up at the ceiling, one black, knee-high boot tapping against the lumpy double mattress.

I hadn't expected a female goblin. I stepped closer trying to spot her pointy red cap and long white beard, or just her facial features, when I got distracted by the guy in the next room orgasming with a final hard pound against the wall and a lusty shout.

There was silence for a minute and then the sound of wet snuffling. I grimaced.

"One minute you're enjoying your tawdry affair in a bed solidified with the sweat of a thousand asses, the next you're laying in a demon wet spot with the niggling suspicion that your kink is a bit too out of hand," said the woman here with me.

I froze, knowing that voice anywhere. "Leo?"

My high school best friend bolted up, allowing me to see her face, and the familiar fall of red hair that spilled over one shoulder. She blinked her brown eyes twice, her small silver eyebrow ring glinting as it caught the light. "Nava? What the shit are you doing here?"

"What are *you* doing here?" My brain failed to compute her presence.

She motioned toward the neighboring room with the sex noises. "I was on a job. P.I. work."

Huh? But the old dude had sent me here because– "You're the goblin?" My heart stuttered. That wasn't possible. This was my Leonie in her trademark black stockings, cut-off shorts, and funky T-shirt worn underneath a cool velvet long-sleeved shirt, accessorized with all her silver jewelry.

Leo scrambled off the bed, looking around frantically. "Is Ari here?"

Ari?! A growl tore from my throat and I slammed my crackling hand right into her chest, knocking her back.

"Psycho!" Leo threw a chair at me.

It winged me in the gut.

"Fuuuhhhck." I ran after her but she'd raced into the bathroom and slammed the door. "You used me for my brother?" I jiggled the knob but it didn't turn so I tried ramming it with my shoulder. Still nothing. Lola had surprisingly good bones.

I pounded on the door. "Come out here and face me, you demon coward."

"Who said I was a demon?"

"Nice try."

She pounded on the door back at me. "Stop pounding!"

My hand was getting red. I considered blasting the door open but didn't want to risk sending all of Lola up in flame. That didn't stop me threatening to do it if Leo didn't open up.

"You pyro cow!" she screeched.

"Practice for what I'll do to your manipulative goblin ass as soon as you unlock this door." I kicked the wood.

"I can stay in here all night," she tossed out in a self-righteous tone.

I pulled a chair up close, straddling it backwards. "As if. You can't go two hours without food."

"I didn't use you for Ari. I didn't even know you existed at first."

"Because that makes it so much better." My heart pounded in my ears. Our entire friendship was a lie. It wasn't that she'd hidden her goblin status from me, or that as a demon, she'd infiltrated my family to spy on my brother, though those ranked close seconds on things I was pissed about. The thing that hurt the most, that knotted my guts and strung my chest tight, was that our friendship hadn't even been real, just another means to an end in the ongoing demon-Rasha war.

I don't know how long we sat there in silence, me white-knuckling the top of the chair. Long enough for Cat Tongue to hit round two with his bed partner in the next room. Long enough for my hurt to harden into rage.

Long enough for Leo to say, miserably, "I'm hungry."

"Then come out," I answered in my sweetest voice.

There was a pause before she spoke. "How are you Rasha anyway? Your balls finally drop and you realized your pathetic rack was really flabby manboobs?"

I kicked the door, relishing her yelp. "I prefer Fallen Angel. My hot badassery could no longer go unrecognized."

Her snort sounded like an asthmatic donkey. Hearing it again, I almost laughed. Almost. "You can't kill me," she said. "Goblin or not, I'm still the one who lent you my favorite shirt for your first date with Stefan and held your hair when you puked your guts out later because he was such a dickhole."

She totally had. "Had you actually been my friend during that time, those points would count in your favor," I snottily replied.

The door flew open. Leonie hopped out, a tiny ball of fury, and winged a roll of toilet paper at me. "There may have been a few facts I left out about my personal history but I was totally your friend. *You* dumped me. *You* stopped calling me." She crossed her arms, her chin jutting out.

That was kind of true, too. "You were spying on my brother." I stroked my chin. "No wonder you always had to pluck your chin hairs. I thought you were part goat, but it was just your goblin heritage."

Leo covered her chin. "Take it back. You know I'm sensitive about that."

I bleated at her.

She smacked me. That's when it descended into the worst of cat-fights.

It was official. I sucked as a demon hunter.

12

Half an hour later, Leo sported a split lip and my scalp was raw from the hair that she'd pulled out, but we'd exhausted our pent-up resentments and called an uneasy truce. We made our way to our favorite diner, the only conversation in the car being Leo's comment that my dad's taste in music still sucked balls.

The Chesterton had gone hipster in the year and a half or so since we'd last been here. Gone were the abundance of spidery ferns and the mini jukeboxes at each booth. Now, a DJ spun electronica in one corner, while an open kitchen showcased the tattooed staff making hand-scratch food and baked goods. At least I didn't have to suffer through the misery of a communal table. A blessing upon the crippling cost of gut-job renos that kept this place from complete desecration.

I studied the collection of kitschy salt and pepper shakers on shelves running the length of one wall, searching for a safe topic of conversation because I wasn't sure how to dive back into the shark-infested waters of our hemorrhaging friendship.

"Leonie? Nava? Ohmigod!"

We both winced at the squeal from the cash register. "Back Rub" Bailey was our high school's most popular everything, with a tendency to get touchy-feely when she got drunk. Bailey was also the sweetest person who ever lived. I think she bottle-fed endangered baby seals in her spare time. Leo and I were just such cynical twats that she grated on us.

But we pasted bright smiles on our faces and gave the requisite hugs.

"What are you guys up to?" she asked.

"Crim major," Leo said.

"Got some things on the go," I replied.

That earned me a pity smile. "That's great."

I nodded gamely. "What about you?"

"I'm dancing with Ballet BC now!"

My smile wavered. Bailey was a bunhead and as determined to make it with her dance career as I'd been. "I'm happy for you." I wasn't petty enough to be catty since it was ballet. Had she been a tapper, shanking may have been involved.

Leo shot me a sideways glance before asking, "Still dating Suki?"

A brilliant smile lit up Bailey's face. She thrust out her hand. "Engaged!"

Leo squinted at the small diamond. "Hmm. Princess cut, nice girth. I grade–"

"H grade," Bailey corrected.

Leo shot her an appraising look. "Half carat. Payment plan?"

Bailey blinked. I could have enlightened her about the whole goblin thing and their gem fetish, but it was just clicking for me why Leo had always made us swing by the jewelry stores at the mall when we were teens to check out the most jewel-encrusted old lady designs.

"Um, cash," Bailey said. "Those interest charges will sneak up on you."

"Find you in a dark alley and try to break your kneecaps," Leo said, nodding sagely.

Bailey's mouth fell open in a horrified "O."

I cut in, leaning my elbow on Leo's shoulder. She tried to jostle me off, but at five-foot-two, her shoulders were perfect resting height, and there my elbow remained. "You picked a winner, Bailey," I said. "We're happy for you."

The hostess motioned to us that our table was ready, so we said our good-byes.

"You think her and Suki have figured out how to make out like normal people yet?" I asked, sliding into the booth across from Leo.

Leo put in her drink order then leaned toward my face in slow motion, her mouth open wide. "Kiss me," she said in a weird distorted voice.

"Yeah, baby," I answered, equally slowly and messed up. Our mouths came closer and we snapped our teeth at each other a few times. Then my anger trumped our jokey solidarity and I dropped the mocking impression, sitting back with a rigid spine.

That set Leo off. "'*We're happy for you.*' Gawd, you *are* Rasha. Earnest bitch."

I slapped my menu down on the green and white marbled arborite tabletop. "All right. You've got one chance to stop me from dusting you after I eat. Asmodeus, what do you know?" I figured the Rasha code of silence didn't apply to demons. Well, not this one.

"Not much beyond he's big time." Leo didn't look up from her menu, but she also didn't scratch the inside of her right wrist so she was telling the truth.

"Can you get a message to him?"

The waitress arrived with Leo's Coke and my water, asking for our orders–pulled pork poutine for me because, bad Jew, and a mushroom burger that I know Leo got so that I wouldn't want a bite. Fungus was a medical condition to clear up with ointment, not food.

Leo took a dainty sip of her Coke. "Are you going to apologize?"

"Why? So you can and it's all better? It doesn't work that way," I said. "You came into my life, into *Ari's* life with the intent to cause harm. It's an unforgivable offense. Plus, you know. Demon. Which, what? Are you glamoured up right now?"

Leo violently crunched a piece of ice. "I'm a half-goblin. From the French fling that led to my existence. Mom still doesn't know and I don't have another form I revert to. So no. No glamour required."

"You're a PD?"

"Yeah, I'm Pissed. Definitely." Leo ripped off a chunk of her burger. "Screw you. I'm not practice."

My best friend from high school was a halfie, a practice demon, though the moment I'd seen Leo's expression, I'd regretted saying it. "I'm sorry about that but it doesn't change the fact that you're a goblin."

"You're a lot of things, Nava," she said, "but I never thought you were prejudiced."

"I'm Rasha. You're evil spawn. It's natural order, not racism." I traced a line through the condensation in my water glass with intense fascination.

"Good luck navigating the demon world with that attitude."

"What's there to navigate?" I toyed with the salt shaker, tilting the salt back and forth between my hands. "Kill. That's it. It's pretty black and white."

Leo plucked the shaker out of my hands, dumped some salt in her palm, and licked it. "Nice try. Also, you're wrong. It's all shades of gray. That's your problem, Nee. You've never seen that. None of the Rasha do."

I slammed my hand against the table. "You lost all rights to that nickname."

She held up her hands, more warding me off than calming me.

The waitress deposited our food without picking up on the tension. We ate in silence for a bit.

I stirred a fry around in the gravy. "What do you mean that none of the Rasha see the gray? Is that relevant to Asmodeus?"

"Could be. Even a villain is a hero in his own story." Leo pulled the pickle off her burger, popping it in her mouth.

I balled up my napkin, frustrated with the lack of concrete information. "The why doesn't matter. Just the what. So tell me, *bestie*, what's Asmodeus up to?"

Leo gave good glare. "It's not like there's a newsletter where the members list their current nefarious plots."

"So much for your stealthy P.I. skills." There was more bite in my voice than I'd intended.

Leonie hit the ketchup bottle with a hard thwack. "Back off. It pays my bills and tuition. Not all of us have Mommy and Daddy footing the bill for our prolonged adolescence."

"If I was still dancing, my scholarship would have taken care of it."

"Nee-Nava, come on. I'm sorry." She raked her hands through her bone-straight hair. "That was super bitchy. You're just not giving me a break here."

"Why should I?" Aside from the fact that I miss you.

"Because I didn't infiltrate your family, okay?" Her cheeks flushed as red as her hair. "Yeah, I did use you for Ari. I was massively in love with him."

"With all the sweet longing that only a thirteen-year-old can have," I mocked. I'd had no clue. That rankled too. "Get a message to Asmodeus. Tell him I'm the one he's looking for and that he can find me at the chapter house. Can you do that?" I wished I could let go of my resentment and just trust her again. Have us pick up where we left off like nothing had changed between us.

But everything had, and given the equal parts anger and hurt in her voice when she snapped, "Enable your death wish, Rasha? Why, I'd like nothing better." Leo wasn't ready to let bygones be bygones either. "Are you sure about this?" she asked a few minutes later.

I speared a cheese curd. "Do you want to be friends with me again?"

She grimaced and took a big bite of mushroom burger, glowering at me until she swallowed. "No, but still. Asmodeus is bad news. And when you upset a demon–"

"Bad things happen, yada yada." I made a talking mouth noise with my hand. "Believe me, I've gotten the spiel."

Just to be certain, Leo went into graphic detail about what he might do to me in payback, using two forks, half a hamburger bun, and the desecration of my poutine to illustrate. "You still want me to pass on this message?"

"No, but yes. It's Ari."

She sighed. "It's Ari."

"And speaking of my darling twin, if you want back in my good graces, you'll also let me read your teen diary."

Leo had been a freak about me never even touching the glittery thing.

She gave this incredibly demony half-growl. Amazing I'd never figured it out before. Then she sighed. "If I bring it over, are we friends again?" She said it like she didn't care, but she was leaving gauges in her remaining burger.

Even if it was Leo and me, it was still demon and Rasha. Talk about complicated. Rohan would never agree to help me with Ari if he found out. Being considered a demon-lover wasn't going to win me any friends–of the human or devil spawn variety. In fact, I'd probably just signed my own death warrant with the Brotherhood.

I snagged one of her fries since she'd rendered my poutine inedible. "Dummy. Your diary better be PG where my brother is concerned."

"Please. I know what you consider PG. I read your fanfic." She handed me the vinegar before I could ask for it.

I grinned for the first time since I'd found her again, remembering the whopper of a bombshell I had yet to drop on her about the inclusion of a certain Rohan Mitra in my life.

Leo narrowed her eyes at me. "I know that look. It preceded my broken arm, three double dates I'd pay to have surgically removed from my memories, and a ride home in a cop car. Forget it. I want an annulment."

I blew her a kiss. "Too late, baby. We're friends." Or would be eventually, I hoped.

I had a lot to think about on my drive home after I dropped Leo off at her apartment. Yes, I'd nearly killed our friendship when I'd been at my lowest, but that had been my screw up. The universe had given me a second chance and no matter how hard repairing it would be, I'd regret it forever if I didn't try.

However, it would take some massive finagling to keep Demon Club from finding out about her. *I* could threaten to kill Leo but no one else could. Xiaoli had known about her for sure, but I doubted any of the new guys did, since they'd have confronted her already if they had. That left Kane. I'd have to find out what he knew.

I floored the gas pedal to catch a yellow light.

These past few days had been a trip, and not a particularly pleasurable one. Would they have treated Ari the same way had our positions been reversed? No, I'd be willing to bet good money that had some dude suddenly found himself one of the Fallen Angels, he'd have been welcomed with open arms. Also hookers, blow, and a giant circle jerk. Not patted on the head, and placed under armed guard, while his fate was decided upon.

My near heart attack today had proven one thing to me. At the end of the day, the only one who could save me *was* me. So I'd play their games. I'd train. I'd fight. I'd study. I may have been a fuck up but I was also a survivor. Whether the Brotherhood liked it or not, I was going to survive them too.

And get my twin fighting beside me where he belonged. That idea just got cooler and cooler.

The car in front of me braked, so I did too, caught in a momentary snarl of traffic headed into downtown to party, the other cars filled with laughing people enjoying life. Good attitude.

With both demons and certain Rasha gunning for me, who knew what tomorrow held? This was my life and, ultimately, I was the one who had to figure out how to live—and live with—this new version of it.

So when Rohan ambushed me at the curb after I'd parked, planning to menace me into submission or apology or something, all I did was grin at him. My talk with Leo hadn't been all Asmodeus-focused. I'd also gotten a tidbit of Samson info from her since I needed something to show for my excursion. Telling Rohan that I'd outed myself to Asmodeus was not going to happen. I'd mention it after the demon was dead.

While Leo hadn't been able to tell me what type of demon Samson was or even that there was any actual confirmation of his evil status since he was that sneaky, she did tell me that she'd heard he had spent time in France. I passed the information on now.

Given how Rohan flattened his lips, he didn't expect that. His expression as I told him what I learned was priceless, cycling through suspicion, disbelief, a momentary flash of impressed approval—which I savored—before veering back to suspicion.

"Let me get this straight," he said. "You managed to find a demon informant who happened to have this knowledge and was willing to give it to you, when Xiaoli could get nothing?"

I nodded.

"You got the intel how?" He smirked at me.

"Not like that, you pig."

"I want to talk to him."

"No!"

"No?" Rohan's voice was a deadly calm. He braced his hand against the car roof, trapping me.

Oy vey. I was walking a serious subordination line here but I couldn't let him get to Leo. "This informant could prove a valuable resource. He trusts me. You guys go storming in and scare him and that'll be the end of it. It can't hurt to check out what I've said. If it turns out to be a crock of shit, then we know not to trust the goblin."

I crossed my fingers behind my back, keeping my gaze steady until he gave a sharp nod. "I had one other thought," I said.

"Give me a minute to brace myself."

"Since Mommy and Daddy demon probably didn't name their bundle of joy Samson, there has to be a reason he chose it. Does the obvious biblical connection get us anywhere?"

Rohan raised an eyebrow. "Us? Did I miss the memo where you were assigned to this mission?"

"Wouldn't you rather have me occupied in a productive manner?"

He looked doubtful at that, but answered me. "We checked out that possibility ages ago. Nothing correlates. But you're thinking along the right lines," he added begrudgingly. "However, you're done fact-finding for tonight. Fact-finding entirely where Samson is concerned. He's dangerous and I don't want him getting even an inkling that you're looking into him."

"Aw. You care." I ducked out from under his arm.

"Yeah. About you blowing all my hard work. Got it?"

"Got it." I headed up the front walk. "See? Going upstairs now."

He stood there, watching me. "No more sneaking out."

"Promise."

I'd tested my limits with Rohan and thus the Brotherhood. Any more unauthorized dealings on my part would undermine my plan and possibly lead to my "retirement" by Demon Club. No, I was smart enough to quit while I was ahead.

There would be no more sneaking out tonight.

This time, when I left the house again about twenty minutes later, I did it pretty blatantly. No way was I jumping out windows in my black three-inch stilettos with the hot pink soles—my one pop of color, save for my equally hot pink lips. Despite the warm weather we'd been having, this early in March it was still a bit too cold to go jacketless, but a coat would have ruined my overall effect and besides, the peaked nipple look really accessorized the outfit.

I sashayed down my front stairs, making a silent bet as to whether I'd make it to the taxi idling at the curb before Rohan found me or if I'd have to go find him first.

His hand clamped on mine before I was halfway down the walk, spinning me around. "Where do you think you're—"

He choked like he'd swallowed his tongue. Highly gratifying.

I pinched his cheek like a maiden aunt. "We're going out."

Not only had I almost died today, I'd also made some very good progress. A treat was in order and a cookie wasn't going to cut it. Balls, babes, and booze it was.

It took a moment for Rohan to register that I'd spoken since he was too busy staring at the silky scrap of black fabric I called a dress. "You should be in bed," he said.

I leaned in close, my orangey perfume teasing the air around us. "Mmm, I should. The question is, with who?"

The taxi driver honked.

"My chariot awaits." I tugged my arm free. "I expect demons will be after me soon and I'm not going to be shut up like a nun for the rest of my life. Now," I strode toward the cab, forcing Rohan to follow me. "I'm off to play pool and get exceedingly drunk." I opened the back door and slid in. "Coming?"

He squatted down out of view of the cabbie and flicked out one of his finger blades. "I could make you stay."

I crossed my bare legs, tantalizingly slow. "Do your worst."

He flicked out another blade.

"In or out?" the pudgy cabbie asked.

Grumbling, Rohan shoved me over, got into the cab, and slammed the door shut.

I laughed. "Neon Paradise," I told the driver. It was my favorite club boasting reasonable-ish priced drinks, pool tables, a low douchebag to normal guy ratio, and good music.

The cabbie grunted in confirmation.

Other than the Bhangra music on the stereo, the ride was pretty quiet. My smile widened with each block away from home. This was the best part of going out, when infinite possibility stretched out before me.

The cab hit the lit up Granville strip in Vancouver's downtown entertainment district, the streets teeming with people in a free-flow of life and music.

I paid the fare, then got out, trusting Rohan to follow.

A quick shake to my mane of curls, then clutch in hand, I waltzed past the people stuck in line, strutting right up to Max, the huge bouncer and keeper of the velvet rope. The red glow of the sign cast a soft filter over us.

"Looking extra fine tonight, Nava," he said, unhooking the rope for me to pass.

"You charmer, Max. I brought a friend. That okay?"

Rohan stood behind me, scowling.

"He's not as pretty but we'll let it go." He winked at me. "Have a good time." The bouncer peered at Rohan. "Do I know you?"

"No." Rohan grabbed my hand.

I barely had time to toss Max a little wave over my shoulder before Rohan dragged me into the club's all-black foyer, the floor vibrating with the pounding bass coming from deeper inside.

I tried to pay for Rohan's admission. "My treat," I said, pushing his wallet away.

He knocked my hand out of the way and handed the cashier a couple of twenties. She practically fell out of her little black dress in her haste to take the money and make skin contact with him.

"That's very sweet, but I forced you down here," I said.

"Don't I know it," he replied.

"So I pay."

"No, I pay."

I shrugged, holding out my hand for the blacklight stamp that would allow me to be re-admitted. "Then the first round is on me."

Rohan made a noncommittal sound as we stepped into the club proper, already busy scanning the room. I did too, trying to see the large space as he did. Pleated curtains framed by multi-colored spotlights illuminated cozy booths along one side. An enormous dance floor separated the seating area from the curved bar and pool tables that ran along the far wall.

A techno remix of a disco classic had the dancers going wild. My foot tapped to the music, my brain automatically finding "one" in the beat as my jumping off point to move to this rhythm. You could take the girl out of dance…

"How long do you plan on being reckless?" Rohan asked, his eyes not leaving the crowd.

"Putting a time frame on it defeats the purpose. Tell me something." I centered myself in his field of vision so he was forced to look at me. "When did you quit going out? Right after you became Rasha? Or was it a gradual slide into boring?" I rested my hand on his bicep, sending a clear message to the statuesque brunette honing in on him.

She sailed past like this had been her direction regardless, though not without a dismissive sniff my way.

Rohan was oblivious. "That's different."

"Why? Because you're male?"

"Because I'm trained."

"Does training keep you from being killed?"

A muscle jumped in his cheek. "It helps."

"But it doesn't prevent it. You said it yourself. You don't expect there to be enough of you to bury. This gig doesn't come with guarantees, Rohan. I know I'm the big shiny prize, but can you honestly say that hasn't been each of you at one time or another?"

From the tight frustration on his face, I'd made my point.

"I'll give this my all," I said, flipping my dark hair off my shoulder. "Prove my worth so that the demons are scared shitless of me and the Brotherhood can't bear to do without me." I jabbed him in the chest. "But I won't give up who I am in the process. Those evil buggers are going to come after me until I die. Don't force me to stop living in the meantime."

He rubbed his hand roughly through his hair.

I curled my fingers into my palms, imagining playing with those silky strands. Toying with them to my heart's content. Toying with *him* in all the most delicious ways.

"I'm supposed to take care of you," he said.

"You're supposed to guard me," I corrected. "I have to take care of myself. But if you really want to be useful?" I pointed to the pool tables across the way. "Rack 'em."

With that I went off to get shots, enjoying all the blatant looks from hot boys. One way or another, I was going to scratch the itchy edge inside me, tomorrow be damned. Which in this crazy new reality was a distinct possibility.

13

From the glowers I got when I arrived at the pool table with our shots, it appeared Rohan had forced a group of frat boys to wrap up their game. While they were too wussy to say anything to him directly, it didn't stop a few hissed "pushy bitch" comments flung my way.

My bodyguard had made himself positively cozy, draping his leather jacket over a tall stool, leaving him in a tailored, short-sleeved charcoal shirt that emphasized his athletic build.

Drinks in hand, I let myself enjoy the vision of him racking for Eight-ball.

He removed the triangle with a deft hand, then seeing me with the drinks, eyed the clear liquid. "No whipped cream?"

"I prefer my shots not remind me of STIs. These are G Bombs." I said, holding one out to him. "Cinnamon schnapps and vodka."

He didn't take the glass.

"Sorry. I didn't even think to ask. Are you an AA member?"

"Hardly."

"You were a rock star. Addictions are within the realm of possibility." I waggled the shot glass at him again.

"I'm on the clock."

I left the drinks on a nearby high round table, licking sticky spicy cinnamon schnapps off my fingers before choosing a cue stick off the wall rack. "Right. Babysitting duty. We'll play for it. Loser drinks."

He tested out some cues as well. "I'll try to contain my excitement."

Rohan offered to let me go first but I wanted to see his form on his break shot, so I waved him over to the table. He bent over, cue held steady, preferring to hit the head ball from slightly off to the left. The racked balls broke with a satisfying crack. He even managed to sink the three-ball, but his five got tangled up in a nasty cluster.

"Not bad." I eyed the table for my best move.

"By all means, do better." He slid past me, his ass deliberately brushing against my hip.

Amateur. I wasn't that easily distracted, though feel free to rub up against me any time. Gripping the cue with a confident hold an earthquake couldn't shake, I sank three balls in rapid succession. I straightened up and smiled. "Better, like that?"

Rohan scratched at his chest. "I was going easy on you, but if that's how you want to play it…"

I picked up the chalk. "It is."

He leaned over the table. "Buckle up, baby."

I learned something very interesting in the next little while. Rohan was exceedingly competitive. There was no banter, no joking around. You'd have thought humanity's survival depended on the outcome of the game, he was so laser-focused.

In the end, though, I sank the eight-ball first. I picked up both shots and made him take one. "L'chaim." I clinked my glass to his and shot the drink back, shivering at the sharp burn of booze hitting my throat, warming a path down to my stomach.

"Rack 'em."

Rohan placed his empty glass next to mine. "What happened to 'loser drinks?'" he asked, as we moved around the pool table removing balls from the pockets.

"I didn't say winner couldn't drink." I rolled balls over to him, hips shaking to the up tempo dance music.

A few people drifted over to watch the next game. I ended up with a small group of interchangeable hipster fanboys–thankfully beardless–alternating between cheering me on with poorly disguised innuendo and offering tips. Neither of which impressed me.

Rohan's posse, on the other hand, consisted of a trio of chicks named after designers, sporting streaked blonde hair and prodigious breasts. Armani, Chanel, and Prada were either incestuous triplets or friends with benefits who didn't like each other. I wasn't sure how to deconstruct their alternate sniping and groping.

About halfway through the game, the girls started buying Rohan drinks. Sure, them, he'd take booze from. I hoped he'd become a sloppy drunk. No such luck. If anything, his playing got better.

"You guys learn to fight wasted, don't you?" I muttered after he slammed back yet another tequila then pocketed the eight-ball with an impressive stroke that won him game two.

He gave me a wide smile and handed me my loser shot.

I fired it back. Good thing I could hold my liquor. I couldn't afford a loss in motor skills.

"Let's make this interesting," Rohan said. "If I win..."

Cuntessa de Spluge woke up, having a vested interest in hearing the rest of that sentence.

"You go home," he finished.

Back to seniors' hours. "All right," I said, "but if I win, we stick around for dancing."

The DJ was winding the crowd higher with a little Usher. How fun would it be to be out there with Rohan? I made a face. "Unless you can't dance." I beckoned him closer. "If you have no rhythm, tell me now."

"My rhythm is bang on," he drawled in my ear.

Cuntessa pulsed.

The two posses took our escalation into betting territory as the green light to place bets with each other. Given the shrieking giggles of the girls, it wasn't hard to guess what was at stake. The trouble was that they now ganged up on poor Rohan and me, deciding that a shot of their choosing (and buying) had to be drunk for each ball missed.

Rohan readily agreed to this. I did too. I could hold my booze and was determined to crush him.

It was on.

I lost track of everything around me. My world narrowed down to the felt, the cue ball, and the occasional fresh cool glass pressed into my hand. Which started happening more and more often as that one drink too many tilted my pool playing abilities into potential epic failure territory. My stomach protested the boozy onslaught.

"Spit or swallow?" Rohan murmured to me, near the end of the final game. We were neck and neck for balls sunk.

I sputtered the water I'd been gulping down. "Beg pardon?"

He nodded at the triplets. "Spit or swallow? What are your boys in for tonight?"

I didn't even need to glance at the girls to answer that one. "Neither. Those girls are not putting their mouths on it."

Rohan gaped at me like door number three wasn't even a reality in his world.

I laughed and patted his shoulder. "Such a sheltered life you've led, Snowflake."

Rohan shot the girls another perplexed glance. They flashed their cleavage while staying primly out of groping reach, resulting in more than one of the hipsters pulling a "trying to adjust myself" shifting side-to-side move in response.

"How can they ask a guy to go down on them if they won't do the same?" he asked.

Cuntessa throbbed at his implied readiness to boldly go where many men would not.

"They don't," I said. "No guy is putting his mouth on it either."

"They're missing out on a whole realm of excellent," Rohan said.

"God, yes," I said, louder and tipsier than I intended.

We grinned at each other in perfect harmony but the conversation had me regretting my choice of bet. Wanting to explore that particular realm of excellent with him. Still. I'd used dancing as foreplay on more than one occasion.

Despite all the drinking, victory was almost mine but I got cocky, using a bit too much force on my final shot. The eight-ball hit the back of the pocket and bounced back.

Cuntessa gave a disgusted grunt.

"It's almost no fun winning this way," Rohan said, not hesitating to sink the ball. He pumped his fist in victory but there was no answering gush of approval from his posse. Come to think of it, no grumbling from mine, either.

We were yesterday's news. The group had already paired off into dry hump partners. One of the pairs had gotten especially frisky. The guy's shirt was pushed halfway up while his partner's tipsy maulings had caused his jeans to slip dangerously low on his ass.

I grabbed my clutch then nudged Rohan, motioning toward the two with a jerk of my chin, notably dude's pale butt. "He could be arrested for possession of that much crack."

Rohan pressed his head close to mine. "'Never back down.'" He read the tattoo written in graphic print at the base of the guy's spine. "Dude," he said with a mournful shake of his head. Booze exaggerated his word into pure Southern Cali drawl.

"Factoring in the placement, those words cover so many possibilities," I said. "Everything from empowerment to grim determination in the face of prison showers. Wonder which it is?"

Rohan smothered a laugh against my hair. It shimmied down to my toes, which curled under to contain the sparkly lightness. He took my slight sway of motion for our cue to leave. "Since I trounced you," he said, handing his stick over to a woman waiting for the table, "it's time for all good little girls to go to bed. You, too."

"To think that wit was wasted in the music industry."

Rohan scooped up his jacket with one hand, placing his other on the small of my back to lead me away from the table.

I skirted the edge of the dance floor with its strobing lights, the alcohol in my system warming me as much as weaving through the press of bodies. Colors were more saturated. Time and my body moved more languidly. The music slithered up from the floor, pulsing into my skin. I stepped toward the other dancers, wanting to join them. To lose myself.

Rohan kept me on course, steering me to the exit with a steady hand.

I had to concentrate on what he was babbling on about to me because words took a bit longer to penetrate. Oooh. Penetrate.

The cool night was a welcome relief. I swayed to the throb of the still-audible bass, watching Rohan grow more and more frustrated trying to flag down a cab.

"Give it up. It's practically impossible on a weekend," I said. "We'll have a better chance a few blocks away."

"So many things wrong with this city," he muttered.

"Follow me," I trilled, pushing through the crowd.

The night had turned unseasonably muggy, the air heavy with that metallic smell promising rain. A born and bred Vancouverite, rain didn't faze me.

Dodging through the late night crowd, we'd just hit the mouth of an alleyway when we heard a hissed, "Wanna blow your mind?" I would have sailed past but Rohan clasped my wrist to stop me. The dealer stepped into view. Your run-of-the-mill slime bucket, he wore a skull and hearts T-shirt under a jean jacket. A crescent-shaped birthmark edged his left cheek.

The dealer jerked his chin at Rohan. "Interested, man?"

Rohan hooked an arm around my neck. "My girlfriend might be. She likes to live on the edge." *Girlfriend?* Under his breath he said,

"Like taking off on her own when ordered otherwise." He pushed me forward. "Show her what you've got."

Slime Bucket's eyes glittered. "Devil's candy. A rush like nothing else."

Evil and unsubtle, a winning combo. I barely refrained from rolling my eyes. "Let's talk." I walked forward.

Thinking he had a customer, the dealer accompanied me into the shadowy alley reeking of urine, Rohan trailing us. The demon led us in through an open door to a small back room with a couple of couches. A naked bulb in a hideous ceramic table lamp cast a dim light, but it was enough to see the young man sprawled out on a couch, pressed close to a willowy, blue-haired female bearing an identical crescent birthmark as the dealer.

What really squicked me out was that the man was sucking on the female's thumb, his face lost in orgiastic delight, even as clumps of his hair fell to the stained concrete. With every moan the guy let out, Blue Hair's skin seemed to plump with an extra layer of collagen, her hair shine and thicken, and the crow's feet by her eyes and lines by her lips vanish.

My head swam from whatever bliss drug she was secreting. I clutched the top of a chair to keep from sinking onto that sofa with them and joining in. Rohan, on the other hand, slouched against the doorframe with his hands jammed in his pockets. Not an ounce of tension in him.

The dealer noted the effect the place was having on me. "Go on," he murmured into my ear as he pried one of my hands off of the chair, "live a little."

"Just say no." I gripped the chair harder and blasted the demon back against the wall with mega-current shot from my eyes.

Oh my God, I had a literal death glare! It was official: I was a badass.

Blue Hair flicked the fingers of her free hand at me, prismic drops of her evil sweat flying through the air to land on me like a gentle spring rain. Well, a gentle spring rain that exploded light into trippy colors and amped oxygen into a liquid happiness rush. My knees buckled and I swayed toward her with a moan.

Rohan slammed the dealer up against the wall, stabbing him through the right palm with a finger blade. With a pop, the dealer dissolved into an oily puddle.

Blue Hair rose up, the man clutching at her leg, his mouth working uselessly, sucking nothing. Fury blazed in her eyes as she snatched her victim up in her arms and blurred past us into the night.

Rohan pulled me into the alley after her but she was gone. I sucked in a head-clearing breath.

"Remember that helplessness the next time you plan on taking off alone," Rohan said.

"I accessed my power."

"Yeah, but you still needed back up."

"Still need babysitting. Got it."

"Hey." He ran his hand along my back, the tension in it lessoning at his touch. "I didn't mean it like that."

I nodded. "So? Why aren't we hauling ass after them?"

Rohan leaned back against the alley wall. "Did you see how far gone he was? Those scum pimp a hallucinatory secretion that induces bliss while they drain the victim's life away. That guy has maybe fifteen minutes left in him tops. And even if we did rush in, save him?" He glowered at the empty room. "Addicts always go back."

I hoped dude's death was painless. Then I blasted a dumpster into a brick wall hard enough to crack it.

Rohan placed a hand on my shoulder. "We don't always win."

Not wanting to go home on that note, I strode into a small urban park, headed for a narrow stream flowing along a concrete channel. It cascaded into a circular pool inset in the ground before gurgling up from a fountain in its center.

Four brick archways flanked the fountain–one at each corner. I picked one at random, sinking onto the bench underneath the over-flowing foliage, which provided a thick leafy canopy. I stretched out my legs, looking up at the stars and focusing on their beauty so I wouldn't lose myself to the ugliness.

Traffic in the background provided a soothing white noise.

I hoped that man had had a full life, short as it was.

"Don't get comfortable," Rohan said.

"Too late." I dug around in my clutch. "Aha." I pulled out my tiny black pot pipe and lit up, holding the smoke in past the initial burn in my lungs.

Rohan plucked the pipe from my fingers and took a deep drag. I was so shocked that I sputtered out all my smoke. I waved a hand in front of my face as he patted me on the back with one hand.

"Thought you were on duty," I said, reclaiming the pipe and drag-ging on it again.

Rohan exhaled in a steady breath. "I've fought more wrecked than this."

I offered him the pipe again but he shook his head. I placed it and the lighter on the bench beside me. "How rock star did you get at the height of things?"

He folded his hands on his stomach, looking up at the few stars visible through the light pollution. "Pretty much every cliché you'd imagine."

That conjured up images of writhing, barely clad bodies that I was either too stoned or not stoned enough to handle. "Why'd you quit?"

He was quiet for a long time. I wasn't sure if I'd pushed one too many times for an answer, or if he was zoned out. "Fame isn't as cool from the inside."

I flicked my eyes sideways at him, feeling every fraction of an in
that my eyeballs moved. So I did it again because shifting them in r
head from side to side was a weirdly wonderful sensation.

It got me thinking about pinball, which morphed into the image
poor Rohan being batted around by giant flippers of fame. "It's li
you were a pinball." I flicked my left hand like a pinball flipper. "Ba
Paparazzi." I flicked my right. "Bam. Managers."

"Bing! Full tilt. Fans," Rohan chimed in.

"Exactly." I wiggled my toes. What other profound insights mig
moving various body parts bring?

Rohan reached up to pluck a low hanging leaf, rubbing it betwe
his fingers. "The need to keep racking up points, to stay in the ga
becomes addictive. But the machine isn't sentimental. If you fall do
the hole out of play, it's got another ball ready to take your pla
It did a number on me and I fucked up." His eyes grew distant a
haunted as he added softly, "Big time."

Before I could ask what he meant, he reached inside his inner jac
pocket and removed a small, disc-like container. Twisting the cl
plastic cover, he shook out a few candy-colored rice grains and popj
them in his mouth. "Coated fennel seeds. Want some?"

A burst of licorice hit my tongue when I crunched into them. I h
out my hand for a few more.

Thunder rumbled in the distance.

Above me, a massive dark raincloud menaced. That wet elec
smell had gotten sharper. It was still muggy though, and I was sto
and comfortable under the canopy of leaves so I didn't bother movi

I glanced at Rohan who still seemed lost in painful memorie
decided not to probe. "You sound remarkably well-adjusted now
brushed the wreckage of the leaf he'd shredded off of his thigh. '
not."

Rohan gave a wry laugh. "This is definitely the well-adjusted v
sion. You should have seen me even a year ago."

"Fucking everything that moved?" I asked, cursing myself for putting images into my very visual brain.

"More like fighting."

"Hence your impressive kill record."

"What about you?" he asked.

I laughed, shaking my head.

"What?"

I repositioned myself, sitting sideways on the bench, my legs tucked up alongside me. "You get this is surreal, right? Sitting here getting stoned with Rohan Mitra while he asks about me?"

He preened. "Your teen fantasy made real. You're overwhelmed."

I shoved his shoulder. He didn't budge, but when he nudged me back, I jostled sideways. Such strength. Bet he could pin me down.

"There's not much to tell." I curled my fingers under the bench to grip it.

Rohan extended the blades on his right hand, bringing them up to eye-level with a waggle. "Ve hav vays of making you talk," he said in a horrible German accent. The blades disappeared. "I know you didn't spring fully formed. You'd have been nicer." He jabbed my side. "Tell me. Ari was the initiate, you were the what?"

I rubbed my arms.

Rohan shrugged off his jacket and draped it over my shoulder, shaking his head at me when I tried to protest.

Feebly.

What can I say? The thing was soft as butter and smelled like him.

"I was going to dance," I said.

"Like around a pole?" I shot him the finger at the giggle that escaped him.

"Like Heather Cornell, Chloe Arnold, Dormeshia Sumbry-Edwards, Lady Di Walker, you asshole. None of whom are Shirley Temple and all of whom are amazing tap dancers."

He held up his hands. "Sorry. So that was your dream?"

I brushed my cheek against the collar, pretending to be scratching my jaw with my shoulder, snuggling into his residual warmth, and letting myself be enveloped in a Rohan cocoon. "Yeah. When I was about three I saw this old Ginger Rogers and Fred Astaire tap number. After that I insisted my dad fix my shoes to 'make those noises,' so he taped pennies to my slippers." I smiled at the memory. "I refused to take them off. They enrolled me in my first class that fall."

"What was the highlight?" I checked to see if he was humoring me but he seemed genuinely interested.

"The summer before grade eleven, I got accepted into a special program where I studied with master tappers and then performed at Lincoln Center. That was pretty fucking mind-blowing. Not sold out concert stadiums though," I said, with a wry grin.

"I never played Lincoln Center. I'm impressed. So, what happened?"

I shrugged, not able to get into it right now. Damn stoner confessions never went anywhere good.

Rohan didn't press me. "Do you miss dancing?"

"Like breathing," I said in a thick voice.

He slung an arm around my shoulder and curled me into him. Nooked into his arm like that, I felt protected. Snug.

Home.

Bad stoner thought. I disengaged from his hold. It was stupid but I missed the warmth of it. The protectiveness. "Do you miss it?"

"Fame? Not even a bit."

"Singing. Your band." I cocked my head to look at him. "Do they know you're Rasha?"

"Zack does. The other three were dicks. We're not in contact anymore."

"And the singing?" No answer.

He'd been a rock superstar and I didn't understand how someone walked away from living the dream. Especially when I'd have given everything for it. "You can't tell *me* of all people that you don't miss something you cared so much about for such a long time."

He shrugged.

"What about the music itself?" I said. "You say the rest of your band are jerks but you guys were together for a few years. There must have been something good about the collaboration."

Rohan raised an eyebrow. "Still dwelling on the wrong members of the band, are you?"

"You never know. I might want to revisit my fanfic." I nudged his leg. "Come on. I'm talking shop with the great Rohan Mitra and you're not gonna tell me?"

He reached over me to pick up the pipe and lighter, sparking up with a flick of his thumb. I waited as he inhaled, watching him leaning forward, his elbows on his knees. He held the smoke in for so long, it had to be a stonewalling tactic. Finally, he exhaled, a long column of smoke that dissolved into the late night mist.

"The writing, the jamming, was one of the best parts." He gazed up at me through his lashes. "I mean performing is always tops, you know that."

I nodded sagely.

"But sitting down with the guys and realizing I could put all the shitty things I was feeling, all the dreams I never thought I'd share with anyone, into words that I wanted to belt out to the world in this incredible music? Having my lyrics come alive for my audience?" He laughed, but it sounded too soft, deflated.

"Sing for me," I blurted out.

"More teen fantasy?" he teased. "I don't think you can handle intimate and interactive."

"Try me." I swear I was still talking about his singing. Not my fault that his lids lowered a fraction over his eyes with a look of simmering desire.

I swallowed, desperately trying to get saliva into my very dry mouth.

Honestly, I didn't expect him to start. I sure as hell wasn't prepared for it to be his first number one hit "Toccata and Fugue." The song jolted me back to being thirteen, to the first time I'd heard it.

It was a hot summer night. Leonie and I were slumped in the backseat of her older cousin's beat-up Jetta that to us seemed like the greatest car in the world because it was owned by a teenager, not a parent. I remember resting my hand out the window and the hot wind rushing through my splayed fingers as we drove back from the beach. Our hair was a wet tangle of salty strands and the faint scent of coconut clung to our skin.

Leo was pissing off her cousin, dusting the sand from her bare feet onto the backseat carpet. Then this song came on the stereo and a guy's raspy voice singing a stream of consciousness love song overrode the bickering in the car.

That voice unnerved and excited me, igniting this wildness that at that tender age, I didn't know how to handle and couldn't name. I'd strained against the seatbelt to push my face and shoulders up to the night air, like the breeze could make the restlessness subside. I don't think I breathed until the song was over.

I caught myself holding my breath the same way now. Rohan's voice called that same wildness to the surface of my skin, dancing over me. His eyes never left mine as he sang the chorus of the girl with the lightning eyes and the boy with demons in his soul.

My stomach plummeted. What the holy fuck were the chances of universe convergence that would make me, him, and those lyrics end up in the same place? It freaked me right out. I'd just learned of one destiny in the past couple days and him singing this song right here, right now, was calling into prophecy something that I wanted no part of.

I'd give freely of my body. My heart was off-limits. Especially to a guy like him. Seriously. I'd take the demons.

Thankfully, I wasn't the only one unnerved. Rohan broke off midway through the second verse, looking like walls were closing in on him. He cleared his throat a couple of times as I stuffed my feet into my shoes, and grabbed my clutch.

"Good thing my eyes are bluish-gray," I joked. "We should get–" I didn't even bother to finish. Just up and bolted along the sidewalk, ready to push anyone out of my way who tried to get between me, a taxi, and home.

I spied the steady "on" light of a cab, waiting at a traffic light a couple of blocks away, and sped up, cutting through the playground to hit the street in time to flag it down.

The ground shook as I passed the swings. I grabbed onto a chain, trying to keep my footing as a massive being winked into existence with a rumble of thunder. Nothing like a demon arrival to sober a girl up.

14

Rohan yanked me away from the swing set, shoving me behind him and blocking my body with his.

"I got your message, Rasha," the demon growled. "So delighted to see who killed my children."

Asmodeus. Oh, shit. Leo wasn't supposed to have been this efficient. He wasn't supposed to have found me until I was safely behind the chapter house wards. At least I had Rohan.

"Message?" Given the cold, flat fury on his face, Snowflake would happily feed me to the demon himself.

I rose onto tiptoe to see over Rohan's shoulder. His body was taut with tension, which was unsurprising since Asmodeus was built somewhere between a tank and a small mountain range and boasted three heads: a bull, a ram, and an ogre. His chest was covered in hardened scales. *Gulp.*

"Kill now, talk later," I muttered.

"If there's anything left of you when I'm done," Rohan murmured back.

Blades snicked out to outline Rohan's entire body, running up from his left ankle, along the outer edge of his leg and arm, over his head and down the other side. Plus the short wicked steel extending from his fingertips. His front and back were still vulnerable but he was pretty fucking intimidating glinting in the moonlight.

Asmodeus sauntered forward, as if giving us puny humans time to marvel. I couldn't see this creature inspiring anyone to lustful thought and deed because he was a ghastly fucker. Prime candidate for needing a glamour. Though it was interesting to see who his spawn took after, in a *huh, would you look at that?* way.

I tossed my purse and Rohan's jacket on a bench with trembling hands, visualized throwing my power switch to on, and stepped out from behind Rohan. "Good of you to reply in person."

Asmodeus stopped, not ten feet away, showing the first glimmer of interest since his arrival. Little clouds of dust swirled around his rooster feet. Then he laughed. At least, his ogre head did. "A female Rasha."

Oooh. Now the lust part made sense. Three boring words spoken in a dark, seductive voice and I'd gone sopping wet. Cuntessa was frantically dog paddling. I flicked my eyes to Rohan's bulge. This was indeed an equal opportunity demon.

Rohan glared at me but I took it as a bonding moment.

"Where's his sweet spot?" I asked, speaking low into Rohan's ear.

"No idea." Officially fucked now. "Watch him fight," Rohan said. "See if he shields any part of himself. That could be a clue."

Asmodeus prowled toward us. For each one of Asmodeus' steps, Rohan forced me back two. I barely registered what he was doing, my attention fully focused on the demon.

Asmodeus reached the swing set, but instead of batting the structure out of his way or sidestepping it, he ripped the thick metal chain right off the frame, tossing the entire swing aside onto the wood chip-covered ground. The disinterest with which he so casually desecrated a piece of kid's playground equipment drove home that nothing was sacred where demons were concerned. They would show up anywhere, go after anyone.

Right now, he was after me. I jumped back another step without any prompting from my bodyguard.

"I could be persuaded to keep you as a plaything," Asmodeus said. "I like new toys."

"Yeah, but there'd be this whole hook-up with your son between us. Best not." I could barely hear myself speak over the crackle of my magic and the pounding of my heart.

Reminding him of his son–and by extension, my role in his demise– was not the smartest move. A cruel smile spread across all three faces simultaneously. "It wasn't up for debate," Ogre head informed me, reaching one fleshy hand out.

Rohan sprang into action, diving to the ground in a roll. With a sharp flick of his neck, he used the blade along the top of his head to slash the tendons of Asmodeus' rooster feet.

Black fluid gooshed out as the entire left side of Asmodeus' body sagged like a landslide, but he didn't die.

Rohan sprang to his feet, then rushed the demon again.

Asmodeus held up a hand, looking almost bored.

Rohan stopped inches from the demon, lips parted, giving breathy gasps, like he was stuck on the verge of an orgasm.

"Bring me the girl," Asmodeus ordered. His eyes glowed as he caressed Rohan's neck with his warty index finger.

Rohan rubbed up against him like a cat. It was the new gold medal standard of creepy. Physical danger from demons was one thing, but I found the psychological threat of being compelled via voice command even more disturbing. Rohan marching toward me with jerky steps, uselessly fighting the demand, unnerved me more.

I sprinted for the section of playground designed for older kids, crossing a small, arched bridge that traversed a blue river painted on the concrete, and swung myself up to the top of a plastic climbing structure. Grabbing the safety rail, I fired a forked blast of electricity at Rohan from my index finger. One day, I'd master this technique from all my fingers simultaneously and have a handy little arsenal going.

It knocked into his right side with a sizzle, but didn't deter him. Rohan came puppet-like, closer and closer, Asmodeus trailing, limping behind him–almost like a bored parent.

Frantic, I scanned the area for some kind of projectile, but these stupid modern playgrounds were made for safety and all the plastic was nailed down tight. Next option. With a running jump, I leapt onto the fireman's pole. In my head, I was super stripper personified as I swung my way down–legs out, core taut–around the pole to kick Rohan. To be fair, I was aiming for his chest, but my sweaty hands slid, knocking me off-balance.

The thud as my foot collided with Rohan's skull jarred me hard enough to rattle my teeth, so no surprise that it was enough to snap him out of his demon-induced spell.

"Wanna not do his job for him?" Rohan bitched, knocking me to the ground as Asmodeus' twisted ram's horn slashed the air where my head had been.

"That's nothing like thank-you." I scrambled to my feet.

"You got that, did you?"

We backed into the grassy field. "You want her?" Rohan asked the demon. "You gotta go through me." I shivered at the menace in his voice.

Asmodeus charged, fiendishly pointy horns thrust front and center.

Rohan grabbed the closest horn before it could do any damage, using momentum to swing himself around. He was amazing to watch, all lethal elegance as he struck the demon with short, fierce blows. He swung his leg around in a brutal roundhouse kick, the blade along his thigh jamming into the neck of the ram's head, lodging there. With a quick jerk of his hip, Rohan popped his leg free, slashing the ram neck in the process.

Viscous goop gushed out in an arc as that head flopped forward onto the demon's chest.

My jaw dropped. "Whoa." I defied anyone to say that move wasn't hot.

Rohan smirked at my reaction.

I narrowed my eyes. No way did he get to have all the fun.

Rohan jumped into my path to block me. "Hey, Dark Menace," he said, "stay back."

I'd sidestepped him before the words finished leaving his mouth, intent on my target. I was still terrified, but then again, becoming blasé around demons would be at my peril. Watching Rohan use his entire body fighting Asmodeus had inspired me so I tried pulsing electric blasts in waves off my body. It was too clunky, depleting, and I didn't yet have the range so I switched it up, flinging lightning balls at Asmodeus, rapid fire like a pitching machine set to eleven.

Rohan grabbed my non-pitching arm, but I shook him off.

Asmodeus lit up as my blue voltage covered him, his flesh smoking. "Is that all you can do?" His laughter boomed, echoing off the trees around us. The demon wasn't shielding shit. He was fearless, taking everything we threw at him without batting an eye.

Rohan swore and jumped back in the fray.

Thunder ripped across the sky, crashing over us. My heart jumped into my throat, and as the skies opened up, my power went into overdrive as if in response to nature's call. The rush was insane. My body tingled, like the explosion of energy inside me needed a way out through my skin. I reached for the electric moisture blanketing me. The rain ran over me in velvet rivulets, dancing over the magic pouring out through every pore.

Everything took on a surreal, dreamy quality–even Asmodeus, swinging back and forth dodging our dual-sided assault. Despite his injuries, he fended us off pretty well, looking almost amused by the entire encounter. Demons were such dicks.

Asmodeus feinted left to avoid Rohan and snatched me up by the back of the neck. That fucking hurt. The sweet release of my magic cutting off mid-stream hurt more. Like having a giant shit suddenly reverse course. My entire body convulsed in wave upon wave of needle-like stabbings.

"Motherfucking, limp-dicked, piece-of-shit," I raged at Asmodeus.

"The first two contradict each other," he said with infuriating condescension. "Watch it, puppy. Keep snapping and you'll get nipped by much larger teeth."

Rohan leapt for me, but Asmodeus backhanded him with a hard crack, winging him halfway across the park to wallop against the post of another brick archway. Rohan crumpled to the ground.

Asmodeus' strength, his compulsion abilities were demonic power on a terrifying scale and I was in his grasp, powerless and unable to stop my shallow panting.

He stroked my cheek, my red-hot agony morphing to a molten heat that consumed me, and lifted me up so that I was eye-level with him. I squirmed, driven by a deep-seated compulsion to do anything he asked of me if he'd satisfy the knife's edge I teetered on. My lips parted in silent plea.

The demon tilted his bull and ogre heads, studying me. All four eyes widened, as if surprised. His bull nostrils flared with a soft snort, he tightened his grip, and the world swung sideways with sudden sharp violence.

Dizzy, unable to summon my magic, I screwed my eyes shut, praying he didn't toy with me too long before I died. Missing the good old days when the loss of a purple bra was the sum total of my worries.

"You want... so much." He touched my face. "Peel back the false layers and embrace your deepest, darkest desires."

Syrup slithered through my bones. *Yes.*

I opened my eyes.

A monster had me. A nightmarish image with too many heads and a horrific mashup body, smirking as I struggled in his grasp. "Help me! Heeeeelllllp!"

A dark-haired man charged us, arms raised. His fingers ended in blades, glinting in the moonlight.

I screamed again.

"Nava!" the man cried out. He skidded to a stop before us. How did he know my name?

I screwed my eyes shut, whimpering, stuck between a nightmare and another nightmare. Wind whooshed against my legs and I was dropped onto the ground.

I cracked an eye to find the man battling the monster. Not on the same team, then?

"Use your magic!" the man barked at me.

I stared at the crazy stranger. Then I did what any sane person would do and ran screaming into the night.

Behind me, I heard the man swear, and the monster laugh.

The stranger caught up with me in the middle of the road. I glanced over my shoulder but the monster was gone.

"Let me go." I tried to tug free.

"I can't." The man's face was tight with frustration. He no longer had blades. Had I imagined them? Imagined everything of the past few minutes? Trying to remember events leading up to the monster's appearance left me clutching my head in agony.

The stranger ignored my distress, hauling me back toward the park. I doubted he'd saved me just to kill me on his own terms but a girl could never be too careful. Another man had scared me recently. This one? I didn't think so, but I couldn't remember.

Running had gotten me nowhere and there was no one else around to help. I really needed some time to process what the fuck had just happened. Preferably at chez Katz because if my knocking knees gave out here, I suspected I might just curl up in the fetal position and be done.

"I'm super grateful for your assistance, but how about we call it a night and go our separate ways?" My feet slid in a puddle of something that didn't match the clear rain water falling around me. I leapt onto the grass.

"I'd love nothing better, Nava," the stranger snapped. "Seeing as how you're a royal pain in my ass."

"Excuse me?!" I planted my hands on my hips. "I have no clue how you know my name but you obviously haven't spent any time around me because I'm a delight."

The bastard actually laughed.

I punched him in the chest hard enough to illicit a satisfying "oomph." Cool. That one kickboxing class I'd taken last year had really paid off.

He grabbed my wrist. "You can do better than that, Rasha."

Rasha? And what was with his tone of voice? Like a taunt? A challenge? No, an order. Big surprise this jerk bossed people around. I tried to break free but he simply stood there, my arm caught in his grasp, one eyebrow cocked arrogantly at me.

That look pushed a major button. Something shifted inside me, like a switch being thrown on. Electricity burst from my palms, causing Rohan to jerk back. My memory was now working just fine. "Asshole," I snarled, lowering my hands.

"There she is." He smiled and I was undone at the tenderness in it.

Our chests heaved in identical rhythms. We were both dirty, our filth ranging in color from demon innard black to demon innard red with a soupçon of purple bruising as an accent. The rain had soaked our clothes and plastered our hair to our heads.

I checked the park but Asmodeus was really gone. The question was, why?

15

"I didn't kill him," Rohan said. "I don't know why he left and I'm certain it wasn't because of anything we did because the two of us on our own had no hope against him. We haven't seen the last of him." He pinched the bridge of his nose. "You used the snitch, didn't you?"

"To be fair, I figured I'd be safely behind the Demon Club wards before he got the message. Before he got to me." I shivered. "What if Asmodeus was right, and all I want is to forget any of this ever happened? I thought I'd been dealing, but…" I blew out my cheeks.

Rohan tipped my chin up, forcing me to meet his eyes. "You are dealing. Brilliantly." He tucked a dripping strand behind my ear.

My chest constricting at this new layer of intensity to an already brain-exploding night, I grasped his hand, intending to brush him off, but found myself leaning into him.

He tilted his head, looking at me oddly. "Your eyes," he said, in a strangled voice. "I can still see lightning in them."

Panic clawed at my throat. I opened my mouth to protest the lightning girl label but the sky above lit up with a brilliant flash that let me see the truth of his words in the reflection of his eyes.

And the heat simmering in their depths. Ironically, that calmed me down. Lust didn't frighten me. Quite the opposite.

Rohan curled his fingers around my waist, ducking his head toward mine.

I slammed my hand over his mouth. "No kissing."

That activity had been kiboshed over a year ago after a spectacularly disappointing session with one Elvis Persig. His fishy-lipped nibbling of my face had felt too much like the time I'd stuck my feet in one of those tanks for squirming, toothless carp to eat my dead skin. Except without the exfoliating benefit.

I loved kissing. Or rather, loved the idea of it as this precious gesture to be shared between two people in love. I just wasn't sure that love existed. Case in point, my ex, Cole, who was supposed to be there for me when I'd learned I had to stop dancing. The one who'd fucked off instead, leaving me to break down alone. Relationships had become hook-ups. While I'd kept the kissing–at first–these hook-ups weren't about tenderness and intimacy.

Easier to let kissing stop being part of the equation.

Rohan shot me a look of disbelief.

I gently cupped his crotch, feeling a cheap thrill at his hard-on. "This isn't romance, baby. It's lust, pure and simple."

"It may be pure but there's nothing simple about it, Lolita. In fact," he traced a finger down my cleavage, "it's rather complicated." He leaned in toward me again and I put a hand on his chest to stop him.

"I'm not dreaming about happily-ever-afters and I'm not your girl with the lightning eyes." I practically sneered that last bit at him.

It took a second for him to believe me. Trust me, I saw the moment that he did because a dark savagery crossed his face. I skittered back, my back hitting a wide tree trunk but Rohan didn't move. He clearly wanted me, so what was the hold up? His eyes were intent on mine, looking for something.

Ah.

"Not backing up because I'm afraid, baby." I winked, throwing a glance at the tree behind me. Though, okay, I did experience a moment of panic about the possibility of another misfire and Cuntessa once more being reduced to a charred nubbin. I wasn't sure her and I could get past it happening twice.

But where Rohan was concerned? No, I'd backed up to get some much needed distance at the lust triggered by the look on his face. My need for him had reached supernova levels. The potential big bang worth any risk. I licked my lips, crooking a finger at him. "Do you need an engraved invitation, Snowflake?"

"Fuck," he ground out, prowling toward me.

My toes curled at the hot look in his eyes that dipped and lingered on the hollow of my neck, only to be replaced by his lips there as he gathered my hair in his fist and tugged it to one side.

His tongue, hot on my cool skin, swirled in tempo with the beats of my heart, now hammering Indy-car fast under the onslaught of his mouth on my collarbone. "Sugar," he murmured.

"Body scrub." I tilted my neck to give him better access, but with a sharp jerk, Rohan spun me around, pressing me against the rough bark. He slammed my hands over my head, gripping them lightly but firmly in one hand. I scrabbled for a hold, my eyes falling on the words "Party like it's 1999" scratched into the trunk, just past the tip of my nose. Rain cascaded down around us like a steamy waterfall, but the leaves made a dry, cozy bubble above us.

Rohan raked his nails up my spine.

I shivered, totally in thrall as he pressed the length of his body against me. Trapped between the tree and him–a near-stranger, and dangerous at that–heat spread like wildfire deep in my core. Flamed high. The unpredictability of it brought out an interesting little kink I had, though it wasn't a case of any guy would do.

My head fell back against his chest and my breathing deepened. A slow legato. How could it sound so languid when my entire being was coiled tight in a dark smolder?

The traffic quieted. We'd hit a lull at this time of night before the bars emptied out, but in this deserted downtown park with a silent city around us, it was easy to believe we were the only two alive.

I closed my eyes, all the better to lose myself to sensation. The scrape of bark against my cheek, his breath gusting my neck, the rough tip of his finger skimming the thin fabric along my hip. Every nerve ending flared to life under his touch. Sweat pooled between my trembling thighs.

Rohan blew a lock of my hair off my neck, ducking his head to nip at my ear.

I twisted my head around, my breath punched out of me at his eyes sparking darkly with need. I tilted my hips back, pressing into his hard-on to get some form of contact.

He hissed, jerking his body away from me.

I arched back, trying to follow him but he kept me in place with a palm between my shoulder blades. My newly-released hands fell limp at my sides. At least now I could touch him, too.

I reached behind Rohan to curve my hand around his hip as he wormed my skirt up from behind to slide his hand between my legs. He gave a satisfied chuckle at how wet I already was. I didn't care. Smirk away, just keep stroking. I closed my thighs around his hand, rocking my hips back and forth.

Rohan moaned into my ear and my belly fluttered.

"Tell me what you want." The rough rasp of his voice scraped over my too-tight skin, kicking my torment up into new stratospheres.

Cuntessa de Spluge swooned. I imagined her screaming like a teenybopper. With my hands still behind me, I roughly caressed his ass. "You. Now."

"That can be arranged."

A whisper of wind hit high on my thigh as my bikini briefs floated to the ground in a scrap of lace. Fuck me, he'd cut them off with one of his finger blades. My knees wobbled. Cool air cascaded over my very flushed nether regions.

Rohan knocked his knee between my legs, nudging them wider. Then he crooked a bladeless finger inside me, rotating it as he thrust it in and out.

I rose onto tiptoes, my stilettos not providing enough height on their own to let him hit *my* sweet spot deep inside. My legs shook and my feet barely touched the ground. Every cell hummed in greedy delight.

"Rohan." The gasp of his name was almost a plea. I was coming undone in his hands.

"Say my name like that again." His voice was hard. Not a problem, since his name was the only thing I was capable of saying right now. I complied.

He swore and leaned away from me. I was about to voice a complaint but then a rip of foil cut through the silence.

"What a Boy Scout," I teased. It came out a bit needier than I'd intended.

"Always prepared," he agreed.

I wished I was facing him to see him roll the sheath over his cock, to see him touching himself, hard and ready and knowing that at least right now, I was the one who'd inspired that reaction, but Rohan kept me in place.

He pushed into me from behind with a hard thrust that stole the breath from my lungs.

Arching back to rest against the hard planes of his chest, I opened my legs wider.

"Is this what you want?" he growled. "Rough and messy where anyone could see us?"

A bolt of lust ripped through me at the image. I grinned over my shoulder at him.

Rohan pulled out long enough to spin me around to face him. The smirk on his face was at odds with his frosty gaze. He gripped my upper arms, once more slamming inside me. I trailed my finger along the hard plane of his stomach. His abs clenched under my touch, resulting in so many delicious contoured ripples that I did it again.

Every thrust knocked me back into the tree, the pitted bark shredding my poor dress and scratching my skin. "Harder."

Rohan's jaw tensed at my command, holding himself in check. He emanated pure, brutal energy, and he was seriously and obviously pissed off.

I caressed his cheek, but he jerked his head to fling my hand off. I shrugged off my unreasonable sting of hurt. I'd set the rules. "No one is forcing you to play with the unclean, Snowflake."

"No, that's on me," he snarled, slowing, teasingly pulling out before thrusting once more inside me. Unleashing himself on me. There was no other way to describe it. He was without an ounce of mercy.

If this was supposed to be some kind of punishment, then I'd happily take double helpings.

Rohan threaded his fingers with mine, using his blades to anchor our two hands to the trunk. An interlacing of dusky brown and pale white skin. He rose up onto his toes, his fucking changing angle and gaining force. The expression on his face was primal.

I clutched at his shirt with my free hand so I didn't try something stupid like tenderly stroke away his anger. These intense coils rippling inside were a new feeling for me. I hooked a leg around his waist, rocking mindlessly against him. My entire body arched in unfettered pleasure.

My hand snuck down to give some love to Cuntessa but he swatted that away too, replacing it with one very capable finger. Go power plays. I happily let him take charge.

My grip on him tightened. I'd have closed my eyes but there was a dare in the hard line of his jaw and in the glint of his eyes that had me hold his gaze in challenge. This wasn't slow and it wasn't gentle. Our fuck was a hard storm. An all-consuming vortex. My hair tangled in sweaty strands; my dress rode higher and higher up my hips. I had to force air into my lungs.

Still I couldn't get enough.

It had been a while since I'd orgasmed from men I'd slept with. Those college guys with their misguided mood music and fumbling chivalrous "No, you come first" that became an obligation I faked my way out of. Mild levels of happy tingle generally constituted a win for me. But here? In this park, with this arrogant boy and his waves of unbridled hostility?

I bucked violently, coming harder than I ever had. Shattering and uncertain that I'd ever be put back together properly again.

The irony? His stunned look and the fierceness of his convulsion made me think he'd experienced the same thing.

The girl with the lightning eyes and the boy with demons in his soul.

Shivers burst across my skin like a mirror shuddering into a thousand pieces. Everything went dark and silent and then the hum of the city rushed back into stereo surround, snapping the bubble of us. Just as I realized I'd fallen against him, one of his arms holding me up and holding me close like the gentlest band of steel, he pulled out. I almost pitched forward at the lack of contact.

Rohan stepped away to strip off the condom and tuck himself back into his pants. He was mere feet away but might as well have been miles.

I tugged down my dress with a wriggle, stuffing the remnants of my underwear into the trash, and struggling to understand how something so tawdry felt anything but.

Disoriented, fluttery, I didn't know if my dizziness stemmed from euphoria or something else I couldn't name. I pinched my cheeks, grateful for the biting pain.

We straightened out our clothes, both so careful not to look at each other. Generally, I was a pro at the après. At bantery fun time that took any weirdness out of the situation and made it clear that I had no expectations. But this? This was awkward beyond all salvaging.

I tried to take a deep breath but I swear my lungs had filled with cold water and it came out as a stuttery hitch. In theory I'd just experienced my dream encounter. So how come I wanted to puke?

"Let's get you home," Rohan said in a flat voice.

Mercifully, I flagged down a taxi as soon as we left the park. The driver didn't even look up when we got into the back seat which was good, since he may have refused us entry had he seen our damp, demon gunkified selves. Apparently reeking of sex didn't matter.

There was no talking on the ride back. I kept sneaking glances over at Rohan but he stared straight ahead into the darkness of the backseat, the occasional slither of passing streetlight over his face letting me know that he wasn't any happier.

I gnawed on the inside of my cheek, my dress drying from soaked through to a more-disgusting clamminess.

No sooner had the taxi pulled up to my front curb than I shoved some money at the driver and bolted inside the house. Thankfully, my family was asleep and I was spared questions and more screaming at the sight of me. I pressed a hand to my cheeks, feeling their warm flush. Probably coming down with a fever. I had to get out of my wet clothes but first I made myself some Neo Citran–perfect for cold symptoms and knocking me out so I couldn't lay there thinking all night.

By the time I got out of my shower, the warm lemony liquid was already kicking in, leaving me groggy. Grateful for the miracles of modern over-the-counter medicine, I crashed. Hard.

16

I woke up Friday morning to the hangover god smashing me in the head with his evil hammer. Groaning, I pressed a hand to my temple, regretting the last four shots.

Wishing I regretted the entire evening.

My mouth tasted of dirt. I scraped my tongue with my teeth but to no avail. That particular flavor was gonna require hella mouthwash to kill.

Ari rapped on my door. "Want some help packing?"

I closed my eyes briefly. Moving day. "Yeah. Give me ten minutes, okay?"

"I'll grab containers," he said, his footfalls getting fainter.

I flung off the covers and stumbled into the bathroom for my morning pee. Awesome. My period had arrived and it was so heavy my vag looked like a *CSI* outtake. The brutal squeezing cramps along my thighs were no great delight either.

Forget looking pretty. Today's fashion highlight? Another pair of black sweats and a faded red Harry Potter tee with "I solemnly swear I am up to no good" spelled out in spiky black letters.

Bedding got stripped and hauled down to the washing machine. I wanted my own sheets with me at Demon Clubhouse.

I popped a couple of much-needed Midol, knowing I'd be fine in twenty minutes when they kicked in. Too bad Rohan found me *fifteen* minutes later, still in pain and taking a stitch ripper to my bras to savagely yank out all the metal underwire. "Not one word," I said, as I pitched another lacy number into a large Rubbermaid container.

"I'm just the help," he said. "What do you want packed up first?"

I exhaled. There'd be no rehashing of last night. Cuntessa shot me the metaphorical finger at the fact that there would probably be no round two either.

"I only need my clothes and my laptop." Between it and my phone I'd have my music, and digital copies of any books and photos I cared about. Damn it. My phone had been confiscated while they waited for my new encrypted model, with my laptop to follow today.

Rohan hesitated. "You're sure that's all you want? Who knows how long you'll be living there."

I didn't know what else he expected me to have. "I'm good." I pointed at a pile on my bed. "Start with those, please."

Ari jogged into the room. "Need more containers?" He stopped as he saw Rohan. "Hey." My brother puffed up as he stepped closer. "I'm Ari. And you are...?"

To his credit, Rohan stuck out his hand for Ari to shake. "Rohan."

Ari shook it. "You're watching Nava."

Rohan tilted his head. "That a problem?"

Ari draped an arm over my shoulder. "Not if you keep my sister safe."

"That's my job," Rohan said in an even tone. "I'm very good at my job."

They stood there, eyeing each other.

I made an "ugh" sound and stepped away from my brother. "Did you put a Rubbermaid in the laundry room for the sheets?" I asked him.

"Yeah. I'll bring them over once they're dry." Ari picked up the first full Rubbermaid. "I'll take this out to the car."

"Put it in mine," Rohan said. "No point in two cars going."

Ari nodded and headed out.

It didn't take long to pack the rest of my stuff. I snapped a hair elastic around my wrist in case I needed to tie my hair back later, then exited the bathroom with my container of make-up, bath products, and hair stuff and dumped it on the bed, looking around my room for anything I'd missed.

"I guess that's it." Five medium Rubbermaids. The sum total of my adult life. I wasn't sure if it was depressing or liberating, so I didn't dwell. I reached for the container with my bathroom items, jerking back at a sharp slicing pain in my middle finger as I caught it on a ragged edge of the lid. Holding my bleeding finger upright, I used my other hand to pull the lid off, rummaging for my Band-Aids. I held out the box to Rohan. "Could you put one on me please?"

He applied the Band-Aid.

Then he kissed my finger. A pointed and deliberate touch of his lips to my skin that went on for several beats too long. He stared at me with those sumptuously lashed eyes, his lips soft and warm.

A giddy bubble danced around in my belly. I snatched my hand back.

Rohan tossed the Band-Aid box into the Rubbermaid, the look on his face daring me to say something.

I bit back a sigh. "Do we need to talk about this?" Much as I didn't want to share my deeply held beliefs around the whole kissing thing, I also didn't want—couldn't afford—weirdness with him.

"We don't need to do anything." His amber eyes were clouded with anger.

I tried to convince myself that not all of it was directed at me but I wasn't that deluded.

"Look, about last night—"

He fit the lid back on the container and hefted it up. "Nope." He popped the "p" for emphasis. "Changed my mind. There is something you need to do."

I smoothed down the edge of the Band-Aid. "Yes?"

"Not talk."

"Ever?"

"Is that an option?" he asked.

I held up my middle finger. "Thanks for the bandage."

He stomped off, grabbing a second container along the way.

"I see," Ari said as he entered, listening to Rohan pound down the stairs.

"No, you really don't." I sank down onto my bed.

He sat down beside me, ticking off items on his fingers. "You had sex, your dysfunctional kissing issues surfaced, and now you're both messed up over it."

"Oh. Guess you do. Except I am neither dysfunctional nor messed up about anything. Everything went according to plan."

We both flinched at the sound of a trunk being slammed much too hard.

Ari's eyes darted over to window. "Yup. It went swimmingly. You get that he's feeling used, right?"

I slapped a hand over my mouth in mock shock. "A man feeling used after a sexual encounter? Oh my God, whatever will we do?" I dropped my hand. "He knew the score. No one forced him."

I sounded a bit pissy but I couldn't believe I had to defend myself. A man had no-strings attached sex, he got high-fived. I did the same, even with the no-kissing, and the entire male gender posse'd up around poor, fragile Snowflake? Screw that.

Ari stood up, stacking the last two containers on top of each other before picking them up. "You're playing with fire."

"I'm not playing with anything. The fire was ignited, blazed, and doused last night. End of story."

He shook his head at me and carried my stuff out.

I pushed thoughts of Rohan out of my mind. I was leaving home. A lump formed in my throat. Going downstairs into the kitchen, I found my mom making my favorite breakfast of waffles and extra-crispy bacon. There was enough for a small army, along with a heaping platter of cut strawberries. She motioned at the coffee pot. "I could warm the milk," she said.

"That would be great." Part of me wanted to rush into her arms but another perverse part of me refused to give her the satisfaction of needing her. I'd learned my lesson with that bullshit vulnerability.

"By the way," Mom said, jerking her spatula toward the counter, "you got a letter."

A letter that she'd already opened. I scanned the contents. It was from the University of British Columbia asking me to contact them about the status of my enrollment.

"I can let Admissions know you're going back," she said.

"Kinda busy with Rasha stuff right now. Might have to hold off for a while longer."

"Being Rasha never kept Ari from his studies."

"Well, Ari was an initiate and he'd had his entire life to adjust to his schedule. Maybe I could have a *whole week* to deal with it before you get on my case about throwing school into the mix," I snapped.

"Don't take that tone with me." Mom turned away to refill the waffle platter.

I balled the paper up in my fist, tossing it into the trash. Though I made sure she didn't see me do it.

To say the meal was strained was a massive understatement. I kept my eyes on my plate. Mom kept hers on her waffles. There was no talking. No bothering to find out how I was doing with moving out.

Dad ambled in trailing citrusy *4711* cologne, a ratty sandal held up in one hand. "Shana, did you already pack the other one?" My parents were leaving for a two-week Caribbean cruise today, originally booked as a celebration post Ari-induction. Not sure what they saw it as now. Funereal?

Mom pointed her spatula at him. "We discussed this."

Dad clutched the sandal to his chest, a mournful expression on his face. "But they're so comfortable."

"I've packed the black ones." She held out her hand for the sandal, but he ignored her to grab a plate and get himself some breakfast, the sandal stuffed defiantly in his waistband.

This Rockwellesque picture was how Rohan and Ari found us.

I met Ari's eyes, miming shooting myself in the temple. He squeezed my shoulder in sympathy as he brushed by to take a seat next to me.

"Eat," Mom said to Rohan, thrusting a plate at him.

He took it, but didn't move to fill it up. "No harm will come to Nava," he said.

"I'm more worried about you boys," Dad joked.

My grip tightened on my fork.

Rohan shot me an uncertain look.

Ari shoved the maple syrup at me. "Eat," he ordered. He tugged on his earlobe, our private twin code for "Relax. I've got your back."

I'm sure it was a delicious breakfast but I barely managed to choke down three bites. "Better hit the road," I said about five minutes later.

My mom glanced at the clock on the stove. "Oh. Yes. I need to finish packing." She came up behind me and kissed the top of my head. "We'll talk soon."

Not if I could help it. I gave her the "I'm wearing my happy face" smile that I'd perfected to get my parents off my back. "Have a great vacation."

Dad walked me to the front door. There was a moment there when I thought he might say something but he just hugged me. "It'll be fine," he assured me.

Again with the "it," not the "you."

"Yup. Have fun, Dad. Drink a mojito for me."

That left Ari as my sole escort to the car, which was perfect. He scooped me up into a giant hug. "Kick demon ass." His voice was shaky. This would be the first time we'd be away from each other for a prolonged period of time.

I grabbed on to him harder.

"We have to go," Rohan said in a gentle voice.

"I'll see you later," Ari said, stepping back. I think his eyes were wet but it was hard to tell through the blurriness of my own.

"And often?"

"And often," he promised.

When he let go of my hand, I stared down at the empty space like I was leaving a limb behind. I'm sure the separation from my twin was healthy. I couldn't give a shit. This sucked. But I dealt, opening the door to Rohan's two-door vintage muscle car with its midnight blue finish and white racing stripe.

The interior had clearly never seen a fast food wrapper. Even the mats were pristine. I relaxed, wondering why I felt so comfortable until I realized that it smelled like Rohan in here.

I rolled down the window.

Rohan fished a pair of sunglasses from his shirt pocket, pushing them up the bridge of his nose before sticking the key into the ignition. Hand on key, he hesitated, shifting toward me.

I got extremely fascinated by my seatbelt. "Nice car."

He gave an insulted snort, stroking the wheel. "This is a fully re-stored '67 Shelby. First thing I bought when the band hit it big. Drove it up here from L.A." With a twist of the key, he started the engine, roaring away from the curb with a sharp left that flung me against the passenger door. His hands rested almost carelessly on the wheel.

I tried very hard not to remember the feel of them on me, but that left my eyes trailing down his work-of-art body to his muscled thighs tensing as he shifted gears.

My mouth went dry.

The middle-aged dad in the minivan next to us glanced over, longing at the total picture of hot girl, hot guy, and hot car written so clearly on his face that I took pity on him and winked cheekily.

He grinned back, swerving toward us before regaining control of his vehicle.

Rohan sped ahead. "Wreaking havoc with traffic, Lolita?"

I reached for the power button to put on some tunes but Rohan swatted my hand away.

"I control the music," he said.

"Fallen angel with domination issues. Shocker."

"Takes one to know one," he replied.

"It *is* a nice car," I said, ignoring his childish retort.

"Best ride I ever had," Rohan said with a sly smile my way.

"You mean best wank." I kicked off my flip flops. "It couldn't be more of a jerk-off machine if you'd painted balls on the back tires."

Rohan gave an amused snort. Ready or not, I was on my way.

17

We carted my things up to my new room in a couple of trips. The bedroom was serviceable, if somewhat masculine. Tolerable queen mattress, wood furniture on the heavy side. This crazy print of two people against a stormy sea sat atop the dresser, propped against the wall. The person on the left was merely a strip of face and neck, as if torn off the person on the right, whose missing strip revealed weird cables and balls. It was the kind of thing Ari would have dug, if not my style. At least the view to the backyard was nice.

The best part was the small ensuite bathroom. I would not have wanted to share with the boys and learn firsthand who missed the toilet seat when he peed.

Rohan took my laptop to give to Ms. Clara.

"Be sure to bring back a receipt," I mocked.

He spread his hands in a "what are you going to do" way. "The Brotherhood is incredibly anal."

"Well," I deadpanned, "anal *is* the new black."

He blinked slowly at me with a fascinated gleam in his eyes. I stumbled back a step, my knees hitting the mattress, but he simply held up the laptop. "Anything you don't want people to see?" he asked.

I checked the heel of my shoe, as if that had been responsible for my lost footing, forgetting I wore flip flops. "You sound positively hopeful."

"Just don't want you to be embarrassed." He paused in the doorway. "More embarrassed."

I grabbed the closest thing handy, which happened to be a boot, and flung it at him. He rocked back on his heels, shaking with laughter, not even flinching as my footwear missed decapitating him by mere millimeters.

"Leave," I ordered.

"Baruch wants you in the Vault," he called back, my computer tucked under one arm.

I popped another Midol and hustled my ass downstairs.

"Yo, Tree Trunk. I'm–" I came to an abrupt stop at the sight of Drio waiting for me in sweats torn off at the knee and a white long-sleeved tee with perfectly placed holes that I swear he paid extra for. The overall effect was mouthwatering. Damn, these boys were annoyingly hot.

"Where's Baruch?" I asked. My previous encounter with Drio had burned up my fear quota, leaving me irritated at his presence.

"You're with me today."

I crossed my arms. "Why?"

Drio cracked a smile at my suspicious tone as he pulled the door shut. "Because I scare you," he said in a stereotypical vamp accent.

"Was that supposed to be a Count Dracula impression? Because you sounded more like Count Chocula."

His brow creased in confusion. I opened my mouth to explain the difference. "No. I don't care enough," he said, crossing the room.

I was about to ask if I should follow but I got distracted by his pants sliding down his hip and the tantalizing glimpse of olive skin revealed. He caught them before things got interesting and tugged them up. Too bad. My dislike of him did not override my voyeuristic tendencies.

Though I hustled to catch up when I saw the vein in his forehead throb at my dawdling.

"Heard you ran into some trouble last night." He flipped a small panel mounted to the wall open, revealing a flat black pad. "Good work pissing Asmodeus off, since it's not like we have enough to do with Samson."

I pulled off the elastic band I wore on my wrist and tied my hair up into a messy ponytail, choosing to ignore his sarcasm. "Here's a question. Last night, Asmodeus compelled me. How do I fight back against–"

I gasped finding Drio with his hands around my neck. He wasn't hurting me, but I hadn't even seen him move. One second he was ten feet away, the next he was behind me.

"Against surprises?" he asked.

I screwed my eyes shut, my heart hammering. "Don't flambé me."

Drio dropped his hands.

I cracked open one eye to see him bring his thumb to the fingers of his right hand, shaking it in what even I recognized as an Italian gesture of frustration. "What are you talking about?" he asked.

"Your fire powers."

He massaged his right temple. "What fire powers?"

I straightened my T-shirt with a sharp tug. "You know, your anger issues that manifest in some kind of elemental flame deal."

His eyes narrowed. "My anger issues? Because I'm Italian, I must be a hothead? Got any other ethnic profiling?"

"Please. You being Italian has zip to do with it. You raging at me since day one on the other hand?" I spread my hands wide, encouraging him to make the tiny jump from A to B. My empirical evidence presented, I rocked back on my heels.

Drio glanced skyward with a pained look, as if seeking divine patience. Then he waved his hands at me. "No flames. Though I'd be happy to find some matches. My power?" He zipped across the room and back in a blink.

"Super speed?"

"Technically, I flash step. I'm not zipping across the city."

"Oh."

"Don't sound so disappointed."

I wasn't disappointed; more confused about how this ability fit in to Ari's theories about personality flaws and power manifestation. I'd have asked but the look on Drio's face made it clear that he was not in a sharing mood. "How do you kill demons then? Flash stepping is hardly attack magic."

Drio looked insulted at the question. "It's still the same inherent Rasha magic. If a bystander stabs a demon in their kill spot, the demon wouldn't die. But when a Rasha zaps that place, touches it directly, or funnels his magic through a weapon to hit that same spot?" He brushed his hands together in an "all done" gesture. "My magic works fine. I don't need fire powers."

"Fine. You weren't going to immolate me. My mistake. What was your point?"

"I lost it in all your..." He made the international symbol for "blah blah blah" with one hand. "For the record, I don't agree with you being here. But Rohan said you deserved it since the make-up artist was your idea and you did pretty well last night. Even if your one-on-one leaves something to be desired."

Had Rohan said something *not* in conjunction with the fight to Drio? I shook it off with a "Let's do this."

"We wouldn't even have to do this if Rohan wasn't so damn stubborn," Drio said.

"Stubborn?" I jabbed his side when he didn't answer. "About what? The difference of opinion between him and the Brotherhood on how to proceed with the mission?"

Drio did a double take. "He told you that?" I didn't even have to fudge the truth about not knowing specific details because Drio was in a mood to rant.

"It's a no-brainer," he said. "Forrest Chang, the director of *Hard Knock Strife* is a huge Fugue State Five fan. He contacted Rohan to do the theme song."

Interesting.

"That doesn't mean Rohan would have the chance to buddy up with Samson."

"Invite King to sing as a cameo. Get in close to the bastard that way. We've tried everyone else in his inner circle. No go." Frustration tightened the corners of his eyes. "It would be so easy for Rohan to get to know Samson. Who'd question a rock star hanging around a bunch of actors?" He pinched his lips together. "But he refuses to step back into that role."

"I think he's afraid of what he could slip back into becoming." Given what Rohan had told me, the scars ran deep, evidenced by the fact that he refused to take on something that would move this assignment forward.

Drio slapped his palm flat against the center of the pad mounted on the wall. "You two have gotten chatty. Why don't you talk some sense into him?" A red light scanned him as he studied me.

If I managed that, the Executive would adore me. Desperate as I was to get Ari confirmed, I couldn't use Rohan like this. It was a million kinds of wrong. "Let's pursue the make-up artist avenue first," I said.

Part of the wall slid away, revealing a smaller room within the larger Vault, its floors and walls made of iron. Drio motioned me through the concealed door. Ignoring my tiny frisson of fear, I stepped inside, the wall sealing shut behind us.

A beautiful Korean woman sat in the middle of the space, duct-taped to a thick iron chair bolted to the floor. Her eyes bugged out, darting around as she strained against the tape covering her mouth and binding her feet and hands to the arms and legs of the chair.

She turned a pleading look on me.

"Oh my God!" I took a step forward to help her but Drio knocked me back with a sigh.

Flashing over to her side, he did some Vulcan neck pinch thing and she transformed into a sleek white fox with multiple tails. Mostly transformed. Her hands, feet, and face–all the bits touching the tape, stayed human. The overall effect was somewhat disconcerting.

"Nine," he said, seeing me count her tails.

I inched closer. "What is she?"

"King's make-up artist, Evelyn. Also a kumiho. A master illusionist usually plying her tricks to seduce men."

"But this one puts hers to use on King?"

"That's the theory."

"How did you know she was a demon?"

He tugged me forward, shoving my face inches away from her neck. "Smell."

This close to her, I accessed my magic just in case, a low level hum under my fingertips, but despite her growling and thrashing, she was bound fast. I sniffed, blinking at the faint smell of strawberries.

"It's her natural scent," Drio said. "She can't disguise it."

I walked around Evelyn, who was struggling against her bindings. "How did you get close enough to smell her?"

"My natural charm."

I poked at a binding. "Duct tape? That holds them?"

He shrugged. "Specially threaded with iron and salt fibers."

"What are you going to do with her?"

His smile bloomed, both terrifying and sexy. "Have some fun."

Evelyn's tails thumped in syncopated agitation against the floor.

I glanced at the demon. "Do I need to worry about sexual misconduct?"

Drio shot me a disgusted look. "I don't do that," he replied in a hard voice. "Even to demons." Just regular torture then.

"This isn't about using her to get close," I said.

"No. She's going to share what she knows about King." He pushed up his sleeves.

The demon's eyes flashed red.

Time to go. I had no desire to watch his methods of fact finding.

"Pussy," he snickered, pressing his hand against the scanner mounted inside the small room to open the iron door on this side.

"You ate your siblings in the womb, didn't you?" I said, pausing in the doorway.

Drio licked his lips with relish.

Riiiight.

I stepped into the Vault, the wall sliding shut between us. On my way upstairs, I ran into Baruch, coming out of Ms. Clara's office, clad in black nylon workout pants and a tank top.

Wonder if they're tearaway. Bet Ms. Clara knows.

"Not interested in seeing Drio work?" he asked.

"I'm skipping today's session of 'Creative Sadism with Batshit Crazy.'" I jogged up to my room, finding a note from Rohan ordering me to the library for study time. First, I allotted myself a few minutes to shower off that unpleasant encounter and root through my still-packed clothing for skinny jeans and my navy tunic embroidered with a brilliant dragonfly. Rohan didn't make an appearance in the library, though he'd set out some books on the long table for me to dive into.

I tried to study. I took notes and everything, in between glances toward the hallway at every footfall and voice. It's not that I care if Rohan shows up, I told myself, as I read a particularly gruesome passage about the damage a se'irim could do, it's just that he should be showing a bit more responsibility in overseeing my studying. What if I have a question about a demon that needs answering?

The hundreds of books surrounding me mocked me in response.

Adopting a less formal study position, away from the table and onto a couch, didn't help me focus. Nor did twisting myself upside down, my head hanging to the floor.

Screw it.

Corralling a laptop I found in a cherrywood cabinet, I logged on, seeing what I could find on Samson King, wanting something that would help Drio. Samson's bio before he hit big–which happened with his first role–was pretty sparse. That gelled if he was a demon, since it would be fake. Out of curiosity, I checked the meaning of his name. I was always curious if a person's name meaning correlated to them. Like Nava meant "beautiful" so bulls-eye, Mom and Dad.

Samson meant "sun." I leaned back against my chair. Sun King. Hang on. Leo had mentioned that King had spent time in France. During a trip with my family to France a few years ago, I'd learned that Louis XIV had called himself the Sun King. He'd been a live large, divine-right conferring narcissist and maybe Samson had modeled himself on this guy. Or, actually picked up few tips from him, since many demons had long life spans.

I drummed my fingers on the tabletop, waiting for the page to load in order to get verification for what I was thinking. Here it was. The original Sun King had been a ruthless bastard whose rule had established France as one of the pre-eminent powers in the world. I leaned back in my chair, fingers steepled together. Since it appeared *this* sun king had similar aspirations, maybe this tie to Louis would reveal what type of demon Samson was, or offer more specificity on the master plan.

I leapt out of my seat, sprinting down to the Vault, then back up the stairs with a frustrated growl, since I didn't have access yet to open the door. Kane did though, and I dragged him with me, insisting that he had to get me to Drio now.

He let me in to the Vault and I pounded on the wall concealing the iron room until the angriest of all Rasha answered. Purple goo was smeared across Drio's temple, and his hair was matted with sweat.

Not wanting Evelyn to hear, I whispered my theory into Drio's ear.

The tight expression on his face sent my stomach plummeting into my toes, doubt at my brilliance slithering through me. Then he gave a sharp nod, his eyes glinting dangerously, and returned inside, the wall whooshing shut behind him.

"Nee?" Ari called out from upstairs.

I sped up so fast to meet him that I practically got lift off, throwing myself into his arms. Hugging him and the overflowing pile of bedding he carried.

"This way," I sang, tugging him up the stairs to my room. "Guess what?" I nattered on about Evelyn and my Samson realizations. "Dump the bedding on the mattress," I said.

He stood in the doorway, stock still, clutching the linens.

"What?" I glanced around in confusion.

"Your room."

"Uh-huh." I tugged him forward. "You're not going to get cooties, bro."

He flung the sheets down. "This was supposed to be *my* room. You got my room."

"I did?" I screwed up my face in puzzlement. He'd never mentioned he'd be moving in.

Ari jerked his chin at the painting. "Magritte. Didn't tip you off?"

I flinched at the anger threading his voice. Examining the art hadn't been a top priority in my short time here. Not sure what I could say to make it better, I opted to go with the tried and true. "Sorry."

"No, you're not."

I blinked at him.

"You're enjoying this. Your training." He waved a hand at me. "Your little realizations."

"My little...?" I unclenched my fists. "I am sorry, Ari. But you know what? I can only apologize so many times. None of this is my fault. I'm doing my best here." I picked up the fitted sheet, shaking it out to unroll it.

He snorted.

"What's that supposed to mean?"

"Doing your best?" he sneered. "You're loving this. You're happy."

I popped the corner of the sheet onto the mattress with a violent snap. "God knows we can't have that. There's only one Katz twin allowed that emotion."

"Hey, don't put your fuck-ups on me," he retorted.

"Then don't put other people's on me!"

A muscle ticked in his jaw. "Enjoy your room." He stalked out.

"Oh, I will!" I threw my pillow against the far wall with a scream. I stomped across the room to retrieve it for scream two, glancing out the window. Ari and Kane were having some kind of intense conversation at the front of the house. At least Kane had put a shirt on. It rode up as he gestured with sharp, angry jabs.

Ari was really going for the gold in pissing people off because while Kane was still speaking, my brother slammed into the Prius and drove off. Kane punched one of the front porch pillars.

Feel your pain, dude. I could clock my passive-aggressive brother for walking out before we'd finished our fight. I threw everything out of my containers looking for my damn phone to call Ari's cell and hash this out once and for all, before I remembered that Ms. Clara still had it. Great. No phone, and now my room looked like a hurricane had torn through it.

The frenzy left me exhausted. Heaving a sigh, I bent down to pick up the pillow, my head jerking up at a shout from outside.

Rohan sprinted up the driveway, favoring one ankle, his shirt torn. No, not just his shirt. His arm was a twisted mass of glistening, ripped open flesh that I could see from the third story.

The pillow tumbled out of my hand to the floor.

I threw the window open to find out what had happened.

The noise made Rohan look up at me. I don't know if it was my twin sense or something about his stricken expression clear to me even three floors up as his eyes met mine but I knew.

Something horrible had happened to Ari.

18

I flew down the front stairs, fear fish-hooking into me. "What—"
Baruch and Drio, huddled around Rohan, looked up at the
sound of my voice. The ensuing gap allowed me a close up look at the
inside of Rohan's right arm. I clapped a hand over my mouth, swallowing hard against the taste of bile. Someone was keening and I had
the sneaking suspicion it was me.

Baruch ripped his shirt off, making a tourniquet to staunch the
bleeding.

"Kane!" Rohan failed to look perturbed at the sight of his tendons
spilling out of his skin but he was mightily annoyed at me swaying on
my feet.

Kane leapt off the bottom front stair, his arms coming around me.
"Inside."

"Where's Ari?"

Rohan's expression softened. "Demons got him. Right outside the
gate."

Outside the wards. "Asmodeus?"

He shook his head. "They were trying to get past the wards. I think
it was just bad timing on his part and opportunity on theirs."

"They think they snatched a Rasha?" Kane asked.

Rohan's shrug turned into more of a flinch as Baruch tightened the
tourniquet.

"If even one of you had bothered to help me convince the Brotherhood to confirm Ari's initiate status…" My voice shook. There was a

good chance that he'd have been inducted by now. That he'd have magic at his disposal.

Rohan limped his way up the stairs, waving off Baruch's offer of assistance.

"If the ritual didn't work, he has no status," Drio said.

"I hate you."

"Va bene. One thing going right in my day."

I lunged for Drio, but Kane strong-armed me inside the house and into a den.

I vibrated so hard that any more delays in getting me info and I might have combusted. It's not that I was unsympathetic to Rohan's giant gaping gash, it's just that Rasha had extra-spiffy healing powers and he seemed calm enough as Baruch tossed the bloody wadded up shirt onto a table, replacing it with a fluffy towel that he must have picked up as they came inside.

"Where's my brother?" I demanded, brushing off Kane's attempt to seat me.

"I don't know," Rohan said. "And I didn't follow because I was busy killing the massive fucker that'd been left on clean up." It was obvious Rohan had to work to keep his voice steady.

Drio entered with a sewing kit and a bottle of vodka.

My butt crashed down onto the chair. Except it wasn't the chair, it was the coffee table, and my tailbone caught the corner. "Fuck!" The bite of pain in my lower back helped keep me from plummeting into full-on hysteria.

Drio had passed the bottle to Rohan, who'd taken a swig, but one look at me and Rohan handed me the booze.

I took a swig or three as well before Drio took it away.

With a deep inhale, Rohan nodded at Baruch, who removed the towel. It had soaked up so much blood that it made a wet splat when he dropped it on the table next to the bloody shirt.

That was Drio's cue to pour the alcohol over the gash.

Rohan convulsed, the breath audibly leaving his lungs.

Baruch pinched the flesh to keep the two edges more or less together as Drio opened the lid on the sewing kit. He threaded the needle.

If I hadn't needed my stupid sheets, Ari would never have been here in the first place. We would never have fought.

He would never have been taken.

I dug the nails of my right arm into my left wrist, welcoming the pain. Welcoming the distraction from my worst nightmare that my brother was in danger. I'd known this was a possibility when Ari joined the Brotherhood as a full hunter, but for it to have played out now in light of what had happened seemed like a needlessly cruel twist of fate.

Drio patted Rohan's cheek gently, piercing Rohan's flesh with the needle, the thread trailing off of it like the end of a comet.

I tore my eyes away.

"Who?" Kane's voice was so low, it was practically a growl. His arms were crossed and his jaw was clenched so hard it could probably cut glass.

"Sakacha and dremla." Rohan winced as Drio sewed up the last few stitches.

I squeezed my hands between my knees, shoulders tense, waiting to hear more, breathing through the antiseptic tang permeating the room.

"Together?" Baruch barked. "Those two are not known for playing with others."

"I don't care what the hell they're known for!" I stamped my foot on the ground. "I want to know who they are and what they did with Ari!" My voice was a panicky screech but for fuck's sake, talk to me like I was a child because I didn't know all the ins and outs here.

Rohan gingerly flexed his arm. "Sakacha are pain demons. Physical pain. Dremla are soul leeches."

"And?"

"I. Don't. Know." His breath rushed out in a hiss.

"Not good enough," I snapped, swiping at my eyes with my hand. "Is he alive?" I could barely choke the words out through my tight throat and I dreaded the answer but I had to know.

Rohan's bleak look conveyed his utter lack of knowledge. "There were five of them. They attacked his car as soon as it left the grounds and pulled him out. I ran over to help but..." He shook his head. "One of them dragged him out of the car, threw him over his back, and bolted."

Kane rubbed his forehead with his fist. "They're on foot."

"But they're fast," Baruch said. "Who knows where they've gotten by now?"

"So I track." Drio cut the thread with a small pair of scissors, tying the loose ends in a small knot.

"Take Baruch," Rohan said.

Baruch was already in the hallway headed for the front door.

"I want to go with Drio," I said.

"You can't. You'll just get in his way." Kane slung an arm over my shoulder. "Why don't you go move your dad's car?"

It wasn't up for debate.

Grabbing my Ryan Tedder sunglasses off the table in the foyer for courage, I jogged down the drive to the abandoned car, parked sideways right outside the gate.

I sidestepped the wreckage of Ari's phone, smashed on the concrete. Even if Ari had still had his special Demon Club phone, Rohan wouldn't have gotten to the scene any faster, but this broken piece of crap was a reminder of how helpless my brother was.

I pounded my fist on the hood.

The incessant chiming of the open driver's side door taunted me. *Gone. Gone. Gone.*

A bloody streak ran from the shredded seat belt along the frame of the driver's side door. I clamped my lips together, very glad my parents had left town and I didn't have to tell them what had happened to their son.

Miserable, I got into the car, Ari's blood literally on my hands as I drew the seat belt across my chest. The engine sputtered when I pushed the ignition button, but caught. My fingers tightened on the wheel, resentment burning hot and deep at being relegated to valet.

A one, a two, you know what to do.

I *did* know what to do. Let the boys pursue their leads, I'd pursue mine. I had to find Leo and get her demon insider knowledge. No one was going to sideline me when it came to Ari's safety. Saving him was the one thing I could do right now.

I'm coming for you, Ace, I vowed. Stay strong.

With a glance up the drive to make sure no one was watching, I backed the car out onto the street. The world sped by in a violent blur as I drove like a madwoman to Leo's place, streaks of traffic and barely-dodged pedestrians set to a cacophonic soundtrack of honking horns. Flicking on my signal, I made the final right turn onto Leo's street. As usual, there was no parking, so I zipped into the alley to double park.

A black SUV T-boned me, spinning the car.

The air bags deployed. One second they weren't there, the next *PHOWOMP*, the bags had exploded out of the front and side of the Prius, blowing my head back with a jarring snap of my neck.

I came to with my ears ringing, and three very cute paramedics crouching beside me. "Hello, boys," I slurred. My arm burned like a son-of-a-bitch, covered in the world's worst case of rug burn. Wrong day to wear short sleeves.

They held up the same three fingers in sync. "How many fingers do you see?" The three spoke in unison really well.

I squinted at them. "Are you guys identical triplets?" I closed my eyes because it was somewhat disorienting every time they moved. Also, my face throbbed.

"You've got a concussion. Do you know your name?"

"Nava. Katz."

"Do you remember what happened?"

Closing my eyes didn't make the world any less spinny-ride, so I opened them again. "I was hit."

Triplet melted down to a duo, his faces furrowed in concern. "Do you know why there's blood on the seatbelt? It doesn't appear to be yours."

That's when everything came rushing back to me. "Ari," I gasped, struggling up out of my seat.

"You need to stay put." Hands grabbed at me. One set since he'd finally snapped into focus. "I'm going to cut you out because the release mechanism got mangled in the crash." He jogged over to his car.

Adrenaline rode me like a little bitch, but struggle as I might the belt had me trapped tight. A quick glance in the rearview mirror showed bruising around my nose and left eye. I probed the puffy skin with a pained hiss. The fine white powder from the deployment that coated me didn't add much to the overall effect, and only half of my beloved sunglasses now sat on my head. The other half was nowhere to be seen.

Neither was the hit-and-run black SUV.

I had to get out of here. There was no way to get past the airbags to try the ignition button and, given the crumpled frame and odd way the door hung open, I doubted the car would start anyway.

Dad was going to lose his shit.

I opted to try and zap my way loose from the seatbelt, since the paramedic was taking too long to get whatever tool he needed. I was so focused on the best way to free myself that I failed to realize he'd returned with what appeared to be a very thin, orange, post-modern stapler-shaped thing.

I shut my magic down with a lame, "It's not what you think."

He frowned at the tool. "The seatbelt cutter?"

No way he hadn't seen my magic. Ignoring the impossible? Dodging that bullet worked for me except something about the way he watched me–his smile a little too bright, his gaze a bit too intense–made the back of my neck prickle.

Paramedic man squatted down, sawing through the belt with one sharp slice.

I pitched sideways. The world swung around me, my hand shooting out to grab the warped doorframe for balance. Out of the corner of my eye, I caught sight of the paramedic. Underneath his image, he was rippling.

A hot, bright burst of panic bloomed in my chest. I slammed my hand into his shoulder.

For a brief second, he transformed from shaggy cuteness to a silvery-blue serpent with an overly large mouth and needle teeth, made entirely of water. My electricity dissipated harmlessly over the surface of him. A weak cloud of steam rose off of the serpent, but that was it. His only reaction was to ask if I needed help standing up.

I doubled over, hyperventilating–not entirely an act–to buy me time.

"Come on. I'll get you to the ambulance." He tugged on my elbow, trying to pull me to my feet.

An icy certainty that I couldn't let him put me in there slithered up my spine. I flashed back on the guy sucking that demon's thumb, unwilling to contemplate what this one might do to me. But if my magic was useless on him, how was I going to get away?

Another tug. "Get checked out and I'll help you find your brother."

My head snapped up at his words. At his encouraging nod, the picture of compassion. Except I'd never said Ari was my brother. The mention of my twin triggered the memory of Ari's concentrated salt-coated blade that had been tossed in the car door pocket. In one fell swoop, I thrust it upward into the demon paramedic's jugular.

His eyes widened and his glamour fell away, leaving his watery serpent self with the knife sliding downstream to his toes.

I jumped to my feet, dizzy, and tense, waiting for the clatter of the knife on the ground. Waiting for his nasty retaliation.

Instead, he puffed up, solidifying into a Jell-O-like state, the knife buried inside him.

I'm not sure which of us was more shocked.

The demon tried to move but the salt content made him unwieldy. He wobbled from side-to-side, exactly how I'd expect a giant gelatin cube to walk.

"Bloating sucks," I said, shooting a fairly decent forked lightning bolt from my eyes, which was so fucking cool. Thanks to his super salt content, he now conducted electricity just fine. His body wobbled back against the attack.

The demon curled into his left side. He had to be protecting his sweet spot. Excellent. That left a lot of him to work on.

"Where's my brother?"

Silence.

Electricity crackling off of my finger, I ran the tip along his wrist, slicing through him like butter. His hand dropped to the ground with a meaty splat. His face tightened but he stayed mum.

The demon snapped at me with his spiky teeth but I sidestepped him, one magic-charged hand held up. "I can do this all day. Ari. Why was he taken?"

The demon edged away from me.

"Who are you afraid of?" I forced myself to voice my deepest fear. "Asmodeus?"

His imperceptible flinch was my answer. All guilt, all terror, I shoved down into a well-buried box to torture myself with later. Then I killed the uncooperative bastard.

The demon convulsed, contorting around himself until he became smaller and smaller and then nothing at all. All that was left of him was a few drops of water splattered on the ground and Ari's knife.

I didn't stick around to gloat, bolting for Leo's place, since I had no phone to call her with. Luckily, she lived around the corner. Hand pressed to my sides, lactic acid burning its way through my muscles, I leaned on Leo's intercom, holding the wall for balance, and praying she was home.

"Hello?"

"Let me in!" I scanned the area for any out-of-place twitch or suspicious person.

It seemed like an eternity before the door buzzed open. I cracked it enough to slide inside then shut it tight, wrenching on it a couple of times to make sure it had locked behind me. With one last look around the lobby, I stumbled into the elevator, hit three, and crashed on my ass to the floor.

I managed to shove my foot into the open door when it reached Leo's floor, but couldn't get up on my own, mostly because everything spun so violently, I wasn't sure which way *was* up.

Leo ran over to me, hooking her arms under my pits. "Your face," she gasped.

"Demons took Ari."

I let her drag me inside. My adrenaline gave out, leaving my legs shaking, and my stomach doing dry heaves. I collapsed onto the round, red brocade chair by the window that she'd brought with her from her bedroom when she moved out. The stories this chair could tell.

"You need to go to the hospital."

"No time." I filled her in on what had happened.

"Shit, Nav, that was a kapasca demon. Psychopathic serpents. If he'd managed to haul you back to the water?" She shivered.

"How do I find Asmodeus?"

"I'm sorry." She shook her head. "No clue even where to begin."

"You got him a message."

"Not directly and no one is going to give up his hideout."

My hopes deflated, leaving me with a gut-level queasiness. I'd been positive Leo would know how to find him. I pressed a hand to my head.

"Got any Tylenol?" If she couldn't help, I had to patch myself up and find Rohan. My accelerated healing powers weren't accelerating fast enough. That, or my concussion was a lot worse than I thought.

"Not Tylenol," she said, handing me a tablet and a glass of water a moment later. "Paracetamol." She took the glass back from me, helping me to sit up.

I didn't question her having the meds on-hand. Leo was a bit of a hypochondriac.

She gave me the bottle in case I needed another pill later. "I'll put out feelers." It was a start.

"Can you drive me back to the chapter house first?" I asked.

She hesitated. "Why don't you just call them?"

"Because the stupid Fallen Angels never bothered to give me their cell numbers." I seethed. "I promise not to let anyone hurt you. Or find out you're a demonette."

"No worries." Leo grabbed her purse, patting it. "Custom made iron switchblade. Very effective. Even on Rasha." She smiled evilly. "Remember that." Then she grabbed her keychain from where she was using it as a bookmark in one of her crim texts.

I groaned at the distinctive logo, pressing a hand to my throbbing head as the sound sent a fresh wave of nausea through me. "Not the Vespa." Given the one second delay between my brain and my body, I'd fall off the damn thing.

"Mom's got my car. This is the fastest way unless you want to wait around for a taxi," she said. She tossed me a spare leather jacket that was too short in the arms and too tight in the boobs, but would keep me warm and protected from any road rash.

The ride back wasn't too bad, with only two stops for me to throw up—once in a box hedge, and the other right into the gutter like the classy kitten I was. We pulled up to the chapter house gate. Tossing her my helmet, I got off the bike to hit the buzzer next to the scanner panel.

"Yes?"

"Yum," Leo mouthed at me, at the sound of Drio's Italian accent.

I squeezed my right fist open and closed twice rapidly, our code for giant anal sphincter.

Her face fell.

"It's me, Drio. Let me in."

"Qui?"

"Nava. Quit screwing around. We don't have time."

"Bella, I assure you," he purred, "You and I have all the time in the world."

Leo shivered. "Could he just be one—" She opened and closed her fist once, indicating a partial anal sphincter personality. "I could deal with that level of douchery."

"Are you fucking kidding me?" The sentiment applied to the two of them.

There was a pause from the intercom, then Drio said, "I'll be out in a minute."

Leo parked the bike, while I leaned up against the gate in a pose I hoped conveyed nonchalance rather than assisted standing.

Drio finally arrived but didn't open the gate. Asshole could have flash stepped outside instead of making us wait. Though he did darken at the sight of me. "Who hurt you?" he asked, pointing at my face.

I rattled the bars which failed to rattle. "Let me in and I'll tell you."

"Tell me and I'll let you in."

Was he really going to do this now? "Where's Kane?" He'd let me in.

Drio braced a hand against the bar. "You're not his type, bella."

"What's your type?" Leo piped up.

He rounded on her with an interested gleam.

"Not the time," I hissed, smacking her across the top of the head. "I know who has Ari."

Drio straightened up, all flirtiness gone, and opened the gate. "You better come talk to Rohan."

I grabbed his wrist, bracing for the worst. "Did you find him?"

Drio glanced down at my hand on his arm. "You dare to wear the hamsa?" he growled in a low voice.

Dread sat in my gut like hot lead. Drio might not like me but he wouldn't joke about me being Rasha. "Don't you know who I am?"

"Problem?" Rohan asked in a silky voice, joining the party. He was not a happy camper.

Leo, however, was ecstatic for about the thirty seconds she fan-gasmed all over him once recognition kicked in.

Rohan bestowed a rock fuck grin on her and said, "Always pleased to meet a fan."

That did it. I let my magic out in full force.

Ordinarily, I'd have loved making the boys' jaws drop in shock at my amazing abilities, but the fact that my powers were news to them meant that *they had no clue who I was.*

I wrapped my arms around myself, a million worst-case scenarios of how this could have happened flashing through my head. Trembling, I started up the drive, needing more than ever to get my fellow Rasha onboard with saving Ari.

Rohan attempted to stop me but I burst into full crackle. "I will go psycho like you've never seen if you don't get yourself, Drio, Baruch, and Kane into the library this very second," I said.

That's when Rohan saw the ring. He grabbed my hand, barely flinching at the electricity scorching his skin. He tugged on it but of course, it didn't move. His hand clamped on my wrist, he dragged me up the driveway without another word.

"Wait for me!" Leo called out.

Reality slowed down into a slow motion "Noooooo." I yanked free of Rohan and sprinted for Leo before she could try to step over the ward and be repelled off of it, visions of Drio dusting my best friend dancing before my eyes.

"Rohan is highly overrated," Drio said. "Allow me." He took her arm, escorting her onto the premises, as I stumbled to a stop. Did he know she was a PD and was toying with us? Or had he inadvertently saved her?

Leo winced, her eyes widening in comprehension, but she regained her composure in an instant, flipping her hair as she assured Drio it would be her pleasure. Not that she had a choice. Drio may have sounded player personified, but the set of his shoulders assured me that neither Leo nor I were going anywhere until they had answers.

Brilliant. A goblin, a Rasha, and two amnesiacs walk into a house— I couldn't begin to imagine where this joke was going to end. Or at whose expense.

So long as it wasn't Ari's.

19

Rohan led me all the way around the house and in through the back door to the kitchen, presumably so I wouldn't see anything I shouldn't. I tried to explain that he was wasting valuable time, but he wasn't inclined to listen.

They really had no idea who I was. How was this even possible?

How could I be so easily erased?

The mean little voice inside my head scoffed. Not that hard, Nava. Other than to Ari, weren't you pretty much incidental to everyone anyway? And he wasn't exactly feeling the love either, was he?

Shut. Up.

Once they had us corralled in the middle of the room, Rohan leaning casually against the back door and Drio lounging in the doorway, blocking our escape, I was ordered to start talking.

"Baruch and Kane," I said. "Where are they?"

"Here. You are who?" Baruch barked at me, lumbering in past Drio. The color drained from Leo's face and she scooted back a few steps. Not surprising. With their height difference, Tree Trunk could drop kick her across the yard. Or snap her in two.

I squeezed her hand. "Get Kane," I insisted. After me, he was the most invested in Ari's well-being.

"He's busy." Rohan's pose didn't change. "Now, who are you?"

"I'm Nava Katz." The guys exchanged a look at my last name. "Look, I know who took Ari."

"Why should we listen to you?" Drio asked.

"If you don't believe that I'm Rasha after seeing my power, maybe this," I pointed upstairs, "will help convince you."

"Power?" Baruch asked, but Drio had already allowed me to pass.

I led everyone up to my bedroom, showing them my stuff which was helpfully strewn across the room after my earlier phone search. "Rasha. I live here. See?"

"Lucky," Leo sighed. She snapped her mouth shut as all three guys conferred identical expressions of barely veiled annoyance on her.

Drio poked at a lacy blue demi-bra.

I smacked his hand away. "I've been here training with you guys for almost a week. The Brotherhood thought Ari was the initiate all this time but when Rabbi Abrams did the second ceremony, it turned out it was me."

They watched me blankly.

I straightened up with steel-spined determination. Remember me or not, all they needed to do was help me get my brother back. "Ari is my twin. You sent me to go pursue a lead," I said, fudging the truth, "and I was ambushed by a bad guy." Emphasis on the last two words.

"Nava is so hush-hush with her new job," Leo joked. "I'd tell you but I'd have to kill you." She broke into a snorting laugh.

I face-palmed.

"Thing is, you've seen her power," Rohan said. "What do you know about that?"

So tempting to slap the re-appearance of rock fuck grin off his face. And hello? How come that grin had never made an appearance with me?

Leo batted her eyelashes at him. "I'm very good at keeping my mouth shut."

An incredulous laugh that I didn't exactly turn into a cough escaped me.

That earned me the finger. Behind her back, so her new friends wouldn't see something so crass. "I wouldn't do anything to endanger my best friend," she said. "Even if she is astoundingly annoying."

Her words made me think of my twin, also astoundingly annoying at times. And the person I wanted most safe in the world. I'd managed to forget about Ace for a quarter of a second and I hated myself for it.

I massaged my temples. "Hold me accountable if she blabs, you know where I live."

Baruch waved a dismissive hand at my belongings. "This means nothing. There is no such thing as a female Rasha."

I appealed to Rohan in desperation. "Last night. We talked about your music. About how incredible it was to sit down with the rest of your band and put all your bad feelings, all your dreams into words for the world to hear. What it was like having your lyrics come alive. You've got to believe me. We're wasting time here."

"Wow," Leo murmured.

Rohan's expression shuttered.

"Ro doesn't talk about those days. With anyone," Drio said. "Nice try." He broke out the psychotic smile that tended to precede Torture Time and stepped closer.

My power didn't convince them. The fact of me living here didn't convince them. Recapping events of the past few days also a big fail. How could I prove I was telling the truth?

"Ari didn't have a twin." Perfect. Kane had shown up, sporting a fine scowl. "I was listening. Might want to do your homework before leading with an easily verifiable lie."

"I'm not–" I stumbled, realizing he'd used the past tense in talking about my brother. I lunged for him, grabbing his shirtfront. "What do you mean 'didn't?' I want to see his body."

He took pity at the desperation in my voice though he pried my fingers off him. "There wasn't enough of him left to see."

"Ari's not dead," I protested. I'd have known. There wasn't a doubt in my mind that Ari, while in danger, still lived. But for how much longer? I had to convince them.

I was about to remind Rohan of how we'd fought together when it hit me. The memory loss. "Asmodeus. He took Ari and he's the reason you can't remember."

"Impossible," Baruch said.

Somehow the demon had compelled the Rasha to forget me. The same way he'd managed to compel me to, well, forget myself. From Rohan's thoughtful expression, he was turning the idea over in his head. How was it possible for a demon to alter someone's memory? Because one, that was terrifying, and two, I was totally going to have words with Ms. Clara about my demon-punching contract not being more upfront about stuff like that.

I kicked Rohan in the head, intending to snap him out of the compulsion like I'd done in the park. It failed to work. He cursed, Drio and Kane tackled me, and I ended up facedown on the floor, sputtering about the demon through a mouthful of carpet.

What Asmodeus had done to me had merely been a taste, weak enough that my anger at Rohan's assholeness had snapped it. Well, these guys were furious and that wasn't snapping shit. Asmodeus had baked the memory loss into them.

"Lock them up," Rohan directed. "Then meet us in the library."

Drio seized Leo and me each by the arm.

Damn it! Why had I told Asmodeus to come after me?

"As your demon master isn't here right now," Drio murmured into my ear, "you'll have to contend with me." He shoved Leo and me out the door. "Resist me, access your power, I so much as feel your muscles tense, and I'll make things very unpleasant for you."

He frog-marched us down to the Vault.

"Drio," I reasoned, half twisting around to face him, despite the pain lancing up my arm, "how could I wear this hamsa if I wasn't

Rasha? You think a demon would be able to wear the ring without repercussion? Isn't the simplest explanation the most logical? That I *am* a hunter and you're all suffering from some kind of demonic spell? I'm telling you, Asmodeus did this. You have to believe me."

He slowed for a second then wrenched my arm up higher. "The simplest explanation is a human obeying a demon," he countered. "Since female Rasha don't exist."

Trying to prove my hunter identity was pointless. I had history and misogyny working against me. I'd have to save Ari another way. Problem was, if everyone believed that Ari was dead, they'd no longer be looking for him.

I had to escape.

Leo broke into a coughing fit halfway down the stairs to the basement. While she looked like staying upright required her full concentration, I'd swear the coughing was fake.

"You okay?" My thoughts were occupied with how we were going to get out of this. Even if I lit up to attack, the chances of Drio zipping away before I could hurt him were high. Payback would not be pretty. I needed to catch him off-guard.

"No talking." Drio tightened his hold on us.

Leo glanced pointedly down at her bag, slung across her chest. It took me a minute to clue in. The switchblade.

I gave the tiniest shake of my head.

Drio locked us up in the room where the kumiho demon had been. There was no longer any trace to show she'd existed. That was creepy and didn't bear thinking about.

He left us there, sealing us in with only a dim bulb for light.

Leo sunk to the ground with a moan. I ran over to her but she held me off. "I'll puke if you touch me." She pressed a hand to her head, the skin at the corners of her eyes tight.

"It's the wards," I said. "I'm sorry. If Drio hadn't pulled you through and you'd been outed?" Unable to punch the solid iron wall for fear of breaking my fist, I gave a loud "fuuck!"

"Forget it. I should have remembered this place was warded." She gave me a faint grin through her pain. "Rohan distracted me."

"He does that."

"Why didn't we take Drio down?" Leo asked.

"He'd have gotten away before you had the knife out. Then we'd really have been screwed." I slid down the wall. "All I wanted was to keep Ari safe until I could give him back his destiny. I failed. Where's the gray area now, Leo?"

She was seated with her arms curled around her knees in a tight ball, as if trying to make the least contact with all the iron, taking deep, even breaths. "Your brother spent his life training to be a hero. Not an insurance agent. He was never going to be safe."

I leaned my head back against the wall, defeated. "But if he'd become a hunter he would have had magic. A fighting chance. He's helpless against them."

"And there will come a time, more than one I bet, that you face demons when you're helpless," she said. I already had with Asmodeus. "Whose fault will it be then? The *Brotherhood* screwed up with Ari. Not you. Stop being so committed to your guilt over this."

"How do you do it?" I asked. "Live in the gray and still have such a strong sense of yourself? You're a good person and yet you still have to balance a demon heritage. No offense."

"None taken. I've known what I was since I was tiny. The goblin used to come visit me when I was small, telling me who I was, what to expect. What I could have if I embraced it. I didn't want it. I like being human. The trick has been figuring out how to use my goblin side to enhance my humanity. Just like you'll have to do as a hunter." She shrugged, her voice growing weaker. "It's a work in progress."

"I think you're amazing as is."

She swayed slightly and I caught her, propping her up with my hand on her back.

"Apparently this much iron and me don't get along," she whispered.

I wasn't ready to absolve myself, but I was more than ready to save my twin and, more immediately, my best friend. I took stock of our surroundings. No windows, a bare bulb, nothing in here other than that chair bolted to the floor. One door that required–

I could have kissed Drio, that "females can't be Rasha" nonbeliever, for putting us in here. Informing Leo I was letting go of her, I scrambled to my feet, blood pumping and pressed my ear to the door, straining to hear if he was gone, but the walls were soundproof.

"Here goes everything." I lay my hand against the scanner, hoping my access had gone through and that I still existed for Demon Club administration.

After the longest second in the world, the light turned green and the door opened, releasing us back into the Vault. We crept up to the ground floor office level. It was slow going because Leo was still shaky but we made it to the outside door without mishap. "Go." I whispered, one eye on Ms. Clara's office.

Leo shook her head.

Still keeping my voice low, I said, "I can be found here. You can't."

"Nee, I told you, you won't find Asmodeus."

"I don't have to. Do you need me to take you back across the wards?"

"No. I'll be okay leaving. It's entering that's the problem."

I hugged her. "I appreciate everything you did. Call me if you learn anything. Now get."

"Call if you need me," she whispered back, and left.

Soon as she'd safely made it across the yard to the trees, I inched my way up the stairs, holding the bannister so it would take most of my weight in case any of the treads were prone to creaking. I expected to be caught at any second, but no hand came down on my shoulder, allowing me to reach the library door, crouch down, and listen.

"I'm sorry about Ari," Rohan was saying.

I peeked through the crack between the open door and the frame to see Rohan lay a hand on Kane's shoulder. Yeah, *he* was the one who needed consoling.

"I'll confirm the demons' location. Then we do clean up." That was Drio. I didn't begrudge him his bloodthirsty tone, though I worried they'd be so focused on killing they'd fail to find Ari. Or worse, hurt him in the carnage.

"Meantime, I'm off to confront Montague." By the growl of Rohan's voice, this wasn't going to be a friendly meeting.

"Nothing he says can justify betraying fellow Rasha," Drio said. "Undoing our wards and letting Asmodeus in."

A *Rasha* had taken down the wards?

Baruch's blink of fury made my stomach plummet into my toes.

"Even though Ari wasn't Rasha..." Kane trailed off.

"He was still a Brother." Really, Baruch? Because he wasn't when I'd been pleading my case to get Ari's initiate status confirmed. Bogus death revisionist history.

Not that Ari was dead. Still, I'd had it with these guys.

"Ms. Clara tapped Montague's phone for GPS inactivity," Rohan said. "We've got his location."

I didn't stick around to hear more. Five minutes later, I was hiding on the floor of the cramped backseat of Rohan's Shelby, curled tight into a ball and silent as a mouse, tagging along to go confront our rogue Rasha. Rohan leadfooted it to our destination, but despite being tossed around, I didn't make a sound.

I gave him some time after he cut the engine to get inside wherever we were before unfolding my stiff joints and scrambling out of the car. I was back in the Motel Shangri-Lola parking lot, site of my reunion with Leo last night. "Fuuuck!" I kicked at the car tire.

Rohan grabbed me by the waist. "How the hell did you get free?"

"I want first crack to see what he knows about Ari." I jerked free. "Room 205."

Rohan stepped around to face me, a dangerous flicker in his icy eyes. "You know this, how?"

I opened my mouth, then snapped it shut, not having a lie ready. If I said I'd met the snitch here, he'd demand to meet him. Her. I would too if I was Rohan. It was an awfully big coincidence on the face of things and I'd need to find out what led Leo to this case. But she was not the bad guy here.

Rohan pinned me against the hood, the warmth of the engine against my back at odds with the cool blade along his forearm pressed across my throat. "Explain."

I swallowed. "You wouldn't kill a fellow Rasha."

"If this alleged Rasha posed a larger threat to the Brotherhood? Try me." He looked a tad too willing for me to take him up on his offer.

"I met an informant here last night. A demon informant."

A muscle jumped in his jaw. "Call him."

I jutted out my chin. "No."

"I'm sorry?" Despite the barely suppressed fury in his voice, the blade wasn't hurting me.

Yet.

Though the stress of the situation had brought my headache back like the cast of *Stomp* had set up shop in my skull. Screwing up my face, I fumbled in my pocket for the pills, holding them blindly out to Rohan.

He took the bottle, releasing me to pop the cap.

I slumped over the hood, my fingertips pressed to my throat but there wasn't any bruising.

Rohan hooked an elbow under me to pull me up. He probed my black eye. "Where's the demon that did that to you?"

"Dead," I said viciously, jerking away from his touch. He'd been gentle but it still hurt.

"Good. He's involved with Katz's death how?" That question would have been brutal to hear spoken aloud if I wasn't sure that Ari lived.

"His abduction," I corrected.

Rohan tilted his head in acknowledgment. "His abduction."

"I'm not sure." I described the accident. "That's how I know it was Asmodeus. He's behind your memory loss, too." I pointed to the pills. "Can I have?"

"You shouldn't need these."

"Tell that to my head."

"How many have you taken already?" Rohan pressed a tablet into my palm.

"I'm a good time on over-the-counter-meds."

"Expired meds."

I held out my hand for the bottle. "Aren't expiry dates just a suggestion?"

"Surprisingly, no." Rohan handed back the bottle, tugging on my ring one more time like he couldn't believe I was actually Rasha. "Ari really is your twin?"

"I swear it with every fiber of my being." I infused my words with as much sincerity as I could and while Rohan studied me, as if weighing their truth, he nodded, convinced. About my sibling connection at least.

Though he shot me one more hard look before stalking off across the parking lot. Gravel crunched under his feet. He still had the slightest limp, courtesy of his earlier injury. "Why do I get the feeling you are all kinds of trouble?"

I scurried after him. "Beats me."

The front desk was unmanned, just like in my first visit, though I did hear a tinny TV set playing some soap opera in a room off back.

Rohan pushed me in front of him. "Lead the way."

Lola didn't reek of tuna fish this time, which was a good thing, but the many oddly colored stains on the cheap beige carpeting running the length of the hallways seemed more pronounced today. The walls were too closed in, the dingy green brocade wallpaper exuding wrongness, though maybe that was me projecting.

It was a good thing that housekeeping was so lax. And that magnetic key cards were an unknown technology in this dump, allowing Rohan to pick the lock. He shouldered open the door, both of us flinging our arms over our noses at the stench. Not from the body. There wasn't enough of Montague left on the bed to stink: several gnawed-on bones, a curled-up strip of skin hanging off the bed like a discarded towel, and a brownish red squishy that might have been part of an intestine. No, the foul stench came from the giant pile of demon cat piss on a wadded up section of bedding. The creature had soaked half the mattress through with its ungodly urination.

"Bhenchod!" That sounded like an excellent curse. I'd have to ask him about it later.

Rohan shoved me out into the hallway, slamming the door closed. "Jax demon. Toxic urine. It ate away the body. This is a relatively fresh kill."

"Ate him out, then ate him. Hope it was worth it."

Rohan grimaced. "Montague fucked that thing? What is it with people and demon sex?"

I shrugged. "Couldn't tell you. Though your subject and object are reversed. Montague being the fuckee and thus the object of the sentence."

He made a call. "Drio? I need a clean up." He filled him in as quickly as possible. "Now," he said in a voice far too sweet, his phone held out to me, "let's try this again."

20

"Leonie is my high school best friend." I slung an arm around her, the two of us huddled together on her sofa under her giant framed poster of Andy Warhol's large multi-colored flowers.

"Best friend *since* high school," she clarified. "On my end, I wasn't on a break."

I elbowed her side. Yeah, but she hadn't called me either so it's not like my existence mattered. No, I couldn't let this memory loss bullshit mess with my head.

"Best friends. With a demon." Rohan paced in front of us, every now and again stopping to shake his head like he couldn't believe the level of stupidity in this room. "Demons and Rasha can't be friends."

Finally. I let out a relieved sigh that he'd conceded I was Rasha.

I threaded my fingers through Leo's. "That's the problem with Rasha males. They see everything in black and white. It's a dangerous way to live."

Rohan was turning "Nava Red" so I quickly added, "Leo is only a half-goblin and I didn't know until last night she was even that. She's also given the Brotherhood a lot of good intel." I had no idea if that was true or not but I psychically willed Leo to confirm it.

She did. "I am a highly valuable informant."

"We'll see." He grabbed a kitchen chair, since Leo's funky open concept apartment was not all that big, and doing his backward straddle, sat down. "Tell me everything about how you got this case and I may let you live."

"You'll totally let her live," I said, squeezing Leo's hand for support. She'd gone a little pale.

"I haven't even decided if I'm going to let *you* live." He grinned at me. All teeth, the way a shark would while contemplating which part of your soft underbelly to rip into in the most painful death strike.

I shrank back into the sofa. "How'd you get the case, Leo?"

Apparently it had been a routine hire. The jax demon contacted Leo by email, the money wired to her account. She'd been given the time and the place of the meeting and told to record it.

"Why?" I asked.

Leo toyed with her long silver necklaces. "He didn't say, but meeting with a Rasha like that? He probably wanted proof of identity in case the hunter wasn't feeling cuddly post-coital."

"Shouldn't Montague have been more worried about the jax?" I said.

Leo shook her head. "It's rare that jax kill."

"He did in this case. On Asmodeus' orders?" I asked Rohan.

"That's my guess. Where's the recording now?" Rohan's hands hung loose and casual at his sides and even his voice sounded relaxed. Pure man candy. But he commanded the room like he was a conquering army of one, so assured of his right and might that all other lesser beings kneeled in his presence.

I fought the desire to present my throat to him like I was a were-wolf and he was my alpha. Okay, yes, I read way too many shape-shifter romances.

Given Leo's fidgeting, her desire to obey warred with her determination to stand her ground. "That recording is confidential. I'm not handing it over to Demon Club."

Rohan smirked at her as if her little show of defiance was cute. He held up a finger. "One." A blade snicked out of the end, startlingly loud in our tense silence. "Two." A second finger and blade followed. There was no doubt in my mind he'd use them on her.

Leo muttered a bunch of expletives under her breath, but got up from the sofa, squeezing her right fist twice at me.

"Totally," I agreed in a low voice, after she'd handed her digital recorder over to him.

"That was for you," she said, "for having led him to my door."

Rohan held up the device. "We'll listen to it here. No one will be the wiser."

Leo blinked at him. "Oh. You're very–Well, thank you."

Ugh. Rock fuck grin alert. "I am very," he agreed.

"I know you are," she said, all injustice forgiven.

"For the love of fuck," I snapped, muscling in between them before they could keep verbally diddling each other, "hit play already."

The recording yielded nothing other than confirmation of Montague's identity and a lot of demon-human porn sounds.

Dusk was falling as Rohan and I headed back across the parking lot to the Shelby. The heavy gray clouds cast an ominous spell over the fading light. Darkness was going to be a step up.

"How do we break this compulsion and get your memories back?" I asked on our drive back.

"The surefire way? Kill Asmodeus."

At least that fit in with my plan to help Ari. I twisted my hair into a bun at the nape of my neck. "How do wards work?"

"The magic in the wards is the same magic that flows through a Rasha's veins," Rohan said in a clipped voice. "As is the blood used."

"So only Rasha can set wards?"

"Yeah. And only Rasha can undo them." Rohan clenched the steering wheel. "Montague let a demon enter a Rasha house." Rohan curled his lip. "Asmodeus had to be close enough for us to hear the memory loss command." The odometer needle inched higher and higher.

I sympathized with his anger, but I didn't want to die in a horrific traffic accident. "Speed limit," I yelped, my death grip on the seat easing up as he slowed the car down. "You think Asmodeus used the sakacha and dremla attack as cover to buy time for Montague to take down the wards? Allowing Asmodeus to get close enough to compel you into forgetting me?"

"Yes."

I rolled down the window, letting the breeze cascade over me. My concussion symptoms were gone and the burn on my arm was starting to fade. Too bad that my Rasha healing didn't cover wounds of the emotional variety, because the painful needles of ice piercing my heart since I'd found out about Ari's disappearance hadn't eased up any.

Rohan took a hand off the wheel to squeeze my shoulder. "We'll fix this."

"How did Asmodeus even know how to find Montague," I said, "if Montague snuck into town for this liaison?"

Rohan braked at a red light, drumming his fingers on the steering wheel. "Prince of Lust. He'd make it his business to know things like this."

I frowned. "I still don't get why he helped Asmodeus at all." How could he betray everything he stood for and help a demon? Even I wouldn't do that and I'd just been Rasha for a few days. Protecting Leo's identity wasn't the same thing. "You think he was compelled?"

"Probably threatened to take away his playmate," Rohan said darkly. The light turned green and we shot forward. "The jax demon. There's a secretion in its tongue that," he made the sound of a bomb going off with the accompanying hand motion. "Provides a very good time."

"What is wrong with you men? You'll strangle yourself, let demon cats lick you, all because you need a bigger bang."

"It's insanely addictive."

I threw him a look.

He threw me a look back. "So I've been told." He slowed the car at the chapter house gate.

"That's no excuse."

"It's not. And if Montague was still alive?" Rohan's finger blades popped out and he studied his hand in a scarily casual way. "I'd kill him myself for the betrayal."

The gate opened, allowing Rohan to swing into the long driveway.

"I made Ari bring my stupid sheets and then fought with him, stupidly forgetting that I'd told a demon out for revenge where I live." I buried my head in my hands. "I should have at least been guarding him."

Rohan braked in front of the house and cut the engine. "You'd have gotten yourself killed fighting the minions off." He flung open his car door. "As a new Rasha you couldn't have taken those demons on your own, so quit beating yourself up about it. Which brings us to last night." Rohan escorted me up the stairs. "Asmodeus learned about you and revamped his plan. That's probably why he left the fight."

"No point killing me when he still planned to toy with me."

Rohan paused at the front door. "Make you hurt the way he does. I think you're right and Ari is still alive. He's worth more to Asmodeus that way."

"Great." My mouth twisted. "My brother is being tortured because of me."

"Tortured isn't dead." A stricken expression flashed over his features. "You can come back from tortured."

"To live what kind of life?" I walked into the foyer, my shoulders hunched tight up around my ears.

"That'll depend on Ari." His clasped my wrist with a feather-light touch, his brows drawing together with an expression of uncertainty. "Last night. It's… blurry. I really spoke to you about my music?"

He sounded so hesitant. So unlike himself. "You really did," I said.

Rohan stalked off. I didn't understand the big deal and honestly, right now, I didn't care. I needed to find my twin.

We assembled in the library where Rohan caught Kane, Baruch, and Drio up on the situation, leaving out Leo's identity, for which I was grateful. And surprised. Though they were super pissed at me for going behind their back with the snitch to begin with.

Also, Drio bristled like he wanted to eye-for-an-eye *me* for getting away on his watch. I stuck close to Rohan because if Drio didn't remember me, he certainly didn't remember his reluctant promise to protect me.

"Pretty genius," Kane said. "At best, the memory loss complicated things for you immensely, at worst, we might have killed you ourselves."

"Still might," Drio said. "We only have her word about who she is."

"The ring and the power are proof," I said.

"We'll see if the Executive thinks so."

"No!" I grabbed Drio's arm as he stood. Baruch caught me with one hand and Drio with the other, pushing us back into our respective seats.

"Maspik." Given Baruch's growl I figured he was telling us to knock it off.

"Tell him not to tattle on me to Big Brother," I said.

"No one is tattling," Kane said.

Drio crossed his arms.

"We done?" Rohan leveled a hard gaze between the two of us. I nodded and Drio sat there stonily, which was the best case scenario.

"Do we know where the demons are holding Ari?" I asked.

Kane's expression gentled. "Ari isn't—"

"Yes," I snapped. "He is. My twin is alive and if it's all the same to you, I'd like to go find him." I jumped to my feet. "Can we do that?"

Baruch nodded. "We can, in fact."

Rohan's hand came down on my shoulder. "That anger? Hold on to it. Don't let it rule you. But let it fuel you."

Count on it.

"It would have to be Riverview." I peered through a copse of trees at the largely abandoned psychiatric hospital located about a half hour drive outside Vancouver.

The looming stone buildings with their iron-barred windows were creepy enough when seen in all the various TV shows that shot here. Onscreen didn't come close to capturing the eerie vibe while actually standing on the edge of the property under an ink-black sky with only the faintest trace of moonlight. Suddenly, that oppressive dusk seemed like the better option.

I'd requested one of those crazy bright flashlights that Scully and Mulder always seemed to have on hand. Instead I'd been clothed in lightweight, fibrous clothing like an armor covering me from neck to ankle that would help deflect demon claws and teeth and given a tight scratchy black cap to tuck my hair under. I resembled a giant black sock with boobs.

The four guys, on the other hand, looked like cool ninja assassins.

It was a good thing I only got the vaguest sense of the buildings. Too much of a close inspection would have played havoc with my already fraught nerves. I'd heard rumors of voices here at Riverview and that was without a demon presence.

Even knowing I was going in with the super mensches and my own magic abilities didn't stop me from jumping at every little sound and obsessively checking over my shoulder.

"Got an idea of what we'll be faced with when we get inside? Based on all the successful demon raids you've led?" I whispered, creeping behind Rohan in the shadows.

"Danger." At a sign from Drio that he was zipping ahead, Rohan put up his own hand to bring the rest of us to a stop.

"That vagueness doesn't inspire confidence."

He flashed me a wry smile. "I rock improvisation."

We waited in tense silence. I sort of wished the demons would hurry up and rush us because the anticipation was awful. At long last, Drio returned, pointing to a building on the west side of the property. "In there."

In another time and place, say on a sunny day in the Deep South, sipping sweet tea while rocking lazily on the front porch, our destination would have been a charming place to hang out. A long staircase led up to a row of two-story columns, supporting the wide balconies on each floor. Now, however, the once-white paint was streaked with black. Clumps of moss clung to the sides of the railings and ferns grew in wild abandonment over the windows.

I shivered, very glad to have Baruch at my back as we stepped inside because my inner things-that-go-bump-in-the-night-o-meter was vibrating hard enough to snap. A coat of silver paint, probably from a film shoot, had been applied, now peeling in huge scabby swathes. Or rather, flaked like something with massive nails had tried to scrabble its way out through the walls. There was junk everywhere, from plaster, wood, and pipes vomited out of the structure itself and strewn around like a bomb blast, to an abandoned shopping cart sitting in an otherwise empty room.

Drio kept zipping off ahead to scout. This time when he came back, he touched Rohan's shoulder to turn us into a large room, then, motioning for Kane to come with him, left.

Rohan, Baruch, and I picked our way over fallen ceiling tiles.

I looked up, then wished I hadn't because the ceiling was rife with gaping holes, perfect for some demon to drop down on us. Say, a seven-foot-high wooden snowman demon, exploding out in a shower of ruptured tiles.

I rocked sideways at the resounding crash of the demon hitting the floor.

The demon's head, the smallest segment, was a good foot and a half in diameter. His eyes took me a moment to find, since his skin was the consistency of weathered bark, but finally I saw the slowly blinking slits. He had no legs and stumpy T-Rex arms. It would have been comical except each of these tiny limbs ended in foot-long, blood-encrusted pincers. He slithered toward us with a scraping sound, each of his segments wobbling in different tempos.

"Sakacha," Baruch said. The pain demon.

This atrocity was one of the creatures that Asmodeus ordered to kidnap Ari? Before I could light up, Baruch stepped in front of me to battle it. The foresty showdown of Tree Trunk versus Segmented Wood Block. Baruch ducked under the demon's snapping left pincer to pop up behind him and snap his head off. He broke off that heavy chunk of wood as easily as if he was breaking off a piece of a cracker.

Being headless didn't deter the demon. The sakacha swiveled his head, now laying sideways on the ground, to watch the fight, turning his body accordingly in order to take Baruch on, like a remote control.

Rohan grabbed my arm.

My neck jolted sideways as he pulled me along. The reverberations of other thunks of wood followed us as we sped through the building, each hit managing to make the floor tremble no matter how far away we got.

I threw a worried glance over my shoulder as we ran, praying Baruch was all right.

"He's fine," Rohan said, as if I'd spoken, because he was a freak that way. "The kill spot is a knot in the center of the lower segment. Baruch has to take him apart to get to it."

"With his bare hands?"

A finger traced down my back. I swung around throwing a voltage-heavy right hook that would have made Baruch proud. But there was no one there. Though I swear I heard a laugh. If that had been Drio with some sick joke, I'd kill him.

I'd never been big on running, but I experienced a sudden deep love for flat-out sprinting. I vaulted down some stairs and skidded to a stop next to Rohan, my chest heaving. Oh. Whatever had touched me before hadn't been Drio. He was otherwise occupied.

Pillars dotted the large room in which we stood. The light coming through the warped window at one end threw slithery shadows that danced along the floor, turning Drio's battle with the half-dozen saka-cha demons present into an eerie ballet.

Kane was nowhere to be seen. I crossed my fingers that he was searching for Ari.

Drio used his flash stepping to dance and weave through their number, disappearing from beside one only to appear next to another. In the seconds it took for *that* sakacha to realize Drio was there, he'd used this small axe blade to slice a piece off it.

Where'd he been storing that thing?

Giant sakacha slivers flew to a soundtrack of axe whistling and wood scraping against the floor. Drio was doing an impressive job holding his own but he was still outnumbered and slicing them apart to get to their knots required time we didn't have.

Rohan pointed to a pillar. "Stay over there. You'll be safe."

I planted my hands on my hips. "Excuse me, Tarzan?"

"We'll find your brother faster if I don't have to worry about you. Don't underestimate these demons."

"What exactly are you going to do against those wood monsters? Carve your initials in them until they beg for mercy?" I pushed Rohan back with a sweeping arm. "Stand back." I struck the nearest demon with a bolt to his middle and like all dry wood, he burst into flame. His pee-wee arm sizzled away, his right pincer clattering to the ground.

My smug triumph lasted about ten seconds.

With a grinding noise, the sakacha demon transformed from wood to stone, dousing the flames and making his skin impenetrable.

Houston, we have a problem.

21

"Um..."

"Stone," Rohan said, pinching the bridge of his nose. "How they react to external threat."

"Like Drio's ax is party time for them?"

"It's iron. It renders them incapable of–" He jabbed a finger at the demon. "That."

Talk about stone-cold killer. Drio's ax now did nothing on the demon, who had, in his rage, seized Drio by the shoulder with his remaining pincer, grinding his long claws into Drio's flesh.

I flinched at the loud snap of Drio's shoulder breaking.

The blood drained from his face and he grit his teeth so hard that the tendons in his neck stood out in sharp relief. His agony must have been incredible but the freak didn't cry out. Using his good hand, Drio awkwardly attempted to jam the axe blade between his skin and the demon's pincer. Like a lever, using it to try and pry the pincers open.

The remaining sakacha converged on them but Rohan jumped into their midst, a human Ginsu knife of slicing and dicing.

Right, his blades were iron.

Three of the demons skittered back out of reach, but one suicidal fucker charged Rohan, the full force of his bulk nailing the Rasha in the small of his back. The jolt should have sent Rohan stumbling forward but the demon caught him by the scruff of his neck with a pincer.

A sly, satisfied smirk spread over the sakacha's face.

I wanted to help but I was scared I'd make things worse. How could I free Rohan if I couldn't use my power?

Didn't matter. Rohan freed himself by jerking away so hard that a chunk of flesh remained in the demon's grasp. Blood streamed down his back. My stomach heaved at the strong coppery stench filling the room.

Drio had yet to unseat his sakacha. One arm hung uselessly at the Rasha's side while the other couldn't get a proper angle to loosen the pincer from his broken shoulder. The demon wormed his claw into Drio's shoulder with an expression of sadistic glee.

A sheen of sweat dotted Drio's face and given his wavery movements, he hovered on the edge of consciousness. Of all the people on Team Rasha, you'd think I'd be most okay with losing him, but I didn't want him to die because I'd messed up.

Thankfully, at that moment, Baruch charged through the door and ripped the entire pincer arm off of the demon torturing Drio. The pincer itself went slack and fell off. Drio's arm hung at a nauseating angle from his broken shoulder, blood flowing from the gauges that the pincer had made. He ignored it to go help Rohan.

In the trauma of losing *his* arm, the sakacha reverted to his natural wood state. My firebomb had done enough damage that once the demon transformed back, he fell apart like cheap particle board.

Tree Trunk thrust his hand into the spongy mass, grabbed the knot–about the size and shape of a large lima bean–and crushed it under his foot.

All that remained of the demon was a pile of sawdust.

With Drio's help, Rohan was able to destroy the sakacha who'd injured him. Baruch seemed to be holding his own against the rest.

As I wasn't needed here, I raced deeper into the creepy building, past water-stained walls with their faint tang of mold, and under graffiti-tagged ceilings, on high alert for Ari.

Having imagined my twin beaten, bloody, and caged, I thought I'd prepared myself for the state in which I'd find him.

Imagining the scene was nothing like seeing it.

Ari was a pulpy mess, his flesh a rainbow of bruising. He sprawled on the filthy floor of a small room so obviously broken that the demons hadn't even bothered to chain him up.

Tears streamed from my eyes as I ran over to him and hooked my hands under his armpits to help him to his feet. "I've got you." My voice cracked.

My brother couldn't even support himself. I staggered under his weight until I managed to find my balance for the both of us. "I wondered when you'd get here." He stared at me blearily, his blinks too slow, his expression too dazed.

My heart stuttered. "Sorry to make you wait." Sorry about everything I ever did to hurt you, intentionally or not. There'd be plenty of time to apologize once we were away from here.

We shuffled to the doorway.

Ari cradled the arm not slung around my neck against his body, his wrist puffy. Blood-encrusted scars were gashed diagonally along his chest and he sported a hell of a black eye. Walking seemed to be a shambling challenge but he wasn't limping.

Shafts of weak moonlight lit our way along the quiet hallway. My scalp prickled. Where was everyone, Fallen Angels and demons both? Being allowed to wander around unchecked had to be part of a massive trap.

It took some time to backtrack but we made it to the large room where the sakacha battle had occurred. The floor was strewn with sawdust though the sakacha were all gone.

A horde of short, fuzzy, pink heart-shaped demons with enormous darkly lashed eyes and arms ending in fat white-gloved hands, things I swear I'd had in pillow form as a kid, greeted us. Sure they were cute, but I wasn't an idiot. They were still demons. If these were the dremla, they were soul leeches.

Careful not to jostle my brother who still clung to me for support, I fired up my left hand—the one farthest from him—with a nice, bright electrical ball.

The demons all burst out into short, nasty quills.

"I'm going to have to let you go now," I said in a low voice, my focus on the demons.

Ari's arm that was slung around my neck tightened to asphyxiating proportions. "I don't think so."

I feebly slapped at my brother with my right hand.

"Take whatever form you want, demon. I'll still kill you."

Huh? Was he talking to me? "Not funny," I managed to gasp.

Ari flipped his poison ring open and threw the contents at me.

I jerked sideways. My poor hair took the brunt of the maybe half teaspoon, but I still screamed, feeling like my scalp was on fire. A clump of charred hair fell to the ground, and my left ear lobe bubbled. My stomach heaved.

"I may not be Rasha," Ari hissed, "but I still trained as one. You hurt me, unholy spawn, I'll hurt you back."

"Unholy spawn" was not a nickname of mine. Ari didn't know who I was.

My blood ran cold.

"Ari," I said in a steady voice, "I'm your sister, Nava. Look at my ring. I'm Rasha."

He laughed mirthlessly. "Good try, but there's no such thing as a female Rasha. And I don't have a sister."

Asmodeus could make the rest of the world forget about me. But not Ari. The demon didn't get that win.

I dropped low, ducking under Ari's arm with a shocked yelp as he kicked me sideways, sending me partway across the room. I smacked the side of a pillar, all air knocked from my lungs. Of course, I had to make sure my darling twin didn't kill me first.

Ari crouched in fighter stance, fists up and a determined look in his eyes. "Make the dremla stand down or I swear I'll kill you. I know your weak spot."

Yeah, idiot. You.

The demons flanked me like an army. *My* army.

My eyes widened. "Oh no. Not mine." I fired at a couple of them.

"We are sorry to disappoint, my Queen," they said in musical voices. Faking, bunny-eyed spawn.

Before I could insist that I had no royalty status among the demonically-inclined, Ari rushed me. I was no match for my brother. The first few hits hurt but it was the punch to my eye that sent me over the top.

I slammed my hand into his chest, spreading my electricity in a fine web around his torso. Ari took deep gasping breaths, his entire body spasming. I kept the voltage low because I had no desire to heart attack him into me being an only child, but I had to make my point. "Who took the blame when you broke the dining room window with your homemade catapult, Ace?"

Still caught in my magic web, Ari raised a shaking hand and shot me the finger.

So much for using my words. I tugged at my non-poisoned earlobe once, in our "I've got your back," code.

His face creased in confusion. Then he tugged back, staring at his hand like he wasn't sure why he'd done that.

I stopped my magic, catching him as he sagged. "Let's get out of here."

Asmodeus stepped into the room, slow clapping, and totally healed from our fight the other night. There were no signs of any of the wounds that Rohan and I had inflicted on him. Not even the slash across his throat. "Good job, catching the prisoner for me, Nava."

Once again, only his ogre head spoke, though he refrained from getting all Lust Master on me.

"As if, you–"

I froze at the look of hatred on Ari's face. "Knew it," he whispered. With that he was ripped out of my arms by the demonic pillow horde and marched away, leaving a couple dremla behind to help Asmodeus.

I faced the demon, jaw tight. Killing his spawn was nothing compared to what I planned to do in retaliation for putting that look on Ari's face.

"So easily forgettable," Asmodeus said. He scratched at the fur on his bull's head, this encounter with me a minor irritant. Hot bovine stank wafted off him. "Your comrades, your own brother? None of them able to remember you."

"Drop their compelled memory loss and their love of me will rush right back in," I countered.

Asmodeus' thick ogre lips drew together in a distorted expression of pity. "Don't you realize how my compulsions function? I work with what people already want. I prefer to deal in lust, but I can affect any desire. I simply amp up that craving, maybe small, maybe buried deep down, but still burning hot and bright inside them. With the memory loss? All those people couldn't wait to forget you. Even you know you shouldn't be Rasha. That's why you wanted to forget the joke of you as a hunter. The joke of your entire existence."

His voice slithered through me, pulling down stone after stone in the wall of my self-confidence that I'd so carefully erected after my dreams went up with the snap of my Achilles. Exposing these bricks as hollow, plastic shells.

"No." I barely choked the word out through the thickness in my throat.

"The Rasha don't want you. Your brother doesn't either. It's your fault he didn't get to take his rightful place."

Shards of my heart cracked off. I clapped my hands over my ears, not wanting to hear the demon's insidious words. Not wanting him to see my hands shake. Not wanting to hear the truth my own experience borne out. The Rasha wanting to forget me I could live with. It sucked, especially from Rohan, but I got it.

Ari, though? Asmodeus killing me over and over again couldn't inflict as much hurt.

He laughed. The same laugh I'd heard in the supposedly empty hallway earlier when he'd also touched me. Creeped out, I skittered backwards.

"I was simply going to leave your brother's body for you to find. But erasing you as his sister altogether? Having him think you're one of us?" The demon hummed in glee. "You've been so entertaining in so many ways."

Head bowed, my hands slid down the side of my head, my palms skimming over my ear lobes. The ongoing searing on my left side was a distant second to my broken heart. I flashed on Ari giving me our secret "got your back" twin code. Asmodeus wanted me devastated. Wanted me to lay down and die. But he'd failed to realize one very important point: even if Ari did hate me right now, he needed me. I wouldn't stop having his back until I was dead.

I straightened up, beckoning the demon forward with my hand.

His three heads looked between each other in amusement. Bulls and rams should never look amused.

"My turn to be entertained. Gonna kill you now." Pushing past all my exhaustion and pain, I dug deep for my anger. Letting my hatred of Asmodeus not rule me, but absolutely fuel me. My magic coated me in a bright blue glow, lightning bolts slithering over my skin like animated tattoos.

"Cute," he said. "But you can't take me on your own and your friends are," he paused for effect, "busy."

I fired a lightning bolt into his side. He didn't get to walk away from doing this to my brother. To me. "Don't be such a coward, Asmodeus."

In the blink of an eye, he dropped what little civility he'd pretended to have. The monster that now faced me was primal, brutal, and very much a deadly prince of his realm. "As you wish." He leapt at me, kicking me in the head.

Light exploded in my brain. If I was going to see stars, it better damn well be from the other kind of hard pounding.

I staggered back only to be caught by the throat with one enormous hand.

The more he squeezed, the harder my power flared up. My vision flickered, white spots dancing before my eyes. Blood seeped from my temple, mingling with my sweat. My inner voltage fluctuated wildly and my heart pounded so hard, I was amazed I didn't crack my rib cage. I had to shut myself down, but since that would leave me powerless in a demon's grasp, I chose to let the needle on my inner meter break and allow my magic voltage to flood me.

Asmodeus roared as I flared bright, releasing me from his grip. Gulping air in heaving breaths, I fell on my butt, my hands sliding in a thick, viscous goop.

I scrambled to my feet, darting away and using every iota of mental strength I had to bring my power levels down. My magic didn't simply dissipate. The electricity bounced around my body before snaking out through the soles of my feet. It didn't hurt though, so that was a step up.

Asmodeus faced me, bits of his flesh blackened and smoking dropping to the ground with sickening thuds. A rat scurried out of the shadows, going to town on this all-it-could-eat demon buffet.

I dry-heaved.

Suddenly, the demon's side went limp.

"You might want to start wearing shoes," Rohan said to the demon. "Because those tendons of yours are baby-sensitive." He reached down and hauled me to my feet, raking an intrigued eye over me. "Magic ink. Nice."

Lightning bolts danced over my still-blue skin. "Took your time."

One of the dremla attached to Baruch like a barb, looking like it was trying to cuddle him to death. Baruch's skin rippled. His eyes rolled back, showing the whites, before he let out a war cry, grabbed the demon by its arms, and ripped it in two.

I expected to be showered in fluff but instead this maggot-like creature fell wriggling to the floor, so I stomped it to gory smithereens. The remaining dremla fled.

Asmodeus regrouped, lashing out.

Baruch tossed me a pair of red ear plugs.

I popped them in and the world fell silent. Which was weird since I should have heard the sounds of the brutal and bloody fight we were engaged in—or Asmodeus using his voice compulsion on us.

His ogre face grew redder and redder as he tried, his features more and more twisted with fury. Drio grinned his unholy grin and mockingly tapped his ears.

The fight raged on. Magic continued to pour out of me with no problem, though my poor meatsack stayed upright through sheer will alone.

Earlier, Baruch had assigned us each a battle zone. A part of Asmodeus' body to focus our attack on. Best case scenario, we'd notice him trying to protect the sweet spot. At the very least, we'd be weakening his body with strikes.

I'd been assigned the demon's back. I wounded him. I even bloodied him but not enough to do real damage. I was tiring far faster than Asmodeus was. True for all of us. With his broken shoulder, Drio looked about ten seconds away from passing out.

Asmodeus had gotten in enough licks that our blood splattered the floor like a Jackson Pollock painting.

Then Rohan managed to slice off one of the hardened scales on the demon's chest. Asmodeus flinched. The tiniest movement but compared to his lack of reaction with the rest of our hits, fairly telling. As if we were Borg, connected by a hive mind, Baruch, Drio, Rohan, and I refocused all our magic on his chest. Drio and Rohan used their ax and blades respectively, Baruch weaved in to rip off scale edges in order to expose more vulnerable flesh, while I blasted any bit of skin uncovered.

That's when Kane, sporting a nasty cut across his temple, hobbled in with Ari. He gave me a sheepish grin, resting Ari carefully against a pillar. *Told you my brother wasn't dead.* Why wasn't Kane jumping into the fight? I did a full-body scan to check if his injuries were more extensive than I could see, but that wasn't it at all. He waited until we'd torn a wide strip of scales off Asmodeus' torso. Kane swaggered up behind him and then, his skin iridescent purple with poison, he hugged the demon.

Asmodeus convulsed.

Kane said something to me but when I shook my head at him, unable to hear, motioned for me to pull out the ear plugs. I did.

He bowed low, with a flourishing arm. "I left you the good part. Care to do the honors?"

Chest heaving, I caught my breath enough to answer. "Hell, yeah. Hey, Asmodeus."

The demon zeroed in on me, the poison rippling through his shriveling frame and tight pain etched across his three faces. His ram's head gave a wounded bleat as he unsuccessfully attempted to protect his right pec. The sweet spot.

I shot him the finger, a perfect forked bolt shooting off that digit to bullseye him. "See who's forgotten now, bitch," I crowed.

Asmodeus fell apart into puzzle pieces, all of him winking out of oblivion with a sucking noise.

It was over.

The lightning bolts disappeared from my skin as I powered down from blue to my usual Snow White pale, though I still reeked of electricity. Despite my bleeding, my bruising, my burned ear, and my bone-deep exhaustion, the knot in my stomach overrode everything else. "Tell me you remember me."

Drio eyed me with distaste. "Sì. I like you even less now." Keeping his shoulder more or less in place with his other hand, he strode out.

"One thing going right in my day," I called out after him.

Still all poisonous, Kane blew me a huge kiss with a "Hola, babyslay." He toed at the floor. "I'll get the sodium peroxide mix to scour off our blood. Don't want demons getting hold of it." Especially not if they used it to take down our wards.

Baruch gave me a proud eye blink.

"Awfully sweet of you, Tree Trunk," I said as they hurried off.

Rohan didn't say much one way or the other. He shot me an inscrutable look and left.

Then there were two.

"Hey, Ace." I slung my arm over his shoulder. Please let Ari remember he comes as a matched set.

"Hey, Nee." Yay! "Sorry for the whole trying to kill you thing."

"No problem." My grip on him tightened. "But do it again and I'll stab you in the tits."

He mussed my hair with more noogie than fondness. "Like you could."

"I so could."

Ari laughed then pressed his hand to his side. He looked like a human punching bag and needed to rest, as did I.

I grabbed him in a hug, practically squeezing the life out of him with my tears falling against his neck. He returned it, just as fiercely.

Just as choked up. I wanted to ask if this meant we were okay or... not. But I wasn't that brave. I'd do it after I got his initiate status confirmed.

I disengaged with a sniff. "Come on," I said and my brother and I trekked out of the darkness and back into the moonlight.

Together.

22

By Sunday, we'd been moved to a new chapter house already fully operational. We could have re-warded the old place but once a ward had been taken down, subsequent wardings were never as strong as the original. Rather than risk vulnerability, the Brotherhood had opted to move us.

The new Demon Club was identical to our previous one, aside from being situated on more land. When I commented on the fact that the Brotherhood could have gone for something different, say a twenty-first century design, Rabbi Abrams answered, "Change is not always a good thing." With a pointed look at me.

Message received, Rabbi.

It was a week since I'd become Rasha, and while my life was totally different, it was also infuriatingly the same. Asmodeus going after Ari wasn't enough to shift the Brotherhood's position, nor was me helping take the demon down. When I'd broached the subject yet again with Rabbi Abrams, he'd simply informed me that killing demons was my job and that the Brotherhood wouldn't look kindly upon me using it as some sort of bargaining chip.

Rohan and Drio were equally frustrated, since even with Drio torturing Evelyn to the best of his ability, she hadn't cracked. Now she was dead and they were no closer to getting into Samson's inner circle. From the snatches I heard around Demon Club, the Executive was not happy.

Meantime, Ari had been sent with us to keep an eye on his recovery in the first crucial forty-eight hour period. Over the next few days, I spent most of my time draped in a chair beside his bed, watching him sleep. Well, watching him thrash under the covers.

While he healed, I did too. Not my physical self: that happened pretty quickly. No, I needed time to get over my hurt and anger that Ari had wanted to forget me. I wasn't a saint. I nursed my grudge and then I got over it.

It wasn't until the following Wednesday that Ari sat up, bitching that he wanted proper food not broth, and looking, on the outside at least, somewhat healed. I brought him chicken noodle soup, filled with chunky pieces of meat.

Ari sat up and took the bowl, eyeing me warily. "Are you going to mother me?"

I shook my head. "After everything that happened, do you still want to be Rasha?"

Ari swallowed a spoonful. "It's not possible. The ceremony didn't work. That means that they were wrong about me from the get-go. You were always the initiate, not me."

The inconsistency made no sense. Besides, he was a natural at this. All these years, he'd carried the quiet confidence of becoming Rasha in his bones. No mistake.

"Not my question."

Ari's shoulders set in a tense line as he answered. "Yes." His eyes glittered dangerously, a contrast to the purple bruising on his face.

"For revenge?"

"Does it matter?"

Absolutely, because that attitude would get him killed faster than any stupid hero impulse. I blinked away the tears threatening to pool in my eyes. "I just want you to be happy."

He relaxed against the headboard. "You can't orchestrate that for me. All you can do is be there."

Yeah, but he needed to be alive for me to be there for him. "Always."

After another couple of spoonfuls, he handed me back the bowl. "I'm going to crash again."

I headed downstairs into the kitchen where I found Rabbi Abrams taking a box of tea from the cupboard. I washed and dried the bowl, then wandered over to the large island in the middle of the room. Opening the box, I sniffed the loose black Darjeeling.

"How can I help you?" Rabbi Abrams leaned against the counter, a green ceramic mug in hand. His black suit smelled of lavender which was an improvement from moth balls.

I eased onto a high bar stool. "Explain something, Rabbi. Why did David call us Rasha? We're not wicked. We fight the wicked."

Rabbi Abrams put the mug down. "Rasha does mean wicked or guilty as sin. But its more literal meaning is one who departs from the path and is lost. This was David's reminder to his hunters how close they are to darkness. How easy it would become for them to truly be Rasha in every way."

I'd had no idea.

All of my fellow Fallen Angels, at least the ones that I'd met, were battling their own demons. Even Ari. "Begs the question if maybe out of all the descendants of the original group of Rasha, those of us who actually become hunters happen to be that much closer to the darkness to begin with."

The rabbi regarded me shrewdly. "Could be, Navela. Could be."

"About Ari?"

He sighed. "I performed the rites. He is not Rasha. We were wrong about him." To be fair, he sounded pained saying it.

I slumped in defeat. "He's going to hunt demons, magic power or not. And we both know how that ends." I grasped the rabbi's hands in mine. "Please."

The kettle let out a shrill whistle. Waves of impatience rolled off me as he poured the steaming water into his mug and filled a tea ball, dropping it in the boiling liquid to steep. "There may be another way to check," he admitted.

"Then–"

He held up a hand. "It is not usually sanctioned by the Brotherhood. In fact, in our entire history, I've only heard of it being allowed once."

"Help me. I'll do anything. Fight more actively or not at all. Whatever they want. Whatever it takes."

Rabbi Abrams got out the honey and a spoon. "Drio learned nothing from Evelyn and everything else we've tried to determine if Samson is a demon has been a dead end. We have one avenue left open to us. Get Rohan to do the theme song and I'll confirm Ari's status."

"Rohan doesn't want to do this."

"He's all we have. Do it and I give you my word." He lay the tea ball on a small saucer, spooning honey into his mug. "I too very much want Ari to be Rasha."

My stomach twisted, but it seemed I had no other choice. "Done."

Ari found me a few hours later, sitting motionless on the edge of my bed, an unfolded pile of laundry next to me. "You okay?" he asked.

I forced a wan smile. "Yeah. What's up?"

"Drive me home? Kane does any more disinterested hovering and I'll kill him."

"Hovering, huh?"

"I'm not up to his game-playing." Ari was disinclined to say any more. He looked around my room, wistfully. "I think it's time for me to go."

Much as I wanted to force him to stay here until he was completely healed, I understood. And honestly, I was glad of the excuse to get away. He came with me downstairs to tell Ms. Clara we were leaving.

She greeted us with a smile. "Feeling better?" She tapped her head.

"Depends," my brother replied. "Unfortunately, I now remember I have a sister."

I licked my finger and stuffed it in his ear. He shoved me away.

"Before you leave," she pulled a new phone out of her desk and tossed it over to me. "I'll have your new laptop put back in your room. Remember, this goes with you everywhere."

I gotta admit, I had a pang or two as I picked up the sleek techno-wonder. "You're not going to be able to find my iPhone anymore," I said to Ari, with a mournful shake of my head.

He smiled. "You forbade me."

"Like you believed me."

Ari took the phone away and smashed it against the desk.

I clutched at his arm. Ms. Clara was going to murder him. "He didn't mean it," I yelped, blocking him from bodily harm.

Ms. Clara laughed.

Ari waved the phone at me, intact and not even dented. "Indestructible. You'll save a bundle on replacements." He dropped the phone in my hand.

I ran a finger over the spot on her desk that he'd whacked to make sure it wasn't dented either, because no way did I want Ms. Clara angry. But, like the rest of her office, it was in perfect, orderly condition.

We said goodbye, then headed out to Dad's Prius, sitting gleaming in the sunlight, scratch-free. Demon Club had restored it to showroom pristine condition.

"Dad's totally gonna know," I said. Ari and I had been driving the car for a couple of years. Pristine had been blown off its list of adjectives in the first two weeks.

We exchanged mischievous grins. He picked up a rock and I got out my key and we proceeded to nick and scratch the thing back to its former state. Five minutes later, we surveyed our handiwork with pride. Much better.

The house was empty when we pulled up, since Mom and Dad weren't due back from their cruise for more than a week. Party animals that we were, Ari went straight to bed and after triple checking that he didn't need anything, I went into my room. Funny how small it seemed. I trailed a finger over my stuff, restless, bored, but not wanting to leave Ari alone until he woke up. I could have watched TV, but daytime programming blew at the best of times. Besides, I was too distracted.

How was I going to convince Rohan to step back into the spotlight and do the theme song? It wasn't my place to force him back into something that had deeply scarred him. He might have stopped singing because he no longer enjoyed it. I'd never gotten an answer out of him one way or the other. On the other hand, if I didn't convince him? Then Ari's chances of becoming Rasha were well and truly dead. As dead as *he* might be if he started hunting.

Absently, I stopped in front of my tap shoes, picking them up to wipe the dust off with my sleeve. Once they were in my hands though? I itched to put them on, something I hadn't done in over two years.

There'd been no dancing in moderation since my dream had come crashing down. My heart couldn't take it. The only way for me to cope had been to go cold turkey. Slam that door forever and padlock it tight. I couldn't handle having something that had been my entire life be relegated to a hobby.

The taste of copper brought me to my senses and I released my poor bottom lip from my teeth, shocked at how strong my urge to slip the shoes on was. Maybe I'd grieved enough. Still, I hesitated, running a hand over my calf. Did my Rasha healing mean I wouldn't relapse into the pain of my dance injury?

I'd do anything to be able to dance on a regular basis again but, for many reasons including my newfound destiny, the ship had sailed on my dreams of dancing professionally. I'd resigned myself to it, believing I couldn't dance anymore. But now?

I wasn't ready to think about the long-term ramifications–or lack thereof.

The ringing metal as I clacked the taps together decided it. Dancing had always helped clear my mind, focus me. Hopefully, it'd provide much needed answers now.

I slipped downstairs, shoes in hand. Flipping on the light in the basement, I felt a nostalgic pang seeing the special wooden tap floor that had been installed in the corner of our rec room so that I could practice. While the floor was worn with black scuff marks from my metal taps, it was clean and polished. Mom may not have been a fan but she wasn't going to let anything get dirty on her watch.

After checking the soles for loose screws and finding the taps tight, I put my shoes on. My feet instantly molded to the worn contouring. I let out a sigh I didn't know had so badly needed to be exhaled.

I grabbed a homemade CD from the tower that had been relegated to the basement about five years ago, starting with a slow swing version of "Caravan" to warm up. Flaps, shuffles, paddle rolls–nothing fancy. I let my body fall into the muscle memory of balance and movement. A small smile crept across my face hearing how clean my moves still sounded.

Next up was the Verve remix of "Sing Sing Sing." I threw myself into it, choosing to improvise to the melody line, playing my own variation of the tune through my feet. A twinge in my left Achilles tendon–literally my own Achilles heel where my dance career had been concerned–had me slow down, testing my foot for further signs of pain.

Tap involved most of my weight being on my toes, with heel stomps aggravating my tendency to swollen tendons. But the pain really was just a twinge. I was good to keep dancing.

It was as if a dam inside me broke. I needed to go hard. To pound the rhythm. Pound out my roller coaster of emotions and stress. I threw on "How You Like Me Now" by The Heavy, craving that driving beat to quell the edge inside me. One-footed wings, syncopated pullbacks, over-the-tops–I pulled out all my moves in addition to the flurry of basic steps rendered at breakneck speed.

Fuck, how I'd missed this.

Barely winded, soaring on adrenaline and happiness, I thumbed through the other CDs in search of what to play next, my hand stilling over the copy of Fugue State Five's first album that Leo had forced on me all those years ago. I smiled when I saw her "Listen to it or I'll kill you, dummy!!!!" written in gold marker on the CD.

Pressing play, I counted down the end of the eight-beat opening of "Toccata and Fugue." In contrast to the raspy growl of Rohan's voice, my steps were lightness themselves. The floatiest soft shoe to counterpoint all the emo feels pouring out of the song.

I'd never danced to this before, but it was the perfect fit. I lost myself in the joy of taking this beautiful piece of music and putting my own stamp on it. While Rohan singing to me in the park had freaked me out, now the song soothed me. My feet twined with his voice to create something altogether new.

I matched the crescendoed ending of the song with a series of turns that propelled me across the floor, my hip bumping into the wall because I ran out of room. I laughed at my spatial miscalculation, the sound ringing clear in the silence.

Then I saw Rohan's face. He stood stock still in the doorway, staring at me like I was an alien. I wrapped my arms around my chest, my gaze sliding away from his. People could be extremely judgmental about tap's place in the dance pantheon. Weirdo might have been offended by my dancing to his song.

"I always thought tap dance was like–"

"Shirley Temple," I interjected dryly. "So, you've said." I crossed the room, cutting off his next song with a push of the button. "What are you doing here?"

I bent over to untie my shoe but he stopped me, stepping forward with one hand up.

"Don't. I mean, don't let me interrupt. I just wanted to tell you I'm leaving. I have to go back to L.A."

A rush of panicky adrenaline speared through me. I clacked over to him, my shoelace trailing on the floor. "You can't go."

"Why not? I haven't been back to my apartment in weeks and Mom wants to take me for pizza at Highland Park Bowl." Rohan pushed me back a couple of steps. "You're all pale. What, don't want to be without your main babysitter?"

Apparently his memory return had come with the return of his anger over our hook-up.

Discussing the theme song right now would only add fuel to that particular fire. I knelt down to take off my shoe. "Have a good trip."

He didn't say good-bye.

I leaned on Leo's buzzer, muttering a steady stream of curses.

She let me in, waiting bleary-eyed in her doorway. My friend appeared crazed: no jewelry, greasy snarled hair, a coffee stain on her denim miniskirt.

"What happened to you?" I asked.

"Huge exam."

"You want me to leave?"

She grabbed my arm, pulling me inside. "No! It's my Ethics course and–"

"Having none, it pains you to understand the concept?" I tossed my bag on her couch, flopping down on the lumpy cushions.

"Something like that." She padded into her kitchen in heavy wool socks with enormous holes in the toes and heels. "Coffee?" She sniffed the pot and recoiled. "Diet coke?"

"Sure, if you have rum. Hold the coke."

Leo took two mismatched mugs out of her cupboard and reaching up on tiptoe, grabbed the bottle of booze sitting on top of her fridge. A generous sloshing of rum into each one and she joined me on the couch. "Ari is doing okay?" she asked. I'd called her once he'd been rescued.

I nodded.

"You're persona grata now?"

Again, a nod. I took a very large slug of rum.

She pursed her lips. "That leaves a guy. Ooh, don't want to let your precious Fallen Angels know you were slutting around?"

I couldn't help myself. I smiled.

Her mouth fell open. "Which one?"

I smiled wider.

Leo launched herself at me, smacking my chest. "Liar!" she howled, her disbelief clear. "Where?"

I held my cup up, out of splash danger. "You know the park by the theater on Seymour?"

"Yeah."

I waggled my eyebrows at her.

Her mouth fell open. "You strumpet."

"Jealous?" I smirked between sips.

"D'uh." She leaned in, a manic gleam in her eyes. "Give me details."

Bless Leo's heart, she embraced her best friend role, listening to me dish and not complaining when I couldn't decide whether I wanted to rant about Rohan or rave about how good he was.

"Yup, better than ever before. I heard you the first four times," she said.

I'd been talking a while, mostly ranting at this point, and Leo had gone back to her homework. She sat at her kitchen table, books spread around her, while I munched salt and vinegar chips on the couch I'd commandeered.

Leo's purple diary lay beside me, a little beat up but still astoundingly glittery. She'd gone to her mom's and dug it out of storage. I'd read a few of the initial goopy entries which had been enough to make me believe her about being in love with Ari. That and all the hearts with their initials doodled over the pages.

"What's the big deal about kissing anyway?" I asked.

She raised an eyebrow at me.

I pointed a chip at her. "It's not the same for guys. It certainly shouldn't matter to Rohan. You know how many girls he must have slept with?" I bit savagely into it.

"You think he's slept with any guys?" she asked.

We both got lost in that image for a moment.

I shook my head. "Don't distract me. I'm ranting about sexual inequality and power dynamics here. The issue is not that he couldn't kiss me. It's about control."

"Boys like him do enjoy control," she said, pencil in her teeth as she marked up her book with a yellow highlighter. "This should not be a surprise."

"Great." I tipped the bag into my mouth, determined to get every last drop of salt and fat. "He's all pissy because I was the one calling the shots." I got lost in the memory of ordering him to go harder, and shivered.

Leo spat out the pencil. "Come on my couch and you're buying me a new one. Scotchgard does not protect against psychological staining."

"Maybe I should have asked him for permission. Guys like that." I pitched my voice an octave higher. "Ooh, Daddy, please may I?"

"That etiquette is especially appreciated when a man thrusts his dick in your face," Leo agreed.

I buried my face in my hands. "I loathe him. But he was so good. I want seconds. Thirds. Thirtieths."

"Sixty-ninths," Leo quipped.

I looked up. "Oh yes. Most definitely sixty-ninths." I sighed. "This is bad. I think I might be addicted to him."

"Eh," she shrugged. "Breathing is an addiction. But once you've stopped for an hour, it's reasonably easy to quit forever. So how hard could this be to kick?"

"And to think I never figured out you were a demon before." I licked my fingers clean.

"It's because you're so self-obsessed."

"Probably." I checked the clock. Time to head back. "'K, babe," I walked over to where she hunched at the table studying, intending to hug her, then decided I didn't want to touch her until she'd showered. "Schmugs."

Leo shook her head at me. I hadn't used our special shortened goodbye of "hugs, schmugs" since we became friends again. "Last time you schumgged me," she said, "I didn't hear from you for over a year. You suck. I have no idea why I accepted you back into my inner circle."

"Because I am your inner circle. Besides, who else is going to get you up close and personal to your teenage masturbatory fantasy?"

Leo blushed.

"Eww. Rubbing one out to thoughts of Rohan Mitra is strictly verboten from this point forward. Besides, don't you have that Madison chick on speed dial?"

Leo gave a dreamy smile. "Ooh, yeah. She does know how to work her tongue. But that doesn't preclude my fondness for boy parts. Hook me up with his friends."

"Schmug me and I'll consider it."

I spent the rest of the week so bored out of my mind that I even adhered to Rohan's stupid schedule. At least it passed the time, since there was nothing else to do right now other than train and study.

Rohan was still in L.A. and even if I figured out the best way to approach him, I wasn't doing it over the phone. Drio wouldn't let me help with investigating Samson. Kane was working a security contract—turns out he was a coder who did a lot of surveillance software development for both the Brotherhood in-house and David Security clients, and Baruch was using the time not spent with me to inventory our equipment and weapons. My brother had decided to go back to class and told me to quit calling and checking up on him.

I'd tried hanging out with Ms. Clara but ten minutes in her office poking at her stuff and she'd threatened to break out the whip. So I was actually excited the following Tuesday when Baruch got me for a conference call with some Executive Rabbis at HQ in Jerusalem wanting a debrief on Asmodeus. Might as well suss out the Powers That Be on their feelings for me.

Of the three men on the other end, Rabbi Simon had been grudgingly complimentary on my performance, Rabbi Ben Moses hadn't said much at all, and the head of the Executive, Rabbi Mandelbaum, a sneering chauvinist who sounded surprisingly young, was clearly never going to be Team Nava, even if I killed every demon in existence single-handedly.

I'd bet money that he was one of the Jewish men who said his morning prayer thanking God for not making him a woman with great sincerity and mean-spirited glee.

It was a no brainer, then when asked if I had any questions for them, to pipe up, "How come you don't bring some female rabbis into the fold?"

Baruch shook his head at me, though his eyes danced in amusement.

Rabbi Mandelbaum, showing great restraint by not declaring outright that that would happen over his dead body, explained that female rabbis weren't really rabbis.

"Pretty sure they are," I said. "You know, on account of having the rabbinical title. It's not something you can send away for on a matchbook. Or wait, can you, Rabbi Mandelbaum?" I asked in breathy sweetness.

Baruch kicked my leg.

The sexist jerk on the other end of the conference call then switched tactics, saying that the few rabbis that worked for the Brotherhood were all descendants of previous rabbis who'd been part of the organization.

"Exactly." I wanted to reach through the phone and throttle him. "You missed me as a potential Rasha. How many other women, rabbis and potentials both, have the Brotherhood missed? All those traditions weren't rules. They were assumptions. Wrong assumptions. Plus, the name needs to go. Brotherhood is no longer applicable. I'm thinking–"

Baruch leaned across the table to cut off my access to the speakerphone, wrapping up the conversation–in Hebrew. Once disconnected, he steepled his fingers together. "Tell me, are you trying to get on their bad side?"

"Nope. It comes naturally."

"Nava." His tone was pure warning.

"Lady Shock and Awe, Tree Trunk," I said brightly. "It's the only way I know how to live." Damn it! Ari had been right.

23

I gave up on the urban fantasy novel that had seemed so engaging a couple weeks ago, tossing my phone on the bed. Fictional supernatural beings failed to hold the same allure given my new career. Chances are Drio and Baruch would go home soon, leaving me with Kane, who was great. But how weird was it going to be living here with just the two of us? What if he was reassigned? How small was my world going to become? Who would train me? Sure, Rabbi Abrams would arrange for someone but I was attached to my Tree Trunk.

This mattress was too hot. I kicked off my covers. Giving in to my loneliness-induced insomnia, I got up to get some water. Everyone was asleep, but I tiptoed down the stairs anyway wearing my black sleeveless nightgown that hit mid-thigh.

An ajar door threw a slash of light into the hallway on the main floor. I veered away from my original destination of the kitchen and toward the door, because it was Rohan's bedroom and I was curious.

I knocked.

"Yeah?" Rohan pulled his sweater up over his head, leaving him in a black button up shirt whose fit left very little to the imagination.

I had a very active imagination.

"You're back." I tore my eyes away from him to take in the space.

The rest of us had rooms together upstairs, all in varying shades of beige, which I planned to paint soon. His room, however, already featured dark green walls with gorgeous black and white framed photography and warm wood furniture all bathed in the soft light of his bedside lamp.

"What's the deal?" I asked. "Me, the local, is in the institution special and you, the transient, gets VIP treatment? What'd you bribe Ms. Clara with?"

One corner of his mouth quirked up. "We have an arrangement." He lifted a small roller board suitcase off the bed, stashing it in his closet, allowing me a glimpse of his clothing arranged just shy of color-coded.

"What kind of arrangement?" Okay, that came out sulkier than I'd intended but gawd, they'd be pretty if they hooked-up.

He threw me a look that was far too shrewd.

Seconds and now, please. I stepped into his room, shutting the door behind me. Then in a move I hoped looked sexy, pulled my nightgown over my head, pitching it to the floor.

Silence, though Rohan did rake a very slow gaze over me.

I leaned back against the door, my palms flat, pushing my rush of nerves into the cool wood and calculating how fast I could grab my nightgown in case I'd made a horrible mistake. "Tell me if I'm being presumptuous."

"About me wanting to fuck you?" He closed his eyes briefly, his "yeah, right" coming out on a rush of pent-up breath.

Cuntessa woke up with a vengeance.

Pushing Rohan onto the bed, I straddled him, rubbing over his very hard cock straining against his pants.

Rohan gripped my hip, gently moving me off of him.

Here it came. His reasons why this was a bad idea and not going to happen. Instead, he leaned over to snap off the light. Moonlight streamed in through his blinds.

Mental fist pump!

"This time, we do this my way." Rohan kneeled at my feet.

"Works for me." I spread my legs but he ignored my invitation to get in and get going.

Cuntessa was not his destination. He took my arm, placing a kiss to the inside of my wrist, massaging his way up the skin with a combination of kisses and his fingertips.

I watched him, a frown puckering my brow. No one had ever paid attention to my arms before. Guys tended to dive in to the sexytime body parts of tits and pussy. Not that that was necessarily successful but if I couldn't will myself into a happy ending with those, what was the point of spending time on an arm?

Rohan acted like those parts didn't exist. He lay me back on his bed, sucking my big toe into his mouth.

I jerked off the bed.

"Should I stop?"

"No." I tried to explain my hesitation. "I'm not sure this is doing anything for me."

Rohan leaned in to lick my clit with a long, slow stroke. "Is this what you want?"

In response, I opened my legs wider, leaning back on my elbows.

He closed my legs. "Tough. Like I said. My way."

"Or not at all?"

Smirking, he squatted back on the balls of his feet.

Bah. I waved a hand at him. "Have at it." My tone made it clear that I didn't think he'd be all that successful doing this his way.

"Turn off your brain."

"What?"

He stared at me, impassively.

I crossed one leg over the other. "Women think about stuff to help them get off."

"Not with me."

Head tilted, I raised my right eyebrow. "Wanna bet?"

"You are not seriously going to fight me about getting you off so hard you can't see straight just to make a point, are you?"

I opened my mouth and then snapped it shut, because, yes, I had been about to do that.

Moron. Cuntessa despaired.

"Shut off everything except the sensation of being in my hands."

"What if your way isn't working for me?"

"I stop. Or," he brushed a hand along my hip, "I have rope." He waggled his eyebrows at me.

I burst out laughing. "Yeah, right, Mr. Grey."

He pretended to look affronted. "Are you mocking me?"

"Incessantly, though if you are a billionaire I'll temper my snark to the occasional gibe." I lay back against his mattress signaling my agreement to do this his way. But I was still tense, dreading orgasmic failure with Rohan. I bunched the pillowy softness of his blanket in my fists.

"I dunno, Nava." Rohan said, in a voice smooth as honey. "I think you're bent that way."

"Come at me with a rope, buster, and find out." Though the idea of tying him up held great appeal.

"Turn." He twirled a finger around and I flipped obediently onto my stomach, my left cheek pressed to his covers, figuring he was going to give me a massage to put me at ease.

Nope. He trailed his finger over my body. That's it. Again and again. He dipped into the hollow of my knee, gliding up along the inside of my thigh only to veer away toward my hip.

At first I found it ridiculous. But after a bit, his caress soothed me, my spine softening, my pliant self sinking deeper in the mattress. He lifted the hair off my back to expose my shoulder blades, writing my name on my back, my body shivering in delight and a small smile tugging my lips. A whisper of a caress, a leisurely stroke along my spine–I craved that single point of contact, his feather-light touch, never knowing where he'd abruptly leave off, only to commence stroking me somewhere else.

Relaxation thrummed into arousal. My skin pulsed a split second behind his touch, my entire body sparking in desire, igniting a long, smoldering burn.

"More," I breathed, wanting anything, even him kissing my arm again.

His hand stilled. "I told you," he said, in a maddeningly calm voice, "my way."

"I have to keep silent?"

He chuckled, the sound spiking my nipples into hard peaks. "You don't like something, you want me to stop? Speak up. You try to direct the action? Game over."

I growled, hating his bossiness, and myself for wanting this enough to put up with it. "This better be worth it, Snowflake."

He raked a nail up my spine.

No. Not a nail. A blade.

I moaned.

The tip of his blade ghosted in long, lazy circles over my body. "What do you feel?"

"It's like sensory phosphorescence trailing in the wake of your touch."

"Cool." He sounded like such an eager little kid that I had to smile.

Rohan rolled me over, continuing his slow exploration, tracing his blade reverently over my left breast, his breath blowing warm gusts over my flushed skin. The focus on his face was absolute. His eyes were molten pools lingering hungrily on my body.

Hypersensitive from his playing, I was wound tight, vibrating with a corked fizziness that was almost too much and not nearly enough. I clamped my mouth shut so I couldn't beg for more.

The feeling of him sucking my tit into his mouth was as intense and amazing as the best orgasm any other guy had ever given me. I clutched his hair, feeling his ragged breathing against my skin. The press of his shirt buttons into my breastbone as I arched against him caused a twinge that did nothing to distract from my pleasure but did remind me he had way too many clothes on. I fumbled at the buttons.

He helped me undress him, shrugging out of his shirt.

"Pants, please."

He lifted his head, his pupils dilated. "I'm busy."

"Multitask." I snapped my fingers at him, figuring that he was too into this to follow through on his "game over" threat at my command.

Rohan rolled his eyes but pretty much ripped his pants and boxers off in record time, leaving him naked and magnificent. "May I return to what I was doing?"

"You may."

He stretched out along side of me, his skin hot against mine.

The air was cool on my back and I wriggled against him, wanting more of his warmth. More of his everything.

He pressed his hand between my shoulder blades, keeping me close as he swirled his tongue along my nipple. My tits grew full and heavy. I placed his palm underneath one to fondle it.

Even during sex, Rohan possessed a graceful elegance, a precision. He veered between an economy of movement that was obscene in its effectiveness on me and a drawn-out languidness that left sensations sinking so deep inside that sparks literally shot off my skin.

One singed his eyebrow. Rohan jerked away.

I blushed beet red.

He gathered me in his arms, turning me to spoon me. "The dangers of lightning girls," he murmured.

How would I ever explain that to any other guy? Was I only going to be able to sleep with Rasha from now on?

Rohan sighed, nudging at my jiggling leg. "Quit thinking." He reached between my legs.

Cuntessa pulsed in a steady slow throb. His stroking was an exquisite torture.

"Fuck, you're wet," he said.

"That's on you."

"Yup," he said in a voice 150% smug.

Our bodies were curved tight around each other. His stubble rasped my skin as he sucked my shoulder. I reached back to stroke his cock, loving its hot, hard fullness. Giddy with anticipation of having him inside me.

Our hips rocked. Rohan hooked his leg over mine to open me wider, a second finger plunging inside me.

"I don't want to come without you inside me," I gasped.

"Tough. Because I need to taste you."

Hello, lucky sixty-nine.

He started with a slow tease of my clit, either forgetting or totally remembering that his dick now hovered over my mouth and two could play that game. I licked the head of his cock, tasting those first salty drops on my tongue. A pioneer in the land of Rohan, I surveyed the length and girth of him with my lips. Not yet taking him into my mouth, simply enjoying a leisurely exploration.

Rohan groaned. There was a squirt of lube and then his finger rimmed my ass.

"Wrong hole." I twisted, all squirmy.

"Or very right if you're up for it."

He pressed some spot at my opening and my stomach clenched in a delicious swoon. Oh. If I could get more of that feeling, I was open to reconsidering my "no buttholes here" stance. Plus, his dirty side was incredibly hot. What the hell. I pushed back against him in answer.

He inched his finger into me.

I gasped, my muscles clenching tight around him.

"Good?" he asked.

"Uh, I don't know?"

Rohan see-sawed his finger in and out.

I practically came right there. A wanton moan ripped from my throat.

He laughed. "You're *so* bent, Lolita."

I deep-throated the smirk out of his voice. Rohan's dick hardened further, jumping to a new level of swollen arousal.

Miracle of miracles, for once in my life my brain shut down. Got to hand it to the guy, it was more fun when I stopped thinking. I was lost in the increasing tempo of his tongue and fingers at play on me, and focused on returning that same level of pleasure to him.

I fumbled on the bed for the bottle of lube he'd tossed there, squirting some into my hand and getting my finger well-oiled up for some play of my own.

Rohan mumbled a whole bunch of words in a language I didn't understand when I slid *my* finger into his ass, but his hips pumped with more urgency so I kept going, almost as heated by my own actions as his.

Behind my eyelids, I saw white. My muscles tightened, my body flushing hotter and hotter. I rocked against his fingers in an ever-spiraling circle of wild abandon, until I shattered.

Every other orgasm prior to this was relegated to a boring black and white, but this was glorious Technicolor. 3D IMAX. And I came not once, but twice! The incredibility of achieving that Holy Grail made me forget everything else–like my name and his cock in my mouth.

Didn't matter though because the second I stopped orgasming, Rohan started, half-arched on the bed above me, biting my hip as he came. He fell back against the bed, his head by my thighs, turning to press a soft kiss against my flesh. "That was round one."

24

Round two? People had those outside of movies? Yowza.

I eyed my nightgown because round one's conclusion was when I should have been getting dressed, but it was way on the other side of the room, and Rohan was lazily stroking my arm, his eyes the color of melted honey, and really how much of a hardship could round two be?

I nestled into the mattress. Even Rohan needed some re-up time so I curled in close, being the one to do nothing more than run my hands over his body.

Gawd, what a beautiful body it was. As the interwebs had shown me–time and time again–plenty of guys were ripped and chiseled. That was their endgame. Rohan was a fighter. He was functionally fit, all sinewy grace. His body had a purpose and while it was obvious in the hard planes of muscle, his tapered torso, and long leanness that he took great care of it, he also displayed an ease and lack of ego in his own skin that I found refreshing.

He had nothing to prove.

Rohan's body wasn't a temple, it was a finely honed weapon. Though that didn't stop me from worshipping it now. I nudged him to turn over, noting the silver scar from his sakacha encounter at the base of his neck. A gorgeous black script was tattooed between his shoulder blades. "Hindi?" I guessed, tracing the letters.

"Yeah. It says 'Kshatriya.' It's the warrior caste."

"It's beautiful." I trailed my hands down his back, rubbing at a patch on the base of his spine that was a bit darker than the rest of his skin.

His gluts tensed. Ooh. Pretty.

I rubbed the spot again, then gave in to my urge and bit his ass cheek.

Rohan yelped, flipping himself flat on his back. "Teeth. Not a kink of mine."

I propped myself up on one elbow, batting my eyelashes at him. "I'm betting that's a very short list, Mr. Mitra."

He grabbed my hips, pulling me across him, while giving my ass a swat. I squealed in laughter which ended in a smothered yelp as his mouth got close to mine.

He froze. "Right," he muttered.

I bit my lip, then wriggled onto my side to face him, running my hands over his body in long strokes. "How was L.A.?" As a distraction technique, my question was only moderately successful. It didn't dissipate the tension that had come over Rohan at the kiss thing, but he did answer and let me keep touching him.

"Got to see my parents, so that was good." The affection in his voice triggered a stab of longing for something I'd never had. "As for the mission? Supposed to be a quick and easy kill. Instead?" He scratched his stubbled chin. "Too much mishegoss."

"You know Yiddish?" I couldn't believe he'd used the slang term for craziness.

"Just the good words. Jewish grandmother."

"Can you imagine if demons spoke Yiddish? Oblivion would be filled with the kvetching of the damned."

Rohan giggled.

I bopped the tip of his nose with my index finger. "Aww. Cute."

He scowled at me, more embarrassed than angry given the way he ducked his head. "I am a former rock god and current Rasha. Not cute."

"So cute." I twisted my body around, reversing my head and feet placement, happy to find him charged again.

Rohan switched on the bedside light, raising his head off the pillow to better take in the sight of his cock filling my mouth.

I raised my eyebrows at him, all the while sucking on the ridge of his penis.

He groaned but didn't stop watching. If anything, his gaze grew more intense.

"Dirty boy, wanting to watch," I said.

He threw his arm behind his head and threw me an unrepentant grin. "Dirty girl," he countered, "liking it."

I couldn't argue.

Rohan caught my leg up by his head, sliding his lips along my calf. "I want to play, too."

"Nope." I angled my body away from him. "I want you in me. Now." Getting onto my knees, I reached into his bedside table drawer and plucked out a condom. It could only mean one thing, since he wouldn't have brought other women to Demon Club. "Look who was hoping I'd stop by?"

"Don't be cocky." He parroted back my earlier words to him. "It's insufferable."

"But I pull it off so well." I tossed the package at him.

He tossed it back. "Put it on me." His command was issued in a husky rumble.

Blood rushed from my brain in a dizzying surge. I ripped the foil packet open with my teeth and rolled the condom over him, so frantic to ease the pressure inside me that I didn't do my usual tease. In fact, I screwed up the direction, cursing when I put the condom on back-ward, essentially short-sheeting his dick.

Rohan rectified the situation with ease. And great haste.

Knowing from previous encounters that this was another place where guys took the opportunity to kiss, I scooted to the edge of the bed still on my knees, my forehead bowed to the bed.

He didn't argue, coming to stand behind me. "Open your knees wider."

I complied and then, finally, he pushed achingly slowly inside me. My eyes rolled into the back of my head at the delicious prolonging. "That feels... yesssss."

Rohan pressed a kiss between my shoulder blades. He rocked back and forth for a second, his hands braced on my hips.

I pushed back against him and that was it. Any thoughts of taking it slow were out of the question. I luxuriated in the feel of him, pounding into me, hard and fast. The top blanket bunched under my calves, our movements making a jumbled mess out of his sheets, every thrust causing my sensitive nipples to brush against the bed. My eyes were wide, my mouth hung open slack, and my fists balled the blanket on either side of my head. Pleasure snaked through me.

I stroked Cuntessa, feeling another orgasm starting to build.

"Not yet," Rohan commanded. He pulled out of me and I whimpered. I'd have begged at this point for more. He rolled onto his back, setting me on top, cowgirl-style.

I groaned as every inch of him slid fully and completely inside me. "I'm at your mercy," I said in a thick voice.

My words kicked him into overdrive. He caressed my breasts, placing one hand on my hips to help bounce me up and down.

I fluttered a look at him from beneath my lashes.

He looked amused so I raised an eyebrow. "Shimmy and bounce," he said. "Very accomplished, Lolita."

"I am a woman of many talents," I replied, staring down at him through eyes half-lidded in lust. I ran my free hand over his heated skin, tightening my knees on either side of his legs, and rocking in tiny rhythmic motions.

"Wide-eyed, breathy, a little off-balance, the look works for you."

Using just enough force to blur the line between pleasure and pain, I raked my nails down his front, marveling at the fullness of him inside me. My lids fluttered closed, startling open again when he released my hand, placing it on my clit.

"I want to watch you," he said. The gravely timbre of it sent shivers of delight spearing through me.

I flushed. This was a whole other level of intimacy.

"Please." Sitting half-curled up, Rohan laced his fingers with mine, squeezing tight.

Who was I to refuse? Our gazes locked, I stroked myself as he continued his forceful thrusts, my other hand held fast in his. The familiar pressure grew and grew. Rohan's free hand moved to my breasts, fondling, kneading.

"You feel so good inside me," I said, the last word coming out as a groan.

I'd had good sex before, my disappointing experiences of the past few months notwithstanding. This was something else entirely. It was more than Rohan knowing what I wanted, or what I needed. He played my body like it was his favorite guitar. Each roll of the hips was a chord progression, every slide of his skin on mine a slow strum. He coaxed a song from my blood and spun lyrics with every fevered caress.

Rohan threw back his head as his orgasm ripped through him.

The vibrations inside me pushed me over the top. My screams were loud enough to wake the dead. Totally spent and deliciously satisfied, I fell across his body, our sweat causing me to slide a bit. We lay there panting a moment. I for one, was mind-whacked.

Rohan held up his hand for a high-five.

Laughing, I returned it.

The room stank of sex. Was he always this vigorous? I shut my thoughts down before I could get weird about the idea of Rohan and other girls. I had no claims on him.

I rolled onto my back, stretching like a cat to enjoy the delicious aftershocks rolling through my body. "Is there a round three?" I looked over at Rohan, his cheeks flushed and his hair sticking up in spiky bedhead and my heart did a little flip.

My throat tightened.

Rohan didn't notice. "You're trying to kill me."

I forced myself to relax. "Not before I get my fill of orgasms from you."

"Humans don't live that long, sweetheart."

I poked him in the side and he squirmed. "You're ticklish?!" I clapped my hands in glee.

He grabbed my wrists, pinning them above my head. "Don't even think it."

I smiled my best feline smile, very much liking our positioning.

"Definitely trying to kill me." He nudged his knee between my legs. "You're a good dancer."

That was the last thing I expected him to say. "I told you, a woman of many talents. You need to remember these things about me, Snowflake."

"And you glow," he said, one hand playing with my hair.

I glanced down at myself.

"Not the magic. When you dance. When I saw you that day?" His eyes went distant. "I remember that look from when I used to perform."

"You could have it again. Do the theme song."

He stiffened, his expression turning to ice. "Is that what this was about?"

"No!" I sounded horrified.

His expression softened. A little. "Then what?"

I screwed up my face. "Rabbi Abrams said if you agreed, he'd find a way to check if Ari is still an initiate."

Rohan laughed bitterly. "Right."

"Wrong." I pushed him down against the mattress, leaning in. "You want to know why I don't tap anymore?"

He frowned at my abrupt topic change. "Why?"

"Remember, I told you about playing Lincoln Center?" Off his nod, I continued, "Out of that, during my junior year, I was invited to audition for a professional tap troupe." I adopted a snooty tone. "New York City, don't you know." I flipped onto my back, staring at the ceiling. "But I got dumb. I pushed myself too hard, got a snapped Achilles, surgery, and physio instead of the bright lights of Broadway."

I ran a hand up my left calf, phantom pain ghosting under my fingers.

"So you missed the audition."

"No. I did all my physical therapy in time to get cleared a week before. I nailed the audition, and I was all set to go."

He propped himself up on his elbow. "Then why didn't you?"

"Because I ruptured it again during spring competitions. There was no way I could join the troupe after grad–I'd just be in and out of hospitals, tearing myself apart."

"I'm sorry."

I shrugged. "They said I could defer until I'd completed rehab, but by that time, my university acceptance letters came in." I wrinkled my nose trying to keep the wetness in my eyes from turning into actual tears. "Let's just say, healing took longer than anticipated. I think my parents were happy for the excuse to steer me back into their comfort zone of academia. Having a tapper for a kid doesn't buy much cred at faculty parties."

"That sucks." His arms came around me. He had very sexy arms.

"Not dancing was like cutting out a piece of my heart." I met his eyes. "I know you feel the same way about singing."

Resounding silence.

"You wanted to know about my heart tattoo?" He lifted his arm up to look at it.

Now it was my turn to adjust to the topic switch. "Who was she?"

He didn't answer so I ran my heel up his leg.

Rohan flinched at the roughness of my heel. "What are you, part dragon?"

"Answer."

"Contrary to your belief that I'm both the world's biggest horn dog and a hopeless romantic whose heart was shattered, this?" He tapped the tattoo. "Has nothing to do with some girl I was in love with."

No? Excellent. Wait, I didn't actually care. "A guy?"

He shot me a wry look. "Not that either." He lay his arm across me, studying the tattoo. "It's a reminder. For my weaker moments when I crave the spotlight again."

"Nothing wrong with the spotlight." I placed his hand on my hair to play with it. His fingers toyed with my strands, massaging tiny circles against my scalp. The effect was almost hypnotic.

"I was young and stupid," he said. "I thought I could put my soul out there with my lyrics and be loved. Turns out people are cruel. The more famous you are, the more the knives come out. Conversely, the more your sense of self gets inflated and you get cruel. *I* got cruel." Rohan gave me a self-deprecating grin. "Imagine that."

That explained his magic turning him into a giant human blade, a reminder to guard his emotional well-being and his lingering regret over the person he became once famous. It made me and my electric powers look positively cuddly.

"That's not the full story though, is it?"

He cleared his throat. "I mentioned in the park that I'd fucked up?" His expression grew tight, but at my nod, he continued. "I had a cousin, Asha."

My stomach twisted at his use of the past tense.

"A year older than me," he said. "Asha was like my sister." His face lit up at the memory of her. "Amazing, hilarious. She was worth a billion of me. And when she needed me most?" He practically spat the next words. "When I could have helped her the most as Rasha? My head was so up my own ass from my rock star trip that I was convinced I knew best. Fuck everyone who didn't agree with me. I let her down."

His silence after that statement was loaded.

"She died?"

Rohan laughed bitterly. "That's the kind way of putting it. There wasn't enough left of her to bury." He echoed the words Kane had mistakenly said earlier to me about Ari. If Rohan had loved his cousin half as much as I loved my brother, his grief and guilt must have been immeasurable.

I eyed the heart tattoo. Still was. "That's why you stopped singing, wasn't it? As a punishment."

"Criticism? From you?" He tensed.

"Hardly," I said.

He relaxed a fraction, but I remained pensive. Bad enough that he'd tattooed this heart on his arm to be slashed–symbolically broken–time and time again, in penance. Destroying his dream on top of that was truly heartbreaking.

More than his agreement to the song, I wanted him to understand.

"My entire life, Ari was the bright shiny twin with a future and a destiny and I wasn't. I had a dream, but it never qualified me for bright shiny status. Except then *I* was Rasha and he wasn't and..."

"You felt guilty."

"Beyond anything."

I sat up, holding the sheet against my chest. "You know why I forgot I was Rasha? Not because I didn't want it. Because I was starting to like it. Coming home that night when I first found Leo, I'd been thinking I had something to offer this gig. That maybe, for the first time since all my life plans had crashed and burned, I'd found something I could excel at again. Except I didn't believe that I had any right to it. Any right to be bright and shiny. And the really fucked up thing? I never considered if maybe that label, that expectation, had weighed Ari down all these years, just as much as lack of expectation had me."

I lost my fight with the tears, but before I could swipe at them, Rohan gently brushed his thumb along my skin to wipe them away.

"Despite what happened, Rohan? You're denying an essential part of yourself. I'm not saying go all rock star again, but you can't stop singing and making music. It's who you are just as much as being Rasha." I cupped his jaw. "Even if you don't do this song, please think about what I've said. You don't need to live with that deep-seated unhappiness. You don't need to live with that guilt. You have the right to decide how you want to live. You have the right to be happy."

Rohan didn't say anything, just held my gaze. Every particle between us was charged with this intense intimacy and, in that moment, I almost broke my rule and kissed him.

Our mutual tensing hit at the same instant.

I dropped my hand. "What are we doing here?"

He sighed. "Fuck if I know."

"Right." I sat up and retrieved my nightgown, pulling it over my head. "Thanks for the sex stuff."

"Any time."

I paused at the doorway. Normally sexytime did not require any clarification because normally I would not be seeing the dude again. However, with Rohan and I being in such close quarters, I figured the laying out of mutual expectations would be appropriate.

"Are you still mad?" I asked.

"About what? Using sex to get what you want, your issues with kissing, or the fact you apparently have never met a personal boundary you care to respect?"

I winced, toeing at a groove in his floor. "Yes."

"No, because I believe you weren't. No, because I'm almost impressed with your level of dysfunction–"

"Your issue shit doesn't smell like roses either," I shot back.

"It would if I had any."

I rolled my eyes at his ability to say that with a straight face.

"And no," he said, "it's annoying, but I'm not mad."

The tightness in my chest relaxed. "Last item. To ensure there is no slap down of a Sexual Harassment 101 course on our," I circled a finger between us, seeking a noun that wasn't *relationship*, "situation by the HR department."

"You mean our resident dominatrix?" Rohan asked.

"Stay professional, Snowflake."

He schooled his features into a serious expression, nodding for me to continue.

I repressed my grin at the amusement in his eyes. "To clarify," I said, ticking the items off on my fingers. "Our future dynamic includes training, dispatching unholy spawn, and doing the horizontal mambo at every opportunity, correct?"

"Except Saturdays," he said. "I rest on Shabbat." The Jewish Sabbath.

My face fell and Rohan laughed. "So easy on so many levels," he teased.

"So mind-blowing on so many levels," I corrected, and left.

25

Our talk didn't bring Rohan to an earth-shattering epiphany. It certainly didn't get me any closer to my goal of having Ari checked. All that happened was that Rohan avoided me the next day. I buried myself in more training, then headed up to my room, stopping in surprise as I entered.

My tap shoes were sitting on my bed. I reached a tentative finger out to touch them. Last time I'd seen them had been at my parents' place. Ari would have mentioned if he'd brought them over. Except he wouldn't have. As far as he was concerned, I'd shut that part of myself down. Only one person was aware that I'd danced again that one time.

I pressed my palms to my cheeks. Was this about me? About him? About us? Not that there was an us.

"Babyslay?" Kane stood in my doorway. "Rabbi Abrams wants to see you in his office."

Hope rising in my chest, I bolted downstairs, skidding to a stop as the rabbi's office door opened and my shell-shocked twin stumbled out.

"I'm still an initiate," Ari said.

Behind his desk. Rabbi Abrams paused his polishing of a gold bar engraved with symbols to throw me a thumbs up. With a whoop, I jumped up and down.

Ari wore the same dazed look all the way out to the car.

"You're happy, right?" I asked.

"Yeah. I just... need to process that it's for real." He sank into the driver's seat, shaking his head. "Listen, Rabbi Abrams wants us to keep this between the three of us for now. Something about figuring out why re-running my induction ceremony didn't work." He popped his seat belt in with a click.

"Okay, but that means no unting-hay emons-day on your end."

Ari started the car. I shut his door, doing my happy dance for the benefit of his rear view mirror until the car had veered out of sight down the drive.

I danced my way up the back stairs into the kitchen where I found Rohan sitting on the counter, texting. "Thankyouthankyouthankyou!" I threw my arms around him.

He jumped down, sliding his phone into his pocket. "I shouldn't have held up the mission like that."

My exuberance leaked out of me and I stepped back. I mean, yeah, it was a perfectly good reason to do the theme song but what about the tap shoes? Weren't they symbolic of well, something?

Before I could ask, Drio bounded into the room and grabbed Rohan in a bear hug, spinning him around.

"Dude. Put me down."

Drio squeezed him one more time then messed up Rohan's hair. "I could kiss you!"

I could watch that.

"We'll have the proof to take Samson down in no time." Drio did a quick one-two step. "Prague, here we come!"

"Why Prague?" I asked.

"The final part of the production is being shot there." Drio eyed me up and down, one hand braced on the counter. "Want to go?"

"Suuuure." I pointed to the stairs. "I'll pack my bags."

"I'm serious." He jerked his index finger up and down my body. "You're attractive enough."

I fluttered my hands in front of my face. "You think so?" I dropped the act. "Attractive enough for what?"

"Yes, Drio," Rohan said. "Whatever are you up to?"

Drio's hands gestured excitedly as the words tumbled out of him. "You doing the song opens up a bunch of new ways to plant more Rasha in the inner circle. As part of your entourage, I'll be vetted by his posse no problem." He jerked his thumb at me. "And any 'friend,'" he used air quotes, "of the great Rohan Mitra's..."

"Hell no," Rohan growled.

I punched Drio. "I'm not whoring out for a demon."

"You don't have to fuck him," he said. "But you're his type. Be a tease. I don't care. The more people we have on him, the faster we take him down. Besides, you're a good Rasha," he added grudgingly.

Wow.

Still, any plan of Drio's to send me in and play nice with a demon needed to be examined inside and out for all the possible ways I could end up dead. I started with Baruch, dropping the comment casually in during a training session the next day. "Drio wants me to go to Prague undercover and get close to Samson for proof he's a demon. What do you think?"

I startled my trainer enough that I managed to land a right hook on his jaw. A first.

"Ben zona," Baruch swore. "No."

"It wasn't a yes or no question, Tree Trunk. I could help." I raised my fists back up to my face.

"You have no experience." He corrected my stance.

I laughed. "Getting guys? That's pretty much the most experience I have."

"Outing demons. You don't have to do this."

Oh, I knew that, but I figured that the Brotherhood would, too. Sure, Ari would be taken care of now but they were still undecided on me. I wanted to change that.

"Scale of one to ten," I asked later, "with one being me coming out unharmed and ten being my grisly remains found twenty years from now. Where do you put this job?"

"Fifty-seven," Kane said. We sat on the front porch, Kane keeping me company "for no reason" but really because Ari was coming over.

"You don't think I could do it?"

"I don't think I could do it and I've pulled straight boys with the best of them." Kane wagged a finger at me. "King is dangerous. And not in the fun way that makes you do that moaning sound that I find highly irritating to have to hear, child who has not processed that my room is directly over Rohan's."

I blushed.

Ari showed up, looking between me still totally embarrassed and Kane, legs splayed in his Adirondack chair. "Do I want to know?" he asked.

"Your sister is being very naughty."

"That would be a no, then."

"Also, she has a death wish." Kane got up. "Talk to her." He swatted me across the top of the head and went inside.

Ari sat down in the vacated chair and held out a gift bag.

"What's this?" I pulled out a giant box from the fancy-ass chocolatier I loved but could never really afford.

"Because you believed in me."

"Aww, Ace." I kissed his cheek.

He allowed one peck before he swatted me off. "What was Kane babbling about?"

"Prague." I explained the situation and why I wanted to do it.

"You're not ready."

"I'm Rasha." I lit up my hand. "I am not without resources." I flexed my fingers. "Ever since I became a hunter, I've been focused on doing this job to survive or prove a point that I wasn't a total fuck up. But I've missed having something to be passionate about and being

Rasha might be it. You were right. I am happy. At least, I'm starting to be."

Ari was silent for a while. "Okay."

"Also, I–wait. Okay?"

He nodded. "You're right. You're Rasha. This wouldn't even be a discussion if you were a guy. And the passion for the gig? I get it."

"We are going to be the coolest super twins ever." I broke open the chocolates. While I chose mine by shape most likely to contain nuts, Ari carefully studied the legend. My first choice contained a macadamia so I nailed it. Next I went for a dark chocolate surprise. "So you don't think the Prague idea is a subtle murder plot by Drio?"

"No. Though once Samson's dead, you might want to watch your back. Sweet! Hedgehog."

"Wait!" I tried to grab the chocolate, but Ari stuffed it in his mouth before I could. "No fair. There was only one of those."

"You snooze, you loose," he said through a mouthful.

"So much for gratitude."

He looked at me like I was insane. "It was a hedgehog. You'd push me into traffic for one." I couldn't argue with that, though I did make sure and eat his second favorite flavor of Mexican hot chocolate truffle next.

Once I had Ari's support, blessing, and common sense take on the matter, I gave Drio my assent. He told me that he was waiting for official permission from the Brotherhood, but that he expected the call soon.

I hurried downstairs to Rohan's room, rapping softly on the door. "Hey, Snowflake." My plan was to keep things professional. He hadn't said word one to me about the tap shoes so I was taking that to mean it had simply been a kind gesture from a colleague.

Rohan stepped out from behind his half-open closet door, dressed in tight black jeans and a white T-shirt, his hair spiky and gelled. And, oh my, he was wearing eyeliner.

He grinned his rock fuck grin.

I clutched the doorframe in support as every bone in my legs dissolved into jelly. "I've decided to go to Prague." My voice came out in a squeak.

"I heard." He advanced on me, pure strut. The light caught the silver of his multiple rings on each hand.

I eeped and held onto the doorframe harder. "Maybe I'll run into you while I'm there."

I prayed that Prague was a big enough city that that absolutely would not happen, because with him dressed like this and in full rock god mode, I didn't stand a chance.

"I'm sticking close to have your back on this assignment." He skimmed his hand over my hip, the warmth of the black leather strap worn with a single fat silver bracelet on his right wrist brushing against my skin.

"Dressed like that?" I stammered. My heart beat a furious tempo at the clear and present danger of this incarnation of Rohan. I flapped a hand at him. "Surely, you don't have to go zero to a billion? Start small."

"I've been thinking a lot about how you missed dancing like breathing." His arrogance fell away, leaving a soft vulnerability that hit me harder than the rock god look. "It made me realize that I'd been holding my breath, too. That, after Asha, I hadn't thought I deserved music in my life." His gaze turned penetrating. "I hadn't admitted that to anyone. Not even myself until now. Until you."

I had to jump start my breathing. "Happy I could help," I squeaked. I tried to step away but he held me fast. Careful what you wish for, idiot. I swallowed, his raw charisma flooding my system.

"I'm meeting with Forrest about the song. And I wrangled an intro to King. Now I need more of an entourage than just Drio." He leaned in, his lips hovering over mine. "You were nominated and won as groupie."

"Mazel tov to me," I murmured, practically pulling the frame off the wall. My mouth was dry and my brain had gone wonky and stupid in the face of his pure male swagger. Oh, how misguided I'd been with my whole "players and their games" insight I'd had on Rohan.

I hadn't even begun to see his game because Rohan Mitra had been slumming in the junior league with me. Nope, I was screwed, and this time, I didn't think I'd get a say in how.

END OF BOOK ONE

Acknowledgments

First and foremost, thank you to my two secret weapons without whom, this book would only have amused me. Alex Yuschik, I officially give you rock star editor status. You always understand what I'm trying to do and then push me to go farther and be better. Rudy Thauberger, my "nerd editor" extraordinaire, you are amazing and insightful and I look forward to many more nerd talks with you.

Big thanks to Dr. Marc Nantel for the magic chats, Ita Margalit for reading this and saying that she enjoyed it like a real book and not just written by her friend, and Bryn Donovan for her eyes on a very early draft.

To my romance peeps who populate my happy corner of the internet, all the good karma and your favorite things to you. You authors keep me sane, make me laugh, and generously share your wealth of knowledge and experience.

And last, but never ever least, thank you to my husband and daughter for not resorting to physical bodily harm when I'm zoned out at the computer yet again. I love you two crazy, ridiculous amounts.

The Unlikeable Demon Hunter: Sting

(Nava Katz, #2)

Deborah Wilde

te da media
vancouver

Publisher's Note: This is a work of fiction. Names, characters, places, and incidents are a product of the author's imagination. Locales and public names are sometimes used for atmospheric purposes. Any resemblance to actual people, living or dead, or to businesses, companies, events, institutions, or locales is completely coincidental.

Book Layout ©2015 BookDesignTemplates.com

Cover design by Damonza

Library and Archives Canada Cataloguing in Publication

Wilde, Deborah, 1970-, author
        The unlikeable demon hunter : sting / Deborah Wilde.

(Nava Katz ; 2)
Issued in print and electronic formats.
ISBN 978-1-988681-01-6 (softcover).--ISBN 978-1-988681-02-3 (EPUB).--ISBN 978-1-988681-03-0 (Kindle)

        I. Title.   II. Title: Sting.

PS8645.I4137U57 2017   C813'.6   C2017-900426-3
                                                 C2017-900427-1

1

"Shove it in already," I said through gritted teeth. My back was freezing from the damp, flaking basement concrete I lay against, while the two-foot-long, rat-shaped demon pinning me down was doing shit for my front.

Rohan Mitra, rock star turned demon hunter, shook his tousled dark hair, his full lips puckering in obvious disgust. "I'm not putting my finger in there. You want it so badly, do it yourself."

I slammed an elbow into the underside of the vral's jaw, whipping her head sideways, intent on keeping the demon's double row of razor-sharp incisors out of my shoulder. One bite and I'd be paralyzed.

And lunch.

"*Now* you're going to get all pussy about sticking your finger places it doesn't belong?"

"I'll reconsider if she begs as nicely as you did, Nava."

The vral snapped her teeth, the sound a loud crack in my ear. Her dank, rotten-meat belch wafted over me.

I tried to plug my nose with my shoulder, my arm muscles straining with the exertion of holding her at bay. "Bite me, Mitra."

He sipped his latte, standing there immaculate and infuriating in a camel-colored trench coat more appropriate to a night at the theater than a demon raid. A raid, it turned out, Rohan had no intention of participating in, deeming it "a training exercise for the newbie."

Overhead, a bulb sizzled and popped out, dimming the light and casting almost-romantic shadows over the warped structural beams and grotty walls.

Rohan had the gall to check his watch.

"Don't let me keep you from anything." I shot lightning bolts at the vral from my eyes and she jerked, her weight almost off me. Hand blasts were so level one. I rolled sideways, but the demon crashed back down on top of me. The two of us tumbled into the shadows, her teeth flashing in and out of the darkness.

"Then finish her," he said.

"I'm trying, but I don't think she's into me that way."

Rohan took another sip. "Make her want it."

Continued grappling with the demon wasn't going to get me anywhere other than exhausted and then dead. Fine, mostly dead. Rohan wouldn't let me be unequivocally taken out.

I wove an electric net around the vral's body, temporarily paralyzing her with my magic so I could scramble free. My problem? The only way to permanently stop a demon involved hitting their weak spot. My other problem? There was a different spot for each demon. With vral, it was their left eye. As in the one that bulged jiggling out toward me from her socket, laden with pus. "If I blast her eyeball, demon goo will splooge everywhere."

"Always about the hard and messy," he chastised. "Gentle has its place, too, you know."

The vral, who I'd thought was still suffering the effects of my magic paralysis, lashed her tail around my arm. Surprise. What looked like smooth fur was actually dozens of tiny barbs. I wrenched free, my stomach heaving at the sight of my flesh that now looked like raw hamburger, and blasted the demon in the chest. "Have at it. *Gently* use one of your blades to puncture—son-of-a-bitch!"

The vral convulsed under the sharp crackle of my power, locking onto me in a spasming hug, her claws shredding my sweater. Eight bleeding gashes were not my idea of body adornment.

The air stank of sizzling fur, which was still a step up from the stale B.O. and garbage juice that had seeped into the walls of this squatter's paradise.

"Stop acting from the flight part of your brain and go to the fight," Rohan said.

Thrashing on the floor, I squeezed my eyes shut against the blood and sweat dripping into them. The vral's claws burrowed into my back. "What do you think I'm doing?"

"Napping? Baruch trained you better than this."

Yeah, for three whole weeks. Muttering an anatomically impossible suggestion Rohan's way, I pulled out a self-defense move that Baruch had drilled into me. Before the demon's tremors could subside, I wrapped my right leg around her left foreleg to trap it, curling my right arm over her body in a tight overhook. My fingers dug deeper into her wiry, scorched fur, hitting something squishy that was matted into her side.

Please don't let that be leftover homeless person from her earlier meal.

I planted my left foot firmly on the floor, bridging up, my hips exploding into the air. The combination of that momentum, along with the pull/push dual action of my arms as I chopped my left hand into the demon, allowed me to swing on top of her.

"That's a start," Rohan said.

Snarling, the vral bucked me off like a seasoned rodeo bull. I flew onto my ass, then scrambled to my feet, panting, my right foot buckling as I stumbled backwards over a piece of ceiling tile.

Rohan tsked me. "We're Fallen Angels, not Falling Angels. Try to stay upright." In a display of rampant egotism, my fellow all-male hunters had dubbed themselves Fallen Angels. I'd graciously been extended the label.

"You're hilarious."

"I am rather," he replied in a put-on posh British accent that intoxicated me like a shot of liquid sex. He gestured to the trash-strewn floor. "Be aware of your surroundings," he directed in his normal voice that was all smoky baritone and velvet Californian curls. "Garbage can be your downfall."

Nodding, I flung a damp lock of curly dark brown hair out of my face.

The vral scrambled back onto all fours, shaking out her fur like she was waking from a nap. Then the man-eating little fucker lunged and sank her two rows of teeth into the toes of my boots.

Steel-toed, but still. These babies were new. Very expensive. Who knew it was such a challenge to find badass boots with reinforced steel, a chunky heel that was far more practical to run in than stilettos, and silver buckles running up the side? It was my consolation gift to myself for having my lovely life of partying, sex, and naps getting shot to hell with the recent discovery that I was the first female Rasha, or demon hunter. I'd been reluctantly inducted into the Brotherhood of David, a dick-swinging secret organization.

Yeah, they weren't thrilled to have their first vag-sporter either.

The vral's eyes locked onto mine. She gave a chittered cackle, her teeth cracking deeper into the leather.

My old tap dance mantra popped into my head. *A one, a two, you know what to do.* Nothing to it but to do it. I blasted the vral's eyeball, shielding myself with a ceiling tile against the putrid pus arcing out of her like a Tarantino kill. The splatter guard worked well, with only a few drops of warm liquid hitting my cheek. It tingled but nothing got in my eyes or mouth so score one, Nava. Which tipped into score the second, as the demon death throe'd down to a single nubbin of fur.

The faintest scuff of claws on metal was our only clue that another demon was present. It flew off an overhead pipe, claws outstretched and the fur on its back raised. A baby vral, much smaller in size, but still deadly.

Before I even had time to gasp, Rohan's hand shot up, one wicked sharp blade extended from his index finger, the movement pulling his coat tight around his astoundingly well-defined shoulders. His magic allowed him to do that party trick with all his fingers, not to mention extend a blade that ran the length of his body like an outline. One time I'd asked him why his clothes didn't get shredded each time he brought out his knives. Maybe I'd said it a little too dejectedly because he'd stopped instructing me on the proper way to punch a chupacabra in the face and raised an amused eyebrow as he said, "It's magic."

He didn't look up when he aimed now, didn't even stop sipping that stupid latte, yet he shish-kabobed the vral right through the neck. Since it wasn't the sweet spot, it wasn't a kill strike, but he still stopped the demon in its tracks.

"Admit it. You're the devil." I trained my eyes on the shadowy corner but didn't see any other movement.

"Nice to see I've risen in the hierarchy of Hell during our brief acquaintance." With a snap of his wrist, Rohan flicked the demon over to me.

Baby vral plopped at my feet with a wet splat, still quivering.

"Don't say I never give you anything," he said.

"I couldn't possibly accept. You caught it. You kill it."

Rohan waved a hand at me. "I insist."

I toed the baby vral. Hmm. I stood behind it, which meant its eyeballs faced Rohan. "I serve at the pleasure of my commanding officer." Barely hiding my snigger, I nailed its eyeball with a concentrated stream of electricity, killing the demon with a tad too much enthusiastic zeal.

Its entire body exploded. An almost impossible amount of pus, guts, and fur flew, dousing our immediate area like the splash zone at SeaWorld. Its various bits then winked into oblivion like they were supposed to when a demon was offed, but the damage had been done.

Rohan remained pristine. He looked like a god and I looked like the aftermath of a Dumpster fire. A dank-ass, gooey, Dumpster fire of demon pus. Awesome.

I strode toward him, my hair dripping with sweat and filth, my skin and clothes not even that clean, determined to make him pay.

He snicked out the blades of one hand as I neared, warding me off.

Ignoring the threat that wasn't, I swiped his coffee cup, tipping it back for those last few swallows. "Mmm, caramel." I licked a drop of foam off my lip with deliberate slowness, gratified by Rohan's nostril flare. Yeah, our attraction was a two-way street, with both of us engaged in a high-octane game of chicken to see who'd blink first.

The first night we'd met, I'd accused Rohan of being a demon because ordinary mortals could not look that good without Photoshop. Only the slight bent of his nose, broken on more than one occasion, marred his perfection. Too bad all of that 'tude poured into the tight package of leanly muscled torso, dark brown hair that curled in thick, sexy locks around his ears, gold eyes, killer cheekbones, firm chin, and light brown skin from his East Indian/Jewish heritage was my personal downfall.

And fall I had. Onto his very fine dick time and time again over the past few weeks of our acquaintance. What can I say? It was worth it.

"Home, Jeeves." I tossed the cup on the ground with the rest of the trash. Ignoring Rohan's sigh, I jumped up the rickety basement steps two at a time without a look back.

Taking the scenic route through the condemned home, I opted for the back door instead of the closer front one in the living room. Even though there were no longer leftovers of the poor desecrated victims, you couldn't pay me to walk back through the site of the people buffet. We Rasha held our own pretty well against the evil spawn found throughout the world, but the hard truth was that we didn't always win. Sometimes we died, and more often innocent victims did.

I gave a wide berth to the stained mattress leaning up against the kitchen wall, teeming with bed bugs. Insidious, unstoppable, blood-sucking demonic parasites. Do all the mattress wrapping and heat treatments you wanted, those bastards could only be killed for good with our help, and it wasn't a service we advertised. Plus, I kept seeing the mangled human arm that one of the vral had been batting around beside the mattress like a cat toy when we'd first entered.

A yellow Post-It note stuck to the back door caught my eye. I smirked at the stick figure woman saying "IOU" to a buffed stick man. My friend, and fellow Rasha, Kane Hashimoto's reminder that I'd be paying for him hauling body bits away. Probably in expensive booze and food. The longer before I was ever trained on clean-up, the better. Badass hunter, I was your girl. Handler of human remains and scourer of blood? Run away very fast. I crushed the note in my hand and stepped outside.

Cold rain pelted the back of my neck, sliding down along my spine into the waistband of my black miniskirt and leggings. The rest of the rain blew right through my tattered sweater, soaking me in less than a minute and burning like acid as it hit the vral claw wounds. Wincing, I sped up, my breath misting the air in sharp puffs.

A March day in Vancouver and rain flowed from the heavens faster than beer down a frat boy's throat. In summertime, my hometown was one of the most beautiful places on the planet, but on days like today where the sky was heavy and gray and the rain incessant, I felt like Mother Nature was sucking out my soul. Not literally. As far I knew there was no Mother Nature demon, soul-sucking or otherwise, though at this point, nothing would surprise me.

Rohan strode past, his coat flapping in the breeze with each of his measured strides, his unique scent of musk and iron teasing my senses. Fishing the keys out of his pocket, he stopped beside the '67 Shelby parked alongside the house. Fully restored, this vintage two-door muscle car with its midnight blue finish and white racing stripe was Rohan's pride and joy.

I dodged a large puddle to catch up, desperate for the car's heat.

The casual observer may have thought it sweet how Rohan lay out a veritable cocoon of towels to wrap me in, but I wasn't fooled. It was to protect the car. Any warmth or comfort on my end was strictly accidental.

Shivering, I pulled the towels around me and slid past him onto the passenger seat. "Such a gentleman."

Rohan gave me a wolfish grin. "You wouldn't want me if I was." He chucked me under the chin. Bastard. Even his door shutting sounded like it was smirking.

I grabbed the sports drink waiting for me in the cup's holder, my stiff fingers fumbling the cap until I gave up, using the edge of one of the towels to open it. I chugged half the bottle in one go. Every time we Rasha used our magic to kill a demon, it took a toll on us physically. Today's little venture was nothing an electrolyte top-up wouldn't fix, but I never looked forward to being zonked out and exhausted post-epic battle.

Rohan started the engine and we headed back to the Brotherhood-owned mansion that served as the Vancouver chapter of Demon Club. The mansion where I now lived.

Beverage consumed, I replaced the empty bottle in the cup holder, and fiddled with the radio dial until I found Radiohead's "Creep." I sang along. "*I'm a winnnneeeeer.*"

"It's 'weirdo,' you weirdo," Rohan said. "Why would he sing he's a winner in a song about self-loathing?"

"I thought it was sarcastic. You know," I dropped into a snarky voice, "*I'm a winner.*" I turned the heat vent to blow directly on my face, holding my hands up to catch more warmth. "As per my basic assumption of how many things are said. *Those jeans look good on you. It's so great to see you again. I love you.*"

If Rohan's eyebrows had knit together any lower, they would have been a V-neck. "Have you ever sought help?"

I snapped off the radio. "Is that an actual question or are you wasting my time with hypotheticals?"

The "Imperial March" from *Star Wars* blasted out. Not because I was such a fan but because most of my calls these days were on Brotherhood business. The only non-Brotherhood people who had the number were my family and my best friend Leonie Hendricks. She'd been assigned Flight of the Conchords' "Too Many Dicks (On the Dance Floor)"–our anthem once we'd started sneaking into clubs.

"Number's blocked." My stomach clenched. This had to be the call from HQ in Jerusalem that I'd been waiting for.

Rohan slowed to a stop at a red light, then laid his hand on the back of my neck. "You've got this."

"Damn straight," I said, though it took me another ring to steady myself and answer. "Hello?"

"Ms. Katz." Rabbi Mandelbaum managed to make my name sound like an insult.

"Hello, Rabbi." My voice remained neutral, despite my clenched jaw.

"Wait," he barked at me in his Russian accent.

I traced a dick in the window's condensation.

There were two sections to the Brotherhood. Rasha, the hunters out there actually fighting, came from every race and religion, descendants of the original men that King David had chosen to magically fight evil. They weren't all Jewish, and it was kind of interesting to see how far-reaching those original bloodlines had traveled.

Then there were the rabbis, the ones who cast the spells involved in finding and inducting hunters. The overall pool of rabbis in turn, voted six of their number to form the Executive to govern and oversee everything to do with the Brotherhood. The Executive wielded a fair bit of power and Mandelbutt, as its de facto leader, had the most power of all.

"Ms. Katz, are you still with us?"

I added horns to my drawing. "Ever your faithful servant, Rabbi."

I swear I could hear him grinding his teeth long distance. "Consider this your official permission."

I sagged against the seat in relief. I'd been waiting for the green light to accompany Rohan and another Rasha called Drio Ricci to Prague and the film set of *Hard Knock Strife*. All to help my Demon Club compadres get proof that mega A-list celebrity Samson King was a demon intent on using humiliation and envy to help achieve his world domination master plan.

Before I could thank the rabbi for allowing me to go, he blew the half point he'd earned in my estimation by adding, "Do exactly what the men say."

My hand tightened on the phone and I punched the seat warmer on with excessive force.

Rohan raised his eyebrows in question but I shook my head at him. He massaged the back of my neck in calming, even strokes.

Religious Jewish men said a daily prayer thanking God for not making them a woman. Rabbi Mandelbaum was probably more effusive than most with that gratitude. Not to mention, the Brotherhood had been a total sausage fest since King David assembled the finest men around him for his secret demon club. Many saw no reason for that to change now.

I had to prove myself a thousand times more than any other new hunter and for most of them, I'd still never be as good as a man. I'd expected to be put on a tight leash with this mission, but this was bullshit. "I'll make sure not to think for myself."

Rohan snorted, returning his hand to the wheel.

"Good." Mandelbutt paused and I seethed. "The Executive will be watching your performance." Meaning he was waiting for a reason to remove me–in whatever form that took.

"I'll do you proud."

He didn't even say good-bye, just hung up on me.

Fuck him. I'd still been given my go ahead and that's all that counted. "Guess who's officially going to Prague?" I crowed.

"I didn't doubt it for a second." Rohan squeezed my thigh. You'd have thought he'd ripped my clothes off, licking his way up my body given the hot, tight coil of lust that wound through me. I was seriously addicted to him. Intervention-level addiction, except for the fact that I didn't believe in interventions. If something didn't kill me, why stop?

I let my legs fall open.

Rohan swung his head my way, his amber eyes molten, until he took in my disarray, grimaced, and focused back on the road.

"Asshole," I said.

"Don't judge."

"But I have no other hobbies."

Rohan grinned at me. "Except poor character judgment since I am a prince among men." He gestured at my towel. "The care I take with you."

We pulled up to Demon Club's gate to be scanned. The house was situated in the Southlands area of the city on a large tract of land, surrounded by forest. Case in point, you couldn't even see the three-story mansion made of chunky stone and large windows or any of its multiple chimneys from the street.

"I'm not deceived by your chivalrous ways, Snowflake." I pulled my fluffy cocoon tighter around me. "I know this is about your car, not me."

His aggrieved sigh was the only indication of how much he hated that nickname, short for Emo Snowflake and an homage to the emo rock band Fugue State Five that he'd been the broody lead singer of in his late teens. Or more precisely, the world-chart dominating musical juggernaut that he'd fronted.

Retiring from that about three years ago at age twenty when he'd been inducted as a hunter hadn't hurt his massive ego one bit. Though he'd dumped the graphic Ts, platinum dye job, and eyeliner for an improved fashion sense and a return to his inherent natural hotness.

The black wrought-iron gate set into the thick stone fence swung silently open.

"Why waste chivalry when I wouldn't even be rewarded with a kiss?" Rohan sported a massive chip on his shoulder about the fact that I refused to kiss him on the lips, during sex or otherwise. One word: hook-up. The sum total of our relationship status and thus, no kissing necessary.

Weirdly, my boundaries offended his control-freak nature.

The rain picked up, lashing the car.

"As if you were sharing sweet kisses with the many girls you screwed in your rock star days."

Windshield wipers on high, Rohan gunned the car up the remainder of the long, winding drive, past well-tended gardens and copses of arbutus and cedar trees. "You're comparing us to tour sex?"

"It's all hook-ups." I zeroed in on the line of muscle flowing from his bicep across to his pec and back to his bicep. A better panorama than anything outside.

Rohan stopped the car in front of the house with enough force that my skull crashed back against the seat. "One-time fucks. No repeat button."

Glowering at him, I rubbed my head. "That doesn't make any difference."

"Doesn't it?" His tone was casual but I sidled sideways to escape the freezer-cold depths of his accompanying smile.

I peeled myself off the passenger door. "Gearing up for a full-scale offensive?"

Rohan cut the engine. Rain pounded on the roof and black thunderclouds seemed to press in from every direction. "If I ever go full-scale, I'll take no prisoners," he said.

He'd have to do better than that.

I let the towel flutter to the seat, giving a sultry head toss, my perky C cups front and center. Despite me still being covered with demon goo, Rohan looked. I leaned in toward him, trailing my finger down his chest. "No quarter. No mercy."

I'd figured our mutual attraction and constant tug-of-war to be a fairly level playing field until I'd seen Rohan in full-on rock god mode, prepping for our upcoming trip to Prague and his return to the spotlight. That's when I'd realized my hot fuck buddy was merely swimming with me in the kiddie pool because he felt like it, and that the deep end was calling again.

I'd had two choices: A) the sane path of ending the mind-blowing sex aspect of our leisure time or B) amping my game. In the animal kingdom, challenging an alpha was a good way to get your throat ripped out. With this kinky boy, dominance games were foreplay. Thing is, despite his bitching about my no-kissing decree, I didn't see him swimming off yet. After the long dry spell of my sexual escapades, Rohan was an oasis I wanted to suck dry. As I'd barely begun to quench my thirst, no way was I the one tapping out first.

Rohan caught my hand before it reached his jeans. Trapping it.

I met his level stare, despite my lungs feeling two sizes too tight. Just because I refused to bow down didn't mean this came easy to me. Still, I shivered in delicious anticipation of what he might do next–like haul me into his room and screw me seven ways from Sunday. Then again, he might drown me in the pool out back then dump me in the forest. Given the wild gleam in the depths of his gold eyes, anything was a go.

That's when both our phones buzzed with texts. It was Drio. *Get the fuck inside.*

2

I scratched at the vral grime coating my skin. A shower would have to wait, because the second we stepped through the front door into the foyer with its cathedral ceiling, Drio snapped, "In here," in a way that left no room for discussion.

We hurried into the TV room with its brown leather mancave couches and comfortable clutter. The one place in the house that didn't feel straight out of *Exclusive British Men's Club Monthly*. Drio was perched on the fat arm of one sofa, staring in bewilderment at the massive flat screen TV mounted to the wall. "King's holding a press conference."

The sexy rumble of Drio's Italian accent combined with his olive skin, blond hair, and startling green eyes made him an irresistible combination. For most. His open loathing of me and sadistic hard-on for demon torture meant I could resist him just fine.

I turned my attention to the screen. Samson King sat at a long table, speaking into the microphone placed in front of him, decked out in a tailored button-down that I'd recently seen on the cover of GQ. His hair was more artfully gelled than a performing boy band's at the Teen Choice Awards. Projected behind him was a huge logo featuring a stylized red SK in the middle of a black diamond. The flurry of flashbulbs were blinding even on my side of the TV.

"He's still in Prague, right?" Standing, since I didn't want to dirty the furniture, I squirmed, trying to relieve the throb in my back from my wounds.

Rohan rummaged amidst the shit on the coffee table for a tin of salve.

"Sì. He's there," said Drio.

Samson had flown from Vancouver to Prague a few days ago to shoot the remaining scenes of *Hard Knock Strife*, with its age-old plot of "childhood buddies get caught up in a gangster lifestyle." His character finds redemption in the end, scarred but wiser. In other words, total fiction.

I sighed as Rohan tugged up the back of my sweater to gently apply the mint-based, healing gel to my skin. The relief as it numbed the area was immediate.

Drio jerked his head toward the TV. "Watch, they're replaying the clip."

Samson had the build and smug handsome looks of a rich-kid college athlete even though he was pushing thirty. The good guy with enough of a bad boy edge to keep from being too All-American, he was always up for a party–that was both his character in this flick and the essence of his brand. He gave people life at its funnest and the masses thirsted for it like water.

Our suspicion was that Samson fed off the envy he inspired and the humiliation he drove people to in their quest to be more like him. Coupled with the number of deaths around him that couldn't be directly linked but were too frequent and too much the inevitable end result of the misery he incited to be accidental, we had probable cause to believe him a demon.

Emphasis on *probable*.

Once we had proof that he was a demon, either his true name, form, or hard evidence about the specifics of his master plan, we'd kill him, because that was what we Rasha did.

I barely registered the feel of Rohan dropping my sweater down, his ministrations finished, listening as Samson announced his retirement from acting to follow his interests behind the scenes. This made no logical sense. He expounded on his plans, pointing to the logo behind him and explaining his new ventures of a record label and management company, with further media expansion to come.

Drio muted the sound, not interested in Samson introducing the two clients he'd already signed, the baby-faced teen boy that I recognized as a viral singing sensation on his left, and on his right, the jet-setting It Girl in her late twenties who was making quite the name for herself as an indie actress. Both of whom wore identical expressions of boredom until it was their turn to speak.

Rohan tossed the salve back on the table with a clatter. "What's King playing at?"

I gnawed on my lip. "Signing a YouTuber hardly lines up with unleashing the apocalypse or enslaving humanity as his minions."

Drio snarled a ferocious torrent of Italian swear words. I was both impressed and unsettled by how long he could go without pausing for air.

"What if we're wrong?" I asked. "If he's not a demon?"

"That's why we don't assume anything until we have irrefutable evidence. We also don't want our assumptions to make us lazy or complacent," Rohan said.

"Or tip our hand. Even if our gut screams 'demon,' we play it smart," Drio added.

"Got it." I scratched at my skin, demon death goo flaking off me, revealing a bumpy red rash.

"Library. Ten minutes," Rohan said.

A shower imperative, I sprinted up the wide, curving staircase to my bedroom on the top floor. Barely a month in to my new living arrangements, moved out of my parents' house for the first time in my life, and I'd yet to choose the paint color to replace the bleh beige adorning my walls. Though the furniture was decent enough dark wood, and at least I had my own tiny bathroom.

The sole personal touch I'd given the room was to hang my large framed poster of Gregory Hines caught by the camera in mid-tap step, his face lit up in glee. I hadn't gotten around to unpacking two of the five Rubbermaids I'd carted my belongings over in, but the other three did a pretty epic job exploding out over every surface. Folding and organizing were for saps. I preferred hunting and rooting, the thrill of the never-ending treasure hunt for my personal belongings.

Stripping down, I tossed my clothes in the trash and stepped under the hot spray in the small black-and-white tiled bathroom. I used to go through clothes because I hated the visual reminder of bad decisions when wearing hook-up togs more than once. At least the wear and tear of killing monsters left me with no regrets. Though demon kills required lube job levels of skin maintenance.

To celebrate the Executive sending me to Prague, I yanked on the T-shirt Leonie had bought for me. Tight, bright, and hot pink, its glittering silver letters proclaimed "50% boobs. 50% sarcasm. 100% new breed of hunter."

What's a girl without a tagline?

Technically, Leo wasn't supposed to know about the Brotherhood. The Mafia were a bunch of gossipy soccer moms compared to the code of silence the Brotherhood demanded. While DSI–David Security International–a.k.a. the global security firm the Brotherhood ran had a respected rep in high powered circles, it was a closely guarded secret that its mancandy employees were demon hunters. Or that demons even existed.

Scrunching some mousse into my hair, I snagged my hair drier for a quick blow so I didn't head downstairs dripping.

Part of our secrecy was maintained by the fine job the Brotherhood did, and part of it was due to natural human desire to explain away anything vaguely monstrous with "rational" explanations, i.e. any reason that wasn't supernatural. Humans' determination to live within our comfort zones was not to be underestimated. It worked in the Brotherhood's favor.

My three-minute patience of hair drying achieved, I threw on some eye make-up.

I would never have told Leo about any of it if our reunion meeting after about a year and a half of radio silence—mostly stemming from the bad place I'd been in after high school—hadn't come with the mind-blowing discovery that she was half-goblin. Goblins were tricksters and smooth talkers, so combined with the sperm donor's glamouring ability to present as human, it left Leo's mom thinking (bitterly and to this day) that she'd succumbed to the charms of a very handsome rogue for an unforgettable one night stand.

Leo, who only had a human form and no glamour abilities of her own, hadn't enlightened her mom. Luckily, her sole visible redcap goblin features were a propensity to white chin hair, shortness, and a fascination for fussy jewels that had never made sense in our teens. Otherwise, her long straight red hair, funky style, and incredible confidence were pure awesome woman.

Given Leo's half-demon status, she was well aware of Rasha. Though she'd been shocked to find out that I, of all people, was the first chick to be among their number.

I glanced back into the bedroom at my alarm clock. Thirty seconds to spare to Rohan's deadline. I hustled out of my room, finger-combing my still damp curls, anxious for this meeting with Rohan and Drio and the specifics of my cover assignment.

Forrest Chang, the film's director and a huge Fugue State Five fan, had invited Rohan to write the theme song. Meanwhile, I was going in under the guise of Rohan's groupie, a role that Rohan was having altogether too much fun lording over me. Supposedly this cover story allowed him to stick close to me as I gained Samson's attention, but I had my doubts. This wasn't the eighteenth century and I wasn't chattel.

Drio was posing as part of Rohan's entourage without the backstory of blowing him on a regular basis, so why couldn't that be true for me as well? Go for fiction not imitating life. By the time I was halfway down the stairs, I'd resolved to bring this matter up at the start of our meeting.

The front door slammed open and Kane stormed in, bleeding from a gash to his temple. Japanese-Canadian and silky-hot with a tendency to shirtlessness, he could have been naked right now and all anyone would have noticed was the anger rolling off him in waves.

I came to a screeching halt.

Kane raked a hand through his spiky black hair. "Swear to God, babyslay, I will kill him myself, he pulls this shit again."

My heart sinking, I braced a hand on the wooden bannister, polished to a high gleam. "How many?"

"One. But it was Abyzou, the psycho spawn. She'd cornered a pregnant woman in a parking lot and was working her evil mojo to cause a miscarriage." He held up his hand at the anxious eep I emitted. "Breeder and fetus are fine."

"Is Ari okay?"

"Your twin is untouched. I, on the other hand?" He tapped his wound. "My perfection is marred." He'd heal quickly like all Rasha did, but Kane loved his dramatic flare.

I exhaled hard, then trotted down the stairs, gesturing at his temple. "Did Abyzou do that?"

"Yep. Compounded by your idiot brother. He clocked me when I stopped him from getting involved." Kane's jaw tightened. "If I hadn't been worried about protecting his ass, I might have taken Abyzou down. As it was, she got away."

A faint sheen of purple iridescence on his forearm caught the light, indicating his arms were still coated in traces of the salt-based poison that was his magic power. Toxic to demons.

Toxic to humans, too. I couldn't touch him until he'd showered.

"What about the pregnant woman?"

"She thought it was some crazy person attacking. Ari and I distracted the demon enough for the breeder to get into her minivan and bolt." Kane took a steadying breath, clearly trying to get his anger under control. "I can't keep babysitting him."

"I know." My stomach knotted itself up. Ever since Ari had been abducted and tortured by a powerful demon a few weeks back, my heroically-inclined twin had become a one-man, monster-slaying vigilante. Sure, he'd trained his whole life for this, but since his Rasha ceremony had gone horribly wrong–inducting me instead of him in the surprise of the century–he hadn't yet been officially made a hunter and therefore, didn't have any magic power. Without that magic, Ari could wound but not kill.

Though he could piss the demons off enough to end up a tragic statistic himself.

In a rare display of cold calculation, my brother was exploiting Kane's feelings for him, dysfunctional as they were. With or without backup, Ari wasn't stopping and Kane was able to make the killing strikes. Payback had twisted my usually rational twin and I was terrified for his well-being.

Kane stomped up the stairs.

I rubbed my temples, sympathetic to Kane's frustration.

"Navela." Rabbi Abrams, Ari's mentor for his entire life, touched my shoulder.

"You heard Kane?"

He nodded, motioning me into the kitchen. Rain hit the windows, wind scattering leaves off the trees.

I took a seat at the island, knowing from previous conversations that he'd speak in his own time. True to form, the rabbi boiled water for his pot of Darjeeling in silence.

The rabbi reached for a large mug. Slowly. No surprise since the guy was ancient. More wrinkles than anything else, he was clad in one of his many black suits, a kippah perched on his thinning white hair. He'd trimmed his beard, which was good since it had been straying into ZZ Top territory.

The only thing that ever seemed to radically change about Rabbi Abrams was his scent, ranging from mothballs to lavender and today... I surreptitiously sniffed him. Lemon candy drops.

"Ready for Prague?" he asked.

"You bet." Ever my helpful self, I retrieved the honey kept in his special cabinet of "rabbi-only" cups, kettle, and kosher tea supplies.

He raised a shaggy eyebrow at me. I was growing on him.

"My mitzvah for the day," I said, referring to the Hebrew word for a good deed. Like certain Hebrew words, it probably had some other literal meaning.

The kettle clicked off. Rabbi Abrams poured the hot water over the tea diffuser in his cup, his hands strong and steady despite his age. "A mitzvah should not come with expectation of reciprocity."

"Then consider my next question totally unrelated. When will you be inducting Ari?"

After a ton of begging and my capitulation to mild blackmail, Rabbi Abrams had confirmed that yes, Ari did indeed still have initiate status. Thing is, re-running the traditional induction ceremony on Ari after I'd been inducted hadn't worked. That's why the Brotherhood believed they'd made a mistake about Ari's status in the first place. With each passing day that my brother remained an initiate and not a full Rasha, the greater the risk that Ari got seriously hurt.

I was worried that my existence had screwed things up, magically speaking, and now the Brotherhood had no clue how to make my twin a hunter.

I leaned on the counter fidgeting, but the rabbi waited for his tea to steep before answering me. "I am not sure that official permission to try alternate methods of inducting Ari as Rasha will be forthcoming," he said.

"You're picking your words rather carefully there." I frowned. "Please. Be straight with me. Did you ask the Executive?"

"It would not be a good idea at this time to seek authorization on this matter." He blew on the steaming liquid before taking a sip.

Clamping my lips shut against my first impulse to shout, "Why the fuck not?" I took a deep breath, forcing myself to lay out my argument in a calm, logical form. "Ari won't be deterred and this won't end well."

The rabbi took another sip. "There is someone I want you to meet in Prague."

Huh? "Who?"

"Dr. Esther Gelman. She's attending an environmental physics conference there." He waved at the miscellaneous drawer across the room. "Get me a pen."

Biddable me, I did as I was told.

He scribbled down Dr. Gelman's name and email but held on to the paper a moment longer. "Send her this message. 'Golem. Alea iacta est.'" He added that to the paper.

I took it from him. "What does it mean?"

"'The die is cast.' Request a meeting. Do not let her say no."

I stuffed the paper in my pocket. "Uh. Okay. Why am I emailing a scientist about a fictional clay monster? Why don't you do it?"

"She doesn't like the Brotherhood." Well, we had that in common. "This isn't about the folkloric version of the golem," he said. "It's the meaning as it appears in the Tehilim. Psalms 139:16. An unformed body."

Like Ari in regards to being Rasha. Rabbi Abrams wasn't ignoring me. He was investigating a way to induct my twin that would not be sanctioned by the Brotherhood. "Way to work the loophole, Rabbi."

He gave me an enigmatic smile. "Ari remains my responsibility. I do not take that lightly," he said. "Get Esther to meet. She will know if there is a way."

"Who is she?"

"That is not for me to share." He pulled a tiny glass bottle out of his pocket, like one used for aromatherapy oils. It was half-full of some brown liquid. "I need your ring."

I held out my right hand with my Rasha ring worn on my index finger. It was a fat gold band with an engraving of a hamsa, a palm-shaped design with two symmetrical thumbs meant to ward off the evil eye. The single open eye etched into the middle of the design boasted a tiny blue sapphire iris. Standard issue. Trust an all-male Brotherhood to ignore the opportunity for a variety of gemstones that could be accessorized at will.

As a hunter, I was incapable of removing the ring. Believe me, I'd tried.

The first night I'd met Rohan, his identical ring had been the only proof that he wasn't a demon. Though if demon power was based on arrogance alone, Rohan would hands down be one of the most dangerous beings to ever live.

Rabbi Abrams unscrewed the cap, flipping the bottle upside down against the pad of his index finger. I tried not to flinch at the feel of his giant old man knuckles as he took my hand and smeared the liquid around my ring, speaking a couple words in Hebrew. The scent of cloves filled the air.

The gold warmed against my skin and from one blink to the next, the rich color leeched to a hard titanium. The hamsa engraving and sapphire iris disappeared, replaced by tiny diamonds encircling the band. "Can I touch it?"

He nodded so I brushed my thumb across the band. There was no sense of any of the diamonds, though I felt the hamsa and iris.

"You glamoured it," I said.

He returned the bottle to his pocket. "You need to be able to get close to Samson without him seeing the true ring. Just make sure he doesn't touch it. Anyone who does will see through the illusion."

"Got it. Is there a time limit on the glamour?"

"No. I'll remove it once you return from Prague." He picked up his tea, indicating our meeting was at an end. "And Nava?"

I paused at the doorway, half turning back. "Yes?"

"Do as Rohan and Drio command. Show the Brotherhood how well you fit in."

I had to unclench my teeth to answer him in the affirmative. Playing nice meant accepting the role of groupie that I'd been designated and that power dynamic did not sit well with me. But if the alternative would cause any trouble in terms of seeing Ari become Rasha, what choice did I have?

I had no idea what to do. Betray my principles or betray my brother? Either my gut-level certainty about what was best for my well-being or that of what was best for my twin's was in jeopardy. I had no idea how to win on both fronts.

I trudged down the hallway, passing airy open rooms with detailed crown molding and gleaming inlaid wood floors. Rohan and Drio were probably stewing in the library waiting for my tardy self to arrive. The faintest hint of furniture polish scented the air, lending a bright note to the decidedly bleak choice I had to make.

Ari had held my hair out of my face the first time I'd thrown up, covered for me when I'd snuck out, and before this Rasha mix-up, never once cut me out of his confidences. I may not have always been the perfect sibling, but I'd lucked into having someone who was always on my side.

Now that the tables had turned, could I really throw Ari to the wolves?

3

L ost in thought, I missed most of Drio's complaint about me taking my sweet time, even though the men were still in the TV room. Though I caught his sneered, "You look... sparkly," as he waved a hand at the glittery silver letters on my shirt.

"I exude sparkly, thank you very much. But in a deadly way."

Rohan cocked his head to read my shirt. "Fifty percent seems generous, Lolita. I'd say more thirty/seventy."

Lolita was the nickname Rohan had bestowed on me the night we met, when he'd learned I wrote self-insert fanfic in my teens about his band. Not him, mind you. Just the rest of them. It hurt Snowflake's terribly fragile ego that he wasn't included, and since those boys were a whopping three years older than me, Rohan had chosen the pet name he thought most likely to piss me off.

I clapped my hands over my boobs as if protecting their delicate sensibilities from his cruelty. "I'll cop to a forty-five, fifty-five spread. And for that insult, you can forget handling these fine representations of womanhood ever again."

Rohan leaned forward and said, nowhere near soft enough for only me to hear, "Tonight."

"Will you do it?" Drio asked Rohan in his Italian-accented English.

"Of course not," I said hotly. "And you're dead wrong if you don't think I get a say."

Drio paused and arched a single elegant eyebrow.

Rohan stifled a laugh. "He means Child's Play." The massive rock concert slated to happen in London next month to raise funds for war orphans.

Ah.

Drio kicked my chair like an obnoxious ten-year-old, which was several years higher than his actual emotional age.

"You got invited?" I swayed at the thought of being backstage with all that rock royalty, since I'd be happy to accompany Rohan as his groupie on that jaunt. My mental list of which rock stars I wanted to meet–and screw–was assembled at light speed. A brief fun escape from more serious matters.

Rohan reached out to steady me with one hand. "Never gonna happen." Spoilsport. "Forrest hoped I'd premiere the theme song there, but it won't be ready."

I'd once read in a years-old interview that when Rohan Mitra got inspired the song flowed out of him all at once. He'd race to write the words down and then he'd tap out beats and hum strings to himself until he had a skeleton he could share with the band to build off of. It'd happen in a day, like a spirit being raised from the dead or lightning being channeled from the heavens, something so powerful you had to do it all at once to do it well.

Given the flatness in his eyes, there was more to his refusal to premiere it than its lack of completion. "You don't want to get back into things at that level, do you?"

He didn't answer. He'd eschewed the musical spotlight once he'd become Rasha. Fame and his own rock star ego had done a number on him, and when his beloved cousin had needed him, he'd failed to save her from demons. Enter his own inner ones. Or rather, *more* of his inner demons given the lyrics to some of his songs. To the point that he'd tattooed a heart on his left bicep as a reminder of his failure and of his character shortcomings whilst famous.

The tattoo lay directly in line with where his outline blade snicked out. Every time he used his power, the heart got slashed. Even *that* metaphor wasn't enough. Nope, in further penance, he'd stopped singing. Yet, a week ago, Rohan had stepped back into the rock star role for the sake of the mission.

At my request.

I wiped my damp palms on my jeans.

"Selfish bastard," Drio said. But he didn't push it. He was fiercely loyal to Rohan, but not out of friendship's sake alone. It was the kind of loyalty that stemmed from something else, something dark and volatile. I wasn't sure what the deal between them was yet, because I'd been busy killing demons and saving Ari and stuff, but mark my words, I was going to find out.

"Now that I'm going to Prague, what's the next step?" I asked. Was there any other way I could help bring down Samson?

"We need hard proof that King is a demon," Drio began.

"I know. Either catching him in the act of using his demon influence or getting him to reveal his true form. Yes, Drio, I've been paying attention at our meetings the past few days."

He peered at me. "Hard to tell how much functioning intelligence is in there."

I kicked at his leg but he moved it before I got near and I ended up smacking my toes on the wooden leg of the chair that he now sat on.

"I still think our best bet is to discover Samson's true name," Rohan said. "We could use that to force the reveal of his demon self."

The way Drio's eyes lit up at that possibility convinced me that method would be incredibly painful for Samson.

"What's the other way?" I asked, massaging my bruised foot.

Rohan snapped the TV off, taking the pearly white smile of some schmo in a coffee ad with it. "Depending on his demon type, he might revert back to his original form under extreme emotion."

"Like Josh before he came." Josh was the first demon I'd ever killed, and boy, finding out his true nature had been a shocker. For him, literally.

Rohan looked at me, his gold eyes sparking with amusement. Damn. Really needed to think before I said the quiet part loud.

Drio mimed jerking off at me. "Feel free to use that technique again."

"Regret *you* can't get close to Samson that way?"

He shrugged and I blinked. What was his deal? Bi or balls-deep dedication to demon killing?

"That won't be happening." Rohan's tone about my up-close-and-personal involvement brooked no argument.

His voice broke me out of the fantasies I was spinning about Drio getting hot and heavy with other Rasha. Like Rohan. Could that be their weird shared history? My clit, Cuntessa de Spluge, throbbed her vote for "please yes."

"Sure it will. If that's what it takes." Drio's voice was just as hard. He tipped his chair back on to two legs, one foot braced on the arm of the nearest couch. "She's Rasha. Let her do her job."

"Actually," I said, "maybe I could be a member of your entourage without being a groupie."

Both the men laughed outright.

I planted my hands on my hips. "Is it such a stretch that a straight, breathing female with an iota of a sex drive might not want to be servicing Mr. Rock God on a regular basis?"

Shut up, Nava, because they're laughing harder and you're not making your case.

I eyed Drio's wobbling chair, so tempted to upend him. "I'm sure there are lots of other options that would still allow me to Mata Hari my way into Samson's life."

Drio's feet thudded onto the floor. He pinned me in his gaze, his green eyes hard emeralds. "You're there for one reason. Bait. Get

Samson interested and get him to work his demon mojo on you so we have proof. That's it. We go with the simplest explanation for your presence and you play that part." He looked at Rohan as if daring him to disagree.

Rohan gave a tight nod. He pushed his sleeves up, revealing the fat silver bracelet with what looked like a stylized "30" inlaid in onyx. He'd been wearing it ever since he'd gone back into his rock star persona. It was supposed to be some kind of talisman, something he'd received before his first tour. At least according to the Fugue State Five message board I'd researched it on.

"Straightforward is best," he said. "You don't reveal yourself. No deaths on this one, okay?"

"Not on my agenda."

Drio tossed me some photos from the coffee table. Given his leer, this did not bode well. "Coloring, looks, build, you're what Samson likes. Mold your undercover persona to that."

Since I needed to go to Prague to meet Dr. Gelman, I pasted a smile on my face and thought "team player." I studied the photos. Drio was right. I did fit the bill. "Luckily for you, you've got just the badass sexpot for the job."

"Sexpot." Drio raked a skeptical gaze over my T-shirt and jeans. "Got anything sluttier?"

Electricity sparked out of my eyes. "Not skanky enough for you, am I?"

Rohan tapped the photos. "It's not us. It's Samson. He prefers short and tight."

Drio warmed to the theme. "One of those dresses with the zipper running the length for easy access. Stick with red and black. Thigh-high stiletto boots."

I waited for them to laugh, because seriously? But they weren't kidding. Rohan fired his fingers like a gun at Drio. "Good idea. You got some?" he asked me.

"Yeah. Tucked away in my closet. I keep them spruced up for my higher-end street corner jaunts."

"Expense them to the Brotherhood if you need a pair." Rohan noted something down, I swear as an excuse not to laugh, because he was biting his lip.

"She'll have to expense a whole wardrobe if she's going to get his attention." Drio looked at me doubtfully. "Try not to speak. It'll ruin the effect."

"I'll dress up real sexy," I said in a breathy voice. I snapped my fingers. "I know. If I shouldn't talk, maybe you could provide a penis-mobile. I could writhe on the hood to a little heavy metal."

"He's more a rap–"

"Fuck off, Drio. I know how to get a guy's attention."

"Ro is hard up," he said.

"Hey!" Rohan and I protested at the same time.

Drio shrugged.

"You'll need a different name," Rohan said. "Something with the same initials so it's easy to remember." He steepled his fingers together. "What about Nicole Kane? Nikki for short?"

Nikki the car-writhing automaton was never going to happen. "Sounds good. I'll put on my big girl pants and make you proud."

The guys chuffed up, pleased at my can-do attitude. I followed them to the library, the photos tucked under my arm and my brain whirring at how to make this assignment more palatable.

Drio and Rohan sat down at the long mahogany table that spanned the back wall under the large windows looking out onto the back garden. Usually tidy, the table was currently a hurricane of papers, photos, and file folders. The thick green curtains were drawn open, allowing misty light into the room. At least the rain had let up.

Floor-to-ceiling bookshelves were built into the other three walls, the higher shelves accessed via rolling ladders. The "old boys' network" decor was evident in the leather club chairs, love seat, and coffee table grouped by the Persian carpets in the reading area.

The room was a librarian's wet dream, filled with every type of book on demons imaginable. Many of the books sported the same publisher's imprint of the white letters BD against a black square. If you were going to keep demonic activity a secret, it made sense to have an in-house printer to keep a lid on how information was disseminated.

The library was woefully light on fiction, though. I kept hoping the Brotherhood would spring my own personal Giles on me, but sadly that had not yet come to pass. *Buffy* had lied big time about the perks of being chosen.

I dropped into a chair. "What's this?" I pulled a highlighted folder over.

"It rules out all the types of demons that Samson isn't," Rohan said. "Either because that demon behavior doesn't fit his M.O.–"

"Like lust," I said, flipping the file open to peruse the columns of densely-typed demon species.

"Like lust," Rohan agreed. "He's not going to be a bottom feeder, like a vral either, acting on base drives."

"Too high a level of intelligence," Drio said.

"He's a master manipulator," I agreed. "He can glamour himself to look human as well." I tapped the folder. "Does this list take that into account?"

Rohan seemed pleased I'd thought of it and even Drio nodded in acknowledgment. "It does." Rohan looked around the library. "We're still left with endless possibilities but ruling these types out helps."

"A lot of things to investigate then." I ticked the list off my fingers. "Name. Unique or a type." As in a one-of-a-kind demon or part of a species. "The specifics and timeline of his master plan. Find someone willing to say word one against him."

"That collective silence is a testament to his abilities," Drio said. "Evelyn didn't crack once."

Evelyn had been Samson's make-up artist. I'd suggested checking her out since actors spent so much time in make-up and she might have known something. Drio had outed her as a kumiho demon, suspected of using her illusionist abilities to help maintain Samson's human appearance.

Since Samson was constantly in the public eye, and maintaining glamours took energy, his having someone to assist him had seemed a reasonable assumption. Even though Drio had given himself a lot of leeway to get answers out of her—he didn't rape demons but he did love his torture—she didn't succumb to his persuasive ways.

And to think that Mandelbutt had made *me* undergo a psych eval to determine my suitability as Rasha. The Hebrew word for wicked, "Rasha" more literally meant one who departs from the path and is lost. A reminder from David about how close we hunters were to darkness.

I eyed Drio. Some of us closer than others.

"Any sense that Samson is suspicious of her disappearance?" Rohan asked.

"No." Drio swung his feet onto the one clear corner of the table. "According to his buddies, he's pissed that 'she's pulled this shit yet again.'" He scanned a page in the file closest to him. "His new make-up artist checks out as human."

"Hold on." That wasn't something you said about an underling you didn't care lived or died. Maybe Leo was right and we Rasha had to cut the black-and-white thinking out. "What if Evelyn stayed silent because she was in love?"

Drio scoffed at the idea.

"Love is just as powerful as terror," I told him. "Maybe more so." Demons did love. Perhaps not as we did but something similar drove them. I'd learned that firsthand when Asmodeus came after me for killing two of his spawn. "'This shit' she's pulling, getting mad at him about something and leaving? That sounds like jilted lover behavior."

"Do we have any intel on Evelyn and Samson having been part-nered up before now?" Rohan asked Drio. "Based on what little we have on him before he hit big in Hollywood?"

"No. But..." Drio tilted his head, studying me as if trying to recall something. "You had me ask her if Samson had spent time in France."

"Yeah. In Versailles at the court of Louis XIV." Louis had called himself the Sun King. Samson meant sun. Sun. King. The similarity was worth pursuing, especially since some demons lived long lives. "Louis wanted to take over the world. Samson could have gotten ideas from him and maybe the location was a clue to Samson's demon iden-tity."

"Yeah, but the French." He pointed at a green folder. "The stapled report."

I glanced at Rohan who shrugged, but retrieved it from the file.

"Check out the second page," Drio said.

I leaned over the table for a better look. It was Drio's findings on his session with Evelyn. The relevant section was a detailed explana-tion of her possessions, including a locket with a French quote en-graved on it that she'd worn around her neck. "On n'aime que ce qu'on ne possède pas tout entier," Rohan read in a terrible French accent.

I giggled.

"It means–" Rohan looked for the translation.

We love only what we do not wholly possess, I thought.

"'We only love what we don't fully possess,'" Drio said. "Could sum up their relationship."

"We done?" I asked. "I want to go over this list."

Rohan handed over a printout of my travel details. "I'm on an ear-lier flight than you two. Your plane lands Thursday morning Prague time, so I want you in the hotel lobby by 2PM. I'll have Samson there so you can meet him."

"Got it." Scooping up the photos and some files, I retired to my room to figure out my plan of attack since the only thing I agreed with them on about me playing groupie was the bait part.

I spent the next couple of hours watching every video online of Samson that I could find. Didn't matter if it was formal interviews, award-show sound bytes, or party footage, I studied it all to see how he handled himself and who he surrounded himself with.

I rearranged the pillows behind my back, sitting against my headboard with my legs stretched out, computer on my lap, scrolling through red carpet snaps and Instagram pics.

Drio had reached out to Samson's posse long before Rohan agreed to do the theme song but they'd rebuffed all attempts to buddy up until learning of Drio's own entourage pedigree, prompting Drio to dub them starfuckers. He could handle them just fine. It was the women that Samson kept company with who were of interest to me. I flipped between windows at the various stills frozen there.

Two things were abundantly clear. One, he was not picking his companions for their scintillating conversation, since he didn't seem to let his dates speak. Every single one of them, from famous swimsuit models to porn stars, always clad in short, tight dresses, mutely let themselves be led around.

This led to the second revelation which was they all possessed a status that I lacked. Drio could tart me up all he wanted, but D-list strumpet wasn't going to cut it. Sadly, there was no way to fabricate any kind of fame for me. Not at this late date.

I'd have to catch Samson's interest another way.

It brought me back to that quote on Evelyn's locket. After Googling it, I learned it was attributed to Marcel Proust, which didn't help any. But the idea kept looping back through my head like a song on repeat. We love only what we do not wholly possess.

Samson worked in envy the way Michelangelo worked in marble. Was it possible to catch his interest through my utter disinterest? Not to make him love me, but to want me? Want to impress me? Physical type aside, he seemed to go for women who didn't present any type of challenge. Hot arm-candy. Not to dismiss the intelligence of his dates, but chances were, when these women were with Samson, they kept pithy insights and witty repartee to a minimum. They knew their role, lesser lights revolving around Samson's bright sun.

Only he was allowed to be the center of the universe with everyone—dates, posse, and general public—being pulled into his gravitational orbit. I expected overt evil from a demon, but Samson wasn't forcing anyone to buy into what he was selling or do his bidding. Merely presenting himself as the de facto pinnacle to aspire to, then exploiting our all-too-mortal weaknesses for his own gain.

I pulled my blanket around my shoulders.

Right or wrong, people worshipped celebrities and would do anything to be like them. Knowing this, Samson was letting us do all the heavy lifting. Simply giving us a final nudge into the misery necessary to achieve whatever his big picture goal was. Shades of gray brilliance.

Though whether that made him a demon or a psychopath remained to be seen.

I stared at his grinning mug on my laptop. "If you're getting everything you ever wanted, Samson, then how do I make you want me? How do I become your own personal challenge to conquer?"

Evelyn had been sexy. She'd been flat-out beautiful. Smart too, I'd bet. She had a Proust quote around her neck, not a pop lyric. Had her intelligence been a turn-off? That would rule out the sexy librarian look. I searched online but couldn't find any photos of the two of them together to determine body language.

My stomach growled, interrupting my investigation. I stretched out my neck and shoulders deciding this was as good a time as any to take a break and headed downstairs into the kitchen to make dinner. Buttered toast and a glass of juice coming right up.

I drummed my fingers on the dark granite countertop waiting for the toast to pop. When it did, I flipped each piece over to examine them, before turning them back over once more.

"Whatever are you doing?" Rohan pulled a bag of pre-cut veggies out of the industrial-sized, stainless steel fridge in the wall of white cabinets.

"Checking for the right-side-up," I said.

"On bread?"

I flipped the piece over for him in show-and-tell fashion. "When you slice bread, that results in a right-side-up and wrong-side-up. Like wood grains. It's important to butter the toast on the correct side."

"Or what? Solar eclipse? Tides out of whack?"

"General fuckery ensues. You can't be eating upside-down bread, Snowflake." I munched on my toast, watching as he chopped up garlic and ginger then fried them up in a pan. "How come you don't just use your own blades to cut the stuff?"

"Because my blades are weapons, not cutlery."

I rolled my eyes. "Sorry." My stomach growled again. "That smells good."

Rohan pulled out a bunch of dried spices from a cupboard. "It'll taste good, too."

He handled the chopping knife with ease and I drank in his relaxed stance with just a frisson of danger in how fast he used the blade. Stubble scruffed along his jaw, and the shadows on his face shifted as he took a sip of wine. It was a good look for him. The look of a guy cooking his date dinner. Satisfying her before he satisfied her.

I dropped my toast on the plate, its taste suddenly lacking. Picking up the wine bottle, I grabbed an empty juice glass and sloshed the liquid in.

Rohan closed his eyes briefly in pain.

"Do we have any photos of Evelyn and Samson together?" The spicy wine hit my palette and went down real smooth. All righty. Liquid dinner it was.

"Yeah. In the red folder in the library. Why?"

"Evelyn possessed a different beauty than the women Samson surrounded himself with, but she'd also been a part of his life for longer than anyone else we could find. I want to know if her feelings were reciprocated, let alone if my love theory is even correct."

"What we have won't help you. They're mostly set photos documenting them working together."

"Damn. Still, I'll check them out." I poured more wine. "Drio might have a point about not talking. Or rather, not appearing too smart in front of Samson."

"That's a safe assumption." Rohan plated the veggies, going back to the fridge for one final item.

"Cilantro? It doesn't need it," I said through a forkful of stir fry.

Rohan lunged for me, wrestling the fork away. "Make your own dinner."

"But yours is so–" I squealed. "No tickling!" Of course that just amped him up further. Silly boy didn't realize that I'd had years of practice suppressing my laughter in such situations, thanks to Ari's merciless tickle torture. Half-bent over, I bit down on my lip, grateful that Rohan attacked from behind and couldn't see my strained expression. "Doesn't even affect me."

"You're a dirty liar," he whispered, wrapping his arms around me and kissing my neck.

I dropped the square ceramic plate on the counter. "More a dirty exaggerator." I tried–and failed–to suppress the shiver that racked my body at the touch of his lips under my ear. I turned in his arms, smoothing the pulse beating in his throat with my finger. Feeling the smooth, soft patch right under the rasp of his jaw-line stubble, like a secret that only I knew. "Wanna really exert yourself over me?"

He pressed his forehead against mine. "I have to go to the studio. Put in some song time."

"It's okay." I patted his cheek as he released me. "Will you be working late?"

"Probably." His regret was genuine.

I picked up my wine, heading for the library and the photos of Evelyn when Rohan pressed the plate of stir fry into my hands. "Eat, Lolita."

I smiled, then gasped. Lolita. That was it. I raced off with my food, the pieces of my plan falling into place.

4

Best teacher I've ever had, but make one dumb mistake and she'll eviscerate you, wrote a commenter on ratemyprofessor. com. I scrolled through the other comments for Dr. Gelman and found similar sentiments. Her academic page at Ben Gurion University in Be'er-Sheva, Israel was populated with lists and lists of her articles on climate change, and her photo showed a woman in her mid-sixties with leathery olive skin, white streaking her black hair, and a no-nonsense expression.

I liked her already.

The rest of my day included last-minute trips to the mall and my parents' place to raid my closet for some Samson-attracting clothes, memorizing the list of demons and their various known traits to the best of my ability, then obsessively checking to see if the scientist had replied to my meeting request.

She hadn't, so I decided to call Leo. My bestie answered the phone sounding more subdued than usual.

"Oh, no. Did your date with the soulful poet go badly?"

Leo gagged. "He had more estrogen than my last girlfriend. I can't be around guys who make me lactate."

"Sorry, pumpkin. Better luck next time."

"There's got to be a group of hot guys who are smart and funny."

"There is." I sorted through my underwear, putting the pairs coming with me into a pile. "They're all sleeping with other guys."

Leo sighed. "I should have been born a gay man."

"Yeah, but then I'd never have a shot with you."

"I like that you dream big. Okay," she said, sounding more cheerful, "gotta go play Switzerland and help broker a transaction between two clients." I didn't bother asking for details, even though I itched to go crash that party. Leo worked part-time as a P.I. with demon clientele. She used much of the info she gathered for good, being an informant to the Brotherhood, much like the Brotherhood used its David Security International front to gain access to high-powered players and secrets that otherwise might elude us.

I tossed my empty suitcase onto my bed. "Good luck and watch your back. I'm off to Prague tomorrow morning."

"That oughta be interesting."

"You have no idea." I filled her in on my hope that I'd soon have a way to get Ari inducted as Rasha. "Can you stay in touch with him while I'm gone? Maybe go out together?"

"Of course." I heard her car door slam. "So long as dickhead doesn't accompany us."

I tried a couple of combinations on the built-in lock before I got the sequence right and the suitcase fell open. "Dickhead is Ari's personal bodyguard right now so please be nice."

Kane and Leo had met while the Nava-guarding Rasha boys were suffering from demon-compelled memory loss about my existence. Had we any *Men in Black* memory-erasing tech, they'd have used it on Leo. But occasionally people did find out about us and it's not like the Brotherhood made them disappear. I didn't think. If they learned about Leo's half-goblin status though? They'd dust her in a heartbeat. It would be my death warrant, too.

Rohan was the one Rasha who knew the truth about Leo, and he was leaving her alone. For that, I'd be forever grateful.

"Gotta book," she said. "Schmugs."

"Schmugs," I replied. My chest got warm and gooey at her matter-of-fact usage of our good-bye, shortened from "Hugs, schmugs." Having Leo back in my life meant everything to me.

Packing took no time at all. I propped my suitcase by the door, casting around for something to distract me, too restless to sleep right now. Grabbing my phone, I scrolled through my music, then set it in my blue and silver bedside speaker dock. After my Achilles tendon snapped in high school on the verge of achieving my dream of tapping professionally, I'd quit dancing. Cold turkey, locked down that part of myself. It had taken becoming Rasha, and more specifically talking with Rohan about his own creative experiences to realize how miserable I'd been without tap in my life.

Kneeling on my fluffy area rug, I rummaged under my bed for the tap shoes that Rohan had brought over from my parents' house as a surprise. A gesture that I didn't want to examine too closely. Sliding my feet in, the worn soles fitting me like a second skin, I hit play. I could have chosen anything to dance to; old swing, modern jazz, pop, even salsa music worked, but right now I wanted Rohan.

Phrasing.

Snowflake's raspy growl filled the room, singing the lyrics of his first hit, "Toccata and Fugue." A stream of consciousness love song, it never failed to fill me with a wild recklessness, an electric flow dancing over my skin that had nothing to do with my newly acquired magic. I tried to stay in the present and not the memory of Rohan singing these lyrics to me in a park late at night a few weeks ago.

The girl with the lightning eyes and the boy with demons in his soul.

As freaked as I'd been at those lyrics, Rohan had practically swallowed his tongue before the second chorus. That didn't seem to stop me from obsessively listening to the song every time I danced these days, however.

Kicking the rug out of the way, I tapped a percussive counterpart rhythm, my heel stamps, open thirds, and five-count riffs landing with gunfire precision on the hardwood floor. A siren's call, the melody swayed through my body, making my blood sing.

I danced until I was too tired to worry about the outcomes of all the balls in motion right now, and then I passed out, laying my head as close as possible to the speakers, with Rohan's voice on repeat, a quiet lullaby to send me into dreamland.

Not even a tendril of light slithered through my blinds when I awoke Wednesday morning. I cracked an eye to look at my alarm clock. 5AM. I flipped over, pulling the covers over my head, but sleep was elusive. Truth be told, I was wound tight, caught between nerves and exhilaration for the trip.

Slipping on a robe and socks, I padded into the kitchen for the first of several coffees. I filled my cup, adding copious amounts of milk and sugar.

Rohan was on his way out, airport bound for his earlier flight. He snapped his suitcase zipper into its built-in lock. "You ready? Got your passport? Your Nikki wardrobe?"

Would he go double-check Drio? Oh wait, I knew that answer.

I slammed my cup down, liquid sloshing onto the counter. "Pass. Port. Is what? For big shiny bird in sky?"

Rohan's lips compressed into a thin line. "This isn't a joke. Get focused on this assignment and your role in it."

"Don't worry," I sneered. "I'll be the picture of adoration."

"Yeah, I'm already feeling the love."

I curled my fingers around the mug, the heat from the coffee seeping through the ceramic. Fucking, fleeing, and fighting, oh my. I'd rather have lions, tigers, and bears.

"Have a good flight." That was the second time in as many weeks that I'd uttered that phrase to cut off a loaded conversation with Rohan.

I brushed past him, taking the coffee with me.

The next few hours dragged by. Drio and I were supposed to ride to the airport in style, but since it became apparent there was no way Drio, me, and our luggage would fit into Kane's Porsche, I called Ari and we all crammed into our dad's Prius instead. I made small talk with my brother in the front seat and tried not to think about how much I regretted drinking that third cup.

This good-bye was far easier than the one my twin and I had said when I'd moved into the chapter house. Still, when we unloaded our luggage in the passenger zone at the Vancouver International Airport, I hugged my brother hard.

"Don't be stupid there." Ari's blue-gray eyes, the only feature my blond twin and I shared, were filled with concern.

"It's not my plan, but you never know."

"I'm serious. Nothing you're doing," he gave me a pointed look indicating he was speaking about Gelman and getting himself Rasha'd up, "is worth you being hurt. Things get hairy, you step away. And by step, I mean run."

I punched him in the arm. "Take your own advice, you hypocrite."

A bleak expression flashed over his face before he rubbed his jaw. "I'm dealing best I can."

My heart shredded into a million pieces at how lost he was. I'd tried yelling, begging, crying–nothing I'd said had stopped Ari. So I'd find Gelman and get the idiot inducted. "Get killed, leave me an only child, and I will find a way to reanimate you, visit humiliation galore upon your zombified corpse, and then kill you again."

That got me a shadow of a grin. I'd take it. One more giant hug for Ari, a smacked kiss on the cheek from Kane, and then it was down to Drio and me wheeling our suitcases into the airport. Being stuck with someone who despised me for the next twelve or so hours as my sole travel companion? Good times.

"I have a very important role for you for the flight over," Drio said as we approached the ticket counter.

Sweet! I cocked my fingers at him like a gun. "You got it. What?"

"Mute." Light glinted off the skull ring on his middle finger, the glamour on his Rasha ring fittingly emblematic of his assholery.

"Look at my face." I waved my hand around it. "Now put all your admittedly limited powers of deduction to the test and tell me if it says 'sass me.'"

Drio bared his teeth at me, while the airport employee was given our passports with a charming grin that had her touching her hair, flustered.

Even then, I might have tried making conversation with him, because I got bored on flights, but upon checking in, I learned that being Rasha meant traveling business class. Time to milk every perk out of this ticket.

I started in the business class passenger lounge in the airport, an enormous rectangle of a room divided into eating and lounging, with one wall of floor-to-ceiling windows providing a view onto the runways. First stop? The booze, of course. It was free and on tap. I liberally doctored an espresso with Bailey's because even I wasn't going to guzzle vodka before 10AM.

On the job.

Then I pretty much skipped the espresso and kept topping up the Irish cream. I found some ice and a splash of milk, and bam! Daily calcium content dealt with. Two plates of waffles, bacon, and sausage for iron helped soak it all up. I finished with a glass of orange juice to keep the scurvy away. All in all, a damn healthy meal.

Belly full, stack of magazines in hand, I moved over to the reading and relaxation area. I wriggled my butt against my comfy chair. This was seriously heaven. I surreptitiously checked out my fellow travelers waiting for their flights to be announced. When it came to being chosen, demon hunters had nothing on the people in this place. Those economy schmucks waiting downstairs in the airport departure areas, stuck sitting on molded plastic with second-rate food-court choices were cattle.

I'd never traveled business class before and this was a revelation. I felt like Eddy Murphy in that old *Saturday Night Live* sketch *White Like Me,* when undercover as a white man on a bus with only Caucasian passengers, the driver puts on "Life is a Cabaret," and a party breaks out complete with cocktails. This was even better because all races and religions were embraced. Cough up the dough, and you too would be welcomed into the promised land.

"Promised land, huh?" A jocular businessman smiled at me.

Too much Irish Cream. "Damn straight, the promised land." I held up my glass in cheers. "L'chaim."

The fun didn't stop there. When we boarded, there was no walk through the fancy part of the plane, eyes downcast, shuffling toward an economy seat that barely fit a child. I had my own roomy, lay-flat seat by the window and it wasn't even next to anyone. I didn't have to make eye contact with a stranger or worse, speak to them about my bladder and bowel needs.

I spent a good twenty minutes figuring out all the buttons on my console, testing everything from seat position to my media center with its plethora of movie choices. Getting the tray out took another five minutes, after which I tore in to my fleece blanket, pillow, and fuzzy slippers–which I put on before we'd even taxied. Items in the complimentary toiletries bag were sorted by fragrance and usefulness. By the time the chef–yes, chef–came around to introduce herself and give me a small printed menu, I'd spread out to the point of looking like I'd lived in my seat for about three years.

My lovely flight attendant Steve didn't judge. Nope. He took my meal order with a smile, enjoying my enthusiastic oohs and aahs when he delivered my appetizer selection via a small cart. I got to pick three different types, plated personally for me onto white china with real utensils.

Movies, food, body lotion, I glutted myself. Forget ridding the world of evil, noble causes, and destiny, I was determined to ace this assignment, if only for more overseas gigs. Despite my desire to catch up on as many Oscar contenders as possible, I fell asleep at some point, until I was gently shaken awake by Steve, asking if I was ready for breakfast. Uh, hells yeah!

But all good things must come to an end, and all too soon, we landed in Heathrow for our transfer flight to Prague. There was no time to sample the delights of the British lounge. I raced after Drio, hauling ass to make our connection.

Much to our mutual dismay, we were seated next to each other for this flight. Drio sprawled out and immediately fell asleep, leaving me to eat all his snacks and the profiterole that came with his meal. At least he smelled nice, kind of woodsy. The final perk of the voyage was our luggage being unloaded first off the carousel at the Prague airport.

Other than the briefest glance to see if I was following him, Drio didn't bother with personal contact.

The wind hit me in the chest the second we stepped outside. I hunched deeper into my coat, sitting on my large, silver, hard-sided suitcase and shivering, while Drio hailed a taxi and gave the driver the name of our hotel.

"Ah. In New Town," the cabbie informed us.

This was my first time in Prague and in the maybe half hour it took to drive into the city, it vaulted to the top of my favorite places list. Prague reminded me of a smaller, more vibrant Paris. It shared the old, fabulous architecture, except while Paris buildings tended to a monotonous cream-gray stone—one of the first things I'd noticed when my family had visited several years back—many of the ones in Prague were colored in soft butterscotch, blues, and pinks. A formidable black gothic castle loomed over the town, while bridges and spires dotted the cityscape.

I had my face pressed to the window for the entire ride.

Our chatty taxi driver was more than happy to point out various neighborhoods and landmarks, like the enormous red metronome on the hill with its swinging arm that was over seventy-five feet long and a reminder of the legacy left by Stalin and communism in the city. He noted the famous pedestrian-only Charles Bridge in the distance as we crossed the Vltava river that snaked through the city.

Finally, the driver turned down alongside a long, skinny square with an imposing statue of a guy on a horse. The plaza gently sloped down, flanked on both sides by more incredible buildings with stores at ground level. "Wenceslas Square," the cabbie said.

"You mean the guy they sing Christmas carols about?" I asked.

"Just so." He stopped at the bottom. Brand name shops lined the bisecting street in either direction, while a pedestrian-only square stood beyond that. The driver pointed along the pedestrian area to the right. "Faster if you walk. About 300 meters."

I took in the architecture that looked pretty much like the rest of the architecture in the city. "Isn't the hotel in the New Town?" Where were the glass and steel skyscrapers?

The driver laughed. "Old Town dates back to 1100 AD. New Town 1300s."

"Upstart neighborhood."

Drio rolled his eyes at me, but to his credit, he gave the driver a healthy tip. We lugged our suitcases over the checkered pavement toward the hotel. I noted a lot of great stores that I'd be hitting up once our mission was completed.

Even my suitcase wheels spun with a cheerful clattering sound.

Drio turned off the pedestrian area and there it was, Praha WS Hotel. A five-story boutique hotel painted vibrant yellow with arched windows, it featured intricate plaster details, and black and cream trim.

"Is Samson staying here?" I asked Drio.

Since it was work related, he didn't grumble at the question. "No. He's at the Four Seasons. Rohan wanted to stay someplace away from our target."

We swerved to avoid a family of weary-looking tourists with broad Aussie accents, bogged down with shopping bags. "Where's King's posse staying?"

"The Four Seasons. As am I. I want to be able to party with the boys. "

"Why are you here then?"

He gave me a tight smile. "I'm delivering Rohan's property."

I looked in confusion at his suitcase until the penny dropped. "Thanks, but I'm good. You can go."

"You have the credit card the reservation was booked under?"

I held out my hand for it. Drio kept walking, pulling the silver handle of the hotel's glass front door open and heading inside.

Since Rohan wasn't due to be here with Samson for a while, I'd been allowed to travel in normal person clothes instead of the easy access zipper-fest the guys were expecting. I kept my coat on and my head down for most of the check-in though, letting Drio handle it.

As baroque as the outside was, the inside was contemporary clean-lines. The black floors gleamed with a high-sheen polish, and the reception desk was a floating slab of the same black. Two long panels backlit in a burnt gold took up most of the wall behind the desk. An elevator bank was situated on the left, while a couple of steps at the back led to white linen tables in a small restaurant.

Drio handed me the keycard along with my room number. "2PM," he reminded me. He checked his phone. "That gives you a couple of hours to eat, unpack, and get ready. Ro is with Samson and his crew right now at the Four Seasons but he's bringing King over here under pretext of giving him some sample tracks for the song."

"He's inviting Samson to sing on it?"

Drio nodded. "Since wherever Samson goes, his two closest buddies follow, I'll hook up with them and make sure I'm here for the meet. In case you need me."

That surprised me and I guess it must have shown because he gave me a crooked grin, only somewhat less psychotic than the one directed at demons. "They take you out, I don't get the pleasure when the Brotherhood gives the order."

It was as good a reassurance as I could have expected from him. "Later, gator," I said, and went to put on my war paint.

My third-floor room wasn't bad. A bit small but bright. The walls, furniture, and linens on the queen bed were gleaming white. Red accents in the curtains and top blanket punched some color into the place. No sexy shower or anything and not much of a view from my room either. I'd been warned that I'd be checked into a basic. Since I was here as Rohan's groupie, common sense dictated I'd be pleasuring the master in his own opulent suite. My place would be more of a dumping ground for my stuff since big time rock stars needed their space. If Samson managed to breach the doorway and visit me, the room wouldn't seem out of place.

I flipped my suitcase open, pulling out the clothing I'd packed on top as my first attack gear. Samson liked the blatant. Red, black, short, tight. I went for white. Pure as the driven snow, me.

I wriggled the black-and-white houndstooth mini skirt that hit mid-thigh up over my white lace bikini briefs. Even if no one else ever saw them, the lingerie was part of my method acting, my from-the-skin-out character build. I'd paired the briefs with a white lace demi bra that pushed my C cups up into lush globes. That bra was a total score. Getting that much support without any metal underwire was a feat but I'd found it. I'd learned the hard way that metal against my body when my electric powers were triggered led to burning and pain. I'd even stopped wearing jewelry other than my Rasha ring, which didn't cause me any problems.

According to Ari, Rasha magic stemmed from personality dysfunction, like how Kane with his poison power was a literal manifestation of him being toxic in relationships. As far as I was concerned, my magic was simply electric awesomeness and not, as Ari had said my "desire to shock others and keep them at bay made tangible."

Next on was a tailored white men's dress shirt, worn with one more button open than polite society would deem decent. The fall of the neckline allowed for a tantalizing glimpse of my rack.

Pointing my toes, I rolled tmy white thigh-high stockings up, adjusting the elastic top so that about an inch of skin showed between their top and the skirt's hem.

Back to the suitcase I went for my hair and make-up bags, then I ported everything into the bathroom. Using a shit-ton of mousse, I finger-styled my curls into a tousled, sexy mane. The kind of hair that guys ached to sink their hands into. I'd used such a style to excellent effect on many an occasion. Lips to match the hair via a scarlet lipstick with plumping properties to get that slightly swollen look. My eyes and cheeks I kept fairly understated, lightly blending concealer and brushing on foundation to brighten my post-travel complexion and adding the smallest pop of eyeliner and pale brown shadow to make my eyes look striking without stealing the show. The effort required to look "natural" was ridiculous.

I slid my feet into Mary Jane stilettos that completed my sexed-up schoolgirl look, then reviewed my reflection, pleased with the results. I checked the clock. I was due to meet Rohan and Samson in five minutes. I slid my keycard into my bra, my hands shaking with the fine edge of jet lag and adrenaline, then headed out.

Rohan was going to freak when he saw me. A silver lining to this suck-ass role after all.

5

I used my time in the empty elevator to close my eyes and center myself. This was no different than any other performance I'd given. When the doors dinged open, I was ready, sashaying into the lobby, my features arranged in an expression of boredom.

Rohan and Samson stood out like two entrenched pillars of testosterone in a sea of frothy high-gleam. Their commanding presence demanded a more majestic surrounding, almost overwhelming the sleek, low lines of the modern furnishings. Rohan had his back to me, all leather jacket and spiked-up hair, the light glinting off his multiple silver rings as he chatted with Samson. I stepped back around the corner, peering out. From this angle, I could see them but they couldn't see me.

Samson, live and in the flesh, was shorter than I expected. Rohan was about six-foot-two and he had a good three inches on Samson. In my stilettos, I'd be eye-level with the actor, which suited me fine.

He sported jeans, a beat-up brown leather jacket, and a T-shirt, all too calculatingly casual to be cheap. I bet myself a hundred bucks he'd smell of that perfect unisex blend of light citrus designed to tease the senses, versus Rohan's more primitive musk and iron scent. I'd have to keep up the mantra of "potential demon" because looking between him and Rohan, Samson wasn't the one registering as the greater threat.

I spotted Drio as promised, hanging with Samson's inner circle. There was actually a largish group with him here in Prague, but Drio had targeted two specific dudes as being the closest to King. Hangers-on, not fellow actors. Too bad. The skinny jittery one in the baggy jeans could have found steady work as a toady hustler in *Hard Knock Strife*. I wondered if he was coked up. His buddy, busy texting, was a straight-up hearts and skulls wearing douchebag with his head buzzed in wavy lines. Sexual predator as higher aspiration.

Drio's eyes widened a fraction but he didn't glare at my deviation from the plan. Instead he looked at Rohan and Samson, his expression thoughtful.

I clicked across the floor, rating a disapproving frown from the buttoned-up desk clerk before he smoothed it into a bland courteous smile as I placed a hand on Rohan's shoulder to let him know I'd arrived.

"Samson," Rohan said, "this is–" He turned toward me for the first time, and I fought hard to keep my bored look in the face of his stunned expression.

"Lolita," I supplied. My voice matched my vibe. Sulky and unimpressed.

Samson scanned my body like a barcode. "Samson King." His attitude was all, "yeah, it's me, be thrilled." Seems I didn't merit the famous charm. Yet.

Sorry to disappoint, asshole. I flicked my gaze away, checking out the lobby as if looking for someone more interesting.

Samson's eyes narrowed.

Rohan's hand curled around my hip. "Lolita," he admonished. It may have come off as him getting me to be polite in the face of this amazing superstar but the growled warning had nothing to do with etiquette.

With a huff, I propped my chin on Rohan's shoulder, half-twisted toward him, but meeting Samson's eyes. Then I raised an eyebrow as if waiting for the star to impress me.

Samson tilted his head and smiled. The look that had landed him *People* magazine's "Sexiest Man Alive" cover. Ugh.

Moving away from Rohan, I raked a hand through my curls, the motion causing my shirt to fall open that much more. Samson obligingly looked.

I trailed my fingers down Rohan's arm. Ignoring Samson. "You done?"

"Text me later," Rohan told Samson. "We'll figure out a set visit."

"For sure." Samson jerked his chin at me. "Bring her."

I squeezed Rohan's wrist, willing him to pick up on that cue and go into caveman mode.

"She's busy." He placed his hand on the small of my back, escorting me off.

Samson stepped sideways, blocking us. Speaking directly to me. "Want to come?"

I shrugged. "Been there. Done that." He could infer the type of set—blockbuster, porn.

"Not like this. Come watch the big chase sequence."

"Stand around and watch your stunt guys?"

Samson puffed up. "I do my own stunts." Said with a touch of annoyance since this was well-documented fact.

I let a flicker of interest leach into my gaze, my turn now to run a slow total perusal of him, while I pursed my lips, like I was considering his offer. "That could be fun." I stepped away from Rohan as I spoke.

Rohan tugged me back into place beside him, his hand hot on my arm. "We'll see."

"You do that," Samson said, not breaking eye contact with Rohan. Sweet. The challenge was on.

One of Samson's friends called over to him and the pissing contest was broken. "Namaste, bitches." A cheeky grin and one more appraising look for me, then he swaggered off.

"Demonstrating a stellar mastery of Eastern teachings, that one," I said.

Rohan planted himself in front of me. "You're pretty pleased with yourself, aren't you?"

"Yup."

"If you can't follow directions, then you're on the next flight home."

I curled my fingers into his belt loops, so no one could tell how deep my nails gouged my palms. "Samson's watching us," I murmured, pouting. "Also, your directions sucked balls. Samson wasn't going to give a shit about a pale imitation nobody of every chick he'd ever bagged."

Rohan nuzzled my ear, his nip hard enough to make me wince. "You should have run it past me."

I leaned in, my hands between our chests, calling my magic up enough so he could feel it thrumming through his shirt, though it wasn't visible to anyone else. "You and Drio wouldn't have listened. You were too busy casting a Whitesnake video."

"Push me one more time." Rohan ran a finger over my lips.

"You wouldn't."

He raised an eyebrow, leaning in until his mouth almost brushed mine.

I stuttered out a breath, stunned into a shocked freeze at his dirty tactics.

"Get a room," Drio called out. I almost did a double take at his perfect American accent. He sounded like any generic TV or film actor. His group burst into raucous laughter, then Samson snapped his fingers, pointing off toward the lounge on the far side of the lobby. They all obediently trotted after him.

Keeping my relief under wraps, I switched off my power and stepped back. "My tactic worked. I was right."

"You were lucky."

"It wasn't luck. I deconstructed that asswipe." I rubbed a hand over my neck. "Trust has to go two ways here, Snowflake. I'm trying to work smart, not hard."

Rohan jabbed a finger at me. "No more going off script. That's a direct order. I won't have you wreck everything Drio and I have done to date."

"Minion. Got it." I patted his cheek. "But do remember that I snagged his interest and keep up the pretense of me belonging to you. He wants what he can't have."

"The chase *is* half the attraction," he replied.

"Then I'll be sure to conduct a lively one."

Before I could hear his retort, a woman called out to him in a voice that was pure Southern California drawl. "Ro? Is that you?"

He turned, his face lighting up as a supermodel launched herself into his arms. Not up to dealing with bitchy models wanting to play possession games over rock stars, I attempted to leave and give them their moment.

Rohan made no move to stop me but the woman smiled at me with genuine friendliness. "Hi."

"Hello." My greeting was a bit more wary. On closer inspection, she didn't fit the supermodel bill. Sure, of East Indian heritage, she was luminous and gorgeous. But her large dark eyes and heart-shaped face were free of make-up, other than lip gloss. Pin-straight silky hair fell to her shoulders. The small rectangle-framed glasses she wore enhanced her beauty as did the loose trousers and cute embroidered coat on her slender frame, but they didn't scream diva.

Cheeks red from the cold, she nudged Rohan with an easy familiarity. "Introduce us, dummy. Maya taught you better." Old family friend, perhaps? Family friends were good.

Rohan slung an arm over her shoulder. Well, he couldn't be rude to her if his mom might hear about it. "This is Dr. Lily Prasad. Lils, this is..." Rohan shifted from side-to-side, his voice flat. "Lolita."

"Doctor?" I did up a button on my shirt.

"Almost doctor," Lily corrected with a laugh. "I'm doing my doctoral dissertation right now. Finishing this summer." She held up her crossed fingers.

Rohan looked at her fondly. "Lily is a geophysicist studying electrostatics." He grinned at her, his even white teeth flashing. "Did I get it right?"

"Yeah. Only took you how many years? It's a pleasure," she said to me.

"Likewise." A geophysicist? Beauty and brains. A smart old family friend then? Like the nerdy girl Rohan had grown up feeling sorry for? I looked at her again. Who was I kidding? This girl had been born a swan.

Still, I couldn't believe how nice she was being to me, especially as it looked like *my* sole area of study was oral fixations. Now I really tried to get away but Rohan removed his arm from Lily to catch my wrist, keeping me trapped here in punishment.

I stood there as they got caught up, with Lily excited to hear that he was singing again, trying to free myself from his grip, but it was like trying to pry loose the safety bar on the roller coaster. No one was getting off this ride until it was finished.

Rohan asked Lily what she was doing here.

She pushed her glasses up her nose. "The hotel I wanted to stay at was overbooked."

He shook his head, chuckling. "Always with the literal, Lils. I meant in Prague."

She blushed. "Shut up."

Was my smile still on my face? Reasonable facsimile. Close enough.

"I'm attending an environmental physics conference," she said.

"What?" Oy vey! It was bad enough meeting this super smart woman under these conditions. If I ran into her at the conference while looking for Dr. Gelman, she might wonder what someone like me could possibly be doing there.

Rohan and Lily turned identical looks of confusion on me.

"I mean, what are you doing there? Giving a speech?"

"I wish. No, I'm attending on behalf of my advisor." Lily's phone beeped. She pulled it out of her jacket. "I swear he's the devil. I mention his name and there's yet another email from him with more work for me."

I cut a sideways glance at Rohan. "I know how you feel."

He smiled sarcastically back at me.

Lily checked the email, rolling her eyes at its contents. "Okay, like the dude is staggeringly brilliant." I smothered a smile at how valley girl she sounded. "But he's also either incredibly passive-aggressive or seriously losing it because he keeps sending me messages in his native French, which he knows I don't speak." She stabbed at the phone. "I had to bookmark Google translate."

"Don't use that. It's lingual soup," I said.

"It totally is, but it's easily accessible."

I held out my free hand. "I can translate it for you."

Rohan released me to cross his arms. "You speak French." He made it sound like the only phrase I could possibly know was "Voulez-vous couchez avec moi."

"I didn't just hatch a pretty blank slate," I snapped. "I was edumacated and everything."

Lily shot me an odd look, her phone held up but not yet handed over. Whoops. Maybe groupies didn't mouth off to their idols? I couldn't think of any way to salvage the moment so I smiled and took her phone. Translating the email was a piece of cake, just some follow up about a panel he wanted her to attend.

I read the translation out to Lily, then handed her phone back.

"You are a superstar, Lolita," she said, already typing her response.

I savored Rohan's dumbfounded look. But it hurt too. "Twelve years of French Immersion, Snowflake," I murmured. "Don't stress yourself."

I'm still outclassed here.

I made my excuses and left, beelining for the lounge and narrowly avoiding Samson and his gang leaving. Drio stood at the bar, paying.

Draping myself over the smooth white bar top, I helped myself to a drinks menu.

"A lemon radler." I smiled at the scruffy bartender. Anyone about to serve me booze or poke me with a needle was deserving of smiles. Them being cute didn't hurt either.

Winking, he acknowledged my order.

Drio scrunched up his face in disgust. "Way to ruin beer," he said in his normal voice.

"Way to get one of my fruit servings." I watched the bartender flick the cap off. "What's with the accent?" I asked Drio.

"Just another good 'ol American boy," he drawled. "Makes more sense I'd know Ro if I'm from the US."

The bartender reached under the bar.

"Don't worry about a glass." I took the bottle, condensation dripping down its sides, savoring the first burst of fruity alcohol on my tongue.

"Who's that? She looks familiar," Drio said, nodding over at Lily and Rohan still talking in the lobby.

"Dr. Lily Prasad. Beautiful genius."

His face lit up with an interested gleam. I braced myself, expecting some comment on her body or stating that he wanted an introduction. "Lightning girl."

My beer hit the ground.

6

I jumped out of the way of the pooling liquid. "What?"

Drio, staring over at her and nodding, was oblivious to my shock. "Yeah. Her glasses threw me. She studies lightning or some shit. A physicist, right?"

"Geophysicist studying electrostatics," I parroted. Lily was the one that Rohan had written "Toccata and Fugue" for? The original lightning girl? The love of his life? I bent down to pick up the bottle shards, cutting my palm on one fat piece. Holding my bleeding hand up, I grabbed the towel that the bartender had brought to sop up the mess. "Sorry," I said.

"Leave it. You need a Band-Aid." The bartender jogged off.

Drio, still checking Lily out, whistled. "She's even better looking now." With that, he left to catch up with Samson.

I wrapped the towel around my hand. Sure, my Rasha healing would take care of this gash in a jiffy but I liked the tourniquet sensation this gave me. A sharp focused pain. I willed myself to move since I couldn't stand here by myself, emotionally exposed like this.

My chest twisted in self-loathing as I caught sight of my reflection in the shiny mirror behind the bar. What had seemed so clever when dealing with Samson seemed so tawdry when compared to Lily.

I forced my breaths to keep time with the steady gurgle of the coffee pot by the bar sink.

The chatter of voices from the lobby washed over me, while the warm air from the register in the ceiling above me ruffled my hair.

I wished I could turn back time. Erase that night in the park with Rohan singing a song neither of us wanted to hear. Maybe without it, our fuck buddy status would have stayed easy and fun. And why force me to witness his reunion with Lily? Some sort of payback for going off-book?

The bartender peeled the towel away, tossing it into the sink behind the bar. He caught my wounded hand, turning it palm up. Although the bleeding had stopped, he pressed the fat, square Band-Aid in place with a feather-light touch. "Are you sure you're fine?" He continued to hold my hand, a smile in his eyes.

I smiled back, my facial muscles on autopilot while my brain stuttered on Lily being lightning girl.

"She's good."

The bartender dropped my hand at Rohan's growl. He gave us a long assessing look, then shrugged. "Just checking." He disappeared into the back depths of the lounge.

I sorted through and discarded a million comments as Rohan stood there taking up far too much room and more than his fair share of oxygen. "Problem?"

He arched an eyebrow. "You tell me."

I ripped off the Band-Aid, tossing it in the trash. The wound would be fully healed in another minute. "Did I miss the memo where I wasn't supposed to talk to other men?"

"You're my groupie first."

That was technically true but to say it here? Now? I expected being made to feel second-best from my parents and from the Brotherhood, both of whom wanted, at least at some point, Ari as the bright shiny twin. No problem. I agreed with them. I was happy to be in his shadow, especially if it took the focus off my own path as Rasha.

But right now, second-best would have been a status upgrade because in the past fifteen minutes, Rohan had succeeded in making me feel like nothing.

No guy was allowed to do that to me.

Looping my fingers into his belt, I jerked his hips to mine. Rohan's breath caught and when I brushed my lips over the shell curves of his ear, his whole body went tense. "Prove you're worth it, baby." Then I pushed him away, stalking off without a look back, mostly sure that he followed.

The second we got inside the empty elevator, Rohan shoved me up against the wall. I groped for the third floor button, leaning into him. He ran his hands feverishly over my body, hot tingles shivering through my breasts like a sexed-up call and answer. The focused hunger in his expression had me craving more, except my rapid breathing wasn't all from arousal.

Given the barely banked rage evident in the tense bunch of Rohan's shoulders, the feeling was mutual. Hopefully, he'd show no mercy in orgasm form and not body count, though I couldn't promise the same right now.

I bit his earlobe, wanting to hurt him. Cuntessa de Spluge purred darkly.

Rohan shot me a cavalier smile in response. Holy fuck. My knees buckled.

The sprint to my room was a blur.

The second the door slammed shut behind us, Rohan edged his face in close to mine, his palm ghosting my cheek in the barest caress that sent slivery shimmers tumbling through me.

I raised my fingers to my mouth, not realizing what I'd done or that I ran them over my lips until Rohan tracked the movement, his eyes glittering dangerously.

His tongue flicked out, wetting his lower lip. He swayed in toward me and–

"No." Taking his hands in mine, I forced them behind me. Forced him to hold me there, his rings biting into my skin. Forced him to make a decision; play by my rules or go.

Alea iacta est. For better or for worse, the die was cast.

The deep raw groan in the back of his throat was his acquiescence. He walked us over to the bed, the two of us stumbling across the carpet until the mattress hit the back of my legs.

I smiled in triumph, pressing my lips against the soft hollow of his throat and suckling the sensitive skin. The press of his body against my front was positively nuclear, but the laugh track of a Czech TV program next door, audible through the thin walls, jarred me. "Next time install me in a better class of room," I said.

"Worried people will hear us?"

"Only if you make me scream." He'd released my hands, so I wormed them under his sweater, my fingers splayed against the hard ridges of his abs.

"Like that's not a given."

I laughed.

"You doubt me?" His hand tangled in my hair and he tilted my head to nip my collarbone. He made a low sound that thrummed through him.

And me. My pulse kicked up in response. Perched on the edge of the bed, I peeled off his sweater, taking the white T-shirt underneath with it. Rohan's body was a work of art: lithe, sculpted, and mouthwatering. I ran my hands over his biceps and around his back to between his shoulders where he had a tattoo of the word "Kshatriya," the warrior caste, scripted in Hindi in midnight black ink. I placed my mouth to his nipple, swirling my tongue, sinking into the familiar taste of him.

Rohan sucked in a breath. He hooked his fingers into the hem of my shirt, rolling it up my sides, buttons popping as the fabric edged up, tracing slow zigzags along my skin. Snapping open my front clasp bra, his calloused hands teased my nipples, giving me a sandpapery spike of pleasure.

Dizzy, my head lolled back, my hair sweeping my shoulder blades. My lids fell half-shut, heat slid down to my stomach. I rolled the heel of my palm over his hard cock. "I love feeling you hard," I sighed.

He nudged my skirt up to my waist. "Allow me to return in kind." His voice rasped against my skin.

I rocked against him. "It might take a while."

"That would be a shame."

"Huh?"

His right hand cupped the back of my neck, his lips trailing up my throat. He sucked my ear lobe, then whispered, "The drapes are open and that apartment building is rather close. Anyone could look inside and see me thrusting into you."

My breath hitched.

One savage tug and my underwear was flung across the room. Rohan plunged two fingers inside me.

I moaned, bracing a hand on the mattress.

"Anyone looking?" He stroked me in long, slow swipes catching my clit on each pass.

I glanced outside. There was no hiding from that window a mere foot away, putting us on display to anyone next door who cared to look. And I swear it had gotten brighter outside, all the better to spotlight us. "No," I squeaked.

"You sure?" His voice was a dark caress.

My legs trembled. I rocked back onto the heel of one stiletto, one stocking falling down like white gossamer to my ankle.

Rohan chuckled. "You like that? The idea of someone watching us. Hidden when you're so very exposed." He nudged my legs wider, his fingers thrusting deeper.

"Whatever." The word ended on a moan as my hips began to rock.

"Bent." He sounded satisfied.

I fumbled with the buckle of his belt but he arched away from me. "Your fault."

"As if."

"I didn't have exhibitionist sex before you," I blurted out in a breathy voice, despite Cuntessa admonishing me to "admit nothing."

"Good." He ran his tongue again and again over the peak of my nipple before scraping his teeth across the tip. The cool air in the hotel room failed to dampen the fever consuming me.

My fingers bit into his biceps, the steel bulge of muscle barely enough to anchor me. Dear holy... "Gonna come," I panted.

He bit my shoulder. "Not yet." He stopped and I mewled. I fucking mewled. I was torn between smacking him for killing my momentum and thanking him for prolonging the delicious pleasure coursing through me. Again I reached for his belt and again he twisted out of reach. But he did start stroking me once more. The multitude of rings he wore added a delicious friction and everywhere his bracelet rubbed against my skin left goosebumps.

I pressed against his palm, convinced I was about to lose my mind.

His mouth was hot against my ear. "I want to fuck you up against the glass of my hotel room with all of Prague laid out before us." He caught my finger, sucking it into his mouth, matching the tempo of his strokes. His tone was so conversational. So mild.

The surge of lust that ripped through me at that image was anything but.

He smirked at my wild shudder.

"Enough." My blood heated at the sight of him remaining so composed, so in control, while I was coming apart. "Get on the bed," I ordered, unbuckling my shoes and kicking them off. They fell sideways on the carpet, my stockings quickly following, topped off with the puddle of my skirt.

Rohan tilted his head to look at me standing there in my open shirt and bra, but didn't move.

"In or out, Snowflake. I'm good either way." Lie, but I'd finished myself off before and I'd do it again if I had to.

"You want to call the shots?" Rohan dropped to his knees before me. "Have at it."

I could barely breathe for the emotion clogging my chest at the sight of him, this disheveled fallen angel giving me carte blanche. I suppressed my first instinct of "suck my clit." I'd learned there were definite advantages to letting Rohan take his sweet time with all parts of my body. "Lick my thigh."

Rohan curled a hand around the back of my knee. Head tilted, he positioned himself between my legs, the soft strands of his hair tickling my inner thighs.

I giggled until, teasingly, achingly slowly, he swiped his tongue along my skin, completing his path with a bite. That's when I shivered. "I didn't order that." My voice sounded thick. My hands tightened in his hair as much for balance as punishment.

He bowed his head in atonement, pressing a kiss to the pale skin showing the faintest press of teeth marks.

"Undo your belt."

He unbuckled it without comment, then waited, his hand on his fly, a question in his eyes.

"That too."

The button popped open, Rohan again still. "The reins of power too much responsibility for you?" he teased when I continued to remain silent.

I caught my bottom lip between my teeth. "Considering my options. Why are you so willingly going along with this?" I didn't trust his motives. Usually Rohan's alphahole tendencies surfaced when I tried to direct the action.

"Because it still gets me what I want," he said.

"What's that?"

With a sharp jerk, he pulled his belt free from the loops. "You."

I tackled him to the ground, tearing at his zipper. His cock sprung free. A quick sheath of latex, two hard strokes inside me, and my orgasm ripped through me. I shattered, pulled apart by the tsunami racking my body. My vision blurred, the world falling away. My head fell back as I cried out.

My cries set him off, jaw locked tight, pupils dilated, a hard shudder racking his body.

Blood pounded in my ears. If I'd had claws, I'd have unsheathed them with a snarl. I never came that fast. Never became raw desire. I'd perfected the art of keeping that side of myself in check. Until now. I didn't want that.

Couldn't have that.

Still laying on top of him, I seethed even as I luxuriated in the feel of him still buried inside me. Rohan was not generally a two-minute wonder. But he wasn't freaking out that in me, he'd met the one person who challenged his precious control, was he?

He brushed aside the strands of my hair draped over us like a curtain and raised his head, moving in for a kiss.

My afterglow blew away. I rolled off of him into sitting position, pulling my shirt closed. No, he'd been in charge the entire time. Gotten exactly what he wanted and pushed me to a new edge in the process. I drew my legs in, resting my head on my bent knees, the only sounds in the room the rustling of his clothing as he dressed.

The buzz of my phone shattered the tense silence. I crawled over to the nightstand, and reached out, fumbling for it. Dr. Gelman had sent me a room number at the Bohemia International Hotel with the words, *twenty minutes. Don't be late.* Brilliant. Ari's best hope rested on an impossible time frame. "You need to go."

Rohan didn't answer. I didn't take my eyes off the screen even though I was desperate to see the look on his face. See if there was longing, or regret. Or tenderness.

But what if this was just another game?

7

I shimmied back into my clothes, tossing on my long coat as I hurried down to the lobby and asked the desk clerk to call me a taxi. He replied it would probably take a good half hour and I'd have better luck heading to Wenceslas Square, so I dashed over. Lo and behold there was one lone taxi pulling up to the curb. A well-dressed man was opening the back door for his wife. "Excuse me." I waved at them. "Could I please have your cab?"

The man smiled at me. "I'm sorry, but—"

"Life or death," I insisted, muscling between him and the now-open door.

"We have a meeting," the woman informed me.

I placed a hand on my stomach, letting out a low moan. "My baby." I used their momentary confusion to throw myself into the back seat and slam the door. "Bohemia International, please."

The cabbie eyed me through the rear view mirror.

"Relax. I'm not going to bust out a placenta on your back seat." Given the breakneck speed of our drive, he didn't believe me, but he did get me there mostly on time.

I pulled out some Czech koruna from my inside coat pocket, careful not to lose my keycard and phone, and thrust it at him. "This enough?" I was too fuzzy to be certain I had the currency exchange right. He grabbed the money out of my hand at "must seize ridiculous overtipping before idiot tourist realizes mistake" speed.

The Bohemia International was about five times the size of my hotel, featuring rows of stone archways at ground level and a couple of spires for good measure. Hurrying into the lobby and through an airy inner courtyard with liberal greenery and small café tables, I grabbed a glass elevator up to room 614. I wiped the sweat off my brows with the back of my sleeve, smoothed down my hair, and knocked.

The door swung open and I was sucked through.

I plummeted downward, crashing in a heap on a cracked stone floor. Pain spiked through my left hip, stealing the air from my lungs. I rolled onto my back to get a sense of my surroundings. Either the overbooked hotel had resorted to renting out musty caverns or... Well, I wasn't sure what the "or" could be. None of my research or training so far had made any mention of alternate dimensions. Especially a musty one encrusted with stalactites and stalagmites, pulsing faintly with a dim red light.

I sat up, every gravity-defying inch upwards drawing a hiss out of me. My hip must have fractured. It wasn't broken because I was able to hobble onto my feet, whereupon my left heel snapped off. I removed my other shoe, tossing them both aside, then took off my stockings as well because they were slippery. Seeing as the ground was rocky but not sharp, I'd manage in my bare feet.

Before I'd taken a half dozen steps, a remarkably well-groomed troll materialized and rushed me, brandishing a spiked club. My arms flew up to block it, which was useless. More helpful was the instinctive full body blast of electricity that forked out toward him. I glowed bright blue from the level of magic I was accessing.

The current snaked around the demon. His body stiffened, convulsing, and he lost his hold on the club. I flinched as it smashed into the ground at my feet, the spike on top splitting the stone to embed itself like Excalibur.

Since the creature was ensnared by my power, I circled it, looking it over. Warty and drab, the sole resemblance this troll bore to its namesake dolls was its shock of bright green hair.

"I'm pressed for time, dude," I said. The troll bared its rotted teeth at me and I threw an arm over my nose. "Where am I?"

The troll snarled out some words in a language I guessed to be of Northern European origin, since to my ears he sounded like the Swedish chef on *The Muppets*.

I tapped my ears. "No babel fish. English?"

He spat a phlegmy glob at my feet.

"That attitude won't get you very far." I peered into the gloom around me. Whatever portal I'd come through was gone, leaving a lot of stone wall behind me. Up ahead, the cave floor sloped down so I limped over to take a closer look. A dank passageway led off into the pitch black. Probably full of monsters, but it was the only way out of this place.

Since the troll wasn't going to play nice, and accessing his weak spot meant a lot of time spent weakening his leathery skin, I shot a bolt at one of the heavy pointed stalactites hanging above him. It crashed onto the top of his skull, and while he was literally too bone-headed for the spike to impale him, it still walloped him hard enough to knock him out. His eyes rolled back into his head and he hit the ground with a thud.

"Good talk."

Keeping one hand on the stone, I hugged the right wall, hoping that I wouldn't come to any forks in the road. I moved at a snail's pace, doing my best to ignore the jarring pain with each carefully placed footfall. My shallow breathing was a creepy horror movie soundtrack and the hair on the back of my neck stood on end. If there was ever a place for a hand to reach out and grab me, this was it.

I lost all sense of time down there, hyper-alert for any danger, my pain pulsing in rhythm with the accelerated beat of my heart. The sharp heat of the tunnels pressed in on me, turning my hair into lank strands. I tied my jacket around my waist. A heavy load but I'd need it again if I ever got out of this place.

When I got out.

Eventually, a faint glow of light shimmered up ahead. Half-convinced it was a mirage, I limped toward it, whimpering and glassy-eyed. I came out into a dim, cavernous space, the floor ending in a giant chasm. It was impossible to jump, and I had no rope to swing across. I glared at the black pit. I hadn't fought demons, and convinced Rohan to do the stupid song, and played nice with the Brotherhood to have my plans for Ari thwarted by a giant hole.

Wings rustled above me.

Fingers of unease slithered down my spine. There was a reason no one ever looked up. I hunched my head into my neck, tilting my entire upper body backward to stare up to the top of the rock wall disappearing in the inky darkness.

I squinted at the pinprick of light at the top. Going back wouldn't get me anywhere and going forward would end in a "Wile E. Coyote off a cliff" impersonation. I considered my options, quickly realized I didn't have any, felt for my first toehold, pulled myself up, and screamed. Fractured hips and rock climbing were not a match made in Heaven.

It was incredibly slow going. Two minutes in and sweat ran in rivulets between my shoulder blades. Three minutes in and my vision started to tunnel. Five minutes in and my entire body shook like a nine-point earthquake. I glanced down, finding myself maybe ten feet from the ground. Nowhere close to where I had to get to, but far enough up that I hugged the wall, frozen. Except for my hip joints that blazed in agony.

I was well and truly screwed. And I didn't mean the fun kind that ended with Rohan's hands on every part of my body. At least the troll wouldn't eat me since given the slight curve of the rock wall, I'd be falling straight into the Pit of Despair. Hopefully the chasm was deep enough for the fall to immediately kill me because if I had to lay at the bottom with a broken neck until I dehydrated to death, I was going to be extremely pissed off.

A deep rumbling shook the cavern, raining a shower of small stones down upon me, and knocking me sideways. I swung out, my left arm windmilling as a zmey, a three-headed dragon demon, roared up out of the darkness.

I curled the fingertips of my right hand into the rock face, willing myself to hang on for a few more seconds. Why climb when I could fly? I whistled sharply. "Taxi!"

The zmey flew closer.

Come on. A bit more.

As it opened one of its mouths to belch fire at me, I launched myself off the wall with a scream. The zmey jerked its head up, its flame going wild above my head.

My hand slid over its scales, slicing open my palm. Slick with blood, I grappled for purchase along its body, managing at the last second to grab a back leg. The hot swampy stench of dragon undercarriage assaulted me. I gagged, swallowing against the metallic bile in my throat, hanging on for dear life, one-handed, my feet dangling over the chasm.

The demon shook me harder and harder, trying to dislodge me.

I blasted sharp bursts of current from the top of my head at its underbelly while tugging on its leg, trying to steer it up to the top of the rock wall.

The zmey roared in anguish and dove into a tight spiral, its screeches decimating my poor ears.

Soupy wind gusted against my face, blowback from the flapping of its massive wings. I squinted against the grit blinding me. Deeper and deeper we descended into the chasm, the light growing darker and more menacing. At least adrenaline had pushed my pain back.

A bit of blackened demon flesh plopped onto the top of my head. I yelped, jerking it off me hard enough to crack my neck. Blood streamed down my arm, now shaking with the exertion of hanging on to its flailing leg one-handed.

Blasting the dragon only encouraged it to speed up.

The zmey kicked at me with its other leg, flexing its talon and catching my firing arm. A sharp heat blazed up my skin, black dots blurring the edges of my sight. With a hard buck, the demon dislodged me. Totally enveloped in darkness, I fell the last few feet to the ground.

I landed on something spongy. Partially eaten corpses. I slid in a nest of bones and decomposing bodies that I couldn't see, but would be able to smell for the rest of my life. It smelled like sulfur and my veggie drawer at home before Mom threw out the broccoli she'd made me promise to eat that I'd let go frothy with mold. Burying my face in my shirt did nothing.

The darkness was so all-encompassing that I started hyperventilating, convinced I couldn't breathe. That did little against the smell and nothing for my dizziness.

The faintest scrape of the demon's talons on bone gave away its position off to my right. Unable to rely on my sight, my hearing was jacked to the point of this merest whisper trumpeting like Dolby surround.

I pushed forward in the opposite direction, hands outstretched, wishing the dragon had feathered its nest with, well, feathers instead of people. I groped blindly for the chasm's wall, but its slime-covered slickness offered no way out.

The zmey changed position, its weight redistribution shifting this garden of people and causing me to sink. Scrabbling for purchase, I seized a rope, using it to pull myself up those precious inches back to the surface.

Not a rope. A length of sweaty, matted hair. Laughter burst out of me like a hyena, wild and manic.

A hot raspy tongue licked up the side of my arm, cleaning away the blood, silencing me mid-chortle. I blasted the giant evil freak. Even if I killed it, I had no clue how I'd climb out of here, but one danger at a time.

The zmey hissed, a sharp pop of sulphur my one warning that I'd displeased it.

I flung a couple of bodies on top of me. Fire rolled over me, the poor corpses I'd pulled over my head barely keeping me from being toasted like a marshmallow. The heat was of an intensity beyond anything I'd ever experienced. I wriggled deeper down into the nest so my clothes wouldn't melt against my skin. Or my skin melt right off. Even with my lids screwed tight, I'd swear my eyeballs were shriveling up in their sockets like raisins.

Dozens of dead people fingers poked at me, some with fleshy touches, others with boney jabs. My whimpers were audible even over the roar of the flames.

The fire stopped as quickly as it had started, leaving the only sounds my ragged breathing and the demon's nasally snorts.

I pushed the bodies off me. They'd been so toasted that by this point, they were merely person-shaped piles of ash that fell apart, coating me. Popping my head up, I inhaled a lungful of hot foul air but as I did, my coat slipped off my waist. I fumbled for it, frantic, until I was able to snag a fistful of fabric and clutch it to my chest. It wasn't a special coat, and I couldn't say why the thought of losing it filled me with such panic.

How long was I trapped listening to the demon snacking away? A minute? An hour? Long enough for death to howl a lonely dirge in my head. I used to think my death would occur after a long life filled with dance. I wasn't stupid enough to think tap would ever make me rich, but between the odd Broadway show, performing globally in festivals, and teaching, I'd be okay. More than that, I'd be happy. Living my dance dreams, I would have taken on the world and soared.

When all that came crashing down due to my torn Achilles, I imagined my death a lot then, too. Probably why, when I became Rasha, the fatality rate didn't freak me out.

Even so, I'd allowed myself to believe that as a hunter, my death would occur in a moment of badass heroism. Hailed and heralded by fellow Rasha for all time, I'd gone so far as to create the perfect "Nava, You Irreplaceable You" playlist. I'd never imagined my death as the pointless end it now seemed fated to be with my disappearance proving a mystery and my body never being recovered. Coldness seeped into every inch of me. I couldn't stop trembling.

I didn't want to die alone in the dark.

Green light filled my vision, bright and shocking against the utter black as the zmey turned all six of its eyes my way. There was enough light from those gleaming peepers to see the puff of smoke from its nostril flare and the many sharp teeth as it opened its mouth, sucked in a breath and–

I fell onto a thick cream carpet.

It was super plush, so I relaxed on it for a second to catch my breath and decide if I was actually alive or in some afterlife waiting room. I blinked, the room swimming into focus. I lay between a bed and a chair with a tiny side table and standing lamp. A flat screen TV stood on a long table across from the bed. Best of all, there was no stone cavern and no demon.

As I struggled to sit up, an invisible force shoved me back onto the ground.

Whoops, spoke too soon.

8

I managed to get off one wild shot at my unseen assailant before my magic sputtered. I didn't feel tapped out. Exhausted, broken, and in desperate need of electrolytes, sure, but my tank wasn't totally empty. I tried to call up my power, but it bubbled up under my skin, and stayed there, trapped. My accelerated Rasha healing abilities may have been working on fixing my hips but they did nothing against this sensation that quickly turned from unpleasant to a torturous searing. Without anywhere to go, magic flooded my nerve endings. A scream tore from my throat and I thrashed against my invisible bindings.

A black shoe stepped into my field of vision. "You are Rasha? How?" I couldn't see the speaker but it was a woman, albeit one with a raspy Israeli accent.

"Bite me, demon," I ground out. Probably not ideal to taunt her, but my skin was starting to blister so my judgment was less than sound.

Dr. Gelman stepped into my field of vision. Gaunt, she'd lost a lot of weight since the photo I'd seen. Her sweater hung off her frame. "You think I'm a demon?"

I couldn't answer her, too busy convulsing at her ongoing magic torture. A head-to-toe spasm racked me with such force that my body bucked off the ground before I bowed backwards, crashing back down head first. My eyes bugged out. I turned my head so she wouldn't see the tears leaking out of my eyes. I'd have done anything to get Ari inducted as Rasha, but hadn't I paid accordingly yet?

I felt a shift in her magic binding and my power shot out of me, dissipating harmlessly into the air. Sweet release, other than the throbbing mess of my post-zmey-encounter body. "Was the zmey going to finish me off too quickly?" I sneered. "Had to fuck with me some more?"

"I should not have left you there so long." A flash of regret passed over her features. "I'm going to let you up," she said. "But if you use your power in any way, you'll be sorry. Understood?"

My tiny head jerk sufficed for a nod. I couldn't sit up. Trying resulted in a whimper. I clutched my hips.

Dr. Gelman placed a hand on either side of me, doing something surprisingly unevil with her magic that relieved much of the pain. Then she propped me onto my feet, where she half-dragged, half-pushed me into the chair.

I sat there, head bowed. Why had Rabbi Abrams sent me here? I hadn't thought he'd wanted me dead, but I'd been wrong so many times before.

The bed creaked as Dr. Gelman sat down on the mattress across from me.

I raised my head to meet her eyes. She leaned forward, arms braced on her thighs. "If you're not a demon," I said, "why did you send me to that alternate dimension?" Exhaustion trumped anger.

"Answer me this first. Who gave you my email? Why did you send me that message?"

I was reluctant to answer because Rabbi Abrams had mentioned she didn't like the Brotherhood but at my hesitation, she conjured up a less intense invisible band to pin me against the chair. Enough to put an uncomfortable pressure on my rib cage. "Rabbi Abrams."

To my shock, she barked out a laugh, which turned into a hacking cough. Able to move again, I rose in concern to help her, but she waved at me to stay where I was.

"That slick talker? He's still alive?" she asked.

I tried to reconcile the rabbi I knew with a slick talker and failed. "Maybe it's a different Rabbi," I said.

"Short? Ancient?" I nodded. "That's him. He dated my sister ages ago. Broke her heart."

"The zmey and the troll?" I prompted. I wriggled my legs. My hips didn't blaze with pain anymore, more of a dull ache.

"That wasn't an alternate dimension. I portalled you under the city. Tons of tunnels crisscrossing Europe. I didn't know what you'd encounter, but after receiving that email, I figured better safe then sorry."

"Got a washcloth?" My hands and forearms were splattered with blood from being sliced by the zmey's scales. Most of it was dried but one gash had opened again and was trickling freely. I looked like I'd been performing open heart surgery with my bare hands.

She jabbed a finger at me. "You look like shit."

I scrubbed the non-bleeding hand over my face. "Seriously?"

"I meant the outfit."

"Don't be fooled by the togs," I said. "They're working attire."

She raised an eyebrow at me.

"Not like that. Actually," I amended, "kind of like that. But I'm undercover."

"I bet you're the picture of elegance normally."

"I have a certain je ne sais quoi style, thank you very much." Since I wasn't dead, I felt justified in returning to my normal mouthiness. "I don't suppose you have a Gatorade?"

"No."

"Water?"

She narrowed her eyes at me then headed into the bathroom.

I sat up, rolling out my neck and shoulders, one tight millimeter at a time. "The reason I'm here is because twenty years ago the Brotherhood identified my twin brother Ari as an initiate. Then at his induction ceremony a few weeks ago, we realized that oops! Wrong twin."

Mom was a direct descendent of King David. Her bloodline meant that when Ari had been born, the Brotherhood had checked to see if he carried the Rasha potential. Since the Brotherhood is big on the "secret" part of secret organization, my parents hadn't been aware of the true purpose of Rabbi Abrams' visit back then. While all male baby descendants of David and those first Rasha were tracked and tested, only a fraction of these potentials passed the first ritual and were bumped up to initiate status. It was only after Ari was confirmed among that number that my parents, much to their shock, were filled in about demons, hunters, and their son's very important destiny.

My brother spent the next twenty years training and studying for the day that he'd be officially inducted as a hunter. The reason for the time delay was twofold. First off, there was a ton of demons to learn about and all their sweet spots to be able to recall. Not to mention fighting, laying wards–all the tricks of the trade.

The second reason was more practical. After a lot of trial and fatal error, the Brotherhood had pronounced age twenty as being the soonest that initiates were strong enough to receive the magic power conferred upon them in their official induction ceremony.

When Ari's ceremony revealed that the Brotherhood had been training the wrong Katz sibling all these years, the shit had hit the fan. My parents were as knocked for a loop as the Brotherhood. Ari had been the golden child with a destiny. I'd had a destiny at one point too, but being a professional tap dancer didn't buy much cred at faculty parties. Neither did being Rasha, since it was top secret, but at least my parents could bask in the glow of clandestine knowledge at their job well done producing such a mensch.

Funny how the glow didn't happen for their little menschette.

Dr. Gelman pressed a glass of room temperature water into my hand, laying a wet washcloth on the table beside me.

"Todah rabah." It couldn't hurt to express my gratitude in her native tongue.

"What do you expect me to do?" she asked.

I fumbled in my skirt pocket for a tiny complimentary package of salt, dumping it in the glass. That little amount of sodium wouldn't deter a demon, but it would help with my electrolytes in case Gatorade wasn't available. Stirring it with one finger, I plugged my nose against the taste and gulped most of the drink back before replying. "His initiate status has been confirmed but re-running the ceremony didn't induct him. Rabbi Abrams thinks you can help."

I swallowed a few times against the disgusting aftertaste of the drink, wiping off my bloody handprint with the wet cloth.

"Thus the golem reference." Dr. Gelman looked me over, tapping her lip with her finger. "The twin factor complicates things." Given the gleam in her eyes, it also made this problem more interesting. "No one ever performed the first ritual on you?"

I shook my head.

"Then your potential had been laying there dormant all this time. Corked up and wanting out. That's how it would have remained had you not been in the right place—the induction ceremony—at the right time of your life to uncork it." Dr. Gelman tossed out the salt package. "Essentially, that ceremony called up all the pressure the magic had built up inside you and the cork popped."

"Like a fine champagne." I cleaned off the blood, dirt, and people ash as much as possible. My movements were slow and careful, my healing not yet complete.

Another coughing fit overtook her. This time I got her a glass of water, taking the opportunity to rinse out the washcloth in the sink. Streaks of red and black swirled down the sink. I handed her the glass and continued cleaning myself off. "How long did you smoke for?"

She frowned. "How'd you know?"

"I had a teacher who died of lung cancer." I scrubbed at a stubborn patch of dried zmey flesh stuck to my leg.

She ran her finger over the rim of the glass. "Why bother quitting? Can't kill me twice. So Isaac re-ran the ceremony and bupkis." It took me a second to realize that Isaac was Rabbi Abrams. I hadn't thought about him having an actual first name.

I tossed the washcloth down. "Do you have a way to help?"

She inclined her head. "I do."

"And Rabbi Abrams," I couldn't bring myself to call him Isaac, "didn't think the Brotherhood would sanction that way. Because you're a... what?" I held up my hands at her glare. "My best friend is a half-demon. I'm not going to judge. Especially if you plan on helping me, but this is about Ari's safety. Please."

Her indignation turned to amusement. "A Rasha with a demon friend. You're an interesting girl."

"Thanks. The Brotherhood fails to see it."

"Yes, well, they are stunningly myopic. I'm not a demon, Nava. I'm a witch."

I laughed. "There's no such thing as witches."

Dr. Gelman's face pinched in prune-faced disapproval. "Says the girl with the magic powers." Her fingers twitched.

"Sorry," I yelped. A touchy witch. Awesome. "Besides, I have *Rasha* magic. Not witch magic. I've never seen anyone go around casting spells."

She grabbed my ring. "What is this, if not a spell?" Her accent grew more pronounced in her anger.

"You knew it was a glamour?"

"You have to wear the Rasha ring. Until I touched it, that ring didn't resemble the hamsa." She shrugged. "A rabbi performed a spell on it. Even mezuzahs have a powerful spell on them. A word, seemingly gibberish, engraved on the back that helps keep demons at bay."

Mezuzahs contained a prayer scroll wrapped in a decorative case. Most Jewish homes had them. In secular ones like ours, they were nailed to the frame of our front door instead of every door. My family home also had wards that used salt, iron, and Rasha blood to keep away fiends but I guess mezuzahs worked well enough for regular folks.

"Those spells, that magic, is wielded by rabbis. Just as you wield magic, inherent rather than spell-based, to kill demons." Dr. Gelman tapped her head. "What did you think was going on?"

"I dunno. Witches are women, not rabbis." Dr. Gelman snorted at me. "Also," I continued, determined to make my point, "I've never heard of a real witch, especially a Jewish one."

She waved a hand at me in barely concealed impatience. "Who do you think performed the first ritual when David gathered his Rasha?" From the look on her face, I knew better than to answer with "a rabbi?"

"I hadn't thought about it," I hedged. "It's not any gospel the Brotherhood preaches."

"This surprises you? History is rife with organized religions, most of which are patriarchal, co-opting celebrations devoted to women's power." She eased back against her chair, her inner professor in full force. "Think about the power of pagan fertility rituals that in Catholicism became the sexless sinless Virgin Mary. Or how Astarte, the Canaanite goddess of fertility and sexual love was condemned as a cult in Judaism and stamped out in favor of the monotheistic Yaweh. The Brotherhood reframed our power, casting us as evil witches."

I leaned forward, fascinated. "Like who?"

"Baba Yaga."

"She's a myth."

"Demons are also a myth," she chided, "but we know better, don't we?" Touché.

"Any other famous witches?" If celebrities could be demons, maybe a few A-listers had other interesting talents.

"Lilith."

"Lilith? The original harlot of history?"

"Yes. There is a strong correlation between sexual immorality and witchcraft in Judaism. To hear the men tell of it, at least."

"No wonder the Brotherhood hates me."

Dr. Gelman cracked a smile. "Have you read the Old Testament?"

"Not my bag, no."

"Exodus 22:17. 'You shall not suffer a witch to live.' Trust me, the Brotherhood knows all about our existence. They hate the fact that we women dare to have a power that they want only for themselves."

I raised my fist in solidarity. "Then right on, witches."

She slapped her thigh. "I like you. All right. I'll help. Beats sitting around waiting to die." She scribbled something down and handed the paper to me. The name and address of a shop in Prague. "Get these."

"Virgin soil from a mountain not dug by men and purified well water? What will you do with them?"

"All in good time. Once you have these things, we'll meet again." She held up a hand like she was making a vow. "No demons this time. I'll take you to my favorite café for the best pastries here in town."

"Yes, please." I tucked the list into my bra, then picked up my coat by two fingers, grimacing at the stink drifting off its various splotchy stains. I wanted the jacket to cover the worst of my dishevelment.

Gelman plucked the coat away and waved a hand over it. The stains disappeared. As she gave it back, I caught a whiff of roses. I wondered how far her guilt extended.

"You wouldn't happen to have a pair of shoes I could borrow, would you? Mine got a tad destroyed down in the cave. Or could you magic mine back up here intact?" Those stilettos had been pricey.

"No. But..." She crossed over to her closet, returning to me with a pair of shower flip flops hooked between two fingers. "My feet are a bit smaller than yours but they should fit well enough to get you home."

Second hand slippers. Lovely.

Dr. Gelman huffed at my expression. Since I didn't want her to toss me around anymore, I took the flip flops and left.

9

Bare-legged, I padded my way into the Praha WS Hotel on ill-fitting sandals, wincing at the twinges afflicting my poor hips. My once sleek outfit lay twisted on my body. Still grimy with dried blood matted into my hair and staining my clothes, I crossed my fingers, hoping that I pulled off the "extra from a low budget zombie movie" look, because, hey, I had on a nice clean coat so the rest had to be wardrobe and make-up, right? Given the looks from the stylish people milling about, I don't think I succeeded. No matter. They'd make up some story to fit my disheveled state. People always found a way to explain things away.

Given the blanched horror of the desk clerk, who I already had strike one with from earlier today, his explanation probably involved alleys, knees, and hourly rates.

Fatigue clawed up the back of my neck, pounding my temples with a tight ache that radiated in my teeth. Cutting diagonally across the lobby, I rubbed my scratchy, dry eyes. Was I really still on day one of my trip? The thought of my pillow incited drooling.

I should have gone straight to the elevator, but I stupidly looked into the lounge. Reflexively checking out the action. Rohan stood at the bar, his rich laughter carrying clear as a bell. In high flirtation mode, he was surrounded by female admirers. Lily wasn't among the throng.

I dug my nails into my palms, having gotten the kick in the ass I needed to keep heading for my room, but Rohan looked up at that moment. His smile slipped.

One of the women, her sweet girl-next-door looks undercut by her aggressive stance, leaned in to say something, resting her hand on his arm. He tilted his head, as if listening to her, toying with his Rasha ring, but ran his eyes over me again, his expression guarded. He pushed away from the bar, shoulders squared. I couldn't hear what his groupies said, but it was clear from their body language that they didn't want him to leave.

I shook my head, motioning for him to stay. Rohan watched me a moment more, then relaxed. Whatever he said in response to the woman had her touch her fingertips to her chest as she tipped her head back and laughed.

Oh, please. I hit the call button.

Boots thudded against the floor, closing in on me. Every step was inordinately loud given the din of chatter in the lobby. Stuck here as my stalker closed in, I stabbed at the button, willing the elevator to descend faster.

The footsteps stopped behind me. "Was it Samson?"

I turned around to face Rohan. "No. Rabbi Abrams asked me to do something."

His brows raised in silent questioning.

"Can we not? I mean, not tonight? I'll fill you in tomorrow, but now," I pushed the button again. "I'm fine."

"You're not." His hand snaked out and pushed up my sleeve revealing the kaleidoscope of yellow and purple bruising.

I shifted uncomfortably under the weight of his all-seeing amber eyes before looking away. Except that landed me on the full glory of the women waiting for the rock god's return. Given their smirks, they didn't expect me to be any great hold-up.

Head groupie caught me staring. She turned with disinterest to her phone.

I ignored the bitter burning in my throat. "Gathering back-ups, are we?"

He clasped his hands behind his back. "Actors Samson thought I'd mesh with." He glanced over at them. "Gifts."

"They're people, Snowflake." Standing up for the sisterhood even if I wanted to return them to sender.

"Not in this reality. We're all commodities and Samson is continually taking inventory."

Peachy. The elevator finally decided to grace me with its presence. I held the door open with one hand. "I need to sleep."

"We can talk tomorrow, just... don't lie to me, okay?" Rohan folded my sleeve back down, his touch so gentle, I barely felt it, even with the sensitive bruising. "Sweet dreams, Nava."

A second of tenderness and three short words and damn sunlight infused my soul.

"Ro," the woman who'd dismissed me called out in a lilting British accent, "my friend got us passes to that VIP room I was telling you about. Let's roll."

"Your wish is my command, Poppy." Between one blink and the next, Rohan swept all warmth away from me to dazzle this Poppy chick with the full force of his charm. He gave her that same cavalier smile bestowed on me in the elevator before we'd dashed to my room.

Dark, malicious tendrils slithered up inside my chest. We might all have been commodities but damned if I was going to be tossed in the junk drawer.

I didn't watch him go back to the bar, shuffling instead into the elevator and down the hall to my room like the walking dead.

It took me three tries to undo my buttons. Stripping my clothes off, I stood under the hot spray, head bowed, watching the combination of human and demon blood circle down the drain in wary fascination.

My bathroom morphed into a steam room, fat water droplets streaking down the walls, before my trembling stopped.

With my last iota of energy, I called Ari from the hotel phone, since mine was dead. It went straight to voice mail. "Hey Ace, tell Abrams I made contact. All good. Adventures galore tomorrow. Can't wait." I think I injected the right note of enthusiasm into my voice to sell the lie. "Crashing now. Stay alive or else. Love you."

Crawling under the covers, I reached out to turn off my bedside lamp and froze, my fingers hovering inches away from the switch. Even knowing the street light would cast a weak glow over the room and keep full darkness at bay, I couldn't bring myself to turn it off. Screw it. I wasn't paying the electric bill. I punched up my pillow into full fluffiness and let exhaustion take me.

What a difference fourteen hours of sleep made. I woke up Friday around noon, refreshed and starving, to find two texts on my newly-charged phone. The first was from Ari who was glad I'd checked in and promised to relay the message. The second was from Rohan with today's agenda. He'd be with Forrest for part of the afternoon, but said I should meet him in his room for dinner around seven and to dress appropriately. We were going out with Samson.

That fit in with my plans for the day, namely eating and finding this shopkeeper. According to the walking map of Prague I'd downloaded onto my phone, the store Gelman had directed me to find was located in Old Town. I noted the tons of small cafés and bakeries on the map to check out along the way, so I skipped the hotel restaurant and headed off to explore Prague and get breakfast.

I popped my earbuds in, choosing an upbeat playlist that contained no danger of playing "Toccata and Fugue" then, soundtrack in place, slid on a pair of red, plastic, heart-shaped sunglasses that I couldn't wait to break out in Rohan's presence. I tugged on my gloves, my breath gusting in tiny puffs in the crisp cold air. It was a lot chillier here than it had been back home.

Sun reflected off diamond sparkles on the frost-covered ground as I wandered the twisted cobblestone streets in dreamy delight, the one downside being the occasional heel snag in the uneven stones. Prague was like a fairyland, a city filled with so many architectural gems that I got a crick in my neck. I passed building after colorful building, paintings and sculptures adorning their facades, some with attic-level arched windows, and wondered what it would be like to regularly wake up to these rooftops?

This time of year, there weren't the throngs of tourists jamming up the streets that I'd have found in summer. I snuggled deeper into my coat, following the scent of sugar, cinnamon, and dough. Turning the corner, I was rewarded with a bakery, its front wall open to the street. Inside, workers wrapped dough around a long stick, roasting it over an open flame until it was golden brown. I hopped inside and glanced up at the filling options painted on the menu board.

I pulled an earbud free, the latest Bruno Mars spilling out. "One Trdelnik please. With whipped cream."

The baker pulled one of the long, hollow pastries off of its cooling stick, filled it to overflowing, wrapped it in a napkin, and handed it over. I bit into it, the cream squishing up over my top lip and nose. Flavor ecstasy burst on my tongue. That's it. I was moving here.

I dawdled in the streets as I ate, checking my map every now and then to make sure I was still on the correct route. There was no hurry and I was happy to gawk at everything.

The map eventually directed me into a narrow courtyard, ringed with tiny shops. The one closest to the entrance was my destination. I peered through the windows expecting some dusty creepfest selling crystals and bits of flotsam best not asked about. Instead a plump, cheerful woman clad in colorful clothing sold children's crafts and the ubiquitous marionettes hawked throughout the city.

The shopkeeper greeted me brightly over the jangle of bells. "Can I help you?"

I glanced around the shelves but my items weren't on display. "Uh, I'm looking for something I hope you stock."

"Yes?"

Feeling half-foolish, half-trepidatious, I said, "Virgin soil from a mountain not dug by men and purified well water."

"Wait here." She disappeared behind a purple beaded curtain.

I didn't believe that it could be this easy. She was going to transform and come out with evil a-blazin', right? Nope. She returned with two stoppered glass vials. One was filled with a rich, dark, soil and one contained clear liquid. "That's it?"

She smiled. "That's it."

I eyed them. "How do I know this isn't backyard dirt and tap water?"

The shopkeeper rang up the purchases. "You don't. Though I'd hardly keep my reputation if that's what I passed off."

Good point. I paid for the vials, thanked her, and tucked them safely into my coat pocket. The fabric still smelled like roses. I exited the store, marveling at how uneventful that had been. Since I had tons of time before I had to get ready for tonight, I pulled out my phone, intending to check my map and see how to get to the Charles Bridge, when a burst of color on a sign in the far back corner of the courtyard caught my attention.

It was a sunburst. A gold stylized sunburst with an androgynous face in the middle, framed by hair streaming out as if blown by the wind. Rays of light, some straight, some wavy extended from the face. One of the rays ended in a fleur-de-lis while another one had a hand, palm forward. I'd seen this design before.

Next to the sunburst was the name of the store. *Karel Tattoo.* I went inside and found another small shop, very clean, with blue walls plastered in artwork. A lone black chair stood off to one side, next to a bookcase with neatly stacked rows of rainbow-colored ink.

Karel, or the guy I figured to be Karel, was a short, burly man with a trim goatee, who was inked up all along his arms and neck. He lounged in the chair, looking up from his phone when I entered. "You want a tattoo?" His English was heavily accented with Czech.

"The sun on the sign. What is it?"

Karel stood up. "You been to Versailles?"

A shiver ran up my spine. "It's his symbol. Louis XIV."

Karel nodded.

"I want it." I didn't, but some deep gut instinct made me say the words. "But..." This was going to sound so lame. "Can you make it temporary?"

"No."

My shoulders slumped. I still had the sense I should do this but it warred with my disinclination to make the sunburst the first tattoo on my body. I didn't want that permanent a reminder of this mission. Besides, if I ever wanted to be buried in a Jewish cemetery, then tattoos were right out.

He pulled a pencil from his back pocket. "I can do it in body paint. Lasts about three or four days if you don't get it wet."

My head snapped up. "Really?"

"Yes. It won't look like a tattoo but it'll look good."

"Can you make it glittery?" Given his scowl, I thought I'd pushed my luck, but he nodded. "You're the best." I placed my hand on my left boob, above my heart. "Here, please. But I don't want the fleur-de-lis or the hand."

He nodded brusquely at me to sit in one of the wooden chairs that constituted the waiting room. "Let me draw it up," he said.

A few hours later, I was the proud recipient of a brilliant, gold, shimmery sunburst. I even had the perfect dress to show it off. I fired off a quick email to Dr. Gelman asking which pastry shop to meet at. Then I got ready for my night out.

I knocked on Rohan's door at seven on the dot. He had a penthouse suite, as much as any room on the fifth floor could be called that.

Rohan opened the door, leaning against the frame to check me out.

I spun on my gold stilettos, knowing I looked fabulous. "You like?"

My pale gold mini dress with spaghetti straps floated out as I twirled. I'd pinned my curls up in a messy, sexy do, with a few tendrils escaping down my back. Gold shimmery eye shadow adorned my lids, with no eyeliner but a ton of mascara. I'd kept my lips nude, with sheer glimmering gloss to pick up the light. My sun design peeked up above the neckline of my dress.

Rohan reached a finger out as if to trace it, but I swatted his hand away. "Don't touch. You might wreck it."

"What's with the body art?"

"Is my entrance contingent on my answer or can I come in?"

Rohan stroked his chin. "I haven't decided." I didn't mind his hesitation because it gave me the opportunity to check him out. He wore a black suit over a moss green T-shirt. There was no eyeliner, no spiky hair. Instead his locks curled softly along the tips of his ears. No rings except his glamoured Rasha one, though he had kept the leather strap tied around his wrist and his single silver bracelet.

I cocked an eyebrow and he shrugged. "Even rock stars can dress up," he said. He stood back, allowing me entrance. As I suspected, the only similarity between his room and mine was the four walls and a floor. I stepped inside his suite, the thick carpet muffling any sound.

Dirty glasses were strewn around the room, with more than one bearing lipstick stains, while a graphic-print scarf was tossed carelessly over the sofa. I picked it up. "The old forget-the-scarf trick?" I loosened my hold on the silky material. Tonight was about the mission, not us.

Rohan took it from me. "Yeah, I'll get it back to her."

I sniffed a half-empty bottle of Glenfiddich. "You had a party and didn't invite me? I'm crushed." My voice was light, airy, totally uncaring.

"It was an impromptu thing this afternoon. It would have been weird to specifically call you."

"So Samson wasn't there?" I guess if he hadn't been around, Rohan didn't need me to play act.

"No, he was. I just didn't need you right then."

Everything he said was plausible and Rohan going out of his way to include me would have seemed suspicious so this could all very well have been true. Still, he was a rock star with self-admitted bad behaviors going back down the rabbit hole.

I decided to give him the benefit of the doubt. "Nice piano."

Neatly stacked sheet music lay on top of the black baby grand that dominated the living room. I peeked at the handwritten notations but Rohan flipped the stack over so I couldn't see what he was working on.

"It's why I stay here," he said.

"If there was a hotel with a tap floor, I'd be so there." I plucked out "Twinkle Twinkle."

Rohan took my lame one-fingered attempt at the tune and upped it, turning the simple nursery rhyme into a haunting melody for a few bars. His strong, elegant fingers flowed over the keys.

I clapped my appreciation.

The modern décor of the lobby continued here in the sleek lines and sharp whites paired with bright pops of accent colors. A large abstract print took up much of one wall. My eyes bounced to the curtains, now closed, and blocking any potential view. Like that of Prague laid out before us. I bit my lip, shutting down any lustful urges with a stern mental directive that tonight was a work night.

"Did Samson want to hang out for a reason or was this a play date?" I asked.

Rohan closed the cover on the keys. "King offered me a recording contract." He laughed at the dumbfounded look on my face. "Yeah. I have no clue either. I'm certain I'm being set up for something, but for the life of me, I can't figure out what it is yet."

"Maybe we'll learn more tonight."

"Hope so." Still seated at the piano bench, Rohan jerked a finger up and down indicating my attire, then shook his head. "Scratch that. Start with what you were up to last night."

I caught him up on what Rabbi Abrams had asked me to do as well as the entire Gelman encounter, speeding through the zmey and troll part, since there seemed to be a direct correlation between that section of the story and the muscle jumping in his jaw.

When I came to the end of the recap, Rohan frowned. "Amazing. In a month, you have me stepping back into the limelight despite swearing up and down never to do it, and get one of the most company men I've ever met going behind the Brotherhood's back."

I gave him an arch look and he held up his hands. "Just that good. I know," he said.

I waited but he didn't say anything else. I jabbed him. "Where's my growl that I'm behaving recklessly? Going off on my own to do something that has nowhere near the importance of this assignment?"

He crossed his legs at the ankles. "You saved me the trouble."

"Can't shut down a rabbi's order to me either, can you?"

He scratched his cheek with his middle finger. "I promise to growl if I don't like what this new look is all about." His voice dropped lower. "Though I'm not sure that's a punishment with you." He watched me with a banked heat.

"Down, boy." I straightened my shoulders and moved away, putting two chairs and a low coffee table between us.

He smirked but let it alone.

Snapping my fingers, I sank onto the sofa. "Drink me."

"Wine?"

"Please."

Rohan uncorked a bottle, holding it up for my approval.

"My favorite kind," I said.

"Merlot?"

"Open." I waited until I had a glass in my hands to explain the sunburst. "When I went to get the supplies for Gelman, I came across this tattoo parlor with a sun on the sign. It's the same design that Louis XIV branded himself with all over Versailles."

The bottle hit the counter harder than warranted.

I drank some wine. It didn't burn like rotgut, so a good vintage. "I saw it and had this overwhelming sense of rightness. I had to get the design."

The jumping jaw muscle was back, but the boy showed remarkable restraint by not speaking. Or locking me into handcuffs. Ooh. Handcuffs.

I forced my thoughts to stay work appropriate. "Up until his retirement weirdness, Samson positioned himself as the sun at the center of the universe and encouraged people with crap lives to fly as close as they could. He pulled the old, 'I'm bright. I'm shiny. Ignore the part where I'm a giant ball of flame that can destroy you.' Well, I'm going to turn the tables on him. Pose as a descendent of old Lou and match Samson's ambition. Because really," I stretched an arm out along the top of the sofa, "even an alleged power-hungry demon needs a consort."

Rohan dropped down beside me. "So you upgraded yourself from bait to queen."

I smiled at him and sipped my wine.

He raked a hand through his hair. "I want to know what you're up to at all times."

I choked on my drink. "You mean I have your permission?"

"Begrudging, but yes." He took my glass, knocking back a long slug, before pressing it back into my hand. "This is a bold move. It might be the thing to crack Samson's facade. Spin it as wanting to get signed by his management company. Figure out what he's up to from that angle." Rohan stared at the sunburst for another brief, intense moment, then snorted. "Jesus."

Sure, I was pleased, but I'd expected more of a fight. Much more. I gave him a once-over, noting the brush of purple under his half-open eyes, and the lines of fatigue sketching his face as he lay on the couch next to me. It was a little too languorous to be just tiredness, a little too carefully disguised to be careless partying. "How you doing there, tiger?" I asked.

Rohan took a breath, looked at me, then looked away. When his smile came back, it was a bit strained, and it seemed like he'd been on the verge of saying something else. "I'd forgotten..."

I leaned forward, awaiting the rest of the sentence. There was a polite knock at the door. Startled, I lost my balance, and tumbled sideways against the sofa cushions. "Samson?" I asked.

"Room service. I ordered in. I hope that's okay. I wanted to eat in peace." He opened the door and a waiter rolled in a cart with two covered plates.

With a flourish, I lifted the first cover and sagged. It was steamed fish with steamed veggies. Ugh with a side of ugh. "This looks–"

Rohan started laughing before I could figure out how to lie my way through the rest of that sentence. "Lift the other cover," he said.

My eyes lit up at the enormous piece of schnitzel accompanied by a heap of gravy-drenched mashed potatoes. No greens in sight.

"I did good?" he asked.

I held my wine glass up to him in cheers.

By mutual unspoken agreement, we didn't discuss work, the Brotherhood, Ari, or us. Instead, Rohan entertained me with music biz gossip.

Wine snorted out my nose at one particularly outrageous anecdote. "She did not!"

Rohan put his hand to his heart. "Swear. Toe hickeys. Her exact instructions were 'Suck them hard enough to open my third eye.' Which was wrong on so many levels."

I screamed in laughter. "What did you do?"

"Told her it was the wrong chakra."

"Was it? The wrong chakra?"

"Fuck if I know." A pious look flitted over his face. "I may have implied that cultural appropriation for western sexual kink purposes was frowned upon by Indian gods and would end in badly blocked energy. Then I blessed her with a namaste and got the hell out."

"How upstanding of you, Mr. Mitra."

"Some of us do have a moral compass."

I jabbed my fork at him. "Hey! I have a moral compass."

"Yeah, with Hell as your true north." But he said it teasingly so I stuck my tongue out at him.

His phone beeped with a text. Rohan glanced at it. "Samson."

I laid down my cutlery and wiped my mouth. "Seems our bubble is broken." I didn't want to go. I hadn't had this much fun with someone other than Ari or Leo in ages.

"Seems so." He didn't sound any happier about it than I did. Rohan pulled his ever-present tiny tin of candied fennel seeds out of his pocket and popped a few in his mouth before offering them to me.

I crunched a few, the sweet licorice freshening my breath. "Pace yourself, baby. I have a feeling it's going to be a long night."

10

"Are you sure this is the right place?" I asked.

We stood at the mouth of an underground passageway that would have looked sketchy by the light of day. At night, with no one around, it looked flat-out disreputable. Small shops with windows filled with tourist crap took up most of the corridor, while a sign pointed the way to the Museum of Torture.

"That looks promising," Rohan deadpanned. He strode into the passageway. "Lolita. It's over here."

I blinked at the name, having forgotten about my persona during dinner. It had been so genuinely Rohan and me, instead of Lolita and rock star. Stiffening my spine, I arranged my expression in Lolita's state of ennui and sashayed after him.

Rohan stopped well before the stairway leading up to the museum, halting next to a nondescript black door with a small sign reading "Chill."

A hostess met us inside. After verifying that our name was on the list for this thirty minute reservation, she fitted us with thermal jackets. "It's roughly minus twenty celsius inside," she informed us. "We're one of the colder ice bars in the world."

I put the jacket on over my own coat, glad the thermal one came almost down to my knees. But I was still bare-legged. "I may not manage the entire visit," I told Rohan quietly. Since Samson had paid for a twenty-minute slot, it would suck to bail and wait outside until they finished up, but frostbite would suck harder.

"Let me know if you need to leave." He placed a hand on the small of my back. "Ready?" His touch helped steady me against my rush of nerves and off we went.

Chill was pretty small. A couple of booths and standing tables carved from ice in addition to the bar itself. Not the floor though. They'd avoided that potential lawsuit. Purple and green strip lights illuminated the larger ice panels on the walls. Shelves had been carved out to display vodka bottles from around the world.

Drio was already there, chatting with Samson's buddies. He nodded as we came in but didn't come over to say hi. Other than them and Samson, I didn't recognize any of the fifteen or so other people.

"Ro darling," came a familiar British lilt as a puffy jacketed figure turned. Poppy, the actress from the other night was here, looking less girl-next-door and more blonde bombshell, with big blown out hair, and sexy smoky eyes. "Thank you for returning my scarf."

Get your own rock star.

"My pleasure," Rohan replied in a rumbly voice. I barely turned my sputter into a cough.

Samson glanced over at our arrival, saluting Rohan with his glass. "All hail the esteemed Rohan Mitra."

"What a douche," Rohan muttered. His smile brightened, his hand slipped from my back, and he crossed over to join the actor. He made it all of ten feet before he was accosted by three men who enthusiastically barked Fugue State Five song titles at him in Czech accents.

Rohan handled them graciously.

I made my way to the bar and ordered a chocolate vodka, shrugging deeper into my double coats. The bartender handed it over saying that drinks were on Samson's tab. It would have been a point in his favor but if your modus operandi was to make people feel bad about themselves, alcohol was a handy tool to speed things along. As was being rich enough to pay the tab for the common people.

The vodka was served in a frozen shot glass. It was so cold in here, that the alcohol, which tasted like a melted chocolate bar, had thickened to a syrup that slid down my throat like silk. I gave a thumbs-up as I handed the glass back, remarking on the experience, and the bartender explained that the cold removed the normal sting when drinking it. Definitely a plus.

Putting my back to the bar, I nursed my drink, checking out the various groups. None of them looked particularly interesting. Other than Samson's posse, who Drio had covered, I doubted anyone had any information that could help us. I wasn't there for small talk, so I crossed over to Rohan and Samson.

I moved into place on Rohan's left in time to see Poppy press a shot into his hand. She maintained physical contact while counting down for them to shoot their drinks back. Snowflake didn't protest the blatant move, nor did he introduce me. Or seem to notice I existed.

Drink downed, Poppy laughed, catching a drop with her tongue that brought both Samson's and Rohan's gaze to her lips. Oh, she was good. Every move she made was calculated to keep their attention on her. Under other circumstances, I'd have bought her a drink in admiration.

I kept my bored look in place, eyes scanning the room as if seeking more interesting climes, while mentally cataloguing all the damage my magic could do to her.

Poppy was even able to keep up with the music discussion the men veered onto. Impressive since they were chatting about some obscure New York band. Since I had nothing to contribute, I did what I did best: objectified the fuck out of the guys. Samson looked smug. He was "on" constantly, a high wattage performance of his cool, funny charm, complete with expansive gestures that were as put on as his perfect tan and artfully tousled hair.

Rohan, on the other hand, with his lazy stance, exuded confidence. His movements came with an economy of motion: a half-grin here, a wry comment there. He upstaged Samson's showmanship with an understated cool. Rohan was every inch the sexy rock star even in that dumb jacket. This wasn't bias. More like objective evidence based on the sidelong glances and awestruck stares he was getting.

With one sly sideways glance from Poppy before she gave me the tiniest smirk. The English Rose showing her thorns.

Time for her to learn the pecking order. I placed Rohan's hand on my ass under my jackets. Samson shot me the briefest glance at that. Rohan didn't. Didn't even pause his lyrical waxings about this one particular band. Though he did idly stroke along the base of my spine as he spoke.

I stared Poppy down, my bored expression unchanging, and my position unmovable until she gave up and moved on under the pretense of greeting a new arrival.

Ooh, being *that* girl was fun.

"Restless Landing opened for you on your last tour, right?" Samson asked. Interesting. Seems he'd researched Rohan.

"Yeah," Rohan said.

"I know Aaron."

"Hell of a drummer." Rohan sipped the beer that one of his three fanboys had pressed into his hand.

I wiggled my toes to keep them from going numb in the cold and pulled my hands up inside my sleeves.

"Not getting much work these days." Samson fired back another vodka shot. "You've been out of the loop so you might not have heard."

"The girls," Rohan said, without missing a beat.

Samson gave Rohan an appraising look. Rohan's bland expression didn't change. Two sharks circling each other, scenting for first blood. "Yeah. You probably ran into that. Teens looking like they were twenty-five." Samson spread his hands wide, like what are you gonna do?

"I did. But then again, I was a teen. Even so, I never screwed fifteen-year-olds." A hot thread of anger laced his voice.

Samson smirked. "You sure? I'm betting you didn't stop the action to do an ID check."

"I'm sure."

Samson clapped Rohan on the back. "Good man."

My eyes swung to Rohan to see how he'd react to such blatant condescension. All he did was take a swig of his beer.

I wasn't the only one who'd been watching the exchange, because with perfect timing, Drio showed up. "Ro, I'm freezing my balls off. Let's find somewhere better, man." I doubted I'd ever get used to that accent coming out of him.

"He's right. I'm over the tundra," Samson announced. "I've got just the place." He gestured to Rohan. "Unless you want to suggest something."

"Go for it."

"It's walkable," Samson said. There was a flurry of activity as we returned the jackets in addition to the normal leaving-a-bar discussion about who was going to this new venue versus who wanted to head somewhere else.

I stomped my feet, trying to get some feeling back into them while the debates raged. About half the group decided to follow Samson, with Poppy welded to Rohan's side.

A security detail had appeared the moment we left the bar. Three "don't fuck with us" men with granite carved jaws and constantly scanning eyes, who fell into a triangular formation around Samson and Rohan. The rest of us were expendable.

The sky was overcast and the wind caused goosebumps on my bare legs, but it was still a lot warmer than the ice bar. I jammed my hands in my pockets, enjoying the lively streets. Everyone high on possibility and good cheer. As for myself, I fell farther and farther back in the group, too busy rubbernecking.

Enough people rubbernecked right back, phones flashing, that Samson, at least, had been recognized, but the bodyguards kept the group moving at a fast clip and no one dared approach.

A group of boisterous Brits celebrating a bachelor party came toward us, singing off-key. The T-shirts they wore marked them as members of "Dave's Stag!" complete with a grainy photo of Dave flying over Prague Castle. One of the guys knocked into my shoulder as he passed.

I wobbled, my heel snagging on the cobblestone. Drio reached out to steady me under the elbow. Dude tossed out a drunken, "Sorry," and stumbled after his friends.

"Thanks," I said to Drio. I lifted up my stiletto. Scratched but not broken. "How's *your* night going?"

"It's already four years of my life I'll never get back."

I laughed and Drio grinned at me. Not his sadistic one. I clutched my heart in shock. "Careful, psycho. I might think you like me."

I wiggled my fingers to lose the residual prickly tingling from Chill.

"Don't worry. I don't." He leaned in, dropping the American accent. "Though I'm very curious about what you're up to."

"Pretensions of royalty. Power plays." I looked up at the sky, in this ancient city spinning out before me and despite the circumstances, felt content. "Ever believe that life was going to work out exactly as you wanted?"

"No."

"Me neither." Not for a long time, anyway. I looked up ahead at Rohan and Samson. At their heads, one dark, one blond, as they chatted. "But I think for tonight, I just might." I flipped a loose curl out of my eyes. "Back to work."

I picked up the pace, intent on displacing Poppy. Should have brought dynamite.

Samson flicked me an unreadable look as I linked arms with his Douchebag minion. "Why, hello," I drawled.

"Hey," Douchebag replied, half his attention on a text.

Samson's other minion, Jittery shot me a weaselly grin and a chin jerk.

I winked at him, then squeezed Douchebag's bicep.

"Like what you see?" he leered.

"I bet you do your own stunts, don't you?" This was said loud enough to carry.

Samson smirked, but Rohan, bless him, knew exactly what I was up to. He stopped dead in his tracks. "Lolita."

I raised an eyebrow at him. Rohan dropped Poppy like a hot potato to fetch me. Yes, I'm just that amazing that rock gods fall over themselves to stay in my good graces. It took everything I had not to bust out laughing.

Poppy fell back with her friends, chattering brightly.

As we passed Samson, my place at Rohan's side cemented, he acknowledged my play with a slow head tilt.

I lifted my chin and sailed on.

Samson's pick of bar was slick, pretentious, and exclusive. Quelle surprise. I handed off my jacket at the coat check and waltzed inside, Rohan by my side. "Gawd. Too much blue lighting, too many high-gloss surfaces, too many high-gloss people," I said.

"And here I had you pegged as such a lover of humanity," Rohan replied.

"Thank you for understanding that when I say I don't like people, I'm not doing it to make polite conversation."

"You know that's not actually considered polite conversation, right?" With a small head shake, he strutted off.

After taking a moment to imprint the image of his tight ass on my retinas, I headed straight to the bar, ordering a shot of vodka from the pouty androgynous bartender. Instinct told me that if Samson didn't approach me here I'd played my hand wrong. I pushed down my anxiety, imagining myself as an empty vessel, filling with confidence. When that didn't work, I knocked back my drink. The booze burned sharp and clear down my throat. I liked it better served cold and smooth, but maybe the bite was for the best.

"Get you another?" Samson appeared at my side. He could have graced any magazine cover in his fitted chocolate brown shirt that made his blue eyes pop. It left me cold. He crowded me into the bar with his wide-legged stance.

Your cock doesn't take up that much room, sugar. I clamped my lips together so I didn't say that out loud and nodded.

He got the bartender's attention, pointing at my drink. "Interesting design you got there." Said casually but his eyes were sharp on my sunburst. "What's the story?"

Alea iacta est. With a mental finger-cross that this roll didn't come up snake eyes, I kept my expression impassive, pulling my neckline down a bit more as if to better see the entire design for myself. I traced a finger around the rays, letting it linger a moment on my cleavage.

Samson only had eyes for the design.

"Ever heard of Louis XIV?" I asked.

"Wrestler, right?" He laughed at my dismay. "Kidding. I manage to break up my Hollywood lifestyle of hookers and blow with the occasional book."

"Phew, because I had no way to politely lead you back from that level of ignorance."

"Politely?" He sounded dubious.

"You got me. You were going to get a shit-ton of scathing." Samson grinned at me and my knees went weak. Was I really that relieved that I was finally getting through to him?

"Okay, smartass," I said, full up on males getting under my skin, "did you know this sunburst was his symbol? Louis was a pioneer in branding."

The bartender slid my booze to me. Craving more of Samson's smile, I wrapped my trembling hands around the drink. No mean feat with a shot glass.

"Put it on my tab," Samson said.

The bartender gave a brusque nod, moving away to help another customer.

Samson leaned an elbow on the bar. "Let me guess," he said. "You went to Versailles and realized there just wasn't enough gilt in modern society."

My heart caught in my throat. Guilt, as in, there needed to be more negativity in our world? No, wait, he meant the other gilt. The gold leaf one. Good catch, self. "Obviously. That and wallpaper. Really busy wallpaper."

"Preferably covered in self-portraits?"

"See, you get it."

His expression turned pensive. "I've been talking to my interior designer about that exact look for my new place. I'm thinking I'd rock portraiture."

I laughed, relaxing. "I actually inherited Louis' innate sense of style, being descended from the guy."

"I hate to break it to you," Samson said, motioning the bartender back over, "but I think Marie Antoinette gets the credit for that."

"Fine, if you're going to be technical about it." I took a sip of my vodka. "One thing that was definitely all him, and that I can totally get behind, were his ideas on world domination. Pretty ballsy."

Samson ordered a scotch for himself. "What's your definition of world domination? *Sports Illustrated* swimsuit edition? Or no. You want to act." He sounded disappointed.

"Dancer, actually. Total stage whore when it comes to performing." The longing infusing my voice was real. "But that's not my plan. I like to think of myself as a taste-maker. People want guidance on what to covet, how to be an early adapter to the newest trend in order to feel cool or relevant, and they want a seal of approval from someone they perceive as infinitely cooler." I gave him a saucy wink. "That's me."

Samson clinked his glass to mine. "Got it."

Bolstered by that small success, I continued. "My job is to show them that I'm the one they want in charge of their tastes and culture." I shrugged. "I just need a larger platform."

A boisterous shout of laughter came from across the bar, interrupting us. Rohan captivated a group with some story while Poppy stood as close to him as she could without Crazy Glue to keep her attached.

"Looks like my co-star is interested in following your lead," King said, jerking his chin at Poppy. Co-star? Fuck me. "Unless of course, she's there by private invitation."

I gave a dismissive flap of my hand, refraining from pointing out that he was the one who'd pushed her into Rohan's path to begin with. "Boys will be boys, and rock stars are definitely boys." I felt like a traitor to my gender even uttering such inane bullshit.

Rohan caught my eye at that moment. I winked at him and he grinned back. Poppy went pinchy-faced.

"Like I said," I told Samson with a smirk, "show them I'm the one they want in charge of their tastes."

"Why Lolita," Samson gasped, "and here I thought you were such a good girl."

"Oh baby, I'm very good. You just don't know me." I put my back to him and knocked back my shot.

Samson pressed up behind me, speaking into my ear. "I stand corrected."

I suppressed my shudder at the feel of his hard-on against my spine. Turning to face him, I pushed him back a few steps, tsking him.

"Maybe Rohan's not the guy for you," he said.

I arched an eyebrow.

"He turned his back on stardom. I find that kind of extreme behavior boring. So black and white when shades of gray make a much more interesting playground."

I willed my racing pulse to slow. Did Samson suspect? Was this a veiled threat against all Rasha or a blatant erotica reference? I got nothing from his expression. Making sure not to let my apprehension show, I shrugged. "I'm not with him for his worldview."

"What's he been up to anyway?" He sipped his scotch, his casual expression at odds with his unwavering gaze. If Rohan hadn't told me that he figured he was being set up, I'd have been insulted by Samson's continued interest in Snowflake instead of me. "I know he said he took a break, did some traveling, but he was on top. You don't walk away from that without a good reason or a scandal." Samson leaned in conspiratorially. "I'll take either."

His reason had been becoming Rasha. Although, I agreed that Rohan shouldn't have walked away from making music. I was so glad that even under duress and the fact this was a mission that he was connecting with his creative side again.

I could have tossed out that Rohan and I didn't do a lot of talking and I didn't know his reasons, but there was a weight behind the way Samson waited for my answer. "Fame fucked him up." If he thought any less of Rohan for it, so be it. Snowflake had nothing to prove.

All the vodka after the wine with dinner was starting to make me wonky, and this verbal sparring without any solid lead was giving me a headache.

He tapped his finger twice on the bar. "Well, I only came over to tell you how much I liked your sun."

"Thanks." Pouring myself a glass of water from a carafe, I winked at him. "Shows you have good taste."

He ran a hand over himself like a show model. "Obviously. But I also appreciate a good ball of flame." He unbuttoned his cuff, rolling up his sleeve to reveal the tattoo on the inside of his elbow.

I gripped my water glass, excitement coursing through me. I'd seen Samson's tattoos. Drio and Rohan had photos of them. They'd studied them trying to connect the designs with any known mythology, demon or otherwise. The designs they'd shown me were pretty generic. But what I was looking at now? A solid black circle sat in the middle of two concentric black rings. The outer ring acted as a frame for the twelve jagged spokes emanating from the center.

"That's a sun? It looks like a swastika with too many arms," I said, because that was true, too. It convinced me further this was a clue. Hitler had been fascinated with the occult and this stylized black sun fit the bill.

Samson stroked it. "I have no time for Nazis." He sounded genuinely disgusted, but his phrasing was odd. As if they'd personally done something to offend him. Was Samson tied to both Louis XIV and Hitler? Too much guesswork, not enough hard proof. "Just got it done."

I was so focused on committing the design to memory so I could tell Drio and Rohan about it, that I missed what he said next. "Sorry?"

He held his hand out to me. In his palm was a small red pill with a happy face on it.

"I don't take candy from strangers." I finished my water.

Samson pressed a hand to his heart with an exaggerated wince. "Strangers? After our chat? Our shared taste in home decorating? You wound me."

"Poor baby. I'm not about to take a random pill that allows you to do God knows what to me."

He broke it in half and popped one piece in his mouth. "Not to. With."

I rolled my eyes. "Right. So I take the red pill and see how far the rabbit hole goes?"

He shot me a crooked grin. "More MDMA, less *Matrix*. Let's see if you've got what it takes to intrigue."

Ecstasy, huh? Leo and I had done our fair share. I wasn't crazy about the touchy-feelies it would induce around him, but Rohan had said that some demons might reveal themselves under extreme emotion. The drug was brilliant for lowering inhibitions and creating intense emotional bonds with whoever you did it with. Plus, if I did intrigue, maybe I'd get to spend more time with him one-on-one.

It sucked that Rasha couldn't communicate via a psychic hotline. I looked over at Rohan, willing him to sense my dilemma, but he was busy holding court, Poppy's hand clamped on his arm like a wheel boot on a tire.

"Go big or go home, kitten."

"Don't call me 'kitten.'" I swiped the other half and swallowed it.

11

"What the fuck did you do?" Rohan hissed into my ear.

"I told you. Took E." I fixed my gloss, wishing the drugs were kicking in. "Consider yourself informed." I looked over to see if Samson had gotten our coats yet, since I'd insisted on going somewhere I could dance.

Rohan shifted to block my view. "Hotel. Now."

"No. We're connecting. He had this tattoo and–"

He blinked rapidly at me, his cheeks flushing red. The very shade my brother had dubbed "Nava Red," in honor of my tendency to bring it out in people. "You took drugs from a suspected demon because of a tattoo? Are you insane?"

"Too bad you were too busy to monitor my every move."

"You've got to be fucking kidding me."

"Language, Snowflake." I waggled my head to the catchy tune playing on the speakers. "Don't wreck all my hard work. You have your role and I have mine."

He leveled me with a mocking gold gaze. "You mean swallowing?"

I threw him a pitying smile. "It's such an easy option for getting what I want."

Drio sidled up beside us, preventing us from coming to blows. Not that I would. Punching was no fun. Swaying my hips was. "Is there a problem?" he said. "Because you two are not playing the agreed upon dynamic."

"Rohan's kvetching over nothing," I said.

"Samson gave her ecstasy," Rohan said. "Or a roofie." What a drama queen.

"You know, Ro, E could actually work." Drio nodded his approval.

I smirked at Rohan. "I don't think roofies come with happy faces on them. Besides, Samson took the other half."

Rohan gripped the edge of the bar.

Across the room, Samson held up my jacket, two of his bodyguards hovering silently behind him. I held up a "hang on one sec" finger. "I need—"

"You need to keep quiet for thirty seconds so I can take that time to convince myself I shouldn't strangle you," Rohan bit out. It seemed prudent to do as requested.

I counted off the time, enjoying the music, then turned to Drio. "I had a breakthrough with Samson. I want to continue pursuing this lead, which I promise to tell you all about tomorrow. But for tonight, will you come with me to this private party? I don't want to go there alone with him."

Rohan pinched the bridge of his nose. "Now she speaks sense."

"I'm supposed to take the Two Stooges to another club," Drio said.

"*I'm* going with you." Rohan grabbed my hand and pulled me through the crowd toward Samson.

Why did the heat of Rohan's hand against mine make me giddier than total nudity with other guys? I stroked my thumb over his.

"Quit it," he snapped.

I barely had time to pluck my jacket out of Samson's hands as we passed. "Rohan's coming."

"Great," Samson said in a voice that made it clear that despite the smile, this was absolutely not great at all.

I, however, thought it was seven kinds of fantastic. So much so that I had to share my delight. I enthusiastically waved good-bye to Poppy.

"Bhenchod," Rohan muttered and pulled me out of the bar, where a limo awaited us.

A brick wall of a driver opened the back door, standing rigidly beside it. I immediately dubbed him Brickie. "Cute cap," I said.

I'm sure that would have kicked off an enthusiastic fashion exchange except one of the bodyguards hustled me into the backseat where I was pinned between Rohan and Samson, the two of them traveling in chilly silence. Whatever. I was buzzed, happy Eurotrash was playing on the speakers, and the ecstasy was tingling my fingers and toes. I was being taken on an adventure in an incredible city. Yay!

Even better, Rohan had my back. He wouldn't let anything happen to me. Big rock star and demon hunter worried about me. I ducked my head so neither of them could see my silly grin. Lovely boy. Under the cover of darkness that the backseat afforded, I slid my left hand over, curling my fingers into the waist of Rohan's pants.

He turned his head to look at me. Still totally pissed.

I blew him a silent kiss. A curious expression crossed his face. Right. But blowing kisses didn't count, so I blew him another one.

Rohan shook his head at me and turned away to stare out the window.

"Kicking in?"

"What?" I looked at Samson.

"You're dancing."

So I was. Grooving away where I sat on the plush leather seat. "It's a good song." I bopped Samson on the tip of his nose.

He laughed, catching my finger and biting gently on it. I rubbed my finger against his teeth for a second because it tickled.

Samson hissed, trailing a finger along my jaw and down my neck.

Party pooper on the other side didn't like that. "We're here." Rohan opened the door and yanked me out.

That won him zero points with Brickie and the security trio, since Samson scooted out, hot on our heels, causing the other four to scramble after us like Keystone Cops from those old silent movies that I'd seen in a film studies class during my brief university stint.

I looked at the nondescript club. More of a warehouse really. Despite the line of sulky beautiful people clamoring to get in, one look at Samson and Rohan now flanking me, and the bouncer lowered the rope. I could get used to this.

Inside the foyer, I handed one of the boys my coat, graciously allowing him to check it. Sashaying down a short hallway, I stepped through a doorway and found myself in a giant black box. Lights pulsed, bass throbbed, and bodies writhed.

Rohan placed his hands on my hips, forcing me to stand still. Even though he'd come up behind me, I knew it was him. I always knew it was him.

"Nava," he said insistently in my ear. "No tapping. Don't give Samson any actual information about yourself."

I froze. Shit. I'd been doing that, hadn't I? I turned around, meeting his eyes. There was none of the anger I expected to find, just an anxious concern.

"Just be careful," he said.

"I know. I'm sorry. I won't screw up. Now you have to have fun, okay?" I smiled, seeing Samson headed toward us. Ecstasy or not, I could stick to the role. I could intrigue.

I swayed my hips, grooving onto the dance floor. They followed like lapdogs, each one making sure the other didn't get too close. Fine by me. Between their posturing and the music, there was no chance to talk and give myself away by saying something stupid.

I made sure not to tap at all.

Eventually, the wusses got tired, drifting off the floor. Not me. No one felt the music as deeply as I did. My heart beat in time to the pulsing lights. I threw my arms high, one with the mass of bodies on the floor, kicking off my shoes and abandoning myself to the music. "Take me higher," the vocalist sang and I obeyed. Blood became melody, heartbeat turned to downbeat. Lighter and lighter and higher and higher I flew.

Rohan pressed a bottle of water into my hand, breaking my trance. I put my hand on his shoulder, leaning in close to speak to him. "You take good care of me." His shoulder felt really nice so I kept rubbing him. Then I drifted that hand down his chest, my other one snaking around his hip, water bottle still hooked between my fingers. I swayed against his body to the music.

"Nava," he groaned. His eyes turned that molten lava that was rapidly becoming my favorite color.

"Ro," I purred. I tilted my face up to his. "You have the best lips."

His face screwed up like he was in pain. I thought he said, "Not like this," and then, body tense, he twisted himself away from me.

I pouted at him, my hips still shimmying. My head still bobbing.

"Drink your water," he ordered and disappeared into the crowd.

I pressed the bottle against my chest for a minute before chugging it back. It didn't matter that I couldn't see Rohan. An invisible thread connected us. Red. No, sunset orange. Winding around the other dancers to anchor deep inside our chests, I could let myself go and I wouldn't fly off. I tipped my head up, grinning.

A pair of hands slid around my waist and I lit up, thinking he'd come back. But it was Samson. He nuzzled my neck.

None of that, demon boy. I disentangled myself, dancing deeper into the press of bodies. Flirting was fine but there wasn't a dose of ecstasy large enough to make me forget myself enough to hook up with him.

Of course he followed me, looking irritated.

Leading him on a chase was all well and good, but the possibility of the catch was important too, so I crooked a finger, beckoning him closer.

He obliged.

I put my hands on his hips. At least this way I could control the distance between us. "Keep up," I shouted over the music.

Then I closed my eyes.

I have no idea how long we danced. Samson didn't press his luck, keeping a slight distance between our fronts. His hands, however ran up and down along my sides. Over and over again. It went with the music so I let him continue.

He smiled at me, his hair plastered to his forehead. His shirt had been discarded at some point and beads of sweat trickled down his abs. A lot of people, men and women both, were doing their share of looking and I had no doubt that a lot of Instagram streams featured new pics of Samson 'dancing fool' King.

I started giggling.

"What's so funny?" he asked.

I bit off my laughter at the sight of Rohan sandwiched between two girls, his jacket discarded. Heat pooled in my belly watching him, one hand splayed against a woman's waist, his hips rolling and grinding in perfect harmony with his partners.

The bass wasn't the only thing throbbing. I fanned myself with the neckline of my dress, realizing that I stood stock still in the middle of the dance floor. I quickly turned my attention back to Samson only to find him fixed on Rohan with an expression of pure hatred. I laced my fingers through his and squeezed to get his attention. Not the hand with my Rasha ring. I had enough presence of mind not to blow the glamour.

Samson focused back on me and I mimed getting water. I had no idea where my shoes were, so I made my way over to the bar in bare feet, keeping a close hold on my target.

We passed a woman in fairy wings reclining on a couch in the back corner, a sensual smile on her face as she watched her girlfriend dance. It was sexy until the dancer turned, revealing the panic in her frozen features. Her movements were jerky, as if she was fighting them. As if she was trying to stop and couldn't.

The woman on the couch tipped her head back, her eyes glazed in cruel lust. Shit! Demon. I sped up, veering for the dancer.

The demon shuddered and the dancer collapsed. That got the attention of the people around her, who came to the fainted woman's aid.

The spawn slunk off through the press of bodies.

"She should have paced herself," Samson said into my ear.

I'd bet a million bucks he knew exactly what had just happened but I didn't let on. "That's why we're hydrating," I said. I prayed the dancer would be okay.

I consumed several glasses of water before pressing one into Samson's hand. "Drink." I wasn't sure if evil fiends suffered from dehydration but in case he was one, I wanted him in good health when we killed him.

Samson ran his fingers over my sunburst. "You're melting." It was true. All my sweat had smeared the sun.

I stared at his hand, drawing small circles over my skin. I didn't want it to feel good but I was on E.

Samson grew bolder, tracing along the neckline of my dress. Then he punched me. Not intentionally, but someone jostled into him, and as he crashed into me, his hands folded over into a fist, bopping me on my right boob.

"Ow!" I rubbed my chest, spinning to berate the clumsy dolt that had hit us.

Rohan gave me a crooked grin, his drink splashing everywhere.

My brow creased. Mr. Control looked plastered. Something about that didn't feel right.

He waved the drink at me, draping an arm around my shoulders. "Found you." His eyes were a bit too bright. His voice a bit too loud. "Time to go."

"Okay, bye," Samson said. To Rohan.

Rohan stumbled between Samson and me, his back to King. The grin fell from his face. His eyes were cold.

He was totally sober and not kidding about us leaving.

I stepped around him with an apologetic smile to Samson. I was tired, and beyond the sun tattoo, I hadn't learned anything useful about our target. "Talk tomorrow?"

Samson's expression hardened. "I'm busy." Adieu, our tenuous connection.

"Maybe we could stay a bit longer," I hedged.

Rohan fell against me, back in drunk-mode. His fingers dug into my skin. "Don't keep me waiting, baby," he slurred.

"Staying or going?" Samson asked when I still hesitated.

The crowd roared as the DJ wound them up, their collective energy rippling through the room in a sinuous pulse.

I threw Rohan's arm off of me, despite his fumbled attempt to keep me close. "I'm still not over my jet lag." I spoke directly into Samson's ear since the music was almost deafening now. "I need to sleep. A rain check. Please? I promise to make it up to you."

"Tomorrow." His barked word was a reprieve and a warning. I'd not get a second chance.

12

"Soon as I wake up, I'll call you," I told Samson.

Rohan waved a hand in farewell and dragged me toward the coat check.

I put on my jacket then tried to go back. "I have no shoes," I explained.

He swung me into his arms, ignoring my yelp of protest. My smacks to his chest were half-hearted since my feet hurt.

I held my tongue until we were safely in a cab going back to the hotel. "You almost ruined everything, you faking bastard."

"I pulled the plug on your night. Tough shit. This isn't about enjoying Samson's attention. Or him enjoying yours."

"Why should it matter? This is just a hook-up."

"I was talking about the job."

"So am I. You shouldn't have made me a groupie if you couldn't deal with me embracing the part."

"*My* groupie."

"As you keep reminding me."

Rohan's grip tightened on the seat belt strapped across his chest. "I've given you a lot of leeway, *Lolita*, but going home with King was not part of the plan. Especially not with you primed to make stupid decisions."

I crossed my arms. "That was never going to happen."

"Apparently neither was a thank you."

There was no talking to him in this mood. I peered bleary-eyed out the window at the silent streets, the occasional passing car disturbing the stillness of deepest night.

My three minutes of good mood ended when we pulled up to the hotel and Rohan unceremoniously scooped me up and carried me inside. He deposited me on the lobby floor, both of us bristling at each other.

That's when we ran into Lily, clad in cute pink sweats, glowing with fresh-faced beauty, hair in a neat bun, and her glasses perched on her nose. Versus the dirty girl vibe I rocked in the all worst ways: sweat-stained hair falling over in a mess, smeared body paint, and lack of shoes.

My night was complete.

"Hey guys! Just getting in?" Her bright smile leeched the last of my energy. "I couldn't sleep. Came to get my fix." She held up a small cellophane-wrapped package of tea, the motion causing the sleeve of her hoodie to shift. A very familiar silver bracelet with a stylized design inlaid in onyx was on her wrist.

"You have the same bracelet?"

Lily glanced down at hers. "The Om? Yeah. I gave it to Ro–"

"Right before his first tour. I heard."

Rohan one-arm hugged her. "I charmed you into buying it for me."

Lily snorted and ducked out from his hold. "You're lucky I didn't throw it at your head. You were such a jerk that day."

"I was cranky from lack of sleep." Rohan gave her a pointed stare and Lily blushed.

Kill me. The E was wearing off, leaving me with an edgy restless thread coursing through my exhaustion. "Well, it was a very long night and it's way past my bedtime."

"It looks like you had fun." I tensed at her words but she didn't sound snarky. In fact, I'd swear a wistful expression crossed over her face. What *was* certain was the brief glance she turned on Rohan.

Ah.

Rohan saw it too. His expression softened. "You wouldn't have enjoyed it, Lils." He took her hands in his. "Besides, I want to hang out where we can talk. I miss that."

I dug my nails into my palms. I'd forgotten that coming off E always left me emotionally wide-open. "I'm off. Have a good night."

"Sleep well, Lolita," Lily called out.

I was really starting to hate that name. At least I'd gotten better about not looking back, though that left me making eye contact with that *darling* desk clerk as I made my way to the elevator. Any pretense of professionalism was beyond him. He scowled at me like I was a plague who'd infested his pristine realm. I'm sure we were both wondering what twist of fate made him present for all my best moments. Sighing, I kept my head held high the entire time it took for the world's slowest elevator to get to the lobby and then crawl up to the third floor. Just because I was alone in the elevator didn't mean I didn't have my pride.

I stepped out to find Rohan waiting for me by the stairwell door. Doing my best not to slump in exhaustion, I stomped past him, the carpet scratchy underfoot.

Rohan's arm shot out to the wall, blocking me. The two of us faced in different directions. How apt.

"Move," I said

He didn't budge.

I stared resolutely ahead.

Finally he dropped his arm.

I pulled my keycard from my coat, walking directly to my room. No passing go. No collecting $200.

"Don't leave." He spoke quietly but in the silence of the corridor, I had no trouble hearing him.

My hands balled up. Hadn't it been enough for one night? That thread between us that had felt so comforting earlier threatened to strangle me now. Anger fueled my turn. I would have welcomed a corresponding anger in him, but the naked longing on his face and the defeat in the slope of his shoulders undid me. That and his sincere, "I love watching you dance."

The hallway was empty but it suddenly felt hard to breathe.

He held out a hand.

I leaned back. The magnetic push/pull between us demanded a certain distance, a certain resistance, as much as attraction. Wrung out on every level, I couldn't afford to let Mr. Force-of-Nature Mitra take advantage of my weakened boundaries to redefine our hook-ups into whatever vision he had of them.

The air conditioning kicked in and I wrapped my arms around myself.

"When you see my shower, you'll thank me." He scrunched up his face, a lock of hair falling boyishly over his eyes. "Nothing happens. Just sleep."

I wasn't sure if that sweetened the offer or not, but I nodded.

We rode in silence up to his floor. A hushed bubble that continued to encapsulate us as we entered his dark suite. Rohan snapped on a light, dimming the brightness down to a more tolerable level. "Want me to start the shower?"

I reached around to the back of my dress and tugged on the zipper. It didn't budge. I grasped the fabric on either side with one hand and tried again. "Help."

He stood behind me. Not touching me at first.

My heart hammered in my throat. I lifted my hair off my neck.

He rested his hands on my dress but it was only to try the zipper. "How attached are you to this?" He ran a finger between the top and my skin. "I might have to rip it."

I swallowed. "Do what you need to." One of his finger blades pressed against me through the thin cloth and then the dress fell open as he cut the zipper away. Tiny goosebumps dotted my skin, cool air rushing against my back. My sweat had gotten to the clammy stage and I really wanted that shower. Really wanted to sleep.

Neither desire was enough to get me moving, my every nerve tensed in anticipation. The yawning nothing that happened as we both stood there was a much better incentive. I dropped my hair, twisting around. "Thanks."

Rohan gripped my hips, keeping me still. With the lightest touch, he hooked his fingers under my straps, sliding them off my shoulders.

My lids shivered closed, my heart practically straining out of my chest waiting for his next move, but there was just the feel of his hands clasping my forearms and his warm exhalations against the back of my neck.

"I'll run the shower." His voice was strained, shaky, but by the time I caught his arm, he was back to his usual level of control.

I let go. "Make it hot."

I stepped out of my dress and under the spray. Another outfit ruined. Oh, well. I sighed in bliss, letting the heat ease my sore muscles. I must have stayed under the water for a good half hour. It took a while to wash the body paint off. Longer than that for my head to clear.

Clean and wrinkled, I stepped onto the bath mat with shaking legs, wrapping a towel around me. Either steam now choked the room or the remnants of the E in my system had turned the world hazy. Spying Rohan's cologne on the counter next to his black toiletries bag, I cracked the cap and sniffed it.

Rohan rapped on the door and I hastily and silently slid the bottle back where I'd found it.

"Do you want a robe?" he asked.

Yes, since I had nothing else to wear right now. I cracked the door, taking the fluffy terry cloth robe from him. I tightened the belt so it was the cloth, and not Rohan's presence wrapped around me, then I stepped into the adjoining bedroom in a billowing cloud of steam, my damp towel in hand. "Should I leave this in the bathroom?"

Rohan had stripped down to boxer shorts and a clean T-shirt. He took the towel from me, going into the bathroom to toss it on the counter. When he returned, he held a dry towel. "Sit." He motioned to the bed. The king-sized bed. Thick and plush, it was piled with cozy blankets, long pillows, and an obscene thread count that I itched to mess up.

I sat down on the edge, smoothing a hand over the pillowcase.

Rohan nudged me into the middle of the mattress then sat down behind me and proceeded to dry my hair. He twisted strands between the towel folds, gently yet briskly drawing off excess moisture. His ministrations slowed, his fingertips massaging my scalp.

I pressed backward into his palms. My hands rested on his calves, his legs splayed out on either side of me. The light dusting of his calf hair was scratchy under my fingers. "How come you never mentioned you provided this service?"

"It's only available to a select clientele," he joked.

Like Lily? "We chosen few appreciate it." I yawned.

"You should crash."

"Do you want me to take the couch?"

"No." He stood up. "I have a few ideas I want to work on."

Didn't have to tell me twice. Still in the robe, I crawled under the covers, half-asleep by the time my head hit the pillow. Out in the living room, Rohan played a soft melody on the piano. It was quiet enough that I had to concentrate to hear it, eyes closed, a caress that lulled me all the way into sleep.

I woke up groggily to find myself laying half on top of him, our legs tangled up together. No light peeked around the curtains yet, the world still slumbering around us. My hand rested on his stomach where his shirt had ridden up to expose a warm strip of skin.

I tensed. He was supposed to stay at the piano. Nap on the couch. Not be here. I didn't *sleep* with guys. Not even after sex. If I wanted to cuddle, I had my pillow. I pulled myself free, needing to kill this incredible intimacy because this type of feels were not part of the fucking deal.

"Stay," he mumbled.

I flung the covers back. I knew where that was coming from. Any body would do at this time of night and I was the closest one. If you can't be with the one you love... Not finishing that. "Because you want company."

I swung my feet onto the floor.

He snagged the back of my robe. "Because I don't want to be alone in the dark."

Rohan let go of me but I didn't move, my head bowed. No one wanted that. It was the reason humans huddled around a flickering fire, pressed close to keep the shadows at bay. But you didn't voice it. You said, "Because you're warm." Because any one of a million excuses that didn't expose your vulnerability.

Rohan never exposed his, so what was this? Another game? Except, that wasn't right. He'd bared his soul to me when he'd admitted that cutting off his music had been denying an essential part of himself. It's why I'd pushed so hard for him to write the theme song.

I had no idea if I wanted to stay or to run away as far as I could. A simple repeat fuck had gotten tangled up and crazy complicated. Icy panic clawed at my throat at what that meant or what I wanted it to mean or hoped it didn't mean.

"Stop thinking." He loosely laced his fingers through mine, but it was clearly my call to stay or go.

I glanced back at him. Big mistake.

Rohan watched me intently, his expression soft and open. His eyes begging me to stay.

Each heartbeat pulsed along my skin from my chest to the top of my head. I forced an exhale, my hand tightening on his.

He tugged me into his side, tucking the covers around us, his head resting on mine. My remaining tension melted away under the steady comfort of his touch.

I snuggled closer. *Because you're warm.*

13

The clock showed mid-afternoon by the time I woke up for good. Alone. I rolled over onto Rohan's side of the bed, pressing my face into his pillow. Even the faint trace of his unique scent smelled better than dark chocolate, clean grass after a heavy rain, or the woodsy musk in the air after two of you have come your brains out. Was it wrong of me to relish this intensely intimate access to him? Or only wrong of me to wonder who else was in this club?

Sitting up with a stretch, I raked my fingers through my curls, tumbling loose on my shoulders, trying to comb them into some sort of style. Then I retied the belt on my robe, and padded out of the bedroom in search of some coffee. I hoped a caffeine jolt would help with my lingering confusion about whatever was going on between Rohan and me.

I followed the sound of music, stopping in the doorway to drink in the sight of Rohan at the piano, head bent, his hair falling into his eyes, fully focused on the keyboard. His white T-shirt was so worn I glimpsed his brown skin through the sheer patches. My fingers twitched, longing to feel the play of hard muscle under soft fabric. "Good morning."

The soft look he gave me was immediately wiped away in favor of a shark-like smile. My heart sped up, thinking this was a prelude to a very good morning.

"Afternoon, actually."

So much for my second chance. I didn't react to the judgment in Samson's voice but any fond thoughts about Rohan fled. I couldn't help but wonder if he'd planned last night to maneuver me here to be found by Samson now.

"I didn't realize you boys had a play date today." I stretched, making sure my robe gaped open enough to flash Samson a bit of boob, then swiped the coffee mug from Samson's hand as I sat down next to him. Thigh to thigh.

A wrong note sounded from the piano. Not sure whose smirk was bigger at that, Samson's or mine. I suffered zero delusions that Samson's cocky glee was about my unique charms. It had everything to do with Rohan and whatever made Samson despise him. But I'd use anything I could to my advantage.

I crossed my legs, my robe riding up to the border of peep show territory. "You're looking good after our late night." He was charmingly rumpled.

Samson ignored my compliment. "Enjoy your sleepover?"

Damage control. With compliments and physical contact both failures I selected and discarded a dozen ways to regain his good graces. No way was I going to be sidelined from this mission.

"She did," Rohan piped up over his playing. "I have a more comfortable bed and Lolita does like her comfort."

I swallowed my sour mouthful of coffee. "But it's morning now. A brand new day."

The barest flash of hurt crossed Rohan's face before he glanced down, testing out a chord. I had no idea if it was real or put on for the sake of the mission but either way, I had to stay in character. Being Rasha came before any irrational desire to spare Rohan's feelings.

"Tell me about your film." I pressed the coffee mug back into Samson's hands, letting my own linger for a moment. "I'd love to come watch you on set. If you'll have me."

"I'm shooting in Český Krumlov the next couple days," Samson said. "Then back here Tuesday for the final day."

"We could work on the tracks after that," Rohan said.

I gripped Samson's thigh. "You're going to sing on the theme song? That will make it epic."

He studied me for a long moment. "You could come Tuesday to watch the big chase scene."

Finally, a freaking bone.

Rohan's song turned from a major to a minor key. I shivered at the darkness that seemed to drive it, but I wasn't stupid enough to take my focus off of Samson. "Hot boys and fast cars? Big yes. Is there going to be a wrap party?"

"That night," Samson said.

I leaned in, my boobs front and center. "What does a girl have to do to get an invite?"

Rohan snorted.

We both looked at him, me to will him to quit disrupting my flow, and Samson to, well, who knew what was in his head.

Rohan seemed to have lost interest in our conversation, erasing something on the sheet music. That placated Samson who didn't notice that Snowflake white-knuckled the pencil.

I trailed my fingers up Samson's arm. "I'd love to help you celebrate wrapping."

Samson broke into a slow smile. "That could be arranged."

I relaxed.

"I'm performing," Rohan said.

Count me in. Though I shrugged as if it didn't matter, conscious of Samson monitoring my reaction.

Samson raised his eyebrows. "Accepted Forrest's invitation, did you?"

"Give the cast and crew a tease of the theme song. Seemed like a no-brainer."

I allowed myself a second to enjoy the excitement that my conjurings of an on-stage Snowflake brought on, then stood up, using Samson's shoulder for balance. If he got a final cheap thrill, all the better. "I need to get dressed."

"Your clothes are in the bedroom," Rohan said.

I stumbled at his words. Had he moved me in? I hustled into his bedroom, breathing a sigh of relief that he'd only brought me up clothes for today. The dress pants and blouse weren't something I'd have worn around Samson normally. Maybe Rohan didn't plan this? Wondering would make me crazy. I slipped into my clothes and the shoes he'd brought. He'd thoughtfully fetched some make-up, too. I needed the mask.

I strolled into the living room, armor in place. "Will you text me later?" Asking not demanding since demon or psychopath, Samson would respond better to being accorded the position of power. "Tuesday is much too far away for further conversations in taste-making."

Samson scratched his head. "Now see, I remember it as further conversations in tasting."

"Lucky for you, I'm rather fluent in tasting."

"I'm quite the linguist myself." He grinned at me and I squirmed like a cat trying to coat itself in a pool of sunshine.

"Don't want to keep you from anything, Lolita," Rohan said.

I dragged my eyes back to his, having forgotten he was in the room. "Right. Stuff to do." Okay, that came out breathier than I intended, but damn.

Samson chuckled softly.

I picked up my coat. "What are you up to?" I asked Rohan.

He tapped his sheet music. "I need to work for a few hours." Perfect. I'd fill him in on Samson's black sun tattoo later.

"Bye, boys. Have fun." I shot Rohan a *behave* look. He busied himself with his music but a half-grin ghosted over his lips.

I escaped before I embarrassed myself, nodding at the bodyguard planted outside Rohan's room and recognizing him as one of Samson's men on duty last night.

Intent on checking my email to see if Dr. Gelman had replied, I headed for the elevator. Both missions–Ari and Samson–had to be completed before we flew home. If Samson wrapped in a few days, that meant the clock had begun to tick in earnest.

Back in my room, I checked my phone to find that she had in fact emailed back. She'd invited me to meet her for breakfast at Café Louvre on Monday morning. I fired off a fast RSVP, then opened the email from Leo entitled "ARE YOU KIDDING?"

The first link contained tabloid photos of me and Samson dancing. His head was thrown back with a wild grin and my hair splayed out in all directions like an open fan. The headline read "Samson King tears it up with Mystery Brunette." I scanned the captions, but none of them identified me by name.

Yet.

I twisted my ring around, running through the ramifications of the media exposure, and therefore Samson finding out my real name. Even if he already knew there was a female Rasha, he wouldn't connect my name to that person. The Brotherhood kept our identities carefully guarded. Same for any personal information, which I'd hope would keep Ari and my parents out of Samson's reach should he prove a demon. The chances of history repeating itself and Samson going after my brother like Asmodeus had done were slim. Though that didn't mean I wouldn't put a back-up plan in place, just in case.

I scanned some of the other links she'd sent, pausing for a long moment on a photo of Samson stroking his finger over my body paint, a focused expression on his face with the caption "Does the King seek a Queen?"

I phoned Leo. "Queen calling. How many jealous comments am I getting?"

"Eh. Haters gonna hate. Enjoy your fifteen minutes, baby."

"Oh, I will. Though Snowflake is gonna have a coronary when he sees this."

"Points for Snowflake," Leo said. "I don't like you getting close to Samson either."

"No. Rohan gets no points. Fuck buddies do not require nor are eligible for points. Unless they're Frequent Flier." I kicked off the flats Rohan had thoughtfully brought up for me and sank onto the mattress. A highly disappointing sensation after Rohan's bed. "I always knew I'd be famous."

"For tap?" Leo snorted in derision.

I massaged my instep. "I'd rock fame. You know how people always say fame wouldn't change them? Screw that. I'd become impossible. Treating everyone like little people. Reminding them they're not worthy, but would be eligible for worthy-status with the appropriate bribe."

"'Kay, you get you're sounding like Samson, right?" Leo asked.

I switched my massage to my other foot. "All right, yes, but unlike him, I'd leave everyone with a warm glow for having been in my presence, instead of misery, humiliation, and world domination. Nava Katz. The gift that keeps on giving."

"Like herpes," Leo agreed cheerfully. "Speaking of STIs, did you sleep with Samson? Because I recognized that *ecstatic* look on your face."

"You did. But nope."

"Too busy servicing your rock star last night?"

"That didn't happen either."

She gasped. "Did you displease him? Were you displaced?"

"Since it doesn't get better than me, I was not displaced." Not yet, Cuntessa whispered. I mentally chucked a rock at her head. "I may have displeased, but that's foreplay with us. What's up with you?"

"Explain something to me, and use small descriptive words so I understand. You're on a top secret mission, very thrilling and adrenaline-inducing, with the boy you've been having hot monkey sex with, under the guise of being the girl who is supposed to be having hot monkey sex with him, while being on ecstasy, and there was no sex to be had?"

"Monkey or otherwise. That is correct."

"What the hell is wrong with you?"

I stretched out my neck and shoulders. "I was fatigued. Even I need a night off now and then."

"Did you not look at him last night?"

"I did, but I'm wondering how you saw him."

"Photos, d'uh. The paparazzi love Rohan."

Putting Leo on speakerphone, I followed the next set of links she texted me. "Rohan's back and more delicious than ever!" read one website. He'd been a busy little beaver last night. No one chick was featured twice in the photos. Commodities indeed.

Please let these photos be the first thing Poppy sees this morning.

I paused over the snaps of Rohan chummy-chummy with Samson. Or, more correctly, Samson chummy with Rohan. I hadn't imagined that look of hatred on his face last night. What was he playing at?

Leo gave a dreamy sigh. "Letting his rock star fly free. I would totally tap that."

"You would have tapped that when you were thirteen. This is not news."

"Nava." Leo wasn't buying my stalling.

I twisted around to prop my feet against my headboard. "Lightning girl is here."

"I know you are. So?"

I gave a strangled laugh. "No, honey. The actual one."

Her sputter was gratifying. "Who is she?"

"A beautiful genius. Very nice."

"Shit. Total nightmare. Are they dating?"

"No. But there is definitely something between them. A tenderness. Which I don't want from him, but sistah, it's messing with me getting some."

Her "then you need to get back on that, beyatch," sounded even less believable.

I tucked my arm underneath my head, staring up at the ceiling. "Ever wish we could hide away until the sun explodes destroying all life as we know it?"

"Would we be hiding out with a lifetime supply of potato chips and vibrator batteries?" Leo asked.

"We could."

"Hmm, still no."

"Why not?" I said.

"Because we are socialized, highly functional human beings who don't hide."

"No, we're not."

Leo snorted her donkey-braying laugh. "Not even a little bit. Still. No hiding."

I sighed. "Fine. Everything good with you? For reals? Get your boy part fix yet?"

"Nope. Last night was all about the delights of girl bits."

"Sweet. Well, I better go prep for my meeting. Got some possible intel to follow up on."

"Good luck. Shmugs." She blew a loud smack into the phone. "Don't let the bastards get you down."

Damn, I loved my bestie. "Schmugs."

The second I hung up, I called Baruch back at the Vancouver chapter house. The top Rasha in terms of weapons and training, Baruch Ya'ari stood about six and half feet tall, with shoulder-length black hair and sharp blue eyes. Combined with the hemp bracelets he wore, he always reminded me of a surfer Special Ops guy.

Rasha weren't just hunters. Their duties involved everything from training initiates and designing weaponry like Baruch did, intelligence gathering on demons like Rohan and Drio did via the in-house intelligence department, or coding surveillance software and top secret databases like Kane.

Baruch had been assigned as my personal fighting instructor, a.k.a. the one with the best chance of quickly giving me moves to keep me alive. I adored him, even though he gave me enough bruises to warrant calling a helpline.

"Shalom."

I smiled at his Israeli accent rumbling over the line.

"Boker tov, Tree Trunk." Baruch bore my nickname for him with the same stoicism he handled everything. Well, everything that wasn't Ms. Clara, the person in charge of all Brotherhood administrative business in Canada. Rasha, rabbi, Executive whether living or visiting dealt with her. She also moonlighted as one of Vancouver's top dominatrixes. Mad whip skills.

Demons were drawn to instability, be it civil unrest or natural disasters. The fault lines along the west coast appealed to them, which was why years ago, Vancouver had founded a chapter. Since then, we'd become the main Canadian hub, overseen by Rabbi Abrams in theory and Ms. Clara in all the ways that counted.

"Tell me you have a plan for dealing with those photos," he said.

I scrunched up my face. "I do." Carry on as planned. "I also have a favor to ask. Can you please keep an eye on Ari until this job is over?"

Tree Trunk sighed. "I'm going back to Jerusalem," he said. "Back to HQ."

"You can't!"

"Maspik, Nava," he said gently. "I can't stay as your personal trainer either. The Brotherhood needs me."

My lip wobbled. I didn't mean to be a wuss, but for the past several weeks, Baruch, Rohan, Drio, and Kane had been my anchors in this funhouse I now called my life. Kane would be sticking around, since he was based out of Vancouver, and I'd be happy for Drio to move to an ice floe in the Arctic, but Baruch? I needed my Tree Trunk. I felt safer knowing he was around, guiding me.

You'd think that being a chosen demon hunter would be broadening my horizons. I felt like it was shrinking my world.

"I'll put Kane on it," he assured me.

Great. Babysitting Ari for yet another reason. If I didn't get Ari Rasha'd soon and all magicked up, I feared the two of them might end in a double homicide.

"Beseder?" he asked.

"Okay," I agreed. I thanked Baruch, making him promise to stay in touch. Tamping down any residual Tree Trunk sadness, I fired up my laptop. One quick call to room service to order a club sandwich, fries, and chocolate cake, since the Brotherhood was paying, and I got to work tracking down the significance, if any, of the black sun. Even without access to Demon Club's databases, the connections I found floored me.

Coming up for air a couple of hours later, I grabbed my pile of notes, stuffing them into my laptop bag to transport them up to Rohan's room in the event Samson was still around, so he wouldn't see them. Bag slung diagonally across my chest, I stepped into the elevator and found Drio. "Nice photos," he smirked. "High much?"

"Took one for the team." I tapped my bag. "Wait and be amazed. Where did you end up last night?"

"Took the boys to an S&M dungeon."

I looked at him with horrified fascination. "Are they still alive?"

"Baby S&M." Such disdain. The place must not have met his standards of true sadism.

"Sucks to be you."

Drio shrugged. "T-Roy spent most of the night with a ball gag in his mouth so that was an improvement."

"You mean Troy?"

"Troy doesn't come with the cred he so desperately craves. He's T-Roy now," he said. I laughed. "Logan is the one constantly texting." He pitched his voice lower in impersonation. "Dope messages bespelling importance, bro."

I stumbled. Drio was cracking me up. What bizarro world had I landed in? "That doesn't even make sense."

"Yeah. I try not to listen when he speaks. My IQ has dropped ten points on this mission."

We stepped out of the elevator, bound for Rohan's suite at the far end of the hall. "You think they're," I pitched my voice lower, "human?"

"I don't know what to think." He shrugged out of his jacket, his quiet tone matching mine. "Part of me thinks the two guys closest to Samson have to be demons. But in all the time I've spent with them, they haven't made a single suspicious move. No sign of any evil agenda."

"Could they be under strict orders to behave? In case they blow Samson's cover?"

"They cause a scandal, Samson gets rid of them. If anything, his celeb status gives them leeway to let their demon tendencies out. Perfect cover for bad behavior. They could be human, but my gut is saying otherwise."

"Could be PDs," I suggested.

Half-demons were known by the pejorative term PD, from the old Rasha joke, "What do you call a half demon? Practice." The only way to tell that they weren't full evil was that when killed, PDs exploded in a shower of gold dust. I'd learned using that term around Leo was at my peril.

"Even so. Something doesn't add up."

"How do they feel about Samson?" I adjusted the weight of the strap on my shoulder.

"Troy doesn't say much unless he's kissing ass. Logan talks a lot of smack about King but never anywhere near him."

I veered around a housekeeping cart piled high with fresh linens. "Does the American accent get tiring?" I asked. "Do you ever slip?"

He shook his head. "Too many years doing Mom impersonations."

"Your mother is American?!"

It was Drio's turn to laugh. "Which part are you struggling with? That she's American or that I have a mother?"

"That you have a mother, obviously. I thought you were spawned."

A door opened revealing Poppy backing out of a suite with a cat-like smile. *Rohan's* suite. He of the rumpled clothes and messed hair framed in the doorway beside her. She trailed her hands down his chest.

I contemplated breaking her fingers. And his balls.

"Quit it. You're short circuiting," Drio grabbed my hand, flinching at the spark that arced off my palm against his.

"Excuse me," Poppy huffed as Drio pushed the two of us into the room, effectively breaking the two of them apart.

Drio flung his coat onto a chair. "You're excused." He made a shooing motion at her.

She looked at Rohan waiting for her knight in shining armor to step in but he'd registered my presence. His face colored in that purple apoplectic way as he opened his mouth, shut it, then jabbed his index finger between me and a chair. "Sit."

Guess he'd seen the photos.

14

Poppy's mood perked right up at Rohan's anger toward me. Smiling, she ran a finger along the outline of her obviously newly reapplied lipstick.

Refusing to sit, I batted my lashes at him. "Punish away, baby." I visibly shivered.

Drio unsuccessfully smothered a laugh.

Rohan murmured bullshit platitudes to Poppy, ushered her out the door, then slammed it shut.

Drio didn't let it bother him. He sank onto the couch. "What's the matter, Ro? True love getting you down?"

"Shut it, Desiderio."

Oh joy! That was his real name? I clapped a hand over my snicker.

"Call me that and die," Drio informed me.

I mouthed his full name at him before broaching the subject of the photos before Rohan could. "Admit it, they got my best side."

"You think this is a joke?" Rohan turned the deadbolt on the door with an ominous click. "I just spent twenty minutes talking Mandelbaum out of putting your ass on the next plane home."

I pushed aside a lipstick-stained wine glass. "You must be quite the multitasker."

"I took the call in the bedroom." His gaze turned flinty. "Don't worry. I made it up to her."

I dumped my bag on the table next to Rohan's laptop with a hard thwack. "On what grounds did the good rabbi want me recalled?"

"Endangering the mission."

"Because of the photos? Why just me? You're all over the web, too." I breathed through my mouth attempting to minimize the cancerous, pervasive reek of Poppy's floral perfume.

"It was a given I'd be recognized. The Brotherhood was prepared for that."

"First off, I haven't been identified." I pulled out my laptop and plug.

"Yet."

"Second, the Brotherhood should have been prepared for me."

"No one can prepare for you," Drio quipped. Pulling out his phone, he pushed the coffee table farther back with his foot. All the better to take up more space. "Not even FEMA."

"That's a bullshit double standard." I pried my fingers off my laptop and placed it gently on the table, wishing all manner of pointy dry anal probing on Mandelbutt. Stupid misogynist douchebag. "I'm hanging around a rock star and a famous actor. I'm not invisible."

"You were supposed to be." Rohan stalked toward me. "Groupie. Background. Furniture."

Drio whistled through his teeth, not looking up from his phone.

Anger ballooned up inside me, my skin tightening from the strain of trying to contain it. "*Furniture*?! I'm not some half-assembled IKEA bookcase!"

"That's your role."

Electric sparks flew off my skin, singeing the carpet. "Is yours asshole?"

Rohan barked a laugh. "Yeah. You think Samson doesn't know about my rep back in the day? Why would I behave other than how everyone expects if that would raise more questions and suspicions?"

I turned around in a circle. "I don't see Samson here so what's your excuse now?"

A vein twitched in Rohan's temple. "Drio, a little back up?"

Drio glanced up from his phone. "Mom always told me not to eavesdrop on this part of the conversation."

Rohan looked at his partner with murder in his eyes. "It's only a matter of time before King learns your name," he said.

"Big deal." Now was not the time to voice any of my concerns about the possibility of discovery. Now was the time to play it like I had nothing to hide. Which honestly, was the only way to play it. With Rohan *and* Samson. "I was introduced to him as Lolita, for fuck's sake. Not even Samson thinks I was born with that name. Should my real identity come out, I'll say I'm reinventing myself." I pulled a sad face. "It was just so boring being good little Jewish girl Nava Katz." I fluttered my eyelashes.

Rohan wasn't amused.

"Relax." I flipped open my laptop and powered it up. "It's all part and parcel of this quest of mine to be famous. This quest you yourself approved last night."

"Much as I hate to agree with Nava," Drio said, "she's right. Samson isn't going to think twice about the fact that she didn't give him her real name. The photos mean squat and don't endanger the mission. Hell, he probably orchestrated them. The only reason King would target her is if he discovers she's Rasha."

Holy shit. Drio defending me? He laughed at my floored expression. "I live to keep you off-balance." He put his phone away. "Now can we get down to business?"

"Happy to." I sat down in the chair, dumping my laptop plug on the ground. It landed next to two odd indentations in the carpet. Something had crushed the pile. Something like...

Poppy's knees? "You forgot to tidy up after your toy."

Rohan was supposed to look blank, not confirm my suspicions with his involuntary glance at that specific spot.

Helpless against the onslaught imagery of red lipstick on specific portions of his anatomy, I shot him a scathing look. "You fucker."

"Not technically," Drio said.

"Working smart, not hard," Rohan fired back at me.

"Five bucks says hard too." Drio smirked, then held up his hands at the death glare I leveled his way.

Rohan grabbed a bottle off the top of the suite's small bar and poured himself a shot of whiskey. "Wasn't that the game plan you set for this mission, Nava? Like I said, why behave other than how I'm expected to?"

The tiny rational slice left in my brain conceded his point. It wouldn't surprise me if Poppy swallowed *and* spilled–the details right back to Samson. So Rohan had gotten a blow job. We weren't exclusive. In fact, this was good. If I ever decided to sleep with him again, and knowing where his dick had been, it was debatable, he'd be in no position to criticize my "no kiss" stance. I forced the part of my brain screaming obscenities at him to return to my best Rasha self and get with the program.

"You're absolutely right." My phone buzzed with a text. "Oh. My date with Samson is a go."

Rohan shot back his whiskey.

"More bonding?" Drio leered.

"More brilliance." I double clicked my notes file on my desktop. "Okay, so here's what I learned last night."

"About time," Rohan said. "Give us something to take the demon bastard down."

"Alleged demon. This is all still conjecture."

"Learned a couple law terms from Daddy, did we?" Rohan poured himself another drink. "You're not running the show here, and I sure as shit don't need you telling me how to think about my mission."

I frowned at him. "I'm not doubting your gut. But you're the one who said we don't think of him as a demon until–"

I flinched as Rohan's glass shattered against the far wall, streaking amber liquid on to the pristine carpet.

Drio jumped to his feet, his hand clamping down on my shoulder. "Go."

No matter how hard I tried, I couldn't get free. He stuffed my laptop, bag, and plug overflowing into my arms, and shoved me into the hallway. I protested the unfairness of the situation the entire time.

Door half-shut at his back, Drio spoke in a low voice so Rohan couldn't hear. "You can share what you learned with us tomorrow."

"But–"

He cast a worried glance back at the suite. "Tomorrow."

I tore into my wardrobe choices, muttering about Rohan needing to get his head out of his ass. If I had been the one costing us precious time in learning something potentially valuable about Samson? Drio would have speed-dialed Mandelbutt to have me exterminated.

I looked at the mismatched red and black shoes that I'd paired with a blue dress. And pulling my own head out in three, two...

Samson hadn't specified the dress code for tonight, but I needed to be the subject of more photos and provide further evidence of me as a taste-maker. Samson's tastes at least. I calmed myself down and dressed with purpose.

A narrow band of black fabric wrapped around my neck like a thick choker. A wider band in the same material covered my breasts like a bandeau. The final part of the outfit consisted of a fitted pencil skirt, also black and the same stretchy material, that hit above the knee. Even my high heels were made of three black fabric bands, the narrowest over my toes, then another over the arch of my foot, with the last above my ankle.

All the training I'd been doing over the past few weeks were toning my body in a different way than when I'd been dancing. I posed in the mirror, arms stretched out, enjoying the sleek line of my limbs. The smooth curve of my silhouette. My legs went on for miles. With my hair down and glossy nude lips, I looked pretty damn exquisite.

According to Samson's text, I had half an hour before he was swinging by to pick me up. I opted to wait in the lobby. Should anybody give me admiring looks, like say rock stars needing to grovel an apology, I'd be fine with that.

I got looks. Even a couple of drink offers. My heart sped up at the sight of a couple that I thought were Rohan and Lily, but it wasn't them. I wondered if they were together, off doing couple things. My mind wandered down that road for a bit but when the woman in my imaginings started looking less like Lily and more like me, I shut that ridiculousness down.

"Mr. King is waiting for you in the car." Showtime.

"Brickie!" I greeted the driver like a long lost friend. "How's it hanging?"

Nothing. He was immune to my many charms. I followed him out to a black Escalade idling at the curb. Brickie opened the door for me and I slid in across from Samson, putting my back to the TV playing a rap video. He was on the phone and didn't look up as I entered, so I blatantly checked him out. He wore a black knit cap along with a black cashmere sweater and dark pants and looked really good in all of it.

"I don't give a shit, Forrest," Samson said. "Work tomorrow's schedule around my conference call or I don't show." My first taste of Samson as temperamental star.

Having never been in an Escalade before, I wanted to examine every customized inch of it, run my hands over the cream leather, see if the tiny lights in the ceiling twinkled, and snoop through all the compartments to reveal their secrets, but Lolita would have been in these a million times so I defaulted back to her general bored disinterest.

I glanced out the window, surprised to see the city speeding by. The ride was so smooth, I hadn't noticed Brickie starting the engine and beginning our drive to dinner.

Samson's laughter drew my attention. Still on the phone, he listened to whatever Forrest was saying, before cutting him off with a sharp, "Deal with it." He hung up, his eyes running over my body.

I got the sense this was more cataloguing than appreciation but I pretended otherwise, preening for him. "Problems?" I motioned at the cell that he'd tossed on the leather seat.

"People forget the pecking order. They need reminding."

"Peons." He missed my sarcasm. "What's your verdict with the photos? Did I intrigue?"

Samson looked at me shrewdly. "Not one for small talk?"

I propped my heels in his lap. "The faster we get business talk out of the way, the faster we get to other lingual pursuits."

"Works for me." Samson scrolled through a few pages on his phone, one hand resting on my shins. "For a first encounter with the general public, you didn't do too badly."

"More lovers than haters? Told you."

"Don't discount the haters," he said. "We need them."

"Why?" I pointed over my shoulder at the TV. "Can you turn that down?"

Samson raised the remote, muting the sound. "People hate to love and love to hate. Makes them want you even more."

"You're very wanted, Samson. So why retire from acting? Tired of the hatred and jealousy?"

"Nah. If I gave a shit about that, I wouldn't be in this game. I just get bored easily. Diversity is everything. What about you?" He stroked up my leg. "Can you handle fame?"

I placed one foot on the floor, the other one propped on the edge of the seat between his knees. "Bring it. Those people don't know me. They know the persona I let them see."

"Lolita."

"Exactly. Fans don't care about who I actually am, only the person they project I am. I simply have to stay one step ahead of them and direct those projections to fall in line with my own goals."

Samson leaned forward and opened a small panel on the side of the vehicle, revealing a small fridge. He pulled out a bottle of champagne and uncorked it, patting the seat next to him.

I slid across the Escalade.

Pouring us each a glass, he handed me mine, clinking his against it in cheers. "Here's to women who understand what it takes to succeed in our build-up/tear-down culture."

"Oh, I understand perfectly." I sipped the bubbly vintage, the fizzy bubbles falling flat in comparison to my rush at having figured out what he was up to.

When I was a little kid celebrating Hanukkah, after lighting the candles and saying the prayers, my parents would make Ari and me sing what felt like the entire catalogue of Hanukkah songs before we were allowed to open our present for that night. It wasn't enough to just sing either. We had to be engaged. Failure to do so, like fidgeting or casting longing glances at the gifts, would be construed as a reason to make us start the song again. Two guesses which twin caused the restarts.

Looking back, demons could learn a thing or two from my parents.

This flirting was fun but I felt like I was back at the Hanukkah table making sure I didn't blow it, when all I really wanted was to get hold of Rohan and Drio and tell them my findings.

If we were correct about his affiliation with Louis XIV and Hitler—and I'd bet we were—then Samson was returning to drawing power from being the one behind the throne. You could get as much light from direct sun as you could from a mirror. Samson was a great mirror builder, building up other people to take the brunt of the fame for him. Slipping in on the sidelines and deriving his power by controlling the world through actors and idols, feeding off both the love and negativity they inspired on their way up *or* down in the public's estimation.

This way, he didn't make himself a target from either Rasha or other demons by taking center stage. Whether through his own orchestrations or a fickle public ready to turn on a dime, as soon as one client, one mirror, fell to another that he also backed, he still won, no downtime, no down*side*. Samson could do this forever, having clients in various stages of fame ascend or descend, and no matter where they were, people would hate to love and love to hate.

I picked up the champagne bottle, studying the label, which incidentally I knew nothing about. What I did know was that Samson would not be a guy to stint on the vintage. "More impressiveness, Mr. King." I topped him up.

He looked at his full glass. "Should I fear for my virtue?"

"Please. Like I'm after anything that easy."

Samson laughed.

"I'm going to get you drunk and find the gaudy chink in your impeccable image to prove how much you need me." I tapped a finger against my lips. "Spiderman underwear."

"I would wear those proudly," he informed me. "You won't find it."

"Bet I will."

He stretched an arm along the seat behind me. "Babe, I never met a bet I couldn't win."

I winked and held out my glass to be refilled. "Bet you've met your match in me."

Under Samson's appraising look, I leaned back, smug.

Samson held up his phone and snapped a photo of me.

"What's that for?"

I leaned over his shoulder in time to see him upload it to his management company's Twitter feed with the tweet, "Intriguing and cocky. Apparently, I've met my match." He'd barely hit send before the likes started coming in.

Samson's social media presence. That would play a huge role in all this as well. If he was a demon, he could very well feed off both his clients' own emotions and those of anyone engaging via print and social media. Every new client he signed put another stone in his well-defended fortress that no one even realized he was building.

Interesting that Samson had offered Rohan, someone he couldn't stand, the chance to be part of this. The chance to toy with him, building the former rock star up before orchestrating his downfall. Banking on Rohan doing the theme song as an indication of his desire to recapture his fame. Samson would have read that situation right, except for one thing.

He wasn't the only one moving pieces on this chessboard.

15

Samson let the champagne bottle fall to the floor. It was just about empty, but a few drops settled onto the lush backseat carpet, staining it. "You've gotten awfully quiet, Lolita. In my experience that means that women are thinking about me in all the wrong ways."

"You're incorrigible."

"I'm positive that is not one of the many adjectives applied to me."

"This oughta be good. Please. Enlighten me." I tipped back the rest of my drink.

"Charming. Gorgeous. Witty. Insanely talented."

I gasped. "You read your fan sites. I knew it."

He covered his face with one hand. The other one, still holding the champagne glass, he raised in the air. "Guilty as charged."

I'd intended to blind Samson by my light but I was remembering why we mere mortals weren't supposed to fly too close to the sun. Even this brief exposure to his undivided attention had left me dizzy, with feverish chills. First-degree emotional sunburn.

Still, that didn't conclusively make him a demon because I suspected that near proximity to Theo James, especially if he spoke in his normal British accent would have the same effect.

Brickie opened the door, revealing a swank-looking steak house. I welcomed the rush of cool night air as I stepped onto the sidewalk.

Samson pressed a hand to my cheek. "Looking a little flushed."

I swallowed, scrambling to pull myself together. "Don't try to distract me. I'm pondering your terrible tastes so that I may rescue you from yourself."

He spread his arms wide as if daring me to try.

"Black silk sheets." I pointed at him. "No. Satin. With mirrored ceiling tiles." I clattered up the walk to the steak house.

"Wow. You think that I—Wow." He held the door open for me. With a smirk, I ducked inside the restaurant that he had booked expressly for our private use. Chandeliers cast warm light over dark wood and crisp white linens.

Our waiter took our coats, pulled out my chair, and brought us more champagne all with perfect aplomb. Just as I was thinking that I needed good help like that, he placed my meal before me. The meal I hadn't yet ordered.

"I was thinking I'd start by seeing a menu," I joked.

"I ordered for you." Samson unfurled his napkin. "Châteaubriand in case you mistakenly slummed it with T-bone."

Subtle. I pressed my hand to my heart. "Now who wounds?" I slugged back another glass of champagne in order to muster up an appropriate level of enthusiasm for the bloody hunk of meat on my plate, topped with two dollops of green foam.

It looked like a demon kill, not dinner.

Samson dug into his steak with relish. "I wasn't wrong about your tastes, was I?"

"Not at all." I eyed the offensive slab, finding a less raw edge to saw at. "Only the best for me."

"Glad to hear it because if you sign with my management company, we'll have some spin to do on your image."

"Such as?"

He laid down his knife. "I'm gonna be blunt. Being Rohan's groupie is not going to inspire anyone to follow you."

I snapped a breadstick in half. "Oh?"

"Is that a touchy subject? I heard you two had a fight. And, well," he placed his hand on mine. "It's worse if you're only his former groupie. We have a lot of work cut out for us."

My face turned hot and tight. Poppy sure knew how to use that mouth of hers. "Not sure where you got your information, but Rohan and I are fine." Other than me wanting to smack him upside the head. "Also, you're wrong." Without even looking the waiter's way, I held up my champagne glass, expecting it to be refilled. "I'm not his groupie."

Samson leaned back, a look of pity on his face.

I took a ladylike sip, enjoying the sensation of cold fizzy liquid. "I'm lightning girl."

"I don't understand."

"'Toccata and Fugue.'"

"Rohan's first hit," Samson said. I raised an eyebrow and waited for him to make the connection. "He wrote it about *you?*"

"Ask him."

"Oh, I will." There was something cruel in his smile.

Sweat broke out along the back of my neck.

There was no bill to settle up. Samson threw his napkin down and the meal was over. Still unnerved, I was about to make some excuse to end the evening when he said, "Wait," busy typing a text.

"We're meeting up with Rohan." He stood up.

Awesome. I shoved my chair back.

Brickie once again drove us to our destination. So far, I'd seen no sign of Samson's security detail. Maybe Brickie was deterrent enough since the restaurant had been empty save for the staff.

This time, there was no chit chat on the ride. Samson watched music videos and I stared out the window into the night, breathing my way through the remnants of feeling humiliated and trying not to dwell on Rohan's potential reaction when he heard what I'd said.

A sign on the cigar bar that we pulled up to announced the establishment closed due to a private party. I had no idea how Rohan had found this gathering but having seen Samson's choice of party last night, I prayed this was more sedate. If not, I'd stick with Drio and–Hell was officially freezing over if that was my upside.

Two hipsters at the front of the line were haggling with the bouncer. "This is shite," one pronounced in a thick Irish accent. "Poppy assured us we were on the guest list. Check again."

Poppy? This was her party? I didn't think my eyebrows could rise any higher.

"Mr. Mitra set the guest list," the bouncer told him.

Nope. My eyebrows climbed another inch. This was Rohan's party.

Hipster number two laughed. "Knowing Pops, she's calling the shots. Check again, man. My bollocks are freezing off."

I shoved past the pair, finding myself momentarily blocked by the muscle in Tom Ford. He could cross his arms all he wanted. No one was stopping me from getting inside. Pointedly I swung my head between him and Samson.

A beat, then recognition crossed over the bouncer's features and he scrambled to let us through.

I sailed in, head held high.

"That Poppy," Samson chuckled from behind me, loud enough to hear over the Latin jazz pumping out through the speakers.

As I glanced back at him, I'd swear his eyes twinkled. My fingers dug into my clutch.

From the mismatched leather vintage furniture to abstract silver flash art stenciled on the walls and the neon-illuminated cigar collection taking up one wall, it was a pretty cool space. The crowd was boisterous, bright eyed, and hammered. Lots of loud laughter, lots of touching.

I couldn't wait to find Poppy and Rohan and make my night complete. I tossed my coat on a chair as someone grabbed my elbow. I tensed thinking it was Rohan, but it was Drio, an uncharacteristic edginess in his stance.

"Oh good, it's you," I said, beyond caring that this was totally weird. He wasn't Samson and he wasn't Rohan and that was good enough for me.

"Whatever happens tonight," he said, "understand that–"

"My man." Samson joined us, fist bumping Drio.

My fellow Rasha snapped back into his laconic persona. "Dude, we can finally get the party started. Come on. Ro's back here." He barreled into the crowd, Samson and I right behind him.

The sight of Rohan, flushed and sitting on a high barstool under a funky glass lighting fixture holding a highball of whiskey, sent my pulse into overdrive.

The sight of Poppy's fingers messing his hair up made me see red. I could have accepted this from Lily. But her? If a blowjob came with personal property rights then I owned every acre of him by now, and there was no such thing as squatter's rights in *this* universe.

Rohan grinned at Samson's appearance. "All hail the esteemed Samson King." Rohan held up a glass in salutation. He shot the booze back, slamming the glass on the table where it joined a half dozen others, then swaggered off his chair, a flash of something I couldn't name in the brief glance he spared me.

"Sit down, love," Poppy said.

Rohan grabbed her around the waist, speaking low into her ear.

My mouth fell open.

"Maybe we shouldn't have come," Samson murmured. Demon or psychopath, the son-of-a-bitch was getting off on my discomfort. Or, more accurately, the hateful thoughts I directed his way for having brought me here. The more I seethed, the more he relaxed. The more space he took up. It was like he was inflating right before my very eyes. Not in a physical way, more on a psychic or subconscious level. His eyes had an extra sparkle; his skin glowed with vitality. The release of my bitterness worked on him like a spa treatment.

How annoyed would Rohan and Drio be if I ended him right now? Except, I couldn't even bring myself to do that. I had this low grade urge to keep giving to him. My gut screamed at me that this was all the proof we needed, but I steeled myself to play it smart. This could simply be a master manipulator at work, in which case this was head games, my buttons being pushed by a pro, and proof of shit. Much as I burned to blast Samson and see what happened, I couldn't take the chance I'd be killing a human.

"I'm here to enjoy myself," I assured Samson.

"Celebrate with me." Rohan threw an unsteady hand over King's shoulder. Snowflake was smashed and I didn't think he was faking this time.

Samson laughed and any mild hold on me snapped. "What are we celebrating?" He plucked a couple of highballs off a tray, handing a glass back to me.

I slugged back half its contents in one go before passing it off to another waiter.

"I'm signing with you." Leading Samson back to the table with a swagger, Rohan snapped his fingers at Drio.

I tensed, waiting for Drio to punch his Royal Imperiousness but he produced two cigars, tips already cut, which he handed over along with a lighter.

Rohan patted his cheek.

Samson took the proffered cigar. "Glad to hear it. You'll be on top of the world again in no time."

I had to warn Rohan about that, about everything Samson was up to, but Rohan's new-found posse closed in on him, leaving me on the outside. I elbowed a couple of men aside and shoved my way into inner circle.

Samson held out a hand to me, puffing away, and I joined him. Lazy circles of spicy-sweet smoke drifted upward.

Poppy and I eyed each other. She smirked like she knew I'd rather switch places with her, then made herself comfortable on Rohan's lap. He didn't push her onto the ground in a quivering heap. Nope, he ran his hand over her arm in long, lazy strokes as he chatted with Samson about record ideas.

Rapid-acting syphilis. It had to be eating away at his brain because What. The. Hell. Rohan would never let anger and control games endanger a mission and whatever was going on here tonight was so off our game plan I felt blindsided.

His fury over the photos hadn't been an act. Was he using that as an excuse to publicly ostracize me as a way for me to get closer to Samson or had I really been banished on both a personal and Rasha level?

If it was the latter scenario, he wasn't going to sideline me that easily.

"Share?" I batted my eyelashes at Samson and he handed the cigar over for me to take a puff. There was one herb I liked smoking and this fell far short, but it was a great way to call attention to my mouth.

Poppy narrowed her eyes and I could tell she wished she'd thought of that move.

Both guys watched my slow suck. Head tilted up, I looked skyward through half-lidded eyes, as if focused on the pleasure of this moment. The angle actually allowed me to see both Samson and Rohan. Samson looked amused.

Rohan brushed Poppy's hair aside to whisper into her ear. She laughed.

Exhaling a perfect smoke ring, I handed the cigar back to Samson. My coy smile hid my teeth grinding.

Samson patted my ass.

"Looks cozy," Rohan joked.

I examined my nails like they were the most fascinating sight in the world, willing my magic to quit crackling under my skin before it erupted.

Samson took a deep puff, his hand still resting on my butt. "You don't mind, do you?"

Rohan shrugged. "Plenty more." He winked at three women standing nearby, who preened under his attention. "Like shooting fish in a barrel."

"That's rather rude," Poppy said.

Rohan raised his eyebrows. "No one's forcing you to stick around."

T-Roy, on Rohan's left, laughed and tried to fist bump him, but Rohan left him hanging. The normally jittery minion pulled up his pants with the first show of swagger I'd seen from him. "Gettin' a drink." He hunched his shoulders and scurried off.

Poppy swallowed any feminist objections and stayed put. Big surprise.

Rohan's behavior was so excessive, and so unlike him, that it had to be an act. But as soon as I convinced myself of that, my inner devil's advocate argued that he was drunk. Cue the lowered inhibitions and bad tendencies. What if he'd fallen back into the worst of his rock star ways? I glanced at his heart tattoo, its edge visible on his left bicep under his shirt sleeve. His reminder of what fame had done to him and who he'd become. The knives were coming out and maybe he was lost to them.

16

I flicked a sideways glance at Drio, busy flirting with some woman on the fringe of the group. The flash of wariness as he met my eyes for an instant clarified nothing.

"I'll take you, Poppy, if Rohan doesn't want you." Samson grinned at her. Her answering smile was faint.

I wasn't sure if I was more insulted on her behalf or mine.

"Here's to women," Rohan toasted. "May they ever flow." He held up his empty glass at a passing server, who replaced it with a full one like he had orders to keep 'em coming. "So, Lolita meeting your needs?"

Meeting his needs? I was hard-pressed not to laugh. Or punch him. I lay a hand on Samson's shoulder. "It's mutual satisfaction."

Samson covered my hand with his. "I foresee a very beneficial professional relationship with her."

Rohan snorted. "Professional, right. Like me and Evelyn."

Samson tensed at her name. Why was Rohan implying he'd had a relationship with Samson's former make-up artist? Why admit to any connection at all with the demon?

I took a gin and tonic from a server circulating with a tray, searching for any sign that the others at this table sensed the same undercurrent of danger at whatever was playing out, but everyone else was oblivious.

Except Drio, who edged closer to Rohan.

Samson lowered his cigar. "Didn't realize you knew her."

Rohan blinked at that. "Really?" He scratched his chin. "I thought she was another one of your gifts." He slung an arm around Poppy's waist.

Samson's fingers picked at the golden band on his cigar. "Did you now?"

Poppy tucked herself into Rohan's side. She either didn't know or didn't care that she'd been pushed into his path in the first place.

"Guess Evelyn just wanted me for me." Rohan held up his glass in cheers before drinking. Five other guys laughed along with him like Rohan was the greatest wit in the world.

"Logan sure thought she came pretty willingly," Drio said.

Samson glared across the room at his buddy smoking a cigar, but he shut that expression down in a blink, back to his easy grin. This was why he hated Rohan. Logan must have seen Evelyn leave with Drio and assumed the minion was there at his rock star overlord's bidding. I wondered how fast he'd gone running back to Samson with the gossip.

Samson exhaled, blowing smoke directly toward Rohan. "Or you were just the next in a very long line up."

Rohan played with the lighter, making it dance over his knuckles. "The next and best. Then again, she has talents worth keeping her around for." He put his own lit cigar out with a grimace. "This tastes like ass. Drio, get us another flavor."

Drio trotted off like an obedient little flunky.

I swirled my ice in my drink, floored that Rohan would imply Evelyn was still with him. Between me, Poppy, and Evelyn, Snowflake had a regular harem going on. Imaginary harem since Evelyn was dead and he hadn't slept with Poppy. Had he? Before Prague, I would have said with absolute certainty that Rohan wouldn't risk the mission getting entangled like that, but after this afternoon? I hadn't anticipated how far Rohan would go *for* the mission.

Rohan's fingers drifted up to play with Poppy's hair.

Or maybe I hadn't anticipated how far Rohan would go, period. I itched to take the half-drunk glass of water on the table and toss it at him to sober him up.

Samson stubbed out his cigar with a forceful jab, believing Rohan's prolific sexual activity. "Lolita told me a fascinating piece of trivia."

The straw bent at the bottom as I jabbed my ice.

"Oh yeah?" Rohan didn't seem to care too much.

"Apparently she's lightning girl? You wrote 'Toccata and Fugue' about her?"

Rohan's hand fell away from Poppy's hair. "She said that, huh?"

Under other circumstances, I'd have relished Poppy's shocked look, but I was too busy trying to decipher Rohan's shuttered expression. All the booze I'd had wasn't helping.

Samson tilted his head. "It's not true?"

"It's true," Rohan said. I made sure not to exhale in relief at his confirmation of my lie. "Why?"

Samson pulled me onto his lap. "She's signing with me. We're working on cleaning up her backstory."

"Really." Rohan's eyes hadn't left my face, but the shutters had dropped, leaving me helpless against the onslaught of a gaze that was too gold. Too blazing.

I slid my arms around Samson's neck, refusing to duck away from his stare. "Really."

Drio returned with more cigars. "Sorry 'bout that, man." He held them out to Rohan, but Snowflake didn't take them.

Drio jerked his thumb subtly at Samson, his eyes flicking to the bar.

I ran my finger around the rim of Samson's now-empty drink, then licked it off. "Get me another one?" I said, picking up on Drio's silent direction. "Whatever you're drinking."

Samson squeezed my side before standing up. "Definitely. After all, this *is* a celebration."

"Best day I've had in a long time," I purred.

Grinning, hands in pockets, Samson strode away.

"I'd say so," Poppy gushed at me. "All that time you'll get to spend with Samson." Her implied "and not Rohan" wasn't even subtle. I hoped she was a demon, too.

"I'll be sure not to forget my old friends," I said.

Rohan watched Samson go, his expression still annoyingly inscrutable.

"Ro? Cigar?" Drio asked.

Rohan took it, then launched into some anecdote about a tour mishap, using expressive gestures to punctuate the story. Everyone was so busy lapping up his every word that no one noticed Drio slip the stub of Samson's cigar into his pocket.

Drio winked at me.

All that business about Evelyn had all been a calculated performance, then? But why not tell me? I turned away and headed into the bathroom. As an armchair celebrity enthusiast, I knew that those in closest orbit to a star tended to indulge any and all bad behavior. What amazed me now, witnessing Rohan's little performance back there was that everyone had taken him seriously. They expected this ridiculous assholery from someone like him and found it acceptable. No wonder Rohan hated who he'd become back in the day.

I couldn't reconcile this version of him with the man I'd gotten to know. Though I couldn't reconcile anything I'd seen of him today with that man either, so what did I know?

A couple of women entered the bathroom, chatting in rapid Czech and snapping me out of my reverie. I reapplied my lipstick and got out of there.

Rohan was coming out of the men's room. The sight of him rocked a fresh wave of anger through me. I planted myself in front of him. "Congratulations, Snowflake. Really became the finest version of yourself back there."

"I can't take all the credit, sweetheart. I wouldn't be here if it wasn't for you." His glittering eyes were at odds with his smirk.

I frowned. That jab was deliberately fired. "Right. Because rock stars are exempt from any personal responsibility."

"Oh, I'm sorry. Were your feelings hurt?" He ran his finger along my bare skin between my bandeau and the pencil skirt. This close in, I could smell the alcohol on him. Warm whiskey spice.

"Don't flatter yourself."

"You chose your role. Play it."

I lifted his hand off me. "I have no problem playing it. But you seem to be forgetting where the act stops and respecting your team member begins."

He looked vaguely uneasy at that. "What about you respecting my personal history, lightning girl?"

Now it was my turn to squirm. "I did what I had to for the mission."

"Is that all it was?"

"Can't imagine anything else it would be about."

The Latin jazz that had been playing smoothed out into a bump and grind bassline under a woman's voice singing about retribution in six-eight time. My kind of lady. I stepped past Rohan but he blocked my hip with his.

"Where are you going?"

"Back to Samson." To have Brickie take me back to my hotel.

"He's a demon, sorry, *alleged* demon, who doesn't give a shit about you."

I white-knuckled my clutch. "Like you do?"

"As a rock star? I'm not supposed to. As Rasha?" He turned away, jaw tight, as if annoyed I even had to ask.

What about as a person? "Then show it and don't play games with your team members."

He braced a hand on the wall by my head. "I'm not the one playing games."

"You've been playing games since day one. I'm the one constantly trying to keep things clear between us." I smacked him once in the chest with my clutch.

"This from the girl who has no idea what she wants."

I blinked at that comment.

"No. Idea."

The groupie/rock star dynamic was abhorrent enough, yet I dealt with the public humiliation because of the mission. But this? This had gotten personal and I refused to become Rohan's personal build-up/tear-down culture.

I tapped his heart tattoo. "Should have made it larger. A big blazing emblem of what you so capably embody."

"*Ro-oo.*" I grit my teeth as Poppy sidled in under his arm. "Everyone was wondering where you got to." She didn't dignify my presence.

I made a show of straightening my skirt and fixing my hair. "Be gentle with him, sugar," I said. "Poor boy is spent." Yeah, now she noticed me, eyes darting between Rohan and myself. I leaned into him as if I was going to kiss him. His eyes widened slightly. Right before my lips brushed his, I turned my cheek, pushing past him with a, "Thanks for the ride, baby."

I swaggered off.

I really thought I'd picked an easy lay. Hot boy. Good sex. Players have fun playing. Instead he'd shot my finely honed plans to hell with prophetic-sounding song lyrics, a connection that gave the finger to our casual hook-up, and game playing at the championship level that had morphed into mutual anger and hurt. To make matters worse, our personal mess was leaching into our professional lives.

I took a moment to compose myself before approaching Samson. Deep in conversation with some couple, he wasn't ready to leave but didn't seem to care much one way or the other what I did. Guess I'd served my payback purpose.

Drio offered to cab back to the hotel with me, claiming that five more minutes and he'd unleash his inner psychopath. A level of self-awareness I had no idea he possessed.

I asked the driver to turn up the music, pretending to love the rock ballad playing. Then I lay my head on Drio's shoulder so I could speak quietly to him. "What was with the cigar?"

"Once we get King's true name, there's a ritual we can do to force his demon form. We needed his DNA in prep and tonight seemed like the perfect opportunity to get it."

"How does the ritual work? Do you take him out right then and there? If we're right about him?"

"Sì. Once we force his demon form, we use the ritual blade to kill him."

"What about the production? Won't they wonder why their lead has gone missing?"

The driver eyed us in the rearview mirror. Drio slung his arm around my shoulder, like a conscientious boyfriend. "Those party photos may prove useful," Drio said. "We could stage an OD."

"Without a body?" There'd be nothing left of Samson once we killed him.

"Morrison's body was never seen," Drio said. "Not that he was a demon," he added at my wide-eyed stare. "Just that there's precedence. Besides, Samson's death will probably boost the box office when *Hard Knock Strife* gets released. It's a shitty film."

Drio pressed the button to roll down his window, sending a hint of cool air into the stuffy backseat. Passing streetlights sent slivers of light over us.

"Wrap is Tuesday," he said. "We could wait the three days. Less of a freak out from production than if they still have to shoot. One less item to manage."

"I can make sure Samson gets trashed at the cast party," I said. "That could help keep him off guard when we lure him to his doom."

"You can't be anywhere near his death." Drio was dead serious. "Not even a hint of it. The media will be asking enough questions about the mystery women in those photos and we don't want you caught up in the scandal."

I opened my mouth to protest but Drio stopped me. "Don't give Mandelbaum more ammunition."

Him having my back like this was a huge step forward between us.

The cab pulled up to the hotel. I pulled out my wallet to pay but Drio waved me off, so I got out. "Thank you. For everything." I shut the door.

Drio immediately rolled down the window. "Rohan had to get drunk tonight. He knew Samson would show up."

"Part of his performance. Big deal."

Drio shook his head. "The only way he'd be able to behave like his old self again."

"Really? Seemed like he fell right into it." I dropped my eyes under the chastising look Drio shot me.

He was quieter when he spoke this time. Musing. "I think it was also the only way he could pretend he wasn't attached."

When I looked up with a harsh laugh, Drio was watching me, his steady green-eyed gaze unnerving. "It's not attachment." I fiddled with my clutch. "It's chemistry and fucked-up power games."

"He has your back."

"I know, but that's not the same." Not like he meant.

"Okay." He rolled up the window, capitulating so easily that I knew he was humoring me.

17

Lack of a full night's sleep plus emotional fuckery led to me crashing the second my head hit the pillow.

Waking up on Sunday morning having had more of an extended nap than a proper rest was all sorts of hideous. Groaning, I cracked an eye open, blinking through the glueyness. I stumbled into the bathroom, cranked the shower to frigid, and scrunching up my face, hopped in.

I yelped at the tiny needles of ice pounding down my back but it did the trick. I was fully awake. Samson was out of town shooting for the next couple of days and time off from Lolita, if only in my wardrobe choices, was welcome. I slid into my modest A-line skirt, thick tights and a pretty pale pink cashmere sweater paired with black boots. At the sight of me as me and not *her*, my entire body relaxed.

My phone rang as I was shrugging into my coat.

"Those photos gave Mom and Dad a coronary," Ari said, skipping hello.

I laughed. "Document it."

"Way ahead of you. I have a pic of Mom gnashing her teeth that should sustain you for weeks."

"My hero. In case you think my life is all jet set and dazzle, I have a meeting tomorrow that I feel very hopeful about." Checking to make sure I had my keycard, I slung my laptop bag across my chest, and left my room, jogging to catch the elevator that was, for a change, present and open on my floor. "How's Kane?"

"Haven't seen him since the airport run," Ari said.

I crossed the lobby into the restaurant. The mouth-watering breakfast spread of fruit platters and baked goods would normally have tempted me but all my belly room was reserved for sampling every flavor of Trdelnik at the bakery down the road. "If you're being coy, I approve. If you're being stupid, stop right now."

The waiter at the espresso station gave me my to-go latte and I charged it to my hotel room.

"I'm not the one groping famous celebs," my brother said. "Mom and Dad are freaking out that someone is going to recognize their wayward daughter."

Just as I was about to step back into the lobby, I heard Rohan's voice. I pressed back, peeking out at him standing less than ten feet away.

Oh good, he looked like death warmed over: unshaven, red-eyed, kind of nauseous, with his hands bundled into his camel trench coat. A little balloon of joy danced its way through me seeing him in the seventh circle of hangover hell.

Ari continued listing our parents' litany of gripes with me. I only half-listened, busy spying.

Lily walked toward Rohan from where she'd been seated at one of the lobby's sofas, a steaming cup of coffee in her hand which she forced on him. Rohan groaned. She zipped up her coat. "You bitch now, but you'll love me in about twenty minutes."

He opened the lid, sniffing at the brew. "I always love you." He kissed the side of her head.

I gripped my own cup so hard the lid popped off.

"Yeah, yeah," Lily teased. "Me and every other breathing female you want to charm."

"You still there?" my brother asked.

"Sorry, yes." I pulled a tissue out of my pocket to wipe coffee off of my fingers.

"How's it going otherwise?" Ari asked.

"Oh you know. Living the dream." Escaping unnoticed was not an option. Even if it had been, I couldn't stop watching them. Couldn't stop wondering where I fit in the spectrum between "always love you" and "every other breathing female."

Rohan pushed Lily's glasses back up her nose. "That's it. We're getting these tightened so you don't embarrass yourself yet again when a pair slips off your face and breaks."

She nudged him with her shoulder. "One time, buddy. You have the memory of an elephant."

"Only when it comes to your most embarrassing moments."

She laughed. "Those would be the Rohan years."

He pressed his hand to his heart with a gasp.

I needed all my awareness to keep stalking so I cut my brother off mid-sentence. "Ace, I gotta run. Love you."

"Love you, too. Later."

I pressed farther behind the leaves of the plant at the restaurant's entrance, peering out to watch Rohan drink, tracking the line of his neck with every swallow.

"Happy?" he asked Lily.

"Ecstatic," she replied dryly. "Now how about some toast?"

Rohan shuddered. "No food." He shifted from foot-to-foot. "Let's go for a walk."

"Without eating first?" She sighed, stroking his back. "Calm down, Ro."

"Then come with me and calm me down. You're best at that anyway." He turned puppy dog eyes on her and I almost stepped forward offering to help with a frying pan to the head.

"Gawd, you're in giant baby mode," Lily said.

Okay, I wasn't as nice as Lily. That much was clear from the quiet care she took of him: from the extra sugar packets she'd known to hand over without him asking to the resettling of his scarf now as it slipped from his neck.

Poppy would never have engaged in those small considerate gestures, which didn't make me her either, or a groupie. I was trying to prove myself as Rasha. I was my own category.

I blinked at the button I'd worried loose on my coat and sighed.

I gave them a moment once they'd left so that I wouldn't run into them outside before going to have breakfast all by my lonesome. Which turned out to be awesome when the sexy baker spent the next half hour flirting and plying me with pastry. By the time Drio texted me to come meet him and Rohan, my mood had improved considerably.

Rohan answered the door to his suite. His walk with Lily must have helped because he no longer looked like crap, the cuffs of his white shirt folded crisply back, with two undone buttons showing a V of dark skin. His worn jeans molded to the long lines of his legs. The sight of him in top form once more sent my blood frothing and churning, dark tentacles lashing hot inside me.

Stripping off my coat, I pulled a sketch of Louis XIV's sunburst that I'd printed out in the tiny hotel business center from a folder in my laptop bag. "If you recall," I said, handing it to Drio, "this was our first break. Samson King. Sun King. Just like Louis XIV. A possible connection."

"The snitch," Rohan said, not outing Leo as my source. "He'd heard a rumor that Samson had spent time in France. It was a potential link."

"Yes. Since some demons have long lifespans." Rohan was being civil, I could, too. "I wondered if maybe Samson had hung out with Louis. Picked up some tips. But I got it all wrong." I picked up the next printout. This one of the black sun. "As you can see—"

Rohan snatched the paper out of my fingers.

"Gee, Mr. Mitra, I was doing my best clipboard impression and everything. Should I be more actual furniture, less office supply?" Nope. Apparently no civility on the menu today.

"Black sun. Occult symbol." He exhaled, a slow controlled breath. "I'm sorry for the furniture crack."

I waited but he didn't add any other items to that apology. I sat on the couch with an unhappy thump. "I don't buy your sincerity. Apology not accepted."

"What's it gonna take?"

I tapped my finger against my lip, thinking. "Get on your knees and grovel."

Drio smothered a laugh.

Rohan narrowed his eyes. "Never gonna happen."

"Fine. Forget it. Drio, tell Mr. Mitra that the black sun–"

"Nazi's co-opted it." Ignoring us both, Drio grabbed my laptop and started typing. "It was on that castle floor in," he peered at the screen, "Wewelsburg."

"Samson recently got that sun inked as a tattoo. He showed it to me the other night in response to seeing my sunburst. I said it looked like a swastika with too many arms. He didn't seem to care much for Nazis." I gnawed on my fingernail. "Something about his response bothered me. It wasn't a general dislike with their ideology. More deep-seated, intimate hate."

"Like they'd pissed him off. Personally," Rohan said.

I didn't want to acknowledge him but Drio looked like he'd brain me with the laptop if I kept this Kindergarten shit up. "Yeah."

"If Samson does have ties to both Versailles and the Nazis, it could be as more than a spectator," Drio said.

Rohan pointed at him. "Hitler and King Louis. Both with delusions of grandeur and plans of world domination." He went over to the mini bar and pulled three bottles of water out of the fridge, handing one to each of us.

I riffled through my notes. "Did you know that at the Palace of Versailles, aristocrats were expected to compete for the privilege of watching the king wake up, eat meals, and prepare for bed? Sound familiar?"

This was the type of envy-inducing humiliation King foisted on contestants on his reality show *Live Like A King*. All for the dubious honor of winning a position in his entourage. Bad enough contestants so willingly debased themselves, Rohan and Drio had tracked players and crew and found that they were exceedingly accident-prone. Fatally so.

"Samson mentored Louis," Rohan said. "We've been assuming the wrong way round."

Drio was already looking something up. "Louis chose the sun as his emblem to cultivate the image of an omniscient and infallible sun-king around whom the entire realm orbited. I'd say this is more than a potential link."

"I don't know if he tried this with any other empire builders." I unscrewed the water bottle cap. "Napoleon or Genghis Khan or Hannibal or whoever." The cold liquid eased the dryness in my throat.

"That brings us back to who Samson actually is." Drio typed as he spoke. "If Louis was his first attempt to control someone and be the power behind the throne, it might have taken him time to get strong enough to position himself."

"Where's he been since Hitler?" I asked.

"Defeat takes a toll," Rohan said, peering over Drio's shoulder at the screen, water bottle in hand, forgotten. "If Samson was behind the Nazi fascination with the occult, tying his own power to theirs, then the end of World War II would have been a huge blow. It might have taken him this long to bounce back."

I shrugged. "He's still not as strong as he once was if he went from partnering with Hitler to being an actor."

Rohan sputtered a laugh as he drank.

"I wasn't being funny."

He wiped a hand across his mouth. "Do you understand how famous Samson is?"

"Yes," I snapped.

He shook his head. "You don't. Not really. You've never experienced it. That level of fame, you're treated like a god. Anything, any*one* you want?" He snapped his fingers. "Yours. There's no door barred to you."

"You'd know."

"I didn't want it," Rohan said.

"What about tasting it again now?"

"I want it even less."

"Even if it gets you your heart's desire?" I asked softly.

Rohan hesitated, his eyes darting away from me for a fraction of a second before he answered. "World domination is not my heart's desire."

Slick avoidance of answering. "No. It's not." Lily was. Maybe I'd arrange for Poppy to meet the good physicist and let her see what she was really up against. I bricked up my sorrow, adding it to the pile of emotions I had no desire to examine or experience.

"There was one last thing I found," I said. "The symbol of the Mesopotamian sun-god Shamash had four straight and four wavy rays. Louis' has both, too. Could Samson be Mesopotamian?"

"Shamash was a god, not a demon. But that sun symbol was present in Babylonian and Assyrian cultures." Drio chugged half his water back in one go.

"That might explain Samson's preference for Semitic-looking women. Personal attraction stemming from point of origin," I said.

"Bhenchod!" Rohan swore, grabbing the laptop away from Drio. The anticipation in the room was palpable as he looked something up. With a shout of victory, Rohan turned the screen around for us to see it.

"Adramelech," I read. "Sun-demon. Is Adramelech his name or his type?"

"Name," Rohan said. "As a sun-demon, he's a Unique." He frowned. "Which means the Brotherhood may not have info on his kill spot. I'll get on that."

Drio leaned back in his chair, nodding. "Babylonian. Nasty bastard. Known for his ambition. Maybe the fact he got burned with politics is influencing his choices now. Like initially he meant to draw power from these charismatic figureheads. When it failed with Louis, Samson tried again with Hitler. Another fail and a new strategy needed."

"Cross-platform." I swirled the plastic bottle, watching the little eddy of water inside while filling them in on my suspicions around why Samson had founded the record label and management company. "Build up. Tear down. With all these available platforms only adding to his power. Social media crosses all national borders and language barriers. For the first time in history, he doesn't require a military leader to allow him to rule the world. He can do it exactly as he is and do it with more reach than any of those rulers ever did. Celebrity trumps politics."

"He's the biggest star with the most reach," Rohan said. "He's in the perfect position to establish himself as an entertainment conglomerate and push his agenda indefinitely." He nodded. "Good work."

Generally his praise warmed me enough to push aside any bullshit between us, but not today. "To figuring it out," I said, hoisting my bottle, and pushing aside my unhappiness.

"To destroying that bastard." Drio clinked his bottle against mine. We looked at Rohan who didn't join in.

"What's wrong? We've got him," I said.

"We've got a name that might be his," Rohan corrected.

"Oh, you mean more conjecture?"

"You were right. Actually," he amended, "I was right in the first place but I had an off day yesterday. No assuming anything until we do the ritual."

"You mean we could still do the ritual and be wrong?"

"Yeah." Rohan closed the laptop which had defaulted into my annoying screensaver of frogs plummeting to the ground. "Though I doubt it."

Drio clapped Rohan on the back. "Playing it smart." The smile he saved for torturing demons bloomed wide. "Then having fun playing."

"Are you still planning to go to set on Tuesday?" Rohan asked.

Off my nod, Drio told me that once I got there, I should arrange a Wednesday meeting with the demon. "I'll give you a time and place as soon as I've made all the arrangements for the ritual."

"How will you get him away from the bodyguards?" I asked.

"We'll take care of them. Piece of cake."

I dropped my voice to a whisper. "You'll kill them?"

Drio looked at me like I'd been dropped on my head.

"Like murder is an unreasonable assumption with you."

"They're human," he said. "We won't hurt them." He stood, stretching his arms over his head and causing his shirt to ride up, giving me a tantalizing glimpse of olive skin and six-pack. "I think a little subtle interrogation is in order today. In case we've missed anything."

"Why get subtle now?" Rohan joked. "Amp up the fact finding. By any means necessary."

Drio snapped off a salute, clearly happy to have free reign. "Ciao, ragazzi." He grabbed his jacket and left.

I stuffed my laptop back into my bag.

Rohan rolled his neck out a couple of times. The corded muscles across his shoulder rippled with the movement. "Nava?"

"What?" I zipped up the bag.

He caught my hand, forcing me to turn toward him. "I'm sorry. There is no universe in which I think you're furniture. I meant the role. And I appreciate you're facing a double standard that sucks balls. That's why I fought Mandelbaum to keep you."

Rasha, rabbis, and Executive alike worshipped Rohan. Him going to bat for me was worth a lot. I focused on that and not the damage he'd done last night. "Accepted and appreciated." I flicked the zipper. "I wish I didn't need anyone to stick up for me."

"I know." He paused. "Anything else you wish?"

"If we weren't committed Rasha doing whatever the mission demands, then that would be quite the loaded question."

I'd made it to the second chorus of "I Will Survive" in my head before he answered. "Is that what we are?"

Now it was my turn to remain silent.

He rubbed a knuckle over his forehead.

"You look tired," I said. He gave me a wan smile. "Do you want a massage?"

A teasing glint lit his eyes. "Are you trying to seduce me?"

"You looked… your neck… tense." I blushed, stammering like an idiot.

"I'd love a massage. It's only fair considering you put half of the knots there." He sat down on the sofa.

Sitting beside him, I stretched out my hands in preparation. I'd given massages a million times with tap friends to work out leg cramps. I was a regular Florence Nightingale here, with the bonus of wiping all traces of Poppy and Lily off of him, branding my scent and my touch into his brain.

"Just a sec." Rohan unbuttoned his shirt, letting it fall off his shoulders.

I swallowed, then warmed up his neck and shoulders, relaxing his muscles. Gradually I applied a deeper pressure on the upward strokes, making circular kneading motions over his entire upper back.

I focused on his tattoo as I worked on the tension in his neck and shoulders, latching on to the black ink as a safe harbor. I pressed the pad of my thumb into his clavicle and he sighed. Still using my thumbs, I applied sustained pressure to the muscles that rotated the shoulder.

His breathing slowed with every touch. In my hands, he became languid, pliant. It would be so easy to lean in and bite the nape of his neck. Let my fingers trail around his front, down the dusting of hair from his navel into his pants.

He'd probably be hard.

Hot.

Rohan groaned, the sound rolling through my hands into my very core. I crossed my legs against the desperate bolt of need that spiked through me. Yes, it would be so easy to turn this into something else, but my brain kept replaying the image of Poppy's cat-like smile and those indentations in the carpet. The memory of him telling Lily he always loved her.

The nightmare of feeling summarily dismissed in every way imaginable last night.

Rohan jerked. "Ow. Careful."

"Sorry." I massaged him a moment longer then patted him between the shoulder blades.

He twisted around to face me. "Done?"

"Yup."

He stretched. "Thanks."

I picked up my bag. "Have a good day." I yawned. "I need a nap."

Rohan frowned. "Big plans?"

"Yeah." Me and the TV. I placed a hand on his now-tense shoulder. "Hey, don't undo all my good massaging."

Are you jealous? Do I care? Fine questions that I had no answers to.

He stood up, regarding me for a long moment. Chin up, I met his gaze, ready to take on any lecture but all he said was, "Be careful."

"Yup." I almost asked him what he was up to, but I didn't want to know. "Later, Snowflake."

"Bye."

I closed the door to his suite behind me, sagging against the door, my head bowed. Then I straightened my spine and headed downstairs to my room.

18

Monday morning, I hustled to go meet Dr. Gelman, banishing all Rohan Mitra thoughts from my mind. Today's weather was more spring than winter. Walking briskly kept me warm, even with my jacket open. I followed the map on my phone to our meeting, eyeing the building in question. Several signs on the ground floor invited people in to a billiards hall, but it did say Café Louvre in giant red neon letters along the second story. Worst case scenario and the place was a dump, I'd grab breakfast from my new favorite bakery on the way back to the hotel.

I hit the second floor and found myself transported. La Belle Époque, indeed. It was an airy, thoroughly charming Parisian café. A long rectangular room, the space was painted salmon pink and cream with rococo plaster touches and ceiling medallions. A long bar ran most of the length.

"Wait until you actually eat something," Dr. Gelman said. She braced a hand on the wall, winded from her climb to the second floor. Once she'd caught her breath, she noted today's outfit in approval. "Better."

With a final longing glance toward the pastry case, I followed her into the farthest reaches of the room. We sat down at a small wood table for two. The waitress handed us our menus and bustled off. There was a good selection of croissants and omelets, but I'd been promised pastry. I pointed back toward the case. "Which one should I have?"

"Go right for the treats, don't you?"

"Always. I want no regrets. You never know when you might die." I clapped a hand over my mouth, realizing that in her condition that might not have been the best thing to say.

"Don't stress yourself, kid."

The waitress came for our order. Dr. Gelman asked for an omelet for herself and the classic sacher for me. "A latte, please," I added.

The scientist looked around the mostly empty restaurant, as if memorizing the few patrons' faces.

"What's wrong?"

"Probably nothing." She pulled out a pack of cigarettes. "You got the supplies?"

"Yes." I reached for my purse to give them to her but she stopped me.

"Keep them. You'll need them for the ritual." She placed the cigarette in her mouth, coughing as she did.

"Really?"

She sighed, annoyed, but dropped the cancer stick on top of the pack.

"Thank you. How does the ritual work?"

"You know the story of the golem?" she asked.

"Clay monster. Rabbi brought it to life." Even if I hadn't vaguely known the tale, the story was set here in Prague. Half the tourist shops displayed books with covers to that effect in their windows.

The waitress deposited our lattes. I sucked my first sip back like a junkie getting her morning fix. Which, let's face it, I was.

"Once the golem had been physically built," Gelman said, "the rabbi needed to write the Hebrew letters aleph, mem, and tav on its forehead to bring it to life. They spelled 'emet,' meaning truth."

I searched my brain for a long-buried memory of Jewish folklore told to me by my grandmother. "Didn't they stop the golem by erasing the word?"

"Not the entire word. The aleph. It changed emet to met. Death."

"I don't want Ari to be erased or die."

The waitress placed my sacher in front of me. A thick slab of chocolate cake. "You're so pretty, face cake!" I clapped my hands.

Gelman and the waitress looked confused.

"It's as big as my head," I explained. "Thus deserving of the moniker." The waitress shot me a weird look like she was wondering if my craziness might interfere with her tip. I beamed at her in reassurance. "Thank you."

She didn't look convinced and after telling us to let her know if we needed anything else, hustled away.

Dr. Gelman cut into her omelet. "Is your twin like you?"

"Not even a little bit. And yes, my parents were overjoyed by that fact. I see the look on your face."

She chuckled.

I dug my fork into the dark rich chocolate, making sure to snag some of the ganache coating and the whipped cream piled high on the side.

Oh, sweet mother of fuckers. I almost wept at the taste. It was the nirvana of chocolate, the perfect sweetness, the perfect moistness, the perfect richness, and then to reward the eater further, the cake was shot through with raspberry. Literally the best pairing in the world.

I dabbed at my eyes. "I'm all verklempt."

She smiled indulgently at me. "I'm glad you like it."

I forced myself to put my fork down and savor this experience. "Ari?"

"The ritual involves invoking aleph mem tav, but it cannot be undone or erased. He's in no danger from that."

"Meaning there are other dangers."

"There are always other dangers, Nava." Her statement reminded me of something Rohan would say. To wipe away the bitter taste in my mouth, I took another bite, still determined not to fall on the cake like an animal.

"Does Rabbi Abrams know the details of this ritual?"

"No. Few do."

Taking another careful look around the restaurant, she pulled something out of her purse. She pressed it into my hand, closing my fingers around it. Paper crinkled over a hard center. She shook her head at me when I turned my hand up to examine what I'd been given.

I casually tucked the small package into my pocket.

Dr. Gelman buttered her toast. She kept a pleasant smile on her face, as if we were chatting about nothing of consequence, but her voice was low and insistent. "Why do you think you can't take your Rasha ring off?"

I caved, needing another bite. "It's part of the magic."

She salted her eggs. "More than that. It's a covenant between Rasha and Brotherhood that the hunter dedicates their life to the cause. The symbol of their willing servitude."

"It sounds like handcuffs." I frowned, tugging on my ring. "No one told me that."

"It wouldn't have mattered if they did. You're not given a choice. The Brotherhood is all about power wrapped up in a cause. The most dangerous sort of fanaticism with very lucrative rewards. They are determined to control every aspect. That's why your existence upsets them so much."

"Not everyone hates me." I felt compelled to defend them. "Some of the Rasha would fight to protect me. Rabbi Abrams is on my side, too." I hoped.

"He is. The fact he sent you to me proves it."

"How so?"

"He hasn't told the Brotherhood about Ari's confirmed status yet, has he?" she said.

"No. And I'd wondered about that." Ari had told me that Rabbi Abrams wanted his status kept under wraps until he figured out why re-running the ceremony hadn't worked. "How did you know?"

Dr. Gelman took a pill case out of her bag, dumped a tiny white tablet into her hand and dry swallowed it. "The Brotherhood could induct Ari, but with their way your magic would be nullified."

"Oh." I dragged my finger through some ganache. "A month ago, I would have been first in line for that option." Save Ari, ditch Nava. I wasn't shocked, though it still was kind of sucky to hear it spoken aloud. I shrugged and licked the chocolate off.

"Your existence has upset the order they've worked centuries to create." She scooped up some omelet. "If my ritual works, the Brotherhood can never know. They must believe that Rabbi Abrams performed the regular ceremony again. That he'd made a mistake with the ritual the previous time. These ceremonies require precision and other factors can interfere with magic. If, for example, your brother was feeling extreme emotion."

"Massive. He was also hammered."

"Perfect. Now, if they know you possess a means of inducting a Rasha without them sanctioning it?"

"We could check for other descendants that the Brotherhood didn't think to."

"Sheket." Dr. Gelman gripped my hand. "You're not listening. They will kill you. Kill Ari."

My fork tumbled to my plate. I dragged my sweaty palms along my skirt. My vision tunneled, the room spinning out impossibly long and distorted. Sound blurred.

I looked down at my fingers clenched in my lap, staring at the crease of my knuckles, the slight bend in my pinky finger, and the tiny patch of dry skin at the base of my thumb. Imagining them bloodied and lifeless on the cold hard ground.

"What if they already know?" I whispered.

"If you bought the supplies and made it here alive then they don't know. You've gone this far. Rabbi Abrams understands the danger and the fact he sent you to me means he's willing to hide the truth. There's no reason not to proceed. Have you told anyone else?"

I shook my head, then stopped. I'd told Rohan.

Her face fell. "Can this person be trusted?"

In this? "I have no doubt."

Dr. Gelman finished her breakfast, but I pushed the dessert around on my plate, appetite gone. She awkwardly patted my hand. "At least you're going to make them work to take you down."

She insisted on paying for breakfast. I slowly descended the stairs with her. I didn't try to help, she was too proud for that, but I did stay close in case she needed me. We got to the bottom without incident.

She promised to give me the step-by-step instructions necessary for the induction ritual after she checked one last detail, though she refused to call or email me, since all my communication might be monitored. Fair enough since my phone had been given to me by the Brotherhood, and my laptop encrypted by them.

"Should I be concerned about them seeing those first few messages between us?" I asked.

"No. But from now on, we should find another way to maintain contact."

Given the schedule for the Samson job, I figured I'd be back in Vancouver by Saturday. We arranged a time for her to phone Leo's place. The Executive didn't know about her. If I wasn't back, she'd phone at the same time each day until she reached me.

"Thank you so much," I said.

She reached a hand up, briefly touching my cheek. "We'll talk when you get home." The conversation was over. Probably a good thing. I'd had my share of bombshells for the day.

I walked back to the hotel, my mind swirling, amazed at the people talking, eating, and shopping around me. Amazed at how normal their lives were. Just over a month. That's how long it had been since my world had been knocked off its axis, and I'd become Rasha. Given such a short adaptation period for such a massive life transition, a transition the rest of them spent twenty years to prepare for, I was not just coping, but thriving.

Thanks to me, we'd cracked the mystery of Samson's identity. Thanks to me, Ari's initiate status had been confirmed and he'd soon be inducted. Not to mention, I'd helped take out the demon Asmodeus, his spawnlings, and the vral. It was fucking unfair then, that every time I found my footing, the floor dropped out from under me.

I stopped at a red light. A little girl in a bright yellow coat watched me. Her dad's hand rested lightly on her head, and her mouth was smeared with chocolate. She grinned at me.

I grinned back. That's how I'd deal. Knowing that doing my job in the dark let kids like her live in the light. We crossed the street and she skipped off ahead with her father. Rohan was wrong about me not knowing what I wanted. Kill demons and get Ari Rasha'd. My personal life had sidetracked me and it was time to reset things to a less complicated state.

Look at that. Meeting Gelman had let me forget about Snowflake for an entire hour. I wasn't to be given a second more, however, because I entered the hotel to find Rohan and Lily, their heads bent close together, cheeks flush with cold, and identical expressions of happiness on their faces as they laughed over a shared joke. A perfect couple.

I tried to sneak past them, but no such luck.

"Where have you been?" Rohan asked.

"Breakfast with a friend at Café Louvre." Let him stew over which friend.

Lily clapped her hands together. "Did you have any of their cakes?"

My heart sank. Not fair. I don't want to like you. "Sacher torte."

She nodded sagely. "That's one of the best." Her phone beeped. Lily checked it. "Oops. Gotta get to the conference." She kissed Rohan's cheek. "See you later."

He kissed hers back. "Have fun listening to physicists, you giant nerd."

She stuck her tongue out at him.

I returned her good-bye wave. "Seems I wasn't the only one breakfasting with friends," I said. "Up early, were we?"

"Up late." Rohan glanced at Lily's departing back.

My stomach twisted. I saw his hand on her naked back. Her face soft and suffused with ecstasy under him. The wicked glint in his eyes as he slid into her. Was he gentle with her? Did he growl her name, the way he did mine?

Rohan snapped his fingers in front of my face. "Hey, spacey. You all right?"

They probably had movie sex: the lightest sheen of non-odorous sweat, low cries, and mutual orgasm. Two beautiful people basking in post-coital radiance together.

"Is there anything you need me for today?" I asked, because if there wasn't, I wanted to go to my room and torture myself further.

"There is," he said.

"What?"

Rohan frowned at my sharp tone. "What crawled up your ass?"

I stuffed my hands into my pockets so I didn't punch him. My fingers brushed the wrapped item I'd been given. Examining it was a much better use of my time than obsessing over the sexual proclivities of the dummy in front of me.

I stalked off into the elevator, Rohan dogging my heels. I didn't speak until we'd gotten inside my room and I'd locked the door. Rohan watched me, confused, as I tossed the vials of dirt and water on the bed. Then I ripped open the package Dr. Gelman had given me.

An amulet. There wasn't much to it. About the size of a Canadian two dollar coin but thicker, it was made of swirled green glass. The only noteworthy detail was a hamsa etched on the inside. I ran my fingers along the edge but there was no clasp, no hinge, no discernible seam.

Rohan leaned in to look at it. "What does it do?"

"I don't know." I tapped the stoppered containers. "We need these for the induction ritual. I'm guessing the amulet is part of it as well, but Dr. Gelman didn't tell me why." I held the disc up to the light, twisting it in between my finger and thumb. "She seemed very concerned that no one see me take it from her."

He held out his hand and I dropped the amulet in his palm. "I've never seen anything like it. Do you want me to research it? Discreetly?"

"No!"

Rohan handed it back. "O-kay."

I gripped his sleeve. "I am trusting you with my life by telling you this."

His expression hardened. "Meaning?"

"Meaning if the Brotherhood finds out that I've discovered a way to induct a Rasha that they haven't sanctioned, they'll kill me and Ari."

Rohan spun off the bed, cursing. I sat there, plucking at a loose thread in my skirt until he ran out of steam.

"You can't tell anyone," I said.

"*Fuck*, Nava." He punched the wall and I flinched. "I think that goes without saying." He rubbed the side of his hand over his forehead. "That's who you were with, wasn't it?"

I nodded, gathering everything up and placing it all in the tiny safe in my closet.

"Is Ari worth it?" he asked.

"Yes," I said, but my hands shook as I locked the safe up.

Rohan turned me into his arms. I tensed again. "I didn't spend the night with her," he said.

"Who?" I asked.

"Anyone."

I lay my cheek against his chest, relaxing into his embrace. Needing this comfort like a balm. "Stick it in whoever you want, Snowflake."

"Your permission is duly noted. For the record, I watched a *Breaking Bad* marathon. Heisenberg is either way scarier or not at all in Czech."

"I know. I couldn't decide either."

His heart beat in time with mine. "The other night..." he began.

I inhaled, letting his presence envelop me on every level. "No point rehashing it."

Rohan tipped my chin up so that I had to meet his eyes. "No more knives. I promise." His voice held a quiet sincerity that led me to believe him. Besides, the faster this was all put behind us, the faster we could continue as I meant us to go on. Fuck buddies and fighters.

"We're good. Drio told me why you had to get drunk." The way he searched my face had me wondering if he was worried that Drio had told me too much.

He slid his hands down my arms, stepping away. "Come on."

"Where?"

He grinned. "Do you trust me?"

"Situationally."

He held out his hand. "Good enough."

19

Rohan pulled a navy knit cap over his hair, slid on a pair of shades and buttoned up his long, wool coat.

"Incognito-level achieved?" I slid on my own heart-shaped sunglasses, keeping my expression bland.

"If I'm lucky." Rohan saw the glasses and mimed having a heart attack. I giggled. He jerked his head to the road running left from the hotel. "This way."

"For someone who hates fame so much, you're not an asshole to fans."

"The other night notwithstanding," he said with a wry twist of his mouth. "My mom made sure I understood what a gift of time, love, and money fans gave me. But this is about you. You've been dealing with a lot and you need a break. Luckily you're in the perfect city, with the perfect tour guide."

"Luckily."

Rohan's disguise worked because we weren't given a second look as we crossed the street into the middle of the rectangular plaza. "Wenceslas Square," he said.

"Of Christmas carol fame."

"Of revolution fame." He pointed up to the top of the square. "Imagine this entire space filled with Communist tanks. That's what happened in the late 60s."

I shivered, imagining row upon row of Soviet tanks looming large under a gray sky. The image faded, replaced with the reality of food trucks and art deco hotels. I cocked my head, taking in the most majestic building. "That hotel is probably a hundred, hundred and fifty years old. Vancouver pre-dates it by a bit. But we don't have anywhere near the sense of history that infuses Europe." I loved the idea of being deeply rooted in something.

He let me admire it for another couple of minutes before cheekily saying, "Stay with the group," and walking off. He led me down to the river and these two weird modern buildings that stuck out amidst the surrounding architecture. The one on the right was a round cylinder with rectangular windows all the way around. The building narrowed at the bottom, a single pole protruding from the bottom like a leg.

The building to the left was made of glass, its middle bent in toward the first building, pressing up against it. A triangle jutted out from the glass toward the cylinder, almost like a hand, while it was supported by struts like legs.

Rohan watched me expectantly.

I bounced on my toes. "It looks like a couple dancing!" The glass building had a woman's shape, and looked like she was about to be swung around by her partner. The energy and dynamism in them was astounding.

"Dancing House. Nicknamed Fred and Ginger."

I pressed a hand to my heart. "Stop. I'm not going to be able to leave this city." I made him take a selfie with me in front of it then took one last fond look at Dancing House before we trekked back to Old Town Square, a huge cobblestoned space whose edges seamlessly blended into numerous restaurant patios. The square was anchored by a bronze commemorative statue of some guy standing on a large stone base. Tourist central on this sunny day.

Rohan dodged the many tour operators marching their charges from attraction to attraction. He might not have been recognized but he was certainly noticed. I was shot more than one dark look at my audacity in being with him.

He stopped in front of this crazy clock tower running up the side of a very old building at one end of the square. Two large clock faces, one a swirl of color, the other gold, were adorned with small figures and astrological symbols. "It's a medieval astronomical clock." He checked his watch. "Give it a sec."

The clock began to ring. Two small panels at the top slid open, revealing a parade of moving figures. Saints or something given the crosses some held. Rohan nudged me, directing my attention to the skeleton ringing a bell along the right side of the tower. "Death."

I pressed my hands together by my cheek. "Awww. That's so sweet."

A minute later it was over. Rohan pointed at the twin gothic spires visible behind the small modern art museum at the opposite end of the square. "Tyn Church."

"It looks like the nightmare version of the Sleeping Beauty castle."

"Some say it was Disney's inspiration." He gazed up at it. "It inspired me. I wrote the song 'Slumber' about it."

One of Fugue State Five's later hits. "'Trapped in a limbo with no way out but down.'" I shook my head at the first line of the chorus. "Hard as it is to believe, you're a ray of sunshine now in comparison."

"I work my issues out in other ways."

"For which we are all thankful."

His eyes roamed my body like tiny licks of flame. "How thankful?"

My stomach growled before I could reply.

"Feeding time," he announced cheerfully.

It took me a second to get my feet to move. How he switched on and off like that was beyond me. Unless, of course, it was more game playing and didn't matter one way or the other to him.

Reset.

We wove our way through twisted streets, coming out at the foot of the Charles Bridge. Passing under a heavy, dark tower, we stepped onto the pedestrian-only bridge that was thronged with tourists taking selfies, browsing the photo and jewelry kiosks that lined either side, having a caricature drawn, or watching the occasional busker do a marionette performance.

It took longer than I expected to walk its length. "Malá Strana," Rohan said, waving a hand at the neighborhood we found ourselves in on the far side. "Lesser Town."

The architecture here was astounding as well. I could have happily wandered the streets for hours staring at the old church spires, red tiled roofs, and arched windows, but Rohan had a specific destination in mind. We entered a nondescript hole-in-the-wall. Dimly lit with rickety wooden tables and chairs, the restaurant was bustling with locals.

Rohan pulled off his knit cap. A lock of hair flopped into his eyes, so he raked his fingers through, pushing back the curl and tousling his hair further.

A harried waiter showed us to the last table, crowded into a back corner. He tossed down a couple of menus.

Rohan handed them back, checking with me. "Did I do well enough the last time I ordered for you that you situationally trust me to do it again?"

"Sure. But if you disappoint, you will be killed."

"Svickova." He held up two fingers. "I'll also have a Pilsner."

"You want a beer?" the waiter asked me.

"Lemon radler." Rohan looked horrified at my order. "Some of us are concerned about getting our daily fruit content," I said.

"Oh no. Not even you can convince yourself of that."

"That's cute. You have no idea what I can convince myself of." I ran my finger over the walls, every inch covered in scratched initials. "Points for local color." I folded my hands primly on the table. "Tell me the history of this fine establishment."

He took a drink of the beer the waiter had brought. "No clue."

"Tour guide fail." I said, before trying my own drink, which was nicely chilled.

"Never enough with you," he grumbled. "Okay. Here's a fun Prague fact. There have been two defenestrations in the town's history."

"Based on the French root in that word, I'm gonna guess it has something to do with windows. Out of windows?"

He clinked his glass against mine. "Very good. The act of throwing someone or something out a window. Don't piss off a Czech unless you're on ground level."

"You're chock full of macabre facts, aren't you?"

"I excel at playing to my audience. Giving them what they want," he leered.

I moved my radler, allowing the server to place my food in front of me. I waited until he'd gone to speak. "You were unbearably arrogant as a rock star, weren't you?"

Rohan picked up his cutlery. "I'm shocked I rate past tense."

"Well, you're old now. You've mellowed into insufferably cocky."

"Thank you. I know how much you appreciate cock...y." He snickered.

"The emotional maturity of a twelve-year-old," I said, cutting into my lunch. A braised beef, it was served in a creamy vegetable sauce with dumplings on the side. I moaned, swallowing my first bite.

Incredibly, he didn't comment.

I decided that I liked a man who didn't need to fill valuable eating time with small talk. Plate cleared and practically licked clean, I sagged back against my chair, my hand on my belly. "If I had a button, I'd totally pop it open right now and nap."

Rohan paid the bill. "Nope. We're going to walk off the carbs."

I groaned but pushed my chair back and followed him outside. "Thank you for lunch."

He tapped his cheek.

I rolled my eyes, then leaned in and gave him a peck. "That was a thank you appropriate to any family member. To be clear."

"You'll be expressing your thanks in a highly inappropriate manner later. To be clear."

I stumbled at his words. But my nipples went rock hard so he wasn't wrong. Necessarily. See this? This was good. Fun easy banter followed up by promises of hot monkey sex. Reset achieved. Poppy could rot in Hell. I let out a breath, my rib cage easing out of its tight lock, and skipped after him to catch up.

Our final stop, Rohan informed me, was Prague Castle. A massive complex, we were herded from line-up to line-up, marveling at the magnificence of St. Vitus Cathedral, the fascination of the palace room covered in painted coats-of-arms, and the delight of the tiny colored houses on Gold Lane.

"Enough," I said at last. "I'm sight-seed out."

We exited the grounds into a large square near the top of the palace. People took photos of the city skyline over to one side, while one especially stunning neighboring building boasting a tiered roof and intricately painted vines and flowers along a high frieze advertised a Baroque art collection.

I tugged on Rohan's sleeve. "Selfie time." He grumbled good-naturedly but obliged, following me as I elbowed our way to the front of the crowd. I held up my phone, adjusting it to get both us and the maximum amount of the city in the shot. "Smile."

A split second before I took the photo Rohan murmured in my ear, "All of Prague laid out before us."

My breath caught. I lowered the phone, not wanting to see the expression on my face in the picture in case I'd embarrassed myself. I also had to step away before I did something bad, here, in this very public place.

I walked back into the center of the plaza, wishing for a distraction. Some higher power decided to take pity on my sexually frustrated state because the perfect one zoomed into view. Waving furiously at Rohan, I broke into a run.

The old-fashioned mini tourist train consisted of the engineer's car pulling two passenger cars with even rows of benches. Open on one side for easy entrance and exit, hard clear plastic formed windows on the outer side.

Rohan eyed the green locomotive. "No."

"Oh yes." I climbed into one of the hard-topped cars, sitting down on the wooden bench. "Come on. The sign on top says it goes back to the square in Old Town." I loved these mini trains, going back to the one in Stanley Park in Vancouver that I rode throughout my childhood. We visited that park year-round and my parents learned to anticipate my pleas to go again. They'd board me with a strip of tickets in my hand so I could ride to my heart's content while they took Ari to feed the goats at the petting zoo next door.

Rohan sat down beside me, unimpressed.

The train started up smoothly enough. Narration about the plaza blasted out through the scratchy speakers. Rohan glowered at me, his hands clapped over his ears.

I laughed. Which escalated to manic hilarity at his death stares as the train clattered through the streets, winding back down the hill. There was no suspension on this beast and combined with the cobblestones, the two of us were flung around like rag dolls, our bones jarring. My teeth rattled hard enough to break. Tears streamed down my face and I was barely able to catch my breath for laughter.

A French family a few rows behind us made loud, disparaging comments about Americans. As a Canadian, I'd seen enough American backpackers sporting Canadian flags that I was happy to reinforce any bad perception of Americans abroad. Payback.

The train jolted over a bump in the road and Rohan gasped. "My balls," he groaned, right as the woman seated ahead recognized him, and squealing, snapped a photo of him.

I lost it, clutching a pole for support.

Rohan glared at me. "I hate you."

By the time the train pulled up in the square, even I had had enough of that ride. Not that I'd admit it. "I'm so happy."

Rohan unfolded himself like an old man. "You don't deserve dinner after that."

Our fellow passenger shyly asked Rohan if she could take her photo with him. I approved of his behavior in complying.

Soon as she was gone, I grabbed his arm, pressing myself against his side. Not ready to let this interlude end. "You're totally going to take me out, aren't you? Do you need to check in with Drio?"

"Nah. He's off sourcing what we need."

My phone buzzed in my pocket with a text. "It's from the Assistant Director giving me directions and call time for Samson's scene tomorrow." Even though Samson was the reason for our trip, I resented his intrusion on my time with Rohan today. "This is good. I can lure him to the ritual location."

Since we were tired and Rohan insisted he was broken, we took a taxi back to the hotel. We agreed to meet in the lobby in an hour for dinner. The second I got to my room, I called Leo, putting her on speakerphone as I changed. "I'm so getting laid tonight," I trilled.

"Been plying your wiles on him?"

I tossed my skirt on the bed. "Not even. But we were sightseeing so–"

"Since when do fuck buddies merit tourist time?"

"Since the assignment is in a momentary lull before the storm. We had a day off and–"

"You played boyfriend and girlfriend?" She sighed.

"Can't we be friends? Friends with benefits. That's a thing." I rooted through my clothing for the right outfit.

"Ten seconds ago he was a fuck buddy."

"Stop twisting everything."

"You haven't let yourself get close to anyone since the great Cole disaster," she said. "Believe me, I get that Rohan is hot, and he fucks like a god, but guys like that don't stick around. Remember how wrecked you were after Cole? What do you think Rohan leaving would do to you?"

I slipped into a cute purple dress made up of overlapping tiers of fabric that had a bit of a flapper vibe going for it. Best of all, no zipper. Pull on, pull off. "We work together. Fight together. It's more than the sex."

Leo made a strangled noise.

"Hence the friend status."

"Nava, you're going to hate me for saying this, but have you considered that maybe you're falling for him and he doesn't feel the same?"

I grabbed the phone, taking it off speaker. "Why not? What's so wrong with me that he wouldn't want me back? Not that I want him for a boyfriend but thanks so much for making me sound like some cast-off you'd find in the ninety-nine cent bin."

There was silence for a moment. I sat down on the bed, wondering why I'd bothered to resume our friendship.

"Sweetie, I think you're the bee's knees," Leo said. I snorted at her corny language.

"I mean it. Far as I'm concerned, you're tops. But from everything you've told me, this guy is the master of mixed signals. Throw in his first love who has suddenly re-appeared in his life?" I'd forgotten about Lily. "I fear for when this issue-ridden boy blasts your world apart like an asteroid hit."

I raked my hands through my hair. "It's not like that. We're reset back to easy and uncomplicated."

Her pause stretched two seconds too long. "I shouldn't have said anything. Lull before the storm. You're right. Enjoy it."

Our good-byes were a tad strained.

.

20

Leo was wrong. I knew what I was getting into with Rohan. Sex. The wolfish smile he conferred on me when I met him in the lobby confirmed it. All good. Still, I was quiet on the ride over to the restaurant located in an industrial complex filled with single story warehouses, most boasting foodie signs. Our destination, SaSaZu, didn't look like much until we got inside.

The restaurant was enormous. A black-and-white patterned wall ran along the right side. The others were painted red, with black exposed pipes traversing the high ceiling. Various table groupings in browns, oranges, and greens filled the space. But the showstopper feature was the myriad of huge lanterns suspended from the ceiling that bathed the room in a warm, low light. Flanking the doors were a live DJ on one side and massive wall map on the other, with pins depicting all the cities that patrons visited from.

Our server explained the philosophy of the South-Asian fusion street food and how we should choose dishes from each of the five sections of the menu to be taken on a culinary journey. He didn't need to tell me twice.

The food was incredible. Rohan didn't ask me what was wrong, but he did make sure the conversation was light-hearted. I felt myself relax, any residual hurt from my talk with Leo disappearing in the enjoyment of the evening.

Ripping off a piece of naan, I dipped it in my lamb and eggplant curry. Some of the spicy sauce dripped on my thumb so I dragged the pad across my teeth, my tongue flicking out to catch the errant drop.

Rohan froze, the grilled shrimp in his chopsticks forgotten, his eyes on my mouth. He cleared his throat. "That curry reminds me of this street vendor that I kept going to in Delhi."

"When was that?"

"I was about fifteen? Before the band hit. Mom was mixing an album for this group that blended traditional instruments like tabla and sitar with electronica. I'd grown up sitting in on her studio sessions but this was the first time she ever asked my opinion about something. Really listened to what I had to say and then incorporated one of my suggestions."

His eyes lighting up as he recounted the story was the sexiest thing about him and trust me, there were a lot of options on the Mitra sex appeal drop down menu.

"Did Maya mix any of your albums?"

"No. She swore there wasn't enough money in the world. Since her teaching me to ride a bike ended in bloodshed, Mom said our level of head-butting would lead to flat-out murder in one session." He held out the last, tiny, tea-infused duck roll in his chopsticks for me to eat.

I leaned across the table, grasping his wrist to tug him closer. The muscles in his arms and chest tensed as he leaned in.

"Open up." His voice was a husky murmur. He placed the roll in my mouth and I obediently chewed.

"Good?" he asked.

"Incredible." I didn't dare shift my weight, worried the sweat trickling down the backs of my thighs would make me creak against the leather seat.

"More tea?" Our friendly server broke the spell.

"Please." I held out my ceramic mug.

Two sips of tea and one bathroom dash to splash water on my face later, I'd regained my composure enough to continue our conversation. "You have to tell me the bike story. Were you pushing her to let you ride it before you were ready?"

He ducked his head, the fringe of his sooty lashes fanned against his cheek. "Not exactly."

"Snowflake," I prompted. "What did you do?"

He lay down his chopsticks. "I told her I wasn't ready but she kept insisting that I was riding my bike just fine." When it was clear I wasn't going to let this drop, he huffed at me. "Okay, but laugh and die."

I crossed my heart.

"To prove my point that I couldn't ride, I rode my bike with expert precision into some very thorny bushes and then screamed bloody murder when I got all scratched up, yelling 'I told you! I can't ride!'"

"My God. Your control issues started so young." I pressed my lips together but couldn't help the laughter escaping me.

"You promised."

I stuffed some noodles in my mouth. "Chewing," I mumbled around a mouthful of food.

Rohan pointed his chopstick at me, an evil twinkle in his eye. "So. Dead." Then he leaned back with an affectionate shake of his head.

Clearly Rohan and I were friends. Possibly better than friends. Friends plus. But why the pressure to quantify it beyond that? Funnily enough, something had shifted. Rohan had gone from being the most obtuse person about the two of us to the only other one to understand us. He did understand, right? I felt like the ugliness of the past couple days had blown things open and allowed us to settle in this happy easy place and hoped he did too.

Dinner stretched out and a delicious state of coiled anticipation about how this night would end grew. Every glance, every touch, every shared bite of food was underscored with the mutual knowledge of two people who wanted each other but wanted to prolong the wanting until it was almost painful.

Truth be told, much as I enjoyed the simmering build, it was time to get on with it already. This European vacation had been lax on the saucy antics.

"I don't want dessert. You?" Rohan asked. He sat back in his chair, eyes hot, voice calm.

"I'm good." My words were at odds with my jittering leg. Once again, he insisted on treating.

I stepped outside while he finished paying, thankful for the brisk wind on my very flushed cheeks. No one else was out here. The night was quiet and still.

Rohan joined me a couple of minutes later. "They called a taxi for us but it's going to be about twenty minutes. Want to stay outside?"

Before I could answer, a demon bobbed into view under one of the parking lot lights. Roughly my height, fuzzy, charcoal-colored, and sausage-shaped, the demon boasted one cyclops eye and a red sneer of a mouth. Both its fingers and toes were long and sloth-like. A two-foot long external metal spine ran down its back with jagged spikes jutting up like a stegosaurus.

The demon swiveled its eye to look at me.

"What is that?" I asked.

"Most of it is a gogota demon," Rohan said. He tossed his jacket on a bench beside the restaurant door, his forearm blade extracting. "Dumb as a sack of rocks, but it'll focus on a task's completion until it's dead. The metal upgrade is new."

"Vashar! Vashar!" The demon screeched in a high reedy voice. It wobbled as if not sure how to accommodate its additional weight.

Rohan swore. "Someone has deliberately messed with it. A gogota's sweet spot is dead center of its back." Where we could no longer access it thanks to the metal spine. "Get it into the shadows."

Right. We didn't want the patrons to look out and see this.

The demon charged us, a blur of motion for such a slug-like shape. Rohan jabbed the blade along his arm into the gogota's belly, forcing it back into the dark reaches of the lot. The demon left a trail of sticky, silver goop that glistened in the moonlight.

Busy slicing and dicing, Rohan blocked the front of the demon from me, so I couldn't blast the gogota without hitting Rohan. I also couldn't sneak up from behind because the demon was backed up against the complex's fence.

It threw Rohan off, angling its body to smash Snowflake's head with one of its spikes. Rohan staggered back and, in that moment, the demon whizzed over to me, wrapping its fingers around my wrist. "Vashar," it insisted. Less like it wanted me dead and more like it wanted me to do something.

Blasting it failed to loosen its grip.

The demon dug its fingers into my jacket pockets. Its hands wandered over my body, probing me.

"Get off!" Even though parts of the demon were starting to shrivel and fall off under my attack, it ignored my demands. The damn thing couldn't even stand upright anymore but that didn't matter.

It pressed up against me, its blobby body expanding, secreting the sticky substance to keep me pinned to it as it continued its exploration of my person. The more I blasted it, the more it expanded, gluing me to its body that much harder.

Rohan tried to rip me off of it, but I was stuck fast.

Closer and closer it pressed into me, smelling of baby powder and sweaty baseball mitt. Soon the gogota would suffocate me, leaving it all the time in the world to violate me with its creepy touches.

My eyes glued shut from its sap. I could hear Rohan's cursing and labored breathing as he tried to free me. The metallic smell of my magic filled the air.

The demon's finger entered my mouth. "Vashar!"

Gagging, I jammed my right fist into the gogota's belly as hard as I could. Then I twisted my fist even deeper into it before firing a blast off my closed hand. A rumbled charge from deep inside me blew through my arm at the motion.

The demon ripped free, fresh air cascading around me. I reached out blindly. "Rohan?"

He grabbed my hand. "Got you."

I leaned on him, my legs rubbery. "Is it dead?" I had to pry my eyes open given the goop coating them. Once I had, it took me a second to figure out what I was looking at.

The gogota was stuck to a metal pole by its spikes. Not just stuck. Its spine was totally mangled, all twisted and melted, leaving the demon half-crushed in the deformation.

"Vashar!" Its fingers wriggled feebly in my direction.

"Why is it stuck to the pole? Is it glued?" Every one of my blinks was sticky with slime. I didn't think I'd hit it hard enough to send it that far back.

"It looked like a giant magnet turned on. The demon shot off you, sucked backward to the lamp post." Rohan approached the creature. Staying out of arm's reach, he examined the spine. "It's not the secretion holding it in place." He pried the tip of one spike off and released it. It immediately clanged back against the lamp as though magnetically charged.

"Did I do that?" Was this some new facet of my power?

"Yes?" He extended a blade from his fingertips. Holding a bent piece of spine away from the demon's body, he stabbed the gogota in the center of its back.

The demon gave one last cry and disappeared in a tiny whirlwind of gray dust. The twisted metal spine remained, attached to the post. Rohan tried to pry it off but it was stuck fast.

I stood there, chest heaving, doing my best to wipe off my face with the hem of my skirt. Beyond caring if anyone saw me with my dress up around my head. "It almost had me. It was unstoppable." A wave of tremors coursed through me.

Rohan draped his arm around me. "It's gone."

"Was this an isolated attack? Did Samson send it? You think he's on to us?"

Rohan scanned the darkness for any other threat. "Don't go tomorrow."

"I have to." I shook my head at him when he looked about to argue. "Samson might not have sent the demon. In which case, standing him up is only going to annoy him. Even if he did send it, there's nothing in his M.O. that shows him directly attacking or killing people. He won't try to take a Rasha down with so many other witnesses around."

"He doesn't have to," Rohan said. "All he has to do is work you into a depressed enough state that you take care of things afterwards."

"Well," I smiled up at him, "you could personally ensure I'm in a good enough mood tonight that it carries me through any bad vibes tomorrow." I got an automatic smile in return but I could tell I'd lost him. Rohan was already thinking through all the ways tomorrow could go wrong, instead of the ways tonight could go right.

The cab pulled around the corner of the restaurant, slowing to a stop before us. Rohan, preoccupied, climbed in. Way to kill sexytime, you dumbass demon.

21

I grew angrier and angrier all the way back because it was clear from the way Rohan handled me with kid gloves that sex was off the table. At this point, I would have taken any handling, kid glove or otherwise. He spent the ride back talking me through various scenarios for tomorrow, spoken in a low voice so the driver wouldn't hear. My only break was when he had the driver stop at a store to get us each a couple of sports drinks, which I downed in no time.

I tried to concentrate on what he was saying but even being attacked by a demon mutant hadn't killed the heady mixture of adrenaline and desire I'd felt in the restaurant. If anything, I needed that release more than ever. I crossed my arms over my boobs, trying to get some relief from their heavy sensitivity without it seeming too obvious what I was up to.

This time when I entered the hotel lobby, I had my shoes. That's about all I could say for my appearance because I looked like an elephant had jizzed on me. Sticky silver slime cobwebbed between my fingers. It had hardened on my face and neck, matting my hair into unsightly white girl dreads.

Unable to help myself, I glanced at the front desk to see who was on duty this evening. Incredibly, it was a different employee, a stylish brunette. Given how she looked at me, like she wished she could snap my photo and pin it to a "do not allow" board, I'm guessing the staff talked. Let the haters hate. I had one objective here: get myself off. Inappropriate? Perhaps. Necessary? Understatement of the year.

Rohan finally finished talking.

"Great. See you tomorrow, boss man."

He narrowed his eyes at me but I didn't care. If he wasn't gonna be a help then he didn't get to be a hindrance. I was outta–

"Hi, Ro. Lolita." Lily bounded over to us.

Sunnydale wasn't the Hellmouth. This lobby was.

Lily's eyes widened at my appearance, one hand smoothing the skirt of her cute blue dress. I looked down at my own dress in dismay. It had been cute once. My hair had been flirty.

"Drunk guy. Science experiment." I widened my hands making an explosion sound.

"Oh. Okay." Lily still looked confused, but screw it. That was as good a lie as I had in me.

I clenched my teeth against a hot spurt of anger at all pretty people. That included Rohan. His shirt had taken the worst of it and since he wore his jacket over top again, he looked just dandy. The bastard. Fuck, I wanted him badly. A rage fuck would have been awesome but I'd settle for a rage wank.

Cuntessa throbbed harder, demanding I do something about her stymied predicament. I mentally fired back that I couldn't exactly rub one out standing here, could I? I had to get through the small talk first.

"Good conferencing today?" I tried to sound like I genuinely cared. Lily was nice and despite the shitty demon interruptus, or her lofty status in Rohan's eyes, she didn't deserve me being bitchy to her.

"It was." Her hands did half the talking for her. "Do you know how many physicists these days are studying cloud movements and wind? It's so cool. Oh, and this morning I got invited to a rocket launch when I get back to the States as part of an experiment they want my expertise on."

That was pretty awesome so I stuck around to ask more about it.

"I was going to get a drink." Lily pointed over to the bar. "Want to join me?" She included both of us in the conversation.

"Love to," I said. I'd drink with Satan himself at this point.

Rohan didn't answer her. He watched us converse with an odd expression on his face. Like this was the first time he'd really looked at us side by side and the differences were staggering.

The world blurred. I tossed off, "Give me half an hour to change," then barreled across the lobby, blinking rapidly. Stuck waiting for the elevator behind a porter and a cart of stacked luggage, and painfully aware of Lily and Rohan standing behind me, I lost my battle with my cool facade. I ran into the washroom next to the restaurant, slamming and locking a cubicle door.

I used a steady stream of toilet paper on my stupid leaking eyes, familiar with this emotional overload. Same thing used to happen to me before a show, when I'd been pushing myself too hard. Breathing was key. I closed my eyes, embracing the emotions, drawing them inside myself to fuel tonight's performance. A good night's sleep and one healthy meal and I'd be dandy.

Three flushes of toilet paper later, I ran dry. Shoulders slumped like Quasimodo, I contemplated opening the lock, not yet ready to walk past Rohan. That moment before I went on stage was an intensely vulnerable one. The last flash of me in my most honest state before I pasted a smile on my face, stepped through the curtains, and dazzled.

Giving myself my "I am fabulous" rallying cry wasn't going to provide the jolt I needed to get out there. Yanking down my underwear, I plunged my fingers inside me. My head tipped back at the sweet ecstasy.

I rubbed Cuntessa, arching my hips for better access.

Someone knocked on the door of the stall.

"Occupied," I said, trying not to moan. God, yes, it was happening. I rubbed faster, harder. My muscles tightened, my body trembled.

Again with the knocking. "Someone in here!" I bit my lip, closing my eyes and trying to keep out all distractions as I reached for the shiny finish.

The woman on the other side of the door rapped again.

"Find a different fucking stall," I snarled. With that, I came hard, muffling my groan with the flush of the toilet. I sat there a second, letting my racing pulse subside enough to be able to pull my underwear up and straighten my dress.

My entire body was infused with a calm, centered clarity. *Now* I was ready to step into my role once more. I flung open the door, my sharp retort dying on my lips at the sight of the elderly man staring at me. Two other guys twisted around from their respective urinals to glance at me.

Whoops.

"Ladies was full." I marched over to the sink, refusing to rush the washing and drying of my hands. The glare the desk clerk shot me as I strode through the lobby to the elevator barely rated. I was re-upped and ready to shine. Except I needed a quick make-up and wardrobe fix.

Once showered and changed, I got to the bar to find Lily sitting alone, checking her phone. I sat down across from her, a red glass lamp casting a mellow glow over us. "Where's Rohan?"

Her perfume, light and sweet, teased my senses, making me feel like I was in a meadow on a bright sunny day. "He got a call from the director about something."

Me and Lily alone? Oh yeah, shots were in order big time. I ordered vodka for me and Lily asked for a rum and coke. Not even diet because she didn't need to worry about the calories.

Meow, Nava.

"How do you know Ro?" she asked.

We'd never prepared an answer to that question since most people weren't interested in how a groupie came into a rock star's life. Lily was not most people.

"We met at an industry thing." You know, amazing chick kills first demon, annoying dude accosts her and presents self as leader forcing chick to show remarkable restraint in not clocking him. That kind of industry thing. "What about you?"

Was I going to satisfy my curiosity about her? You bet.

"We went to school together. I've known him since first grade."

Thank God, the drinks were here. "Was he a dark-haired charmer on the playground?"

Lily rolled her eyes. "He was a total brat. Such a tyrant if he didn't get his way."

"Yet he seems so easygoing, now," I remarked.

Lily clinked her glass to mine with a wry smile.

Over the next little while, I learned all kinds of things about Rohan Mitra. His favorite color was green and he preferred savory to sweet. He'd also been a huge D&D nerd. Probably had a constant hard-on getting to actually fight demons in clandestine situations. I finished another drink, the burn helping with Lily's walk down memory lane.

Lily swirled her straw around in her second rum and coke. "His middle name is Liam."

Rohan Liam Mitra. It had a nice ring to it. "Where did Liam come from?"

"His dad's best friend," she replied, crunching a piece of ice between her even white teeth. "Ro's godfather." I couldn't help wonder with Lily knowing all about his past, and me knowing the secret of him being Rasha, which one of us truly knew him? Or with all his inner demons, if anyone really did?

I was intrigued to learn that she hadn't been a big Fugue State Five fan either.

"Too emo for my tastes," she admitted. "Though he'd been writing his depressing poetry even when he was young and runty. He had a growth spurt at fourteen and suddenly he was 'mysterious.'" Her eyes gleamed. "Girls found him quite attractive after that."

"'Quite attractive' like panties in his locker?"

She giggled. "There were rumors."

Girls throwing themselves at him, what a surprise. That struck a little too close to home. This entire conversation, learning the mysteries of Rohan was a bit too fangirl, a bit *too* groupie for comfort. I brushed my shredded napkin into a pile.

Besides, one could only talk about a guy for so long. The conversation veered onto other topics. We discovered that we could both sing the *Grease* soundtrack by heart. I'd pegged her for good girl Sandy, but her favorite song on it surprisingly, was not "Hopelessly Devoted to You" but "Beauty School Dropout." Mine unsurprisingly was "There Are Worse Things I Could Do."

We bonded over sucking at our respective religions with Lily being a Hindu who never met a hamburger she didn't like, and me, the Jew, believing bacon was a food group.

Lily even explained a bit about geophysics and her specific research with lightning. She was sweet, smart, and as much a person of the light as that little girl I'd seen in the street this morning. I liked her.

She yawned, her hand flying up to her mouth. "Sorry. I should go. Another early morning at the conference tomorrow."

I signaled for the bill. "Yeah, I'm going to set."

"You act?"

Constantly. "Me? Ha, no. I'm watching Samson's chase sequence."

Her eyes bugged out of her head. "Samson King?!" She looked at me, envy written all over her face. "I'm hoping to meet him at the wrap party."

Of course she was going. "If Rohan can't wrangle you an intro, what good is he?"

"Yeah, but it's not the same as hanging out with him. You are the luckiest girl alive."

Oh, those deceptive appearances.

Even though my contact with Samson today would be limited since he'd be filming, I was still uneasy. I didn't know if Samson expected me as Lolita, client of interest, or Rasha, public enemy number one.

While I brushed my teeth, I checked the hotel phone hoping for a message from Dr. Gelman. I even checked my cell though she wouldn't risk calling it. I'd left her a message last night about turning the demon into a magnet and asking if she had any insights. She understood magic. Maybe she could explain why I'd suddenly acquired a new dimension to my power, one that none of the Rasha had told me to expect. I'd written everything down that I could remember about the fight to deconstruct it with her.

Even though I'd been pretty insistent about speaking with her, she hadn't called back. She was probably at the physics conference. A mounting feeling of dread hooked in between my shoulder blades. She'd been so skittish when we met at Café Louvre. I kneaded feeling into my fingertips, pulled on an extra pair of socks. Wormed into a sweater.

Preoccupied with concerns over her safety, I barely registered Rohan and Lily breakfasting together in the hotel restaurant.

I used the phone in the lobby to try her but once more it went straight to voice mail, so I left another message asking her to contact me via the reception desk here. I even looked up the conference, calling the contact number on the website and asking if there was any way to page her. There wasn't, but the person I spoke with informed me that

Dr. Gelman was participating on a panel this morning. I thanked the woman for her help, somewhat relieved.

Pushing any lingering concerns aside, I took the time in the taxi to prep for this next Samson encounter. I had to secure a meeting with him tomorrow at the ritual location Drio had texted, so that he and Rohan could finally, irrefutably determine if Samson was a demon.

The taxi pulled up to a hive of activity, the driver conferring with some woman in a yellow safety vest directing traffic. All manner of tents and trailers were set up in a giant gravel field. Beyond it was a stretch of winding highway that had been blocked off.

There was a moment of confusion until the helpful Assistant Director was informed that I'd arrived. She came over to take charge of me, a welcoming smile on her face, a walkie talkie stuck in her waist band, and a massive steaming cup of coffee in the hand not holding a clipboard. A petite blonde force to be reckoned with, she introduced herself as Anya.

About a half dozen people stopped Anya to inquire about one thing or another as she led me over to a large white tent. "Will I be watching from here?" I asked.

"No. You're going to be outside for a while. I thought you might appreciate grabbing something from craft services first."

"I get to eat while I'm here?"

She leaned in with a conspiratorial smile. "To your heart's content."

If I'd known that, I'd have visited Samson sooner. I filled one Styrofoam cup up with hot, sweet, milky caffeine and another up with M&M's from the array of snacks laid out.

"Are you tap dancing?" she asked.

I froze, candy halfway to my mouth and guiltily looked down at my feet. I'd been doing paddle rolls. "Yeah."

"I tapped. How many years?"

"Fifteen. You?"

"Eleven." We chatted dance for a few minutes. "Forgive me asking," she said, "but you don't seem like Samson's regular type of guest."

I refilled my candy cup. "Strange times."

Her walkie talkie squawked to life. "Go for channel six," she said. A stream of instructions in Czech came at her. "Let me take you to video village."

We wove past scurrying crew members, including two paint-splattered women working on a flat. Anya assured me that I'd picked the right day to watch them film. "Going out on a high note with the car chase."

"Samson's finished after today?"

"Shooting, yeah. A couple tiny commitments for the production left. Well, until the film comes out and the press junket begins."

Video village turned out to be a grouping of directors' chairs around several monitors with all kinds of cables snaking out from them. Men and woman stood around the screens discussing everything from camera angles to make-up needs. I recognized Forrest Chang, the director, right away. Not because he was one of the few Asian people, but because he exuded an air of quiet authority, giving due consideration to each question posed to him.

Anya led me to the chair with Samson's name on it. "Front row seat," she said. I thanked her, sorry to see her go. From the curious looks shot my way, I could only imagine how people assumed I'd managed to get this guest pass.

Another hour went by. The craft services guy passed out some yummy sandwiches so it wasn't all bad. At long last, Forrest nodded in satisfaction, his slight smile giving him a boyish air as he watched Samson be led out to the classic hot rod he'd be driving. The actor looked good, dressed in black leather, a helmet tucked under one arm. He tilted his face down for the make-up artist to brush powder across his forehead, but only suffered her ministrations for a minute before stepping back.

He raised his head, looking directly into the camera. At me?

I was kinda far away from him, so I wasn't sure he could see me, but I stood up and waved a gloved hand at him. Onscreen, he grinned. It was all too bizarre. I sat back down, cradling my coffee between my hands.

Forrest called action and the magic started.

I was glued to the screens, twitching at every sharp turn of the wheel, every dodge, every crazy maneuver Samson pulled. For someone who wasn't a stuntman, the boy was crazy good.

After the seventh take, Forrest decided he'd gotten what he needed and everyone broke out into applause. Since I didn't want to get in anyone's way as they dismantled the monitors to move them to another spot, I stayed in my chair.

Anya eventually came and got me. "He wants to see you."

I tossed the dregs of my fourth coffee out and followed her.

Samson's trailer was nicer than Leo's apartment. Bigger too. Two stories with leather furniture, granite counters in the kitchen, and a freaking screening area, he even had his own make-up room so he didn't have to share oxygen with lesser cast.

He greeted me clad in a towel, freshly showered. He shook his wet hair, drops of water trailing down his perfect abs. This wasn't the first time a guy had greeted me this way but it was the first time I felt like I was watching a performance. Disconnected and watching the technical steps involved in "sexy dude" trope play out.

His towel is going to slip now.

Sure enough, there it went, an inch further down his hips. Samson caught it at the last second with an unrepentant grin. But there was no heat in his eyes, only cold appraisal, like a deadly snake.

The hair on the back of my neck rose. Did he know what I was? I raised my eyebrows, taking in the line where the towel met skin. Demon or psycho, he didn't fool me. I didn't chalk it up to some higher intelligence on my part or even a Rasha talent for seeing through demon bullshit. We didn't have that. But I'd had Rohan. I knew what hot and raw and need looked like.

Samson didn't want me. This was calculated.

"You don't play fair," I pouted, pretending to buy it.

"What did you think of the chase?" he asked.

"You were phenomenal." Truth.

"Yeah, I was." He looked at me with such a cocky grin that I was almost tempted to shoot him down. "I'm going to get dressed," he said. "Make yourself comfortable."

By the time I'd taken off my jacket, gloves, and sweater, he'd already returned. He'd only thrown on a pair of jeans, so not a huge wardrobe change. I glanced down at his feet. Bare. Big surprise.

"You look different," he commented.

"It's the fifty-seven percent more clothing. I get cold easily and didn't want to freeze." I sat down, the leather butter soft.

Samson took a seat next to me, placing his hand on my arm. I looked pointedly between his fingers and his eyes. "You know how many women would kill to be in your position? Show a little gratitude." He unbuckled his belt.

That was the moment I decided that the gogota had been some random attack. King didn't know I was Rasha. This was about one thing and one thing only. Now, what would it take for Samson to think he'd achieved full payback for Evelyn? A revenge fuck? My disappearance? Neither was going to happen.

"I'm not interested in a quick screw." I sent a withering glance at his pants, as he popped the top button of his jeans. "You're not either, so let's skip the bullshit."

Samson sat back, his gaze shrewd. "Negotiations, huh?" I hadn't meant my words that way but if it got him to back off, I'd take it. "What's to stop me from a hostile takeover?"

I smiled sweetly. "I'll rip your balls off."

He smirked but not quickly enough to hide his surprise.

I pressed on in a husky voice. "That said, I'm open to the possibility of a merger."

"What's in it for me?"

I leaned in close, resting my hand on his upper thigh. "You have that blond, good-looking charm going for you, but Rohan is something else altogether. Bad. Dangerous." His nostrils flared. "You wouldn't have offered him a record deal if you weren't exactly aware of how bright he burns."

"I stand to make a lot of money off him," he replied. "I don't need to stoop to his left-overs."

I blinked away the tears that instantly flooded my eyes fast enough that I'm pretty sure he didn't see them. "You think I'm a left-over? Give Rohan six months. Babe, you'll be a vague memory. Everyone knows rock stars trump actors. Especially actors out of the spotlight."

The air around us charged with an undercurrent of violence. I braced myself for some show of demonic power. When was the last time anyone had openly mocked him? The danger of claiming to be the center of the universe was being a victim of your own PR.

Samson stood up, grabbing himself a water from the bar fridge. "Mitra doesn't give a damn about you."

"Don't believe everything that you see. The other morning? He wanted you to see me leaving his bed. And at the cigar bar, he allowed you to be with me and everyone saw it except you. He likes his power games." I leaned back against the leather, my arms splayed along the top. "People forget the pecking order. They need reminding."

I thought I was being so clever. A guy who'd believed he'd been cuckolded was capable of some pretty ugly behavior. A potential demon who got off on misery on a good day? Let's just say, I hadn't thought this through.

"We can't have that."

I barely processed the menace in Samson's voice before a bolt of despair ripped through me. It left me cold and bereft, in ravenous pain, desperate to please him.

"I'm sorry." I jumped to my feet, my voice reedy and pleading. I couldn't seem to get enough air into my lungs and my muscles felt locked into place.

"Better." He prowled toward me. "You may be right about Mitra. He was drunk that night and from what I saw the other times? Yeah, I think you have some value to him. Some value to me."

He slid his arms around my waist. "Give me something."

His words warmed me into submission. I hadn't messed up. Whatever he wanted, I'd give. I ran my hands around to the small of his back. "Anything."

Samson's fingers bit into my hips. "Make him hurt."

I didn't even need to think about how. Rising onto tiptoe, I kissed Samson.

My fingers tangled in his hair. Nipping, licking, tongues tangling, moans that vibrated through me.

Say what you will about my issues, they brought me to my senses, blowing away Samson's hold on me. I pushed against his chest.

Samson let me go, staring in bafflement.

Using his demonic compulsion on me, because I had no doubts about his status anymore, wasn't what had me racing for the door, lightheaded. It wasn't even thinking a kiss was the one thing that could hurt Rohan. It was the fact that I'd broken my kiss embargo with someone who *wasn't* Rohan and wanted to cry over the loss.

I fumbled for the door handle needing air. Needing to collect myself because, just no. I ran out, my legs giving out on me about ten feet outside the door.

Anya caught up to me. "Are you all right?" She shot a concerned glance at Samson's trailer.

Not in any reality. "Can you get me a taxi?"

"I'll get you a driver. Come." I followed her on shaky legs over to a bearded Teamster who introduced himself as Jan and offered to drive me back to the Praha WS.

I zipped up my coat with clumsy trembling fingers, not able to get away from there fast enough. Only once I was halfway back to the hotel did I realize I'd failed to get the meet-up for tomorrow.

22

D rio answered my frantic knock on Rohan's door.
      "I messed up."

He pulled me inside. Rohan wasn't there.

Drio didn't say a word, just let me sit down and waited. The story tumbled out of me. "I knew intellectually what Samson was capable of. But I hadn't truly understood. He made me feel things."

My hand shook on the shot of bourbon Drio had given me. Between the bitter ache of my failure, the fading rush of adrenaline, and my brain trying to lockdown replays of my epiphany, it was a miracle my motor skills worked at all. "I had to get out of there and I didn't get the meeting for tomorrow."

"It's a setback. It's not the end of the world."

"I should have handled the situation better. I know I didn't have the ritual blade to kill him and I couldn't use my magic and tip our hand, but I should have–"

"Screw that." Drio was furious. Weirdly, not at me, but on my behalf. "We fight evil. That means we do whatever necessary to stay alive and fight another day. A plan is not worth your life. Not worth any part of your body or well-being." His eyes narrowed at the way the glass shook as I held it in my lap. "You ever feel threatened like that? Go off-book and flambé his dick."

I was starting to realize that off-book and me might not be the best pairing. I'd gone off-book contacting Gelman, resulting in my possession of a secret ritual that could get me and my brother killed. I'd gone off-book by creating Lolita, resulting in...

I shot back the booze.

"We're so close," I said. "I was scared to blow it. If the Brotherhood learned I was responsible for Samson getting away?" I rubbed my temples.

"We've all screwed up."

"You get more leeway than I do."

"True." Drio took my glass, holding it up in question. I shook my head. "Doing what we do, it's easy to get caught up in the rush and charge forward into danger. It's fun and hell, the Brotherhood encourages it." He rubbed his finger over his glamoured up Rasha ring. "Battling darkness, we become convinced that light shines out our ass." He tapped his head. "It fucks with us because if our big heroic quest is the only thing that matters, failure stops being an option. Any action, any emotion not related to the cause pales in comparison. Then one day we get a harsh reality check and understand what failure really is."

I barely dared to breathe, more curious than ever about his story.

His cell went off, ending sharing time. Drio glanced at the screen, then tapped it a couple of times. "Hey Ro, you're on speakerphone."

"Lolita there?" In addition to voices in the background, I heard snatches of musical instruments.

I pressed my palms into the tops of my thighs with a brief irrational fear that he'd forgotten my real name. "Yeah. I didn't get the meeting. I'm sorry."

There was silence on the other end. "We'll Plan B it."

"Ro, I got you some water." Lily was with him.

"Gotta run. See you both later." Rohan disconnected.

Drio nudged me with his shoulder. "Put this out of your mind. Go pretty up. Ro performing?" He whistled. "A lot of women wanting a piece of that. You'll want to look good."

"He can do what he likes."

"Yeah, sure. You're both free agents." He snorted.

I shot him the finger and went to get my glam on.

The production had rented out a large, stylish art deco lounge with a plush interior for the wrap party. Everyone glittered, ready and willing to have a good time.

I wore a midnight blue sheath dress that hit below my knees and hugged my curves–very pin-up girl. Mesh connected the sweetheart neckline to sequined blue fabric around my throat and arms. I'd paired it with what I termed my dominatrix heels: four-inch red stilettos lacing up the front that I'd found in an exclusive shop near the hotel. My hair was pulled back into a sleek bun at the nape of my neck and I had on very little make-up other than mascara and red lips.

I looked chic and confident, a taste-maker. Exactly how Samson needed to see me tonight. *Just Samson?* I ignored my bitch of an inner voice. The wrap party was my only chance to get the demon to agree to meet me tomorrow and I wasn't about to blow it with self-doubt. Rohan would be busy performing, which probably wouldn't endear him to Samson, and it would be odd for Drio to ask Samson for a meeting, which meant this was all on me.

I wandered through the space, taking in the curved built-in booths and tin ceiling, and making it all the way to where a DJ spun tunes on a low stage without any sign of my team. For a while I was content to hang out by the bar, people watching, letting the music and loud chatter wash over me. Watching Samson's group with particular interest.

Decked out in a flashy suit, the demon held court, standing in the middle of a group wanting to bask in his magnificence. That wasn't sarcasm, most of the people around him wore expressions of slight desperation, smiling too broadly at whatever he said. Jostling each other to stand next to him.

Samson put his drink on the high bar table beside him but when he reached for it again, it was gone. I hadn't seen a waiter take it away. He frowned, studying everyone in his vicinity but they all held wine-glasses as opposed to his highball.

Samson excused himself, headed toward me. Well, toward the bar, his progress hampered by everyone wanting a word. I finally intercepted him, holding out the drink I'd procured. "This is me saying sorry, and hoping you'll let me bribe you into forgiving me for acting like a complete weirdo earlier."

He didn't answer me or take the drink, so I placed it on the bar. "When I kissed you?" I shivered. "You made me feel things and I freaked. Forgive me?" I tilted my head, my eyes wide.

"You're not in the clear yet." He looked down for the drink but once again, it was gone. His lips compressed into thin white lines.

Wanting his attention on me instead of some overly enthusiastic server who was removing glasses with invisible aplomb, I ran a hand over his arm. "I want to make it up to you." I looked at him through my lashes, running my finger along his chest. "I know you're busy to-night and everyone is gonna want a piece of you. Tomorrow. Meet me."

Still nothing.

I caught his hand, playing my last card. "Please. I can give you what you want to make Rohan hurt. *Who* you want. Just don't let one mistake ruin everything for me."

Samson nodded. "Text me the details."

I kept a relieved smile on my face as he moved over to the bar-tender to place an order. Mission accomplished. My gamble that the one thing that would convince him was Lolita's burning desire for the spotlight, combined with her insider knowledge of all things Rohan had paid off. The fact everything I'd said was a lie wouldn't matter so long as he showed.

Speaking of Rohan, I needed to find him. The kiss epiphany had freaked me out to the point of paralysis. In the same way that people who were afraid of spiders were given tarantulas to hold to desensitize them to their fears, I needed to see him and remind myself that there was only one thing I wanted from him.

I spotted Anya standing hand-in-hand with a willowy redhead, so went over to say hello. She introduced me to her girlfriend Fiona, who had a posh British accent.

"Have you seen Rohan?" I asked. "The guy who is supposed to perform tonight."

Anya shook her head but Fiona lit up. "I saw him. Wouldn't kick him out of bed for eating crackers." Anya stared at her girlfriend incredulously but Fiona simply tossed her hair. "Please. He's yummy." She winked at me.

Anya pointed at a door next to the bar. "There's a small green room for performers. He might be in there."

I thanked her and headed over. The door was unlocked and no one seemed to care that I was about to enter, so enter I did. It wasn't much of a green room. There was a lame cut-fruit platter and some bottles of water on the table.

A leather jacket was thrown over a chair. Feeling only moderately stupid, I sniffed it. Iron and musk, the unique pairing of blades and spicy cologne that was Rohan's signature scent. He'd been here, so where was he now? Another door led off this one. I checked it out, but it was a supply closet.

I was about to close the door when I heard Lily say, "Today has been perfect."

I slipped inside, keeping the closet door open a crack. Enough to spy on her and Rohan as they entered the room. I couldn't see him from where I hid, but I heard him teasing her about a cheesy set of souvenir magnets that she'd bought.

Lily, however, was in clear view. Close enough that I could reach out and touch her. She wore a super cool pink cocktail dress that looked as if it had been made from sari material. "I've missed you," she said.

"Me too, Lils."

My hand tightened on the door knob.

"If you're going to be jet-setting around the world now, the least you could do is come rescue me from my dissertation from time to time." She twirled a lock of hair around her finger. Her eyes without her glasses seemed huge as she blinked up at him.

"Take you to Paris for dessert?"

She laughed. I might have laughed too at the farfetched suggestion until she said, "You have no idea how much mileage I still get out of that story."

Excuse me?! He took her to Paris for dessert? From California? I thunked my head against the door but they were too busy chatting to hear me. Too busy engaging in a gentle flirtation that bore no resemblance to any interaction that Rohan and I had ever had.

I think I had late onset claustrophobia. I tugged on my neckline, desperate enough to get away that I considered texting Drio to come for Rohan so I could sneak out. I peered out through the crack.

Lily motioned for him to turn around. "You know the drill."

He chuckled but I'm guessing did as he was told as I still couldn't see him. "My pre-show check. You realize I haven't caught my shirt in my zipper in years."

"I concede that you might know how to dress yourself now."

"I'm much better at undressing."

Lily stilled, caught under the weight of his blazing gold stare. I didn't need to see Rohan to know what made her sway in toward him, her lips softly parting.

My phone hit the tile floor with a loud clatter.

Lily's head jerked up. I flattened myself back into the shadows and closed my eyes.

There was a loud knock on the green room door. "Rohan, I have some people I want you to meet." Bless Forrest.

Rohan hesitated before answering and I held my breath, certain I was about to be discovered. "Sure," he finally said. "Come on, Lils."

I waited an extra few minutes to make sure they were gone. And because my fist was stuffed in my mouth so I wouldn't scream. This was so stupid. *I* was so stupid. Rohan and I weren't dating. Big deal, I'd lose a fuck buddy. A phenomenal fuck buddy but it wasn't the end of the world. There was absolutely no reason for my irrational anger and even more irrational yearning and damn it! I yanked my fingers away from my lips.

Rohan and I had run our course and as the chic, confident woman I was, I wanted to be the one to end things. I smoothed down my dress, picked up my phone, and stepped back out into the green room.

"Spying?"

I screamed, fumbling my phone at hearing Drio's voice by my ear. He'd flash stepped to sneak up on me, and now leaned against the wall, looking cool and polished in a deep blue suit, his blond hair slicked back. Very *Mad Men.*

I shoved at his shoulder. "Give a girl a heart attack, why don't you? Who said I was spying, anyway?"

"You didn't leave with the rest of them. Where were you hiding?" He glanced around and saw the closet. "Ah. How close were you to getting caught?"

I grimaced. "If I'd breathed out at the wrong time, it would have been a threesome."

He threw back his head and laughed. I shoved him again, then headed back into the main lounge. Drio caught me around the waist, steering me in a different direction. "They're at the far end of the bar. Go this way."

"Will you get me a drink?"

"There's another bar." He pushed through the crowd. I lost sight of him for a moment, startling when he appeared at my side, holding a half-drunk highball, a cheeky grin on his face.

"Have you been using your powers to steal Samson's drinks?"

"All night."

"That's so petty of you." I high-fived him but, of course, he left me hanging. Jerk. I was tempted to make a Speedy Gonzales crack because the comparison turned him a particularly rich shade of "Nava Red" but then I'd have to listen to him go off on the difference between short bursts of super speed and the ridiculousness of anyone racing around the planet at the speed of light.

We arrived at the much smaller bar in the back corner. A handwritten menu propped on a stand listed a number of different absinthe drinks.

"I've always wanted to try this stuff." I pushed close for a better view as the bartender made two drinks for the couple ahead of us and set the alcohol on fire.

"Way to waste booze." Drio's American accent was back.

"A good show though." When it was our turn, I ordered an absinthe mojito.

"No. Old school," he told the bartender.

The bartender pulled out a green glass bottle from under the bar and showed it to us. Drio read the label, nodding in approval. The bartender poured a generous slug of pale yellow liquid into two glasses, then he placed a slotted spoon with a sugar cube on top of each.

"This is what got all those artists and writers tripping balls, isn't it?"

Drio rolled his eyes.

The bartender put an old fashioned water fountain with two spigots on the bar. Sliding the glasses under the spigots, he turned them on, water dripping into the absinthe, before dropping dry ice into the fountain at the top. Smoke billowed out, curling around the entire apparatus.

"Unnecessary," Drio said. I, however, appreciated the theatricality. Our glasses filled with water, turning the absinthe cloudy. The bartender handed them over.

I raised mine to Drio. "L'chaim."

"Salut." We clinked. "Sip, don't chug," he ordered.

"Mmm. Licorice."

The music cut out to boos. Forrest stepped onto the stage which I noticed had been outfitted with a drum kit. Also a drummer, a bassist, a guitarist, and a keyboard player. It wasn't actually Fugue State Five, but it was the same set up.

The director held up his hand for silence but people kept talking until someone in the crowd let out an ear-piercing whistle. "Thank you, Anya," he said. "Tonight, I have a treat for you. Rohan Mitra, lead singer of Fugue State Five, is here to perform a few numbers for you, including a bit of the theme song for *Hard Knock Strife*."

The room erupted into cheers and applause.

I edged my way forward to be closer to the stage, making sure to stay on the opposite side from Lily. I just couldn't.

"Without further ado, let's get him out here. Rohan!"

Rohan came out and man-hugged Forrest. Then the director stepped off the stage, leaving Rohan to take the mic.

Hel-*lo*, rock god.

23

Rohan wore a slim-fitting black velvet jacket, cut to precision to show off the broad line of his shoulders. It tapered down the V of his torso over a partially unbuttoned black shirt with Hindi script in metallic silver across the front. A silver chain hung low around his neck, the braided leather and silver circle hanging from it drawing the eye down to his black leather pants. His ass was going to look incredible when he turned.

He'd forgone spikes for his natural curl, messed enough that he'd been raking his fingers through his locks. He looked like he'd rolled out of bed, and given the dreamy stares cast up at him, plenty of people here would be very happy to roll back into it with him. His eyes burned deep amber, his smoky eyeliner causing them to pop with a fiery intensity.

I was really going to miss getting a piece of that. I sagged against the wall, the movement putting Lily directly in my eyeline, my slug of absinthe bracing me as much as my hip. I rubbed the heel of my palm against my chest. Seems I wasn't the only one watching Lily. Poppy stood off to her left, glaring daggers.

Rohan's leather strap and silver bracelet slid up his arm as he adjusted the mic stand, his rings glinting off the stage lights. "For my first song, I thought I'd sing something I wrote here in this incredible city." The crowd loved that.

The music kicked in, my pulse kicked up, and Rohan kicked off "Slumber." He started off slow, working the crowd up to the chorus.

A lot of people sang along. There was something intensely compelling about him. Stage presence on steroids. I'd never seen Fugue State Five live in concert and as good as he must have been then, this was cult-leader charismatic.

His next number "Falling Sideways" was more upbeat. A bass-heavy number.

Rohan slunk across the stage like a panther. Jim Morrison was a toddler compared to the sinuous sexuality that Rohan exuded. He revved the audience into a frenzy with small ass shakes and hip shimmies, like the music lived inside him. The melody poured out of his blood and his heart.

All around me people danced, rapt looks of delight on their faces as they watched him. With one pissed off exception. Samson.

"Told you he was something," Drio said.

Rohan posed, hip popped out, arrogant smirk on his face.

I swooned.

He gripped the mic stand, swinging it in toward him as he stretched out a hand. "Falling sideways, help me land," he sang.

The audience roared in approval, reaching out for him. Lily practically glowed with adoration.

I tipped back my glass only to find that I'd already finished my drink.

Rohan tossed his jacket off to the side, his biceps flexing as he grabbed the mic stand. For the third and final Fugue State Five song, he announced he'd be singing their last number one hit, "Trainwreck of Lost Saturdays." He hit the ground running, jumping up and down, the audience moshing along with him.

I threw myself into dancing with as much abandon as everyone else. I flung my arms up to the ceiling, the absinthe seeping through me like a languid high. Colors were sharper, more intense, from the flash of a woman's silver sequins to the pop of Drio's green eyes. He was one of the few people who didn't dance but even he looked captivated.

Watching Rohan on stage, it was clear that he ruled this room. He told us to jump, we shook the floor when we thudded back to earth. He held the mic out to us and we sang his words back to him with fervor. He was mesmerizing.

Magnetic.

Mine.

My arms dropped to my side. He wasn't though, was he?

The song ended and the cast and crew went nuts. Rohan grinned at us, king of all he surveyed. Then he held up his hands for quiet. Unlike when Forrest had tried the same thing, for Rohan, it went from frenzy to could-hear-a-pin-drop in seconds.

"Thank you. It's been a while and well," he ducked his head, "I was nervous."

I snorted. If the room could have group hugged the boy, they would have. Rohan grabbed a stool that he put in the middle of the stage, moving aside the mic stand. He went over to the guitarist and spoke a few words to him. The guitarist nodded and handed over an acoustic guitar propped on the stage behind him.

Rohan sat down on the stool, adjusting the guitar strap around his neck. He blinked coyly at us. "Do you want to hear the theme song?"

I put my hands over my ears against the deafening roar.

That earned us a Cheshire Cat smile. Foregoing the microphone, he rested his hands on top of his guitar. The lights dimmed, an expectant hush falling over the room. Even the club's staff had stopped working, with nary a tinkle of glass daring to break the moment. I waited for the band to start up but he sang a capella.

His deep baritone rang out pure and clear through the first verse.

Hard fists they strike/ Still not the stone my heart entombed lies beating

Scoring big/ I pay my dreams in blood/ Rush like a knife

Strike a match blaze/ Seize the bright lights/ Give me some illumination

In the end Hell will come calling/ Crown me king of hard knock strife.

Rohan growled the last line, his famous rasp front and center. He stretched out the final word impossibly long, the rest of us collectively holding our breaths.

With the first three songs, he'd given us a show.

With this one, he gave us magic.

The silence when the note finished was absolute; the chord he struck for the start of the chorus was shocking in comparison. The dark majesty of it resonated through the room after the clarity of his voice. I shivered.

Rohan didn't play the next note. The crowd wailed in protest. He shot us a sleek, satisfied smile. "I live to tease," he drawled.

The woman next to me fanned herself.

Rohan stood up. "That's all you get... for now." He winked and walked off the stage.

Samson immediately jumped on it, clapping. "Big hand for Rohan. Now let's party." Points for effort, but the audience demanded their idol back.

"Encore," they chanted, stomping their feet.

A darkness slithered behind Samson's eyes. I doubt anyone else noticed but I was close up and besides, Rasha. I was watching more intently than most. He covered it with a big grin. "Ro, get your ass back out here."

Behind me, Drio chuckled.

Rohan came out, shaking hands with Samson like they were the best of friends. After presenting Rohan with an arm flourish, Samson jumped off the stage and Rohan once more sat down on the stool. He slung the guitar around to his front, then spread his hands wide as he raised an eyebrow, as if saying "you got me, now what do you want me to do?"

"Toccata and Fugue," Samson yelled out.

My breath hitched. It hadn't occurred to me that this song would be played. That I'd have to listen to Rohan sing it to Lily.

Rohan's eyes flicked to mine for the briefest second, the genuine concern in them causing me to step back. "What about–" he said. Any potential suggestion was drowned out by the demon rallying the rest of the crowd into picking up the "Toccata and Fugue" chant.

As one, Rohan and I turned toward Lily. She beamed, nodding at him. Dancing hearts couldn't have conveyed her feelings any clearer. He smiled at her, the kind of smile bestowed on a woman by a man who is powerless to deny her anything.

I'd seen those smiles. In movies.

I flinched, my gaze clashing with Samson's. A mocking smile on his face, he held up a glass in cheers. I looked away.

Rohan strummed the opening chord, his head bent forward in concentration, cocking a hip to better adjust for the weight of the guitar. Looking down at the instrument through half-lowered lashes, his hair falling forward, he had the tiniest smile on his face.

Barely blinking, barely breathing, I let the song flow over me, forcing myself to remember with every word flaying my soul, that these lyrics were not for me and never had been. Forcing myself to watch the bond between Rohan and Lily, my head bouncing from his face back to hers. The entire audience were voyeurs on an incredibly intimate moment between the two but, for me, there was no titillation in the spectacle.

Standing rooted to the spot as Rohan sang of the girl with lightning in her eyes and the boy with demons in his soul to the actual fucking lightning girl, I learned exactly how deep my masochism ran.

At some point Drio took my arm trying to pull me out of there, but I tugged free.

It was the rawest version of the song I'd ever heard. My stomach twisted with the irony that as much as that song had freaked me out when he'd first sung it, now it broke my heart.

Rohan's bow when he finished the song was more subdued this time. He disappeared off the stage. Further demands for another song were ignored. The show was over.

People wandered back to the bars or stayed on the dance floor as the band brought out the funk. I raced toward the green room. If I was going to have any hope of facing myself in the mirror again, this ended now.

I found him leaning against the wall, eyes closed. His head was tipped back, hair sweaty and sticking up in tiny spikes. One leg was bent, his foot planted on the wall. A mostly empty water bottle dangled from his hand.

His eyes snapped open, pinning me in place. The blazing naked hunger in them stole my breath. He peeled himself off the wall. I stepped forward, powerless to resist his gravitational pull. Rohan inhaled, a harsh shaky sound and–

"That was so good," Lily squealed, bounding into the room and breaking the spell. She leapt on him, kissing him squarely on the lips. Rohan tensed for a second, then his arms came around Lily and he kissed her back. Short and sweetly everything.

I shut down. Eviscerated. There were parts of my heart and my brain that I wouldn't–*couldn't*–visit right now. I cauterized them just to make sure.

Other people poured into the room and I slipped away.

Drio caught up with me outside the club. He fell into step beside me, telling me some stupid story about Samson's posse. I didn't know when things had shifted between us for him to become my guardian angel, but I was very happy to have him there distracting me.

Back at the hotel, I went straight to the bar. Drio matched me drink for drink. Eventually I'd consumed enough that he had me laughing. I poked his shoulder. "I like you."

"I'm likeable. You're a hot mess."

I curled an errant strand of hair around my finger. "Yeah, but you're trouble and I bet you love hot messes. We don't come with strings."

He cocked an eyebrow in interest. "No strings?"

I licked a drop of vodka off my lip. "None at all."

Drio's nostrils flared.

I ran a hand over his pecs. These Rasha boys had such nice bodies.

Drio grabbed my hand. We practically sprinted over to the elevator. Inside, he pushed me up against the wall, sucking on my neck. I pulled his shirt out of his pants to get closer to his skin. To feel his heat.

To feel something.

The second the elevator door opened, he flash-stepped me down the hall, slamming me up against my door. Giggling, lightheaded from the jaunt, I nipped at the underside of his jaw. "Speedy."

Drio leaned into me, his erection hard between my thighs. "No, bella," he purred, "it's going to be a very long night."

My knees buckled. I wove my hands into the silky strands of his blond hair as he made his way down my body, his mouth hot and sloppy through the fabric of my dress. My head thunked back against the door and I closed my eyes to better lose myself to the tingling along my skin.

Drio pushed my dress up, his breath ghosting over Cuntessa. She voiced her approval with ripples of hot pleasure. With a wicked glint up at me, he nipped the inside of my thigh.

An electric sizzle caught at the base of my spine, arcing up through me. Holy yes, Batman! I fumbled in my clutch for my keycard, yanking him to his feet. "Inside," I breathed. "Now."

His eyes, fiery emeralds, locked onto mine. Using his powers so absolutely for good, he had me inside on the bed with my dress off my shoulders before I could blink.

"More skin." I wrapped my leg around his waist, tearing at his shirt buttons.

Drio dragged his finger up my side. The sharp smell of his arousal pushed me into overdrive.

I moaned, rocking against him.

"I don't kiss," he murmured in my ear.

"What?"

He raised his head. "I don't kiss."

His words were like a douse of freezing water. Ice seeped through my veins, making everything numb when I should have been on fire.

I pushed Drio off of me.

"Does it matter?" he asked.

I rubbed my hands over my arms, thoroughly unnerved by this of all similarities between us. "I'm sorry. I can't do this."

He wasn't angry. In fact, the look he gave me was heavily laced with compassion. He shrugged. "Sometimes you just want to feel something else, you know?"

I nodded. Yeah, I knew. I pulled my dress back onto my shoulders.

Drio made himself presentable once more. "Will you be all right?"

"Yes." I squeezed his hand. "Thank you."

He was already opening my door. "Yeah, yeah."

I figured that I'd toss and turn all night, but sleep claimed me pretty fast. The next morning, I woke up to a moment of horror for what I'd almost done. That turned into a moment of horror that I felt horrified about *being* horrified when Rohan and I weren't in a relationship. Whatever had not happened with Drio was none of Rohan's business. Just like whether or not Rohan spent the night with Lily was none of mine.

Then I sprinted to the bathroom and vomited.

24

I'd always thought battling demons involved physical fights, but Samson was the second demon I'd faced who'd unleashed emotional wreckage and mind game fuckery on a brutal scale. I almost blinded myself with my mascara wand, lost in the grip of my savage urge to destroy him for loosing that encore on me.

So when Drio and not Rohan called me with the details of the location for the meeting, I needed more than a few steady breaths to calm down. Rohan didn't get to start avoiding me now. Not before I'd had my say and officially ended our penile paradigm.

I armored up in all-black.

The one good thing in my morning was a message waiting at reception for me from Dr. Gelman saying her panel had gone well. Her check-in calmed me down a bit.

Using Rasha connections, Rohan and Drio arranged for us to have use of a cool underground bar. I'd texted Samson the time and address, receiving confirmation that he'd be there.

I paced at the top of the stairs leading down to the bar for a good ten minutes before I felt psyched enough to go meet up with my team, though I was surprised to descend the stone stairs and find other patrons inside. The bartender looked up from drying a glass, studying me with more curiosity than my presence warranted. Then he nodded, raising his hand to show his Rasha ring. Ah. He'd looked a bit too ripped to spend his time slinging booze. Each of the half dozen or so other men here were hunters as well, providing background so Samson didn't get suspicious by walking into a deserted bar.

I took a seat at one of the high tables, taking the chair that put my back to the wall. The bartender brought me over a can of dark beer. "I shouldn't."

"Root beer," he said.

Neither Drio nor Rohan showed themselves. I wished that I had some understanding of what would happen but I guess they couldn't risk Samson walking in and seeing them.

Samson kept me waiting for twenty minutes. Long enough to make me sweat that he wasn't going to show. He skipped hello to go straight for the jugular. "Guess you've been replaced. I hear she's smart, too." A mean sort of smile slid across his face.

I ran the edge of my thumb over the can's tab. "Does that change things?"

Samson shrugged, watching me with a feigned casualness. "You tell me."

"If you were only interested in me for Rohan, then you should have skipped the middle man and fucked him yourself. You'd have enjoyed it. Evelyn sure did."

White spots of rage appeared on his cheeks. "You cunt," he hissed.

A low chanting filled the room. A call to Adramelech.

Samson hopped off his chair, but was blocked by Rohan. The other Rasha, including the bartender, had slipped out. Samson tried to knock Rohan aside, but Rohan wrenched Samson's arm up his back, planting him facedown against the table.

"Going somewhere?" Rohan asked.

Samson's eyes darted to the door, being locked shut by Drio.

The source of the chanting, Drio held a small blade, using it to trace a complicated pattern in the air.

"Hey man, I'm not into Satan shit." Samson laughed as he struggled against Rohan's grasp.

Rohan's eyes met mine, twins of the doubt I felt. Why wasn't Samson's form changing? I was positive that after our encounter in his trailer that I'd correctly pegged him as a demon. Had we gotten his true name wrong? If so, we were screwed. We'd never get another chance to get close enough to do this ritual.

"You know, if you didn't like the terms of the recording contract, you could have just said." Samson was way too blasé.

Rohan slammed the blade of his middle finger through Samson's palm. Samson howled. His face flickered, revealing black charred skin.

I exhaled.

Rohan held the demon down as he struggled.

Closer and closer Drio came, chanting and tracing the pattern. The demon's skin rippled and bubbled. Tendons strained in his neck. An eyeball bulged out. His teeth ground together trying to fight his transformation.

Rohan yanked his blade from Samson's palm. The demon snapped upright, clearly not of his own volition.

"Hear me, Adramelech," Drio said. "Before me now, I use your name, demand your form." Drio slit his own palm with the ritual blade. Blood dripped onto the floor.

Samson's glamour fell away, leaving a humanoid creature covered in ruined, burned flesh. Not unexpected for a sun-demon. But he also had a gorgeous peacock's tail, rising six feet high, and swaying behind him in a vivid swirl of iridescent greens, blues, and golds.

"You think you can take me, Rasha?" the demon sneered. He turned a look of unadulterated loathing on me. "Puppet."

He didn't know I was Rasha. That was a refreshing first. Before I could enlighten him, there was a resounding crash of breaking glass. I looked over at the window, confused. Logan, Samson's flunky, had just burst inside. Glass dotted his skin, blood streaming from a dozen cuts.

Drio grabbed the demon's tail, lifting the blade to plunge into the base of his spine.

Logan flicked his fingers and it felt like all the oxygen was sucked out of the room. Drio's knife clattered to the floor.

I doubled over, gasping, my lungs burning. My head was being squeezed in an invisible vise. Drio coughed, swearing, which snapped my attention up.

Samson and Logan were gone.

I looked over at Drio, who held a handful of peacock feathers, and blinked. There was Drio, but *I* stood next to him. I shook my head. That wasn't right. Neither was the stunned expression on my face as I stared back at me.

I pointed at myself. This wasn't my hand. This was too big and too male to be my hand.

Eyes wide, I looked down. "Oh shit," I said in Rohan's voice.

"Shit," he echoed in mine.

The next hour was surreal. While Drio and Rohan, as me, commanded the other Rasha on hunting down Samson and Logan, I went into the washroom to stare at my new face. Planting myself in front of the dingy mirror, I examined every feature of Rohan's with more thoroughness than I ever had, but I couldn't reconcile my brain with reality. Again and again, I touched a fingertip to his nose, his tongue, his lashes, but no matter how much I willed the face to change back into my own, it didn't.

I trailed his fingers over the silver taps. Solid. Cool. Back up along his arm to the reflection staring out at me, sweat breaking out over his skin at the disorientation of being there but not.

I shifted, aware of a pressing on my bladder. Were these insides still mine? Unbuckling his jeans, I gripped his dick. So freaking weird, feeling his hand and his cock at the same time. I pointed it at the toilet but that felt wrong too, so I ended up sitting down, giving his dick a firm yank to shake it off. I tucked it back in his jeans and washed his hands.

Bad enough walking back into the bar that I had to find my balance, learn how this body moved, I kept having to adjust his balls because the jeans pinched. How did men get anything done?

"Are you wearing butt floss?" Rohan's words said in my voice, stopped me in my tracks, every Rasha in the bar swinging his head my way. The bartender even halted the phone conversation in rapid Czech he was having.

So. Dead. So not answering him.

I marched over and swiped Rohan's bottle of water away. "You don't eat or drink anything until we've switched back." I was not having Rohan wipe my ass.

He glowered at me. Wow, I gave really good glower. I tried to glower back but hadn't perfected the movement with these facial muscles so I'm not sure what the overall effect was.

"Ro," the bartender said, hanging up, "get a move on. The bar needs to open for real and we need to get the window replaced."

Rohan stalked over to my jacket, one hand held across my chest.

"This is no time for your cheap thrills," I informed him.

"They bounce. You need a better bra."

"They bounce because they're real. That's what women's boobs do." I adjusted his stupid balls again shaking out his leg in my attempt to make everything lay properly.

"You're going to chafe them," Rohan said. "Men's genitals are very sensitive. Unlike some who require a battering ram."

Baring his teeth at him, I tugged on his cock. He winced, but I did too at the pain that spiked through me. Spectacular backfire.

A sharp whistle cut through our hostility. Drio muscled between us like a ref at a boxing match. "You two need to go back to the hotel and stay there."

Rohan tried to argue the point, but I agreed with Drio. I didn't want any unnecessary further harm to my meatsack and I didn't trust

Rohan to take proper care of it. Rohan's-*my*-eyes spat electricity. A spark landed on the sweater I'd worn this morning.

I slapped at it before it could do any actual damage but in my anxiety, I triggered one of his finger blades. It slit the fabric, drawing a fine line of blood along my actual body's skin.

Rohan hissed in pain and jerked his arm away. My arm. The arm of the body he was in. Both of us limited to feeling sensations in the form that we were each trapped in.

We glared daggers at each other.

"You're both too much of a disaster to be out and about. I'll take charge of finding the demons so we can switch you back." Drio shoved us toward the door.

The bartender, Mirek, drove us back to the hotel. I took the front seat, forcing Rohan to crawl into the back. Petty pleasure since it was a two-door Citroen.

I followed Rohan back to his suite. "You got any food?"

"If you eat, I eat." Jeez, he made me sound pissy.

"Forget it." I sat down on the couch, pulling his long legs in to his chest and wrapping his arms around them, his chin propped on top.

Rohan leaned back against his chair with my legs extended carelessly, and my arms crossed over my chest. Dude managed to take up a lot of room with my slender self.

I ran his hands over his arms, feeling his biceps tense and the light sprinkling of hair. I'd felt them with my hand many times, but it was weird and fascinating to feel them with his.

Rohan stood up.

"Where are you going?"

"To your room." He shook my head. "Watching myself is wrong. No masturbating," he ordered, one hand on the doorknob.

"Huh?"

He pointed at his crotch. "I know you, Nava. You'll be all over that the second this door closes." It hadn't occurred to me to do that, but now I was curious. "I'm serious," he snarled in my voice. "I'll know." He smiled innocently. "Unlike you."

"Fine," I spat.

He slammed the door behind him.

Great. Given Rohan's mood, who knew what condition I'd get myself back in? He'd probably cut off all my hair or something just to spite me. I hadn't had a chance to have our talk, either. I couldn't call anyone, couldn't do anything. I paced the room like a caged animal, catching sight of him in the oval mirror mounted on one wall.

I was invisible. Sure, I existed but where was the proof? Where had been the proof of me on this entire trip? I'd been playing a role and now it had swallowed me. Nava was gone. I glanced in the mirror. Literally. His chest tightened. I waved his arms over his head, but that did nothing against my escalating sense of panic. Being outside my body was seriously screwing me up.

There was a knock at the door. I ran to open it, praying it was Drio with good news.

It was Lily.

"Are you all right? You look pale," she said.

I stared at her unable to find my voice. Which wasn't mine at all.

"Ro?"

I cleared Rohan's throat, wanting to tell her this wasn't a good time, come back later but Lily took the sound for permission to enter. I shut the door, wishing I could bash Rohan's brains against the wood instead of enduring this social call.

Lily sat down. She picked at a cuticle, her eyes staring off to the side, her words rushed. "I know that our first attempt at dating didn't work. But being with you again? It's so easy."

I gripped the top of the sofa. Lily was here to have the "let's get back together" talk. I didn't hear much of what she said after that. Her words blurred over me like Charlie Brown wah wah wahs.

At some point I found that I'd sat down. That I was nodding along.

"When we kissed?" Her eyes found mine, bright with hope. "That spark was there. It's always been there with us."

"It was pretty brief," I said. Lily was sweet, but how naive was she if a five-second kiss was proof of romance?

She smoothed out her skirt. "Don't be coy. You know I mean the other one."

I squinted at her, forcing a smile. Other kiss. Right. I crossed Rohan's arms. "Sure." Uncrossed them. Crossed his legs. Stretched them out. Stood up and beelined for the suite's bar.

I poured a glass of water.

"You can't be surprised by this."

No, surprised wasn't the word. Furious, that was more appropriate. At the universe for putting me in this position. At Rohan for well, so much.

I almost dropped the glass because the sight of those hands that weren't my own unnerved me. I gripped the counter, head bowed, needing some sense of myself instead of this Shakespearean mistaken identity that was anything but comedic.

"Say something," she said.

I had no claim on Rohan. Sleeping with him for a few weeks didn't give me any rights, even if I'd wanted them. I was the last person to stand in the way of his happiness. Of him rekindling his first love for their happily-ever-after.

"It's not you. Long day." I sat down again and smiled at her. "Talk to me."

As she poured out her heart, all I kept thinking was how easy it would be for me to sabotage this. Destroy any hopes she had and drive her away. Do it right and she'd never even bring it up with Rohan. She'd be too embarrassed. I wouldn't get caught.

I couldn't do it.

I covered her hand with Rohan's. "I want to talk about this, Lils. Because it's important, but I have somewhere I have to be."

She slipped free. "I get it."

Wishing I was undergoing hot pokers up my ass rather than this, I gently lifted her chin up, forcing her to meet my eyes. Rohan's eyes. Damn it! "No. You don't. Promise me you'll find me tomorrow." I hoped that would give Rohan and me enough time to switch back so he could be the one to talk to her.

I squeezed her hand. "Please."

Her smile was bright enough to light up the room. "I promise." Talk about a mitzvah with no expectation of reciprocity. She left soon after.

I lay on the sofa, staring blankly out the window at the darkening sky. Willing my mind to remain empty. At long last there was another rap on the door.

"Open up." It was Drio.

"You got them?" I spoke in little more than a whisper.

"Logan. Not Samson. Ro is waiting for us."

I nodded, letting myself be led. As long as I kept staring out into the middle distance, I'd be fine. I rested against the car window, feeling the cold glass under Rohan's cheek and keeping my stare into the darkness level. I had to hold on to that emptiness. Let the enormity of outside fill me up, leaving no room for anything else. Force my tangled emotions into the tiniest atom instead of the wall of barbed wire they wanted to be.

Drio left the city, driving for a while until he turned onto a narrow dirt road. At the long, winding end stood a decrepit stone farmhouse. The car bumped over the ground as he drove around back, the headlights illuminating Rohan-as-me, arms crossed, standing at the back door which hung half off its hinges.

"Took you long enough," Rohan said in my voice as we got out.

I rubbed his eyes with his fists. If I had to live like this for much longer, I was going to go insane. "He's in the house?" I asked.

"Under it. Imprisoned," Rohan said. "Ready?" he asked out to the darkness.

"Ready," came Mirek's low voice. I peered into the gloom and made out a couple of figures. I assumed there were other Rasha out there as well, guarding the place in case Samson showed up.

Drio went in first, slipping through the door. Rohan insisted I go next, leaving him to bring up the rear. I needed a minute to adjust to the gloom, but there were enough cracks in the walls to provide a dim light. I wrinkled Rohan's nose against the must and dust tickling it. The house smelled old and unused. It had also been gutted. Empty spaces, wires with no appliances, and partial cupboards made up the kitchen.

Drio opened a door at one end of the room, flipping on a tiny flashlight. "Stick close."

We went down the stairs, feeling our way. At least the basement floor was hard, packed dirt with nothing to trip over.

Drio shifted sideways to fit through a skinny hole in the wall. Going through after him in Rohan's body was a tight squeeze. I wrenched on his shoulders to get them through. "Careful," Rohan said.

I grit his teeth and pulled free. For the second time on this trip, I found myself in a stone tunnel. No monsters showed themselves as we hugged right wall. It wasn't a hard slog, just a boring one. I sang "I Will Survive" on repeat loudly in my head so I couldn't dwell on anything. Eventually, a soft glow spilled from up ahead.

We followed it into a large opening, the walls and floors made up of rough salt crystals, the smell sharp enough to clear my sinuses. The ceiling was something else entirely. All around me lights twinkled in soft clusters. An incredible phosphorescence.

"Cool, huh?" Logan sat in a busted lawn chair, a silhouette, his head tipped up.

Drio ran the flashlight over him. Logan wasn't even in demon form, though he didn't look too great. His face was puffy and bruised. His nose had been broken and dried blood crusted his nostrils. A half dozen beer bottles littered the ground around him.

Logan pulled a fresh brew out of a torn box. "Want one?" He cracked it open without waiting for our answer, chugging it back and then tossing it on the ground with a soft clunk, accompanied by a belch. "Cheap shit. Couldn't pony up for the good stuff, bro?" he asked Drio. Then he eyed me up and down. Me. Not my body. "Bet you like the good stuff, Lolita," he leered. "Heard you were pretty willing to play musical cock for a sweeter gig."

I had the blades of Rohan's left hand extended in an instant, but Drio punched Logan on the side of his head before I could get close.

The demon flickered.

"Why'd you have to wreck it?" He asked in a whiny voice. Not Logan's. T-Roy's. He sat there in the same seat, the same position that Logan had been in a second before, his leg jittering.

"Shut it," Logan snarled, appearing once more as T-Roy disappeared.

What. The. Unholy. Fuck.

"A gemini." Rohan didn't sound scared. Just mildly irritated.

"Astrological signs are demon types?" I really didn't want to meet a cancer.

Logan placed his foot over a bottle. I tensed but all he did was roll it back and forth under his dirty sneaker. "Having a twin sucks balls." Had to disagree with you there, bro.

"Switch them back, Logan." Drio spoke in his normal voice.

Logan squinted over at Drio. "What's up with the weird accent?" He got himself a fresh drink, waving it drunkenly at Drio. "I'm already dying. Not a lot of incentive to do as I'm told."

I snuck closer to Rohan, picking my way over jagged salt clusters. "Dying?"

"His duality has collapsed."

"All his energy was going into maintaining his two forms," Drio explained to me. That explained the boys' lack of bad behavior.

"Switching you two accelerated the process," Logan said. "No choice though. Tied to the fucker's well-being. Soon as I felt Samson take his true form, I had to rush to his rescue." He drowned his bitterness with another drink.

Rohan walked over to Logan, kicking his legs off the beer bottle. "King's dumped you, hasn't he?"

"Asshole. Said he could save me."

"Maybe he can." That was T-Roy, back for a desperate second.

A beer bottle whizzed past my head, shattering on a fat bunch of crystals behind me. "It's your fault," Logan raged. "Weak. Pathetic." He punched himself in the head. This took twin dysfunction to a whole new level.

Drio rolled his eyes. "Ro." Nobody moved. "Rohan body," he said pointedly. "Encourage Logan to behave."

Rohan poked me in the back to get me moving. I crossed over to Drio who tapped a spot on the back of his own neck.

I snicked out a blade, pressing the tip into the same spot on Logan. "Where's Samson?"

"Like I'd tell you."

"Your loyalty is touching." I dug the blade in hard enough to draw blood. "Misplaced but touching."

Logan made a sound that almost sounded like a laugh. "Fuck loyalty. I don't want that psycho coming after me in whatever afterlife I'm doomed to." He pressed his neck back against the blade. The tip slid in.

I smacked him on top of his head. "What is wrong with you? Why aren't you fighting?"

Logan took another sip.

"Suicidal," Drio said. "Chemical side effect of his collapse. Change them," he ordered again.

Logan ignored him and kept drinking.

Rohan fired a blast of electricity into Logan's crotch. The demon fell out of the chair, doubled over, howling in pain. We waited for his cries to die down.

"A girl Rasha? Fucking hell, bitch. You're crazy." In his pain, he seemed to have forgotten he was really speaking to Rohan.

Rohan rolled him over with my foot, a ball of electricity crackling off of my fingertips. "You have no idea." Damn, I was impressive. Also, was Rohan's agreement some not-so-veiled commentary on the real me?

Logan muttered something under his breath.

"What was that?" Rohan asked sweetly in my voice.

"Promise me you'll make Samson hurt and I'll change you."

Rohan agreed to Logan's request.

A sucking pull stretched out the skin I was currently in. Any second now Rohan's eyeballs were going to pop like bubble wrap, but as suddenly as the pulling sensation came on, it stopped.

I held out a hand. Mine. It trembled and I pressed it down against my leg.

I met Rohan's eyes, needing the assurance of looking into steely gold, not sparkling blue-gray. He looked back at me with, not intimacy exactly. More a melding. A time-stopping moment with no sense of where he started and I stopped. We shared one heart, breathed one breath.

It was staggeringly disorienting, but not in the same way I'd felt all day.

Drio finished Logan off. It was pretty sweet how the gemini sputtered in alternating flashes between himself and T-Roy before he disappeared into oblivion.

We trudged back up to the surface in silence. Drio and Rohan had a brief conversation with Mirek then we left. I willingly sat in the back seat for the ride back.

"Can you deal?" Rohan asked Drio as we got out of the car in front of the hotel.

He nodded. "No problem."

"Anything pressing, you call."

I wandered off, totally spent and beyond ready for this night to end. Rohan followed me into the elevator. When I went to hit three, he blocked me, hitting five instead. The barely leashed savagery on his face dared me to protest.

I almost did. Because of Lily. But she was going to get Rohan for the rest of their lives. I was weak enough to want him for one more night. I nodded.

Alea iacta est.

25

Rohan kicked the door to his suite shut, but didn't touch me. Moonlight slashed his features through the opened drapes. "You left." I startled at the thickness in his voice.

I didn't need to ask him when he meant. After his show. "I didn't think I was needed."

"You thought wrong."

Today's events had left me emotionally strung out and unable to understand his cryptic statement. I thought wrong because he needed me? Or because he'd needed someone to take the edge off the adrenaline coursing through him and I was the best option? Since he didn't know how Lily felt at that point, since they hadn't yet kissed again.

"I'm here now." A bead of sweat trickled down my spine.

Rohan came toward me. His eyes glittered hotly enough to be made out even through the press of darkness. "Wanna see my view?"

A lick of heat unfurled in my gut. I managed a nod.

Rohan slid the glass door to his balcony open and stepped outside. He led me past the table and two chairs that took up most of the space to the solid front panel where he wrapped my hands around the metal railing on top. The bar pressed into my navel.

"Keep your hands on the railing." His voice was a rough purr against my neck. "No matter what."

Not a problem since I suspected I'd need the support.

"Beautiful, isn't it?" His voice ghosted over my ear. The city lay before us like a glittering jewel.

"Yes." I could have demanded he speed things up. I often did, but tonight was about savoring and prolonging. Dawn would come soon enough.

We stood like that, an almost magnetic force vibrating between our bodies. I closed my eyes, not giving a damn about the view. I wanted my other senses to kick in to cocoon his touch around me, fill my veins with his scent.

Rohan pressed into every inch of me without a single point of contact. I was hyper-alert, attuned to the slightest nuance in his breathing over the distant wash of traffic and how the smallest shift in his position behind me sent a tiny current of air along my shoulder blades. He slid his arms around me and it was almost overwhelming. Resting his head on my shoulder, he popped the button on my jeans, tugging them down.

He traced the curve of my ass. "I may have been hasty in dissing this thong."

"Told you." I gripped the railing tighter, its metal a weighty curve in my palm. A breeze whispered against the front of my shirt, teasing my nipples into even stiffer peaks.

"But it has to go." He cut it free, slipping it off from behind, running the fabric over my clit. Glorious friction against my growing wetness.

I gasped. A sugary syrup of desire slid through my bones.

He removed his hands and I heard his belt unbuckling. Heard a rustle of foil.

"Widen your legs."

My chest rose and fell in ragged breaths. Strung tight with anticipation, I did as I was told. With a single thrust, Rohan slid inside me. My head fell forward.

"Enjoy the view, Nava." He nipped my shoulder. "I am." His hands flattened on the railing on either side of me, trapping me as much as the gentle rhythm of his hips.

My breasts were heavy. Cuntessa clamored for attention, but I didn't remove my hands from the rails. The deliciousness building inside me was enough of a reason to hold off.

The energy crackling off my skin wasn't my magic but an invisible force licking and dancing between us. I offered no resistance, happy to let it spark higher. To consume me.

Of course, when Rohan reached around to stroke my clit, I didn't exactly complain. "Five floors isn't that high up," he said. "Someone must see what we're doing here." He jerked his hips, my own hitting the panel wall with a rhythmic thumping. The movement a dead give-away to anyone watching us. "See me fucking you."

My eyes snapped open and I twisted around so I could see that too, see the truth of us reflected in his expression. It was fierce and gorgeous.

He lifted his hand from my clit and sucked his finger into his mouth. "See me tasting you," he said. I whimpered at the blatant carnality. He chuckled. "I love how easy it is to get you aroused." He teased Cuntessa once more.

Tonight was the end of us and I'd hold nothing back. I slammed my hips back against him. "Then let them see you really fucking me."

Rohan pulled out of me. "Inside," he growled.

I spun to face him. He took my hand, laying it against his cheek. "Inside," he repeated in a softer voice.

His washboard abs clenched as he bent over to retrieve the clothing we'd shed so far, obscuring the thin line of dark hair running down to his pelvis. I looked my fill before leaving the balcony.

Once inside, I finished stripping while Rohan ran the shower for us. He nudged me toward the roomy stall, his still-hard cock pointing the way.

Did he sense this was our last time together?

I stepped under the hot spray to combat the twist of my stomach. Already tightly coiled, the heat of the shower and the massaging circles of his hands as he lathered me up wound me into a near delirium. What I'd forgotten about shower sex though, was that it kind of sucked. I kept being jostled into the cold air. Twice Rohan whacked his skull on the shower head. Half the time, the water sluiced down on us like drowned rats.

This was not doing it for me so I dropped to my knees, the river rock on the shower floor pebbling my skin. What I was about to do would turn me on as much as it did him. Except, I hesitated, seeing Poppy in this exact same position.

Rohan tilted my chin up to face him, understanding written clear on his features. "Nava–" I shook my head, banishing her from this moment. Sincerity and sorrow shone out of his eyes.

I liked going down on him and I wasn't about to let anything, or anyone, wreck that. Not on our final night together. I ripped off the condom, tossing it out onto the floor, then took Rohan's thick length into my mouth, sucking gently on the head of his cock, licking off the salty pre-cum.

He sighed, bracing one hand against the sandstone shower tiles.

I swirled my tongue over the tip before intensifying the pressure, taking in more of him.

Rohan hissed, his fingers threading into my hair. His dilated pupils burned with an unholy intensity. "Touch yourself," he ordered.

Happily. I slid my fingers over my clit with aching slowness. Rohan watched me with darkening eyes.

I sucked his balls into my mouth. He gripped my hair tighter, his hips starting to rock. He white-knuckled the safety bar mounted to the wall, his harsh groans almost swallowed by the sound of the spray. His cock jerked, hardened further.

I licked my way up the length of his dick.

Rohan gave a desperate wanton moan that made my blood run hot.

"Bed." It was my turn to give orders.

The shower was abandoned in haste.

He stretched himself out dead center on the mattress. Grinning, naked, and stroking himself. Absolute sin on pure white sheets. I forgot how to breathe. "How do you want it?" he asked. "We can do anything we've ever done before." A mischievous glint lit his eyes. "Or try something new."

Déja vu hit hard at the sight of Rohan once again offering himself to me. The first time, in my hotel room, I'd hesitated, suspicious of his motives. Now I failed to answer for an entirely different reason. My imagination was up to the challenge. My emotions weren't. "I want to quit thinking."

He tilted his head, studying me for a moment with a cat-like curiosity. "Then lay on your back." The darkness in his voice made me shudder.

Rohan stretched out on top of me, pressing me into the mattress and the cloudlike softness of a billion thread count sheets. I ran my foot along his calf, his toes flexing at my touch. He pressed hot kisses down my neck and along my collar bone, then sucked my tit into his mouth, his teeth scraping along my sensitive skin.

I arched up under him.

Rohan caressed every inch of my body, whispering my name between breaths. I tried to burn this moment into my brain: the slight rasp of his voice when he was aroused, the scratch of his stubble when he turned his cheek to my belly, the heavy warmth of his hands cradling me like I was his birthday present. I willed myself to focus on the heat spreading like wildfire with every touch and not the tightness in my chest.

He licked my clit and I bucked off the bed. "Nicely played, Snowflake."

"Not everything between us is a game." Another lick. The delightful sound of a second condom package opening.

"Isn't it?"

He crawled up my body, pinning my hands over my head as he rocked against me. Not yet inside. "Is it a game how badly I want you?"

I dug my heels into the blankets. The heavy ache between my legs grew. "I don't know."

Rohan sank bank onto his calves, jerking my legs up to ninety degrees as he planted himself deep inside me. "Does this feel like a game?" He gripped my ass, tilting my hips up, filling me more completely.

My legs trembled. Rohan adjusted them so they'd rest against his chest. He sucked my toe into his mouth, his hand sliding along my calf with a possessive glide. "It's not," he said, when I didn't answer.

It didn't make it real though, either. Still, he'd been honest and he was deeper inside me, connected more intimately than anyone had ever been. He deserved honesty, too. I met his eyes. "I don't want to be alone in the dark either."

He groaned helplessly and surged up against me. His fingers biting into my hips, he claimed me. Strong. Lethal. Fucking ruthless.

We'd both been ruthless with each other. It amped my desire and broke my heart.

I writhed in sheer wanton abandonment as he fucked me into the mattress. Still-damp strands plastered to my face. The blood roared in my veins, the emptiness I'd clung to all day blown away by the storm raging inside me, bringing with it impending bliss.

Our bodies were fever hot. A primordial fire, all-consuming. I fell into the tensing and clenching of my core. Into that fine edge of pleasure and pain that only Rohan properly satisfied.

He gave a wicked groan and called my name, his orgasm triggering my own. These mutual orgasms were a recurrence between us that bewildered, delighted, and terrified me in equal measure. Stars danced under my closed lids, my body shuddering, then slowing to stillness. He fell against me and kissed my forehead. The lazy smile he gave me was my personal Aurora Borealis, wondrous, mysterious, and lighting up my world. Anything Samson had ever made me feel, even with all his sorcery, had been nothing in comparison.

I craved Rohan again so badly it physically hurt. I balled my hands into the mattress.

He slid his hands around my back, cradling me to him before reaching past me to pull the covers up over us.

"You want me to stay?"

He nudged his leg between mine. "Back to thinking," he chided. His arms tightened around me. I took it as a yes.

The first time we woke up, we were a tangle of limbs that slid into a sleepy lazy fuck. The second time, Rohan woke up first but given what he was doing with his tongue, I didn't sleep much longer.

The third time, I woke up before him, watching him sleep on his stomach. Dawn was breaking, a soft hazy light infusing the room. Rohan's hair had fallen into his eyes, and one arm was thrown off the bed. The blanket had ridden down, a spill of cloth bunching at the base of his spine. I traced a finger over his heart tattoo on his bicep, memorizing the lines of his muscles. Sure, I'd see him shirtless again when we trained, but not in bed like this. I'd be able to fight him, but I'd never again be allowed this gentleness.

I moved my hand up his arm, along his shoulders, my fingers ghosting over his body. Trailing my hand down to his Kshatriya tattoo on his back, I placed my hand against his skin, feeling the soft rise and fall of his breathing under my palm as he slept.

Even if I'd considered a relationship with him for a second, I wasn't the one for him. It was one thing for him to want me in the dark, in the dead of night, but I saw how he looked at Lily. He needed the light she brought him. I wasn't capable of that, and even if I was or I wanted it, I had enough on my plate with the demon hunting gig. No, I had no desire to be Rohan's sun.

He knew it, too. Rohan hadn't tried to kiss me, hadn't done anything last night except give me exactly what I'd wanted. I brushed a lock of hair off of his face, smoothing it away.

Good-bye, Snowflake.

I pressed a kiss between his shoulder blades, my vision blurring.

Rohan opened his eyes, scrunching up his face against the sunlight streaming into the room. "Quite the workout last night."

Blinking to get rid of any telltale moisture, I pulled the blanket up my chest. "I totally Debbie Allen'd you."

"Huh?"

"Made you start paying. In sweat."

For a second I didn't think he'd gotten my bad *Fame* joke, but then he laughed, smacking me with a pillow. "That's terrible." His smile worked its way into the cracks of my soul, warming me up like patches of sunshine that I wanted to curl up around.

I scrambled out of bed.

Rohan didn't notice my haste. He sat up, scratching his chest. "There's a word for people like you."

I hopped around the bedroom searching for my clothes. "Incredible?"

"Not what I was thinking." He picked up his phone and frowned. "A dozen Rasha out tracking and no sign of Samson yet. And the production office isn't answering."

I considered the problem as I got dressed. "Anya mentioned some other commitment Samson had. He might be hiding in plain sight." I found my phone and called her.

She answered, sounding harried. "Hello?"

"Anya, hi. It's Lolita." I couldn't wait to be rid of that name. "Sorry to bother you but I was wondering if you knew where Samson was today?"

"I'm with him right now. You want to talk to him?"

I gave Rohan a thumbs up that my hunch had paid off. "No. I, uh, want to surprise him. Where are you?"

"A very drafty warehouse. He's doing a photo shoot with Poppy."

A lot of people around. It might be tough to lure him away. "Is he up to anything later?"

"One sec." I heard paper rustling. Her ever-present clipboard. "Yeah. He has a radio interview."

I got the interview time and station address, thanked her and hung up. Rohan applauded me. "Work smart, not hard," I said. I sat down on the edge of my bed to put on my boots, while Rohan texted Drio to set a guard on Samson.

I checked my phone, even called in to my room for messages, but there was nothing from Dr. Gelman.

"Where are you going?" Rohan was back in Rasha mode.

I chewed on my bottom lip. "You don't need me right now, do you? We can't get to Samson until later."

"You're not going anywhere alone."

"Why not?"

Rohan swung his feet onto the ground, wrapping the sheet low on his hips. "Samson knows we're Rasha. Buddy system until he's dead." He rubbed a hand over the back of his neck. "I have an uneasy feeling."

"I have an uneasy feeling, too. About Dr. Gelman. Will you come with me to make sure she's safe?"

"Yeah. Give me ten minutes." He grabbed some clothes and headed into the bathroom.

I used those ten minutes to phone Leo, calling from the hotel phone instead of mine. Gelman had me paranoid about who might be listening in.

Leo answered on the first ring.

"I'm sorry," I said.

"Me too. I had no right to go off on you like that."

"It's over now, so it doesn't matter."

"Aw, babe. What did he say?"

I listened to make sure Rohan was still in the shower. "No words necessary." Yeah, I'd chickened out of actually saying it, but after last night it seemed apparent. "Listen, I've got a favor to ask."

"Shoot."

I explained about Dr. Gelman phoning on Saturday. "If I'm not back yet, you'll need to be home at the same time for the next few days until she and I connect." I dug around in my purse for a spare elastic and bobby pins to pull my hair back.

Leo checked her schedule and then assured me it wouldn't be a problem.

"You going to be okay?" she asked.

I scraped some loose strands back. "Sure." At least until the first time I saw Lily and Rohan together. "You know me. Besides, now we can go trolling for boys together." She didn't answer. "Unless of course you've caught one?"

"Catch and release, but what a spectacular expedition."

"Do tell." I twisted my ponytail into the elastic band.

"Kane and I bonded," she said meaningfully.

I stabbed my head with a bobby pin. "Huh? But he…? What about Ari?" I couldn't figure out which part of her statement to get more indignant over.

She snorted. "I went out with Kane *and* Ari. Drinks were had. Kane decided he loved me."

"Bitch. I'm his love bug."

"Tough titties. You've been displaced. He introduced me to a friend of his."

"Who?"

The fridge open and shut on her end. "A Lucas, Marcus, someone. Maybe it was Jason. What's important is that I could pick his mana-conda out of a police line-up."

"Never use that word again." I tightened my ponytail. "How were my boys?"

"Ari is playing hard-to-get. He's got game. When did that happen?"

"No idea. But it's about time."

Rohan came out of the shower, hair damp, but dressed and ready to go.

"Gotta run. Schmugs, babe."

"Schmugs," she said and hung up.

"Schmugs?" Rohan asked.

"Leo. It's an old goblin word for good-bye."

"You are so full of shit," he said.

"Good thing I'm cute. Come on, Rasha, let's go make sure Gelman's all right."

Her trashed hotel room and signs of struggle proved that nothing was all right. I sank onto the bed with a low moan. "This is my fault."

Rohan sat down beside me. "Nava, we don't even know what *this* is. There could be any number of explanations for what happened. Gelman is a witch. Who knows what else she was involved in? You don't know much about her."

"You're wrong. This was on me." I walked over to the window, fingering the torn curtain dangling precariously from the broken rod to peer outside, as if I'd catch her down on the street strolling back to the hotel without a care in the world. When I released the fabric, my hand was sticky. I grabbed the edge, twisting the curtain into the light.

"Oh." The fabric glistened with a familiar silver substance. It trailed down the wall, hardening in a small pool on the carpet.

Rohan caught me before my knees hit the ground. "What?" He inhaled in a hiss when he saw the secretion.

I looked at him bleakly. "The Brotherhood is using demons."

26

I sat on the floor, next to the gogota's slime. I couldn't stop poking at it. If I did it enough times, maybe it would become something else. Take away the fierce sting of hurt. I'd barely been Rasha for any time at all, and still, the magnitude of this betrayal stole my breath away.

We killed demons. We didn't modify them to be more effective and send them after our enemies. Except, it seemed we did. Someone in the Brotherhood did and it didn't take a genius to figure out who'd be able to pull something like that off.

If I was devastated, Rohan was shell-shocked. He stood in the middle of the room, just blank. It scared me. "You're right," I babbled, watching him desperately for signs that somebody was home in there. "I didn't know much about her. This could have been anyone—"

With a silent roar, Rohan tore down the curtain rod. He threw it like a spear, the decorative tip embedding itself in the wall across from me.

I flinched.

Rohan raged. Overturning the mattress, punching furniture until his fists turned bloody. All in a silent, cold fury.

I curled up into a ball, my hands thrown up protectively around my face. He wasn't going to hurt me, but that didn't mean I couldn't get injured from the fallout.

Eyes wild, Rohan spun around the room, looking for another way to vent but there was nothing left to destroy. He stood there, panting, his blades out.

I waited. I wasn't going to leave him alone but I didn't think I could get through to him yet. I counted guests coming and going on the floor outside. I'd gotten to seventeen before the savage light left Rohan's face and something resembling him returned.

I grabbed the edge of the windowsill above me, using it to pull myself up. With hands up placatingly, the same way I'd treat a feral animal, I spoke. "What you said before about not knowing–"

"Stop." A muscle jumped in his jaw. His eyes practically sparked and I could feel the wildness emanating from him. Rohan was still very much lost in the dark.

Not that I could blame him, but seeing him like this freaked me out. Especially knowing it was my determination to see Ari inducted that had led to this horrific moment. I'd say anything to make Rohan better. "Gelman was a witch. An enemy to the Brotherhood. I don't understand how they could use demons but if she was considered the greater threat..." I pulled my sweater sleeves down over my hands, shifting at the look he threw me. "What?"

"The first gogota. They sent it after you. A Rasha." The rage in his voice was absolute.

I thought about the Brotherhood. "I don't really count, though."

"You *count*, Nava." His impatience was palpable.

It triggered my own fury. I wrapped the emotion around me, drawing fuel from it. "No shit I *count*, Rohan. I'm not fishing for compliments and validation. My ego is fine, thanks. But I am a female Rasha and to the ones who would stoop to doing this," I waved a hand around the room, close to tears and hating myself for having no other way to express my angry frustration, "*bullshit* to begin with? No. I. Don't. Count."

My outburst defused him. He got himself under control with a visible effort, his blades sliding back into his skin.

Kneeling down, Rohan examined the gogota slime again. Maybe he thought things would turn out differently this time. When that failed to happen, he pulled out his phone, clenching his hand around it. "We can't even call any other Rasha in."

"No."

"Not even Drio? You still don't trust him?"

"With my life? I do. With Ari's?" I shook my head.

Rohan paced in a tight circle. "You really think the Brotherhood is behind this?"

"If you have another explanation, then please, lay it on me."

"You don't leave my side. I'm serious."

I set an overturned table back to rights. "For how long? The rest of my life? That's not realistic and we both know it. Look, I'm still alive."

"Barely."

"But I am. Whoever sent the first gogota after me, obviously sent this one after Gelman afterwards. She was still unharmed early yesterday. There's been plenty of time to grab me or kill me since then. Maybe they want me alive and behaving for now." I pushed the chair I'd sat in when I'd visited back up to the table, picked up Dr. Gelman's sweater that had fallen, and carefully hung it over the back. "Meantime, I'm going to hope she's still alive, she'll phone me like she's supposed to, and that we'll know more then."

Dr. Gelman was a powerful witch and I wanted to believe she'd escaped this and was hiding out. Safe. I added this to the growing list of things I couldn't think too closely about. Not until Samson was dead. Maybe not even then.

"I need to call Ari." There was nothing more to see here. Housekeeping would find the mess and report a missing guest to the police but this wasn't something Rohan could cover up.

I used a hotel phone in the atrium to phone my brother. "Ari?"

"Nee, what's wrong? Why do you sound like that?"

I took a shaky breath.

Rohan placed his hand on the small of my back. A tiny touch but enough to draw strength from. He wasn't even watching me as he did it, intent on scanning the lobby for anything suspicious.

I closed my eyes against the sucky knowledge that him being with Lily was going to change everything. He'd be faithful to her, careful with his affections to any other woman. Especially an ex-lover. Touches like this, even in a comrade-in-arms moment would be history. Well, he'd be going back to Los Angeles soon and we'd never see each other again.

I clung to that uplifting thought.

"Thistleton, Ace." Mrs. Thistleton had been a neighbor of ours when we were kids. If we disagreed with anything she said, even a difference of opinion on the weather, her face fell like we'd driven a knife through her heart. Plus, she'd always had a million "requests." Help her with the groceries. Walk her dog. It was impossible to refuse her without feeling like the worst person in the world.

Ari and I had appropriated her name, turning it into a joke password between us. Whenever one of us wanted the other to do something, no questions asked, we said "Thistleton," and the other had to obey or endure guilt galore. I'd used it most, usually to get my brother's help in sneaking me in or out of the house.

"Fuck that. You sound terrible."

"Thistleton," I repeated. This time in a steely voice.

He sighed. "Thistleton."

"Remember when you wrecked the Beamer? Go."

When Ari was sixteen, he'd fallen in love for the first time. The boy in question didn't deserve it. To be fair, he wasn't ready to come out. He'd humiliated my brother. Hurt beyond measure, Ari had run away in my mom's car, a freshly waxed BMW 328i with buttery leather seats and a finely tuned engine. There had been an accident. He was fine and not the driver at fault, but Mom's brand new birthday present, the car she'd been not-so-subtly dropping hints about for years, had been totaled. Ari had fled to our older cousin Yael's place. Third cousin actually and the perfect hideout now. Distant enough that no one would look for him there, close enough to the two of us that he'd be welcome in her fancy, security-heavy apartment building without question.

He was quiet for a moment. "Is someone watching your back?"

I glanced at Rohan, standing guard over me. "Yeah."

"I'm gone," he said and disconnected.

Now Rohan's phone rang. "Drio?" He listened for a moment, his expression hardening. I hovered anxiously, but didn't get to find out what had happened because my own phone rang.

"Hello?"

"Hello, Nava."

Chills ran up my spine. "Samson."

Rohan told Drio to hang on, motioning for me to keep the demon talking. He moved next to me and I tilted the phone so he could hear both sides of the conversation.

"You had me fooled with that little act of yours," Samson said. Before I could say something glib in response he added, "I don't like being fooled, Rasha."

"Poor baby."

"I'll admit, you're far more interesting this way. I've never met a female hunter before. You should have led with that."

"But then we would have missed out on all our good times."

He laughed. "The best is yet to come."

"Quit jerking around, Adramelech," I said. "Tell me where you are and let's finish this."

"Are you that impatient to end things with Rohan? Oh wait. That was an act, too. Should have known. You're not exactly in his league."

I may have caused a scorch mark on the floor with the electricity that spat from my eyes, but I didn't respond to his taunt.

Rohan snatched the phone from me and hung up, resuming his call with Drio. "Come get us. We'll be out front." He tossed me my phone and walked off.

I jogged after him, holding my questions until we'd gotten outside. The front of the hotel was busy, all tourists and luggage. No one paid any attention to us. Still, we stood off to the side of all the activity, speaking quietly.

"Samson killed the two Rasha who abducted him after his radio interview," he told me. I had no doubt Rohan would make him pay for that.

I clutched his arm. "Mirek?"

"No. Two of the guys from the bar. I'd only met them a couple of times. Still." He touched his glamoured Rasha ring, an expression of grim determination on his face.

There was nothing more to add. Two Rasha were dead. More death was a certainty.

Drio picked us up. He looked up at the hotel with curiosity. "What brought you here?"

"Later," Rohan said. Drio didn't press him.

We drove out of town once more. Given the importance of the job ahead, of keeping my shit together, now was not the time to brood over what we'd learned back in Gelman's room. I failed. Spectacularly. I leaned forward to see if Rohan was doing any better up in the passenger seat. His jaw as he stared straight ahead could have been carved from granite.

Once again, we turned onto the dirt road leading to the farmhouse. The fact we came in mid-afternoon this time, when it was still light, wasn't a plus. It was desolate out here. Even the sunlight seemed stark. Trees ran along both sides of the road, their naked branches stretching out like witch's fingers, casting twisted shadows inside the car.

The light did nothing to enhance the deserted two-story farmhouse either. The stone work on the first floor was black with dirt and age, while the horizontal wood siding that had been added up top was leached of all color. The rotting roof looked ready to cave in at any second. Only one window on the upper floor still had a pane of glass; the others had been blown out through time or Rasha encounters.

I got out of the car, sidestepping a pile of loose rock by my foot. If there were neighbors, they were far away and on the other side of the woods that bordered the property on three sides. "Why would Samson give us the home court advantage?" I asked.

"He said he wanted to kill us where we'd killed the gemini." Drio stuffed the car keys in his pocket. "I'm sure he does, since the other Rasha warded up the farmhouse, imprisoning him."

Ah. He needed our blood to break the ward and get free. "He couldn't compel them into breaking the ward?"

"No," Rohan said, as we tromped over the weed-choked front lawn. "The ritual affected that ability."

"Then why not use the Rasha blood to break free once he'd killed them?"

Drio's mouth flattened into a hard line. He pointed out into the field between the house and the woods. About thirty feet away lay two blackened lumps that I'd mistaken for burned hay bales. My hand flew to my mouth.

The stairs leading up to the front door were warped, twisting away from the house as if trying to escape. Smart stairs. A moldy sofa in a hideous brown velvet stood in the otherwise empty living room. Some-one should have burned it and put it out of its misery.

A creepy whistled tune came from everywhere at once, as if broad-cast on a state-of-the-art speaker system. There was a sick clutch in my stomach as I recognized the tune. "I've Got No Strings On Me" from Disney's *Pinocchio.*

Drio flicked his eyes to the living room door. Rohan nodded. A flash of iron caught the weak sunlight as Drio flicked the ritual blade from some kind of wrist sheath. Then he zipped off. With his speed, he'd be able to search the house for Samson in seconds.

Rohan and I crept into the hallway, following it toward the center of the house where it opened up to the second floor with a wide staircase. While Rohan went into the kitchen, I glanced up at the cathedral ceiling and the grimy skylight.

In the second that it took me to look up, Samson appeared in human form. I shivered at the way his eyes tried to pierce my skin. Determined not to give him the upper hand, I called my magic up, letting it coat me in a bright blue glow. Lightning bolts slithered over my skin like animated tattoos.

Gathering electricity between my fingers, I played with the strings of crackling blue and silver current, twisting and stretching them like they were taffy. Then I flung my magic at Samson. The current caught him across the face and chest like a net. His glamour fell away in patches, revealing the ravaged skin of his demon form, now bleeding from my attack.

Samson whistled a few more notes at me.

"Hardly a puppet." With another ball ready to go, letting it dance over my fingers, I moved close.

Samson laughed. A cruel sound. "You have no idea how many people are pulling your strings."

I chose to take his words as game playing of his own and not some demon intel about more people with me on their hit list. I patted his bloody cheek in mock affection. "I'd give a shit, Samson, but I ran out a while back and haven't restocked."

Red eyes narrowed thoughtfully. "Come to save the damsel in distress?"

"Nah," Rohan said from behind me. "Just watch your ass get pounded by a girl."

The demon's glamour fell away. As his peacock feathers majestically unfolded behind his humanoid demon form, there was a rush of air and a blur of motion. Adramelech flew across the room, smashing into the back wall hard enough to partially break through it.

I blinked. Drio now stood beside me, his fist still raised from the blow he'd dealt the demon. Note to self: being hit by speedster Rasha, bad.

Drio's lips curved in a sadistic smile. "I didn't want to miss any of the fun."

Adramelech disappeared, leaving a demon-shaped imprint in the wall, and a handful of bent peacock feathers fluttering to the ground.

The damn whistling started up again. Rohan and Drio ran upstairs, while I retraced our steps here on the main floor. I'd cleared every room and skidded back into the stairway area when a commotion overhead caught my attention.

Adramelech managed to fight pretty well given the giant tail he carted around. He executed a low spinning kick, intended to take Rohan out, but Rohan jumped it, landing on the other side of the demon.

Drio blurred toward Adramelech but the demon judged the approach correctly, managing to jump up and nail Drio with a two-footed kick in the chest. The hunter flew backward, but recovered quickly, springing forward into two consecutive handsprings, his legs jackknifing out in front of him.

He caught Adramelech around the neck, twisting to pin him to the ground. The demon's tail twitched once, twice, and then Drio's skin started to bubble. Drio roared, trying to pull free as his arm burst into flame, but he was stuck until Rohan kicked him clear of the demon.

Rohan decked Adramelech, catapulting him backwards over the low second-story railing. The demon crashed onto his back at my feet.

He threw me a wink, hooked a hand around my ankle, and we disappeared.

He'd transported us to a low-ceilinged attic. Patchy sunlight trickled through the gaps in the roof. I rushed him but he caught my hands in one wrist. My skin heated painfully under his touch. Electricity crackled between my skin and his, but he only laughed. "Knock yourself out. Can't feel a thing for all the scarring."

I jerked free. "You're a douchebag and should be plowed under like mulch."

"Volunteering for the gig?" Hearing Samson's all-American accent coming out of this ruined flesh was disorienting to say the least.

"Yeah. I'm a real humanitarian."

"You're a real little actress. I'm impressed with your performance."

"Thought you didn't like being fooled."

"Oh, I don't. You're going to die for that. But I appreciate showmanship. I've left you a gift. Rohan's gig was... illuminating. In so many ways."

I eyed the stairs but Adramelech blocked my escape.

He glared at me. "Are you listening?"

"Not really. But don't stress yourself. Long-winded villain plans are generally where I leave to go to the bathroom."

I feinted sideways and dashed forward. The demon caught me. Perfect. Now up close and personal, I wrapped my arms around his waist, brushed his tail away, and fired a burst of electricity into his sweet spot.

Since we'd forced his true form using the ritual blade, only the use of that blade on his kill spot would end him, but my blast surprised him enough to give me a chance. Adramelech instinctively jerked backward at the feel of my magic. I pulled free, yelling for Drio as I sprinted down the stairs.

The whoosh of wind against my skin was Drio blowing past me. Adramelech shot a blast of fire at him, and had Drio not had super speed, he'd have been flambéed. "Only need one Rasha to get free," the demon taunted.

I poked my head back up the attic stairwell to see he'd disappeared again. Cursing, Drio spun and was gone, hunting him. I followed, skidding to a stop in the atrium at the top of the stairs that led down to the main floor.

Below, Rohan had Adramelech pinned facedown on the ground, Drio chanting as he stood over them. Rohan pressed the blade along his elbow against the demon's spine, his knee resting on the peacock feathers, bending them out of the way.

Adramelech burst into flame.

Rohan kept his arm on the demon's back, despite the flames engulfing his sleeve. Pain etched his features as he waited for Drio to finish the chant.

I leaned over the low railing for a better look.

Drio nodded at Rohan, who shifted, allowing Drio to plunge the ritual blade into the demon's sweet spot. Adramelech winked out of existence, dead. All that was left was a single peacock feather.

Rohan sank back on his calves, beating his still-flaming arm against the stone floor.

As I stepped onto the top stair, headed for the pair, a black ball of smoke blazed up from the spot where the demon had lain.

Drio barely managed to pull Rohan out of the way. The farmhouse went from zero to inferno in a second, smoke and flame billowing up toward me. Not a normal fire, this was oily and vicious, snapping in evil tendrils, sparking and hissing. The demon's "gift."

The staircase collapsed in a rumbling roar. To jump down would be to jump into the heart of the fire. Blackness curled and danced around me, sucking more and more light from the world. I felt my way along the wall, my lungs burning from the incessant heat, looking for a window. The smoke slithered inside me, defiling me. I spat it out as best I could, throwing my arm over my mouth and nose to make a filter.

I couldn't see, couldn't hear anything except the roar and crackle of the flames licking at the walls and floor behind me. The flames had a languid quality, as if they had all the time in the world to devour me. As a gift, this one sucked balls.

My fingers brushed a doorframe and I almost wept. Granted, I was already weeping from the fire, my tears leaving sticky streaks on my cheeks. The faintest trickle of cool breeze swept over me and I turned toward it in relief. It had to be coming from one of the empty window panes. I could make it out of here. Safe. Not a second too soon, either, because out from the hallway came a deafening crash. I suspected the roof had caved in.

I was almost to the window when I heard it. A thin, plaintive, *terrified* cry for help from another room. The person cried out again. Definitely female. When she cried out for a third time, this time for Rohan, I knew who it was.

Lily.

27

Swearing viciously under my breath, I detoured away from the window and towards Lily. I tried to call out that I was coming, to reassure her she wasn't going to die, but I only coughed.

I was willing to believe that the guys had escaped, anything else was unthinkable, but if no one was coming for me, it was because they absolutely couldn't. That they were trusting me to make it out alive.

That meant they had no idea that Lily was here. Was it my fault Adramelech had brought her here, by implying on the night of the wrap party that I could give him the person who could make Rohan hurt? The demon had said that night was illuminating. I'd never meant for him to turn his sights on Lily, but I'd done exactly that.

Too bad I hadn't put Poppy in his sights. I would have been outside already.

Probably.

Groping my way back toward the door, my fingers brushed a smooth basin with a familiar curve. I fumbled around, thanking all the gods and fates when I felt the tap. Only the tiniest trickle of coppery smelling water came out but it was the richest treasure ever. I ripped off my shirt and immersed it in the water as much as possible. Tying it around my head like a scarf, I then wet my bra and upper body as much as I could.

Eyes screwed shut, I advanced inch by inch. Flaming bits of ceiling rained down on me, burning my skin. But the wet shirt kept my hair from catching on fire. I held one sleeve in place across my nose and mouth, sucking on the water, desperate for cool air in my desert-dry mouth.

Once in the hallway, my progress slowed further. I had to feel for each step before I placed my weight. I didn't know where the roof had collapsed and I didn't want to plunge down to the main floor.

Lily cried out again, sobbing.

I stepped into the room that sounded like the source and carefully cracked one eye. The fire was in here as well, but there was a flame-free circle. Lily sat in the middle of it, tied to a chair with rope. She'd fallen over in her attempts to wriggle free and her left ankle had puffed up to twice its size. Flames licked at the boards, millimeters from her hair. A gag was tied around her mouth with enough of it slipped down for me to have heard her cry out.

"Nava?" she hiccuped.

I ran over to her, pulling the gag all the way off. "Do you remember how you got here?" Her face was streaked with soot, as were my hands.

"It was Samson. He told me Rohan wanted to see me. I felt like I had to come."

She babbled as I untied her ropes. "He said that when it came to envy, we humans were the architects of our own misery and it never ceased to amaze him the lengths people would go to to achieve their heart's desire. What was he talking about?"

Me. *Lily* was my gift. One to save or destroy and both choices came with a price. Fucking demons.

I helped her to her feet, taking her weight as she hobbled unsteadily. "We need to get out of here."

I eyed the window. Of course, it had to be the one that still had glass. But the outside wall brushed the edge of the circle so we had a chance of escaping without being burned alive. I hoisted the chair and heaved it out the window.

Behind me, Lily shrieked. The rush of oxygen had fed the fire. She was still safe inside the circle but all around it flames blazed hotter and higher.

I stepped to the window. Outside, on the ground, Rohan and Drio turned their faces up to look at me. It seemed like Drio was holding Rohan back from racing inside.

"Jump," Rohan yelled at me. He and Drio moved into position to catch me.

I held up one finger. When I returned, Rohan was glaring at me.

"Jump," he yelled again.

I moved Lily to the window. His face drained of all color.

Yeah, I get that I'm not the priority anymore, but thanks for sparing my feelings. I used my fist to smash out any glass along the bottom of the pane, ignoring the bloody gashes welling along my skin. "Lily, you need to do exactly as I say."

Her pupils were dilated in fear and she clung to me, paralyzed.

"Okay, we'll do this together." I maneuvered her so she sat on the pane. "I'm going to swing your legs out and—Shit!"

She grabbed my shoulders, her fingers digging in like talons, snagging my hair in the process.

"Rohan will catch you. You know that."

She nodded. Shaky and with more than a hint of disbelief, but she pried her fingers off of my flesh.

While the magic circle kept the flames out, the heat flayed the skin on my back. I couldn't stay in here another second, so I swung Lily's legs out the window and essentially shoved her out. I checked to make sure she'd landed safely, then, without waiting to see who'd be there to catch me, I hung off the window sill, pushed off the house, and dropped.

I looked at my rescuer. Drio held me, not Rohan. He was busy comforting Lily as she was examined by a Rasha paramedic. The two dead hunters from earlier now lay in body bags on the ground.

"Thank you." I rested my head against his chest, exhausted.

Keeping me in his arms, Drio walked in the opposite direction of the paramedic.

"Shouldn't I get checked out?"

"You will be. By the Rasha doctor on standby. We'll drive you over to him." He carried me to a yellow ambulance with red stripes. Mirek opened the door for us and helped position me on my stomach, inside on a gurney, before spreading some kind of cool salve on my back.

I grit my teeth against the million pinpricks of pain, simultaneously flushing hot and shivering with cold. It made me think of the vral claws fondly. The salve helped, numbing my skin somewhat. I propped my head on my chin, having a clear line of sight outside as Drio hopped out of the van. I tracked him over to Rohan. Drio said something and Rohan nodded, all his attention on Lily.

Mirek shut the ambulance door. The passenger door in front opened and closed and then the motor started and off we drove. I wasn't sure if I was happy or disappointed that I couldn't watch Rohan and Lily disappear from view.

I was kept at the doctor's clinic over the next few days so he could keep an eye on me. I slept a lot and let my healing abilities do their thing.

Rohan didn't visit me. Drio did once, after he left me in the doctor's care. A brief stop to bring my things over from the hotel.

"How's Lily?" I asked.

"Good as could be expected. She was worried about you."

I plucked at my blanket. "That's sweet of her. What did you tell her?"

"Nothing about demons. She thinks Samson had a grudge against Rohan." The best lies always had a grain of truth. Drio explained that he and Rohan had to deal with clean up and debrief and would see me back in Vancouver. They'd be busy providing evidence of Samson's death for the world. I got that.

Guess Rohan wasn't worried that I'd be targeted by the Brotherhood any more. Still, I couldn't help but wonder if he had made time for Lily. I tortured myself obsessing over whether they'd had their talk yet. Then I coughed up more vile black shit, tired myself out, and fell asleep again. The joys of having a routine.

Since my flight out wasn't until Monday night, I called Leo on Saturday, Sunday, and Monday morning to check if she'd heard from Dr. Gelman. She hadn't.

The flight back was business class as well, but I was a lot more subdued on the way home. I was the only one, it seemed. In the airport and on the plane, everyone was buzzing with the news of Samson King's tragic demise in a fiery car crash. His burned remains had been found outside Prague in a Ferrari that had been wrapped around a tree. Speculation was that he was still partying after the wrap of *Hard Knock Strife*. I would have been more amazed that the Brotherhood had been able to produce a corpse if I hadn't known that they, or some of them anyway, were dealing in demons.

I was thankful that no photos of Samson and me were rerun in light of his death. My name or past association wasn't mentioned either. The Executive had a long reach. It was a chilling reminder of what I was up against and made me wonder if the reason they'd sent the gogota after me was as much about me putting myself in the public eye without their approval as meeting with Gelman.

I spent the flight back staring at my personal entertainment screen, watching movie after movie with no real memory of any plot. The one thing that did pierce the haze of my brain was yet another story on some entertainment show about Samson's demise. Poppy was interviewed, the grief stricken co-star in elegant black, off to Ireland to shoot a new picture. When asked about rumors of her getting cozy with Rohan, she gave a coy smile and said they were just friends.

That meant Rohan was back in Rasha mode and done with her. I couldn't muster up enough energy to care.

With the time difference going back to Canada, I landed in Vancouver late Monday night local time. A week and a half and a lifetime since I'd left. The chapter house was silent when I entered. I left my suitcase in the foyer and climbed the stairs. Baruch's door was open, so I knocked softly. "Tree Trunk, you up?"

I tiptoed inside, listening for any sound of deep, even breathing, until I remembered with a pang that he'd gone back to Jerusalem. I pushed his door open to make sure, taking in the empty hangers in his closet. Feeling like a hole was punched inside me, I sank onto his bed, crying. Big gulping sobs, my face pressed into my hands. The harder I tried to keep quiet, to stuff this sloppiness back inside, the more I shook.

"There's no crying in Rashaland." Kane sat down beside me, yawning, and pulled me into his chest.

"Long trip?"

"Yes," I wailed.

"He'll be back. Baruch wants me. Seriously, there's no other reason for how often he flies out here."

I laughed through my sobs, knowing it was Ms. Clara that kept Tree Trunk coming back. And on his toes.

"That's better." He brushed away my tears. "Let's get you to bed." He waited until he'd tucked me in, airplane clothes and all, and kissed my forehead to ask, "Any idea where your wayward twin is?"

"He's at home." With Samson out of the way and any immediate danger to Ari gone, he'd left our cousin's apartment. I was sure he had his reasons for still avoiding Kane but if I learned it was so he could chase demons without a babysitter, he was toast. I'd find out when I spoke to him in the morning.

"Uh-huh." With a huff, Kane went back to bed.

I lay in the dark listening to the clock tick. Baruch gone. Rohan gone. The Brotherhood playing a waiting game for reasons unknown. I turned over, my fingers brushing something furry in the darkness.

Sebastian. I clutched my battered black panther stuffie to my chest. Ari must have brought him over while I'd been gone. I cuddled the toy, sorry that I'd ever forgotten about him. He'd languished in a closet the past couple of years, but growing up I'd slept with him every night.

A tiny ray of hope cracked through the sorrow tightening my chest. Maybe Dr. Gelman would phone tomorrow. Maybe, finally, I'd have my brother fighting by my side. It wasn't much, but I clung to it for all it was worth.

I got to Leo's the next morning a half hour before the hoped-for 11AM phone call. My friend took one look at me and poured a giant cup of milky sweet coffee, pressing it into my hand.

I pulled her into a hug. "I'm so happy to see you." I'd been a giant idiot letting our friendship slide.

"Pffft. You're just a slut for the many services I provide." She pushed her straight red hair off of her shoulder, busy hopping around the living room gathering up all her funky silver jewelry to put on.

Sinking onto the sofa beneath the colorful print of Warhol's flowers, I waggled my eyebrows at her. "Are we broadening our friendship boundaries?"

Leo ran a hand along herself in fine show model form. "You couldn't handle this much woman."

"A little goes a long way," I teased, alluding to her height.

"So I've been told on many an occasion." She winked lewdly at me.

11AM came and went.

As did 11:10, 11:20, and 11:30.

I placed my cup in the sink. "She's not phoning."

"We'll try again tomorrow. Come on," Leo hooked her arm in mine. "I'll walk you out. I need to check my mailbox." We'd said our schmugs, and I had the front door to the building open when Leo called me back. She held a letter up. "It's for you."

There was no return address and the postmark was smudged. We ran back to her apartment and I tore it open. A faint hint of cigarette smoke clung to it like perfume.

Dear Nava,

If the cancer hasn't killed me, you can be sure the Brotherhood won't. It'll take more than some mutant fiend to rid them of me. I promised you the ritual, and you'll have it, but first: remember that Vashar amulet I gave you?

I stopped reading aloud. "Vashar. That's what the gogota kept saying when it attacked me. Why the amulet?"

Leo jogged my elbow to get me to resume reading.

It's a powerful artifact. In fact, it's the only thing capable of stopping a...

I trailed off as I read the next word.

"I get if you don't want to share that with me." Leo didn't look perturbed.

There were so many reasons to keep this information from her. She wasn't Rasha. She *was* a half-goblin. This information could seriously harm the Brotherhood if it got out to the demon world. It *would* get me killed if I was seen as the source of the leak. There was only one reason to tell her. After Ari and Rohan, Leo was the person I trusted most with my life. I kept reading aloud.

...stopping a Rasha induction. Use the amulet during a traditional ceremony and it sucks the magic into itself.

Leo whistled.

The Brotherhood knows you have it. They also know that you've been causing trouble for Isaac, insisting that there is no point in testing your brother further. That you are the only rightful Rasha in your family.

"Isaac?" Leo asked.

"Rabbi Abrams."

"That's ballsy of them. Make the Brotherhood think you're a whiny, petty bitch, which they're probably inclined to think anyway. Then you team up with a witch who gives you an amulet capable of stopping Rashas from being made."

"Yup." I squinted at the postmark again but its point of origin remained a mystery. "When Ari proves to be Rasha, the Brotherhood will believe it happened via the usual ceremony and if I'm not happy about it, that will make them very happy."

I'd have to turn the amulet over to Rabbi Abrams, but I could have kissed Dr. Gelman and her devious mind. The gogota wasn't sent to kill me because of the secret ritual. It was sent to kill me for the Vashar. Well, I'd be handing over the amulet soon. Eliminating one strike against me. I might live awhile after all. Even better, Ari was safe. I was the bad guy in this situation.

The rest of the letter detailed the ritual. How to prepare for it, what to say, how to use the vials of water and dirt that I'd brought back from Prague. The rabbi would have no problem following it.

Final item and I can't stress its importance enough. You must be the one to perform this ritual. The fact that the first ceremony to determine initiate status was never performed on you, combined with your Rasha essence asserting itself during Ari's induction has caused any division between you and your twin to disappear in this matter. This ceremony will separate you both as it inducts your brother. It is simple to follow, but know this. If the ceremony fails—

"It'll kill me?! What the fuck?" I glared at the letter but there was no "Psych! Kidding!"

Leo squeezed my shoulder.

I realize this may not seem different from Brotherhood actions, but there is a difference. If this works, and I believe it will, then you and Ari will both have magic with no harm done. But more importantly, now it's your choice. For once, you should be the deciding factor in your fate.

She'd underlined "your choice" twice. The letter ended with Gelman wryly admitting that should I live, she expected to see me live and in person to yell at her. We'd also discuss that other matter at that time.

"What other matter?" Leo shook out the envelope but there was nothing else in it.

"I might have more magic tricks than previously assumed," I said.

"The force is strong in you?"

"Apparently." I peered into my mug as if more caffeine might magically appear. Or rum.

Leo tucked her legs under her on the couch. "Are you gonna go through with it?"

"Do I have a choice?"

"D'uh. She didn't say you'd die if you did nothing."

"Leo," I sighed. "Do I have a choice?"

Scowling, she jabbed a finger at me. "Fine. But if you die, I am going to screw all memory of you out of Rohan's brain."

I snorted. "Good luck getting him away from Lily."

"Let me have my revenge fantasy here." She shoved me and I fell backward against the sofa.

"Fine. I die, you screw, and I won't spend eternity haunting you." I tucked the letter in my pocket. "Before I meet my alleged demise, I think I better chat with Rabbi Abrams."

I found him in the kitchen back at the chapter house, almost as if he'd been waiting for me. Or waiting for his kettle to boil. I slid the amulet across the dark granite counter to him as he poured boiling water into his mug. "No, no, don't take this from me."

He pocketed the amulet, stroking his beard. "You leave me no choice. Shame on you, Nava. I'm incredibly disappointed in your behavior. Such mishegoss." His eyes twinkled at me.

I retrieved his honey from the cupboard. "Yeah, I'd be sorry, but what can I say? I'm the only Katz twin who deserves this. My brother's a loser and unworthy of the title."

He stirred the honey into his tea. "And to partner up with such a bitter witch."

"Desperate times, Rabbi. Desperate times."

He took hold of my hand, running his thumb over my glamoured Rasha ring, and spoke a few words. The ring transformed to its normal state. "There."

"Rabbi?" He looked at me. "Thank you."

He patted my hand. "Navela, you understand the danger?"

"I do."

"You still want to go ahead with this?"

I nodded. "You won't tell Ari, will you?"

"No. You should. You must."

Agree to disagree, Rabbi. I was the one in danger. My body, my choice. Ari would never be part of the ceremony if he knew. He was always conservative with his bets, whereas I could happily let it all ride on one hand and let the chips fall where they may.

"Alea iacta est," I said.

I pulled my phone out of my pocket to fire off a quick text to my brother that the ceremony was a go and that I'd phone him later with the details. By the time I'd finished, the rabbi had gone. But I wasn't alone.

Rohan watched me, lounging inside the room. I drank him in, freshly shaven with his sweater and black trousers molding to every muscle. His eyes were alight with amusement. "Why were you quoting Latin, Lolita?"

My hand tightened on my phone. "That name is done. Got it?"

Rohan gave a confused nod.

I stomped out of the kitchen and up the stairs to my room. Of course he followed me. He never knew when to leave things alone.

He stopped in the doorway. "The Latin?"

My head had started to throb. "It means–"

"I know what it means. I'm asking why you said it."

"Is it any of your business?"

"Does it have to do with the scientist whose hotel room was trashed? Because if it does?" He crossed his arms, propping one hip against the wood. Settling in for the long-haul of being annoying and making this his business.

Really? Now he was concerned about that? About me? "Dr. Gelman gave me the instructions for the ritual. I'll be the one performing it."

"She's alive?"

I nodded. "Hiding out, but alive." I untangled the mess of blankets on my bed, hoping he'd see I was busy and leave.

"Good. What did Abrams want you to tell Ari?"

I smoothed out the top cover, keeping my back to him. "Eavesdropping is a nasty habit."

"Around you it's a requirement. Spill."

I plumped the pillow up. *Pound. Pound. Pound.* "There's a slight chance I could die."

"If you do the ceremony."

Still working on the pillow, I faced him. "Yes."

Rohan smiled, a glittering dangerous smile. I scooted backward a couple of steps. My knees hit the boxspring. "Ari wouldn't let you do anything to endanger yourself," Rohan said.

I flung the pillow at him. Rohan wasn't expecting that. It bounced off his face and hit the ground. "You rat me out and I'll never forgive you."

He pushed off the wall. I sensed that same wildness in him as the day we'd learned about the Brotherhood using demons. "I can live with that." His words were silky and more lethal sounding for it.

I stepped up to him, toe to toe. "You have no say in my life or my decisions."

It took everything in me not to smack his arrogant eyebrow lift off of his face.

"I'm in charge of you," he said. "Your main babysitter, remember?" Babysitter. Right. Just the poor schmuck stuck watching my pathetic ass.

I punched him in the stomach. Rohan grunted. "That's for not even saying 'thank you' for saving Lily," I said. "I had third degree burns on my back and had to spend *three freaking days in an iron lung*!" A total lie but the doctor had given me oxygen. "I didn't even merit 'a good job, Nava' from you. Your leadership skills suck balls."

I shoved at him, craving a physical target for my anger, but he grabbed my wrist, jerking me up against him. "Thank you, Nava," he growled. "For saving someone so important to me, when I failed to realize she was even in danger. Thank you, Nava, for risking your life when all I did was leave her wide open to be taken by a demon."

He released his hold, the fight going out of him.

I'd never seen the expression on his face before so it took me a minute to figure it out. Shame. With a healthy heap of guilt. Shit. His cousin Asha. What kind of flashback hell had Rohan spent the past few days reliving, believing his failings had caused yet another person he loved to be hurt?

I reached out to place my hand on his cheek, then remembered that gesture wasn't on the approved list anymore and curled my fingers into my palm. "Rohan, if you were to blame for her being there, then I was just as much to blame."

His eyes lit up like I'd thrown him a lifeline. Then he shook his head. "That doesn't make any sense. It wasn't your fault." Truth be told, it was probably more my fault than his. Lily was my gift from Samson after all. It was my lie about being lightning girl that started it. Plus, he'd seen me replaced by her at the concert. The pissed off demon had gifted me with my chance for payback, convinced I'd take it.

However, I'd shared as much as I was going to. "Absolve yourself. I do, and I'm sure Lily does."

I walked over to my doorway and paused, one hand on the wall. "The thing about living in the dark? It doesn't exist without light. That means you can step into that light, if you want. Only you can choose how you live your life, Rohan, just like only I can choose how I live mine."

I was halfway down the hall when I heard his soft, "good luck."

28

I never did enlighten Ari that he might be an only child when this was over. He looked nervous enough to puke, or bolt, as it was. Dressed all in white, as per Dr. Gelman's instructions, he sat on the sofa in our family's living room, drumming his fingers on the modular coffee table. Both our parents were at the university teaching so I'd commandeered the room. It seemed appropriate given this was where his induction ceremony had gone so wrong the first time.

Outwardly, I was the picture of calm as I poured the dirt and water into separate small clay bowls, but his drumming set my teeth on edge. Luckily, right before I concussed my sibling with the decanter, there was a firm knock on the front door. "That's the rabbi. Go help him."

Ari jumped up to answer it.

I ran a critical eye over myself to ensure that I'd properly adhered to the clothing specifications. I wore an ankle-length white cotton skirt and long sleeved white cotton blouse. My feet were bare, my hair was down, and I wore no make-up or jewelry other than my Rasha ring. Gelman had been clear about both the purity of color and fabric for this ceremony. I was to be as natural as possible to ensure nothing could contaminate the ritual. Ari and I being bound was complication enough.

My brother returned a moment later, leading Rabbi Abrams into the room.

"Rabbi, where are all the ritual items?" He'd promised to get me everything on Gelman's list, insisting they were easy enough for him to procure without raising any suspicion.

With Ari's help, the rabbi lowered himself into a chair. He sighed in pleasure, rubbing his knee, and looked over toward the hallway. "My helpers." As if on cue, Kane and Rohan walked into the room, each carrying a box.

I pointed to the ground next to the coffee table. "Set them there, then you can leave."

Kane put his box down. He flung himself onto the sofa, pulling Ari down next to him by both hands. "Nervous? Excited?"

"This isn't a spectator event. Invited guests only." I snapped my fingers at him. "Out. That goes for you too, Mitra." I rushed Rohan as he sat down, trying to knock him out of the chair he'd reached for. He got comfortable and I barely escaped falling into his lap.

"Rabbi," I appealed, "I'm nervous enough about performing this ritual correctly without a home audience."

The rabbi reached into his pocket, pulling out three simple white cloth kippahs, which he distributed to the men. "It's better to have witnesses for this. They can attest that I performed the Brotherhood's induction ceremony which, thanks to God, worked properly this time." I'm glad he believed it would work.

Or was at least faking really well.

He pointed to the box that Kane had put down. "That one contains the Brotherhood ceremony items."

The Brotherhood's anal corporate tendencies worked in our favor. Every time a rabbi performed a ritual, he had to request the necessary items through the Brotherhood. In Rabbi Abrams' case, that meant having Ms. Clara take the candles, wine, and ceremonial cloth from inventoried stock. If anyone checked, they'd see that the rabbi had indeed requested them to re-run Ari's induction ceremony. The box Kane had brought over was the dummy box full of Brotherhood-mandated ritual props.

For the ceremony that I was going to perform, however, other than the dirt and water that I'd purchased specifically in Prague, it didn't matter where the other items came from.

Rohan reached into the box at his feet and pulled out a white tablecloth. "Where do you want this?"

I snatched it out of his hands and lay it back in the box. "If you two are going to stay then keep out of the way and don't touch anything." I planned to follow Gelman's instructions to a T, not intending to drop dead because of some minor procedural screw up. "Sit on the sofa, both of you."

At least they did as they were told.

"Navela." Rabbi Abrams pulled a small, intricately carved box out of his pocket and held it out. Inside was the same Rasha ring that I wore, a gold band, engraved with a hamsa and dotted with a tiny blue sapphire. If the ceremony worked, the ring would fit itself to my brother's finger. I had him hold onto it for a bit longer.

I pulled Ari to his feet and positioned him in the center of the room. "Don't move."

I'd read and re-read Gelman's instructions. Could recite them backward and forward and still I wiped damp palms against my skirt in fear that I'd accidentally do something in the wrong order.

First, I positioned four white pillar candles on glass bases in a wide circle around Ari to delineate north, south, east, and west. I'd used an old compass earlier to mark out the correct directions. Moving the coffee table by the north candle, I spread the white tablecloth on it then placed my clay bowls on top of the fabric. Beside them went a shofar, a hollowed-out, carved ram's horn that I'd blow through to make a kind of trumpeting noise. Shofars were most closely associated with the Jewish new year, Rosh Hashanah, but also with mitzvahs and were part of my instructions now.

From the box I removed two white talleisim; knotted, fringed prayer shawls, which I placed next to the shofar. The ring box was the final item needed. I took it from the rabbi, but instead of placing it on the tablecloth, handed it, lid open, to my brother.

Ari was still fidgeting so I took both his hands in mine best I could with the ring box, looking deep into his eyes. Affirming our connection. He straightened his shoulders and nodded. He was ready.

Was I? I looked at my twin, standing tall and smiling at me, implicit trust in his eyes. I felt his love wash over me and knew, come what may, that I was. Taking a deep breath, I placed one tallis over Ari's shoulders and the other over mine to signal the beginning of the ritual. A symbolic garment to denote placing ourselves in a space conducive to sacred work.

Reaching into my skirt pocket for a book of wood matches, I lit each candle, starting with the north-most one and turning clockwise from there. Under my breath, I invoked the blessing Gelman had sent, transforming this space from profane to sacred.

I picked up the shofar, running a hand over the smooth, curved surface. Standing tall, shoulders back, I raised the shofar, starting the ceremony. I pursed my lips, keeping the upper one tight and the lower one loose as the rabbi had instructed. Rabbi Abrams had coached me on how to sound it last night. Or attempted to. The noise I'd produced was closer to a constipated moose than the clear sound he'd demonstrated but he'd insisted it was good enough for purposes of the ritual.

Right before I blew into it, I glanced over at Rohan and Kane expecting some snarky look. An eye roll at the very least. But the two of them were treating this ceremony with the solemnity and dignity it deserved. Kane leaned forward, his forearms on his thighs, watching me, rapt. Rohan's gold gaze was more hawk-like but just as captivated.

A single pure note trumpeted out of the horn when I blew into it. Hearing it, my heart soared.

I dipped my fingers into the clay bowl containing the purified well water, flicking three drops over first my head and then over Ari's. A ritual immersion. Keeping that bowl in my right hand, I picked up the bowl with the virgin soil from a mountain not dug by men and added it to the water. It formed gloopy clumps. I set the empty bowl back on the tablecloth, then stepped in close to Ari.

"Aleph, mem, tav." I smeared a line of watery dirt across his forehead with my right hand. "Aleph, mem, tav." Another line down his left cheek. Again and again, I recited the letters. The ones which spelled "emet"–truth in Hebrew–and which, according to legend, had brought the golem to life. I recited them until I'd outlined Ari with the dirt. My brother was the golem, the unformed substance that I prayed this ritual would complete.

I took a moment to center myself. This was the last step. The make or break moment. Quite literally.

Pulling a Swiss army knife out of my skirt pocket, I extracted the blade which I'd previously cleansed in fire. Holding it in my soil-smeared hand, I slashed my other palm in a diagonal line. "Emet." I flinched against the stab of pain.

A bright line of blood swelled on my skin.

Rabbi Abrams inhaled sharply. Every muscle in Rohan's body was tense. Kane had half-risen off of the sofa, perched on the arm.

I slashed another line perpendicular to the first. "Met." The word for death. The second slash burned a million times worse. I pressed my bloody palm to Ari's heart. "Rasha!"

Ari's heart beat slow and steady through his shirt. The sound traveled through my palm, up along my arm, vibrating from the heavy thrum. My arm shook, his heartbeat growing in strength as mine grew weaker and more fluttery.

There was a great sucking whoosh inside my head. White spots danced and spiraled in front of my eyes. Ari's heartbeat was joined by a sparking noise. A clicking sound like a lighter not quite catching.

My chest constricted. I was blinded by the white filling my vision. The clicking morphed into the explosion of a single spark, so loud it deafened, so tangible it snapped my head forward. My magic burst free wrapping my body like barbed wire. A million agonizing bites tore into my flesh.

I couldn't pull away. Ari's heart pounded in my skull drowning out all other sound, throbbing through my teeth as my magic tightened around me. I smelled blood.

The magic wire outside my body tightened and tightened; the magic knot within threatened to rip me in half as it fought its unraveling. I sagged, unable to breathe, unable to support myself. Propped up solely by the magic killing me.

"Met." A chorus of women's voices chanted in my head. Death and death and death.

The world went dark. Gelman hadn't prepared me for this but it was beautiful. Nothingness and totality. Peace at last.

Compelling, but it wasn't *my* choice.

"Chai," I whispered. Life.

My eyes snapped open. I gasped and surged to my feet from where I'd been crumpled on the floor.

The ring flew from the box to fit itself onto Ari's ring finger on his right hand. The silence in the room was absolute. My brother held up his hand, looking from it to me in wonder. "You did it."

He crushed me into his arms.

"Told you so." I buried my head against his chest, holding him tightly.

Kane whooped, breaking the spell. He bounded over to us, joining in the hug.

"Exiting now." I ached all over and the boys' adoration, while appreciated, hurt.

Rabbi Abrams patted Ari on the back in congratulations. Rohan was busy welcoming my twin into the fold as well.

"This calls for a celebration," Kane said.

Ari and I exchanged grins. "Balls inside," he said.

I picked my tallis up off the floor where it had fallen, folding it carefully. "It's always about the balls inside with you."

"Is this rabbi appropriate?" Rohan asked.

"I enjoy the balls inside myself," Rabbi Abrams said, winking at us. I snorted. Go, Rabbi.

Rohan's and Kane's double take was a thing of beauty.

Snickering, Ari explained to the poor gobsmacked men. "St. Honoré cakes? The ones with the little cream balls on top? Our baker makes one with the balls both on top and inside, instead of just sponge cake inside."

"Ari requests it for every occasion." One of the best things my parents ever did was to let Ari and me each choose our favorite cake on our joint birthday. That meant I didn't have to give up my more-chocolate-per-square-inch extravaganza to enjoy balls inside.

"Very delicious," Rabbi Abrams pronounced. "Nava, may I have some water?"

"Of course." I escorted him to get a drink, leaving Kane taking bets on what Ari's magic power would be.

My parents hadn't known about the ceremony today so the kitchen wasn't in the pristine state my mom normally demanded for rabbi visits. A couple of dirty mugs in the sink, magazines on the counter, and the miscellaneous cork board a disaster of notes, flyers, and postcards. They were going to freak out that they'd missed Ari's induction, and even better, since they'd believe that Rabbi Abrams ran it, I was in the clear.

I sat down at the table with the rabbi as he drank.

"Mazel tov. I'm very proud of you," he said.

"Thank you." I debated telling him about the gogota, letting him know what the Brotherhood was up to because I'd be willing to bet he had no idea. But I didn't. Today was about celebration. Plenty of time to fight again tomorrow.

Placing one hand on the table, he pushed to his feet. "I'm going to speak with Ari and then update the Brotherhood." His eyes crinkled in a smile. "So glad I correctly performed the induction with your brother in the proper frame of mind this time." Movements slow but full of dignity, he left.

I lay my head on the table, exhausted. All the terror I'd held in both before and during the ceremony kicked in, leaving me shaky. It wasn't that I could have died but that I could have screwed up and hurt Ari somehow. There were so many ways this could have gone wrong, and the fact that it went right kind of overwhelmed me.

I'd done it. Me. I'd stuck to my convictions and Ari was now Rasha. Once more on track for his destiny. I couldn't believe that I'd be getting my brother back down the hall from me, fighting with me and I couldn't wait to see what magic power he manifested. Like all Rasha, it would be tied to some aspect of his personality. I stood, wondering if I'd learn some deep dark secret about my twin when it did.

"That was incredible," Rohan said.

"Thanks," I mugged. I carried Rabbi Abram's glass over to the sink. "I was pretty fucking glorious if I do say so myself."

That got the requisite smile as Rohan walked over to me. "Agreed." He shifted. "Nava." Ah man, that was the reluctant solemn tone that signaled the start of "we need to talk." I knew I should have officially broken things off. I'd stupidly assumed he'd do the gentlemanly thing after his talk with Lily and go away so I never had to see him again.

Bring it, Snowflake. "Yes?"

"I'm not doing this anymore."

Join the club. "It was a good ride while it lasted." What was this brutal disappointment coursing through me? *We only love what we don't fully possess.* Maybe that was it. Not love, obviously, but we'd both possessed and been possessed. There was nothing left to want. We had an expiration date, and this was it.

"A good ride," he repeated.

"Yeah," I said. "Our hook-up was the ultimate in escapism. This admittedly amazing–" I decided to soften the blow to his ego because he was staring at me incredulously, "orgasmic drug I'd been using to keep myself happy in the face of my life turning upside down."

My words hit me with the force of an epiphany. Wow. I really and truly didn't need Rohan to help me escape my reality anymore. No matter what the future held, demons, misogynistic rabbis, I'd face it head on. Maybe it would be lonely, maybe not, but I wouldn't be alone in the dark. I'd have me. If only all of Samson's victims had realized the same thing about themselves. He'd never have been able to peddle his lifestyle as the only game in town, never have been able to feed off the envy and misery he inspired.

I'd told myself a million times that it was over between Rohan and myself, but I'd been saying it for all the wrong reasons. Lily's presence in his life was irrelevant. I'd miss it, miss him in that way, but I didn't need him to fill some void or fear. "I don't need this anymore."

"No, you don't." Rohan's lips curved up in a small smile. "But this isn't about need."

"Then what is it about?"

He braced his hands on the cabinets behind me, one on either side of my head, trapping me.

I flattened myself against the bamboo wood. No. He couldn't. He wouldn't.

He did.

Rohan kissed me. My body stiffened with the first touch of his lips. Alarm bells clanged in my head.

He knew the rules.

And I knew what I did when people broke the rules: run away very fast. But I couldn't move. Not because he was forcing me, though I'd have been very happy to blame my inaction on some kind of paralytic in his lips. No, I could have easily broken off the kiss, but I was powerless to do so.

Rohan didn't touch any other part of me, making me focus on the sensation of his mouth on mine. He kissed me leisurely, like we had all the time in the world and not like the merest brush of his lips had lit me up like a pinball machine on full tilt.

The kiss was uncomplicated and all the more shocking because of it.

I tentatively relaxed, kissing him back. His hand cupping the back of my neck, Rohan kissed me like I was precious. I was a dry river bed flooded by a giddy rush. The sensation tore mercilessly through me, ripping through all my defenses leaving them broken dams.

I leaned into him, gripping his shoulders.

Rohan groaned, his hand on my hip, jerking me to him. He boldly thrust his tongue into my mouth, demanding complete control, tasting of candied fennel seeds and raw need.

The kiss turned reckless, as seductively dark as it was exhilaratingly bright. It slowed and lingered before once more turning feverish. A river of whirling eddies and slow, lazy drifts.

Rohan kissed me harder and rougher, absolutely presumptuous, his hands fisting in my hair. I pressed my palms against the small of his back, drawing him even closer. I wanted no delineation between where he stopped and I started.

I was delirious, lost in a live-wire crackle. My blood was rocket fuel, my heart lifting off under this hot breathlessness. Nothing had ever prepared me for this kiss. It demanded everything. Gave everything.

Rohan planted a lingering kiss beneath my jaw before pulling away. I reached out blindly for him, my fingers closing on air. Opening my eyes, I found him watching me. He didn't give me a smug smile like I expected. In fact, he looked troubled, like maybe he'd gotten more than he expected and wished he could take it back.

I placed my fingers against my swollen lips, my heart hammering in my ears.

Any qualms of his vanished between one blink and the next, as with the arch of an eyebrow, Rohan tucked a lock of hair behind my ear, his arrogance back in full form. "Any questions?"

END OF BOOK TWO

Acknowledgments

Thank you to my dear friend, Dr. Kim Binsted, for her insights on both superpowers and physics. Any mistakes are my own.

Tina Suraci, big hugs for your ice bar knowledge and, most especially, my first ice bar experience. There's no one else I would rather have gone with.

Alex Yuschik, my rock star editor, I honestly have no words. These books would be pretty pathetic without you and you have all my gratitude.

To my family, can I tell you how lucky I am to have you? None of this means anything without you.

Finally, thank you so much to everyone who followed me from my Tellulah Darling YA romcoms to take a chance on these new, more adult books, and those of you new readers who've embraced Nava, Rohan, and the gang. Thank you for promoting me and jetting these books to the top of your TBR pile to review. I am so humbled by this gift you have given me.

This book is for all of you, especially all you fabulously mouthy, funny, brilliant women.

THE UNLIKEABLE DEMON

HUNTER: NEED

(Nava Katz, #3)

DEBORAH WILDE

te da media
vancouver

Publisher's Note: This is a work of fiction. Names, characters, places, and incidents are a product of the author's imagination. Locales and public names are sometimes used for atmospheric purposes. Any resemblance to actual people, living or dead, or to businesses, companies, events, institutions, or locales is completely coincidental.

Book Layout ©2015 BookDesignTemplates.com

Cover design by Damonza

Library and Archives Canada Cataloguing in Publication

Wilde, Deborah, 1970-, author
        The unlikeable demon hunter : need / Deborah Wilde.

(Nava Katz ; 3)
Issued in print and electronic formats.
ISBN 978-1-988681-04-7 (softcover).--ISBN 978-1-988681-05-4 (EPUB).--ISBN 978-1-988681-06-1 (Kindle)

        I. Title.   II. Title: Need.

PS8645.I4137U56 2017   C813'.6   C2017-901640-7
                                               C2017-901641-5

1

"I could do with a boy or a burrito." I rubbed my belly, the silky material of the long-sleeved tunic that I wore as a mini dress sliding under my fingers. Were TV shows and book covers to be believed, I'd stake out my prey with a sleek fall of hair, clad in head-to-toe leather. Too bad my curls were allergic to flat irons and tight leather pants gave me yeast infections. Learned that the hard way.

"In that order?" My twin brother Ari was a disembodied voice in the shadows.

I side-stepped the run-off dripping from the broken rain spout onto the alley's cobblestones, thinking fondly of my double-breasted, classic trench coat back inside the bar. "Depends on how good the burrito is."

The bar's dented back door crashed open, releasing a spill of music, a sharp blast of chatter, and two demons glamoured up to look human.

I jerked my chin at them. "Took you long enough."

The taller of the two, Zale, swaggered toward me in his white shitcatcher pants, his white vest stretched tight across his wiry torso, and his fedora perched rakishly atop his bald black head. He cocked his finger and thumb at me like a gun. "All right, all right, all right."

Fucking Matthew McConaughey wannabe. The original was more than enough.

Skirting the edge of the dim pool of light cast by the sole bulb over the door, I sashayed forward on my three-inch heels, a whisper of a breeze rippling my hem. "You promised me witches." I trailed a finger down his chest. "Gonna deliver?"

His friend Dmitri barked a laugh.

Zale shot him an amused smile. "You want the goods? Pony up." He reached for his elastic waistband.

I reached for my magic.

Look at that. I was faster. Electricity snaked out of my fingertips in a forked bolt.

"My implication that I was willing to blow you for their whereabouts?" I smiled sweetly and cracked open the concrete beside his shell-toe shoes. "Total fabrication."

Zale blurred out of sight. I wasn't concerned because this raku demon only had short range flash stepping ability and a dark shadow had disengaged itself from the gloom to give chase. Ari, my fellow demon hunter.

My brother's smirk, sharp as a razor's edge as he tracked the demon, made it all too clear how hunting suited him.

"What are you?" Dmitri's perplexed and vacant blink at me fit right in with his dishwater blond man bun and tapered floral pants, but was still insulting.

"I'm Rasha."

He laughed. "You can't be a hunter, you're a girl."

I grabbed my boobs with a shocked gasp. "*That's what this means?*" Damn, I had a good rack. "I can't sing either, but that doesn't stop me practicing for *The Voice* auditions. So, yup. Girl and Rasha."

He made a sound of disgust.

I didn't need that kind of disrespect today, so I flicked a bolt of electricity into his crotch.

The felan demon dropped to his knees, his wheezed exhale a pretty good dying bagpipe impression.

"You were saying?" I asked.

Five tentacles sprang from his chest like Shiva's arms, the one closest to me striking the ground with a sticky slurp. The air fogged with the stench of patchouli and fungus.

I swiped at my watering eyes. "You're missing a tentacle."

"I'm perfect the way I am." His snarled—and issue-laden—response made the hair on the back of my neck stand up, but the real kicker was his front tentacle lashing across my forearm.

Take the precision of a bee sting and magnify it by the mass destructive power of a nuclear bomb. That was close to the searing fire that his paralytic touch shot along every nerve ending in my body. I wheezed a gasp, my arm dropping to my side.

The felan snickered.

"Shut it, asswipe. At least I'm not wearing floral pants." I tried to move my arm, receiving a wet noodle dangle for my efforts.

He fingered his fabric. "I'm wearing these pants ironically."

"Not paired with that hair abomination you're not. Might as well wear a button that says, 'I'm a demon, ask me how!'" My arm felt like my mouth after a dental procedure—numb, swollen, and clunky. Had my elbow been able to drool, I'm sure it would have.

A sliver of moonlight guided me as I fired my magic at Dmitri, but the paralytic was already taking root, thick and sticky as molasses. My stream of blue and silver current stuttered out of me, the demon dodging it with ease.

Dmitri swaggered in closer, locked a tentacle around my ankle, and pulled. I crashed down on my ass, my legs wobbling like the finest Jell-O. "Cute panties," he said.

I'd have killed him just for the use of that horrid word but my heart hammering at an unsustainable speed was all I was capable of. He pinned me down and wrapped a tentacle around each appendage like I was Gulliver imprisoned by the Lilliputians.

I stiffened out like a surfboard. My breath punched out of me in a scream, my pain spiking like I was coated in bubbling lava. I was half-convinced my flesh was melting from my bones. Gritting my teeth, I forced my magic out. Animated lightning bolts danced over my now-blue skin and a wave of current burst from my entire body to wrap around the demon like barbed wire.

It knocked the felan back a whopping half-step, but at least it broke his hold. I still couldn't move, but I could take a deep breath.

"Witches. How do I find them?" I tightened my magic net on him, taking perverse satisfaction in his eyes bugging out of his head.

"Urban. Myth." He flailed his tentacles, caught tight in my web. "There are no witches, you moron."

My vision kaleidoscoped into black blobs, the paralytic sinking its hooks into every inch of me. Lungs burning, nervous system in a Code Red panic, I had to finish him off, except I was now seeing multiples of the lemon-colored tentacle tip indicative of his weak spot. His Achilles heel and the place I needed to direct my magic in order to kill him.

I dug down into my last molecule of energy and nuked Dmitri with so much magic that he charred like a well-done steak. The air reeked of fetid BBQ, but I'd hit his sweet spot and dispatched him into oblivion with a puff of lemon-colored-yet-hippy-scented-dust. At least I didn't have to clean up after myself. Lack of a corpse, the sole public service that demons provided.

Fumbling for the edge of my Spanx with spasming fingers, I pulled out the modified EpiPen tucked against my hip and blue-to-the-sky'd it in my thigh. Thanks to the fast-acting antidote, the pain in my body subsided from "rip my skin off" to "whimper madly." Much better. I twitched my fingers, happy to note they still moved, then flopped over, hands braced on the cobblestones. Luckily, the stones were dry. Landing in an unidentifiable puddle would have been an indignity too far.

The bulb over the back door cracked and sizzled out. I turned my head away from flying shards and sat up.

Zale blurred into the alley, eyes wide. Shadows pressed in as if they had weight and heft, tinged with an ashy smell. The raku backed away but he was cornered on all sides by darkness.

There was a languid elegance to my brother's magic.

Zale spewed some super homophobic insults involving Ari's interactions with his fellow hunters in a way I was almost positive was
impossible.

The shadows expanded, like they were taking a deep breath, before
wrapping themselves around each of Zale's arms and his upper torso.
They jerked the demon back against the brick wall, the crack of his
skull momentarily shutting him up.

I yanked out the doctored-up EpiPen still sticking out of my leg. It
contained a felan antidote provided by the Brotherhood of David, the
testosterone-laden secret society of demon hunters that I had become
the first female member of. The antidote had dealt with the worst of
the poison–the fatality part–leaving me merely battered and bruised.
A run-of-the-mill Wednesday.

Zale struggled as Ari strolled closer, a pale blue silhouette. The
raku's tendons popped along his skin as he strained against his bonds.
"Fucking psycho."

Ari stilled. Flexed his fingers. The shadows holding Zale gave a
sharp jerk, snapping both his arms out of their sockets. The demon's
roar cut off in a cough as a shadow slithered up his chest, wound
around his neck, and strangled him.

"*Ari.*" I scrambled to my feet.

My brother's eyes glittered dangerously. He edged his face close in
to Zale's and Zale flinched.

"Boo," Ari said with a hard smile and fired a shadow like a punch
into Zale's abs. His sweet spot. The raku gasped and disappeared,
dead.

With a flick of his hand, Ari caught Zale's fedora before it hit the
ground and flipped it onto his head.

Ugh. I winged my used EpiPen at him, where it hit his shoulder
and then clattered to the ground. "Seriously?"

Ari cocked his head at the bar's back door. "Ready to go in?"

Not hardly after his baby Drio torture impersonation.

Picking up the EpiPen, I exchanged it for a nubby joint from the tiny purse slung across my body, slid a bobby pin from my hair, and fastened it on as a holder before lighting up.

I exhaled a long column of smoke into the warm May night, my skin returned to its normal Snow White complexion.

"We'll find the witches another way," Ari said.

"I know." But I was running low on ideas. Over the past month, we'd sussed out campus wicca groups and employees of the new age bookstore Acacia Books. When neither of those avenues had panned out, we'd done what Rasha do best, worked our way up, okay, killed our way up, one demon at a time until we'd found this duo. I'd been certain Zale and Dmitri were our ticket to sniffing out actual witches instead of women who celebrated the goddess via pricey bamboo clothing and new age bush beating.

Insert sad trombone sound.

Ari made a "hand it over" motion and surprised, I did. All of my life, my handsome, serious twin had been the good to my not-so-much. Our parental unit's "golden boy" to my "big disappointment." Blond to my dark, the only thing we shared were our blue-gray eyes and absolute bond.

When I'd managed to get Ari inducted in his rightful place as Rasha, I'd bet that his power, reflecting an aspect of the user's personality, would manifest as some type of earth magic. Steady. Stable. Grounding.

I'd lost fifty bucks.

Ari lit up, practically deep throating the joint.

"Your technique needs work." Our friend and fellow Rasha, Kane Hashimoto, had joined us from inside the bar, hands jammed in the pockets of his dark jeans, his shock of black spiky hair even more explosive than usual.

Ari raised his eyebrows and sucked deep enough to hollow out his cheeks before passing the joint to me.

"Ew. I almost don't want it after that."

My brother offered it to Kane who shook his head.

"Uh, excuse me," I said, snagging the joint. "I said almost." I took a drag, letting the burn spear my lungs.

A group of friends passed by our alley with a clatter of heels on concrete and shrill drunken laughter. Once, before all the demon-hunting, I'd been that carefree. That oblivious. I held on to the sound of their laughter, wistfully wrapping it around me before letting it flutter free.

"How did the fact-finding mission go?" Kane asked. He'd agreed with my assessment that Ari and I could dispatch the felan and raku just fine.

"Dead end." I contemplated the hissing, glowing joint tip, the sweet smoke curling around us a definite upgrade from the rotting garbage emanating out of the nearby dumpster.

Ari clapped my shoulder in sympathy. He'd help me keep looking for the witches to make contact with the woman I'd hoped might become a mentor. I wanted a friend and a guide who both possessed magic *and* was female, the Brotherhood being sorely lacking in that department.

That was the reason I'd given Ari and Kane for my search anyway.

My brother patted his head. "I got a hat."

Kane grimaced. "Demon cooties."

"The demon was bald," Ari said.

The explanation didn't win Kane over. He grabbed the fedora and pitched it into the dumpster. "You're welcome."

Ari shook his head, his lips a flat line.

"At least you got to add another kill to your scoreboard, brother dear, making you still in second place to moi," I said.

"Only in your cheating reality." He snagged the joint.

Kane laughed. Japanese-Canadian with chiseled cheekbones and a tight body, he had two modes of dressing: barely and horribly. Tonight was door number two, featuring a Technicolor Eurotrash-striped nightmare. He rolled up his sleeves, carelessly folding up the cuffs.

"Look at you, big boy," I said, "you're still wearing a shirt."

"The night is young, babyslay." He peered at me. "You look like shit."

I flicked the lighter a few times. "And here I was going for utter shit."

Ari took one more hit then held out the joint to me. I waved his offer off. If I was considering the rainbow bruising on my arms a pretty accessory, I'd had enough.

Shouting broke out from a crack deal going down at the end of the alley. Since it involved all human players and the buyer took off, I didn't mix in, though the pricey cover I'd paid earlier tonight that could have gone towards getting the addict some food didn't sit well. In this neck of Vancouver, lush gentrification butted against low-income neighborhoods and the uneasy mix was sickening to anyone with a conscience. Or me.

Kane strode over to the dealer, now smoking a cigarette by the wall.

Ari frowned at the man, as if trying to place him. "Fuck." He ground out the joint and hurried after Kane, me at his heels, trying to get my brother's attention and have him fill me in.

Ari got to Kane before Kane got to the dealer. He stepped between Kane and the man, but Kane neatly sidestepped him, his eyes trained on the pusher.

"You ought to rethink your line of work." Kane smiled, dagger-sharp.

"Yeah?" The dealer flicked his lit butt at Kane.

Kane caught it, crushed it in his hand, and winged it back. The butt beaned the dealer on the nose. In retaliation, the dealer pulled a knife and lunged, but Kane deflected the strike, an almost bored expression on his face as he slammed the attacker's arm back into the wall, over and over again, until the knife clattered to the ground.

Kane shoved his palm into the dealer's cheek, pinning the guy's head back against the bricks. The Rasha's skin coated with a purple iridescent sheen.

My nose stung from the sharp tang of salt.

Ari made a tch noise.

The dealer threw his hands up. "Take it easy, man."

Kane casually ripped the dude's ear off.

My hands flew up to block the blood spray, but there wasn't any. The dealer's skin simply split open, droopy speckled gills popping out. He struggled, but Kane held him fast.

"Should have taken me up on my offer." Kane slapped his poison-covered hand against the gills. The demon just sort of dissolved under Kane's toxic touch and disappeared, dead.

Kane swayed on his feet, one hand shooting out for balance. Ari tried to grab his shoulder and steady him but Kane brushed him off. "Leave it. I'm good."

"Sure. Until your kidneys fail, idiot."

Kane shot us a bright smile. "But like all things about me, even my failure shall be glorious."

2

Ari filled me in about Kane being pulled off active duty for a while because of dangerously high salt levels in his blood after too many kills in too short a period of time. The cost of his particular magic, just like mine was risk of heart attack. Much as I wished otherwise, there'd be no point berating Kane.

"What kind of demon was that?" I asked, with a glance back.

"A fix. They feed off addiction." Ari shook his head, staring musingly at the bar's back door that Kane had already gone through. "Rare though. The only way to identify them is by a thickness in their throat where the gills are hidden."

I flung the bar's door open. "How the hell did he spot that all the way back in a dark alley?"

"He spots everything." I couldn't tell if Ari sounded annoyed or impressed.

If the witch-seeking fail wasn't enough, the bar was an irritating insult to injury. Too many bodies pressed too close together in hopes of getting even closer before night's end.

We muscled our way to the rickety metal table we'd secured with our jackets. For the amount this place charged to get in, the owners could have refurbished this old watering hole. The floor was sticky in patches, and the ceiling fans couldn't overpower the stench of stale beer and brittle desperation.

I crashed my ass onto the chair, grateful to be sitting down, then grabbed the muscled arm of a passing server. "There is a massive tip for you if you get us a pitcher of beer and a large order of wings in five minutes." The bar didn't do burritos but their miso-glazed wings were to die for.

Kane dropped down next to me, all iridescence and salt tang gone from his skin. He must have washed the poison off.

The saucy waiter pursed his mouth. "Sweetheart, we're under-staffed. I'm good but I'm no miracle worker."

I motioned to my two companions. "I'll throw in the phone number of the boy of your choosing."

Ari craned his neck to check out the beers on tap. "Whoring your own brother for food. Wow."

"Yes," I said. "Because for years women had to bear that burden. Feminism. Get on board."

"I'll take the non-whiny one," the server said.

Kane preened. "If you want me to call you back, you'll give me extra ginger dipping sauce."

The server winked at him. "Done."

Kane tracked the guy's ass as he walked away and Ari tracked Kane. This is what I'd been living with for the past month. Ignor-ing, longing, sexual tension, and more ignoring. I was living in a CW teen soap as the sassy best friend without any foreseeable love inter-est in my storyline. It was time to get these two together already so I could star in my own spin-off. Besides, they'd be adorable together. Provided they didn't turn their magic on each other leaving either a poisoned corpse or one eviscerated by shadows; but hey, every couple had their problems.

Tonight's plan to wisen these two the fuck up? Beer. That fine liba-tion that had kicked off many a beautiful romance.

The waiter was back in three minutes with tall glasses and an icy pitcher. "Wings in two." He pointed at a table of customers playing a loud drunken game of "I never." "I switched their order with yours. The McRude ones can wait."

I waved the lager he'd poured for me in benediction. "Bless you, my son. Drink up, boys," I said to Ari and Kane.

Holding my dark curls off my neck with my free hand, I pressed the pint glass to my forehead, sighing at the nip of condensation against my skin. "It's great to kick back with good friends."

Silence. I'd lost them to their phones. I snapped my fingers. "Social time, gentlemen. Be social."

They grumbled, but the wings arrived, and that did the trick. I dug in with a munchie-induced fervor, happy to eat and people watch. "If my life was a movie, I'd fire whoever cast the extras. These people are blech." I jerked a chicken wing at a couple engaged in a nauseating display of PDA. "Especially them. I can't stand them."

I sucked the rich, slightly spicy glaze off chicken skin that was so crispy, it crackled when I bit it.

Kane looked over. "You know them?"

I dipped another wing in the tangy ginger sauce. "No."

"Nava hates lots of people she doesn't know." Ari nodded his thanks as I topped us all off with more beer. "It's her special talent."

"I'd settle for them turning off the baseball game and *Grease*." Kane glanced at the muted TV screens hung above the bar, dipping his sauce-coated fingers in the small bowl of warm water that had come with our order. "Sports and musicals, the seventh level of Hell."

I gasped, hand to my heart.

Ari facepalmed. "Now you've done it."

"*Grease* is the seminal cinematic exploration of teen culture," I said.

Kane grabbed a napkin. "No way. *Cruel Intentions*."

I eyeballed the remaining wings, pulling my generously estimated third into a pile. "Wanting to fuck late 90s Ryan Phillipe does not make something seminal."

Kane and Ari both leaned back, arms identically crossed. "Says you," they said in unison.

Perhaps bonding over their mutual interest in screwing a third party was not the way to foster romance. Hmm. Further thought was required.

I nibbled on a wing. "I'd argue that contrary to popular belief, *Grease* doesn't have a happy ending."

Ari paused, his glass halfway to his mouth. "Criticizing the movie? Are you concussed?"

"No. It's still a mostly perfect film. I'm merely older and wiser," I said. "See, it ends with Sandy sewing herself into a catsuit that makes peeing impossible. She'd totally rather be in her ponytail and poodle skirt but she's so sweet that she's not going to say anything, letting her bitterness build until it manifests in a brain aneurysm." I pulled the dipping sauce away from Ari. "Don't hog the sauce."

"Much as I cannot believe I'm encouraging this conversation," Kane said, "I'd say they both compromised and got their happily-ever-after."

"Please. The second Danny saw he'd broken her, he had that stupid letterman's sweater ripped off. Couldn't even make it through the first verse of 'You're the One that I Want.' Greedy bastard wanting things how he wanted them." I tossed the bones onto the plate. "The only sane one was Rizzo. She would have taken one look at the indignity of the catsuit and the flying car and said 'Fuck this, I'm out.'"

In a move of stealthy beauty, Ari exchanged a runty wing in his pile for a majestic specimen in mine. "Rizzo wouldn't have been asked into the car in the first place."

I picked up a fork, holding it tynes-out above my remaining wings. "Right? The guys knew that. She's fierce. She wasn't going to change for anyone. I am Rizzo. Hear me roar." I ran a finger along the tynes. "I got distracted by the bullshit car and forgot I was Rizzo."

"Jesus," my brother muttered.

"Ah." Kane's voice was gentle. "You got distracted by a lot more than the car, babyslay. Ro–"

I jabbed the fork at him. "Say his name and I'll kick your ass six ways to Sunday."

Kane patted his butt. "I see through your pathetic excuse to touch it."

My stoner brain was taking over and I was about to get maudlin. Nope. Time to put happy sloshy brain back in the driver's seat. I motioned to our server for another pitcher, but he was super harried and didn't see me, so I nudged my brother, who was busy eye-fucking some guy at the bar.

That was wrong. He should have been eye-fucking Kane. No. Ew. "Less catting around, more paying attention to your tablemates."

"You're just jealous you can't sample what is so readily available," Ari replied, twirling a finger around the bar.

Excuse me? I tapped my fork dangerously against my plate. "Because I accidentally crazy-glued my legs shut?"

"Because of he-who-shall-not-be-named," Kane said, disarming my weapon before swiping a wing from me.

The men fist-bumped.

"Voldemort?" Peeved, I stabbed the wing back. "No problem. We're just good friends."

Ari rolled his eyes, accompanied by an aggrieved sigh that had totally been my signature move. When I was fourteen.

"Oh, for the days when you were still a nice guy. Demon torture really changed you, bro."

Ari held up his glass in cheers.

"Nice guys are only good for one thing," Kane said.

"What?" I licked glaze off my fingers.

"Corrupting. And when done right?" Kane drank some beer. I suspected it was more for effect than thirst. "Highly rewarding."

Ari made a derogatory sound.

"I'm sure you've had loads of experience with that," I said.

Kane shook his head. "Just one."

I wadded up my napkin. "Somebody shoot me."

My brother gave Kane a lazy smile. "Except you weren't rewarded that time, were you? Guess you're not the irresistible sex god you think you are." He pushed his chair away from the table and sauntered off.

Kane flicked beer droplets at his back. "That's rude. I'm exactly the irresistible sex god I think I am." He left as well, swaggering in the opposite direction from Ari.

What was *actually* rude? Me sitting here still drinkless. I elbowed my way through the packed room, following Ari's path to the bar.

"What can I get you?" The scruffy bartender trained a polite smile on me.

I bit down on my bottom lip, wondering what his stubbled jaw would taste like. "Pepper," I sighed.

"Pardon?"

I tore my eyes away from his chin.

"G bombs." I amended. My favorite shot of cinnamon schnapps and vodka. I held up two fingers, eavesdropping on the conversation next to me while I waited.

To be fair, it was more of a monologue, punctuated by vague agreement from the other party. I suspected his lack of participation was because his IQ, like mine, was plummeting at the inanity spewing out of the main speaker. I almost had to bail on my eavesdropping to preserve what little brain function I had left when the monologuist said, "...and then I sobered up and *didn't* get the Harry Styles tat."

"Wise move," Ari said to the beautiful boy without a hint of sarcasm.

"You cannot be this hard up," I said into my twin's ear.

Loud laughter from the far end of the bar flitted over to us. I caught Kane licking salt off rock hard abs, an empty shot glass in his hand and a Cheshire Cat smile on his face.

"Next round's on–" But Ari and Pretty Boy were gone. I was all for no-strings attached hook-ups, but that had never been my brother's style. Somebody had to be the good twin in our dynamic and since he'd perfected the role, I'd appreciate him staying out of my theatre of shock and awe. That was *my* leading lady material.

"Here you go." The bartender lined my drinks up.

I paid him, added a generous tip, and slammed the first shot back. The booze warmed my throat, making my battle pain, if not obsolete, then well-obscured. Kudos to my accelerated Rasha healing abilities. I'd still be bruised for a while though, hence the long sleeves tonight.

"That looks good." A plus-sized chick on the stool to my left tapped her French manicured nail in front of my remaining shot. She propped her elbow on the bar, head in hand, and tilted her face to mine, her eyes endless pools of brown. Her black hair was pinned in a messy chignon, and she was all curves in her pencil skirt and white tank top.

"It is," I said. "Provided you like cinnamon."

"Fortunately, I do."

The *Entertainment Tonight* segment on the TV mounted above the bar caught my eye. Specifically the footage of the famous singer on the red carpet last night for some party at Child's Play, the music fest happening in London to benefit war orphans.

A flurry of light bulbs flashed in his smug face as he grinned his rock fuck grin for the cameras, decked out in black leather pants and a metallic black T-shirt, his hair spiked up and eyeliner ringing his gold eyes.

Rohan Liam Mitra, ladies and gentlemen, the asshole who hadn't replied to any of my texts because he was on a mission but who now was, apparently, back on the grid and just ghosting me. I downed my second shot, slamming the glass back on the bar hard enough that I checked I hadn't cracked it.

"Bad night?" the girl asked.

"You could say that." Weeks ago, Rohan had left on a last-minute assignment to Pakistan to hunt down the demons that had killed four Rasha. Fine, had to go where the Powers That Be sent you, I got that. But you didn't just fire off an arrogant "any questions?" and leave my stunned-yet-perfect self without so much as a third party "Rohan says 'hey.'"

I smiled at the woman. "Thanks for asking about my night. It's more than I can say for my charming companions, wherever they went." I held out my hand. "Nava."

"Audrey." Her grip was firm, her skin warm against mine.

As quite the peen aficionado, girls didn't generally light me up, but there was something heady about her. "Could I buy you a drink?"

A feline smile spread across her face. "I'd like that."

Audrey was smart and funny and mostly kept me from sneaking glances at the TV every three seconds, where Paul McCartney mugged with Rohan as they gave some interview outside the party. Did they not have any other performers to focus on at this stupid event?

"...and the best part was just jumping off the boat every morning into the tropical waters, in this endless bay of blue."

I leaned in closer to catch Audrey's description of her Vietnam travels over the noise of the bar, her vanilla scent teasing my senses. "That sounds amazing."

Her hand skimmed my arm. "It was."

Onscreen, the photo frenzy had intensified to the point of me having to blink against the strobing white light. Freaking Shakira was giving Rohan a giant hug. He said something to make her laugh then squeezed her shoulder.

My supposed fuck buddy had upended my life, smashing through my "no kissing" rule with a kiss that had lit up my soul and quenched an ache inside me. I'd been like a woman so dehydrated, she hadn't even realized she was dying of thirst.

Rohan didn't need to call. I didn't need to call.

I eyed the smattering of freckles across Audrey's collarbone that I intended to lick my way across like a map to nirvana. "Wanna get out of here?"

She licked a drop of G Bomb off her lower lip, her smile blooming wide and filthy. Excellent.

3

"Get out of here" was a relative term. We made it as far as the bathroom, crashing into an empty stall, our lips locked together. I moaned, licking into the corner of her mouth.

Rohan had left me with a simmering need that my new vibrator couldn't satisfy, erotic dreams that I couldn't escape, and a desperate yearning that frequent underwear changes couldn't accommodate. I craved the glide of skin on skin, fingers plunging, and the taste and feel of lips on mine.

Kissing was definitely back in my world.

Audrey rocked her hips against me. I palmed her breast, hot and heavy in my hands, thick-headed with lust.

The main bathroom door crashed open, Kane's cheery "Incoming," booming through the space. There was some giggled shrieking from the women at the sinks and a "Watch the hands," from my brother.

The giggling continued through the women's departure.

Audrey bit my lower lip, her fingers inching their way up my thigh.

A stall door banged. Then another one.

Then ours, catching me in the shoulder as it swung open. "*Hel-lo,* cherry ChapStick."

"Piss off, Kane," I snapped, not taking my focus off Audrey.

Audrey twined her leg around my ankle. "What she said."

"What the hell is wrong with you?" Ari asked.

I slammed the graffiti-covered cubicle door shut with my ass and crushed my lips to Audrey's, sucking on her tongue, the taste of cinnamon driving me wild.

Ari pounded on the stall door.

"Boyfriend?" Audrey asked, pulling out of the action.

I gagged. "Annoying brother."

"Who will get more annoying if you don't stop what you're doing," he said from the other side of the stall.

"That's rather homophobic of you, Ari," Kane said. "And hypocritical given what you were up to ten minutes ago. Huh. Maybe hypocritical should have gone first?"

"Your dad forgot to give him 'the talk,'" Audrey murmured, her lips trailing up my throat.

I snickered, then shivered as she sucked a sensitive spot under my ear.

Another pound on the stall door.

Growling, I flung it open. "*What*?!"

Ari braced his hand on the door so I couldn't slam it again. "You don't kiss."

"I beg to differ," Audrey purred. Oh, I liked her.

"It's your golden rule," Ari said.

"I never met a rule I couldn't break." I shooed him off.

He went nowhere.

Kane splayed a hand on the counter, gave a horrified look at whatever he'd touched, and washed his hands. "So she wants to open her legs and not her heart. So what?"

"Aren't you a charmer?" Audrey drawled.

"Your place?" I asked Audrey. She nodded and I grabbed her hand, ducking past the assholes in our path, and leading her out of the bathroom.

Kane strolled alongside Audrey. "It's not judgment." He shot a pointed look at Ari keeping pace with me. Stupid Rasha wouldn't recognize a brush off if it bit them in the ass. "I'm all for living life on one's own terms."

"I know what happened with you and Ro," Ari said.

I cut through a knot of women crowding the bar, hoping to ditch him in the fray.

"Ro?" Audrey said. "Is that your boyfriend?"

"Ha! No."

"He kissed you," Ari said, rejoining us on the other side of the people cluster. "Then took off. That's why you've been throwing yourself into your work this past month."

A server backed into our path.

Audrey ducked under his drink-laden tray. "Am I being used to punish some guy?"

"*No.*" At least, I didn't think so. "This is none of your business," I informed Ari. I stopped at our table and grabbed my trench coat.

"I have to live and work with both of you," he said. "I don't want to fucking deal with your collateral damage. Not when I finally got here."

I, of all people, understood why being Rasha without further complication mattered so much to him. But it wasn't fair to assume that, once again, I'd be the roadblock. "There's nothing to deal with."

Ari shifted to block me.

Kane mimed hitting a bell. "*Ding.* Corners." He manhandled a glowering Ari and me onto opposite sides of the table. Audrey came too, since I still had hold of her hand.

A couple at the next table turned our way as if waiting to be entertained by our drama.

"Do *this*," Kane wagged a finger between me and Audrey, "all you want, babyslay, but after the talk which must be had."

"You wouldn't say that if I were a guy," I said. Audrey snickered, helping me put on my coat. Chivalry, always a turn-on. "And since

Rohan is partying halfway across the world, consider the talk unnecessary."

Audrey stepped back. "Wait. Rohan, as in Mitra? As in lead singer
of the global chart-topping emo superband Fugue State Five?" she
squealed. We all stared at her and she shrugged. "I may have had three
or four of their albums. That's why you couldn't stop ogling him on
TV?"

"No. I mean, yes, but not like—"

"You want an introduction?" Ari asked Audrey.

I stepped on my brother's foot.

Kane slapped his hand over his mouth several seconds too late to
cover the laugh that burst out of him.

"I'm more a Janelle Monáe girl now." Audrey's hand slipped from
my grasp. She pulled the clip from her disheveled chignon, her hair
dropping like a curtain to her shoulders and hiding the sexy curve of
her throat. "We could have had fun but—"

I reached for her. "No past tense. Present tense."

She shook her head, keeping her hands out of reach. "Too much
drama for me. Hope things work out for you."

"Audrey, please. At least give me your number."

She waggled a wave at me over her shoulder and was swallowed up
by the crowd.

I whirled around to face Ari. "Happy?"

"Just sort your shit out." On that note, Ari left.

I lunged for him, Kane catching me around the waist as I batted
at the air between me and my brother's retreating back. "Can you
believe him?"

"He's scared and lashing out," Kane said, clapping a hand over my
mouth when I opened it to protest. "Think of what he's been through."

I yanked his hand off. "Like I don't know? I was the one who did
everything to get him inducted again."

He dropped down into a chair, waving our empty pitcher at a passing server. "Via witchcraft. Not the regular Brotherhood ceremony. Sit. You're giving me a crick."

I pulled off my coat and sat down. "He's being ridiculous."

"His entire life he'd been told he was a chosen one. Then he wasn't. You were. None of the regular rituals worked on him and the one thing that did make him Rasha was some witchy ceremony. Half of him is convinced it's temporary and the other half is terrified that even if it isn't, the Brotherhood will find out and take the magic away." Kane fixed a strand of his black spiky hair. "He doesn't want anything that might draw attention or reflect badly on him. As your twin, that includes you."

"Like you guys had some big heart to heart?"

"I don't do those." Kane patted his cheeks. "Excess emotion causes age spots." He beamed at the waitress who had returned with a sloshing pitcher and two clean glasses. "You do get that I've known Ari most of his life, right?"

"Uh, well, no."

Kane poured me a drink. "We grew up here. Were initiates together. Yeah, I'm five years older so mostly Ari was an annoyance underfoot, but for a lot of the time, me and him were the sole non-Rasha around."

"I hadn't thought about it like that." I accepted the proffered drink.

"No kidding. Ari was a perfectionist before all this happened. Now?" He whistled.

"Not fair. I want to be mad at him."

"Cheer up. If he goes on for too long like this, I'll help you kick his ass."

The rest of the evening was a bust, though our rousing duet of "Enough is Enough" on the cab ride back lifted my spirits. I made a fine Babs and Kane's Donna Summer smacked of sass.

Once back at Demon Club, a.k.a. the Brotherhood-owned mansion that served as the Vancouver chapter, I took a bag of BBQ chips into Kane's room.

"What do you think you're doing?" Kane glanced up from his computer, its two monitor set-up casting an eerie glow over him.

"Cutting my sexual frustration with a salt overdose."

Kane arched an eyebrow. "Okay, tactless. Care to rephrase?"

"Sorry," I said sheepishly.

He snorted. "Get crumbs in here and die."

"Whatcha doing?" I peered over his shoulder.

"Software patch to Orwell. Been having problems with it crashing."

"Who's Orwell?"

"What. Not who. Brotherhood in-house intelligence."

I laughed. "Do they know you call it that?"

He pushed me back a couple of steps. "They don't not know."

Hunters underwent a three-part process to become Rasha, starting with the Brotherhood tracking all male Rasha descendants, designating these babies "potentials." A rabbi performed a special ceremony on them when they were less than a week old and if that determined they carried the Rasha gene, the boys were elevated to initiate status.

Cue the next twenty years of studying all aspects of demon hunting, from demons types to fighting and ward building. At age twenty, decided upon because that's how long it took to complete training, have stopped growing, and be in the prime of health to accept the magic, the final induction ceremony occurred.

For some, hunting demons was all they stuck with, but others continued with school or specialized training, using that expertise in service of the Brotherhood. Ridding the world of evil spawn required a huge infrastructure. I'd recently learned much to my absolute shock, that another Rasha, Drio Ricci, had a degree in psychology. Kane had one in computer science, which he put to use developing and refining surveillance software. In fact, he spent more time doing that than actual hunting these days, which now made a lot more sense. He also did custom jobs for clients at David Security International, the Brotherhood's public persona.

"Question." I licked BBQ seasoning off my fingers. "Why live here at Demon Club? Wouldn't you rather have your own place?" Living and working together intensified all the relationship drama–romantic, sexual, or other–but I certainly hadn't been given a choice of housing.

I got comfy on his bed, careful to eat over the bag.

"I save a bundle in rent. But even better, I have a built-in reason to never bring anyone home." Kane swore under his breath and typed in a short series of commands. "Don't reroute, you bastard."

"What do you tell them?" My phone vibrated with a series of Twitter alerts for #RohanMitra. Huh. I had a blurry memory of setting that up sometime during pitcher number three. I flipped the screen face down on the bed.

Kane double-clicked the mouse pad and quiet acid jazz flowed out of the speakers in the corner of the room. "I drop the DSI name, invoke vague-yet-sensitive security issues that preclude me from bringing them to my place, and steer us back to theirs. Boys eat that James Bond shit up."

"That's cold. Maybe I want to invite people over and saying I live at DSI is weird." If I ever decided that anyone other than my bestie Leonie Hendricks was worth socializing with.

My stupid phone kept vibrating so I opened the damn Twitter stream to shut it up.

Rohan was trending. I crammed a handful of chips into my mouth.

"It's practical. Don't have friends who aren't Rasha." Kane watched the monitor a moment longer before he hummed in satisfaction, spun his chair away, and pulled his shirt off.

"You can't be serious. I need friends who aren't just men. Or hunters." I did a double take at one of the many Tweeted propositions for

Rohan from his diehard fans, the Ro-mantics. "Jeez, lady, his dick isn't magic."

"That's not what I've heard." Kane rolled his chair over to his dresser, opened a middle drawer, and pulled out a pair of manicure scissors. "Free advice. Keep the Muggle world at arms' length and you don't have to cut them off when the lies get too hard to keep track of."

I scrolled through photos of the Child's Play party. Someone had had a good time. I wadded up the empty bag of chips and hurled it at the trash.

Kane tensed, but as I made the shot, didn't comment. He stuck the scissors point up into one of his nipple rings and opened the blades. The bead that had been holding the ring closed popped off.

I winced. "That's how you deal? Cut the Muggles off when it gets too messy?"

"*That* would be cold. I don't discriminate between Muggle and wizard. I'm equal opportunity cut 'em off." He winked.

I navigated over to one of the myriad of Fugue State Five fan boards. The first several threads were devoted to speculation on what Rohan was doing. And who he was doing it with.

"While I applaud the sentiment, the sheer incestuousness of an all-Rasha environment is stifling. Twenty-four/seven Rasha *is* the messy part." I said.

Kane applied a drop of Astroglide to each side of the nipple piercing before rotating the ring, removing it. "Sucks to be you."

I stuck my tongue out at him, knowing he was teasing. "Don't distress me, Kane. You wouldn't want Ari learning that you're making his twin unhappy."

He brightened, unscrewed a new bead from the end of a short straight barbell, and slipped the body jewelry through his piercing. "Blackmail? Oooh, I love this game. Let's see who can disturb Ari more next time we see him, shall we?"

"Let's shall."

Kane secured the barbell in place. "How about this for sheer trauma value?" He broke into a series of high-pitched moans, waggling his eyebrows at me. Never letting me live down the fact that his bedroom was over Rohan's and he'd heard us. Many times.

My blush-avoidance failure made me cranky, not the thirty-seven comments on the fan boards with zero speculation on *my* inclusion in Rohan's life. "You sound like a cow giving birth. My sex noises are sexy."

I tossed the phone on the bed.

"No sex noises are sexy. Except for mine. But I'm the exception that proves all rules." He switched out his other nipple ring, beginning the process all over again.

"You're lucky I love you."

"My blessing and my curse. Now to convince the other twin."

My eyes bugged out. "You want Ari to *love* you?!"

"As if." Nipple rings switched out for new jewelry, Kane tugged on each barbell.

"You looooove him. You want to marry him," I sang.

"How adorable. No, I want to bend him over a sofa." He shot me a look of pure exasperation. "What is it with Katz twins thinking my intentions are honorable?"

"Is that what turned Ari off you before?" My brother was infuriatingly tight-lipped about his personal life. I had to share enough for the both of us.

"You assume he's turned off."

"Whatever." My eyes darted back to my screen, compelled to reach for the vibrating phone once more. Fools. Taylor Swift was not Rohan's type.

I smirked at the next few ridiculous pairings, then froze. @MainMitraMistress had posted a grainy photo of Rohan and his first love Dr. Lily Prasad breakfasting together. I recognized the restaurant as part of the hotel we'd all stayed in back in Prague last month. The Ro-mantic poster wondered if Rohan had reunited with lightning girl.

Kane pulled the phone out of my hand. "Quit torturing yourself."

I sank back against his mattress. "Help me, Obi Wan."

Kane lay down beside me, folding his arm under his head. "You're looking at this all wrong. Jettisoning flotsam is not a sacrifice."

I lay my head on his shoulder. "What about when you end up jettisoning someone who isn't flotsam?"

"If they cross a line and they should have known better?" The song ended, leaving Kane's next words quiet musings in the silence. "Tell yourself that's not a sacrifice either."

"Like that's so easy."

"It's a rough business, babyslay. I'm not going to say it won't hurt, but you have to look out for yourself. At the end of the day, no one else will." His expression was distant.

The two of us hung out in comfortable silence listening to music, until too tired to move, I passed out still-clothed on his bed. I'd planned to sleep late Thursday, though I'd swear I'd only had the shortest of naps when someone shook me awake, with my gummy eyes, coated mouth, and all.

"Nava," said a breathy voice.

I squinted up at my assailant to find our resident admin Ms. Clara standing over me. She was like a mini ray of sunshine with her blonde hair, bright blue eyes, and golden skin.

"Later." I jammed a pillow on top of my head.

"Get up," she snapped in the commanding tone that made her one of Vancouver's most in-demand dominatrixes on her time off.

Weighing the risks to my personal safety, I decided sleep overrode finding myself on the wrong end of her famous whip and flopped over to face the wall.

She grabbed my arm, hauling me to my feet with surprising strength given her petite frame. "Rabbi Mandelbaum is here."

I blinked. The head of the Brotherhood and man who wanted me dead lived in Jerusalem. "Huh?"

"Nava Katz," a Russian-accented voice said. A man in his mid-forties wearing a kippah, with peyot sidelocks and a curled lip stopped just inside Kane's door. "We meet at last."

It was one thing to mock Rabbi Mandelbaum with a couple of continents between us but there was no ignoring the way the air itself seemed to charge with the power he embodied.

I swallowed, pushing my rat's nest of curls out of my face. Shit.

4

Rabbi Mandelbutt ordered me to meet him in the conference room once I'd made myself presentable. I swear he used air quotes on that word. Small mercies that Kane hadn't still been asleep in the bed. The rabbi would have ordered a giant scarlet "A" to be sewn on all my clothing.

He gave Kane a hearty handshake and headed downstairs.

I hopped into the hallway, tugging off a sock, shower bound. "Holy shit, are you okay?"

Kane looked down at his sedate green sweater and black pants. "I spy with my little eye something that looks like perfection. To what do you refer?"

"You're dressed like a normal human being." I jumped onto my other foot, ripped off my sock, and gasped. "You knew Mandelbaum was coming and didn't tell me."

"I found out yesterday and there was no point. You'd have stressed all day and I don't like drama." His lips quirked.

I chucked my free sock at him. "You can't even say that with a straight face."

"Obviously." Kane waved his hand around his head. "As no part of me may be denigrated as such." He pushed me into my bedroom. "Hurry up. You don't want to make a bad impression." He pursed his lips. "Worse impression."

Kane didn't know the half of it.

The Brotherhood was well aware that I'd gone to a witch for help. The question I couldn't answer then but hoped to now was: what else had come to light about my activities in Prague?

I made it downstairs to the conference room in time to get the full view of Rabbi Mandelbaum man-hugging my brother. I de-scowled my expression. Tried counting to ten. My twin embracing my mortal enemy was not something I could handle without coffee, much less breakfast.

The rabbi's face was alight–as alight as a bearded, sanctimonious douchebag could get–and I didn't think he was faking it. On the one hand, this was great since it meant he'd bought the lie hook, line, and sinker that Ari had been inducted via the normal ritual. On the other hand, the Eau de Boys' Club wafting off them made me want to hurl into the tasteful ficus beside the doorway. But if it meant Mandelbaum wasn't about to breathe down my neck about the witches, then I'd grimace and bear it.

"Our brilliant initiate is now Rasha! Mazel tov!" He gave Ari a final man-slap on the back.

My brother preened.

I cleared my throat.

With that telltale curl of his lip back in full force, the rabbi grunted at me and motioned for us all to sit down.

I took a seat next to Ari and across the table from the rabbi, smoothing a hand over my black, long-sleeved shirt with DSI printed in neat white letters over the heart. DSI was the most current incarnation of the Brotherhood's public face, both providing the organization with a cover and allowing them access to high level places and people that might provide valuable intel for their real business of demon hunting. Not that I'd done any work for that side of the society yet, but it couldn't hurt to look like a team player.

The rabbi distributed folders to us, then leaned back in his chair, fingers steepled together. The motion pulled his tailored navy suit tight across his broad shoulders. Rabbis were allowed to hit the gym. Who knew? "Rohan and Drio said your efforts to take Samson King down were invaluable."

"I think so," I said, examining his words for any trap.

Mandelbaum waved my comment off like what I thought was irrelevant. Which, let's face it, it was. The very fact of me being Rasha was an abomination to him. "Rabbi Abrams assures me that this business with the Vashar has been put to rest and you've learned your place."

I'd *earned* my place but I let the dig pass, giving myself a mental high-five that I'd at least swayed the head of the Vancouver chapter to my side. One Brotherhood rabbi down, dozens to go.

Ari frowned. "Vashar?"

"Did your sister not tell you about that? She got hold of an amulet imbued with dark magic, capable of stopping initiates from being inducted as full hunters."

Ari fumbled his folder for the briefest second before his expression smoothed out. "I see."

He didn't see at all but points to Mandelbaum for shit-disturbing.

In a brilliant bit of misdirection, Dr. Gelman, the witch I'd gone to for assistance, had given me a Vashar. The Brotherhood, specifically the six rabbis who made up the Executive that ran the organization, were convinced that I'd taken the amulet in a jealous attempt to stop Ari from becoming a hunter. Their focus on *that* violation meant they'd missed the real crime—Gelman giving me the magic ceremony to induct Ari as Rasha.

"I love my brother," I said to Rabbi Mandelbaum. I hoped I sounded contrite and not relieved. The Brotherhood would kill Ari for having been inducted via "witchcraft" and kill me if they discovered I possessed induction magic. I mean, what if I decided to look for other females that had been missed as potentials and make them hunters as well? The horror. "My actions were ill-advised."

Where was that John Williams swell of uplifting music when you needed it?

"She's learned her lesson," Ari affirmed. "Nava realizes how lucky she is to be one of us."

Sarcasm or sincerity?

"Women like her are never satisfied with what they're given." Fabulous. Mandelbaum had been wronged by some female and I got to be the living embodiment of his gripes now.

I dropped my eyes to the high-gloss gleam of the mahogany conference table. Not because I was chastened, because I couldn't control the hate spitting from my eyes. I gouged my palms with my nails as hard as I could to get myself together enough to school my features into the epitome of contrition. "All I want, Rabbi, is to show you how devoted to the cause I am. Earn your praise."

True fact. I wanted to hear him acknowledge my worth right before I exposed him and all his Machiavellian ideas around doing whatever it took to win the war of good versus evil.

"I hope so," he said, smoothing his beard with one hand, "because your accomplice is dead."

I gripped the table. "What?"

"Esther Gelman," he sneered.

I bowed my head, willing my heart to start. I thought he'd meant Rohan. "De–dead?" My abashed quiver was a nice touch.

"She was killed by a gogota."

Back on my last assigned mission in Prague, versus the "self-directed demon slaughtering path" I was currently on, I'd been attacked by a modified gogota demon. The same type of demon had later gone after Dr. Gelman, making me positive the Brotherhood was behind it. After that incident, she'd gone on sabbatical from her tenured physics prof post at Ben Gurion University in Israel, put her email on auto-respond, and dumped her cell, given the "not in service" messages I kept getting.

Saying she was dead was the final nail in the rabbi's full-of-shit coffin. She'd sent me a letter *after* she'd been attacked. Off-line, in deep hiding, sure. But she wasn't dead. Also, interesting that he didn't mention my attack. Though he had balls for bringing the demon up, I'd give him that.

Then his balls turned brass because he went on. "Yes, your witch co-conspirator was killed by a gogota. A gogota that was modified with a metal spine rendering its kill spot inaccessible."

Ari shot me a pointed look because this was the first he'd heard of it. I frowned, unable to believe the rabbi would admit to the existence of the modified demon.

"Really?" Ari said.

"Yes," Mandelbaum said. "The witches are armoring demons for some reason and one retaliated. Who knows what fallout the Brotherhood will have to deal with as a result of their hubris?"

I fiddled with the fat gold band engraved with a hamsa that I wore, marking me as Rasha. Dr. Gelman had told me that the Brotherhood historically had painted witches as evil. It wasn't like my own personal experience with the Brotherhood had been that great, so I was inclined to think more kindly of the witches than my fellow Rasha. But still, Gelman's version of the witch-Brotherhood feud comprised the sum total of my knowledge about the conflict. Rohan had been devastated at the idea that the Brotherhood was modifying demons and sending them after their enemies.

Did I have this all wrong?

A muscle jumped in Ari's jaw, his eyes flint gray with only a sliver of blue. "If that's the case, then I'll personally see that these witches are brought down."

While Ari's reaction wasn't unexpected, it made me realize that more than ever, I needed proof of my suspicions. That was my actual agenda this past month and why I'd gone after Dmitri and Zale to tap into the witch network and contact Gelman. Though after the rabbi's bombshell, it might be a smart idea to put contact with the witches on hold and find proof on my own until I determined who was behind the rigged demons and the attacks.

Mandelbutt mistook my dismay for well, dismay, but for the wrong reasons. "You are Rasha. Have you nothing to say about this, Nava?"

Don't get me started. "It's a lot to take in."

The rabbi nodded. "Luckily, you have Ari to guide you."

"Nava is doing great. She's helped me take down a number of demons over the past few weeks," Ari said.

Helped? I'd dusted dozens of those suckers without Ari lifting a finger. The strain of keeping my lips clamped together caused a muscle to jump in my jaw.

Rabbi Mandelbaum braced his elbows on the table, speaking directly to my brother. "While I appreciate your commitment to fighting evil since you became Rasha, I'd like to officially present you with your first assignment."

Was that a thing? Funny, this was the first I'd heard of it.

"Thank you," Ari said. Had I not spoken with Kane, I might have missed the flash of relief across Ari's face.

Had my brother bothered to look my way even once while Mandelbaum verbally fingered him, he'd have noticed the too-toothy smile pasted on mine.

The rabbi indicated we should open our folders. "Our internal intelligence found a spike of people dying of supposed heart attacks here in Vancouver."

"How?" I asked.

For a second I didn't think he was going to answer me. "We have software that monitors 911 calls in all cities with chapters. Certain keywords trigger a deeper look."

Very cool. I flipped my yellow folder open and scanned the overview. "Could the heart attacks be just that? Aren't they one of the leading causes of death?"

"These deaths are suspicious." Rabbi Mandelbaum pulled out his buzzing phone, glancing at the screen before sliding it back inside his suit jacket. "Look at the ages."

I checked the file. Twenties to forties. Six victims in under two weeks. A notation indicated that none of them were smokers or overweight. No family history of heart disease, no sign of coronary artery disease, heart defects, high blood pressure, or high cholesterol.

"So the autopsies found no reason for the sudden heart failure," I said.

"As these deaths fall outside the scope of medical science, they wouldn't have, would they?"

My grip on my pen tightened in proportion to the blandness of my smile.

"Figure out what's causing this," the rabbi said.

"Who do I report to?" Ari asked.

I raised startled eyes to his. "Who do we both report to?" I mean, if we were going to get technical about this, and, why yes we were, I was the one with seniority. I was the one who'd actually participated in missions.

Both the rabbi and my brother shook their heads in identical motions, like I'd said something amusing.

Mandelbaum wasn't speaking to me when he answered. "Report to the Brotherhood via regular channels, in as much as any CO does. Make us proud." There were channels? A reporting system?

"I will." Ari and the rabbi shook hands.

Look at that. More Boys Club by Sausage Fest fogging up the joint.

Since I was nothing if not an awesome team player, and I preferred to lay into my twin with no witnesses, I held out my hand to shake as well. "Put me in, coach."

Mandelbutt ignored it. Right, I might be menstruating and therefore unclean. Like all religious Jewish men, he wouldn't ask and he wouldn't shake and risk contamination. "Dealing with the witches was strike one," he said to me. "Find the demon responsible for these deaths and perhaps the scoreboard can be reset."

"You're too kind," I said, biting the inside of my cheek hard enough to draw blood.

He clapped Ari on the shoulder one more time and left.

Ari flipped through the contents of the folder. "Give me a minute to divvy up the victims and then you can amass a list of suspected demons. Type or Uniques, whatever fits."

"Just because you pushed your way out of Mom first doesn't actually give you the right to pull rank on this."

"Someone has to be in charge."

"So it's automatically the one with the dick?"

He grabbed a pen out of a box on the table, jotting down some notes on the cover of the folder. "How about it's the one who trained for this his whole life?"

I took a pen as well, testing its ink with the words "Ari," "sucks," "rotten," "smelly", and "eggs." "How about this assignment is an equal partnership?"

"How about guess again because it was given to me?" Ari placed my half of the victims' list in front of me.

"How about go fuck yourself? I'm the one with actual field experience."

He drummed the pen on the table. "Explain what Mandelbaum was talking about."

I threw my hands up. "You're not even going to pretend to consider my viewpoint?" Screw the sob story Kane had given me about Ari being freaked out about his Rasha status. This was not supposed to be bros over Navas. Our twinship meant Nava über alles.

Ari sat there, waiting.

I squeezed the pen, its faceted edges digging into my skin. "You got me. With you already *not* inducted, I went to a whole bunch of trouble to get a magic amulet just in case anyone else bothered to find a way to make you Rasha so I could then undermine it. Mwah ha ha."

"Not the Vashar. Don't be an idiot. I know why you went to Dr. Gelman."

"Then what?"

"The gogota. You already knew about the modified demon. How?"

I tried to protest but he stared me down. "One attacked me in Prague."

"And you didn't tell me?" Ari pursed his lips. "Interesting."

"What is?" I pulled the pen away from where I'd been gouging it into the table.

"From the moment my induction went wrong, you made all the decisions about me. Deciding what I could and couldn't handle."

My fingers twitched as I fought the urge to jam the pen in his eye. That condescending tone of his masquerading as rational got under my skin. It always made me lose it, which always let Ari win any argument. At least my parents weren't around to tell me not to be so sensitive. "Is that how you see it?"

"You don't?" Ari waved it off as if that point was unimportant. He was so our lawyer father's son. "But now I find out that even knowing what the witches were up to, you still used one of their rituals on me."

I slammed my hand on the table. "*They* weren't up to anything."

That earned me a look of pity. "Even you can't believe that."

I jutted my chin out. "Can't I?"

"What possible reason would the Brotherhood have to modify demons?"

"The spine made the gogota harder to kill."

"No harder than a lot of other kill spots," he said. "You're grasping."

"No harder for a Rasha maybe," I said, "but they sent it after Dr. Gelman as well. Yes, she has magic but could she take down a demon? Especially one that was armored up?" The external metal spine blocked the sweet spot on the demons' backs. And the stegosaurus spikes running the length of the modification did serious damage in their own right.

I jabbed a finger at him. "Maybe the Brotherhood is sending demons after anyone who opposes their goals? You can't tell me that people high up in the shadowiest corners of government don't know about us. Some either aren't going to fall in line with what we do, or want to do things their way. You think the Brotherhood wouldn't go after them?"

I'd learned a few things from Dad, too. Like how to present a counterargument.

"They might," Ari said. "But not with demons. Demons don't work for humans."

"Not willingly. But they can be summoned and bound to do a person's bidding."

Ari rolled his eyes. "Stories, not fact. There is no way to bind a demon to your will. They might choose to work with another demon but they never, ever take orders from a human."

"What about Montague and the jax?" Jacob Montague, a Rasha, had engaged in a sexual encounter with a jax demon.

"That wasn't coercion. The jax needed that release to survive. Whatever prompted those gogota attacks stemmed from some demon agenda. Not a human one and definitely not a Brotherhood one."

"What reason would a gogota have to attack both me and Dr. Gelman? No, the Brotherhood is behind this. I just have to find the spine that was left behind after my attack and prove it."

I wished I'd examined that spine, but the metal had been so mangled and scorched that it hadn't looked like much. Then again, I was half-blind with gogota slime and rocking an après-battle shock, so I could have missed something. I'd magnetized the spine onto a lamp post with so much force even Rohan hadn't been able to pry it off. So there we'd left it.

Even though I'd emailed the restaurant next to where the attack had occurred to ask about it, by that time, the "art installation" was gone. I doubted some enthusiastic Czech sanitation worker had taken it. That meant it was either in the possession of the Brotherhood or the witches. Either way, finding it was my number one priority.

Followed closely by finding a way to test it for any traces of magic indicating the demon had been bound.

"Even if witches can't force a demon to do their bidding," Ari said, "doesn't mean they're not doctoring them in hopes of being able to use them for some other end."

"So witches are stupid *and* bad?"

Ari waved a hand at me. "Come on, Nava. The Brotherhood is a centuries-old organization dedicated to destroying evil and you think they're the potential villains here? Not some bunch of power-hungry women?"

I opened my mouth. Closed it. Looked at my twin and at the features as familiar to me as my own–the way his mouth pulled down slightly when he was annoyed, the two freckles high on his left cheek, the scar on his right forearm that he got when he broke my fall out of a tree–and for the first time in my life, I saw a stranger.

My choices were "all evidence to the contrary" versus my gut-level certainty and personal experience of misogyny that the Brotherhood was to blame. Sure, I had my doubts.

But he had none at all.

The low hum of the heat kicking in was the only sound in the room.

I scooped up my folder. "I better get to it, then."

Ari shot me an unsparing look. "Good."

Two hours later, hunkered down in the library, neither of us had apologized. An unwelcome first.

We worked in silence to compile a massive list of potential demons. Any demon who conformed to any aspect of the crimes, no matter how tenuous a connection went on it.

I'd cross-referenced the shit out of these crimes, giving 200% to the task, and refusing to give Ari any more real estate for his moral high ground. "Both genders. Different vocations," I said. "Different races, religions, times, and locations of deaths. Even one Jane Doe. A lot of possibilities."

I tapped my pen, perusing the list of victims: Ellen Chen, 40, mystery author, found at home, Davide Garza, 21, a student at Simon Fraser University also found at home, Max Bader, 30, a stockbroker, at a club, Jakayla Malhotra, 35, a mature student, found in her teaching assistant office, Reuben Epstein, 29, discovered after-hours at the restaurant where he worked as a pastry chef, and a Jane Doe about 23 or 24, in a low rent hotel, found yesterday morning. "You wouldn't happen to know the T.A., would you? Malhotra? She goes to UBC."

Ari was on summer vacation halfway through his chem major–with a biology minor–at the University of British Columbia where our mom, Shana, taught history and our dad, Dov, taught law. Me and university, on the other hand, were on a time-out to review our relationship.

He polished off his turkey sandwich. "Considering UBC has like fifty thousand students? Nope."

I rubbed the kinks out of my neck with fingers stiff from typing on my laptop. "There's no common factor in these deaths."

"There's one. The deaths themselves."

I stood up, pacing long lengths along the floor-to-ceiling bookshelves and masculine groupings of furniture. "How? There's nothing to help us identify how they were killed."

"Exactly." Ari pushed our lunch plates aside to fan out photos of the victims showing various angles of their bodies in the positions they were found. I no longer marveled at the information the Brotherhood was able to access. Having been around since King David's time, they'd entrenched themselves into all kinds of places. "The lack of wounds are the common factor. What demons kill without leaving a trace?"

I narrowed my eyes at him but he was already checking the online database in answer to his question. It hadn't been a test for me alone. I dropped back into my seat, pulling a fat tome towards me. Even with their database there was no beating the details found in the books the Brotherhood had amassed. "The felan do. If I hadn't had the antidote, I'd have left a beautiful unblemished corpse in that alley."

"Except for the patch of back hair you shave," he said dryly.

"One time when I was twelve." I jutted my chin up. "I outgrew my Sasquatch soul strip years ago thank you very much, and even if I hadn't, no shaming the Jewess for minor beauty flaws. Unlike some with their 'dry hands' requiring Vaseline kept under the bed."

"I have sensitive skin," he said.

The index didn't yield any entries for my searches related to "lack of a trace when killing" so I ploughed in to the book proper to check the demon entries one-by-one. "Blame circumcision."

His shuddered "ew" and punch to my arm was our reset to normal. I pushed my anger down with the silent vow that I'd gloat like crazy once I had proof that the witches weren't to blame for the gogota.

And when I cracked our assignment and destroyed this demonic serial killer first.

"I'd lose the poison demons," he said. "Or ones that freeze or strangle the life out of their victims."

"Why?"

He studied the victims' photos. "The vics look too peaceful. Before you took the antidote, you looked like you were trying to shit boulders."

"Lovely." But I deleted those demon types from our list.

Hours passed in which we narrowed down the list further.

I thunked my head on the table, my eyes achy and throbbing from print that now swum before me. Darkness pressed in against the windows and I'd missed a meal somewhere in there. "Have mercy."

Ari folded a piece of paper into an airplane. "It's down to soul suckers or energy leeches." He compared the wing sizes with mathematical precision. "Still leaves more possibilities than I'd like."

"Something's bugging me. Rasha are concerned with keeping demons a secret. Demons don't care. Not that they're hell-bent on outing themselves, but both soul suckers and energy leeches could kill a victim in the middle of a packed dance floor with no one the wiser. So why the discretion to isolate these people?" I cross-checked the revised demon list against the overview page. "Even the deaths in public places were done in shadowy corners: an empty office, a closed restaurant with the other staff gone. So what if the demon got caught in the act? Most would just kill whoever caught him as well."

"Unless the demon is vulnerable in that moment?"

I drummed my fingers on the table, watching the curser pulse. "Like an incubus or succubus? Feeding off sexual energy can kill, but won't leave a trace. And when those demons climax, they'd be wide open."

Ari shook his head. "Except we've got men *and* women dead. That would mean an incubus and a succubus working together. Never heard of that happening."

"Before me, you'd never heard of a female Rasha, either."

"You were an anomaly."

"Or the Brotherhood was short-sighted. Like you're being now. Way to endanger the mission right out of the gate."

"Don't like it? I can find someone else to work this with me."

Rabbi Mandelbaum popped his head in. "Off to a good start?"

My eyes darted to Ari, only half-certain he wouldn't get me booted.

"We've got some promising leads," he assured the rabbi.

Rabbi Mandelbaum nodded. "Good," he said, and left.

Ari fired the paper airplane, bonking me on the side of my head. "You're such an idiot."

I retrieved the airplane, placing it on the table. "Long day, little sleep. I'm getting testy."

With pouty lip and faux-concerned voice he asked, "Does Nava need a snack?"

"Like you need a shower, buddy. What's that cologne? Eau du glory hole?"

He pulled out his phone, waving it at me. "I'm telling Mom you're not following the 'if you can't say something nice' rule."

I scratched my cheek with my middle finger.

"If Nava had to follow that rule, people would think she was mute," a voice said from the doorway.

"Only mostly mute." Despite my "couldn't care less" intentions, my head whipped toward the speaker.

Rohan was back.

5

Rohan Mitra was 6'2" of broad shoulders, lean muscled torso, and a swagger to his hips as they propped against the doorframe. His dark brown hair curled in thick, sexy locks around his ears. It was almost as striking as the combo of his gold eyes and brown skin from his East Indian/Jewish heritage. Less appealing was the enough-arrogance-per-square-inch that left me amazed there was any room for his internal organs.

Thankfully, he wasn't in full rock god mode, like eyeliner and a smile dripping with killer lyrics and promises he'd be only too happy to keep. No, his quirked lips, worn jeans, and untucked white shirt with its cuffs rolled up to expose strong forearms were more rock god casual Friday. That meant a sliver of my brain was able to keep functioning even if most of it was busy envisioning ripping his clothes off.

Or figuring out the most painful use of my magic on his person.

"You're sputtering, Nava," he said.

"It's just... Did anyone else feel that disturbance?" I jumped to my feet, making a big show of looking around the room, brows knit together. "Like something just showed up where it wasn't supposed to." My gaze landed on Rohan. "If this was a movie, this would totally be the point where reality jumped the tracks into a horrible alternate universe and the main character, her hot not-boyfriend, and her dog had to go back in time and fix the original mistake that loosed this irritant upon our world."

"Too bad you don't have a dog," Rohan said.

"That's easily remedied," I replied. "But good of you to assume I've acquired a hot not-boyfriend."

"For fuck's sake." Ari scraped his chair back. "Hey, Ro. Welcome back." He stood up and pushed me closer to Rohan. "Here. She's all yours."

"Hardly," I said.

Rohan looked at me thoughtfully. "Can I do whatever I want to her?"

I glared at him with narrowed eyes. "Try it."

"Define 'whatever,'" Ari said.

"Geneva convention? Ish?" Rohan rolled his shoulder, stretched out his neck, and generally acted like he'd been upstairs for a couple of hours instead of gone for a month having kissed me, ditched me, then been all famous and not even texted me. On top of that, I blamed his existence for my kiboshed hook-up.

"Works for me. Eat then we'll resume," Ari said to me as he left. I'd time machine his ungrateful ass too, if I could.

"Go find someone else to play with. I'm done." I rapped my fist twice against the table.

Rohan pushed off the doorframe. "You think that's what I came here for?"

"I don't presume to think anything about you anymore. I have better things to do with my time."

"Right. What with the dog and the boyfriend." Rohan's voice was quiet. Upon closer inspection, which I couldn't exactly help since he was only about five feet away, he had purple smudges under his eyes.

My heart gave the pained "awww" indicative of level one stupid girl. I hated myself for caring one way or the other about his well-being. Because more than I'd replayed the kiss this past month I'd replayed the look on his face right after it.

Like he wished he could take the kiss back.

He took a step closer, and I braced myself for his touch, but he didn't close the distance between us to lay his palm tenderly on my cheek.

I didn't trail my fingers along the ridge of his abs, feeling them clench under my touch.

He didn't clasp my arms to pull my hands away from my body, holding them fast as he propelled me backward, up against the bookshelf.

I didn't feel the edge of the shelf grind into my shoulder blades as he pressed me into the bookcase, his body fitted in a hard, long line against mine. He didn't inch one calloused palm along the delicate skin on the inside of my wrist to interlace his fingers with mine and I wasn't enveloped in the scent of spicy cologne with an underbite of iron that was pure Rohan.

He didn't nip the hollow of my collarbone. Didn't slide his hand along my hip, dragging up my shirt for the heated glide of his skin on mine. And he didn't kiss me hot and rough, his stubble rasping my skin, his mouth demanding, almost cruel.

I snatched up the paper airplane and winged it at him. It hit Rohan square in the chest before fluttering to the ground. "What are you waiting for? Official orders? We're over. Finished." I mimed breaking a stick in half and tossing the pieces away.

The summer Ari and I were thirteen, we'd been on this beach vacation, body surfing, when something soft had brushed across my chest, along the edge of my bikini top. A jellyfish. The coolness of the waves had ratcheted into a burning pain.

My first love bailing on me when my tap dance dreams had blown up had brought that same pain with it. Except more an incessant stabbing than a brief sting. A ten to the jellyfish's six.

Neither a sting nor a stabbing, that look from Rohan after our kiss had smashed the relativity scale to smithereens.

To be fair, that expression had flashed across his face really fast, and I'd still been in shock from the kiss itself, so I could have been wrong, but the fact that he wasn't arguing with me now about us being done? That he merely pushed away from me, his steady gait nothing like the whoosh that rocked me as he removed his presence from mine, leaving me bereft?

Score one, for me. It was too bad I was only right about shitty things, but a point was a point.

As soon as he was out of the room, I collapsed against the table, pressing my forehead into the cool wood. I dragged in a deep breath, but couldn't get the air deep enough into my constricted chest to fill my lungs.

The antique clock mounted on the library wall ticked off the seconds. Saddle the fuck up, Nava.

Why kiss a person if you were going to regret it? Especially given how pushy and cranky he'd been about not getting to kiss me in the first place. And hello? How was kissing me regrettable? I was an amazing kisser.

I yanked the pen out of the mahogany table where I'd jammed in the tip like Excalibur. Even if he did regret it, basic etiquette demanded that he fake an expression of delight after his lips touched mine.

Now he'd returned and there'd been no "I'm back" hug, an "I missed you," or the grabbing of my hand, dragging of me to his bedroom and banging of my brains out. Which I would not have allowed to happen but damn, watching him beg for it would have rocked. Nope, all that time apart and not even a handshake.

Or a "sorry."

Had Lily met up with him in London? Were they finally back together?

Scorched, melted pen shards fell to the ground. I kicked them into a pile.

Rohan had found a crack in my highly-fortified shields and wormed his way in, eroding them with our growing connection, then blowing the rubble away with that kiss. He'd capped it all off by giving me the look of regret, effectively turning me into the fallout from his scorched earth policy. I'd spent the past month attempting to put out the fires and salve my emotional third degree burn.

No more.

I gathered up my folder and left, just in time to witness Rabbi Mandelbaum clasp a hand to the side of Rohan's head. Seriously, was the rabbi staging our encounters for maximum annoyance? "Excellent work in Pakistan." His eyes narrowed. "We'll forgive your unauthorized playtime, yes?"

My foot squeaked on the floorboard.

Rohan glanced past the rabbi at me. He didn't offer an excuse for his side trip. Not to the rabbi and certainly not to me. No, in his unrepentant gaze was the death of my faint hope that the sole reason Rohan had been in London was as some sort of mandated follow up to our Samson mission.

"Nava? You need help with something?"

"No, Rabbi," I replied. "Everything is crystal clear." I swept past them up the stairs, done with the she-who-pines-over-unsuitable-guy cliché. There was a veritable buffet of boy options out there and this girl was now all-you-can-eat.

"Stick this on." I pulled a tiny round adhesive bandage out of my purse and handed it to my best friend Leonie Hendricks.

She rolled up the wide sleeve of her funky velvet dress, the motion setting her mass of silver bangles jingling as she slapped it onto the inside of her elbow. "Affixed."

I stuck mine onto the top of my hand. "Juice box?" I asked, pulling an apple juice from my purse.

"I'm good."

Ripping out the straw with my teeth, I spat out the plastic wrapper and jammed the straw in the box. I took a few sips, keeping the straw between my teeth. "Try to look altruistic."

We strolled into the ballroom of the student union building at the University of British Columbia, currently set up for the campus blood drive. A fact gleaned from my dad's text that had woken me up a couple of hours ago, reminding me to give.

Waving our Band-Aids at the sign-in table like a couple of night-club re-entry stamps, we walked past the rows of students earning good karma through bleeding. I figured I bled enough on a regular basis for the good of humanity to reap the rewards of blood drives now and then.

"What's your take?" I asked.

When Leo and I had resumed our friendship a couple of months ago after some idiocy on my part, we'd both gotten the shock of the century. Her at learning I was the first female Rasha and me that she was a half-goblin. I'd stumbled upon her the night I was looking for a demon informant. Leo was it. She had passed on a lot of good intel to Demon Club previously. Though none of its current residents knew of her true heritage.

Well, almost none of them.

I'd had to do some clever dodging to keep my brother from coming with me today as I went to meet with the snitch. Ari hadn't been thrilled about not coming to meet the informant given he was "in charge," but I'd convinced him that the snitch only trusted me and his presence would complicate things. Understatement.

A student volunteer came by, spotted our Band-Aids, and stuck a smiling blood drop sticker on each of us. "Thanks for donating."

"Wouldn't miss it," I said. "Where do we get our meal tickets?"

She pointed at the line-up at the far end of the ballroom.

Leo and I made our way there. "I can't say off the top of my head which of those demons are in town," she said.

"In that case..." We joined the line-up and I pulled a folded paper out of my purse. "These are the victims. Any chance you know either of the students on it?" I indicated the names I meant.

Leo blinked. "I do."

"Brilliant. Who?" We shuffled forward.

She pushed her fall of red straight hair off her shoulder, her face screwed up. "Here's the thing."

I raised an eyebrow. "Yes?"

"Davide Garza? He went to SFU with me."

"And?" I slurped my juice.

"He was friends with Cole. Harper," she added, as if I'd somehow misunderstood who she meant.

I stilled, lowering the juice box. "This is where you tell me that you would never have kept in touch with that rat bastard."

"I would never have kept in touch with that rat bastard."

"I see." I gave her my sweetest smile. Which maybe was a bit feral because she flinched.

"Next!" The bored volunteer handed over our tickets for a free meal and beer at the student pub.

I grabbed Leo's before she could. "I'll just hang on to these, shall I? Thanks so much," I told the volunteer and strode out the door, slamming my juice box into the trash.

Leo raced after me, tackling me in the hallway, and smashing my cheek into the wall. She was a pushy little thing. "Gimme my ticket."

"I don't negotiate with terrorists."

She planted her hands on her hips and glared at me. "It's a small campus and when Cole and I run into each other, we chat. It's polite small talk, not detonating car bombs."

"Wow."

"The point is," she said, "he was buddies with Davide. So if you called him?"

I dropped my head into my hands. As a Rasha, I'd had my fair share of trials. Made sacrifices. Calling my ex might not have been the worst one, but damn, it sucked hard. I allowed myself a count of ten and five deep breaths before I reached into my pocket, pulled out my phone, and punched in the number that I could still reel off three years later. Mostly because the last four digits spelled "cute."

"Hello?" Cole's rich baritone had been one of his best features, at odds with his adorkableness. It had always given me a little rush. Still did, though not for the same reason.

I wiped my damp palms on my skirt at this first contact since our horrible blow-up fight when he'd walked out of my life in the waiting room at physio because he couldn't handle my "dance shit." Cleared my throat a couple of times. "Hey, Cole. It's Nava."

Dead silence except for the sound of a video game on TV in the background. I could picture his owlish blink of surprise behind his glasses. "Hi. How are you?"

"Great. Listen, I was wondering if we could meet up?"

"I dunno, Avon."

My heart clutched at the sound of his old nickname for me. My name, Nava, backwards that had mutated into Avon somehow. "It's not about us. I'm doing some work for my dad."

"Yeah? That's great. Following the old man into the legal profession?"

"Yes. I am justice system affiliated."

Leo facepalmed.

"Anyways, your friend Davide? I'm really sorry for your loss, but there are questions about..." Wide-eyed, I mouthed "help."

"A potential medical condition being missed," she whispered. Thank you, private investigator bestie.

"A potential medical condition being missed that could have contributed to his death," I said. "If I could find out a bit more about him, it might mean his family getting insurance money." Dad always said people were open to talking if money was involved.

"Oh. Sure."

"Great. Could we meet?"

He paused before answering with a reluctant, "I guess so. You know Beta house up at Simon Fraser?"

"Yup."

"They're having a party tonight. Meet me there around nine."

I mimed shooting myself in the head. "Thanks."

"No problem." There was a weighted silence. "It'll be good to see you."

"You too." I hung up, throwing the phone at Leo.

"Scale of one to ten awful?" she asked, catching it before it shattered against the wall.

"Six and counting. For the record," I handed her a meal and drink ticket. "I hate you."

She smooched my cheek and hustled off, my misery forgotten in her quest for food. Goblins had extremely fast metabolisms packed into tiny bodies.

Reuniting with my ex at a frat party. If disembowelment wasn't an option, I couldn't come up with a better way to spend a Friday night.

When I got back to the chapter house later, I updated Ari that he'd get to spend tonight around two of his least favorite things: Cole and frat boys. Then I headed into the kitchen and switched on the electric kettle to make myself some chamomile tea. Coffee would make me postal and I was jittery enough. 14,200 seconds until I saw Cole again. I stared at a point on the tree outside the window to keep my mind blank, filling the infuser with loose tea.

I was assaulted with images of the greatest hits of our relationship, like our endless exchange of notes before the day I found him in front of my locker with a crumpled paper that he'd stuffed into my hand before racing off. I'd had just enough time to see it was a heart with a time, place, and question mark on it, and yell "yes" before he'd disappeared around the corner. He'd popped his head back around, a giant grin on his face, and given me a thumbs up. Or our first kiss in the snow under a streetlamp, after which he'd wrapped his scarf around my neck and I'd floated home. The time we'd ditched school one hot June day and snuck off to the waterslides, laughing and singing only the cheesiest of boy band songs all the way out there in his mom's car.

The whistling kettle snapped me out of my failure of a meditative state. Waving off the steam, I poured the boiling water into my mug, took a sip, and immediately spat it out. The chamomile tasted of lawn clippings and Mother Nature's pubes.

I fished a bag of berries from the freezer, dumping some in the blender along with vanilla yogurt, orange juice, and ice cubes. I flicked the power on, then broke off a hunk of cheddar, nibbling on it for my protein fix.

While Ms. Clara kept our kitchen fully stocked, being Rasha didn't come with an on-site chef and I sucked balls at feeding myself. However, with Ari and me on an official mission, I vowed to take better care of my person. There could be no slip-ups on this job.

Thirty seconds later, I flicked off the blender, opened the lid and dipped my finger in. "Un peu plus."

"You're mad I didn't take you to Child's Play." Rohan leaned his elbows on the counter, infringing on my personal space. Jeez silent ninja, wear a bell or something.

I took my time fitting the lid on the blender, scrambling to jump from memories of Cole to Rohan's arrogant assumptions. "Is that the impression you got? Interesting."

I jabbed the "on" button, my hand on the lid. Staring at him with a customer service smile. No wonder Ari pulled this cool questioning shit on me, because Rohan's tight expression was intensely satisfying.

Rohan crossed his arms, waiting until the blender morphed from grinding noise to death throes wheeze and I was forced to shut it off. "Nava–"

Face impassive, I let 'er rip again.

Rohan yanked the plug out of the wall, holding the cord hostage. "I think we should discuss what happens next."

I poured my smoothie into a glass. "Do you."

"You don't?" His bland tone made my hackles rise.

My hand tightened on the glass. "As I'm working with Ari now, you're not my CO anymore. Plus, we're done, so we don't have anything to talk about."

Rohan prowled closer. "I can think of one or two topics."

I put up a hand to stop his progress, my motion bringing him up short a scant inch from my palm. Did his heart race as furiously as mine? "Such as?"

"The attacks in Prague."

Only years of performance training kept my shoulders from sagging. "They're not your concern."

He bristled. "That's not your call."

"Wanna bet? This conversation is over."

Rohan took my hand. I leaned back, having caught myself swaying in to smell him, but all he did was press the blender plug into my palm, folding my fingers over it. "Not by a long shot," he said.

"Hold your breath and wait for it to happen." My anger was so thick it choked me and yet, one kind word, one tender gesture might have diffused it.

Rohan spun on his heel, yanked the fridge open and pulled out a can of root beer. He popped the tab with a sharp snap.

I busied myself washing the blender and pretending I didn't feel the weight of his stare on my back. Drying it off, I crossed the kitchen to put the appliance back on its base on the counter.

"Damn it." Rohan grabbed my wrist. "Nava."

"I swear, I'm getting that dog. Today." I jerked free and kept walking.

"Please." His voice was soft and gentle.

I closed my eyes briefly as I returned the blender to its proper place. "What?"

"I need…"

I turned to catch the fire of his gold gaze. "What?" It came out in a whisper.

Rohan stepped forward. The air between us thickened with the gravity of his expression and my ache to have him finish that sentence with one simple word.

My every muscle strained with the effort of keeping still.

His voice dropped to a growl. "To know." He raked a hand through his hair. "About the Brotherhood."

Hollow disappointment kicked through my chest. "Like I said, there's nothing to talk about."

Only once he'd left did I spin away from the blender, open the cupboard over the fridge, and reach up for the bottle of vodka stashed there. I poured a generous slug of booze into my drink, raised it in cheers to the universe, and chugged it back.

6

Putting on clothing applicable for this frat party was akin to willingly inviting in chlamydia. Cole had texted me to say that the theme was "naughty schoolgirl." Really? "All you need is love" was a theme. "No man is an island" was a theme. "Naughty schoolgirl" was a reminder not to leave my drink unattended.

And yet, here I was.

The frat party was less annoying than expected. Though I came to that conclusion after the delicate soufflé of cannabis, a shot of McCallum's, and the half of an Atavan that I'd found in a medicine cabinet had kicked in.

I waited for my ex to arrive, appreciating the "art imitates life" moment as I stood on a sticky patch in the corner trying to fend off some guy pushing me to dance and wishing I was at home, while Alessia Cara sang about being in that exact situation over the stereo in "Here."

I'd just managed to rid myself of him when from across the room, atmospherically decorated with multicolored Christmas lights, Ari met my eyes. He'd forgone a costume, and honestly, the rest of us in our sexed-up high school get ups looked ridiculous next to his all-black badassery. His chin jerk and glance sideways indicated "incoming."

I steeled myself.

A cold Coke was shoved into my hand. "I'm not actually an asshole," Cole said.

"Evidence to the contrary." I frowned at the pop.

"Did you want something else?" he asked. "I know you don't drink because of–"

I swiped the red Solo Cup he was holding and knocked a third back, before sticking him with the Coke.

"...Dance," he finished up.

"Things change." I tapped the cup. "Unlike your disgusting habit of mixing 7Up with beer, you lightweight."

He grinned at me.

My eyes trailed down his school boy tie and along the V of his fitted shirt and vest, looking for the connection between the guy standing before me with the gelled hair, his glasses replaced with contacts that made his green eyes pop, and my first love.

It was still Cole, but sexy Cole. I wasn't sure if that made this encounter easier or not.

"You gonna try to man me up?" His eyes warmed and I laughed.

"Yeah, remember how well that went the last time."

When we were sixteen, he'd gotten so bummed about his skinny frame that he'd enrolled in extreme boot camp. I remembered him moaning on the ground, telling me he'd die if he had to do another sit-up.

Then I remembered him moaning for other, more pleasant reasons. I got lost in the memory of him propped above me, biting his lip when we'd lost our virginity together because he was so worried that he was hurting me–which he had, and talk about lackluster first time.

Still.

I curled a lock around my finger. "I dunno. Do you need manning up?"

He hooked a finger into his belt loop. "Do you think I do?"

And wouldn't that be the massive win I'd been after, to bang my ex's brains out, to have sex and not have to think a damn thing about it if I didn't want to, and then to walk away first. Hot not-boyfriend achieved. Also closure. A shit-ton of that.

He smirked and I snapped my gaze away, taking a long drink. As I lowered the cup, I caught Ari frowning at me, before he nodded absently at something one of the people in his group was saying.

"You look good." Cole's eyes lingered on me. More precisely, lingered on the old schoolgirl tap costume that had been conservative when I was fourteen, but was "thematically" appropriate for tonight. My white button down shirt strained across my breasts, ending in a knot under my rib cage, while my bare thighs peeked out from the red plaid skirt that sat low on my hips. "Really good."

"Yeah, I do." Suck it, buddy. I'd be lying if I hadn't planned this outfit knowing that Cole would be picturing me in dance sweats.

He ducked his head. "I'm sorry, Avon."

As apology gestures went, it wasn't what I'd dreamed of. That had been more him falling prostrate in remorse at my feet before I kicked him in the balls then stepped over his body to drive off into the sunset in my hot boy toy's '67 Shelby Mustang. I shook my head. His *Maserati*.

Cole did that nose scrunch thing that I'd once found so adorable. "I freaked out when you got hurt and that's no excuse. Trust me, my ex–" He swallowed the rest of that sentence.

I set the cup down on the window ledge. The hits I took for this gig. "You dated after me. You can say it. I'll even go so far as to assure you that I don't require your eternal monkdom in atonement." 'Course I wouldn't have said no to castration.

"Consider me grateful."

The 70s classic "Ain't No Sunshine" pumping out of the speakers morphed into a mash-up with "Toccata and Fugue." Rohan's first hit and the song that had come to represent everything confusing and tangled up about our relationship. Such as it was. Or, as of yesterday, wasn't.

"How about you?" Cole fiddled with the tab on the pop can. "Seeing anyone?

"Nope. Though I was screwing the lead singer of Fugue State Five on a regular basis."

"Even in fantasy land, as if." Cole laughed and put the Coke down. "Remember the impressions you used to do of him performing with a giant ego-inflated head like it was a helium balloon?"

I laughed too. Weaker.

The lush bassline of this funky remix slid through my veins, leaving me wide open for Rohan's famous singing rasp to wrap around my bones and shiver up my spine.

"The girl with the lightning eyes and the boy with demons in his soul," Rohan sang.

"All kidding aside," I pressed Cole's hand between my own. "I'm not seeing anyone right now."

A slow lazy smile spread across his face. "Good."

My heart didn't do a flip precisely but nostalgia did snag it, sinking in a hook and making it twinge. "Isn't it just? Tell me what you've been up to."

While he caught me up on the past couple of years, mostly filling me in about his business courses and the cabin his parents had finally bought on one of the nearby Gulf islands, I traced my fingers over his palms. Once upon a time, I'd memorized the feel of them roaming over my body. Now the totality of Rohan crowded out memories of other men.

"Ow." Cole pulled his hand away, shaking out his fingers that I'd been crushing. "Iron grip there, lady."

"Sorry." My breathy giggle and head toss were pathetic but Cole didn't comment.

Luckily, it was a new day with plenty of room for new memories. I shifted closer to Cole. Partially for privacy but partially to make him lean in.

Ari made a "get on with it" motion from his side of the room.

"What can you tell me about Davide?" I tapped my index finger against my lips, drawing his gaze to my mouth. "Could he have been high or drunk that night?" Certain demons preferred their victims unconscious so if Davide had blacked out after attending some campus party, like say, one here at this frat, that might narrow the list of possibilities.

Cole gave a chin jerk and a "hey" to some frat boys. "Davide smoked pot occasionally but he didn't drink. Kept him too hungover to rock climb. And he was super stoked about climbing the Chief the next day, so he was probably sober." The Chief was a nearby mountain and popular rock climbing destination. "Didn't you say something about an undiagnosed medical condition?"

It didn't even occur to him that I might be lying to him about why I was here. About who I was.

"Uh, yeah. I'm just ruling things out."

There was a bright burst of laughter over to our left from a couple utterly wrapped up in each other. I drank in their easy familiarity, the way their bodies angled towards each other, their pinky fingers hooked together. That need to be connected at all times. Cole and I had had that once. That underlying thrum of awareness that I was his and he was mine.

Unlike Rohan and I. Except... I flashed back to our time in Prague: Rohan's excitement at showing me Dancing House, the blazing hunger on his face when he'd seen me after his performance, his fury when he'd realized that the Brotherhood had sent the gogota after me. And the kind of kiss I'd never even dreamed was possible.

"I wonder if it could have been a side effect of the meds he was on." Cole hadn't noticed me lost in my thoughts.

I pulled my hand away from my lips. "What meds?"

"Sleeping pills."

The back of my neck prickled.

Cole nudged my drink aside to sit on the ledge, patting the spot next to him.

I sat down. "What was the problem?"

"Not sure," he said, "but he'd started going to some sleep clinic over on the west side."

Nightmare demon? It would fit the crimes and a sleep clinic was the perfect place to troll for victims.

Cole lay his hand on my thigh, the warmth of his skin seeping into mine. "I don't want to talk about Davide anymore."

"Hmm. Whatever topic could interest you, Mr. Harper?"

"Let's roll." Ari showed up, not even pretending to acknowledge Cole.

"Hey, Ari," Cole said, with a friendly smile. "How are you?"

Ari trained a fake smile back at him. "I'm great, Cole. How are you? Good? Great. We done?" Ari and Cole hadn't gotten along before he'd dumped me. Now? Yikes.

Cole laughed. "Wow. Golden boy not minding his manners. Shocking."

"Cole." I shook my head at the use of his old nickname for my perfect twin, but Ari didn't need me standing up for him.

"You never knew me, Harper. Don't act like you do now."

Cole blinked at the silky menace in Ari's voice.

My stomach dropped and I pushed in between them. "Ari is my ride so…"

Cole nodded, keeping a wary eye on my brother. "Glad I could help."

"Me too. Maybe we could get together for a coffee sometime?"

Ari tapped his foot.

"We could. I'll text you," Cole said.

Ari was already dragging me off so I shot Cole an apologetic look and a wave. My brother barely made it out the front door of the frat house before voicing his opinion. "No."

"You don't get a vote."

He laughed. "Me and Leo are the only vote casters. Are you high?"

"You don't want me with Rohan. You don't want me with Cole. Stop killing my fun."

"Yeah, getting tangled up with Cole is gonna be so fun. For all of us. Here's a thought. Pick a guy you don't have emotional baggage with."

"Where's the fun in that? Now, can I tell you what I learned or not?"

"You mean douchecanoe is good for something?"

I laughed. "Douchecanoe is and will be good for a series of limited run somethings."

Ari gagged. Then brightened. "New plan. Unleash your finest self on him."

"That's the idea, though why are you suddenly onboard?"

"Thinking this through, I anticipate much amusement at his expense."

"Uh, okay." I filled Ari in on the sleep clinic as we crossed campus, the sounds of the party fading away, replaced by dark silent forest pressing in on us from all sides. Towering Douglas fir reached up for the stars, while the night air was laced with the scent of cedar.

I shivered, wrapping my arms around myself. Simon Fraser University was located on top of Burnaby Mountain and it was chilly up here. My short fake-leather jacket looked good but did zip against the elements.

I'd had to get somewhat creative with what I'd told Ari in terms of the information that had led us to Cole in the first place, given he had no clue that Leo was a half-goblin, or, in Rasha terms, a PD. Named for the old hunter joke "What do you call a half-demon? Practice." I'd learned not to call Leo a practice demon at my peril. I'd ended up saying that while the snitch had been a dead-end, I'd asked Leo about Davide since they both went to Simon Fraser University together.

She'd led me to Cole which, in turn, had brought us to this possible break of the sleep clinic.

We stepped into the half-empty parking lot. There was a whistling hiss and then a black whirlwind burst from the shadows. It funneled counterclockwise a couple of times before flying apart into about a half-dozen tiny, red, demonic bats. They'd have been cute if it weren't for the needle-sharp fangs.

Ari stepped into the shadows, drawing the darkness up into his hands like the swell of a wave before rolling it out to envelop a few of the demons, curling the darkness around them with weight and force. Their wings beat frantically as his magic tightened until sufficient pressure was applied on their weak spot on the underside of their left wings to kill them.

Three of them choked out wheezed death rattles and poofed out of existence.

I wrinkled my nose at the ashy scent filling the air, but disposed of a couple myself, taking sadistic glee in toying with one little bugger who had nipped my finger. "Come here, my pretty," I cackled, sending out a wave of electric magic like a net to trap it.

The demon hovered in mid-air, struggling to get away, but I pinned it in place. I waved my hands like a conductor, directing it in sluggish loops. The link was strong and magic sang in my blood. The demon glared red murderous hate at me, straining to pull itself out of my web but I steered that puppy all over the parking lot, laughing in delight at making a demon dance to my tune. The novelty ran out soon enough, so I put it out of its misery and hurried toward the car, shivering.

One last demon bat whizzed out of the darkness, its claws outstretched as it flew for my face. I flung up an arm to deflect it, right as the wind picked up. My loose curls, so sexy at the start of the evening, now whipped around me like Medusa's snakes, and the bat became entangled.

I screamed like my five-year-old self when Ari had dropped a spider down my back. "Get it off me." Arms windmilling, I spun in circles, batting at the demon to dislodge it.

Ari grabbed my arm. "You're making it worse."

The demon chittered in a creepy high scream, its teeth snapping too close to my ears for comfort and its little feet spasming against my head.

I wrenched free of my brother. Hand blazing with magic, I seized one of the demon's legs, shrieking when the bat licked my still-bleeding finger, courtesy of its vampiric friend. I flung the bat to the concrete, ripping out an impressive amount of hair along with it.

I fired a stream of magic into its heart, but the demon wasn't dead given it hadn't disappeared. I'd incapacitated it but the weak spot was the only thing to finish them off.

The demon lay there like it was taking a little nap. Except for the part where my continued magic flow was ballooning its body out to grotesque proportions.

I still shook with residual shudders at the memory of it tangled in my hair. "You like that?" I increased my power.

"It's not a zit," Ari said. "Don't pop it."

The demon's eyes bugged out; its body rippled and bulged as my magic crackled inside it.

"Spoilsport." I tried to disengage but my magic stretched between the demon and me like taffy. We were stuck fast.

The demon's skin tore with a squishy rip.

"Oh, shit." Ari grabbed my hand and pulled. The world twisted sideways in a vertigo-inducing lurch.

Eventually I was able to open my eyes without wanting to vomit. We stood on the flat stones which skipped across the reflecting pond in the academic quad at SFU on the far side of campus from the parking lot, flanked by wide lawns and neat hedges. Long rectangular buildings supported on fat pillars formed a "U" around us.

The world was bathed in a weird green light like I was viewing my surroundings through night vision goggles. A green version of the real world.

Jaw dropping, I spun in a slow circle. "What...?"

"Welcome to Emerald City. I shadow-ported you." Correction. A hidden green version, accessed by my brother.

"No points for originality, but many for portalling, O, great and powerful Oz."

"Thanks. Hadn't realized I could bring passengers." Ari laughed. "Fear and surprise. Chief weapons."

"Don't forget that fanatical devotion to the Pope," I said. "So how does this work?" I fanned out my shirt, sticky with sweat. "And why is it so hot?"

"It's always like this. Near as I can figure, it's the energy I'm generating manifesting this pathway. Emerald City conforms to our spatial universe but lets me jump across our world in leaps and bounds. Have shadow, will travel. Watch."

Ari winked into existence on the far side of the quad by a large concrete flower pot. The dark outlines of the North Shore Mountains were visible in the distance.

He was back with me a second later. "Cool, huh?"

"Very. But if it's shadow-port, and we did that, how come we're still stuck in this green light place?

"I need shadows to enter Emerald City but once I'm in, I stay in until I choose to leave. It uses up less energy than going in and out between EC and normal reality."

I let out a low whistle. "Someone's been practicing. And keeping secrets." Perhaps it was hypocritical of me, given that I hadn't owned up to my real agenda with the witches, but it stung that he hadn't told me about this. Ari and I had never kept secrets from each other. Not before we'd become Rasha.

A cold shiver ran up my spine. Was our being Rasha together going to strengthen our crazy twin bond or drive us apart? I hunched deeper into my jacket, for all the good it did.

"I wanted to figure out some stuff first," Ari said. "I've researched the archives on Rasha magic. No one has ever had the ability to teleport. Drio can flash step, but it's not the same thing." He shrugged.

Ari didn't know if this magic was a result of the witchcraft we'd used to induct him. If it was and he was already anxious about standing out? I rubbed the side of my hand over my forehead. "No matter how you got it, Ace, it's all kinds of awesome."

A security guard came around the corner.

I edged behind Ari but he wasn't fazed. "He can't see us."

It was weird how through the lens of Ari's magic every single detail on the guard's uniform was apparent even from a hundred feet away, down to the neat cross-stitching of his company's logo.

Closer and closer the guard silently came, a jaunty spring in his step. Completely oblivious to our presence. Also whistling given his pursed mouth, even if I didn't hear anything.

"Enhanced vision but no sound?"

"No smells either," Ari said. "No clue if that's the magic itself or me not having a handle on it."

Sweat ran down the backs of my knees. "What happens if you knock into someone while you're in EC view?"

Ari shadow-ported.

The guard stumbled left, avoiding Ari's sudden appearance. The guard frowned, looked right through Ari, then checked his shoe.

"The magic forms a buffer." The guard didn't hear my brother even though he stood right there.

Ari jumped back to my side, looking a little pale. "I'd better take us back." He grabbed my hand and, with another sickening lurch, the world snapped back into color.

We'd returned to the parking lot, next to the second-hand Honda that Dad had bought us. He'd said it was because we'd needed our own transport living at the chapter house, but I suspected he was relieved his Prius wasn't going to suffer any more damage at our hands.

Ari rubbed his hand over his chest.

"You okay?"

"If we're being flexible with the definition, then sure." He fumbled the key into the door, opened the glove compartment, pulled out a bottle of Tylenol, and popped a couple pills, dry-swallowing them.

Since I was now sober enough to drive, I let him rest for the ride home.

The magic we received when we were inducted was derived from an aspect of the Rasha's personality. My prickliness, as Ari called my behavior after my dance dreams were shot, had resulted in my Lady Shock and Awe abilities. Kane, toxic in relationships, was literally poison, his skin turning into the ultimate bad touch, while Rohan had his knives. Enough said.

I'd chalked the nature of Ari's powers up to damage suffered from being tortured by demons and the shock of having his Rasha dreams put on hold when I was the one inducted at his initial ceremony. But was that all it was?

Maybe the invisibility as we'd stood there-but-not-there wasn't inherent to Emerald City but came from the fact that all these years Ari had longed to be a little less bright and shiny. That his deep-seated desire to be a little less seen had been made tangible.

I glanced sideways at him, eyes closed, sprawled in the passenger seat, and wondered how far his resentment extended. The combination of dark forest and my own spiraling musings was not a good one, and I was glad once I turned off the winding road that led down the mountain back onto the light traffic at the base on Lougheed Highway.

Forty-five minutes later, I drove through a black, wrought-iron gate set into a thick stone fence forming the perimeter of Demon Club's property. The chapter house was located on a large tract of land in the Southlands area of Vancouver's west side surrounded by woods. I cut the engine in front of the stately three-story mansion with its wide front stairs, large beveled windows with stained-glass accents, and multiple chimneys pointed up at the sky like divining rods.

I shut the driver's door, waiting for Ari to get out before beeping the fob at the car to lock it. A basketball thumped steadily against the pavement from out back, and Kane whooped as another of his shots went in.

Thanks to the glow of the LEDs lighting up the court, his shirtless-ness was on display, so the night wasn't a total write-off.

The ball bounced off the rim.

"Come play." He fired the ball at Ari. "Twenty-one."

"With your shitty layup? Fast game," Ari said.

"Watch it, son. I have five years of experience on you." Kane jogged backward to the center line.

"Five years of bad habits. At least my dad taught me how to shoot." Kane froze. Only for an instant, but still.

"Aw, man." Ari strode toward him. "K, I didn't mean–"

Kane stole the ball away from Ari. "Shut up and play."

"Kane."

Kane raised his eyebrows at Ari, as if daring him to continue down that path.

"All right, but you're going down," Ari said.

Kane dribbled the ball. "Other twin?"

"No, thanks." I didn't want to get in the middle of whatever old wound had just been opened. "I'm headed for ice cream."

"Seeing the ex not go well?" It was as if all sound stopped just in time for him to drop those words with a loud thud.

I glanced at Rohan's bedroom window, his *open* window, exhaustion seeping into every inch of me. Working together, sleeping together, my time with Rohan was over. I wanted him gone so I could focus on my future. Which, admittedly might involve elements of my past, but in a new futuristic dynamic that was solely on my terms.

Kane shot, missed, then patted my shoulder on his way to retrieve the ball.

Leaving the guys, I marched through the back door and dug out the mint chocolate chip ice cream, sucking on a spoonful, and letting the icy crystals melt on my tongue.

My eyes narrowed on the car keys to Rohan's precious Shelby Mustang that were tossed on the counter and I couldn't help once more replaying his look of regret. I stuffed the lid back on the ice cream tub and jammed it in the freezer, letting the cold blast of air steel my shards of ruined pride. I wanted to put that look back on Rohan's face now, but for very different reasons. I was a free agent and after reconnecting with Cole, I wasn't about to have our mutuals get all up in my business. Or kill any further hook-ups. Once and for all, Rohan needed to realize we were done.

I waltzed through most of the main floor with my Brotherhood phone pressed to my ear, faking a conversation with some guy. By the time I got to Rohan's door, I was running out of ways to turn my imaginary lover down, so I hoped he was in his room and not down in the Vault working out.

Jackpot. His door was ajar enough to see him laying on his stomach across his bed, a low stream of chill music issuing out of his speakers. I strode back and forth in front of the door, giggling that it was late and I couldn't possibly meet my pretend hook-up now.

As soon as Rohan indicated by word or deed that he'd overheard, I'd set him straight with absolutely no room for doubt. It was time for him to go back to Los Angeles so I could get my sex life back.

By my third pass of Rohan's door, I peeked in to see how my conversation was going down. In case I needed to adjust my volume.

Rohan hadn't moved. I crept around the side of his bed, doing my damnedest not to think of the many varied and deliciously filthy acts we'd partaken of on his mattress and ignoring my clit, Cuntessa de Spluge's throbbing vote for one more round.

His head lolled over the edge of the bed, his hair falling forward, blocking my view of his eyes.

I touched his shoulder. "You asleep?"

He flipped over, one hand shooting out to grab me by the throat, his iron blades snicking out from his fingertips to gouge my skin before his eyes even opened.

My phone clattered to the floor. I froze, not daring to breathe until he blinked through his confusion into recognition.

He jerked his hand away from me, scrambling back wide-eyed.

Harsh breaths stuttering out of me, I grabbed my phone and fled. I didn't stop running until I'd locked my bedroom door, sliding down the wall to sit with my knees drawn in to my chest. Shaking, I touched my fingertips to my throat and the tiny drops of blood that came away a shocking red.

Lizzo's "Good As Hell" rang out from my phone, jarring in the silence. I'd assigned that ringtone to Rohan as a reminder to myself to be hair flip girl with razors underneath. Well, my metaphorical razors had just met his very real blades and I wasn't sure hair flip girl was up to the task of speaking to him.

My hand hovered over my phone, my decision on whether to answer up in the air until the last note.

"I'm so sorry." Rohan's voice was bleak. "I'd never–I wouldn't hurt you."

I didn't answer. Couldn't answer because I wasn't so sure anymore. I rested my head on my knees until I could speak with a steady voice. "Did you hear what I said in the library yesterday?"

"Yeah."

"Good. You need to go home."

He laughed quietly, the sound laced with a bitter edge. "Don't I just."

"Rohan."

"I'll let you go." The fatigue in his voice called up the smudges under his eyes and whatever was haunting him enough to put him on the attack before he was even fully awake.

"Wait, what happened?" I asked before he hung up. I screwed my face up into a scowl. Why did I have to ask?

There was a pause. "You caught me off-guard."

I toyed with the edge of my fluffy throw rug. "Something bad went down when you were away, huh?"

His "yeah" was a long time coming. There was no point asking him about what. If he was reluctant to admit this much, I'd get no further answers out of him.

"I saw my ex tonight," I blurted out. I mimed shooting myself in the head. Hang up, idiot.

"On purpose?"

"Intel gathering. He was friends with one of the victims on this mission Ari and I are on."

"Ah. So who won for shittiest encounter?" Rohan asked. "The guy who ripped out your heart or the one who almost ripped out your throat?"

Same guy. I fumbled my phone. "I have to go," I said, and hung up, wishing I'd listened to myself ten seconds earlier.

7

"What crawled up your ass?" Ari asked Saturday morning, as he drove us to the Westside Sleep Disorders clinic.

While this clinic wasn't the nearest one to Davide's apartment, we'd decided to investigate it first. The closer one was affiliated with Vancouver General Hospital and required jumping through a lot more bureaucratic hoops to get into. That probably ruled it out for demons to troll for victims. Besides, we could swing by that one later if need be.

"Nothing." I placed my venti latte in the Honda's cup holder. Rain streaked down the front windshield, the slick streets amplifying the traffic to a dull roar. "Did you research your supposed symptoms?"

He tapped the steering wheel absent-mindedly. "Yeah. If we don't get anything here, we need to talk to the families of the other victims."

"Sure. We can rule out whether others complained of night terrors."

We snagged a parking spot in front of the clinic with about five minutes to spare before Ari's appointment.

The reception area was fairly generic: abstract art on the walls, chairs and couches in muted greens and blacks. A bland soothing comfort. The receptionist's red bow tie was the brightest pop of color in the place. He handed over a clipboard with paperwork for Ari to fill out, his smile a bit brighter than polite patient care warranted. I got the hairy eyeball.

Ari didn't seem to notice, so once we'd sat down, I pointed out in a hushed voice that Gay Cutie was jonsing for him. My brother didn't answer, concentrating on the questionnaire to be completed.

When he'd finished, I volunteered to take it up to the counter. "Here you go."

I scouted the reception area. Or, rather, the files lining the bookshelves along one wall.

"Thanks. Dr. Alphonse will be out to see your…" Gay Cutie arched an eyebrow.

"Brother," I supplied.

"Brother," he replied more cheerfully, "in a minute."

Another employee dumped more files next to the receptionist. "Risking life and limb in the name of health care," she said.

"Better you than me," Gay Cutie said. "I swear one day we'll be found like the Wicked Witch of the East in there."

His coworker laughed. A phone rang. "I'll get it," she said, answering the phone on a second desk.

"So, how long has the clinic been in business?" I asked.

Gay Cutie sorted the new files. "About three years now. Doctors Stewart and Alphonse founded it."

"Big staff?"

He cut me an unimpressed look over the stack that he straightened with a sharp smack against the desk.

"Sorry," I said. "It's just that the other place we tried was a bunch of quacks and if Ari doesn't get his sleep problems resolved soon?" I sighed.

"Well, we're professionals." His tone was clipped.

Before I could thaw his icy demeanor, Ari called out that he was headed in to his appointment with Dr. Alphonse. He stood beside a fifty-something woman in a smart pantsuit with white streaks in her frizzy hair.

I nodded then asked Gay Cutie where the restroom was. He directed me down the hall with a lazy wave of his hand, eyes already back on his computer screen.

The first open door off the corridor lead to a sparse consult room decorated with a large illustrated poster asking "What type of sleeper are you?" The cupboards were locked and there was nothing else of interest so I moved on. The next door was closed and I didn't want to risk interrupting someone's session.

One more door before the bathroom.

Jackpot. Files were stuffed into a filled-to-bursting bookshelf, while various clinic supplies from boxes of printer paper to neatly folded linens were stacked in haphazard rows. I pulled out the list of victims' names and began scanning the folders, grateful that they were in alphabetical order.

Unfortunately, the files were also all old. I examined a stack on a battered desk that was jammed into the corner beside an ancient Mac, its laboring fan sounding like a bag of angry bees. The top file was open and, given some of the notes in pencil, it looked like the employees were transferring these files to an electronic database.

I moved the mouse and the monitor came to life. Good. One less level of security to get through. I gained entry to the system with the clinic's address. Kane had imparted all kinds of useful tips regarding common passwords.

The database of patient records popped up, but there were no files for Bader or Chen. I continued my search with Epstein.

"Ari, why don't you tell me in your own words what you've been experiencing?"

I fumbled to catch the keyboard before it hit the ground, but the doctor's voice had come from a vent. I exhaled. Then cocked my head to hear how well Ari could pull off this ruse.

"I'm only sleeping for a few hours a night," he said. "When I wake up I see this dark figure at the foot of my bed. I'm powerless. My vocal chords are frozen, my limbs don't move. I'm stuck there watching it watch me."

I barely caught that last quiet statement.

Night terror symptoms were essentially the same as a visit from a nightmare demon. He wasn't describing an actual nightmare demon since the wards around Demon Club precluded that. What made me uneasy was that I didn't think his recitation of the medical condition was an act. The way he rushed his words, the break in his voice as he'd said he was powerless; my brother wasn't that good an actor.

"Do you feel too hot or too cold during this process?"

"Both. I'm sweating but I'm shivering, too."

I had to double-check the last batch of patient records listed on screen, having no memory of what names I'd just read. Even an initial visit by any of the victims would have produced paperwork. But there were no files for anyone other than Davide who had only recently started treatment with Dr. Alphonse.

"Do you feel paralyzed?" she asked. "Like there's a pressure on your chest?"

"Yes."

"Terrified?"

A pause.

I stared down at my feet. He'd had nightmares when we were kids. On a scale of one to awful, how bad did me not considering how investigating this place would affect him rate?

"What you're experiencing are classic sleep terrors," she said. "Any history of substance abuse?"

"No."

"Have you had any stressful situations in your life lately?"

Ari laughed, a devastating sound. "You could say that."

"Night terrors can manifest as a result of post-traumatic stress disorder. It's a paralyzing experience where the sleeper feels helpless, unable to scream or open their eyes." There was way too much compassion in this woman's voice for her to be a demon. "Those symptoms are called 'felt presence.'"

"Huh," Ari said. "Didn't some cultures attribute these symptoms to demons?"

"Yes," I could practically hear her smile. "If you meet Mara, you can ask her about it. She lives for those tales."

I stiffened because a mara was a type of nightmare demon.

"I'd love to hear them. Is she around?" he asked.

"Not right now." Dr. Alphonse went on to explain some of the physical attributes of sleep paralysis, such as difficulty breathing due to the controlled respiration of REM sleep. From there she outlined some of the ways that her clinic could help alleviate the symptoms.

Minimizing the database, I poked around until I found a Word doc helpfully labeled "Employee contacts" and snapped a photo of Mara's information. The clinic was closed on Sunday and Monday so tomorrow morning would be the perfect time to try and catch her.

I hurriedly concluded my search, restored the screen to the way that I'd found it and hustled out of there. Gay Cutie gave me an odd look, like going into the bathroom after me was probably going to require nose plugs, but I hadn't been caught.

I flipped through half a magazine without seeing a single page, practically grabbing Ari by the elbow when he emerged to hustle him out the door faster.

I thrust the photo of Mara's address at him.

"Not bad, newb."

"What are those?" I fished my keys out of my pocket, casually craning my neck to take in the title of one of the pamphlets he held–*Sleep Disorders*–before he just as casually stuffed them in his pocket.

"Convinced her," he said.

"Great." I started the car. If Ari wanted to discuss this, he would.

I lasted three blocks.

"Why didn't you tell me the nightmares never stopped?" I pinched my lips together.

Ari jabbed a finger at me. "Because of that."

I flicked on my right turn signal, waiting for the crosswalk to clear of pedestrians. "Are you considering seeing Dr. Alphonse?"

"I'll deal." His voice was flat.

I slowed to a stop at the red light. This was one of the longest lights in Vancouver and with my hands not needed on the wheel, I worried I might do something I'd regret, like haul off and clobber the stubborn bastard. PTSD had to be pretty common amongst our bunch. I'd bet good money Rohan was neck deep in it after Pakistan.

"If the Brotherhood has massage therapists on call, they must have someone you can speak to. A Rasha psychiatrist or something." The second the light changed to green, I gunned the car forward.

Ari was quiet for a long time, staring out at the rain. "That's part of how they train us."

"You need to be a bit less cryptic. I never got the program."

He rummaged in the leather messenger bag that lay at his feet. "When we initiates hit our teens, we're exposed to the harsh realities of demon hunting. Shown photos of carnage, hear firsthand testimony about demon attacks. We work with specially trained Rasha on how to live with the stress."

I clenched the wheel. Another thing I'd missed out on. "That's what you were doing each spring break in high school? That intensive you did?" It explained why my brother had always come back quieter than usual from "Camp Rasha."

Not finding whatever he was looking for, Ari opened the glove compartment and rooted through it. "They flew me out to different crime scenes or to spend one-on-one time with hunters describing what they'd lived through," he said. "What they'd lost."

Who they'd lost?

"If they took the trouble to prepare you before you started hunting then they've got to have Rasha on staff to help you cope now," I said.

"They do." He fished out a black pen and dropped it into the messenger bag.

"But you won't go see them."

"No. And not because I'm stubborn, which is what you're thinking right now." He slammed the glove compartment shut. "If we went into therapy for every single thing that was going to mess with our heads? We'd never be out there. So we deal with it. We talk to each other and do whatever we have to to claw some sunshine back into the world."

"You could talk to me. As well."

"It's not the same. Kane has gone through everything with me. So much about our lives are similar. Initiates, being gay."

Fascinating that Ari's general "all Rasha talking to each other" had suddenly gotten so specific. I shrugged off my sting of hurt and renewed my commitment to seeing him and Kane together. If they could figure out their bullshit, they'd be good for each other.

"I'm glad you have someone to confide in," I said. "As for me, I managed to get into their files. Only Davide was a patient."

"It was worth a shot. Turn left here. Ellen Chen's family should be at the end of the block."

I slowed to a stop in front of the house he indicated and cut the engine.

"I'm going to take this one on my own." He fished a pair of glasses out of his jacket and slid them on, then picked up the messenger bag.

"Why?"

"They believe I'm her agent's assistant in town to settle up some paperwork." He rummaged in the bag and pulled out a business card.

"Millner and Associates Literary," I read. It had an embossed logo and everything. "Is this for real?"

He nodded and tapped the name. "Right down to Simon Kelly. Her actual agent's assistant."

"Well, go get 'em, Simon."

"Thanks. I'll make my own way home."

I hadn't expected to be on my own this afternoon but maybe that was for the best. I could get on with my plan to track down the spine. "Hey, Ace, the contact guy for the snitch? You wouldn't happen to have his phone number, would you?"

I could have asked Leo, but I felt kind of weird asking for that favor from her.

"No clue. Why?"

I started the engine. "Doesn't matter."

"Is this about the witches? I'm not helping you bite off more than you can chew and accidentally endanger my brothers. Especially not after you lied to me about what the witches are up to."

"Montague *deliberately* endangered you, endangered the entire chapter house, when he took down the wards." In addition to his intimate and interactive time with the jax, Montague had been the Rasha who took down the wards around our original place at the bidding of Asmodeus, Prince of Lust. Ari had been captured and tortured in the fallout. "You're focusing on the wrong loyalties, bro."

"So are you." He opened the door.

I released the parking brake, muttering under my breath about deliberately obtuse individuals.

Ari slid out of the car. "I know what you meant, Nee. I always do when it comes to you. But sometimes I wonder if the reverse is ever true." With that, he shut the car door and walked away.

What a ridiculous thing to say. So I hadn't realized his insecurities around the way he'd been inducted until Kane had told me. Why would I have assumed that he was bent out of shape about it? What did it matter that his becoming Rasha hadn't happened exactly according to plan? It had still happened, hadn't it? I'd risked my life to get him exactly where he wanted to be and he was going to pout about it?

And he had the gall to doubt my loyalty?

I sped back to Demon Club, making one quick stop.

"A mocha latte no whip," I said, presenting one of the two cups I held to Ms. Clara with a flourish. She was in her office, located on the ground floor of the chapter house next to the conference room and other offices kept for visiting Rasha or rabbis.

Tasteful photographic prints of the city from Pacific Spirit Park to neon signs in Chinatown framed her white walls. The office wasn't large but it was bright and organized with a near mania.

While the Brotherhood was a secret organization, it wasn't secret from families of the rabbis and Rasha. That's how Ms. Clara had come to work for us. Her dad had been Rasha.

She was dressed in iron-gray slacks and a matching sweater that she managed to make soft and feminine looking. "Thanks, doll. What do you need?"

"That obvious?" I sat down.

"Kind of." Ms. Clara leaned back in her black and brushed steel Aeron chair that matched her desk and sipped her coffee. "Mmm."

"There's this guy."

Ms. Clara raised an eyebrow.

"Really not like that. This old guy. Obsessed with UFOs." I drank some more of my own mocha.

She nodded. "Harry. Our go-between with the informant."

"I need to find him." I paused, ready with a lie, but she simply drank some more coffee, waiting for me to continue. "Ari was the one who'd originally gotten me to him, but when I swung by Harry's house, he'd moved and Ari doesn't have a number for him."

I'd hoped Harry could get me to the witches. Now I hoped he could find the spine.

"I'm not sure how to reach him. Why don't you just ask Leonie?"

I spat mocha all over her desk. Still coughing, I grabbed a handful of tissue from the box and mopped up the liquid before she broke out some dominatrix moves for messing up the sanctity of The Desk. "Leonie?" I squeaked. "Why would I do that?"

"Nava, I know she's half-goblin. And our resident informant."

I shook my head "no" hard enough to rattle my brain. My heart thudded in my ears.

Ms. Clara came around to my side of the desk and, grasping my shoulders, crouched down to meet my eyes. "Breathe, doll. She's in no danger."

"How did you find out?"

"Xiaoli." The previous head Rasha here in Vancouver.

"Who else knows?"

"No one." She stood up, opened her top drawer and peered inside. "I'm sorry I couldn't help you."

I knew a dismissal when I heard it. I threw the soggy tissues out into the trash, praying I could trust her about Leo. "Yeah, sure. Sorry to have bothered you."

She brushed past me, headed for the door, coffee in hand. "Not a problem. I'm going upstairs to get a cookie to go with my mocha."

I pointed at her desk. "You left your drawer open."

"Did I? I'm opening and closing that thing *three hundred* times a day." She left the room.

I edged around the desk warily, not sure what I'd find given that blatant set-up. There was a plastic cube containing paperclips, a bundle of multi-colored pens and a neat stack of pastel Post-Its. Also an envelope filled with petty cash.

I smiled and plucked out three crisp one hundred dollar bills. Harry liked his payouts. And Ms. Clara was truly a bad-ass mofo.

I texted Leo to see if she was around. I'd made it up to the foyer, rooting through my bag for my lipstick when she texted back a photo of a bunch of red squares.

I sent her a series of question marks. Seconds later my phone rang.

"Tell me you're downtown," she said.

"I'm headed that way in a minute." I applied the Rebel pink, running a finger along the edge of my lips to wipe off any excess lipstick.

She squealed. "Really? How come?"

"Coming to see you." I stepped outside onto the front porch, squinting against the sun's glare. My favorite pair of sunglasses had been broken in a demon encounter and my back up heart-shaped ones had been dumped in the Great Lolita Purge when I'd rid myself of the undercover persona I'd used in Prague–and Rohan's nickname for me.

"Good. Paint chip 911. Can you come to the hardware store by my place?"

"Sure. Be there soon." This visit necessitated yet another stop. The bribe train just kept adding more cars.

Leo had commandeered the two high school employees into holding about thirty-seven paint chip samples up to the front window and was barking commands at them to turn this way and that.

"I'll take it from here," I assured the terrified kids. They fled, scattering paint chips in their wake.

"Argh!" Leo pulled on her hair. She looked about sixteen in her striped jumper with the cap sleeves and a jean jacket. Not that I was stupid enough to mention that.

I waved the giant, fake, shiny ruby ring surrounded by "diamonds" that I'd purchased at the dollar store down the block. "Look deep into the gemstone. Let its cut edges–"

"Facets," Leo said primly. Goblins and their gem fetishes.

I rolled my eyes. "Let its facets calm you, you psycho."

She snatched the ring from me and slid it on her finger, admiring it.

"Working?" I asked.

"As a placebo, sure." She regarded the rows of paint chip samples and whimpered. "Or not."

Ten minutes later we'd narrowed the selection down to seven different shades of red and one green. "You know my vote," I said.

"I can't paint my wall this color just because it's called 'Olive-ia Newton John.'" She was beginning to vibrate.

I slung an arm over her shoulders. "I'm going to say this with as much love as I can, okay?" She nodded. "Your bedroom trim is white. And if you paint the walls red, my diminutive demon friend, you will look like you live in a toadstool."

She snatched the green chip out of my hand and marched up to the front counter.

I waited until she'd placed her order for a gallon of paint and we were browsing the aisles to ask my favor. "So, hey. I was wondering if I could get Harry's phone number."

Leo picked up a utility knife. Casually examined it. "Why do you know his name?"

"Uh, Ms. Clara told me."

"I see."

"No one else knows any identifying info on him." She didn't put her weapon down so I picked up a wide putty knife and brandished it in front of me. "The guy obviously consorts with demons so I'm hardly a threat."

"What do you need to talk to him about?" She popped the blade out.

I scrunched up my face. "Witches."

"Right. I can't see how pulling my friend into whatever this Brotherhood-witch animosity is could possibly be a problem."

I brushed the blade she jabbed at me aside with my putty knife. "I promise you–"

"Maybe I don't trust your promises." Leo threw the knife back onto the shelf and stalked out of the aisle.

I laid down the putty knife and followed her, cornering her in the back by the bookcase of wallpaper samples. "I was a shitty friend, okay? There are not apologies enough for cutting you out of my life, but the number of people I trust are pretty much standing in front of me."

"Don't be such a drama queen. You have Ari."

"He's pretty firmly committed to Team Brotherhood right now. That's part of why I need to talk to Harry. He seems connected in certain circles...?"

Leo gave a slight nod.

No one was nearby, still, I lowered my voice. "The demon that attacked me in Prague had been modified. I'm hoping if I find the external spine that had been rigged onto it, I can do some kind of spell to test for magic indicating binding and use that to figure out if the attack was ordered by the witches or the Brotherhood." I rubbed my forehead. "I know you help fight the good fight, and believe it or not, I'm really conscious of not crossing this line between us. I don't want you to think that I'm using you for your friends and contacts, but I don't know where else to turn."

"The thing is, Nee, it's not just your life that you're playing with anymore. It's not even just mine." Leo flipped through a rack of shower curtains, each one cheaper and uglier than the last.

"I wouldn't do anything to hurt you again."

"Not consciously. But you've changed. You're a lot more willing to cut and run."

I willed myself to respect what she was saying and swallowed the snarky comment I wanted to make about some people willing to give up on others pretty fast. "Okay. You need time to trust this again. Trust us. Forget I asked."

This wasn't worth my friendship.

"Really?"

"Really."

The employee called out that Leo's paint was ready.

"Go pay," I said. "I'll help you prime your walls."

Leo fiddled with the fake ring. The employee called her to the counter again. She took two steps, stopped, and pressed her phone into my hand. "Two seven three three one six," she said and headed for the counter.

27-33-16. The combination to the locker we'd shared in grade twelve. I smiled.

I unlocked her cell, and got Harry's number from her contacts, leaving him a message using the burner phone I'd purchased when I'd gotten back from Prague. The Brotherhood had given me an encrypted phone which they could track and probably use to monitor all my calls, so I'd bought another cell.

We lugged all the paint and supplies back to Leo's apartment, threw open the windows, blasted her Girl Power playlist, moved her furniture away from the walls under plastic sheets, and rollered our little hearts out.

"What is Harry to you?"

Pouring more primer into the tray, Leo wiggled her hips to the Beyoncé playing. "My boss."

"He owns the P.I. firm?" I dipped my roller in the primer, slapping it against the tray to get rid of the excess.

"Yup. Is that good?"

"It's even better than I expected." I'd been hoping that he could get me to someone who could get me to someone who could find out what had happened to the spine, but if he was a seasoned P.I., he could very well be able to get it for me himself.

"Nee." I glanced up at Leo, holding an angled corner brush in her hand. "I'm conscious of the line, too." She resumed painting, singing "Crazy In Love" at top volume.

I hugged her and went to work on my own wall.

8

Just as we were finishing up, Ari texted me to come back to Demon Club. I scratched my cheek with primer-covered fingers. "I gotta book. You okay for the rest of this?"

Leo tapped the lid back onto the paint can. "Yeah. Go."

I washed off my roller, we wished each other "schmugs," and I returned home.

Ari was in the library, plugging in his laptop. He'd brought Szechuan take-out for dinner and the room was filled with the smell of chilies and sesame.

"Did you learn anything useful from Ellen's family?" I pulled off the first lid, inhaling the delights of ginger beef.

"Not really."

He pushed a package of Twizzlers my way without looking over. His go-to peace offering with me since we were kids. The tension in my shoulders eased.

"Strawberry. Good boy." I opened the other two Chinese food containers to find shrimp fried rice and spicy green beans.

"Like I was gonna buy you the black ones and watch you throw them in the garbage."

"It only took one lesson for you to learn."

He dug out his phone. "I swung by Mara's place—"

"You went without me?" I shoved the licorice back at him.

He tossed the package at me again. It landed on the table with a thump and a crinkle. "It was on the way home. I just wanted to do an initial recon. See what I could scope out."

"Without me." I scooped rice onto my plate. "After I was the one that got her address to begin with."

"Will you stop bitching and look?" He shoved his phone at me.

Sure, this was no big deal to him because he was the one getting to call the shots. I probably wouldn't even have minded if he'd given me a heads up *before* he'd gone over there. Note to self: less of the free and easy with anything I learned in the future.

I looked at his stupid photo. "It's an ugly butterfly. Mazel tov."

"It's a sphinx moth."

That got my attention. Certain types of mara demons were reputed to take the form of sphinx moths. I examined the insect more closely but unless mottled and brown had become synonymous with evil, there was nothing to definitively ID it. "Why didn't you capture the thing?"

"It flew away before I could get close. Tomorrow morning, when we go back there, if we can catch her transforming or better still, force a transformation?"

"Then we've got her. Is that possible? To force it?" When Rohan, Drio, and I had taken down Samson in Prague, we'd performed a ritual to force his transformation back to his true body, but in that case, we'd had his demon name and, besides, moths were a shape these demons shifted into, not their natural form.

"I don't know, but it can't hurt to check the library."

We spent the next couple of hours hunting through the library and Brotherhood database for any references to inducing a mara demon transformation.

"I guess it was too much to hope for." Between us, we'd inhaled all the food, so with no leftovers to place in containers, I dumped my dirty dishes in the dishwasher, then ripped into a bag of tortilla chips for our after-dinner-after-dessert-after-snack snack.

"I need to think about how I want us to play this when we go tomorrow." Ari removed a tub of guacamole from the industrial-sized fridge, snapped off the lid, and, tearing off the plastic sealant, dumped the entire thing into a mixing bowl.

I smooshed up the tortilla chips, added them to the guacamole, and stirred, not saying a word. He could strategize; I could strategize. It had taken both of us to get this far: Ari learning about Mara in the first place and his keen eye for detail that had him spot the sphinx moth, coupled with me getting the connection between Davide and the clinic as well as Mara's address. He wasn't going to shut me out now.

I tossed him a spoon and we dug into the guac and chips like it was a crunchy cereal. "We'll get her," I said around a mouthful.

Kane wandered into the kitchen, peered into our bowl, and grimaced. "That's disgusting."

"Disgustingly good." Ari held up a spoonful. "Try it."

"No. That's a line too far even for me."

Ari and I shrugged. Kane's comments didn't come close to our parents' very vocal feelings on our culinary masterpiece, created by us at the tender age of six.

"It's comfort food," I said, savoring the creamy, lemony texture with its crispy surprises in every bite.

"It's chunky sacrilege." Kane tossed a package of popcorn into the microwave. "I'm going to watch *Deadpool*. You're invited. That bowl is not."

Ari's taste may have run to crime dramas not superhero flicks, but his gaze lingered on Kane speculatively when Kane's back was turned. "Sure," Ari said. He grabbed some beer and headed into the TV room.

"Gonna get cozy?" I asked Kane, rifling through the cupboards for the stash of M&M's that Ms. Clara had hidden away.

Kane placed his hands on my shoulders. "For the last time, babys-lay, I am not interested in your brother as a boyfriend. I don't do those." He smirked. "Well, yes, I do, but only other people's." He smacked my ass. "Movie in five."

I brought my empty calorie hoard into the TV room and got comfy under my favorite blanket next to Kane and my brother on the couch, wearing my "I'm sarcastic because punching people is frowned upon" pajama top and black boxers with a giant yellow happy face that I'd won as some door prize. I seriously needed to do laundry soon. It was a massive injustice that I lived a reality in which demons existed and house elves didn't.

I arranged the snacks by proximity and order in which I planned to eat them: the salt and vinegar chips and one of the two-party sized bags of M&M's stayed in front of me. The popcorn and other candy bag was positioned for the guys to eat.

Where Rohan was, I had no idea, nor did I care.

We'd just gotten to the pegging scene, with Ryan Reynolds on the receiving end of a strap-on dildo in a hilarious celebration of Interna-tional Women's Day, when Kane gave this breathy sigh.

Awkward.

He let out a somewhat more gutteral moan. Ari and I stared at him in confusion.

"Oooh," Kane gasped in a high voice. He smirked at me.

That. Bastard.

"Uhhhhhhhh," I groaned in a lower register.

"Ah. Ah. Ah," Kane continued in falsetto.

"Yeah, baby," I said in my most manly voice, thrusting my hips, and pumping the cushions.

"Oooh. More." Kane sloppily thrust his tongue in and out of his mouth.

"The fuck is wrong with you two?" Ari asked, turning up the vol-ume on the movie.

Kane stuck his tongue in his cheek, miming a blowjob while panting, which, for the record, sounded nothing like me.

I bent over the sofa and slapped my own ass. "Do me."

Kane whipped a pillow at me. "The hell I'm bottoming."

My jump of triumph due to him breaking first became a stumble when Ari tossed out, "You'd bottom for me," without even taking his eyes off the screen.

Kane's mouth fell open.

I curled into a ball in the corner of the couch, and spent the rest of *Deadpool* that way, all thrill of victory gone, as I tried to concentrate on the movie and not on the absolutely serious way my brother had said that. Partway through *The Avengers*, I was yawning so hard I had to bail. I gathered up the detritus of the snacks when I left and loaded up the dishwasher.

I shuffled down the hallway, headed for the back stairs and bed.

Rohan's door was half-open. I couldn't escape the lure, much like a mouse to a cheese-laden trap, or an alien enthusiast to an anal-probe-promising light beam. Just a quick peek from a safe, stalkerish distance.

The light from his bedside lamp cast a warm pool over him. He sat on his bed in boxers and a faded green T-shirt, his hands pressing down on the mattress and earbuds in his ears. A broken piece of pale curved bone lay tossed beside him. He didn't speak, didn't give any sign of my presence, lost to the thoughts responsible for his blank stare.

I stepped toward the door, my hand raised to knock.

Stepped back, dropping my hand.

Maybe if I hadn't ended things, I would have asked him what was going on, given the nightmares and now this. We'd been friends if nothing else. But I'd set our boundaries and to muddy things up now wouldn't be to anyone's advantage.

I went up to my bedroom, clutching my phone, unable to banish the image of him. I thunked my head back against my headboard twice before dialing his number, praying it went to voicemail so I could hang up guilt-free.

"Hello?"

"It's me. Nava."

"Oh. I didn't recognize the number." He sounded... empty. Running on autopilot.

"It's a burner phone." I arranged the covers over my feet.

"Prepping for your drug dealer debut?"

Even that level of lame teasing from him sent relief swimming down to my toes. "Or adulterer. Keeping my options open." I cast about for something to say as our silence stretched on for a beat too long. "Uh, what were you listening to? I saw you when I was walking past a minute ago."

His bed creaked. "Albinoni's 'Adagio in G Minor.'"

"Ah. I'm not a classical music person. Jazz and big band."

"Because of tap."

"Yeah. Did you get into classical from your mom?"

"My dad, actually. It's all he listens to. He whistles a mean concerto."

"Impressive."

More silence.

"You okay?" I asked.

"Yup."

All righty, then. Compassion quota satisfied. "It's late. I should let you–"

"Have you been dancing a lot lately?"

I jerked my head with a double blink. "Uh... Trying to."

"How's it going?"

I lay back on my mattress, allowing the call to play out. My initial caution quickly disappeared because when we weren't at each other's throats, Rohan and I could talk for ages without running out of topics. We discussed a dozen inconsequential things, from a Saturday Night Live sketch that had gone viral to whether the Empress of China had owned pugs (related to the sketch), until the conversation turned to Rohan telling me he had no idea what to buy his mom as a belated Mother's Day present.

I tucked the edge of the blanket cocoon I'd made for myself under my hip. "Ari and I bought ours a spa gift certificate, but that's because I have zero desire to have an actual conversation with her and find out if she's developed any interests outside her field of study and Ari's lazy. But your mom is Maya Mitra."

A quiet chuckle cut across the line at my blatant squee. Rohan was well aware of how in awe I was of his music producer mother. "She's impossible to shop for. If she wants something, chances are she's already bought it. Or Dad has. I've never figured out if he loves to spoil her or he just really loves the fact that his engineering firm is successful enough that he can buy stuff without worrying about the cost."

I wrapped the sound of his fond laughter around me as tightly as my covers and tried not to wonder if his sharing mood meant I was something more than a convenient cover for a mission and a fuck buddy. It didn't matter anymore.

"You're Maya's only child and you actually like her," I said sternly. "You do not get to descend into gift certificate territory. Write her a song. I'm sure you can think up something insightful."

I swear I wasn't dredging up the whole "Toccata and Fugue" debacle but both of us must have gone to that place because I didn't imagine how the silence went from the easy familiarity we'd achieved to loaded. I cleared my throat. "It's the perfect gift for her."

"Hell no."

"Why not? Done that too many times?"

"Actually," he admitted, "I never have."

"Rohan Liam Mitra, what is your problem?"

There was a rustle of sheets through the phone. "You know how scary her rep is," he said. "She'll mock it."

I smiled, switching the phone to my other ear. "Aww, kitten. She won't mock it. She'll love it because it's something thoughtful from you to her."

Rohan growled in frustration. "Fine. I'll write her a song." His voice was warmer when he said, "You're good. I will be exploiting you further."

I had a flash of Rohan bending me over the nearest surface and exploiting me until stars exploded overhead. I shivered. "I'm sure that sounds more intriguing than it will be."

"Perhaps it will be precisely that intriguing."

His cocky tone made my nipples harden. I screamed silently into my pillow. "What is that on the international intrigue scale?" I said.

"Hmmm. Halfway between mysterious and illicit."

"That sounds positively naked."

"That's your smutty mind," he said in a prim voice. "I was only talking about help with gift options." He yawned. "I should go."

"Okay." I snuggled deeper under my blankets, my eyes falling shut. "Hang up."

"Ladies first."

"So I could keep you on the line all night if I refused?" I teased.

His "you could," made me catch my breath.

"We can talk about Prague," I said. "If you want."

"I want." His words were only in relation to this mission and not us.

A pang speared my chest.

I want, too.

The line went dead. Uh, okay.

Two minutes later there was a soft knock at my door. "Nava?"

I sprang out of bed like it was on fire, placing my palm against the wood as if I could feel Rohan on the other side, but I didn't open the door. "What?"

"You said we could talk."

My eyes darted to my bed. The one that Rohan had never been in and wasn't going to sit on now. After Cole and I self-destructed, I'd had a shit time sleeping because I had all these memories of him on my bed: goofy, sexy, and just hanging out being a best friend. It had taken me forever to uncouple him from that place.

It was all too easy for me to picture Rohan sitting there, taking up space and acting like he belonged there, like he belonged in my life.

"Acting" being the key word. "Now?" I gripped the knob, holding it fast, not that he was trying to open the door.

"Yes, now," he said.

"It's really late." I yawned loudly, the doorknob still in a death grip.

"Oh. Yeah. I guess it is. Tomorrow?"

I rested my forehead against the door. "Sure. Buy me lunch at Lotus." Lotus was one of the most expensive and insanely delicious sushi restaurants in the city. I'd only been once but dreamed of going back many times.

"Isn't that kind of public?" he said.

Exactly my intent. Years of tap performances had taught me how to keep a brave face in front of an audience. The attacks on me and Gelman in Prague were too bound up with all the other baggage that had gone down between Rohan and me. Given some of the things I expected to hear, I wouldn't be able to keep it together if we were alone.

Or say "no" if he wanted us to try being an "us." Unless, of course, that position was already filled by Lily.

"It's private enough," I said.

"Lotus it is."

"Good-night, Rohan."

"Good-morning, Nava."

Right. Technically it was Sunday. The day that the two of us would have our talk. The day that could definitively settle things between us one way or another.

I cracked the door to watch his back disappear down the stairs, wrapping my arms around myself to hide my trembling hands, even though there was no one there to see them.

9

Ari and I headed out for Mara's place at the ungodly hour of 7AM. There was a chill in the air and I bundled into my coat, shivering and sipping my steaming café latte until both the car and I warmed up. Whoever had bought this over-roasted crap needed to pony up for a better quality of bean because sour java and cow juice was stomach turning. Desperate times.

Ari hadn't come up with any kind of brilliant strategy beyond arming us with bug catching nets and a zapper fly swatter, but to be fair, neither had I. My chat with Rohan had kind of fried my brain. All that was forgotten, however when we pulled up to her aluminum-siding bungalow in a modest neighborhood and found an ambulance parked outside.

Ari and I exchanged glances. "Did she kill someone at her house?" I said.

"Do we have a folder or envelope or something?" he asked.

We found a glossy UBC course catalogue of Ari's that had slid under the front seat. Ari grabbed it and strode over to a small knot of bystanders.

I followed him.

"Did something happen to Mara?" he asked a blonde woman rolling a stroller back and forth.

"Are you a friend of hers?"

"We work together at the clinic." He held up the catalogue, his thumb covering the mailing label with his name on it. "She left this at work and called me last night asking me to swing by before my shift."

Her face crumpled. "I'm so sorry. Mara passed away."

"What?" His shock wasn't faked. Neither was mine.

"Heart attack."

"Holy sh–" I swallowed the curse in the face of the mom's disapproving stare.

"Are you a coworker, too?" She popped the soother back into her fussing baby's mouth.

I nodded. If Mara wasn't the demon, then who was? And why was the clinic the common factor between Davide and Mara when none of the other victims had ever frequented it?

"Is any of her family here?" Ari asked.

"No. But that's her roommate." The woman pointed out a shellshocked man of Asian heritage in his late-twenties, standing on the concrete front steps with a paramedic. "Daniel."

"Thank you." Ari and I walked toward Mara's front sidewalk.

"How do you want to play this?" I asked. "The roommate might have met Mara's colleagues before."

"Tell him you're here to pick up the gift for Dr. Alphonse that Mara was arranging. See if you can get into her room. Search for anything out of place."

"What are you going to do?"

Ari glanced at the paramedic, now walking back to his ambulance. "Have a little chat."

"Good luck." I headed up the walk, catching the roommate before he shut the door. "Daniel?"

He looked at me with red-rimmed eyes. A couple of inches taller than me, his fitted black T-shirt reading *Policing with Pride* showed off his hella tight biceps. "Yes?"

"I'm Alison. I've been doing a practicum at the clinic."

He screwed up his face. "Was work notified already?"

"No. I came to pick up Dr. Alphonse's gift. For the surprise party?" I wrung my hands together. "I'm so sorry for your loss."

"I got back from my swim, and..." He brushed a hand over his hair plastered in wet strands to his scalp. "I don't know about any gift."

"That's okay."

Daniel nodded distractedly, swaying on his feet. He gripped the front door frame. "They gave me a shot."

I touched his hand. "Do you want to sit down? Have some water or something?"

"Tea." He smiled faintly. "Mara drank gallons of the stuff." He shuffled into the house, lowering himself into a chair as I filled the electric kettle.

A clanking noise vibrated up from the basement. "Water tank," Daniel said, seeing my puzzled look. "It's old."

I gestured at his T-shirt. "Are you a cop?"

He nodded. "Serve and protect." His pride was evident even through his grief.

"This is such a shock," I said. "She was so young. Was there any history of heart trouble in her family?"

"Diabetes but not heart problems." Daniel toyed with the spoon in the bright yellow ceramic honey pot that matched the walls. "The paramedic said it could have been an undiagnosed condition or just brought on by stress." He directed me to the appropriate homey wooden cupboards.

I pulled out a mug covered in painted sunflowers, its cheeriness a slap in the face to how awful I felt. I filled it with boiling water, then let it steep, keeping an eye on him. Pretending to have known Mara, known her personal history and be exploiting it during this tragedy to further the investigation, was one of the ickiest things I'd done as Rasha.

"Was there anything going on at work? Mara didn't say anything but you know how cheerful she was. Never complained." Daniel was starting to slur his words.

"Nothing out of the ordinary," I said.

Daniel slumped further down in his chair. "How could Mara be here one moment and gone the next?"

I dumped the soggy tea bag in the sink. "When did you last see her?"

"This morning. She was asleep. I mean, I thought she was, except the paramedic estimates that's when the heart attack happened." He buried his head in his hands. "What if I could have saved her?"

"There was probably nothing you could have done."

He shook his head almost violently. I wished I could tell him the truth, though learning about demons would hardly be a comfort.

I placed the mug down in front of him. "Here. Drink your tea."

He shot me a grateful look. I squirmed, wishing he'd denounce me as a liar instead of acting all indebted when I'd entered his house under false pretenses and was about to go snooping in his dead room-mate's stuff. Fighting the good fight could be such shit. "Can I use your bathroom?"

He gave a slow wave behind him. "First left."

I tiptoed down the hallway, peering into doors until I found Mara's room since I doubted Daniel was the one with the fanatical love of Daenerys cosplay. Not that I'd judge, but his shoulders were too broad for the costumes hanging on the wall rack. Each outfit was neatly stored in its own plastic garment bag, with long blonde wigs arranged on Styrofoam manikin heads. There was no handy demon evidence, unfortunately, though her swirly green bedspread was really cute.

When I returned to the kitchen, Daniel was slack-jawed and asleep, his head on the table next to the mug.

Ari was checking his breathing. "Find anything?" He shot Daniel one last sidelong glance as we left.

I elbowed my brother. "Quit macking on the mourner. How inappropriate."

"I was making sure he was okay."

"Keep telling yourself that."

"Well?" He edged me out of the way to claim the driver's side.

"Other than a deep Mother of Dragons obsession? No. You?" I walked around the front bumper to the passenger side.

Ari filled me in as he drove. "Mara had a symbol drawn on her in felt pen." He retrieved his phone from the cup holder and tossed it to me. "Took a photo." The symbol looked like a distorted small "w" with a dot underneath the left side. "It's the Arabic word for love," he said.

"We didn't see anything like this on the other vics."

"Not like we have full nudes of them. This was drawn on the back of Mara's neck, hidden by her hair. We need to see other bodies."

"Is that possible?"

"Maybe. I need to make some calls."

I poked his arm. "And then fill me in immediately."

"Yeah, yeah." That sounded so believable.

Well, at least this morning's shock hadn't left time for me to obsess over my impending lunch. After going home and armoring up in a form-fitting raspberry knit dress and my favorite sparkly purple nail polish, I drove over to Lotus. I arrived at noon on the dot, the soothing noise of the water feature inside the front door making me breathe easier. The interior was elegant, minimalist, and smelled like fresh linens.

Servers flitted about, attentive without hovering.

A lithe waiter in all white showed me to a table. My lunch date wasn't here yet so I took the seat that would allow me full view of Rohan's arrival. I was idly perusing the menu, the thousand volts thrumming through my veins undercut by a sharp curl of dread, when the other patrons shifted in a rippled wave.

If Rohan was aware of the electric jolt his presence charged the room with, he gave no sign of it. His stride past the well-heeled crowd, their hungry eyes feasting on his progress, was leisurely and self-assured.

My greedy little heart chanted "mine" almost loud enough to drown out the stutter of my brain's grand mal seizure at the sight of him.

Rohan wasn't dressed flashy. In fact, in a slim, black suit tailored to his frame and silver cufflinks winking discreetly at his wrists, it was his very understatedness that packed a punch. There was a certain beauty about a man clad in a sharp suit during daylight hours, dressed to impress.

I curled my fingers into my palm, scared I'd reach for his ear-length dark curls that were raked back in wavy locks. And then almost drew blood when I looked at the face I'd saved to savor last.

He'd shaved his scruff into a mustache-goatee combo. It made him look so wicked that when he smiled that pirate smile, I almost came in my seat. Hot disappointment rushed in, filling my chest. This wasn't about gaining my approval. My adversary had chosen his initial weapons with calculated brilliance.

I would not underestimate him again.

He strolled toward me, hands in pockets. "See something you like?" Nodding his thanks to the waiter, he eased into his seat across from me with fluid grace.

I tilted my head, studying him. "I've never noticed before, but in this light, you're not bad looking."

He grinned, picking up a menu. "I get that a lot. Order whatever you want. They've got my card on file, and you're easy when you're well-fed."

Sadly, around Rohan, I was easy most of the time. *Had* been easy. I snapped my menu into submission.

We decided to share a number of dishes, from tuna tataki to salmon sashimi and an assortment of nigiri. The waiter took our menus, promising to return with our drinks.

"How's your training going?"

"Okay. Not as good obviously without Tree Trunk." Baruch Ya'ari was the Brotherhood's weapons and fight specialist. He was the first Rasha I'd met when they sent him to take charge of me and train me in fight moves to keep me alive until the Brotherhood decided whether or not they wanted a sister. An official decision had yet to be handed down but Baruch had been recalled to HQ in Jerusalem while I was on assignment in Prague. Huh. Maybe that *was* the decision, though it was a toss-up whether they trusted me enough to stay alive on my own, or they didn't care if I died.

Regardless, I missed him with a fierce ache.

Polite small talk continued through our tataki appetizer. It was excruciating. I poured some soya sauce into the dish, which was adorned with tiny ink brush outlines of fish swimming under a crackly glaze, and cast around for my opening gambit. Something blasé to ease into the topic of the gogota.

"You kissed Lily." I jabbed wasabi into the soya sauce. "Twice."

Damn it!

Rohan nodded. "I did." He didn't bother rationalizing that for at least one of those kisses Dr. Lily Prasad, that sweet, beautiful physicist, had kissed *him*.

"I get it." To be clear, I meant that in the literal logistics way involving facial muscle movement and not with any emotional understanding known to mankind. "Lily was your first love. The original lightning girl."

"And yet you claimed I'd written the song for you."

The waiter set down our first platter of nigiri sushi.

I cooed appreciatively. Each of the pieces presented on individual flourishes of daikon were such sumptuous works of art that it was almost sacrilege to eat them. I silently thanked the sushi for their sacrifice to the greater cause. "Please. I said that for the mission."

"Are you sure?"

"Obviously. Since I'm the one who said it." Fresh and light, the fish melted in my mouth. This sushi was gonna ruin me for all other sushi. I eyed my companion and snorted.

"When Logan body-switched us, and Lily came to see me about getting back together, you could have wrecked things." He mixed a smear of wasabi into his soya sauce, his chopsticks clattering faintly against the ceramic as the bright green blob dissolved into the dark liquid. "Lils had no clue she was speaking to you. But you didn't. How come?"

"It wasn't for me to wreck. Besides, I like Lily." Enough that I'd saved her from a demon's clutches. Though I'd sort of put her there so that might not tally in my "go Nava" column.

Rohan nodded. "You were kind to her. I appreciated that."

"Is that what our kiss was? A thank you? Because gratitude doesn't usually involve tongue." I pried my fingers off my blue lacquered chopsticks, folding my hands in my lap and away from the pointy projectiles.

A muscle jumped in his jaw but he didn't say anything.

Amazing how provoking him brought my appetite roaring back. "Regardless, there was no reason for Lily to get hurt." I dipped a piece of mango-wrapped salmon in the soya sauce, eyes seemingly on my meal, but watching Rohan through my lashes. "We're off topic."

"Have you heard from Gelman?" Rohan asked as the waiter placed a small carafe of warm sake and two tiny jade green ceramic cups in front of us.

"No."

"Is that why you and Ari have been targeting specific demons this past month?" he asked in his Southern-Cali drawl, all velvet curls and smooth baritone. His gold eyes, on the other hand, had the predatory gleam of a jungle cat.

"Yeah. I was hoping they'd lead me to some local witches who would in turn get me to Gelman." There was no point lying to him.

He'd been with me when the gogota attacked me and when I found Gelman's trashed hotel room with no sign of her.

"Did they?"

"No. I'm not pursuing that avenue anymore." I sipped some sake, wrinkling my nose at the taste.

Rohan leaned in. "Why not?"

The memory of Ari's utter conviction that the witches had to be the bad guys flashed in my head. I opened my mouth, shaping my lie, when Rohan added, "Don't even think it." In a rumble that sent shivers up my spine and had Cuntessa willing my knees to spread-eagle.

I crossed my legs and went for a secondary truth to appease him. "I want the gogota spine as proof of what the Brotherhood is up to."

"Despite Mandelbaum's claim that the witches are behind it."

"Heard that, did you?"

"You'd be amazed at what I hear." His eyes narrowed. "And?"

"And nothing. I don't have the spine yet. But I don't think the witches are to blame. Hence me checking. If the spine is the mechanism by which someone is binding demons, then there'll be magic traces on it."

"So you want to perform a spell on it?" Rohan snagged a piece of paper-thin ginger, his strong fingers handling his chopsticks with deftness and certainty.

Shoot me now. I was envious of condiments.

I grasped my sushi too hard and it slipped with a plop onto my plate. "Yeah. I'm hoping that will give more insight as to who orchestrated all of this. Like the Brotherhood."

"Unless the witches *have* figured out a way to control demons," Rohan said. "Their abilities are a giant question mark."

"Maybe if the Brotherhood had played nicely with them, they wouldn't be such strangers." I reached for my water.

He gave an exasperated huff.

I expected a lot of bad behaviors from Rohan, but sexism was not one of them. I took a sip, feeling oddly disappointed. "You're right. The women must automatically be at fault."

He lay his chopsticks down. "Could you stop being so damned prickly for a second? If the Brotherhood could control demons, why wouldn't they pass that info on to their hunters?"

"Because they want it for their own nefarious plans."

"Which are what?"

"Gee, how about taking out a Rasha who doesn't want to go quietly?" I clamped my lips shut.

His expression softened. "That is never going to happen."

"Don't make promises you can't keep. Besides, you'll be back in L.A. soon."

Rohan's mouth pulled tight with frustration as the waiter arrived with our final dish, a beautiful piece of marinated sablefish.

"Back in Gelman's hotel room," I said. "You believed it was the Brotherhood behind the attacks, didn't you?"

His "yes" was a pained exhale.

I ticked items off on my fingers. "Because the attack wasn't random, it wasn't on Samson's orders, and it didn't make sense that other witches would attack me or Dr. Gelman. Our gut instincts were pointing us to the same culprit. The Brotherhood."

"We do nothing without hard proof. Making assumptions could get you killed." He took half of the sablefish, chewing thoughtfully. "Does Ari know about any of this?"

I shifted in my seat in order to jiggle room in my belly. "He doesn't want to be involved."

"Who else knows?" The gleam in his eyes inched a few more points up the "Danger, Danger, Will Robinson" thermometer.

Unconcerned, I fit a last piece of sushi into my stomach like the Tetris Grandmistress of Food that I was. It was taking me longer to set him off. Either he was getting inured to me or I was losing my touch. "Other than certain pushy people at this table, no one. I have a burner phone and I've been careful. I know what's at stake here. Give me some credit."

"I'm giving you sweet fuck all."

I blinked at his words.

"You want to blow either the Brotherhood or a cabal of dangerous witches wide open and you're going to do it on your own?" He leaned in, his voice low and hard as steel. "Are you crazy or just psychopathically egotistical?"

I sat up ramrod straight. "How dare you? This isn't ego. I'll bring people in when it's safe to do so. When I have proof."

"Right. When you have the spine. When you do a spell that, by the way, you have no training in. You tell yourself that you'll bring people in, but you'll find another reason to keep all of us out of the loop and you want to know why?"

"Mansplain it to me, would you?" My magic frothed inside me like a million pinpricks.

"Because you want to do everything, *have* everything, on your terms."

Yes! Exactly! I was arranging my life to my satisfaction after so many years of feeling like I was at the mercy of the universal goddess of suck-ass. That was a good thing, not the rampant narcissism that Rohan made it sound like.

Blood pounded in my temples. Rohan had walked away from his dreams, not had them ripped from his grasp like I had. Even becoming Rasha had happened with the full support of his family and the Brotherhood. While the demon-slaying lifestyle hadn't been my choice, it could still be my opportunity, provided I was able to oust Mandelbaum and get some real change in the organization. I'd made a plan, I was collecting evidence, and I was going to see it through one careful step at a time. As the lone female in this situation, I knew better than anyone how this had to be played and if Rohan couldn't deal with that, that was his problem.

I gripped the table and counted to ten. "Like I said, I need proof. I won't risk bringing anyone into it until then."

"You can't bring me into it? I was there."

My skin stretched tight from the strain of containing the wild hum of my magic. "You were gone," I shot back.

"I was on assignment–"

"Child's Play wasn't your assignment!"

Rohan's blades slid out of his fingertips for a fraction of a second before he forced them back under his skin with visible effort. "And you're pissed that I didn't bring you along to screw your way through the performer list."

"Fuck you." I jabbed a chopstick at him. "You don't get to be mad because I didn't tell you what I was up to when you didn't even bother dropping me a line to, I dunno, say hello. Let me know you were alive. Since I'm fairly certain London has means of communication."

"I was going to contact–"

"But what? A kraken ate your letter? Well, I'm here now so lay it on me. What happened with Lily to make you come running back and kiss me?"

Silence reigned.

I pushed the eighteen grains of soya-saturated rice on my plate into a passable small "n." "Feel free to speak."

"What's the point? You've obviously figured it all out."

I nodded. "I did have a month to come to my conclusions."

Rohan spread his hands wide, his suit jacket bunching tight around his flexed biceps. "Enlighten me."

"I can't bring you into the light and I don't want to stay in the darkness anymore just because you want company. I can't fix you."

Two white spots appeared on his cheeks, his eyes going hard. "You think I need a crutch? Or saving?" He laughed an exhale. "I can't tell if you think less of me or yourself."

"Trust me." I smiled sweetly. "I don't think less of myself."

"No?" He cocked an eyebrow, tossing his linen napkin on the table, and reaching for the sake. "Not even if you were my second choice?"

Only sheer gritty tenacity kept me from flinching. "Aw, baby," I purred. "You don't think you were mine?"

Rohan froze in mid-pour, setting the carafe down with careful precision. "Meaning?"

I tossed my hair, a hard smile sliding across my face. "I hooked up with Drio. In Prague. The night of your wrap party performance."

Rohan pushed away from the table, standing over me. Of all the responses he could have given me—anger, outrage, betrayal—the last one I expected was a smirk. "Drio told me the next morning." His lips brushed my ear as he whispered, "Didn't conclude that, did you, baby?" and was gone.

10

Slamming my car door wasn't particularly satisfying. Rohan had known about me and Drio and hadn't cared enough to comment. I was such a fool. I really had been his second choice. Beating on my steering wheel and screaming curse words was slightly better.

Drio and I may have started out as the worst of enemies but we'd grown into an odd sort of friendship and mutual respect. Yet boy, had he killed it with his blabbermouthing to Rohan.

I hit speed dial, not bothering with greetings. "You kissing and telling motherfucker!"

"What is your problem now?" Drio's Italian-accented English was a low rasp, his voice thick with sleep. Even given the time difference between Vancouver and Rome, where he was currently on a mission, it wasn't that late. Wonder what he'd been up to?

"You told Rohan about us?"

There was silence for a moment. "Oh. Not much of an us considering my blue balls that night." He scratched some part of his body with a loud scritch. "That upset you?" Given the glee in those words, he'd unleashed the sadistic grin that always preceded demon torture time and was bestowed on *me* about thirty-five percent of the time. He and I had come a long way from the ninety-nine percent I'd first rated.

I repeatedly shot the phone the finger. "It was none of his business! Do something useful for a change and make him go back to Los Angeles."

"He should be soon. Rabbi Mandelbaum always personally greets new Rasha so he came to see your brother–"

"And me. My greeting was definitely personal." I wrenched the ignition key on.

"...and since Ro had to go back to Vancouver to pick up his things, they had the debrief there."

Debrief and clothing retrieval. I gripped the wheel, not yet releasing the parking brake lest I drive off in a homicidal rage. "As we've both moved on from our little fling, the sooner he leaves, the better."

"Quit toying with him."

"Other way round."

He gave a pffft of disbelief.

"What's the deal with you two?" His loyalty to Rohan was a dark fierce bond. One day I'd figure out their relationship which I'd short-listed down to a top three of blood brothers, lovers in a hard, rough one night stand, or co-perpetrators in some heinous crime. God knows, I had my preference.

"I'd tell you but then I'd have to kill you, bella," he purred.

All righty, I was one twisted dudette because fan me now, that was hot. "I hate you."

He laughed and hung up. Death by testosterone. It was pretty much a given in my future.

Enough of him and his annoying BFF. I called Cole, snorting at the irony that he was my least stressful dynamic these days. "Come bowling with me. Now."

"What's with the sudden need for five-pin, Avon? Feeling sentimental?"

"Just felt like flinging some balls, looking for an easy score."

"Not so easy anymore."

Truthfully, we'd both been pretty terrible bowlers. I should have met up with Ari and kept investigating but he'd text me if he had any leads. Probably. Until I worked off some of the anger pumping through my veins, I'd be no good to him. Plus, I couldn't be responsible for what might happen if Ari looked at me sideways when I was in this mood.

"In or out, Harper?"

He chuckled. "See you there."

Once I'd exchanged my heels for bowling shoes, I headed up the narrow staircase, grinning at the disco music growing louder. I stepped into the darkened room. Glow-in-the-dark flowers and paisleys painted on the wall and a dim purple light were the only illumination for the ten lanes up here. I sidestepped the gaggle of small children that seemed to be here for a birthday party given their identical pirate hats, and headed for Cole, already waiting for me at our lane by the far wall.

"Should have said the dress code was semi-formal," he teased.

I smoothed down my dress, about to reply that he looked just fine in the T-shirt stretched tight across his pecs when my brain got past these new changes to Cole's frame enough to process it was a Twenty-One Pilots concert tee. I growled.

His brows creased in a feigned look of confusion.

"Oh, you bastard. You did steal my shirt." I jumped on his back. "Give it."

We wrestled for it, me laughing and beating on him.

"Ouch!" Cole shook out his arm. "Electric shock."

I slid off him hands clasped behind my back. "Yeah. Ouch."

The curve of his spine and his head dipped close to the score keeping machine as he typed in our names was a familiar and comforting sight, as was the TV screen mounted above us lighting up with Avon and Cold-Hearted, the bowling moniker I'd given him due to his constant refusal to let me use kiddie bumpers.

I smiled and motioned him to the balls with an arm flourish. "Prepare to meet your doom."

Forty-five minutes later, Cole bowled his third straight strike, annihilating me.

"Huh," I said, watching the fallen pins reset, "that didn't go as planned."

"Did I forget to mention I'm on a bowling league?" He strutted back to the hard orange plastic seats.

"Awwwww. Do you wear matching button-ups with your names embroidered on them?"

He shook his head. "Strike Force wears black T-shirts, thank you very much."

"Of course they do." I toed off my shoes.

He jabbed a finger at me. "For that diss, you're buying me a double scoop."

We hit up my favorite gelato place in separate cars. Walking inside, Cole shook his head at the panels behind the counters boasting colorful chalk murals of the Seven Wonders of the World. "Tacky as ever," he said.

"Fabulous as ever." I trailed Cole around the store.

"How's it going getting Davide's family some money?" he asked, sampling some moccachino chip.

"We're pursuing some very promising avenues." With every lie today, my place in Hell was that much more assured.

"I'm glad. His family are good people. They deserve something out of this loss." He gazed off, a wistful expression on his face, the tiny pink sample spoon clutched in his fist. "It's so crazy. Davide was convinced that if he ever died young it would be because he fell in a climb. I guess dying at home is better than your family having to identify bits of you at a morgue."

"The morgue!"

"What?" He tossed out the spoon.

Okay, yes, I had said that with a bit too much enthusiasm, but Cole had just given me an excellent idea. I schooled my features to look chagrined and somber. "I just thought… how awful for them to have to go to the morgue and see him in any circumstance. Sometimes working on cases like this really brings it home." I shook my head. "You must miss Davide a lot."

He tucked an errant curl behind my ear. "I do." He met my eyes. "I didn't realize how much until he was gone."

"Yeah, it's pretty awful when people go away."

Cole dropped his hand.

Transitional. "So what flavors do you want?" I asked brightly.

He settled on cherry cheesecake and coffee.

"My grandfather used to really like that combo, too," I said.

"At least I try new things." Cole pushed me toward a case on the other side of the store. "Stop drooling. Go get the chocolate raspberry."

"Nope," I said, quelling a longing glance at my favorite flavor. "I'm all about new experiences these days." I ordered a lemon sorbetto, my second favorite, but what he didn't know couldn't hurt me.

We stood in the store, munching on our cones, and watching the blustery clouds through the glass doors. "You and Ari still play that disgusting 'what's that flavor?' game?"

"It's the best game and not lately. We've both been busy."

"Yeah? Is Ari doing summer semester?"

"Kind of a work study thing," I hedged. Really mastering the art of spewing utter bullshit, Nava. Thankfully, Cole had no idea that I was, and probably wouldn't have challenged me if he had.

I never thought I'd need to prepare a cover story because I was hanging out with him again. Our interactions were going to have to get a lot less verbal.

I finished the last bite of my sorbetto. "Thanks for the bowling. I needed this break."

"Play hooky. We can grab dinner later."

"I can't. Work beckons even on a Sunday. How about tomorrow?"

"Tomorrow it is. I'll text you."

"Sounds good." I paused, my hand on the door. "Hey, Cole?" He looked over at me, the sight of his tongue darting out to catch a drip on his cone distracting me for a second. "I will be getting that shirt back."

He grinned. "We'll see."

I bounded out to my car in a much better mood.

The Sunday evening plans I wouldn't break for Cole involved a light bout of B&E at our local neighborhood morgue.

To be fair, I would have told my brother but his phone kept going to voicemail and when I went back to Demon Club to find him, Kane was surprised that I wasn't with him, given Ari had gone off to do something around the investigation. I didn't need to be in charge but his refusal to even treat me as an equal was going to end up biting him in the ass when I cracked this case first. The look on both his face and Mandelbutt's would be worth savoring.

And capturing in photo form for multiple viewings and possibly a Hanukkah card.

A few hours later, I drove past the row of buildings comprising the large Vancouver General Hospital complex in mid-town, parking the car around the corner from the entrance to the emergency ward. I tucked my key inside my bra under the nurse's scrubs I'd purchased after leaving Cole, and put a fake employee lanyard around my neck.

Walking with purpose, I crossed the small drop-off area, past the couple of ambulances parked there and entered the sliding glass doors under the neon Emergency sign with a measured stride. The sting of disinfectant with a top note of vomit assaulted my nostrils.

From my own visits here when I'd been dealing with my Achilles injuries, I knew that the security doors immediately to the left of the admittance desk led to the ER ward itself while to the right was a waiting area.

I curved around the desk, skirting the plastic lounge chairs that at 3AM on a Monday morning were only a quarter full.

A janitor mopped up a puddle of something I had no desire to identify.

Not having a magnetic access card to get me through the double doors where the elevators were, I checked for any security camera and finding none, zapped the keypad. A small current snaked over the pad before it shorted out. I pushed through the metal doors, finding myself in a quiet hallway with linoleum floors painted with multi-colored lines leading to different departments. I headed for the bank of elevators at the end of the hall, passing more exam rooms.

A nurse turned into the hallway from an X-ray room, pushing a bed with a patient on it, but other than a nod, took no notice of me.

Once inside the elevator, I pushed the button for the next level down, figuring the staff would want the shortest distance possible to take the bodies. If I was wrong, well, I'd go through each floor one by one.

I expected creepy flickering and buzzing fluorescents, but the hallway was surprisingly well-lit. Dead silent. A good sign. Halfway down the corridor, I found the morgue. A bright, open room with lots of stainless steel sinks and tables.

On one wall was a list of body parts including Thyroid, Lung R, Lung L, and Heart written on plastic signs and tacked along one side of a chalkboard. Next to the board was a scale. Empty, I was happy to note, though the orange "biohazard" buckets under a couple of the tables were disconcerting.

A grizzled middle-aged man in plain scrubs and a disposable surgical cap stepped out of a doorway. "Can I help you?"

I jumped. "Oh. Hi. You've got a Jane Doe here? Early twenties, red hair? Heart attack." I rubbed my hands over the goosebumps springing up on my skin.

He twirled a finger around the room. "Constant current of cool air. Prevents smells from stagnating. Has our JD been identified?"

"Possibly. I was sent to check for a tattoo."

"No kidding." He handed me a surgical cap and latex gloves. "Put these on. We don't want to contaminate her remains."

He led me into a huge cooler where sheeted bodies were stacked in rows on refrigeration shelving, kind of like an IKEA of the dearly departed. Along one wall were the latched drawers I'd expected from years of crime show watching.

"That's where we keep the rotters," the attendant said.

I gagged, tasting bleach.

He unlatched a drawer, sliding out the slab with the Jane Doe, our first victim. I braced myself but she didn't stink. He smirked. "We also seal certain bodies to preserve evidence." He grasped the sheet covering her. "Ready?"

"Go for it."

He uncovered her and left me to check. My excitement at getting a leg up on Ari dimmed in the face of my first human corpse. Jane had only been dead a short time and since she'd been in the cooler, decomposition had yet to set in. She looked exactly like bodies in the movies did except what was dismissible up on the silver screen packed a punch when I was close enough to see the ragged cuticles that she must have had a habit of biting, and the small scar cutting diagonally through her left eyebrow. When I was close enough to see the chipped purple polish that was eerily close to my own.

I curled my latex-covered fingers into my palm.

Her entire right side was covered in an elaborate tattoo of tropical flowers in brilliant colors running from her shoulder down past her hip. No wonder the attendant had laughed. Pretty distinct ID.

I wondered how she'd spent her last hours. Had she lived her life to the fullest, burning brightly, believing the world was hers for the taking? Or was her life a mess of failed dreams and half-formed regrets?

My chest grew tight.

Since there was no sign of the Arabic word for love anywhere on her front, I reached out to turn her over. My fingers froze inches from her body. It was the nail polish: the sight of her lifeless hands so similar to mine. Dizzy, I gripped the door to her drawer, my fingers tingling.

Pull your shit together.

Had this been part of Ari's training? I'd cycled through a lot of emotions on missing out on the twenty years of being an initiate but jealousy had never been one of them. This probably wouldn't have been his first corpse. He wouldn't have frozen up.

The image of his smirking face kicked my butt into gear. I pinched my arm until pain dissipated any panic, then, steeling myself, rolled her over.

There it was. Once more in felt pen, woven through the stem of one of the flowers curving around her hip. I snapped a photo of it and, with a whispered promise that I'd avenge her life that had been cut far, far too short, pitched my gloves into the trash, and got the hell out.

I barreled through the corridors, car-bound. Two wrong turns later, I found a service elevator that took me down into the underground parking garage. I stepped out and pushed the bar to open the door to the garage but nothing happened. Tried again. Still nothing.

I threw my weight against it, hysteria dancing over my skin. I needed out of this building of death. Eyes darting around, I found a scanner requiring an access card to get out, but the lights on it were cycling from red through to green. It was broken and zapping it didn't make a difference. Which meant my choices were go the long way through the hospital, out the door open this late at night to the street, and down the block to the garage entrance or…

Making a fist, I rotated it clockwise, and blew the door into the garage.

That had been louder than I'd anticipated, but given it was the middle of the night, no one was around to raise any alarm. I raced across to my car in the far corner, the skin between my shoulder blades prickling.

A figure jumped out of the shadows.

I let out a sound somewhere between a gasp and a scream and threw a right hook that should have done some serious windpipe damage.

My assailant dodged my blow and flipped me onto my hood, pinning me in place with his hip.

Rohan ripped my surgical cap off. "Getting a jump on the day?"

I shook out my curls, calming my beating heart. "I'm bringing my C game. It's like my A game but bigger and more supple."

His eyes darted down to my boobs.

I pushed him off. "Are you following me?"

"Yes."

I blinked, not expecting him to be honest about it. "Well quit it, stalker. I have work to do."

"Can't let anything happen to my partner before we retrieve the spine."

I wiggled all my bits, checking for damage. "We're not partners."

Rohan sat on my hood. "I'm not totally useless at this. Kinda have a lifetime of training in assessing character and making judgment calls about life or death situations."

"I don't want you making judgment calls. I want you doing what you're told."

"Right. In Nava-land, my role is 'dance, monkey, dance.'"

I beeped the fob at my car to unlock it, my fingers squeezed tight around the plastic. "Au contraire, Rohan, you have *no* role in Nava-land anymore."

He didn't react. "Why are you in scrubs?"

"I was pursuing a lead with the serial killer demon." I let out a stuttery breath.

Rohan jumped off the hood. "Hey." He lay his hand on my shoulder. "What happened?"

"Corpse. Unnerving. Go figure." I traced the rough edge of my fake employee ID.

"Was this your first dead body?"

"Yeah. Does it get easier?" Please tell me it gets easier.

He nodded. "But you'll never forget this one. Every detail down to where you were standing when you saw it." He skimmed his hand along my back. "You shouldn't have had to face that alone. Or unprepared."

I blinked away the tears pooling in my eyes, refusing to break down. "Get me a coffee and I'll be good to go."

Three figures stepped out from between two minivans to circle us. "Wallets," the leader demanded.

Baggy jeans, hoodies, shaved heads, and dull stares, the trio were the Huey, Dewey, and Louie of thug life. They were exactly what I needed to shake off the past hour.

"In my car." I bounced on my toes.

"Put the bloodlust away," Rohan murmured. He turned to the thugs and held up his wallet. "You want this? It is pretty flush with cash, but no can do, dude. This lovely lady needs a coffee and I need money to buy it for her."

"Such a gentleman." I stepped away from the thug leering at me.

"We'll take the lady, too." The leader jerked his head at Sir Leers-A-Lot, who grabbed my arm.

I broke his hold, then broke his nose. Big thanks to Baruch for teaching me how to keep from telegraphing my moves because damn, had I taken him by surprise. I fist pumped.

The thug stumbled back, his hand failing to contain the blood spurting from his big honker. "Bitch."

He didn't unleash his inner demon which meant these were human assailants. Oh well.

Rohan tossed his wallet up in the air, catching it one-handed. "I'd say that's a no."

"You'll fucking pay for that," the thug said. The three pulled out switchblades, flicking them open in synch like they practiced.

Rohan snorted. "Those are barely knives."

"Boys and their blades," I said, sliding onto the hood of my car to watch the show. I prodded my knuckle. That was gonna swell.

"Not gonna play?" Rohan asked.

"Nope." Breaking the guy's nose had improved my mood considerably. I examined my fingernails. "Show me what you've got to offer, partner." This wasn't me relenting; I just wanted to watch Rohan fight. "I'm the helpless female that needs protecting."

"Role playing, are we?"

I tried to hide my grin, but Rohan caught it, winked, and beckoned the asshats forward.

A minute later it was over. The crook with the broken nose now also sported a badly broken arm. The second guy had run off after Rohan stabbed him in the thigh with his own switchblade, and Rohan had the leader in a chokehold. He applied more pressure and the leader crumpled to the ground, unconscious.

Rohan slapped the last thug standing across the head with his wallet. "Get lost."

The thug hesitated.

Rohan broke his other arm. Howling, he ran off the way his friend had. Rohan pocketed his wallet.

I jumped off the hood. "Not so fast. You're buying me coffee."

"I saved your life at great risk to my own. You're buying."

"Get real." Ripping off the lanyard, I slid into my seat and started the car.

Rohan didn't speak again until we were at a twenty-four hour Starbucks drive-through, halfway to our next destination. He reached across me to hand the money to the cashier. I closed my eyes briefly, inhaling his signature scent of his iron blades cut with a spicy musk. My tension melting away as essence of Rohan curled inside me.

"Where are we headed?"

I handed over his disgusting black coffee, taking a generous sip of my mocha latte with extra whip before setting it in the cupholder. "You can go find a rock to slither back under. I've got a cranky old man to delight with my presence." Harry had never phoned me back but Leo had had his home address in her contacts and I may have taken that, too.

Rohan frowned. "It's the middle of the night."

"Very astute." I patted his cheek. "I don't require as much beauty sleep as some."

He caught my hand, biting gently into the fleshy part of my palm. "Beauty sleep for this body would be too much of a good thing."

I pulled my hand away, changing the cheesy love song playing on the stereo.

A Blur song started up, Rohan bobbing his head along with the beat before launching into a falsetto "whoo hoo" along with the singer. I laughed and he met my eyes with a half-grin. The private one he only ever trained on me, then a full smile emerged, almost like it had burst out of its own accord.

Fizzy heart-shaped bubbles danced in my chest, pouring forth fast and furious, no matter how much I mentally whack-a-moled the bastards into oblivion. I was pretty sure I was still sitting up straight despite all my atoms listing sideways toward him with a magnetic pull, but I checked my alignment to make sure.

Wrenching the wheel, I pulled into a spot outside Harry's new place, a war-era bungalow on the east side, sending Rohan careening against the passenger door. "We're here."

I didn't bother checking if he would follow me, because when had he ever done otherwise, and also because of each steady footfall behind me.

I leaned on the bell until Harry answered, bleary-eyed, his white hair sticking up every which way.

He was a vision in plaid, from his pajamas peeking out under his robe, to the blanket slung over his bony shoulders. A lit cigarette hung from the corner of his mouth.

At the sight of me, he took a deep pull on the cigarette, exhaling a thick white column of smoke into the frosty night sky. "My lack of a response was supposed to be a clue. What's with the scrubs?"

"I'm a ministering angel," I said.

Harry flicked a gaze over Rohan. "Who are you? The sidekick?"

Rohan's incredulity was a beautiful thing.

I put my hand on the door. "Let us in. I've got a job for you."

Harry shifted to block my entrance. "You can't afford me."

"Sidekick," Rohan grumbled.

I shot him a "move on" look and pulled the cash from Ms. Clara out of my pocket.

Harry slowly and deliberately closed the door.

I shoved my body between the door and the frame before it was half-shut, fanning away his disgusting smoke. "Help me because this could have ramifications for Leo."

Harry gave me a hard look, then stepped aside. "Five minutes."

His old place had been tatty: yellowed clippings of UFO sightings on the walls and ceiling, UFO models on every available surface, outdated and worn furniture, and the stench of decades-old cigarette smoke baked into every particle.

This place had white walls, new furniture, and no UFOs. "Aw, Harry."

His gaze shuttered. "What's the job?" He eased into his newish leather recliner.

I held out the money. "Take it. That way you're on retainer and bound by confidentiality rules."

"I'm not bound by anything I don't want to be bound by, missy," Harry said, snatching the money from my hand. He thumbed the bills. "It's a start."

"It's plenty." Rohan's tone was deceptively mild.

Harry was no fool. He gave a snarky nod.

I told Harry all about the gogota attack in Prague and the metal spine that had been left behind that I was hiring him to find.

"I'm not hearing how this impacts Leo," Harry said.

"It might be how demons are bound," Rohan said.

Harry whistled. "Someone wants to force demons to do their bidding?" His expression changed from cantankerous old man to a shrewd conniver who'd seen far too much for his years. "I've got a dealer who, well, let's just say if it can be found, Baskerville'll find it. Got a nose for black market items, especially ones purported to be occult."

"Great." I stood up.

"Not so fast," Harry said. "You and Boy Wonder here need to do something."

I'm not sure whose self-control was more commendable: Rohan's for not stabbing Harry the way he so clearly wanted to, or mine for not laughing. Okay, it was totally Rohan's. My snorting coughs weren't fooling anyone.

"Baskerville isn't going to help you without something in return," Harry said.

"I'll pay him." I'd get the money somehow.

"Cash won't cut it. There is a trinket, however, that will. A dog collar. Go get it."

"Why can't you?" I asked. "The three hundred should cover you doing that."

"I don't like the dog that has it." He readjusted the blanket around his shoulders.

"Fine."

"Watch out," he said, scribbling down the address, "the dog senses fear." With that he practically manhandled us out the door.

Rohan raised his eyebrows. "Asking for help? What an idea."

"Isn't it?" I jogged down the front stairs.

Rohan grabbed me around the waist before I reached the car, swinging me around. "Not the sidekick," he insisted. I giggled and sang the Batman theme at him. He pretended to drop me. "Take it back."

"I'm Batman," I said in a growly voice.

"You suck." He set me back on the ground.

"You must have something better to do than come with me," I said, unlocking the car. Like pack.

"Nope. I'm off active duty for a while after that last mission." Yawning, Rohan slumped in his seat and took a sip of his now-cold coffee. "Can we skip ahead to you accepting that I'm working with you on this?"

No, we could not, but forcibly removing the lunkhead from my car would take more energy than I had. "If you have dog allergies or anything, say something–"

He twirled his finger in a "get on with it" motion.

"Awesome."

11

If there was anything of value in the abandoned warehouse that Harry had sent us to in the industrial area outside the city, then demons had to be involved. A misty haze draped the sunrise like a net. The air was cold, dank, and stank of open sewer.

The left third of the desolate single-story building was unfinished and missing most of its roof. Broken scaffolding drooped, in contrast to the concrete exterior tagged in colorful graffiti, including over the bricked-up window frames. Greenish-black ribbons of mildew ran riot over the concrete.

A dented metal sign proclaimed the premises patrolled by a guard dog.

The wind bit at my skin and I pulled my coat tighter around me.

We checked the perimeter for any hostiles. A couple of white rats with rheumy eyes and abscesses mottling their patchy fur haunted the nearby makeshift garbage dump, overflowing with plastic bags, stained mattresses, and broken furniture. Otherwise, the area was clear, but we still approached the warehouse with caution. Why this place necessitated a guard dog given the exposed walls and lack of a front door was a mystery.

A fluff of a white dog with a pink ribbon tied at the end of its cute braided tail jumped out from the shadows, barking furiously. Yippy little thing. Around its neck was a matching pink leather collar with a sparkly pink stone. The only thing that could have made it less scary was if its toenails had also been painted pink. It was totally a demon.

I knelt down. "Come here, evil mop."

The dog growled. The same "arr-ruff" sound I used to have my black panther stuffie Sebastian make when I was kid.

I wasn't a demon dog person at the best of times. "Get over here." I lunged for it but it bounded off, leading Rohan and me on a merry chase through the trash-strewn warehouse. After many frustrating minutes, we managed to corner it.

"All right, mutt–" I jumped back as the dog snapped at my fingers.

Rohan nudged me aside and knelt down, his hand outstretched. "Who's a good dog?" he cooed, edging closer until he was able to scratch it under the chin.

The demon's growls changed to happy yips as it licked Rohan with near-ecstatic fervor.

"It's a she, isn't it?" I said. Rohan smirked. "Just get the collar."

"Already on–"

The room swung sideways with a sickening snap, and from one blink to the next, the warehouse disappeared, replaced by jungle.

"Is this an illusion or have we been portalled somewhere?" I asked.

The air was rich with rot and a heavy lushness. Twisted trees in a million shades of green jutted up from the ground, their gnarled roots protruding from the dark soil.

I tied my coat around my waist, a hot moist breeze washing over me.

"Illusion." Rohan did the same with his leather jacket. "The dog was a cù-sith."

Now Harry's warning made sense. This particular type of demon dog would feed our fears to us before going for our souls. I scrunched my head into my neck, keeping my mind utterly blank. "You didn't think to give me a heads-up it was mega hellhound level evil?"

Rohan steered me around a wide patch of mud. "No point. We need the collar. Like you said, this business could have consequences for Leo. If anyone has figured out how to bind demons we've got to put a stop to it."

Rohan was supposed to be providing a myriad of reasons why I wanted him gone. Not this. "You are *such* an asshole."

Rohan blinked at me. "Because I don't want Leo hurt?"

"Yes."

"Right. What a dick."

I refused to laugh at his wry tone. "Be verwy, verwy qwuiet. We're hunting demons."

Rohan let out a bang-on impression of Elmer Fudd's stuttering laugh. Double asshole. He tilted his face up to the sunlight filtering through the tree canopy, sighing in delight.

"Probably nice and hot in Los Angeles this time of year."

He cut me a sideways look loaded with disapproval.

"What about your family? Your friends? Don't you miss them?" I jumped a rotted log.

"I have friends all over the world."

"Great. Go visit them."

"I'm here until we find the spine. Deal with it."

"Look, I may be biased against the Brotherhood," I said. Rohan snorted. "But the rest of you have dedicated your lives to this organization. How much is that going to temper your need for answers? Or affect your actions if you can't reconcile your loyalties with whatever we find out?"

"It won't."

"God, you're infuriating."

He gave a small smile, his eyes constantly scanning, keenly assessing our environment. "You've rubbed off on me."

"No, that's all innately you." I sidestepped a leafy fern, unseen birds and monkeys calling out overhead.

We crashed through a dense press of trees and stopped. Before us lay a stone temple in the process of being reclaimed by jungle. The uneven, rust-colored flagstones were rough and pocketed with spongy patches of dark-green moss.

A bird screeched overhead.

"Why are we in *Raiders of the Lost Ark*?" Rohan said. "I barely remember the movie, much less was scared by it. You?"

"Nope. It's one of my faves." Repeated viewings with my dad was one of my happiest times with him. I pushed a sweaty curl out of my eyes. "How are you with spiders?"

"Why is that a question?"

"Replete-with-tarantulas-assistant, dude. If he shows up, you get to deal with him."

"Don't even joke about anything you're scared of. Put it out of your head."

We walked up to the open doorway, our footprints in the thick layer of dust as clear as tracks in the snow. Flaming torches cast flickering tongues of light, the corners falling off to cobwebbed shadows. It was just bright enough to see the row of bolt holes indicative of arrow traps for those foolhardy enough to cross the floor.

Stairs lead to a huge stone dais at the front of the cavern. Light glinted off the pink dog collar, now positioned on top of a boulder at the back of the dais. A plethora of deadly arrows waiting to be fired stood between it and us.

I toed at some dirt on the flagstones. "Thoughts on surviving the arrows?"

Rohan studied the bolt holes visible from our position. "Or the giant boulder?"

"That's on the way out. Stick with the script, Snowflake."

Rohan gave a half-grin, turning away like he didn't want me to see it.

"What?"

"Hadn't heard that nickname in a few weeks. I forgot how much I hated it."

"Yeah, that grin screams deep loathing."

He crouched down, slamming his fist down in the center of the one of the stones. An arrow shot over our heads.

"Follow me. Exactly." He stepped onto the first stone with supreme confidence.

When nothing happened, I stepped on the same spot he'd just been.

An arrow narrowly missed my shoulder.

I jumped back, triggering some motion sensor that released the rest of the arsenal. Well, this sucks, I thought before I was ripped apart.

Or was saved by Rohan crashing me to the floor, blocking my body with his as arrows whizzed overhead embedding into the walls on either side.

"Fancy meeting you here," he joked.

The edge of a flagstone jabbed into my shoulder blade, so I shifted, wanting up, but ended up pressed against Rohan instead. Our first full-body encounter since he'd returned. I arched up into him more and his leg shifted between my knees, the hard line of his body fitted to mine. My cheek grazed his, and I nuzzled into his neck.

My body sighed in recognition and something else I didn't want to examine too closely. I ran my hands along his biceps, Rohan catching my fingers and gently squeezing them. Enveloped by him as I was, the only reason I noticed that the arrows had stopped was because I could now hear my thudding heart. "We should keep going," I said.

Rohan pushed away from me, so slow and pained it was as if he had to physically snap our connection. The fiery gold of his eyes sparked an answering shiver of bliss in me.

He stretched out a hand and pulled me up, dragging a thumb along the inside of my wrist.

I stumbled up the stairs to the dais.

A beautiful mermaid dragged herself out of the shadows near the collar. *Clump. Click.* Her fish tail ended in bloody knives. They struck the flagstones off-beat with the haunting, ethereal melody she sang that made me yearn to offer myself up to her, even though I knew that would be the last thing I'd ever do.

Rohan looked at her. Looked at me. Opened his mouth. Shut it.

"That's the Little Mermaid," I explained.

"Why the hell would you think of her now?"

I planted my hands on my hips. "Way to assume I'm responsible."

"It wasn't me. I didn't even know what she was." He pinched the bridge of his nose. "You just Stay-Puft Marshmallow Man'd us. Death by mermaid. Bhenchod," he swore in Hindi.

The mermaid clumped back and forth in front of the boulder, singing all the while. Beckoning us to come take the collar. If we could.

"I didn't conjure her up."

"Then why did she manifest? What's her deal?" Rohan asked.

"The original story isn't singing crabs and catchy melodies. It's this graceful mermaid who trades her tongue for legs that feel like she's walking on knives with every step."

"It *was* you," he said. "Your fears of losing the ability to dance."

"Lived it already. Can't happen twice. So nope. Not my fear."

The mermaid stuck close to the boulder. Those knives of hers would do serious damage as soon as we got within striking range.

"How do we kill her?" Rohan asked.

"We need a prince who with a single rejection, which, let's face it, is the most likely outcome, will turn her into sea foam."

Rohan was staring at me with something suspiciously akin to pity. My face grew hot. No way. This wasn't on me.

I stomped toward the mermaid.

Eyes blazing, she slithered over to us in an inhuman burst of speed, flinging drops of sea foam from her fingertips.

I barely had time to shoot a crippling bolt of magic. The mermaid lurched as my strike found its mark. Her tail thwacked the ground, the floor now visible through the impressive hole I'd created in her gut.

Unbalanced yet undeterred, she roared, her stumpy tongue waggling at us, her knives flicking back and forth like a metronome.

A gob of sea foam hit Rohan square in the face. He grimaced and wiped himself off with his sleeve but he didn't turn Hulk, freak out, or seem to be tripping balls, so that was good.

He partially extended his own blade along the length of his right leg and cut the bottom half of her tail off with a jumping spinning kick that was a thing of beauty in its execution. The tail fell to the stones with a meaty plop and a clatter of knives.

I jumped over her writhing body, snatched the collar off the boulder, and tucked it into my pocket.

Whoosh! Thump!

Rohan pressed down on my back, forcing me to duck, just as a volley of spears shot out of the walls, passing so close overhead that I patted my head to make sure I hadn't been scalped.

A blood-curdling howl raised the hair along my arms. The mermaid raised her voice in answer, but wriggling on the ground as she was, she was the least of our worries right now.

The cù-sìth were soul reapers. We had until the demon dog's third howl to reach safety or our lives were forfeit, and since its baying could be heard for miles, it didn't even need to face us, robbing us of the chance to kill it.

And if we didn't kill it, we'd be trapped in this illusion forever.

We raced through the temple's corridor, a now endless stretch of hallway, the exit elusive.

The mermaid had been left far behind, but my back warmed with the splat of sea foam, and then her whisper of a laugh shivered inside my head.

I grabbed Rohan's arm, stumbling after him. He was going to leave me. I'd be alone and deserted and I couldn't do this. I clutched his arm tighter, one last touch before he went back to L.A. and his life there. His loves there.

My knees buckled.

Rohan yanked me up. "What's wrong?"

We weren't going to make it. We wouldn't outrun the cù-sith's howls. I'd doomed my lover, my best guy friend.

I tried to pull free and curl into a ball.

The second howl set birds wailing in alarm.

I forced myself to run, one hand pressed against my burning side doing my best to ignore the insidious voice still gnawing away at me.

A pair of eyes glowed bright in the shadows to one side, then with a blink and a swish of a tail, were gone.

Positive I could feel the cù-sith's teeth at my back, I sucked in a breath, feeling like my insides had hit a brick wall. After what felt like an eternity, we rounded a corner, the temple's exit just up ahead. Fresh air and sunlight wafted toward us.

With a bone-rattling rumble, the earth rent apart into a jagged pit. Rohan and I stumbled to a stop at its edge, kicking small stones and loose dirt tumbling down into the dark void.

A skimpy vine hung down for us to swing across.

I stepped back.

"I'll go first. Prove it's safe." Rohan grabbed the vine, tensed, then faced me. "Give me the collar."

"No way." He wasn't leaving me. Wasn't using me and then throwing me away.

"Come on, Nava," he coaxed in a purr, "you might lose it. This isn't the time for you to be stubborn."

I slapped my hand over the pocket where it was stuffed.

He grabbed my arm with his free hand, yanking me close. "Hand it over." His eyes were narrowed, a thread of panic lacing his voice.

A gigantic shadow flew up from the void. The demon landed on the ground behind us with a thud that almost rocked us off our feet. Pure white with shaggy fur and a densely muscled body, her muzzle was slightly open, revealing wickedly sharp teeth. As a dog, she'd been a mop of fur, now she was a monster. Bull-sized with a still-braided tail and massive paws, her red slits of eyes shone out of the avalanche of white. She trotted toward us, about to howl for the third and final time.

Rohan's blades snicked out on one hand, five sharp points gouging my skin. "The collar."

I fired into his hand; just a shock. Enough to break free, creeping sideways out from between him and the demon dog.

"I want it, Nava," he growled.

I clutched my head, the voices hammering at me. This was what happened when no one thought you were worth keeping around. You went on and on until suddenly you died.

No. I was the one calling the shots. I wasn't some loser that got left. I wasn't going to die here. I grabbed the vine and jogged a few steps backward to get a running start to swing over the pit.

Rohan caught me in an ironclad grip. He raised his arm, blades out and swiped.

I whimpered.

Rohan flinched at the sound, jerking his knives away violently.

The demon's dirge of a third howl filled the sky.

Rohan trained horrified eyes on me. "Run." He grabbed me around the waist and hurled me over the pit.

The howl abruptly cut off. The second my toes touched ground on the far side of the pit, I spun around, my heart encased in an icy grip, positive Rohan was dead.

Rohan had the cù-sith pinned to the ground, his expression caught in a tight snarl as he smashed his fist into the dog's face over and over again. The demon emitted a single high-pitched whine before Rohan snapped her neck. He'd hit her kill spot because she disappeared.

Whelp, I wasn't getting a dog that way.

With the cù-sith dead, the illusion's power had been broken. The temple and jungle disappeared, leaving us in a deserted warehouse with rain sluicing down on us through the gaps in the roof. Getting soaked to the skin helped to clear my mind of the mermaid's evil whispers, the means by which the demon dog had played on my fears. Well, cleared it somewhat. And speaking of fears...

"Rohan." I stepped toward him, the collar spilling from my hand. "In the temple. The re-enactment of the betraying assistant by the pit. That was your fear, wasn't it? What happened to you on that assignment?"

"Demons killed Rasha. I killed the demons." He used his "don't push it" voice.

Except I deserved better than that.

No, you don't.

My hands balled into fists. "What. Happened?"

"What happened to *you* in the temple? You were holding me like you'd die if I left." He prowled close, his eyes glinting dangerously. "Would you have?"

"Don't flatter yourself." It took everything I had not to sprint when I left the warehouse.

Wind howled around me, dark clouds lending an ominous weight to the sky. My hair snapped in tendrils around my face. I hugged the collar to my body, half-hunched over, plodding toward the car.

Rain plastered my clothes to my body, my hair sticking to my skin in wet strands. Fumbling the keys in my icy fingers, I finally opened the car door and threw my filthy coat in the back seat.

Rohan's hand came down on the door, preventing me from closing it. Water streaming down his scalp, he turned his face to mine, his expression bleak. "I need to know if everything I've ever believed I was fighting for still holds true." The pain in his voice punched into me.

I cupped my palm to his jaw. "Oh, Rohan."

He framed my face with his hands. "I'm sorry."

I winced at the cloth melted to his wrist from where I'd shot my magic into him. It had been more than a mere shock. "I hurt you worse."

He gave a pained laugh. "Stop being so competitive."

I couldn't stop spinning the sensation of his fingers splayed against my cheek, a steady warmth offsetting the rain sticking to my lashes, and rolling across me in a million cold drops. The tenderness in his eyes sped my heart and made the tips of my ears tingle. I didn't want tender. I wanted every part of him to fill me up, his hands pinning me down, and a hungry focus on his face for me and only me.

I pushed him into the back seat, falling on top of him. His palm brushed the scratched skin of my hip through my torn shirt and I winced.

He stilled. "I'll hurt you." His lips compressed in a flat line, self-disgust etched on his face. "Again."

"Probably." I sucked on his neck and he moaned. "Right now I don't care." I rubbed myself against his erection.

"You're going to kill me," he ground out, fumbling at my scrubs. I helped him peel the wet pants off, Rohan growling and me laughing at his frustration. The second my legs were free, Rohan rolled me off of him onto the seat, his mouth hot and desperate as he kissed his way down my body.

The rasp of his goatee on my skin wound me tight, heightening everything into a honed, hard clarity that was almost too much to bear. I dug my fingers into his wavy locks, my fingers tightening against his scalp.

His fingertips dragged along a curve of muscle, his soft hair tickled my belly, and his lips skipped up the inside of my thigh. His touch stoked embers that I wanted to coax into an all-consuming blaze.

Rain pounded on the roof in a wild drumbeat, lashing across the back seat. I'd swear it was sizzling and turning to steam as it hit my skin, like the hiss of water over sauna rocks.

Rohan hooked a finger under the elastic of my underwear, ripped them off, and licked my clit, a long slow tease.

Moaning, I reached overhead and clutched the door handle, Rohan's fingers pushing deep inside me, his tongue stroking harder and faster. My body tensed in waves: thighs, abs, core.

Fingers still curled in his hair, I tugged him up. "Fuck me, Rohan."

He rested his head against my stomach. "I don't have a condom."

"I do. Purse. Floor. Front."

Rohan found it, dropped his jeans to his knees, and sheathed himself in record time. "Your wish. My command." Switching places with me, he sat on the edge of the seat, his feet planted on the concrete.

I straddled him, sinking down on top of his hard cock with a loud groan. Requiring a moment to steady myself against the tangle of need and want.

"I thought I'd remembered it wrong. That you couldn't feel this good," he said. "God, Nava." His hips snapped off the seat, one hand clutching my ass, making me ride him hard. He ran his fingertips, blades out, up and down along my spine.

Hips thrusting upwards, he pounded into me. Every time he pulled back, I chased him, my hands clutching his biceps, forcing him to bury himself inside me, over and over again.

He clasped the back of my neck with one hand, my blood singing under his relentless desire.

My curls snarled, Rohan running his hands through them with fingers that started out steady but soon were trembling. He claimed every inch of me, his breath coming in ragged pants, and those gorgeous eyes burning for me. I grinned, thrilled at reducing him to a shaky, needy mess.

I pushed down on his shoulders, gripping the hard lines of muscle, reveling in the feel of bottoming out against him. He sucked a tit into his mouth, the pressure almost painful. My body buzzed, my hands and feet pulsing. I felt brutally, intensely, electrically alive.

My orgasm ripped through me and I shattered. My vision blurred, the world falling away from me. My head tumbled back as I cried out, Rohan joining me seconds later.

With the car door open, we were soaked, and the wind bit viciously into my back, but lazy satisfaction glowed deep inside me and heat burned through my chest.

He smoothed away my hair, resting his forehead against mine. "Hi."

"Hi." I splayed my palm against his chest, taking in the staccato beat of his heart.

"Someone came prepared." He carefully lifted me off of him.

"Hmmm? Oh, yeah." Reaching for my pants on the floor of the back seat, I smiled at him, covering the guilt twisting my stomach into knots. I'd tossed those condoms in my purse after I'd accepted Cole's dinner invitation. I slipped back into the wet, dirty scrubs. Shit. How was I supposed to go to dinner with him now? Traces of the mermaid's whispering still bounced around in my brain; traces of Rohan's scent branded my skin.

I scrubbed a hand over my face as my phone trilled a reminder. Oh no. Rohan reached my cell before I could, picking it up off the floor of the car to hand it to me.

"Here." His smile turned to confusion as he put the phone in my hand and caught sight of the screen. "Cole? Isn't that your ex?"

"Yeah. I ran into him because of the investigation? He was friends with one of the victims?" I was babbling. Fuck this. I wasn't betraying Rohan. I had nothing to feel guilty about. "We're having dinner tonight."

Make of that what you will, Mitra. The waistband of my scrubs snapped hard against my hip.

Rohan tugged his jeans on. "Make him take you somewhere fancy." That was it. No scowl, no show of possessiveness.

It wasn't the reaction I wanted but it was the only one I was going to get.

12

We made a brief stop at Harry's to give him the collar. Rohan wouldn't even touch it, leaving me to drop it off. Harry grimaced when he saw my disheveled, drowned rat appearance.

"Don't say a word." I placed the collar in his hand. "Is there some doggie owner going to come after us for theft and destruction of property?"

"No."

"Good. Talk to your dealer and get me the location of that spine asap or I swear on my friendship with Leo, I will come back and hurt you."

"No need to get mean," he grumbled and shut the door.

Rohan and I didn't speak for the ride back to Demon Club. I put on some random station and turned the volume up.

Once home, I stood under the shower for a good twenty minutes getting feeling back into my extremities. My skin was turning lobster red but I still hadn't unraveled the cold knot in the pit of my stomach. I argued myself back into and out of the date for the length of my shower and the time it took to get dressed. The internal debate continued while I cornered my brother in his room.

I shoved my phone with the open photo of Jane Doe into his hand. "Two of seven victims have the symbol. Not quite a hard link but a start."

Ari looked at it for a long time before handing it back. "You shouldn't have gone by yourself."

"When are you going to admit I have something to contribute to this?"

He walked into his bathroom, returning with a small bottle of sleeping pills which he pressed into my hand. "You might need these for a few nights. Okay?"

Oh. "Okay." I put them in my purse.

"You're right. Two bodies aren't enough, but I've arranged to see another one. How do you feel about gravedigging?"

I groaned.

Ari clapped me on the shoulder. "That's the spirit."

"Can we not do it tonight?" Not that I was blowing work off because of Cole. "I don't think I can handle two dead people in one day."

"Sure. Let's spend tomorrow going over the files. See if we missed anything in light of this new connection. We'll hit up the cemetery at night."

I hugged him. "Thank you."

I was almost at his door when he called out, "Hey, Nee?"

I turned back. "Yeah?"

"I get not wanting to be alone after what you went through today, but don't let douchecanoe take advantage of you."

"Wait. How did you know?"

He laughed and waved good-bye.

I sat in the car for five minutes before I'd pulled myself together enough to meet Cole inside the upscale burger joint he'd chosen. It wasn't fancy, but he knew my weakness for a good burger and this place was reputed to have the best in the city.

Cole was already seated at a window table, but he got up to give me a big hug.

I grit my teeth at the pain that flashed through my shoulder. My accelerated healing abilities were doing wonders for the damage I'd incurred while fighting the cù-sith, but the still-visible knife scars on my skin weren't something I had a ready lie to explain away.

"I'm glad we could meet tonight," he said.

"Me too." I picked up the extensive menu. "Do you want to share some appies?" Cole laughed. I peered at him over the menu. "What?"

"You are the worst sharer ever."

"That's harsh, Harper."

He thrust his index finger out, pointing at a miniscule silver scar. "Onion rings, your teeth. Yes or no?"

"I have no memory of that," I said piously.

Our waiter came over and we placed our orders, with separate appetizers.

"What were you up to today?" Cole asked. "Spa date? You look pretty relaxed."

Well-fucked will do that. I fiddled with the vinegar bottle, lining it up neatly with the napkin dispenser. "Some work stuff. You?"

"The frat had a mixer with our sister sorority, but I bailed early."

"And dozens of women deflated with disappointment."

He pressed a hand to his heart. "You wound."

Is Rohan okay? I forced a grin. "What exactly does one do on a mixer? Not being of the Greek persuasion."

"We were handcuff bowling today. Plastic handcuffs," he added. "It's harder than you'd think."

Try fighting demon dogs and insane mermaids. Or seeing dead bodies. "Sounds fun. Did they mind you ditched them to come see me?"

"Nah. Everyone's pretty cool. You? Your job must be pretty intense. It seems you're always working. Anyone give you grief?"

"Not even a little bit." I downed the last third of my beer, and motioned to the waiter for another before pushing my plate closer to Cole. "Potato skin?" He looked at me suspiciously so I made a big show of leaning back, hands up, and mouth firmly closed. He snorted, took one and then spun his plate to me so I could eat all his calamari with legs, since he only ever ate the ones that were ring-shaped.

Over burgers, we caught up on old friends; he told me about a river rafting trip he'd taken. Our conversation was light and easy. Easy was good, right? A refreshing change where I didn't have to wonder about ulterior motives or power plays. Cole was an open book. Adorable. The perfect transitional.

"I heard you were at UBC for a while. After…" Cole dragged a fry through the blob of ketchup on the corner of his plate but didn't eat it. "Should I be talking about this?"

I scooped up the fried onions that had fallen off my burger, stuffing them back on the fat grilled patty. "After what? After I almost permanently messed up my leg trying to dance on it when I knew I couldn't take it? After you dumped me when I needed you most?"

He took my hand. "I'm not that guy anymore and I promise you, I'm not going to hurt you."

I don't trust your promises. But that didn't matter, right? I smiled, looking up at him through my lashes. "Regardless, I think you should make it up to me. Take away the hurt."

"You weren't the only one hurt."

I yanked my hand away. "Excuse me?"

"You shut me out. And I'm not using that as an excuse to justify my behavior. I'm just saying, there you were, going through one of the worst things ever and I went from being the guy you shared everything with to getting nothing from you. No matter how I tried to engage."

"Oh, forgive me for not being articulate and considerate of your needs when my life was crashing down around me."

His face suffused with pity. "You never used to be this sarcastic."

"And you used to be smart enough to differentiate between sarcasm and truth. Guess we've both changed." I hastily wiped my fingers off and grabbed my purse.

Cole caught my arm before I could get up. "You're just going to run away? Can't we discuss this like adults?"

My body tensed with the urge to rip his hand off me and storm off except Leo's accusations about me cutting and running trumpeted in my head. I slapped my purse back on the table. "Okay. Let's discuss the fact that you were supposed to know that I needed you."

"I did, but I had no idea how to comfort you. It takes two people to be in a relationship and you weren't there." He reached up for glasses he no longer wore, his fingers closing on air, then dropped them back to the table. He'd always obsessively cleaned his lenses when he got upset.

Part of me wanted to take his hand in comfort but anger kept me locked in place.

"I didn't know how to express myself," he said, "and it bottled up. What I did was awful. But I'm not the only one to blame for the break up."

I stared at my hands folded in my lap, rubbing my thumb over my knuckle in agitated strokes, my thoughts an uneasy jumble. This didn't have to change anything. Mutual hurt, lack of trust, none of that mattered. Cole was perfect for what I wanted tonight. For what I needed. I didn't want to be alone in the dark.

"Do-over?" I said.

"I'd like that." In the warm glow of his eyes and the firm squeeze of his hands was a promise that he'd take care of me in all the right ways this evening.

He called for the bill, pulling out his card to pay at the table.

I wondered how our bodies would fit together now. If there were still secrets to be learned about each other. I smiled, picturing Cole above me.

Green eyes morphed to a vision of blazing gold and Rohan's hard, hot strength pounding into me. The half-grin he'd given me when I'd come. His comfort and understanding at what I'd faced today.

"Nava?" Cole tucked his wallet away. His anticipation turned to resignation when he looked at me. "Ah. Is this a rain check or so long, farewell?"

"Rain check." I gave Cole a peck on the cheek and called it a night.

"How many did you take?" Ari set a fresh mug of coffee in front of me in the library the next morning. I held up one finger. "Lights on or off?"

"On." I cradled my hands around the mug, savoring the warmth and that first inhale of java. Covering the previous coffee package in biohazard symbols had done the trick. This brew was rich and smooth.

"I kept a flashlight in my bed after I saw my first dead body. Slept with it on for a week so no one would know."

"Did your nightmares get worse?"

Ari looked off out the window, his gaze distant before he flipped his laptop open with a brusque gesture. "Social media profiles. Let's start there."

Despite searching through a zillion selfies on all the major social media sites and several dozen more obscure ones, we didn't find anything connecting our victims—not interests or even sexual preference. Though they'd all been attractive individuals in their own way.

I stared at the list that Ari had written on a whiteboard. Of our six vics to date, Davide lived for rock climbing, Jakayla was big on animal rights activism, Reuben's world revolved around pastry-making, Ellen was a moderately successful author busy with book signings and promo, and Max was a stockbroker who spent his downtime at flashy restaurants and clubs with different men. The Jane Doe remained the only question mark.

Ari drew a line along the table with his finger. "Imagine this is the demon. It moves forward and at some point along this line, each of the victims comes into contact with it." His hand closed into a fist. "Except we have nothing to anchor its movements except the victims' deaths and there's no pattern there."

"With that love symbol, I'd say maybe a dating app or site?"

Ari tapped the blue dry-erase marker against the table. "Ellen's sister told me she was still getting over a divorce. Not dating. Maybe a hook-up? Trouble is, a lot of those profiles don't use real names. We could ask Kane if there is some kind of software he could run to search according to their photos but that's going to take time because he's away."

"She made a convincing Daenerys." Of the multiple Daenerys cosplayers in the photo from the fan convention Mara had attended last weekend, she was the only one wearing Dany's Dothraki riding outfit. I stifled a yawn as we scrolled back further, past *Game of Thrones* memes, and a series of photos of her and Daniel mugging at a pho restaurant. They were adorable, him all hot cop, and Mara with her Harry Potter glasses and sassy grin.

Ari rubbed his temples.

I clicked to load more photos, going back about two weeks now on her feed.

"Stop. Go back." Ari stopped drumming. I scrolled up. "That one."

It was an innocuous photo of Mara at some club in front of a curved bar covered in silver mirrored tiles, like a giant dissected disco ball. She'd captioned it "Playing wingman."

"She's at Labyrinth," Ari said.

"The club Max was found at." I opened another tab to pull up his profile, flipping back to photos of the night in question. He'd posted a number of them before he died. "What's Electric Sands?" I pointed to a logo projected on the back wall of the dance floor in one of Max's photos.

"Holy shit." Marker between his teeth, Ari grabbed the laptop, pulling up the club's homepage. He jabbed a finger at the screen.

"'Labyrinth's bi-weekly celebration of Arabic electronica, deep lounge, and trance with DJ Isra. Wednesdays,'" I read. I clicked back to Mara's profile to see when she'd posted that photo. "Same night Max died."

Ari grinned at me and held up his hand for a high-five. This was huge. Two victims attending the same place on the same night. "Pull up our suspected demon list, then make a new column and add any demons of Arab origin that fit," he said. "We don't need to bother with ghouls or demons taking on animal forms. They wouldn't have done this."

"Or ifrit," I said. "They don't glamour and winged fire beasts would not go unnoticed."

Ari swung the screen around to study the list. "Some subsets of daeva might fit."

"I still think we're looking at an incubus or a succubus. Jinns pull that sex shit," I said. "And we do have two victims connected by a nightclub."

"What if they'd been blackout drunk or high? Still unconscious and open to nightmares."

"Max maybe, but Mara doesn't strike me as the type to go on benders. Sex though? Anytime, any place."

Ari ran his finger over the delete key but didn't tap it. "You'd know."

"As would you lately."

He shot me the finger. "Male and female vics. I'm still bumping on an incubus and succubus working together. There's a lot of enmity between those two."

"Unless we've got a bisexual demon."

Ari tossed a dry-erase marker up, catching it one-handed. "No such thing."

"There are exceptions to every rule." I pointed to myself. "Exhibit A."

"True, but when it comes to incubi and succubi, they're strictly hetero in their victim choices."

"Which brings us back to a team," I said.

"Maybe." He tossed the dry-erase marker on to the table. "You up for some clubbing tomorrow night?"

"Sounds like a plan. We can take the victims' photos there, ask around."

"See who they were with," Ari said. "Hopefully we'll narrow things down more once we suss out the place. For now," my brother stood up, cracking his neck. "Eat and get some rest. We won't be going in to the cemetery until late tonight."

The second he left the library, I hit the shelves, bent on some spell-finding recon for my other mission. Once I had the gogota spine, I needed a way to test it for magic since binding would involve spell-work.

I grabbed one of the huge demon overview texts off the shelf, lugged it back to the long table by the windows, and dropped it with a thud. No cloud of dust rose off the covers, though I coughed at the musty smell emanating from the pages. There was nothing in the index under "binding" and searching "compulsions" just got me a list of demons that had that ability in their arsenal.

While both were a means of exerting control magically, compulsion was an innate ability done by a demon on a human, while binding, if at all possible, involved a spell done by a human on a demon. Ari believed binding to be an urban myth and that forcing demons to do our bidding was impossible, but the spine had to be indicative of something more than making it harder to access the kill spot.

Hmm. Dr. Gelman had told me that the first Rasha were created by witches. The magic we used to kill demons and that the rabbis used to induct us had originally come from them. Maybe there was some clue in that? I grabbed all the historical texts I could find and hauled them over to the table.

Six deadly dull books later, I shoved aside the heavy tome I'd been plowing through on the magnificence of King David. Not only was there no mention of witches in any of these books, there was no real mention of women at all, which was surprising since Jewish history was rife with important women playing a part in saving our people. From Judith, who hacked off the head of Holofernes, a massive evil asshat and enemy of Israel, to Deborah, a kick-ass judge, prophet, and warrior, to Yael, that sly babe who'd killed Sisera, the captain of the Cannonite army. While important Jewish male figures were mentioned on a regular basis in these books, the women were absent.

But nah, the Brotherhood wasn't sexist and my suspicions couldn't be right.

I opened the final text, inhaling a lungful of old glue and dry parchment, and struck a nugget of gold in one of the footnotes. Before David, it was still mostly men that hunted demons but, not having magic themselves, they'd needed witches to kill the spawn. David had decided to cut out the middleman. He made a deal with a powerful witch to create the first group of Rasha. Himself included. She'd agreed. There weren't that many demons and so there weren't that many men given the Rasha magic.

Apparently, witches weren't all that into hunting demons, preferring to focus on keeping up the wards between our world and the demon realm and stave off a full-scale invasion instead of one-spawn-at-a-timing it. The author bitched about how, in typical suspicious, mistrustful witch fashion, she'd only given Rasha a fraction of the magic that witches had. Just the bit pertaining to killing demons and not a drop more. So much for gratitude.

I sat back, my mind blown. Wards on a global scale? Rasha magic only encompassing a sliver of what witches possessed? How powerful were they?

Hang on. Wards involved magic, as did the ritual Drio had performed when he was trying to make Samson King reveal his true form. So where were those spell books?

I studied each bookcase, the texts grouped by subject. Most of the space was taken up by all things demony, with a smaller section on history and... Aha! On the bottom of one of the bookcases was a slim volume on wards.

And a giant empty space. I knelt down and snatched up the only other book there: a tattered children's picture book called "Witchy Witch and her no good, spooky bad spells!" featuring a crazy cartoon witch and her bubbling caldron. "Looking for something, partner?" was written in red pen across the cover.

"Rohan!" I charged out of the library but he was nowhere to be found. He'd even put a lock on his room so I couldn't search it for the missing spell books. If Ms. Clara wouldn't have killed me, I totally would have blown the damn thing off its hinges.

I was still fuming when I met up with Ari that night.

"Two of the bodies were already cremated so we can't check them." He tossed a couple of shovels into the trunk. "But there is one other one we have access to."

"Who?" I'd spent the past couple of hours punching things in the Vault and the back of my shirt was plastered to my shoulder blades. No point changing just to dig up a grave. Letting Ari drive, I strapped in on the passenger side and rolled down the car window.

"Reuben Epstein was buried in the Jewish cemetery and Cantor Abrams is on the board that oversees it." Ari turned down the volume on the upbeat pop song playing on the radio.

Moonlight swirled around the trees lining either side of the street. I lifted my hair off my neck, resting my head against the window frame. "No way he condoned exhuming a burial plot." As Rabbi Abrams' son, the Cantor may have been sympathetic to the Brotherhood but for sure he'd draw the line at desecration.

We skirted the edge of the city on a wide six-lane road, traffic practically non-existent as we left the boundaries of Vancouver proper.

"It's a 'don't ask, don't tell' policy," Ari said. "The board had recently changed the locks on the cemetery so I had to contact him and arrange for new keys. We usually have a set in our possession."

"Why? We don't bury demons."

"There are some unmarked graves kept for us. Sometimes we need to bury other things."

Like human remains from victims we couldn't afford to be found? I swallowed hard, picturing Jane Doe's face.

Unlocking the cemetery gate, hiking over to the correct grave, it was all fairly banal. Even the moon provided just enough light to see what we were doing but allowed us to hide if necessary. Ari stopped in front of a recently interred grave and handed me a shovel. There was no tombstone yet. Most of the Jews I knew unveiled the tombstone on the year anniversary of the person's passing.

For the next little while, the only sounds were the crisp snap of our shovels hitting the earth, our laboured breaths sending puffs of white air into the cool night sky, and the occasional hoot of an owl.

The rhythmic digging was calming in a weird way, so long as I didn't dwell on why we were doing it. By the time the plain pine coffin was exposed, our sweat-soaked T-shirts were streaked with dirt. I stretched on a cramp in my poor, pampered first world hands, which rocked massive blisters.

We pulled the lid off and scrambled out of the gravesite, hands clamped firmly over our mouths and noses. The stench wafting out of the bloated, distorted cadaver was redolent of rotten egg that had enjoyed a trip through Satan's sphincter along with the aftermath of a large meal of beans then been steeped once more in a putrid eggy bath.

It was unfortunate that this was the moment my grade eight science teacher's fact about how scent particles went up our noses popped into my head. Vomiting on the guy wouldn't have hurt his appearance much at this point, but I still did my best to keep the splatter off him.

"The maggots are a nice touch," Ari said, peering down at the body.

Poor Reuben didn't look too hot after two weeks of decomposition with his blistered marbled skin, bugged out eyes and tongue, and his hair slipping away from the scalp.

"You okay?" Ari said.

I wiped off my mouth. "Yeah. It's gross, but not freaky. Second body desensitivity?"

"Less human-looking."

That too. Nose firmly plugged, I motioned for my brother to have at 'er.

"You need the field experience," he said. "You do it. That's an order."

"Make me." I punched him in the arm.

Ari laughed, turning it into a cough at my scowl. "Oh. You were serious."

"Skeerred?" I clucked at him.

He made a pffft sound and strode over to a stretch of grass. "Standard terms?"

These terms had been set when we were seven years old and our dad, tired of our complaining, had said that if we were going to fight then we had to establish rules and abide by them. Hits to Ari's crotch and my face were off-limits, otherwise it was anything goes. At some point, we'd decided that there should be some kind of spoils of war to the winner.

"Standard terms," I agreed. "When I win, you drop the commanding officer bullshit and treat me as your equal partner."

"Agreed. And when I win, you admit that I am the superior Rasha while you search Reuben."

I ground my teeth hard enough to take a layer of enamel off. "Agreed."

We crouched down facing each other. "One, two, three, four," we chanted, "I declare a twin war."

The words weren't even out of our mouths before we both let our magic fly.

Our epic battle lasted all of three seconds. I knew that my brother would use his shadow magic to swipe my feet out from under me because knocking me flat so he could sit on me and pummel me was his favorite move.

Except he knew that my favorite fight tactic was throwing something into his eyes to blind him and get the jump on him.

So in a brilliant bit of reverse expectations, he wrapped his shadows around my eyes like aviator shades, blinding me, while I blasted his feet out from under him, pinning him to the ground.

"Say uncle," I said, trying to pull the shadows off. Yeah, that's not a thing. I spun too far and whacked my kneecap on the corner of a tombstone, resulting in a two minute run of my favorite curse word.

"You," he said.

My magic singed the hairs on his arms and legs, while the pressure in my eyeballs was growing to splat proportions. We released each other, panting in our respective corners. Then we attacked.

In the exact same way.

Three more times.

"I hit you first." I lay on my back, probing the puffy, bruised skin around my eyes.

"Dream on." Ari beat his smoldering arm into the pile of dirt we'd excavated. "We'll do this together."

I got to my feet and shuffled to the edge of the pit, a wary eye on Ari.

"One, two," he said.

On three, each of us whacked the other person into the open grave.

"Aaaaahhh! I touched rotted corpse!" I squealed, hopping up and down and wiping my hand on my brother's back.

He flinched, hip checking the coffin, and rocking the corpse onto his side.

We gagged at the fresh wave of putrescence unleashed at the movement. But it jiggled Reuben's foot out of the coffin. On the bottom of the heel was the Arabic word for love.

"Mara, Jane Doe, and Reuben. That's three," Ari said. "I'm calling it an official link."

"Works for me."

Any lasting animosity was put aside in our mutual desire to quickly rebury him. We patted down the last of the earth as the moon disappeared behind the clouds, signalling it was time to leave.

Pity that the ghoul who jumped us hadn't gotten the memo.

13

P ale with catlike features, the ghoul bared his fangs, hissing with a forked tongue that brushed my cheek as the demon caught me around the neck. I jabbed my shovel backward at his head, but he plucked it from my hands before I made contact and flung it away.

When shovels didn't work, go with plan B. A wave of electricity rolled off my body. That dislodged the bloodsucking fiend.

Ari wrenched me into the shadows with him, backing us up against the cemetery fence. He wove the darkness up to bob in front of us like a living shield.

I peered through the gloom at the ghoul, batting at the shadows with his elongated claws like a cat with a toy. "That's not a thing," I told him.

"Smooth as a baby's bottom," Ari observed of the demon's naked, humanoid form. "Even his balls are wrinkle free. It's like he got a full-body Botox."

With a satisfied shriek, the ghoul tore through Ari's shadows, claws out.

There may have been one of him and two of us, but our resulting fight was bloody and brutal. Forty-five minutes later, two tombstones were broken, three of my ribs were cracked, and Ari's left arm was dislocated at an awkward angle. Both of us were bleeding, which drove the ghoul into a bloodlust frenzy that sharpened his senses, yet we couldn't get a hold of the slippery bastard with our magic.

Pain fogged my brain, slowing my reaction time. I tripped over the corner of one of the broken tombstones, my knees hitting the ground hard.

The ghoul jerked my head to the side and punctured my neck with his fangs.

My head lolled back. Oooohhhh, niiiice.

I had just enough presence of mind to remember that in seconds his blissful hold on me meant I'd let him exsanguinate me and wear a smile on my face while he did so. I snapped my elbow back in a vicious strike, breaking the demon's nose with an audible crunch. He staggered back, then lowered his head and rushed me, breaking mine in payback.

"Owwww!" My blood spurted through the air, splattering on Ari like a Rorschach test. Hissing sharply, Ari jerked his hand to his own nose. Twin thing.

I wheezed through the rivers of agony bubbling along my shattered cartilage. That area had still been tender from our earlier twin war. Now? My entire face was a tight throbbing mass. Blue and white spots danced through my watery vision, my magic pulsing and crackling in starts and fits.

The ghoul backed away from me, taking a bite out of Ari's dislocated arm. We both howled. I swore blood ran hot over my arm and down my wrist and it took a second for my brain to realize only Ari had been hurt. Still, I gagged as the demon chewed and swallowed my brother's flesh.

Using our last reserves, the two of us managed to wrestle him to the ground and pin him there long enough to send Ari's shadow magic to the ghoul's kill spot, conveniently located inside his mouth. Yeah, universe, put the cannibalistic bloodsucker's weak spot inside him.

I kicked the single fang left of him when he died through a hole in the fence, then we limped back to the car.

An acrid burning smell redolent of a match when you've just blown it out lingered in the air. This wasn't a hint of sulfur crossed with a soupçon of burning wood. More like a freaking quarry of the chemical shit hitting a blazing forest.

The back of my throat burned and my eyes watered.

I opened the trunk and unzipped the first aid kit that Dad had provided us with, wrapping Ari's arm with a tensor bandage like a tourniquet to staunch the bleeding. The ghoul's teeth marks were ragged gashes against his skin.

Using a package of baby wipes, I wiped the blood off me as best I could, yelping against the dozen little antiseptic stings.

I had no idea what had happened to our shovels, nor did I care. Whoever unlocked the gates could blame the same vandals they'd deem responsible for the broken tombstones. The damage would cover up any evidence of our gravedigging.

Despite my nose being four sizes too large, I had to drive because Ari's arm was shot to hell.

"What the fuck?" I panted. "How does the ghoul fit into this? We deliberately didn't include them on our list." Ghouls were bloodsuckers who wouldn't leave their victim with an unblemished corpse. Or potentially any corpse if one was feeling peckish.

Ari cradled his injured arm to his chest with his good hand. "They're Arab. Beyond that, no clue."

"That ambush wasn't a coincidence." Like much of this case, the pieces of the puzzle were taking their sweet time to fit together. I smacked my hand on the wheel.

My brother's head lolled back against the seat rest, his exhale a soft pained hiss. He directed me to the home of a Rasha-approved physician to get my nose checked out in case it needed to be set. My healing abilities would fix the break but magic wasn't exactly concerned with cosmetic appeal and I didn't want a matching crooked nose to Rohan's.

The doctor examined it then told me I'd been lucky. There was no displacement due to trauma. My septum was intact which meant I shouldn't have any breathing problems and since there appeared to be no change to function or appearance, I could let my Rasha healing do its thing with no further intervention.

That was a relief. Exhausted and in pain, I pulled into Demon Club, hoping to slip inside without running into anyone. Best laid plans, right?

Rohan lay on the hood of his Shelby, staring up at the stars, earbuds in his ears, rolling the piece of curved bone between his index finger and thumb. The slight widening of his eyes was his only reaction to us. He swiped at his phone, removed the headphones and stuffed both in his pocket along with the bone fragment.

"One twin that looks like a raccoon. And one that smells like he was set on fire." He shook his head. "Is this normal for you two?"

"Ha!" I fist pumped. "I totally won our twin war."

"Twin war?" Rohan looked confused. "What are you talking about?"

"Often hard to know with Nava," Ari said.

"True," Rohan agreed. "She's very confusing."

"What you mean boys," I said, "is, 'Aren't we lucky Nava provides a certain je ne sais quoi to liven up our otherwise stultifyingly dull routines?'"

"'Je ne sais quoi?'" Rohan said.

"That certain something? That elusive pleasing quality?" I waved my hand in a 'get with it' gesture. "Bilingual, Snowflake. Nevermind. Don't tax yourself."

"The French wasn't the part I had trouble with."

Ari braced a hand against the hood, his skin ghastly pale.

I pulled a package of ginger chews to combat nausea out of my pocket, and dropped one into the palm he'd outstretched without looking at me.

"Can I have one?" Rohan asked.

Ari and I cocked our heads to the right, blinking at Rohan until we both said, "Oh, the chews." I gave him one.

"Freaky," Rohan said. "I hadn't seen your twin thing before."

"We learned to tone it down," I said.

"Unnerved the parents," Ari added. We both snickered.

"Can't imagine why," Rohan said.

I brushed my fingers over Ari's wound. "You want help changing that?"

"I'm good." Ari shuffled up the back stairs, blood seeping through his bandaged arm.

I made sure that he made it inside okay, then planted myself in front of Rohan. "You're a total bastard."

"You'll need to be clearer with your complaints than that."

I shoved his arm. "Witchy Witch?"

Rohan chuckled. His gold hamsa ring caught the moonlight, flashing against the deep black of his bulky sweater. "You gonna quit wasting time trying to be in charge and just admit it's better if we're partners on this?"

"Will you give me the books?"

"Under supervision, yes."

I cocked my fingers at him like a gun. "Great. Partners."

"Liar."

Obviously. "Not at all. I need to test the spine for magic and if that means we need to be partners, I won't fight it. Let's get a-spellin'."

He scooted over. "What happened to your face?"

"How quickly we forget accusing *me* of control issues, person who is not producing the spell books."

"This isn't controlling things. It's important bonding talk between partners."

"I stand corrected. You're a total bastard, intractable, *and* full of shit." I huffed a laugh, and sat next to him so he could get the full glory of my broken, swollen, blood-clogged nose. "Ghoul."

"You live a full and exciting life." He one-arm hugged me.

Disgust with myself at how badly I was drawn to his touch, his steady presence, and yeah, his concern, didn't prevent me from cuddling into him. I was a moth to his flame. And that always worked out so well for the moth.

I craned my neck to take in the night sky. Thanks to light pollution, only a few stars twinkled overhead, but the moon cast a cool, serene glow. The deep pull of a tugboat's horn far out in the water floated over to us. "Did you think about me this past month?" I asked.

"Maybe."

Unable to stop myself, I nipped at his goatee, feeling his sharp inhale vibrate between our bodies. "Liar." I leaned back against the hood, desperate to redirect the adrenaline bouncing around inside me. Desperate for his fingers biting into my shoulders as he made my body sing. "Fuck me on the Shelby."

He looked aghast. "It'll scratch."

I sat up, smacking his shoulder. "*It'll scratch?*"

"It's a custom paint job."

"Wow." I jumped off the hood. "You lost your shot at the ultimate wet dream made real, buster."

"Nava," he purred. He leveled his rock fuck grin at me. The one I generally stood zero chance of withstanding.

"Forget it. The offer is rescinded."

I breathed out, trying to regain control, an impossible feat with him standing so close and filling my vision. Plus, the pain still riding me like I was its prison bitch.

He amped the ante, standing up and shooting me a smoldering look.

"Don't you work your sex eye voodoo on me," I said waspishly.

Rohan nudged me back against the bumper, gently pushing my butt onto the hood. He knocked my legs aside to stand between them, one hand braced on either side of me, shutting out the rest of the world. His spicy scent washed over me in tantalizing waves. It almost neutralized the dead corpse smell still burning my nose hairs.

He slid his hands into the back pockets of my jeans and tugged me closer. "I thought about you."

I curled my fingers into his belt loops. "Yeah? Doing what?"

That earned me a wolfish grin. He skimmed his hands up my sides.

"Tease." I ran my hands over his muscles strung tight across his corded torso. Drank in that volcanic gaze he trained on me leaving no doubt that despite this other crap between us, this mutual need and want was so real.

"What are you going to do about it?" He nipped my fingertip hard, amping the wanton ripples cascading inside me.

"Punish you. Five minutes in the penalty box," I said. "And by penalty box, I mean pussy."

"Sounds like a serious infraction." He pushed up my shirt to run his tongue over my nipple before scraping his teeth across the tip.

I shivered. There it was. That hot, delicious fire spiraling out from deep inside me. I tangled my hands in his hair. He ground his thigh against my crotch and my hips rocked in abandon. I rode a knife's edge and I needed it to cut deep.

His hot wet mouth brushed along my ear. "Is this what you want, Nava? Rough and messy where anyone could see?"

He'd asked me that same question the first time we'd had sex and the answer had been an unequivocal yes. Had Cuntessa had her way, it would have been yes now and given the tight curl of need unfurling inside me, yes *should* have been my answer. It had been enough yesterday, and would have been enough now, if the feel of his lips against my skin coupled with his tender concern for my well-being hadn't made me remember the kiss that had upended my world.

I jerked sidewise. The heat of our connection dowsed like a bucket of cold water had been tossed on it.

"What's wrong?" Rohan asked. "Your boyfriend have a better car?"

I flinched. Then I straightened both my shirt and my spine, and marched inside without a look back. Slamming my bedroom door, I yanked open the bedside table drawer, and pulled out Snake Clitspin, my S-shaped vibrator. No slender milk snake was my Clitspin; he had the hardy girth of a well-fed boa and I needed release more than ever.

Pushing aside my heap of unfolded laundry just enough to make room for a Nava-sized body, I lay down on top of the mattress, wriggled out of my filthy T-shirt and jeans, letting my legs fall open, and eased Snake into my underwear, teasing Cuntessa with him. My eyes shuddered closed, my desire burrowing deeper, glowing hotter.

"Nava." Light streamed in as the door swung open.

"Shut the door!" I burrowed under the blanket.

Rohan kicked the door shut then snatched Snake from my hand.

My full body blush transformed into a deeper red. I sprung up, jumping for Snake but he held it out of reach. "Get the hell out of my bedroom."

He waved Snake at me. "Cole not doing it for you?"

"This is about me getting off. Without *you*. Or is that not allowed?"

Snake buzzed away in his hand. So near and yet so far.

"Oh, it's allowed," he said. "In fact, I encourage it. Thinking about the look on your face when you come? Thinking about what I wish I was doing to you with my tongue?"

He licked up my neck.

A stuttery breath left my lungs.

"About what I wish I was doing to you with my fingers." His hand ghosted up my spine, each vertebrae lighting up under his touch.

I leaned into him.

"With my cock." Rohan rocked his hips against mine, so I could feel how hard he was.

I swallowed, my voice thick. "What are you waiting for?"

He skipped Snake up my thigh, inch by tantalizing inch. I moaned, jerking his hand up until he rubbed the vibe against my clit through my bikini briefs.

I clutched at his chest, wet and breathless.

"Ask for it." Shadows flickered over his face, lending a dark edge to the anger in his voice. He nipped my bottom lip. "You don't even need to use your words."

All I had to do was close the fraction of an inch between our mouths and I'd get everything he'd promised and more. I clasped my shaking hands behind my back, unable to forget his visual reminder of what happened when I left myself open to more.

"Well?"

I tried to get my throat to work. Tried to make myself move under threat of losing that intense, gorgeous focus forever. Big deal. I'd kissed before. I could do this.

Except, if I kissed him and he pulled away, face pained, it wouldn't just be me falling asleep unsatisfied and wrecked from my ghoul fight.

That kind of rejection would destroy me.

I stepped back. Rohan speared me with a hard look and left. He took Snake with him.

14

It took me ages to fall asleep, so when Harry called bright and early on Wednesday morning to say that Baskerville had come through, I was tempted to blow him off. Instead, I pounded on Rohan's bedroom door.

He poked his head out. Still surly. "Yes?"

"Harry called."

It took him two blinks to understand this olive branch. He nodded. "Meet you at the car in ten."

The only interesting thing about the low slung, single-story house that Rohan and I pulled up to was the fact that it was protected by a Rasha ward. I crossed my fingers that it was protecting the spine. After ensuring there was no vehicle in the carport or parked directly out front, we crept around back and silently unlatched the gate.

The ward's faint pulsing drew me to it like a siren's song.

"Need more proof the Brotherhood has their fingerprints all over this mess?" I asked, as we followed the round paving stones through the slightly overgrown back lawn.

"Yes."

Grr. Argh.

The closer we got to the ward line that lay at the bottom of the back stairs, the more intense the wave of nausea and dizziness coursing through me became. This ward hadn't been created to simply repel demons, it was intended to repel everyone. With each footfall, my entire body strained to turn around but I forced myself to put one foot in front of the other and keep going.

By the time I reached the ward line, I was swallowing convulsively to keep the bile down. Even though the demarcation was invisible, I pinpointed exactly where it started.

Rohan jerked his chin at me. "You feel confident undoing it?"

I'd had some rudimentary training in ward making, but I was still getting the hang of this aspect of my magic. "You do it."

Rohan positioned himself outside of the ward line and slashed his palm open with one of his finger blades, dripping blood while uttering a Hebrew chant.

Nothing happened.

I frowned at the blood seeping into the dirt. "You sure you did it right?"

Rohan shot me an unimpressed look. "Knock yourself out."

I couldn't do worse than he had, right? Reciting the Hebrew, I held out my hand, hissing as he sliced open the fleshy part of my palm. I dropped into a crouch so my blood could get nice and close to the ward line. The second the fluid connected with the ward magic, my eyes widened. While Rasha could sense a ward set by another Rasha, there was no way to tell whose blood had been used to create it.

Except I could and I did.

The ward magic slunk up against me like a cat demanding affection from its owner. Its thrum was a purr that vibrated from my head to my toes. Another magic joined it, dark and sinuous, probing. I'd swear it was sniffing me out.

The ward dissipated.

I flattened my hand against the dirt, bracing myself against the sucking pull threatening to flip my organs from internal to external from this new magic. A shockwave ripped through me, my head snapping back.

"What the—" Rohan lunged for me, his hands closing on empty air as the world seemed to stretch impossibly long between us.

My stomach fell into my toes as I went into free fall, landing seconds later with a teeth-jarring thud. I blinked rapidly, trying to clear my vision against the flash that had blinded me.

"Took you long enough, kid," a familiar voice said.

Dr. Gelman.

We stood in the center of a long, narrow, open concept kitchen and living room with a sliding glass door to the backyard. Even though the room was white-walled and sparsely furnished, brightly colored cushions and an enormous photographic print of a spice market added warmth. Rohan was nowhere to be seen. Not here, not out back.

"You didn't do anything to my friend, did you?"

"He's fine. I just wanted some privacy for our conversation." In her mid-sixties with olive leathery skin, she looked way better than the last time I'd seen her. She'd even colored out the white in her black hair. She was the picture of health. Had her cancer gone into remission?

"You okay?" I asked.

"I'm still alive, so yes. Thanks so much for asking." Her snark was sharp enough to sting.

I tsked her. "You don't call. You don't write."

"Snippy today, are we? Why are you breaking in to my sister's place?"

"Sister?"

She pointed to a group of photos hanging on the wall. Most showed a woman who looked remarkably similar to Dr. Gelman, just older. Several of them featured my Gelman as well. The first time we'd met, she'd said that her sister had dated Rabbi Abrams years ago, I'd just never imagined she meant in Vancouver.

"I came for a gogota spine," I said. "Got one or both?" I was no longer certain of the spine's proximity. Gelman might have created the ward to protect herself while she hid out.

She dropped into a chair with a lithe movement. It was great to see her so healthy. "You've been a busy little worker bee. Yes, I have the spine, but I want something in return."

"What?"

"The Vashar."

"I don't have it anymore," I said. "I had to hand it over to Rabbi Abrams."

"Right." She rubbed her forehead. "But you can get it back. You will get it back if you want the spine."

"I can't and it's unreasonable of you to keep that spine from me. I'm trying to help you. Prove the witches' innocence."

"I need the amulet." Her Israeli accent got much thicker when she was mad.

The sliding glass door exploded inward.

Screaming, I ducked, throwing my hands up over my face. Glass bit into my exposed flesh and lodged in my curls. Dozens of drops of blood welled up on the backs of my hands, calves, and the skin at the V of my throat. Bad day to wear a skirt.

Two figures in head-to-toe black stepped into the room.

Gelman chanted. The couches flew together stacking one above the other and barricading us from our ambushers before bursting into flame.

The two stepped through the flaming sofa wreckage like the fire was a gentle summer's mist.

Gelman grabbed my arm and pushed me down the hallway into an office. Her hands trembled as she slammed the door and locked it. "You've led the Brotherhood to me."

"I didn't! I swear."

Her fingers bit into my wrist, her panic palpable. "The Vashar. We need to get it, now."

"The spine first."

"After."

The back of my neck prickled. I looked from Gelman to the locked door. The locked door beyond which I heard nothing. Not intruders. Not even a fire alarm. I sniffed. No burning sofa, just the faint tang of lemon polish.

The attack had been an illusion.

I blasted whoever–or whatever–this was back against the far wall.

Fake Gelman's glamour fell away, revealing a whip thin demon with a pronounced Adam's apple. His expertly tailored pinstripe suit even had a pressed triangle of a handkerchief in the pocket. The picture of a 1950's Southern gentleman, except for the snout and iridescent blue skin.

"Baskerville, I presume. Good idea faking me out but you dropped the follow through."

The demon pushed to his feet. "It was worth a try."

I pulled my sleeve over my hand, brushing at the glass embedded in me. Too bad that exploding door part had been all too real. When that didn't work, I called my magic up, letting it build under the surface of my skin. Closing my eyes, I pushed the magic out through my pores, envisioning it pushing the slivers out of me. A throbbing buzz shook me from head to toe like a swarm of bees being expelled from my body, stingers first. I blinked my tears away, shaking myself off like a dog to get the last of the glass out. "How did you know about the Vashar?"

"I wouldn't be worth my weight in blood if I didn't, child." Baskerville's voice was honey-smooth, tinged with a hint of the Deep South.

"Didn't you get the collar we retrieved for you?"

He gave an elegant one-shouldered shrug. "I did. But it lost its luster once I possessed it."

"Tough titties. Where's the real Dr. Gelman? Or her sister?" Until I knew for certain whether the witches were innocent, I still wasn't ready to see Gelman, but I didn't want her hurt either.

"Out?" the demon said. "I have no idea. The house was empty."

"So how did you get in?"

"That was all you, chérie." He tugged on his pressed cuffs. "You so helpfully dropped Dr. Gelman's ward, allowing me to waltz right in."

Except I'd felt a second magic. "You overlaid her ward with some kind of spell of your own to bring me to you, didn't you?"

"Very good."

I made a "wrap it up" motion. "Is the spine here or not?"

He flashed me an enigmatic smile and snapped two of his three fingers. The air shimmered and then crumpled like a veil falling to the floor, revealing a modified gogota demon standing between the desk and the bookshelf.

I shrieked.

Baskerville clamped his hands over his large flappy ears, similar in appearance to those of Wallace from *Wallace and Gromit*.

My feet, legs, torso, all went concrete-heavy. The sensation crawled up my throat, clogging my airways.

"Sensitive hearing," he said. "Please keep it down."

I blinked my eyes to indicate my agreement, since I couldn't move my head to nod. His eyes narrowed, then the feeling just kind of fell away. I sucked in a breath, the jittery motion jump starting my heart, and sidled closer to the gogota.

Evil dude was not looking too hot. About my height, his body was no longer a plump sausage–more shriveled like a leftover wiener past its expiration date. A dull sheen lay over his charcoal gray fur which had acquired mottled white streaks. He vibrated seizure-fast but remained rooted to the spot, his long, sloth-like fingers and toes twitching. The demon stood half-bowed over as if succumbing to the weight of the metal spine that was no longer shiny.

"This is the demon that attacked Gelman?" I said. Baskerville nodded. "How did you get it?"

"Not important."

He'd totally kidnapped it.

I circled the gogota, ready to access the magic humming under my skin, choking on the dubious pairing of baby powder and sweaty baseball mitt undercut with rot that poured off the demon.

The gogota's single glassy eye tracked my progress and his blood red lips seemed to be mouthing something over and over again.

Having the entire modified demon and not just its spine might go a long way toward determining once and for all whether the Brotherhood was involved. This demon was my one lead to expose Mandelbaum, heal the rift between Ari and myself, and show up all the hypocrisy within the Brotherhood–starting with the second-class status of yours truly.

"We good here? The gogota for the collar?"

Baskerville pursed his lips. "Very well."

I left the gogota locked in the office, counting on it not having the fine motor skills with those sausage fingers to turn the tiny tab in the knob and unlock the door.

"Pleasure doing business with you." This was the point where I should have killed Baskerville since the only good demon was a dead one, Leo excepted, but his resourcefulness might prove useful another time. "Lucky you, you get to live."

Life became a little bit more gray with each passing day.

I escorted him out the shattered sliding door, glass crunching underfoot. The couches were intact, however.

The back gate banged open and Rohan stormed in, his face and arms covered in scratches. Twigs and bits of frothy leaves were stuck in his hair. As soon as he saw the demon, he broke into a run, blades out.

"And that's my cue." Baskerville disappeared.

Rohan swiped at the empty air, swore, and then glared at me. "You let him get away?"

"His future value outweighed killing him."

"Based on your decades of experience."

"Based on my gut. I'm not completely useless at this either. Besides, if you're jonsing that hard for a demon, I've got another one."

"Of course you do." He raked his fingers through his hair, dislodging shrubbery.

I snickered. "Where did he teleport you?"

Rohan's gaze flicked to the neighbor's hedges peeking up above the fence. He rubbed the side of his head. "The old lady that lives there is really mean. She clocked me for disturbing her stupid Viburnums. Don't laugh," he said, jabbing a finger at me, then chuckled, bowing his head so I could pluck the remaining foliage off him.

"Come on." I took his arm. "You'll want to see this."

Unlocking the office door was as easy as one, two, three, blast. The door crashed open into the wall. I grimaced. That was going to leave a dent. Though it was still hanging on its hinges so my master control had reached new heights.

The gogota rushed Rohan, grabbing him around the neck with his long, sticky fingers.

Rohan's iron blades shot out of his body.

"Don't kill it!" I shoved Rohan off-balance.

"Why not?" Rohan failed to disengage from the demon.

"Because having all of the demon to examine could give us a total picture of what was done to it and how." My eyes watered from the demon's stench. Grunting, I heaved on the window clasp, wrenching it open and gulping down fresh air.

Rohan sliced off the gogota's arm. It came off the demon but remained stuck around Rohan's throat like the ultimate goth accessory.

The gogota started freaking out, yelling "Gel. Man. Gel. Man." and running in circles, his head swiveling around looking for his target.

"He's still trying to kill her," I said. Once fixated on a task, a gogota would try to complete it until he was dead, and given that this one was probably bound by magic to carry it out, the impulse must have been twice as strong.

"Gel. Man. Gel. Man." The gogota's cries increased.

The front door opened. Oh shit. Gelman's sister was back. If she was a witch like Gelman, this B&E was not what I wanted my first impression to be.

There was a shriek of rage. That would be the destroyed sliding door.

"We need to get out of here," I hissed.

Rohan plowed into the gogota with his shoulder like a linebacker, knocking him back a half-dozen feet. Of course, thanks to the glue-like slime the demon secreted, Rohan was once more stuck to the damn thing, but that did help him steer the gogota toward the window which was our only way out.

Footsteps thudded closer. "I'm calling the cops."

I slammed the office door, blasting the heavy filing cabinet across the room to block it.

Rohan punched the gogota in the face. It didn't shut the demon up.

Gelman's sister banged on the door. "Open up."

We attempted to wrestle the demon out the ground floor window. Get a five-foot-eight moving sausage with flailing arms, okay, arm, and try to shove it through a half-open window while your partner is stuck to it. See how far you get.

"Fuck this," Rohan said, and jerked himself, me, and the demon sideways out the window.

We landed in a pillowy heap. Pillowy for me. Less so for Rohan and absolutely not at all for the demon, who'd ended up at the bottom of our dog pile.

We wrestled the demon out the side gate and over to Rohan's car. He had to cut himself free of the gogota, the two of us stuffing the demon into his trunk with our magic and a tire iron. Rohan bitched about the damage to his precious Shelby until we'd screeched out of the alley when he switched it up to bitching about my driving.

My reminder that his eyes were stuck together with gogota goop and I was the better driver option was scoffed at.

I stuck to five kilometers below the speed limit, my eyes darting to the rearview mirror in time with the thumps emanating from the trunk and jolting the entire car. "The mandated procedure for being pulled over with a decaying irate demon in the trunk would be what?"

Rohan laughed, more pained than in hilarity, prying his sticky eyelashes open. His entire front was coated in a rapidly hardening sticky goo, every little movement going "crack."

The gogota shrieked. I glanced into the windows of the neighboring cars but no one seemed to notice. Or they just didn't care. Blessings on human indifference. "I could call Leo. She might know somewhere safe to stash it."

"No." Rohan wiped more demon goo off with his sleeve. "We'll put him in the iron room where we can keep an eye on him."

"Are you insane? We can't bring him into the house." My voice had risen about two-octaves.

Rohan patted my back like I was going to panic. I opened my mouth to snap at him, except my lungs had constricted and my vision had blurred and yup, he was right. I was about to panic. I leaned in to his touch.

"Freaking out?" he said.

"Yes. Jump in, the water's fine."

"Just get my baby home in one piece."

I crafted a taunt about his concern for my well-being, then didn't bother. He was talking about the car.

"That room is the safest place for the demon," he said. "Rabbi Abrams doesn't go in there and the room is soundproofed so no one in the Vault will hear the gogota screaming. Besides," he ripped a strip of goo off his arm and winced, "maybe the demon will break free and kill us before we get back to Demon Club and we won't have to worry about sneaking him in."

I patted his knee. "Your cynicism is catching up to mine. It's so close it's passing me a baton."

"Yeah, you're a real gold medalist that way." He rolled down the window and flung the hardened goo out.

Incredibly, we were neither ambushed nor arrested on the drive home. The demon even shut up once I'd crossed the wards onto our property. Demons couldn't come through on their own, but we could bring them through if we chose. Being on our side of the wards was painful and draining for them.

"I'll check the ground floor. If it's clear, we'll take him in that way." Rohan jogged inside.

I tried to find some music to distract me from the banging inside the trunk, while searching for an explanation in case we got caught. The others would be curious enough about us bringing this demon here without the added complication of why it had a metal spine welded to its back. Oh no, that didn't scream sketchy.

Five minutes later, Rohan rapped on my window to get my attention. "It's clear."

Rohan snicked his blades out while I had a nice ball of electricity at the ready. We opened the trunk, bracing for an attack. The demon lay on his side, snoring.

"You've got to be kidding." I said.

"Don't knock it. It'll be easier carrying him like this," Rohan said. "Grab a side."

I pitched the demon's disembodied arm that Rohan had torn off his throat and tossed into the trunk earlier into the rosebushes. The arm sailed over the dense, thorny bush, and landed on the grass. A crow hopped off a branch to take a closer look, cawed, and pecked at it, which was when I decided I didn't need to see any more.

We lugged the dead weight in through the ground floor door and down the stairs. Rohan had propped open the Vault's door so we didn't have to wait for the hand scanner.

"Hurry." I adjusted my hold on the gogota. "He weighs a ton." He also sputtered phlegm as he snored and my shirt was getting disgustingly damp.

We carried the demon across the room and dropped him onto the Vault's blue padded floor. Rohan slapped his hand on the scanner for the small iron room while I shook out my arms, waiting for the light to change from red to green.

The demon was back in our arms, the wall sliding away to allow access into the iron room, when the stupid thing woke up and started thrashing. Limbs flailed: his, mine, Rohan's. The gogota wound various body parts around each of us. My face was stuck to his armpit, his remaining arm bouncing off the top of my head. Rohan was swearing from somewhere in the vicinity of his shoulder blades.

"Need a hand?" Ari said. "Or is that just the demon?"

"Fuck my life," I said.

Ari ripped me off the demon.

I swore, bidding adieu to my first few layers of facial epidermis.

Rohan cut himself free and shoved the demon into the iron room so hard that the gogota hit the far wall. With his head. He slid down onto the floor in slow motion. KO'd.

Rohan hit the scanner again and the iron door clicked shut, the wall sliding back into place to conceal him.

Panting, I braced my hands on my thighs. "Nothing to see. Run along."

"Why'd you bring a modified gogota demon here, Nee?"

"I asked it 'your place or mine?'" I spread my hands wide.

Ari glared at me.

"Since we're asking questions," Rohan said, "why did the ward react to your blood and not mine?"

"What ward?" Ari asked.

Rohan oh-so-helpfully filled him in. Two pairs of eyes lasered me, waiting for my answer.

Being resigned to the truth didn't make sharing any easier. "Okay, so..." I scratched my neck. "I know who the Rasha blood came from to make that ward."

"Who?" they asked in unison, their expressions grim.

I scrunched up my face. "Me."

I didn't expect that news to be greeted with cupcakes and a parade but it wasn't as if I'd deliberately handed my blood over, so my brother's many variations on "How could you be so stupid?" was not, in my opinion, deserved.

"It was a mistake," I said for the umpteenth time, Rohan and I following Ari into his room. Near as I could figure, Dr. Gelman had used blood that she'd gotten off me in Prague when I was injured to set the ward on her sister's house. That was one way to create a Rasha ward. Let them bleed on your linens in the name of hospitality, add magic and voilà. "How was I to know she could extract my blood from a washcloth and save it for use at a later date?"

"Why do you think we scour shit if our blood is spilled?" Ari sniffed a T-shirt, pitching it into his hamper in the corner. "You can't leave any trace of your blood."

"I understand that now, but at the time, I was coming off almost dying by dragon and preoccupied with whether or not she could help get your stupid ass inducted."

Rohan smirked, but Ari was still mad at me. "You bitch about the fact that you didn't have your whole life to train and study like the rest of us," he said, "but that never seems to stop you from doing whatever you want instead of remembering that you know squat."

"Give her a break," Rohan said.

"Am I the only one who sees sense around here?" Ari jabbed a finger at me. "You've been stumbling around above your pay grade from day one and you can't see how badly this is all going to blow up. Christ, it already has. You've brought that demon here."

"What do you want me to say? I fucked up and should have taken it somewhere else?"

"You *didn't* fuck up, Nee. You *are* fucked up. The past few years you've been this tornado of bad decisions. It's been exhausting to live with and I figured that being Rasha, being part of something bigger might rein you in, but it's done the opposite. You're more hell-bent than ever on just doing things however you want." He shook his head, trying to shove me out his door. "Forget it."

I grabbed onto the doorframe, throwing my weight against him. If I contaminated him with demon phlegm, all the better. "Is this where I'm supposed to apologize for wanting to live life on my terms?"

"This is where you leave shit alone. Hunt demons. Save humanity. Stay away from witches and for fuck's sake, stop pissing off the Brotherhood." Ari released me so suddenly that I stumbled. He pushed past me and stomped down the stairs.

I jogged after him. "No. They don't get to decide my worth and they absolutely don't get to hurt innocent people, pulling this 'end justifies the means' shit."

We wrestled for control of the library door that he tried to shut in my face.

"But you do?" he said. "You're doing the exact same thing."

"I'm not modifying demons." I balled my hands into fists.

"Don't be dense." The two of us were nose-to-nose by this point, bristling at each other.

"Enough." Rohan stepped in between us and pushed Ari away from me. "Back off."

"Says the guy who lets her do whatever she wants. Newsflash, Ro, fucking my sister doesn't mean you know what's best for her and it sure as hell doesn't give you any say in this conversation."

"Excuse me?" A dangerous smile lurked at the corner of Rohan's mouth.

Ari took a step back, scrubbing a hand over his face. Had I not seen the sheepish flash as he flicked his eyes to me, I'd have clobbered my twin for that comment. His maiming was still on the table.

But he'd be injured at my hands, not Rohan's. I placed my palm on Rohan's chest because as good a fighter as my brother was, Snowflake would wipe the floor with him. "Everyone take a mindful freaking moment here."

I wanted to wait until the tension in the room had ratcheted down a notch before I continued but Rohan shot me a sharp glance before it'd gone down even half a degree. "You going to stay and listen to this?"

I bit my lip.

He didn't even give me a second to decide. "Your life," he said in a tight voice and left.

"Rohan," I called after him.

His footsteps faded away. Great.

I shoved my brother. "For someone who kiboshed my make-out session with Audrey because he didn't want to 'fucking deal with the collateral damage?'" I saluted Ari. "Well played."

Storming off was immature and petty, but damn did it feel good.

15

After a quick shirt change, I barged into Rohan's room. Unlike mine, it was painted a tasteful green with framed photography on the wall courtesy of Ms. Clara. His clothes hung in a color-coded line in his open closet and his toiletries were still neatly arranged on the counter in his small en suite bathroom. No sign of a man packing up to leave.

"Listen," I said. "I appreciate your concern but you have no idea what it means to be a twin. You can't get mad at me for my decisions around Ari. Things are tough between us right now and it's not something either of us are used to."

Rohan finished typing on his phone, then slid it into his pocket. "It annoyed me to hear him speak to you that way. But you're right and I'm sorry. It wasn't my place to mix in."

"Thank you. Now let me see the spell books."

Rohan pointed at the small stack on his dresser. "There are actually very few spells in these books because Rasha don't have a lot of cause to use them. If witches can do all kinds of spellwork, it's not something we're taught. That said, check the blue one on top. I marked the page."

I flipped open the book. "This is what we need but the list of ingredients has been redacted."

"I know. We could search the database? See if we find the spell there."

"The search would be logged. No point sending up a flare saying "Yoo hoo! Over here! Your least favorite Rasha knows what you're up to.""

There was no way around it, I needed Kane's assistance. If anyone could comb through the database and not leave a fingerprint, it was him. Except bringing him in to this would mean sharing my beliefs. Trusting him not to turn around and tell the Brotherhood what I was doing. I was safe trusting Rohan, even before he'd had his own doubts, and Ari, no matter how much he disagreed with me, would never compromise my safety. Had this been Drio, I wouldn't have risked it, but Kane was still an unknown in a lot of ways to me.

I was pretty certain he'd do this if it was for Ari, and while he didn't actively wish me harm, that was different than going behind his Brotherhood's back on my behalf.

I stood there, book in hand, weighing the risks. In the end, I could see no other way of finding a spell for detecting magic traces in a timely fashion. Being able to prove Rohan wrong about me not ever bringing in others to help was merely an added bonus. "We need Kane."

"Asking for help, again? I'm rubbing off on you," Rohan said.

"Ha. Ha." Loath as I was to admit it, he was right. I couldn't do this on my own. I went in search of Kane, my mind in overdrive at the best way to share minimum information and achieve maximum results.

I'd checked his bedroom, the entire main floor, the Vault, and had hit the offices on the ground floor in case he was talking to Ms. Clara, when his Porsche roared up. I sprinted upstairs to greet him.

Kane stepped into the foyer, dropped his large, leather carry-on bag on the ground, and shrugged out of his coat.

"You were away?"

"And evidently desperately missed." He hung his coat in the front closet.

I smooched his cheek. "I pined."

He swatted me off of him. "Troweling it on implies you want something." He shoved the bag at me.

I lugged it up the stairs. "Where were you?"

"Mongolia." He stopped inside his doorway, causing me to walk into him. He rolled his eyes with an aggrieved sigh.

"Why?"

"Caught some rays in the Gobi Desert, kicking my Seasonal Affective Disorder in the ass." He unzipped the carry-on. "Why do you think?"

"If you're going to be sarcastic, dude-who-isn't-supposed-to-be-on-active-duty, I won't give you this prize mystery to solve." I shut the door.

Kane raised an eyebrow at that, then went into his bathroom to unpack his toiletries bag. "Mongolian Death Worm."

I planted my hands on my hips. "They shouldn't have sent you. Do you feel okay?"

He dismissed my concerns with a wave of his hand. "My poison trumped his. They needed me and I was happy to get back in the field. Besides, my salt levels tested back within normal range."

"So it's less coding, more killing, now?"

"I like coding." He rubbed a hand over the back of his neck. "Offsets the high burn-out rates with our bunch, but, yeah. Something like that. Now, what's the mystery, Velma?"

Had he called me Daphne, I'd have protested, but I'd always liked Velma. The show had just caught her at an awkward stage. "Keep an open mind."

Kane walked back into the bedroom. "You're up to something involving either witches or the Brotherhood and you don't want either aware of what you're doing."

My mouth fell open.

Kane chuckled. "Tell me if I'm getting close."

I crossed my arms. "Lucky guess."

"Aww." He patted my head, then continued unpacking, tossing clothing from his bag into his hamper. "Pique my interest or leave."

I searched his face, my gut saying it was okay to trust him, but my paranoia forced me to swallow a few times before I was able to get the words out. If I was crossing one of Kane's lines with this, what would he do? Jettison me or throw me to the wolves? "You need to come down to the Vault."

I would have really enjoyed the dumbfounded look on Kane's face at the sight of the gogota had there not been so much on the line.

The demon sat placidly in the corner. Between his already-weakened state and all the iron in here, we didn't even need to strap him into the iron chair.

Kane crouched down beside him. "How did they get the spine on him?"

"That's part of what I want to find out. These modified gogotas were used in two attacks that I know of. One on me and one on Dr. Gelman, the witch who gave me Ari's induction ritual. If I'm correct, the Brotherhood was behind them and the spines are how they've gotten the demons to do their bidding."

"You think they've figured out how to bind demons?" Kane whistled. I was profoundly grateful that he didn't question the idea that the Brotherhood would stoop to such a thing. "When were you attacked?"

"In Prague."

He crossed his arms. "So Ro and Drio know about this?"

"Just Rohan."

"And Ari?" His voice was as tight as his jaw.

"He's not a fan of my theory."

He didn't speak for a very long moment.

I wiped my sweaty palms on my thighs. Twice. Fuck it. If I couldn't trust anyone, I was going to go insane. "Get everyone and meet me downstairs. It's time for a debrief and I need you all there. Okay?"

"Okay."

I only crossed two sets of fingers that I didn't live to regret this.

Looking around at the four of us in the kitchen: me, Ari, Kane, and Rohan, I was reminded of the quote about how three people could keep a secret only if two were dead, and wondered if maybe I needed to take some of them out.

"Nothing goes farther than this group." I trusted the nods I got.

Marginally.

I started with Ari's first failed induction ceremony and Rabbi Abrams getting me to contact Dr. Gelman, through trying to find the witches and up to Baskerville and the spell with the missing ingredients. I'd brought a bottle of blue nail polish with me so I'd have an excuse not to look anyone in the eye as I spoke, but the story took so long that I was finished painting all of mine and was on to Rohan's second hand before I'd caught everyone up.

"Oy vey," Kane said, sitting on the counter and swinging his legs. "You've been busy."

I nudged my brother's foot. He'd apologized to me for his earlier comments but I wanted a clear declaration of his standing by my side. "You onboard?"

Ari toyed with the handle of his coffee mug. "I won't interfere. For now."

How magnanimous.

"Kane, I need you to find those ingredients," I said. "Check the database."

"I'll whip up an algorithm."

"Okay?" I nudged Rohan.

He nodded, examining his nails. "Needs a second coat."

I shook the polish up, giving Kane a stern look. "No one can know that you're looking into this."

"I'll be a ghost in the system."

"No showing off and leaving a sneaky signature or Easter egg or something in there either," Ari said.

Kane waggled his fingers at my brother. "Ooooo," he said in a scary voice. He did it two more times until Ari laughed and called him an idiot.

Ari wasn't laughing when he spoke to me. "Even if you find a spell to test the spine and it shows what you're hoping, that's not proof that the Brotherhood is behind it."

"Let's worry about that when we come to it," Rohan said. "Nava, promise me you won't do any spells without me there."

Every fiber of my being screamed "no." It didn't matter that still believing this goal was mine to prove and mine to handle was immature, especially considering that I'd called this meeting. And sure, there was something really comforting about having all these guys in my corner, not to mention that this thing had spiraled beyond my capabilities. It's just that the self-reliance and self-protective instincts I'd honed over the past couple of years were hard to shake.

"I promise," I said. "Meantime, Ari and I will stick with our investigation." It was doubly imperative if the Brotherhood was keeping tabs on my and Ari's progress.

The meeting broke up after that. I pulled Rohan aside. "You and Ari okay now?"

"He apologized." That didn't answer my question but whatever. They were big boys.

"Don't smudge your nails," I called after him, answering my phone without checking who was calling. "Hello?"

"Hey, Avon."

I lowered my voice. "Hi, Cole."

"Did I catch you at work?"

"Yeah." I headed into the farthest back corner of the kitchen, one eye on the door. "What's up?"

I turned on the tap so the water would drown out the conversation.

"Just wondering if you wanted to get together tonight."

"Oh. Uh, well, I promised Ari I'd go out with him tonight to Electric Sands. Playing wingman. Woman." I facepalmed.

"Ah."

The silence ate at me. As did lying to him. "But it probably won't go too late," I said. "How about I call you after?"

"I'd really like that."

"Me too."

Half an hour at the club that night and I was already three G&Ts in. Drink one was purchased and consumed upon seeing the line of cages suspended over the dance floor that contained contortionists twisting themselves into pseudo-lewd positions with each strobe of the giant silver disco ball. All the performers dripped with ennui. Quite the emotional conveyance when one's foot was wrapped around one's head.

Drink two: the sleek, beautiful clientele, not to be outdone in world-weary cynicism.

I jabbed at my ice with the straw. "The pretension levels in here are puckering my anus."

Leo wiggled her hips to the Arabic-infused electronica pulsing over the speakers, whose curling horns and sinuous percussion conjured up warm nights in a Moroccan town on the edge of the Sahara. "Eye on the goal, Nee." Hers were on Kane and Rohan, ensconced on a couple of sofas in a far corner.

My oh my, did those boys clean up well.

Kind of. Kane sported red skinny jeans with a white shirt featuring a hideous zebra pattern which he'd paired with a red tie. I wished I could dissect his brain to better understand the thought process that went into his clothing choices.

Then there was Rohan, in dark wash jeans, a navy pinstripe vest, white and navy plaid shirt, cuffs rolled up to his elbows, and a dark fedora perched jauntily on his head. His clothes molded to his every muscle, almost like a sentient being doing its damnedest to keep earning Rohan's approval by showing him off in the most flattering light.

Drink three, right there.

Leo snickered at my blatant ogling. "How goes things with Le Mitra?"

I wrinkled my nose, stirring my drink. I'd invited her along to offset the testosterone when Ari brought the other men along as props. Just a bunch of friends going out in a group. When she poked my side, determined to have an answer, I regretted the invitation. "Ancient history."

She made a mocking sound. "When's Drio coming back?"

"Please find another guy to mack on and rethink this possible demonicide." Ever since Leo had met Drio, she'd been bugging me to hook them up while I'd done everything in my power to keep them apart. This girl had a death wish because if Drio found out about her halfie status, he'd dust her in a heartbeat, and I wanted no part of it.

My bestie licked her lips. "I'm sure it would be worth it."

I munched on some ice. "True. He knows his way around the female body just fine."

Her head whipped toward me. "You say that with such certainty, why?"

Right. I'd never actually told her about my little make-out session in Prague. I slid small snapshots of the victims showing them in happier–read: *alive*–times out of my purse. "Must work." With that I scampered off, ignoring her demands to "get back here."

Since the bartender and I were old friends by now, plus I'd been tipping like a baller, she was happy to take a look at the pictures, but the only person she recognized was Max. Even Mara didn't look familiar, though if she'd only ever been here once or twice there was no reason for her to stand out.

Sulky dancers, men in metrosexual cologne and pricey suits, burly bouncers, no one yielded any results. Ari and I leaned against the second floor railing, surveying the club.

"Now what?" I asked.

"I dunno." He stole my gin and tonic away from me and finished it off. "The patrons here are so slicked up that any of them could be an incubus or succubus. No one person stands out."

"They're all working what their mama gave 'em. Wanna do one more tour of the place?"

"Sure. But let's get another drink first. Props make for a good cover."

We hit the bar up on this level since it was less crowded. Leo was chatting with Kane, her hand on his arm and the tilt of her head making her seem particularly small and cute. Her bite-sized snack look. Her wisp of a dress didn't hurt her appeal.

Even Team "Up With Dicks" Kane was enjoying flirting with her.

I'd just taken the first sip of my new drink when Ari elbowed me in the back. "Goblin."

I spat out G&T, shooting a panicked look at Leo. "What?"

He motioned to a short, red-haired man headed our way.

"Because he's a short ginger?"

"That and he's doing a shit job of glamouring his ears. Look at the tips. A bit too pointy."

The goblin raised a hand in greeting at someone. My best someone who'd just smiled back at him, from where she stood next to Kane: the man who Ari had said spotted everything, who was the go-to guy to take out *death* worms, and who had zero compunction jettisoning flotsam.

I shoved my way down the bar and spilled my drink all over Kane's abomination of a shirt.

"Oops," I giggled, swaying.

He grabbed a cocktail napkin and dabbed at the cloth. "You're a menace." No, I was a godsend, saving Leo, and providing a service to humanity in destroying that shirt.

Leo stared at me in confusion until the goblin joined our party.

"Leonie," he said. "Long time no see."

"No way," Ari breathed, his head swinging between the two of them.

Kane shot Ari a puzzled look. He turned in the direction Ari was staring and–

I stumbled against Kane, knocking him backwards.

Kane bitched about me being a crazy person and elbowed me out of the way. "If I don't get to the bathroom and rinse this, this silk is going to be a write-off."

I babbled profuse apologies as I helped him through the crowd.

The second the restroom door shut behind him, I raced back to the bar, practically tossing people out of my path. The goblin was gone and Leo and Ari were engaged in a game of Am Not/Are Too.

"Nava," Leo said through clenched teeth. "Ari is high. For the last time, I am not a mythical creature."

Ari inspected my bristling friend from head to toe. "No. You're not a goblin."

"Told you."

"You're a PD."

"Fuck you, I'm not practice." Leo clapped her hand over her mouth.

I muscled in between the two of them. "Here's the thing."

My brother swung his too-calm gaze my way and I wondered if perhaps I should have spilled that drink over *his* shirt instead. No, I was reasonably certain Ari wouldn't kill Leo.

In public.

I threw my hands up. "Surprise?"

"It doesn't change who I am," Leo said.

"Why didn't you tell me?" he asked me.

"I only found out when Leo and I reconnected a couple months ago and to be fair, she had her reasons for not telling us in high school."

"Thank you," Leo said.

Ari pinched the bridge of his nose. "You're the snitch, aren't you? That's how Nee and you reunited."

"Told you he wasn't just a pretty face," I said.

"I prefer informant." Leo jabbed him in the chest with her finger. "I work part time as a P.I. for a mostly demon clientele to fund my crim degree." She jabbed him again and he swatted her hand away. "I passed on a ton of good intel to Xiaoli when he was still based here, so back off."

"Ace," I warned, "no one can know about Leo. Xiaoli may have recognized her worth and allowed her to live–" Leo flinched, but it was what it was. "But other Rasha won't be so understanding."

"My silence has a price. Point out all the demons in this club." Ari pulled out his most commanding tone.

Leo wasn't fazed. Guess my brother's menace didn't scare someone who'd been around for the three months of squeaky cracking when his voice was changing. "It doesn't work that way." She reapplied her lipstick. "I'm not some kind of Hellspawn detector and we don't have secret handshakes."

"Sucks for you," Ari said, downing the last of his drink.

Leo grabbed his hand, pressing it against the kill spot on her left hip.

I swallowed my "eep" and even refrained from knocking his hand away, recognizing that this was Leo's to have out with Ari. Maybe she could get some iron plating, though. Just in case.

"Dust me or shut up already," she said.

"There a problem?" Kane leaned his elbow on the bar.

Ari tore his hand off her.

Leo smiled up at Kane. "Nothing a drink can't fix."

"My pleasure." He waved at the bartender to get her attention, then looked at Ari. "Twin the elder? You look like you could use a couple of drinks yourself."

Tight-lipped, Ari shook his head and strode off.

Leo squeezed her fist twice at me. Our code for someone being a giant douchebag.

Not entirely sure which Katz twin it was directed at, I shot her an apologetic look and hurried after my brother, catching up to him halfway down the stairs. "Why are you so mad? She's no different than she's always been."

Ari stopped on the last tread so abruptly that I ran into his back. "It's only going to be so long before she turns on you for her own ends," he said.

"She'd never."

He shook his head, his eyes hard in the club's low light. "How much intel have you handed over to her? Fuck, Nava. What have you done?"

"I've reconnected with my best friend. Your friend, too."

"She's a demon."

"She's Leo." He opened his mouth to argue and I held up a hand. "Spare me the 'Rasha and demons can't be friends' bullshit. I'm familiar with the party line. It's up there with women can't be Rasha. The Brotherhood has laid down a lot of absolutes that–"

"Not now," he said.

"Yes, now. You and I are going to have this out."

He clasped my shoulders and spun me around. "Mara's roommate, Daniel. Three o'clock. Talking to sex on a stick."

Smoldering dark eyes, lush red lips, stubble meandering into beard territory–I swear Cuntessa whimpered. My hips involuntarily thrust forward, my body's attempt to get closer to this stranger's orbit. "Yum. And he could be Arab."

Though if he was an incubus, why was he hitting on Daniel?

The sexy man smiled wickedly at something that Daniel said. The punch from that was like being railroad spiked with lust. "Definitely an incubus," I said through gritted teeth.

"He's something else." I thought Ari was saying that in admiration, until I took in the tight strain in his muscles and the slight flush on his cheeks. He literally meant this man was some other type of demon because he was affecting the both of us–and Daniel–and bisexual incubi were not a thing.

Ari and I groaned in tandem, shifting.

"Demon," my brother said. "Not our faults."

I certainly hoped so, because if we weren't being affected by some evil compulsion, our sibling relationship was about to get extremely awkward.

16

Our suspected demon lounged on a sofa, one arm stretched along the back, his legs splayed, owning his gunmetal black suit that had to cost a small fortune. His black hair was styled in a Caesar cut. Ninety-nine percent of all men with that cut could not pull it off. This man was absolutely the one percent.

I ran my eyes over every inch of him in thorough investigation. Giving my all to this job. Tugging on my red halter top to straighten it, I sat down on the high bar stools we'd commandeered to better scope him out. "Hello, billionaire BDSM romance cover."

"He could tie me up," Ari said.

My brother was a switch? I desperately looked around for a drink to magically appear, though if alcohol got Ari dishing facts like this, he was cut off. "Over-sharing between us only goes the other way, bro. Don't fuck with a perfectly acceptable system."

With his eager expression and black-and-white striped sweater, Daniel made an incongruous sight next to this other man. He was a kitten playing with a panther. A panther who reached out a hand to stroke the kitten's cheek.

"They seem to know each other," I said. "Which makes sense because of Mara."

"Right." Ari looked pained as he tore his eyes away from our target. "We need to keep Daniel away from the demon."

"Good luck with that. Look at him. That boy is jonsing hard for a taste of tall, evil, and ride-me-hard."

Ari shifted his stool a couple of inches to the left in order to see around the couple now blocking us. "Not like we can pull Daniel aside and warn him off. He wouldn't believe us."

"Even if he did, it might not matter," I pointed out. "My many warnings to Leo about Drio have failed to douse her interest."

Daniel pressed close to the other man.

"The libido wants what the libido wants," I said.

Ari leaned back, head bobbing to the music. "Think Daniel was already under this guy's thrall? I mean, Mara only died a few days ago. A bit fast to go clubbing, isn't it?"

"No kidding. But we need proof." I slid off the stool. "I am the best sister ever. I'll handle Daniel. You sample Yummytimes and report back."

I pasted on my brightest smile as I approached. "Daniel, right?" He looked up with the blatant scowl of someone not wanting company. I kept my attention on him and not the potential demon studying Ari and me with hooded eyes. "Alison, remember?" I said.

"Right."

I dropped onto the seat next to him. "I'm glad to see you out. After Mara's sudden passing." I glanced at our target but he showed no reaction to her name.

"I had to get out of the house," Daniel said.

I nodded. "Totally understandable."

While I babbled on to Daniel, ignoring his crossed arms, frowning, and curt answers, Ari had moved in on the other guy. I was having trouble hearing both conversations over the music, but then Sexy placed a hand on Daniel's shoulder, interrupting us.

"Excuse me." I gripped the top of the sofa because, dear lord, he had a posh British accent. Could he get any more delectable? "We're going for a drink."

There was no invitation for Daniel to join them.

I raked an objective eye over my twin. Blond, buff, and owning the bad boy vibe. I wasn't thrilled with his constant penchant for all-black these days but it suited him.

Daniel didn't stand a chance.

Ari and the target left. Daniel tried to follow but I stopped him, clasping his hands and mouthing platitudes about how much Mara was missed at the clinic. I sent her a silent apology and hoped that wherever she was, she understood that this was for the greater good of saving her roommate's ass.

I kept up my verbal barrage until Daniel extricated himself to join some other friends that had arrived. After ensuring to the best of my ability that they were human, I wove through the patrons, tossing off "excuse me," as I circled the club searching for Ari. There was no sign of him or Sexy anywhere on this level.

Kane and Rohan were in the same back corner as the beginning of the evening, but there were a lot more glasses on their table now. Rohan sprawled in the chair. His slack posture changed as I approached; the intensity on his face made my skin tingle and he gazed at me like I needed devouring.

Eat me. Please and thank you. I pinched the inside of my arm. "We need to find Ari."

Kane tossed a handful of peanuts into his mouth. "What's the wayward twin up to now?"

"She's standing right here," Rohan joked.

"Yes, yes, you're both hilarious. He's with a potentially incubus-esque thing."

"Incubi are hetero," Rohan said.

"Hence the 'esque,'" I replied. "We should find him."

Kane rolled his eyes and stood up. "You think?"

After another check of the ground floor, we started up the stairs, Rohan's fingers ghosting across the exposed skin on my lower back. I clutched the railing, focusing on the treads beneath my feet and not the whisper of contact along my sacrum. Rohan wasn't drunk. Unlike the one time I'd seen him soused, there was no glittering edge to him tonight. He was just relaxed.

Oh, the things I could do with a pliant Rohan.

We found my brother upstairs, slumped over a table. "Ace!" I shook his shoulders.

He raised his head. "Crazy strong power. Conversation alone was..." He dropped his head back down. "I got Malik's number."

Malik was an Arabic name, which fit the pattern we were looking at, but right now we had a more pressing concern. "We need to go after him," I said.

"Nope."

I frowned. Kane and Rohan exchanged amused smiles.

Kane chucked my brother under the chin. "Need a moment there, sport?"

"Get lost," he groaned.

"Oh my god," I sputtered. "Will down the hard-on and move. We can't let him get away."

"Demon-induced erections. Got a good hour before it comes off crowbar status." Kane jammed his hands in his pockets, rocking back on his heels. "What?" he said at my look. "Hunter. Shit happens."

"Boys and their stupid genitals," I said. "Fine. I'll find him."

"Buddy system." Rohan grinned at me, placing his hand flat against my shoulder blades. His warmth sunk into me like a hot stone massage, unraveling me. I rued my choice of halter top which left so much of me exposed.

I wrenched myself out of touching range. "You're... no. You?" I boffed my brother across the head. "Also no. Kane. You're with me."

"No way, babyslay." He tugged on his waistband. "These pants don't stretch."

"Ugh."

"The demon isn't going to be able to hurt anyone for a few days," Ari said, shifting with a wince. "I put ground labradorite in his drink."

Kane clapped him on the shoulder. "Nice work."

I shook my head, uncomprehending.

"It protects against ill will and negative energy," Rohan explained. "By getting him to ingest it, Ari has bought a couple days of this Malik not being able to hurt anyone."

"Didn't know that, did you?" Ari asked in a smug voice.

Bastard. I hadn't. "How's your dick, brother dear?" *Phrasing.* I grimaced. "Retract that. Because we're not *Flowers in the Attic* type of twins."

The more the guys stared at me, Ari horrified, Kane incredulous, and Rohan shaking with silent laughter, the less control I seemed to have over my mouth. Or maybe it was the fourth G&T that I'd had.

"No sir," I said, laughing heartily. "Only perfectly normal interactions in our family."

"Can you please leave me alone?" Ari said.

"I mean our mom used to make us share baths," I rambled as Rohan ran his fingers along my hip, the flimsy material of my silver hip huggers an inconsequential barrier to his searing touch. "But that ended before Kindergarten. Though I did accidentally see his penis once when we were twelve but we were at a pool and–"

"Keep babbling," Rohan said. "It's stupidly cute."

I snapped my mouth shut.

"And what?" Kane prompted. "We were just getting to the good part."

"And I need a drink," I said.

"Make mine a double," Ari instructed.

"What do you want?" Kane's hand slid up to the back of Ari's neck.

Ari turned half-lidded eyes to Kane.

Now I needed two drinks. My vision of them together was *Sweet Valley High* not *50 Shades*. Why couldn't people stay in the boxes I put them?

"You're paying," I informed Rohan as we muscled our way to the bar. It was the least he could do.

I'd just put in my order when some guy in a flashy suit and overinflated ego offered to pay for my drink. I thanked him, refusing.

He wouldn't take "no" for an answer. His buddies chimed in, intent on convincing me.

Rohan raised an eyebrow. He'd step in and help if I required it, but ignoring pushy men was a skill set most women sadly had to acquire at a young age. I shook my head, took my drink, and steered Snowflake away from the group, their slanderous comments growing meaner and louder as I left.

They weren't worth any more energy.

I sank onto a sofa. "What a bunch of twats." I sipped my icy G&T, fanning myself with one hand. It must have been ninety degrees in here.

Rohan took off his fedora, using it to fan me.

"What would you call a bunch of twats? A pride?" I asked.

He plopped the fedora on my head, a grin catching one corner of his mouth. "A murder?"

"A crash," I countered.

"A fuck load." He adjusted the hat to a more rakish angle, his grin crumpling into a naughty smile. His eyes met mine, easy and alight with amusement.

I leaned in—

"Avon."

I jerked away from Rohan, breaking into a smile to hide my brain stuttering on Cole showing up now. Here. "Cole."

Rohan's lips flattened out. "That's twice."

Huh? "Hey, you. I thought I was supposed to call you. Later."

Cole leaned over to kiss my cheek. "I was excited to see you."

Rohan snorted.

"That's sweet," I said with a pointed look at Rohan.

Cole stuck his hand out. "Hey, sorry, man. I'm Cole."

"Rohan." He shook Cole's hand. I tensed but there were no breaking of bones. So this didn't bother Rohan?

Cole failed to recognize Rohan. To be fair, he'd never been a Fugue State Five fan and back then, Rohan had had platinum hair that fell into his face, eyes rung with eyeliner, and graphic vintage Ts. He was not that boy anymore.

Objectively there was no comparison between the two of them. Cole's attractiveness caused hearts to beat 70% faster but Rohan's sent them into cardiac arrest. Then again, Cole had broken my heart and I couldn't help but dock his attractiveness factor for that. Though he got points because I'd loved him. Argh.

The two of them looked to me, like I should be furthering the conversation, making some kind of decision, or doing some action. Yes. Taking action.

I finished my drink.

Rohan clapped Cole on the back. "Good meeting you." He left, getting about ten feet before some other chick stopped to talk to him.

Oh no, she didn't.

Rohan placed his hand on the small of her back and led her away, his head bent close to hers to catch what she was saying. Lasering the crowd didn't lead to X-ray vision and thus eyes on his activities.

Cole took my hand in his. "I've been thinking about you."

This was where I twisted a curl around my finger, batted my eyes, and purred that I'd been thinking about him, too. I pulled on a chunk of hair with my free hand, blinked owlishly, and squeaked, "Okay."

"Give me a second chance. Being with you is so—"

"Easy."

He laughed, a puzzled frown between his brows. "That too, I guess. You said you wanted a do-over. Did you mean it?"

I'd only meant it in the context of that one night, but with our fingers intertwined and all of him focused so completely on me, I knew that part of me would always fit perfectly with him.

I squeezed his hand.

"Then give us another shot," he said.

It didn't matter that my brain was chanting "Bastard. Broke your heart. Stomp on his head." Cole was letting this be my call and once upon a time, before dashed dreams and demon hunting, there had been a boy and a girl wrapped up in a shiny uncomplicated love.

Maybe there was still a sliver of that left.

The flash of a fedora caught my eye but it wasn't Rohan.

Cole glanced in the direction I'd been looking but there was nothing to see. He leaned in toward me, his lids falling half-shut, pausing until I gave the tiniest nod, and kissed me.

His kiss melted like sugar on my lips. It was sweet and tender, his hand on the back of my head. It was Cole and it was me and I was floating. I wound my hands into his hair, tasting Tic Tacs, innocence, and lost love.

I broke the kiss.

"Did I convince you?" he asked with a cheeky grin.

"You devastated me."

The grin disappeared. "I know." He let out a slow steady breath. "Is that a no? Tell me the truth."

"The truth is…" I hunt demons and am trying to blow open a patriarchal secret society and there's this other guy who… I sighed. "… I'm not sure."

"Fair enough. I'll wait."

Talk about things getting messy. I patted his knee and left. I didn't see Rohan on my way out.

17

Leo didn't answer any of the messages I left on the cab ride home. Trying–and failing–not to read too much into it, I proceeded into my bedroom, changed into loose cut-off sweats and a faded T-shirt saying "tap dancing is my superpower," grabbed my tap shoes, and headed into the basement. While most of the space down there was taken up by the Vault, I'd commandeered a little-used room as my own personal studio, setting up a small portable tap floor. Ms. Clara had procured me a plush sofa, a nicked up coffee table, and a docking station. I loved it.

The creaks and ticks of the old house settling were already as familiar to me after my short time living here as those at my parents' place had been. I didn't bother turning on the lights. There was enough moonlight to make my way downstairs without crashing into anything.

I slowed as I passed the thick iron door to the Vault, tempted to check on the gogota, but I decided to leave well enough alone. Up ahead a spill of light came from my little studio. As did the soft strains of an unfamiliar song. Hell no. Whoever was in there didn't get to drive me out of the sole girl refuge in this place. I strode in to the room. "No boys allowed."

"Yeah, well, some of the boys in your life are assholes." Was that a Cole dig? Rohan sat on the sofa, hair mussed, wearing only a pair of gray pajama bottoms. He had a guitar slung across his lap, his bare foot perched on the edge of the coffee table. He hadn't removed the polish and even more than his tight six-pack, it was the blue nails on those strong fingers strumming softly that made my insides all gooey.

Still holding my tap shoes, I clasped my hands behind my back. "Did you make a new friend at the club?"

He glanced up at me, still playing. "Did you make an old one?"

"I didn't tell you to leave."

"Not in words."

He was right. I should have handled Cole's arrival better. "Can we agree upon mutual horribleness and call a truce?"

"We can."

I dropped my shoes on the ground.

His strumming stopped. "You came down here to dance?"

"Yeah." A pencil and sheet music lay scattered in front of him. "Are you writing original music?" I craned my neck to see if it was the song for his mom but he flipped the page over.

"Mmm hmm. Should I leave?"

"You suck." I sat down next to him and slid my tap shoes on.

"Can I watch?"

The way he asked sent a dark thrill coursing through me. "You'll have to work for it."

His lips quirked in a grin. "Yeah? What do I have to do?"

"Accompany me." Ever since I'd started dancing again, I'd used his songs at least once a session. Having him here live? It was too good an opportunity to pass up.

Rohan rubbed his hamsa ring against his lip. "How do you want it? Fast or slow?"

"Fast." I trailed my fingers along the top of his guitar. "Funky." Along the back of his hand. "Freeing."

Rohan's eyes flashed. He steadied the guitar.

I moved into the middle of my tap floor and signaled him with a "bring it" flick of my fingers.

He launched into the song and I laughed. "'Start Me Up.' That's not yours," I said.

"You didn't specify," he chided.

"Negotiation failure. Shame on me." I could work with this. I listened to the intro, deciding on a straight percussion to his melody. Dancing was bliss; I exalted in the vibrations from my metal taps rolling through my body and the fat sounds bouncing off the walls.

Listening to music, making music, being music. My body thrummed, my cheeks aching from grinning as I moved.

Rohan whistled at my one-footed wings, launching from The Stones into "Smells Like Teen Spirit." From there it was a wild ride through "Paradise City" and "Seven Nation Army." It was the weirdest playlist I'd ever improv'd to, but it was also really fun, forcing me outside my comfort zone. And how par for the course was that with him?

Our relationship, such as it was, was the antithesis that Cole's and mine had been. It was exhausting.

Exasperating.

Exhilarating.

It would have been so much easier if all I felt for Rohan was sexual attraction, but I respected his intellect and abilities. He made me laugh and he pushed me to grow. I'd been challenged as a dancer but never to find my full potential overall.

Halfway through "Pumped Up Kicks," I waved my hands for mercy.

"Noooo," he wailed. "Don't stop. You're amazing."

I blushed and wiped my forehead with the hem of my shirt. "I'm also dying."

"One more." He pressed his hands together in supplication. "Very slow. I promise."

"One more." I clapped my hands at the opening chords, instantly recognizing them. "'Rainbow Connection.' That was my favorite song as a kid."

"Me too." He adjusted the guitar. "Dance with me?"

My cheeks hit maximum blush under his steady scrutiny. "Yes."

Rohan sang to me about the lovers and the dreamers, drinking in every step of my soft shoe, his voice wrapping around me. A current of recognition for a kindred soul arced between us. That whole not knowing where he stopped and I started? I'd had that with him during sex. That had been freaky enough since I'd never experienced it with anyone else. But the twining of his singing and my dancing was an intimacy I didn't even know I could feel.

Or have.

Or want.

The final chord rang out, my drumming heels fading out along with it. In the charged silence I asked him the one thing he didn't expect. "What happened in Pakistan?"

His harsh exhale reminded me of knives. Ironic since his superpower was turning himself into a human blade and his internal demons involved slashing himself with guilt over the death of his cousin and the person he'd become at the height of his fame. I thought I'd been helping him with those demons by getting him to return to his music, but this didn't look like progress.

He gazed off, his features lapsing into blankness. "Does it matter?"

"I dunno," I flopped onto the couch and untied my shoes, kicking them off, and wriggling my toes. "I'm trying to figure out what does."

"To what end?"

"Does it matter?" I grabbed my tap shoes and headed upstairs.

Taking my second shower of the day, I scrubbed at my skin with the loofah hard enough that I emerged pink as a newborn. I'd brought a clean pair of pjs into the bathroom with me and I guess on some level I'd been expecting to find Rohan in my room when I came out because I wasn't surprised to see him sitting on the edge of my bed.

I unscrewed the lid of my coconut oil, rubbing a dollop along my arms. "You need to talk to someone."

He nodded, though whether in actual agreement or to placate me, I couldn't tell, since from where I stood, only the back of his head and the tense line of his shoulders was visible.

I kept an eye on him as I moisturized. He didn't relax. Not even by the time I'd returned the glass jar to my bathroom and brushed my teeth. This boy needed Prozac stat. But since I didn't have that...

"Do you want to sleep here tonight?"

That startled him out of his trance. "What?"

"Don't get ahead of yourself. Just sleep." See Nava slide a bit farther down the slippery slope. "Ari used to crash in my room when he had nightmares as a kid. It helped." Not that Rohan would be sleeping in a sleeping bag on the floor.

"No." He swung himself off the bed, walking to the door with balled fists.

I rubbed my chin, my brows scrunching together. He liked sleeping next to me, so what...? Ah. "You're not going to hurt me."

He stopped in the doorway, his cool gaze tipped with gold. "You don't know that."

No. I didn't. I busied myself retying the string in my waistband to refrain from touching the spot where he'd nicked my throat when I'd woken him from his nightmare. A frisson of fear danced down my spine, but I'd offered and I wasn't going to renege. "Eh. What's life without danger?" I folded back the covers and patted the bed.

An odd expression came over his face. Oh, no. Quit looking at me like I'm throwing you a lifeline. Now I wanted to renege for a whole other host of reasons.

I snapped off the overhead light and crawled into bed, feeling like I was stepping into wildly uncharted territory. Rohan was just as hesitant as he slid in next to me.

"Good-night, Snowflake."

"Good-night."

I stared up at the ceiling. Why did his presence make me feel both steadier and shakier? I inched my hand toward the heat he was generating, brushing his. He hooked our pinky fingers together.

I swallowed. Okay. I edged my body closer. He did too. Beyond that, neither of us moved. Neither of us instigated anything sexual and it was fine. Better than fine. When had he become my zone o' contentment? I was so caught up in the implications of that terrifying thought that I almost missed what he said.

"The other Rasha." Rohan's eyes were fixed on the ceiling. "They died hunting yaksas demons. Do you know what those are?"

It was a fair question given I was playing catch up on twenty years of demon studies, but I'd actually studied this type. Fanged, horned, and nasty. That explained the bone fragment Rohan had. He must have broken it off one of the demons before he killed him. "Yeah."

"The demons had been crossing the border into India from their base in Nepal and from there trekking to the Gilgit-Baltistan region in Pakistan. They were targeting Askuchar, which is this isolated village in the mountains." He smiled. "Village is a flattering term. Less than two thousand people. Stone houses, half of them falling into rubble. But the air?" He gave a happy rumble. "The sweetest, freshest air I've ever breathed. And that view." He swept a hand out, drawing the panorama for me. "Sharp white-peaked mountains tinged with blue. One of the most beautiful places I've ever seen."

"It sounds gorgeous. But the demons weren't coming for the scenery. What was the draw?"

"We never figured out why they were attracted to this particular place. Random choice, because of its isolation, or something else?" He punched his pillow with steady pounds as he spoke, beating all the puff out of it. "The demons were using it like their personal buffet. Coming back night after night feeding off these people and tossing aside any parts they didn't feel like eating."

My hand flew to my mouth. "Kids?"

"Everyone. The villagers were terrified."

"But the Rasha stopped the demons, so why were you sent overseas?"

"Because one of the demons was a female and it was spring. That meant there were eggs somewhere. Those creatures mature fast, so my buddy Mahmud who's usually based out of Kabul, asked me and another hunter Michel to come help track."

"Did you find the eggs?"

"After a couple of weeks. They'd hatched but we got the babies before they were strong enough to be doing more than foraging small animals locally."

"That put a stop to it, right?"

Another harsh laugh and lapse into silence. I'd lost him again and I really didn't want to hear the reason why.

Practically holding my breath, I curled into him, resting my head on his shoulder. Stroking his arm in comfort.

Rohan released my hand. I tensed, but he slid his arm under me to pull me even closer. "All our books and databases and we're still fumbling around with our heads up our asses so much of the time." His hold on me tightened. "Fun new fact. Yaksas divide their eggs into *two* stashes before hiding them."

"Shit," I whispered.

"Yeah." Rohan looked away. I was glad I couldn't see the pain in his eyes.

"You don't have to keep talking."

"She says that now," he muttered, but he angled his body in to mine, resting his chin on the top of my head. I wouldn't have moved for all the money in the world, his heartbeat slow and steady under my cheek. "We got back to the village, expecting to assure them all was well only to find it ravaged. Everyone—" His voice caught. "Everyone was dead."

I tightened my grip on his shirt.

"The Brotherhood ordered us to burn every shred of their existence then cause a landslide to obliterate all trace of the village. Thwart any rescue effort." He rubbed his forehead with his fist. "The smell. It was in my nose, my eyes." His hands bunched and flexed on the edge of the blankets. "You haven't faced Hell until you've put a baby's corpse into flames."

I was a Pantone expert in all the shades of Rohan's gold eyes, but the hard darkness edging them now as they glittered against the shadowed plains of his face was new to me. I couldn't imagine the horror and couldn't think of anything to say that wouldn't sound like a hollow cliché. Rohan's extreme sense of responsibility resulted in a massive burden of guilt he placed on himself, fairly or not. I based this on the little he'd told me about his cousin Asha, and my first-hand experience of it when Samson had kidnapped Lily in Prague. If Rohan was tormenting himself because he'd failed those villagers? Let babies die? I'm amazed he wasn't catatonic.

I kissed his T-shirt right over his heart.

He cleared his throat. "From a tactical standpoint, keeping the existence of demons secret, the order was logical, but it was issued so coldly. We may be Fallen Angels," he said, referring to the Rashas' self-appointed nickname, "but I'd have sworn we were on the side of light."

"How did you end up in London if the Brotherhood didn't send you?" I said. "No way would you have gone partying after that."

Rohan pulled away, laying back against my mattress.

I splayed my hand out over his chest.

He folded his hand over mine. "Forrest wanted to meet in person in the studio with his notes for 'Hard Knock Strife' and he's based out of London."

"You finished the theme song." I gave an excited bounce. I'd only ever heard a teaser and couldn't wait to hear the whole thing. "But doing the song was part of the mission when we took down Samson, so why was Mandelbaum unhappy you'd gone?"

"It was only authorized while the mission was active. The Brotherhood wants me to get out of the rest of the contract obligations."

"No!" I practically crushed Rohan, leaning on top of him so he could see how serious I was. "You can't quit making music again."

He touched his forehead to mine. "I won't. Not after all your hard work to get me writing and singing again."

"Damn straight." I slid back down onto the pillow, my head next to his.

"As for going to Child's Play? I hadn't slept for days, replaying everything over and over again. Mahmud had handled a lot of bad shit in Afghanistan and he told me that sometimes the only jolt to the system strong enough to knock you out of the darkness was to immerse yourself in the most superficial candy-ass reality you could. The festival was surreal, that's for sure."

"Why didn't you call anyone? Talk to your friends?" Maybe I wasn't inner circle enough but he hadn't called anyone. Not even Drio.

"I didn't want to taint any of you." He propped himself up on his elbows, his lashes falling across his cheeks as he slanted me a look. "Especially you."

"Jesus, Ro." What was I supposed to say in the face of that? *Have the talk*, the grown-up voice in my head insisted. *Ask him why he regretted the kiss.* I didn't recognize that voice at first because, well. And no way. I tugged at my neckline assuring myself the room still contained oxygen.

He brushed a curl behind my ear. "The night you did E with Samson," he said, "you called me 'Ro' for the first time. You haven't done it again until now."

I'd needed the emotional distance created by using his full name. Sure, I could call him Snowflake, but for some reason, shortening his name was an intimacy too far. "I guess I haven't."

"So it takes you on drugs or me sharing things that no one else knows for you to stop being formal with me?" He said it teasingly.

Sharing things that *no one else* knows? My throat closed up, a light sheen of sweat breaking out over my body. How much of a bitch would I be if I ran from my room? Would my bad karma at abandoning a friend in need be tempered by the fact that I was only fleeing in self-preservation?

Instead of my legs pumping cartoon-style, leaving a cloud of dust in my wake, I pulled him into a hug. My brain was so stunned at my body's rogue impulse that I was left speechless.

Rohan tensed for a second when my arms came around him, then he relaxed against me.

Our hug went on and on until it stopped being clear who was comforting who. Staring into the shadowy corners of the room, listening to Rohan's breathing slow into slumber, I spun a fantasy of falling asleep every night with this man. Of waking up to lazy lovemaking or laughter that made me snort.

Rohan Mitra was not the type to stick around and play house. Even taking the rock star angle out of it, his Rasha duties kept him globe hopping. Besides, what kind of house would it be with all our testosterone-laden roommates, like the Lost Boys on steroids? I wasn't Wendy and had no desire to play the little woman. Even while dating Cole, my dance dreams had trumped visions of white picket fences. Now I had a Rashadom to conquer. A Brotherhood to expose.

I stroked a hand through Rohan's tousled hair and down his back, feeling the long line of his body totally languid as he slumbered against me, his breathing soft and measured. There were times that I looked over at Rohan, amazed at how deceptively relaxed he seemed. Almost insolently lazily, but he was always on high alert. Nothing got past him. In this moment, at least, he'd let down his guard, letting me see to his well-being.

I was so screwed.

18

Night tipped into the perfect stillness of pre-dawn. At some point my manic obsessing had quieted enough for me to fall asleep because I woke up in a pool of sunshine, feeling utterly content. Like multiple-orgasm content. I smiled drowsily and snuggled into my pillows, wrapping my foot around blankets and a familiar leg.

A familiar leg, wait.

I bolted up because the reason I was so calm and relaxed was simply from sleeping next to Rohan. I peered over the side of the mattress to see my beloved body pillow and usual recipient of my night-time snuggles on the floor, all bereft.

"And she's up." My pillow-substitute scratched the dark scruff under his jaw. That soft patch of skin I'd discovered the first time I'd licked my way across his body. A secret Rohan treasure.

I gripped the covers.

"Is this where you panic? Or insult me?"

"No," I huffed.

He blinked up at me, amused, like a cat. If I could bottle warm, sleepy Rohan, I'd wear it as my new perfume.

My black panther stuffie Sebastian had rolled into the crook of Rohan's neck. He patted the toy absently before moving Sebastian to sit on the pillow on his other side.

I wrenched my gaze away from the disgustingly cute sight and touched the skin under his eyes with my fingertip. "Thirty percent less bags, Snowflake. You slept?"

"Yeah." His expression was pure amazement. He trained that golden stare on me with wonder and something that looked like expectation before he flicked it away, rubbing his palms over his goatee. "This itches."

"Don't you dare shave it." I wanted it scraping over me again, its edge kicking up my pulse, making my skin buzz. I flapped a hand at him. "Or do what you want."

Rohan shifted to pull his arm free, brushing his impressive erection against me.

My shiver turned to a groan.

He smirked, but didn't make a second move. So this wasn't going to be a repeat of what had happened after the cù-sith. How much was Cole's arrival at the club a factor in all this?

I wasn't stupid. I knew what it would take to get a replay and if I wasn't ready to ask Rohan about the kiss, I wasn't ready to give him one. Well, that was that. I brushed off my hands, then threw back the covers, ready to get on with my day.

"Do you want to go out sometime?" I said. Rohan may have been shocked at those words issuing forth from my lips but I was dumbstruck. I quickly glanced around the room to confirm that yes, that had been me that had spoken.

His eyes flared bright, then dulled, a cautious expression crossing his face. "Like a date?"

I scrambled out of bed. "Do we have to label it? It's food and conversation at an agreed upon time."

I'd been possessed. That was the only explanation for this insanity spewing out of me. I made a mental note to perform some kind of ritual and find out.

Rohan grabbed me by my pj top and tumbled me back into his chest. "Buy me breakfast."

Well, damn.

I jutted out my chin. "I can do that."

He laughed, burying his face between my shoulder blades. "Only you could turn your own meal invitation into a to-the-death challenge."

"Yes, well, I'm special."

"Too easy." He winked at me and left.

I dressed for my date in skinny jeans and a warm chocolate brown, cowl neck sweater that invited touching, Shakira's "She Wolf" blasting out of my speakers. I'd forgiven her hugging Rohan. Dressed, groomed, and satisfied with the results, I swiped mascara over my lashes and headed downstairs.

Rohan was waiting for me in the foyer. He'd paired his bulky black sweater with black pants and not shaved the goatee. I rolled onto the outside edges of my feet, taking a moment from the safety of the hallway to watch him–the strong column of his throat as he tipped his head back and laughed at something he'd read on his phone, the steady strength he projected.

If we hadn't been interrupted right after the kiss with his new marching orders, I'm mostly sure that I would have asked him what exactly his problem had been in regards to that lip-lock, but too much time had passed. Too much obsessing had occurred over what had gone down with Lily. There'd been too much hurt that yeah, I *was* his second choice. I could take on a hoard of demons but adult communication left me wanting to run away very fast.

Problem was, our "finished and done with" status had gotten a tad blurred. We needed a tectonic upheaval to fix that, which made this outing perfect. I'd catch him off-guard with weirdness and underline that he'd be better off in Los Angeles.

I stepped forward. "Ready?"

Rohan smiled. "You better be taking me somewhere good because I'm starving."

I grabbed my black trench coat from the closet, pleasantly surprised when he took it from me to help me put it on. "Better than good."

Rohan dug his car keys out of his pocket. "I'll drive."

"Nope." I held out my hand. "Keys, please." His hand tightened on the keychain. I blinked up at him with my widest, cutest eyes. "Pretty please? I did just fine driving the last time."

He looked visibly pained as he unclenched his fist, allowing the keys to fall into my hand.

I patted his cheek. "Good Snowflake."

Rohan sighed in defeat and followed me out to the Shelby. His instructions started the second I sat down: seat placement, how to shift gears, the best way to brake. "Be gentle putting in the key. Shelby has a very sensitive ignition."

"Oh my god, you anthropomorphized her. Do I need to rethink this date?"

"So it is a date." His eyes gleamed in triumph.

I tossed my hair back. "An unforgettable date."

He steepled his fingers together. "That's a bold claim."

"I'm a bold girl. And my claims are not without merit."

"I'll be the judge of that. Where are you taking me?"

"We're going to a fight and then you will be fed delicious food. Happy?"

"I wouldn't have pegged you for a boxing aficionado. All right." He rubbed his hands together. "Let's go." He motioned for me to start the car. To his credit, he tried not to flinch as I did.

I patted the dashboard as the car roared to life. "We're going to be great friends, aren't we, sweetheart?"

Now for the best part. As the driver, I got to control the music. Rohan ground his teeth but didn't dispute my choice. Not like the Chet Baker CD wasn't his to begin with.

All was well as I drove down the driveway and waited for the gate to open. Rohan's shoulders even descended a fraction of a millimeter, though that may have been wishful thinking. The trouble came when the gate opened revealing a baby barghest, a demon resembling a mangy black lab puppy with large, glowing eyes. It was trying to cross our wards and failing, bouncing off the ward's invisible shield at our property line.

Luckily, the curve of the road and the press of trees between houses ensured that only someone directly at the foot of our driveway would see these demon attacks on the ward line.

Visitors were discouraged.

The barghest planted himself in the middle of our path and growled.

"Can I keep him?" I asked.

Rohan draped his arm over my shoulders. "A date, a dog. Are you angling for me as the hot not-boyfriend?"

I shifted into gear and ran the demon over. There was a bump, an audible crunch, and a yelp.

The last from Rohan. "I'm driving," he announced with a steely glare.

I shrugged, amazed I'd even made it this far. We switched places and were off.

Rohan looked a little dubious when I directed him into the strip mall parking lot with the large Asian supermarket anchoring one end. "Did you need to get something?"

"Nope." I tamped down on my grin, leading him inside past the heaping displays of cookie tins and ramen noodles. I hip checked him out of the way of a petite, elderly Chinese woman, barreling down on us with her grocery cart. "You gotta pay attention," I admonished. "These women let nothing and no one get in the way of their efficient shopping strategies."

We veered off from the produce section selling everything from smooth, dark green bok choy to pyramids of earthy taro root, past soya sauce and rice cookers, headed all the way to the back to where bags of frozen gyoza and dim sum dumplings lay stacked in open coolers. Rohan had slowed down, bafflement clear on his face.

I tugged on his sleeve. "This way."

I stopped in front of a massive lobster tank, part of the live fish section running the length of the back wall. The suckers were going at it in no-holds-barred grappling, dancing back and forth trying to get purchase and take their opponent down.

His dumbfounded look was the most priceless thing I'd ever seen. I half expected him to pull out his phone and start searching flights right then and there.

"This is the fight?" His voice was a perverse mixture of horror and delight.

"Yup." I pointed to the two largest lobsters occupying the center of the tank. "On the left, we have Anchorage Al, the comeback kid. He had a bad couple of years." I mimed glugging back a bottle. "But he's hungry to regain his title. Thing is, Claws Kowalski over here?"

"Not ready to relinquish the title?" Rohan asked.

"Not even a bit. He's mean, too. Look at his right hook. Hooks," I corrected, as the lobster in question waved three legs. "Last chump who got in the ring with Claws lost an eye."

A beat passed. And another one. And another one. I tamped down my smug grin. Yup, I'm a weirdo, run away.

Except he didn't. Rohan broke into a deep, rich belly laugh, unlike any I'd ever heard from him. He wrapped one arm around his midsection, shoulders shaking, partially bent over. His laughter echoed through the room, an infectious rumble that had shoppers looking our way, smiles on their own faces.

The young female employee manning the long counter threw me a thumbs up.

Huh?

His laughter rolled through me, stealing the breath from my lungs, and when his sexy, deep laugh mellowed to a sputtering giggle, I put my hand to my heart.

"Lobsters," he snickered. He shot me a look of pure glee. "Brilliant."

I recovered with amazing aplomb, rocking back on my heels and hoping it came off as smug and not unmoored. "Told you."

Rohan waved a hand at the rest of the tanks. "Some real shifty characters taking in the fight today. Like the bookies over here." He strode over to the tilapia, flashing silver scales as they swam, spinning a story about these low level minions working for the shuffling crabs crammed in one tank over.

He pointed at one crab wedged on the bottom jamming his rubber band-wrapped pincers upwards, trying to get on top of the pyramid. "Trying to *claw* his way to the top. And this guy?" A runty crab had separated from the pile, wriggling away in the corner. "He likes to go dancing but he pulled a mussel."

He waggled his eyebrows at me like Fozzie Bear.

Nope. No. Uh-uh.

Snickering as he made crustacean puns was not supposed to be a thing. Hot and broody, easily dismissible, rock god demon hunter. That's it. No facets. No being able to get nerdy and silly and into this ridiculous date that I'd always wanted to share with someone.

I followed him in growing agitation as he punned his way through the rest of the fish. When we reached the end of the row, I was so worked up that I needed a time out to collect myself. "You hungry?"

He nodded. "Starving."

"Then I shall feed you. Go outside and look to the right. There's a bench. Wait for me there." When he was safely out of visual range, I stuck my face in a freezer, wondering what Pandora's Box I'd opened here and trying to remember whether or not that particular myth had ended well.

I joined Rohan a few minutes later, bearing two huge white bakery bags which I set on the bench between us. "For your dining pleasure." I motioned at the odd little housewares store whose window was filled with row upon row of ceramic Japanese welcoming cats, their paws waving. "Note the enticing view." I pointed up at the speakers of the nearby dollar store, blasting up-tempo K-pop. "The infectious soundtrack. And…" I tore open one of the bags, delicious pork and yeast-scented steam curling out. "The best BBQ pork buns you've ever had in your life."

Rohan helped himself to one. "I'm from L.A., sweetheart. Not sure this is gonna top the pork buns I can get there."

"Ye of little faith. This is Vancouver. Our Asian food is second to none."

His eyes fluttered shut at his first bite, his tongue darting out to catch an errant drop of sauce.

I crammed a piece of the soft bun into my mouth as a decoy for any embarrassing noises about to spill out of me.

Rohan took another bite, his white even teeth flashing. "It's delicious. Go ahead. Be smug."

"Nope. I'm giving you new experiences, not revisiting old ones."

We ate our way through the stash I'd purchased in compatible silence.

"More?" He looked hopefully at the second bag.

I shook my head and his face fell. Laughing, I tore that bag open to reveal the coconut buns inside, which were also still warm. "Dessert."

"Yes! I love these." He helped himself to two right off the bat, polishing them off faster than I did, which was no mean feat.

I smacked his hand when he reached for a third. "Step down, cowboy. That one's mine."

"Fine," he grumbled, stretching an arm along the back of the bench. His eyes remained fixated on the bun.

Growling, I tore off a piece and held it out to him.

Instead of taking it from my hand, he leaned in, his mouth closing around my fingers, all heat and wetness as he slowly sucked the piece away from me. Neither of us blinked. He swallowed, then grasped my wrist, turning my fingers from side-to-side to lick coconut cream off.

I may have forgotten how to breathe.

"Yum." His voice was rather husky. Sexy.

"That's nothing. Second dessert time now." Mine was husky, too, except I sounded like Gollum. I crumpled the bags, jumping up to throw them in the trash. "Come on."

I barreled off to his car. This date was not a good idea. I'd been wrong about tectonic upheavals. They were dangerous. Much carnage.

"Nava." Rohan snapped his fingers at me.

I blinked at the door he held open for me. "Huh?"

He smirked.

And then there were the things that never changed.

It may have been the middle of the week, but it was also a sunny spring day and the gelato place was a local favorite. The giant pink store was bustling. Cars spilled out of the parking lot and the cobblestoned outdoor seating area was full of people munching cones under leafy trees.

Rohan's eyes lit up at the promise of two hundred flavors on the sign.

"Wait until you see inside." I tried not to snicker. Even Ari, who loved the gelato, could have done without their choice of interior decorating. I held open the door for him with a "ta da!"

Rohan spun in a slow circle, taking in the full glory of the bright chalk murals. "Whoa. This place rocks." He bounded off to explore the gelato selection.

"Uh, yeah." I stumbled up to the cash register and paid for our ice creams before we ordered, scanning the room for my date.

"Wasabi?" he asked, pointing at a tub of green gelato. "Really?"

I held up the poker chip he'd have to exchange for a single scoop cone. "Before I give you your token, you must play a round of 'what's that flavor?'" Another chance to make this date memorable for all the wrong reasons and make Rohan want to go home.

To someone like Lily.

The guy behind the counter stepped back. I smoothed my snarl into a smile.

Rohan glanced at the wasabi container one more time, rolled his shoulders back and cracked his neck. "Lay it on me."

"We each choose one sample for the other person to taste. Then we guess."

"What do I get if I win?" His eyes twinkled, smug certainty rolling off him. I held up the token. His face fell. "You're holding my ice cream hostage to my correct guess?"

Not really, but it was fun taunting him, so I nodded. I twirled my finger around the room.

"Pick wisely, grasshopper." I skipped off to get the perfect flavor.

We met in the middle of the room with our offerings.

"Ladies first." He held out the tiny plastic sample spoon with what looked like vanilla gelato on it.

Bracing myself, I swallowed it and acked like a cat spewing a hairball. "It tastes like feet."

"Is that your guess?"

"No." I sorted through the disgusting aftertaste of cold, salty cheese. "Parmesan."

His eyes narrowed. "You've tried it before."

"Have not." I waggled my token at him. "It was too obvious. You can't just go for gross out. Try subtlety. You boys."

"You've done this with a lot of guys?" he asked. Geez, grumpy.

"Just Ari." He cheered up at that. "Your turn."

He eyed the pale green hit of durian chili ice cream that I held out, snatched the spoon from me, and knocked it back. "Oh fuck," he gagged. "It's spicy frozen vomit."

I tried not to laugh, but not very hard. "Is that your final answer?"

"I hate you."

"You really don't." I held up his token. "The stakes are high. Make your guess."

"You've burned my taste buds off. How about we rock paper scissors instead? I win, you give me my token."

"What's in it for me?"

"Anything you want. But you won't win."

As if. There was only one thing guys like him ever threw. "Count of three." I laid down paper, right as he threw scissors. "You got lucky," I said.

"Nope. You profiled me as the type of guy to throw rock. That hurts, babe. I'm way more secure in my manhood than that."

"*Babe*? I think not."

He grinned at me, swiping his token from my hand. "I'm trying out new nicknames since Lolita was retired. What do you think about 'Sparky?'"

"Not much."

"It's cute." He swaggered off to the counter.

I was not being put in the cute zone. No, the only zone I intended to share with him was the Pacific Time Zone and that only with an international border and two states between us.

We ate outside, crammed together on one of the benches, Rohan's leg pressed against mine. I tilted my face up to the sun, taking lazy licks of my gelato. Rohan was smart enough to share his coconut chocolate chip with me, while I graciously allowed him to try my chocolate raspberry.

Such a couple tableau we made. Except we weren't. I bit into my cone.

"I'll always love Lily," he said.

"What?" My thumb punched a hole in my waffle cone and I had to suck out a glob to keep it from spilling. Why volunteer information I had no interest in? And bring it up now on our date? Had all those feels of the past little while been strictly one-sided?

"If you're figuring out what matters, this does. Besides, you asked about her," he said. "At lunch last week."

I refrained from pointing out that whether or not he loved her hadn't exactly been my wording. "Yes. You love Lily. Maybe you should stop flirting with me and run back to L.A. to be with her."

"Even though I'll always love her–" Okay, he could stop repeating that. He swallowed his last bite of cone. "I don't want to get back together with her. We're different people now."

Throwing my arms up in victory would be bad, right? In despair. Throwing them up in despair. "Can you not tell her about being Rasha? Would it be too hard?"

"I think in general, any relationship with her would be easy."

Like Cole.

He licked a smear of ice cream off of his finger. "It's not what I want anymore."

Which meant what? I was difficult? Was he even talking about me? I glanced at him to see if he planned to offer up any more information, but he watched me like it was my turn to speak.

Finishing up my cone, I silently repeated the words thundering in my brain until I was capable of saying them aloud. "I don't know how to move forward and I can't go back."

"Me neither," he admitted.

Great talk.

Chet Baker's mournful jazz trumpet washed over us on the ride back. No matter how many times I snuck glances at him, Rohan remained unreadable as he drove us home. This was impossible. *We* were impossible. I wasn't even sure I wanted a "we" but I wasn't sure I didn't. Life was so much simpler when everything was black and white.

The end of the date loomed large and potentially awkward. First off, my dates didn't usually live in the same house as me so I wasn't sure about proper protocol, second, I still wasn't ready to kiss him, which was the traditional parting gesture, and third, given our last conversation, maybe the only thing to do was toss off a "nice knowing you."

I fiddled with my purse strap, wondering if I should try for some formal pronouncement or just walk away when Rohan said, "Unforgettable date, Sparky," fist-bumped me and went inside.

19

I was still standing there dumbfounded over Rohan's exit when Ari cornered me, snagging my arm and hauling me to our car. "Where have you been? We need to figure out how best to approach Malik. You can buy me Waffles at Stacked."

"Why would I want to do that?"

He held up his phone. "So I don't call Mom and tell her you're involved with both a co-worker and your ex." Ari pitched his voice into a pretty good imitation of our mother's. "Nava Liron Katz, I'm so disappointed in you."

I eeped because Stacked, while delicious, was pricey and the Brotherhood didn't pay its newbies all that well. But Mom would submit me to a litany of lectures. "Done."

Ari wasn't finished. "This being the first of three breakfasts, the last one to be bought no later than two months from now."

"You are your father's son. That's not a compliment," I added at his laugh.

Ari hit speed dial. "Hey Mom. You around to make Nee and me breakfast? There's so much to catch up on." He put her on speakerphone so I could hear that he'd really called her.

"Mama's boy," I whispered. "Fine. I give in to your demands."

My agreement came just as our mom said she couldn't, remember? She was at a conference all day, but to give her a call this weekend. Ari promised he would, snickering as he hung up.

"Now I'm going to have to visit her." I shoved him. "And you knew she wouldn't be around to begin with."

"Yup." He slid his phone into his pocket. "Never negotiate without all the facts. You know better."

"I plead mental distress."

Over really yummy Belgian waffles, Ari and I combed once more through the victims' social media profiles, this time looking for any photos or connection to Malik. Our break, odd as it was, came on Jakayla's feed. The animal rights' activist and mature student had posted a photo of a painting donated for some charity event that she'd organized. The artist? Malik Irfan.

Further searching led us to his modest website and yes, it was the same person. We scrolled through his online portfolio of vibrant abstract oil paintings. Kinetic and bold, these did not look like the work of evil spawn.

I poured more Jack Daniels maple syrup over my light and crispy Brussels-style waffles. "He *is* a demon, right?"

Ari frowned at the screen as if trying to make it conform to a logic he understood. "Has to be. There's no way I psychosomatically exaggerated my reaction to him." He motioned to our server for more coffee. "He's got a studio. We can check out if it's for real or a front. First let's find out more about the connection with Jakayla."

"Sounds good."

The server came round and topped up our coffee mugs.

"So. Stringing Ro and Cole along." Ari gave me a pointed look and dove into his all-pork sausage. Jew fail.

I kicked him under the table, smiling at the lovely man who kept the caffeine coming in timely fashion. "Any nightmares lately?"

"What did Harper say when you told him he wasn't welcome in your life anymore?" My brother cut his waffle into squares with surgical precision.

I squirted cream into my mug and ate one of my raggedly sawed-off pieces of waffle. "I haven't. Rohan and I aren't dating and Cole is merely a transitional."

"Rohan hasn't been in a relationship the entire time he's been Rasha."

"You gossipy old woman. Who'd you pump? And why'd you bother? According to you, I'm the Sheriff of Hot Mess Township, relationship-wise."

"Mayor of Hot Mess Metropolis at least." Polishing off his last bite, he eyed my plate.

I pushed it closer to him, allowing him access, since he'd gone for the thicker Liege-style waffles. He, in turn, spun his plate so I could get at his hashbrowns. "Spill, already," I said.

He chewed thoughtfully. "Him not being in a relationship makes sense. Adjusting to hunting full time is big enough, never mind his years of being the guy who could and probably did have anyone he wanted."

"Works for me." I spread my arms wide like I was drawing a rainbow. "Be free, little bird."

"It means there haven't even been any repeat performances on his part. Not until now."

I spit out my coffee. "Oh no. Repeat away."

"So you're okay with Ro seeing other people?"

"Obviously. Since I'm hardly going to be hypocritical about it." I stabbed at my waffle.

Ari opened his mouth to argue some more, but at my glare, shrugged.

Stupid twin planting stupid ideas in my brain. I obsessed over this the entire way to the offices of A.L.E.R.T., the animal activist 'zine that Jakayla had co-founded.

The 'zine's offices were located through a side door in a shabby building upstairs from a pet store and a dubious-looking tanning salon. Landlines rang and volunteers ran around dropping off papers on one of two editors' desks. The walls were covered in corkboards with dozens of photos thumb tacked to them, from gruesome photos of chicken factories to sun-bleached posters announcing International Bears' Day.

One of the volunteers, a man in his late thirties who looked like a Burning Man-refugee with his striped cords and low slung leather utility belt, looked up from the desk nearest the doorway, vaping away, which was totally illegal indoors but I doubt this crowd cared. "Can I help you?"

"Hi," I said. "We'd like to speak with someone involved in coordinating the wildlife rescue fundraiser a couple of months back?"

"That'd be Zaph." He waved us over to a couple of rickety wooden chairs. "Have a seat."

I thanked him, taking the chair farthest from the burnt popcorn-scented smoke curling around his head.

Zaph, single-monikered and non-binary, as they informed us upon our meeting, had a rangy frame matching their energy, and long dreads.

"How would you describe working with Malik?" Ari asked. He stood by the edge of Zaph's desk, a wary eye on the tottering pile of folders threatening to topple onto his feet at any moment.

"Very professional." Zaph spoke in a lilting Jamaican accent, sorting through their desk. "I have no hesitation recommending him as your artist in residence." Yeah, we'd kind of lied, presenting ourselves as the executive assistants to the chancellor of the local art college, sent to check references and narrow down our list of candidates.

"You met him how?" I asked.

"Through my co-founder, Jakayla Malhotra." Zaph spun a red file toward us, labeled as the fundraiser in question.

"Had she worked with him before?"

"No. They were in a relationship."

The Burner volunteer working on his computer at the next desk scowled at Zaph, caught me looking, and strode away, his e-cig clamped between his teeth.

"Impossible," Ari said.

"Like they hooked up a bunch?" I flipped the folder open. The idea of an incubusy thing in a relationship was too much for me to wrap my head around.

Zaph closed the folder's cover before I could examine the contents. "What does this have to do with anything?"

"Speaks to conduct," Ari said. "The college has a strict no-fraternization policy between staff. Even guest instructors."

"I had no issues with Malik and I'm not going to gossip about a friend's private life." Zaph wriggled their desk drawer open and placed the folder inside.

Further entreaties were met with stony silence. Reluctantly we took our leave.

Ari stopped in the restroom, so I waited in the hall for him. Burner guy sat on a bench, head bowed, rolling his e-cig between his fingers. He reminded me of Rohan with his piece of curved bone.

I sat down beside him. "Hi."

"Hey. Get what you needed?"

"Not really. Zaph was very politic in their choice of words."

"Yeah, well."

"Jakayla seemed like a real sweetheart," I said. "Trying to do some good in this world. Were you close?"

He gave a "kind of" wave with his hand, his shoulders tensing as he hunched inward.

"It's hard to lose people like that."

Ari stepped out of the bathroom and I gave the tiniest shake of my head. He stayed at the far end of the corridor checking his phone.

There was no heat in this hallway. I pulled my unlined black trench coat tighter around me, wishing I'd gone for something a bit warmer. "Is there anything you could tell me about Malik?"

The guy sucked in some more e-juice, sorrow aging his features. "Yeah." He was quiet for a moment. "Malik snowed all of us. Talented artist, real charmer, good looking." I didn't begrudge him his bitterness. No one could compete with a demon for charm factor. "But he was a bastard. They'd only been together a couple of weeks and he screwed around on her the entire time. She kept making excuses for him but, well... It was like she was addicted."

Exactly like.

"What is it with the bad boys?" He jabbed the e-cig at me.

"Pardon?"

"I mean really. Emotionally unavailable, game playing, where's the appeal?"

"Nice guys have a lot to recommend them."

He groaned. "You're not selling it."

I shrugged. "I've had the nicest guy be a bastard when I needed him most and someone who has that mad, bad, and dangerous vibe be there for me again and again."

Aw, crap. I dropped my head into my hands.

"Maybe it's too simplistic to say men are nice or they're bad boys. Maybe you just gotta judge each one on their individual character," he said.

I raised my head to glare at him.

"Debate club alum. Sorry."

I picked up my purse. "Thanks for the help. If it's any consolation, not only will we not hire Malik, I have a feeling that he's going to get everything he deserves."

Burner gave me a sad smile. "Karma is just a fantasy. Guys like Malik arrange their lives exactly as they want them and nothing gets in their way." He stood up, making his way back to the office, then paused and turned back to me. "If I were you, I'd dump them both and start fresh."

"Noted."

"Get anything?" Ari asked when we got outside.

More than I'd bargained for. "Not really."

The artists' collective where Malik painted out of was a three-story building adorned with a colorful mural depicting its vibrant Mount Pleasant neighborhood that was loaded with cafés, local designers, antique shops, and a diverse population.

Ari and I entered the small gallery on the ground floor. It featured a selection of work by the artists in the group, from black and white portraiture to landscapes in soft watercolors and video installations.

We stopped to admire a selection of delicate filigree jewelry displayed in a case to one side. I nudged my brother, drawing his attention to an elegant handcrafted ring. "That star pattern really screams 'this way there be evil,' huh?"

"It could be deliberately deceptive. All malignant jewelry presents as beautiful."

"Yeah, they also tend to boast big ass diamonds or something blatantly worth coveting. I doubt that this," I checked the description, "celebration of Gaia's bounty is gonna elicit some Faustian bargain."

"They couldn't just give us a demon spidey sense." Ari wandered over to the lone volunteer, engaging him in conversation.

I strolled through the space looking for Malik's work, finding it in a single large canvas hanging on a far wall, depicting the merest suggestion of a female form. Arms stretched above her, she faced the spectator. A fall of black to denote hair. Facial features dashed off as haphazard circles and smudges that still managed to convey incredible personality. Here was a woman who wouldn't back down. The artist's warm regard for her was evident. I checked the title. "Lila: on waking."

I hoped this Lila wasn't another victim of his, because, grisly.

Ari rejoined me. "Malik has been a member of this collective for five years now."

"Quiet guy? Last person in the world they'd peg as a serial killer?"

"Nope. Mr. Personality. The other artists adore him."

I gestured to the painting. "He's really talented, too. Is he around?"

Ari nodded. "He's upstairs in his studio but apparently he's painting and not to be disturbed. When I phone him I'll see if I can get a tour. His workspace might yield some insight."

Tempting as it was to go in with magic a-blazin', we needed concrete proof of his demon status. Antagonizing him off the bat without it wouldn't help our cause. There was nothing more to be learned here so we ran back to the car, dodging puddles as the rain pelted down on us.

"This entire case has been so random," Ari said. "Even when we do get a break? I feel like we go one step forward two steps back. A demon artist? Is that relevant to the deaths? A weird personality quirk? What?"

I turned on the motor so that we could get some heat. "Leo said something interesting to me the night I discovered she was the snitch. She said that all Rasha saw things in terms of black and white and that we'd never navigate the demon world with that attitude. And she's been right. Asmodeus came after me because I'd killed his kids. Revenge as a demon agenda? Sure. But it was more personal than that. He'd meant to hurt me the way I'd hurt him." My eyes slid away from my brother.

"What happened to me wasn't your fault."

I nodded, grateful he could say that with a straight face. "Anyhow, his actions implied love on his part or as close to that as demons get."

"What about Samson?"

"His agenda was pretty straightforward, feeding off the envy he so carefully cultivated. But he had this make-up artist Evelyn. She was a kumiho demon and she helped keep his glamour intact. Drio killed her but he never managed to break her."

"Loyalty." Ari cupped his hands over the vent to catch the hot air.

"In part. I think she loved him. Samson felt something for her as well because his plans for Rohan were payback for believing Evelyn had left Samson to hook up with Ro."

Ari shook his head. "Even if we've been wrong about only ascribing negative emotions to demons instead of examining their motives through other lenses, it doesn't change the fact that demons are evil. Doesn't matter what drives them. In the end, evil is all there is."

"What about Leo?"

Ari stared out the window. Silent.

"Will you come with me to see her?"

"I'm not ready."

My heart sank. "We've got a situation with a demon artist creating beautiful paintings. Motive does matter, because to understand this demon is to perhaps stop another one in the future. If Malik is the one responsible then we need to figure out his reasons beyond 'sucks the life out of his victims.'"

"That's very open-minded of you."

I shrieked at the words spoken by Malik from our back seat. The demon, because only a demon could have manifested back there, had muted his sex appeal somehow. Sure, he was still dark and luscious, with sparkling black eyes, wearing rumpled, paint-splattered, casual clothes. A look that would have won him the internet. But it was regular sexy, not "take me now" demonic compulsion.

Ari, furious, lunged for him, but Malik eased him back into the passenger seat. "Relax, Rasha. I'm not here to hurt you. If I were, you'd be dead already. Especially since there are few shadows in here for you to draw from." He chuckled at our twin expressions of stupefaction. "I keep track of who and what is in my city. Now you, petal." He wagged a finger at me. "You're really stirring things up."

I let my magic coat my hands, keeping them below the window so any passersby couldn't see. "Is that a good thing or a bad thing?"

"I haven't decided yet. Though sending the Brotherhood into a tizzy is a point in your favor."

"Who are you?" Ari asked.

"*What* are you and how can you possibly know all this about us? Because if you are some kind of incubi-offshoot, they aren't even that high up in the demon hierarchy, never mind privy to Rasha business. No offense," I said.

"None taken." Malik slung an arm along the top of the back seat. "Succubi get all the glory whereas incubi are seen as the second-rate gigolos of the demon world. Suffice it to say, I'm not the one you're looking for. I don't kill humans." His lips quirked. "Anymore."

"Right," I said. "You've discovered a deep love of humanity." I snapped my fingers. "Or wait. You're lonely. Looking for companionship. Wouldn't hurt a fly."

Malik scratched at a dried patch of yellow paint on his cheek. "Hardly. Don't ascribe some romantic notion to me." His gaze turned shrewd. "Love troubles getting you down?"

"Hardly," I said. "Don't presume you know me."

"Back at you," he said.

"Fact. You drain your partners dry," Ari said. "It's how demons with sexual compulsions survive."

"Rasha have all the answers, don't they?" Malik smoothed a hand over his shirt. "We'll discuss exactly what it is you think you know at dinner tonight, Ari. Eight sharp. La Bella Trattoria."

The roll of his "R's" in that upper-crust accent sent a small shiver through me.

"Hold your breath," Ari said.

Malik smiled. "You'll be there. Besides, you owe me for that little labradorite stunt." His smile widened, his eyes licking over my brother's body. "Clever boy."

I punched off the heat, deeply uncomfortable watching this. Especially since Ari's eyes darkened, just a fraction, but still.

"You can make it up to me with scintillating conversation. I'll even pay for the extremely expensive Italian cuisine." Malik clapped his hands together, the sound sharp as gunfire in the tense car. "All right. Enough lolling about. This painting won't finish itself."

Malik hopped out of the car, slamming the door behind him. His gait back to his studio across three lanes of traffic was hands-in-pockets leisurely, even drivers of the big-ass SUVs scrambling to stop for him–presumably recognizing him on some level as the greater threat.

"Why would he bother to protest his innocence?" I said. "Evil reps are oxygen to demons."

"Do we know Malik is telling the truth and he doesn't kill humans? I doubt it. No, he's the most likely culprit. Some twisted sentiment towards humanity evidenced by writing the Arabic word for love on his victims before murdering them." Ari opened his door. "Come on. We're going up to his studio and finish our chat in private." A hard smile slid across his face.

I bounded out of the car. I liked chats that ended in bloodshed. And even better, started that way, too.

We practically collided with Daniel at the front door to the artists' collective, dressed in his navy police uniform. He jerked back. "What are you doing here?"

"We're in the mood for some art," I said.

Ari cocked an eyebrow. "And you?"

Daniel reddened. "No reason." He stomped off.

My brother watched him leave, a thoughtful look on his face.

"That boy has it bad. Five bucks says he would have told Malik he was just in the neighborhood," I said. The grown-up version of cutting class to detour three floors up to a crush's locker. "Is he our next victim?"

Ari broke into a run, giving me my answer.

I looked down at my heeled boots, sighed, and ran after him, cursing that stupid emotion that was just as dangerous as demons. You think we humans would learn.

Daniel hadn't spotted us trailing him. He got into his cruiser, sitting in the passenger seat and staring out the front window.

From behind a mail truck where we crouched, Ari and I had a clear view of him. Daniel's partner, a wiry blonde showed up about five minutes later bearing a cardboard take-out tray with coffees, a brown bag balanced on top of the cups.

"What time is it?" Ari asked.

I checked my phone. "Two-thirty. Why?"

"Daniel won't be off shift until seven. He's safe until then." And we'd be at dinner with Malik soon after.

"I'm trying very hard to come up with a reasonable explanation for you knowing police shift times and can't get any further than loving a man in uniform. Literally."

Ari shot me a "stage two trying my patience" look. Since I was good to provoke until at least stage four, I ignored him.

"The VPD lists the various shifts on-line," he said. "Twenty-four hour serve and protect coverage from our fine men and women in blue. I had to memorize certain operational details about them as part of my training. In case we had to call someone in."

We waited for the cops to drive off, then stormed Malik's studio. The dimly lit corridor on that floor provided Ari with tons of shadows to draw upon, while I stepped through the doorway with my electricity blasting.

The demon must have heard or sensed us coming because our magic was absorbed by a fire shield around him. The blaze didn't spread, didn't cause any of the multitude of paint tubes or turpentine splatters on the concrete to catch flame, just crackled away, pouring off incredible amounts of heat and keeping us from him.

Holy. Fuck.

"Now," Malik said, not even looking up from his easel, "I really do need to finish this painting today, so if you could get on with whatever futile errand you came here for?"

"Killing you. Ridding the world of another evil spawn. Pretty opposite of futile," I said. Ari and I tried to attack him with our magic through the flames. Each time, the fire rose up to harmlessly absorb our hits. Totally and absolutely futile.

Inside the ring, brush between his teeth, Malik grabbed a small knife, scooping tiny amounts of blue to mix into the yellow blob in the middle of the palette he held in one hand. His quick flicks were reminiscent of a longtime artist comfortable with all aspects of his craft. He possessed that same lazy assurance that I'd had with my dancing. A way of holding oneself, of quickly yet efficiently doing a movement that was as familiar to the body as breathing, and requiring as little conscious thought.

But to stay so focused on that task while holding us at bay? This was some crazy strong power. No matter what we tried, we couldn't breach the fire. Couldn't reach Malik. The air heated to blistering proportions, forcing Ari and me to look away or risk eyeball meltage.

Too bad there was no way to prevent the familiar acrid burning smell from doing permanent damage to my nose hairs.

Ari jerked his head toward the hallway.

"Until tonight, Ari," Malik called after us.

We stopped halfway down the corridor. I wiped my still-streaming eyes, pitching my voice low. "Um..."

"Yeah." Ari pulled me into the stairwell. "Best guess? He's a marid. Kill spot, right shoulder." Marids' nefarious activities had a larger scope than merely that of an incubus. The root of their name "mar" meant ocean, or in English "mer" like "mermaid." They had water magic in addition to their fire abilities, but dealing in sex was fairly common for them.

I sniffed, hoping for some fresher air to clear out my nose. "He was also at the graveyard. I recognized his scent. He probably sent the ghoul after us. Now what?"

Ari's booted heels made ringing thuds as he headed downstairs. "We figure out how to kill him before cocktails are served."

20

La Bella Trattoria was an upscale Italian restaurant, all gleaming gold accents and plush leather seats. I gave Malik's name to the hostess and was immediately ushered into a private dining room that boasted an enormous temperature-controlled wine rack and a long table seating twenty but set for two, positioned under inset spotlights throwing off a muted glow.

The hostess shut the door behind her as she left, giving us our privacy. And leaving me alone with Malik, who stood by the window, drink in hand, framed by the soft indigos and oranges of dusk.

Malik had cleaned up, once more wearing what had to be a tailor-made suit. He quirked an eyebrow, so carelessly arrogant. "You're not the one I invited."

"Yet here I am." I whistled. "Private back room and everything. How schmancy."

While Malik got top marks for the lengths he was going to to charm Ari, I kind of felt bad for the demon, because no way was my brother ever going to get involved with his kind. At the same time, this full-court press was incredibly flattering, and if anyone could get Ari to fall, it was probably Malik. Which, back off, buddy, because Kane.

I glanced out the window. "Nice view of False Creek. Now, be a gracious host and offer me a drink."

"I'd rather not." He shooed me away.

I eased onto the maroon leather banquette against the window, slapping my purse down beside me. "Come on. Let's chat. You can give me your best villain monologue and then try to kill me." I arranged my features in a suitable expression of rapt interest, folded my hands, and propped my chin on them.

Malik laughed. "Fair enough." He sank into a chair across from me with feline grace. "I assume as the 'hero'–"

"You don't need the air quotes, dude. Also, get your genders straight."

"Apologies. 'Heroine' of this little interlude, that you have a question you want answered?"

I cleared my throat and shook out an imaginary list. Malik's lips quirked as I pretended to read. "Why did you send the ghoul after us?"

"Guess." Malik winked at me. "It's ever so much more fun, petal."

"Was it as simple as we'd figured out the connection between your victims or were you raging at us finding something so private with the word you'd penned on their bodies?"

Malik took a sip of wine. "You can't expect a scorpion to change its nature."

Seems I couldn't expect a straightforward answer either but I kept trying. "Jane Doe. What's her name?" I wanted to give any family or friends of hers closure so they wouldn't spend their lives wondering what had happened. Where she was.

"I couldn't tell you." He ripped off a piece of focaccia bread.

I grabbed his arm before he could dip it in the plate of olive oil and balsamic. "Couldn't be bothered to find out who she was before you killed her?"

Malik's eyes flashed then he smoothed out his expression. "Something like that." He removed my hand.

"Now, that's a shame. Ari?"

My brother appeared, having used his EC teleport abilities and my location hints over our open phone line to catch Malik off-guard. He drove his shadow magic like a spear into the demon's kill spot on his right shoulder.

Malik dissolved into pure flame before the magic hit him, a dancing blaze of gold and orange contained within a human outline with the merest suggestion of a face. It was surreal and beautiful and I locked my knees together so the demon couldn't see them knocking in the presence of his incredible power, even as I added my magic to Ari's.

Malik burned brighter, hotter, our power infusing his. He was like a glorious sun, dazzling, fearsome, but in no danger of losing control.

Of the three of us, only two gaped open-mouthed.

Malik laughed. "I can stay this way indefinitely but it might scare the serving staff."

Ari and I turned as one to the door, still closed for our privacy. It was too thin a barrier between the danger in here and all the innocent people in the rest of the trattoria.

We dropped our magic.

"Sit down." Malik's body returned to his corporeal state with nary a mark on the chair or his suit, just that same acrid burning in the air. "We'll share some food, enjoy some conversation, and then you'll be free to go, no harm to anyone." The marid popped a balsamic-glazed fig in his mouth from the platter of assorted antipasto on the table.

Outwardly, I remained calm, but I scanned him for any evidence that he'd been a demon tiki torch just seconds ago. I'd seen demon glamours fall away, I'd even seen transformations, but nothing on this level. What kind of power did it take to not leave a single drop of soot on anything? Or you know, not turn this restaurant into an inferno?

"What if I don't want to sit and chat?" Ari asked. "Will you compel me?"

"I don't compel." Malik reached for a prosciutto-wrapped breadstick, shrugging when Ari didn't move. "Suit yourself. But I assure you the food is delicious."

"Right." Ari said. "When you sexually drain people, it's all free will on their part."

Malik arched an eyebrow. "It is rather. Curious?"

Ari jerked a chair out and sat down. "Not in the slightest."

"Mmmm." Malik's lips quirked up in a half-smile and he waggled the breadstick at me. "Eat, Nava. You seem like a girl who knows exactly what she likes."

I helped myself to a fig. "It's nothing to be ashamed of."

"That wasn't an insult, petal. The excesses of human confidence are wondrous to behold."

Ari crossed his arms. "You mean we're greedy. Which works out perfectly for demons to take advantage of."

Malik bit into the breadstick. "Aren't you judgmental?" I snickered at his assessment, earning me a hard look from Ari. "What's wrong with wanting more?" the demon asked. "More money, more fame, more power, more sex."

He said that last bit in a low rumble and I reached for the closest water glass because, holy Hannah, my nipples had gone hard.

Malik smirked. "That drive is exactly what has propelled mankind to some of its greatest achievements."

"Or its worst depths," Ari said.

"True. But you don't get one without the other." He tilted his head. "Don't you want more, Rasha?"

"More dead demons?" Ari raised a hand. "Guilty as charged."

Yeah, I'd really picked the wrong hunter to spill my drink on back at the club. Once we'd dealt with Malik, I had to resolve the Leo situation.

"No," Malik said. "Just… more."

Ari tried to hold his stare but he broke first.

Malik ate another fig punctuating his words with expressive gestures. "And to speak to your earlier point, I don't take advantage of humans. I'm charming, I'm good looking, and when I need someone,

I enjoy that need. As do they. I may take some of their energy but in the long run I leave them much better off than I found them."

I nibbled on the end of a breadstick. "Don't sell yourself short or anything, Malik."

He smiled. "I never do."

"Jakayla's behavior was described as addictive," I said. "How is that better off? Or not compelled?"

"Have you never been addicted to anyone? That deep-seated craving for a particular individual who you just can't get enough of?" I squirmed under the weight of his stare. "Did he compel you?" I flushed. "Lucky man," he said. "Though not his fault for how you felt."

Ari huffed an incredulous laugh. "Is that why you drew the symbol for love on your victims? You imitating this confidence you admire? Your twisted love resulting in sociopathic killing? Or just plain old demon evil?"

A waiter knocked on the door.

I tensed.

"Come in," Malik called.

The waiter entered bearing a bottle of wine. He presented it for Malik's approval, then poured a taster amount into a wine glass.

Malik tried it and nodded. The waiter poured some into the glass in front of Ari.

"I don't need any."

"He most certainly does," Malik said. "Top him up."

"Would you like a glass?" the waiter asked me.

"No, thanks," I said.

"Very good." The waiter took his leave. As he shut the door, the smell of garlic and roasted meat wafted into our private dining room.

My stomach growled. "Can we go now?"

We needed to find some other way to kill Malik since surprising him was impossible.

Malik picked up Ari's glass and held it out. "Don't waste a great Merlot."

When Ari didn't take it, Malik set Ari's glass down, and picked up his own. "No drink, then. Let's talk about you. I'm fascinated by that topic."

I put my tongue back in my mouth at the absolutely filthy smile that Malik trained on my brother.

The clouds darkening the sky over False Creek had nothing on my brother's expression. Ari pushed his chair back, but before he could stand, Malik's hand had shot out to clamp down on his arm.

"Let. Go."

"Tell me, Ari, if it's all so black-and-white, where on that moral spectrum do you fall?"

Ari jerked his hand away. "Pretty obvious."

"Is it?" The marid brushed a speck of lint off of his cuffs. "Portalling in was a cute twist, but did you really think you could surprise me enough to overcome my millennia of honed instincts? You know what I am, Rasha. You know my kind have walked this planet since the building of the first pyramid, since the Great Ziggurat of Ur. Admit it. You knew that you and your lovely sister could never take me down, yet did you show up with a gang of hunters to erase me from the earth?" Malik sipped his wine. "Or did you just go for it anyway?"

Ari flushed red. "Fuck you."

"Probably not tonight. Enjoying the appetizers, petal?"

I froze mid-reach for my fourth fig. Refused to feel embarrassed and took two. "Yup."

"See? Your sister is honest. I find that refreshing."

Hearing that approval from him made my self-empowerment feel sketchy. I drank some of Ari's wine.

Out in the main part of the restaurant, there was a loud crash of glass and applause for the dropped tray. Why did patrons do that? A man called out, "Sorry."

Malik tapped his index finger against his chin. "Tell me, Nava, what have you sought in your short life? Fame?"

"Sure."

"Accolades, respect?"

"Who wouldn't? Hardly brilliant insights." I drank some more wine, his smirk getting under my skin.

"Mmm," Malik said. Geez, this demon was as irritating as my brother. "Love?" he asked.

"Why have love when I can have fun? Ari, seriously. Let's go." I shoved my chair back.

Malik's chair scraped across the wood planking. He caught up to me in a second, spinning me to face him. "You want it all."

I tossed my head. "So what if I do?"

The demon tilted his head down to meet my challenging stare. His eyes were an ordinary brown and yet I had the distinct impression that some ancient intelligence saw right through all my plans, outmaneuvering me in games I hadn't realized we were playing yet.

I shivered, my lips parting with a soft sigh.

"Nava," Ari said. "Stop talking to him."

Malik flicked his fingers. Still trapped in the depths of his regard, I heard a meaty thwack and my brother's grunt.

"Go on," Malik urged. He glanced past me, his eyes delighted and cruel. "Tell me. What would you sacrifice to have your life exactly as you want it?"

His damn eyes forced the truth from me. All-seeing, exposing me, and making my continued silence impossible.

"Everything." The answer tore out of me. Chest heaving, I spun away from the demon...

...and right into Rohan, who caught me. He jerked back as if burned.

"I didn't mean it like that," I said.

"I think you did rather." Malik held up his hands at my glare. Winking, he disappeared. Cue flame, blinding light, searing heat, yadda yadda yadda.

I blinked against the bright afterimage on my corneas.

Ari swore, cradling his shoulder and running out of the room as if he could catch Malik. I ran after him. Clearing up Rohan's misunderstanding would have to wait until after we'd found the marid.

I got halfway through the main dining room, when I heard Leo's assigned ringtone coming from my purse. Before I could answer it, I was cornered by our waiter, steering me towards the bar and insisting that I pay the obscene amount this restaurant charged for the appetizers and wine that Malik had ordered.

All my protests about needing to go after my brother and promises to come back and pay fell on deaf ears. Hoping Ari was able to keep up with the demon, I pulled my credit card out and handed it over.

It was declined.

There was a whoosh from the open kitchen and a flame shot up on the stove. The chef smothered it with a lid. I craned my neck trying to spot the towering mound of dirty dishes that I'd now most likely be required to wash.

"Here." Rohan handed over his card which covered the bill no problem.

I shook my head. Freaking fabulous. But he had saved me from dish duty. "Thank you."

We hurried outside but Ari and Malik were gone. At least my car was still in the packed lot. I strode towards it, Rohan keeping pace. "About what I said," I began.

A Smart Car slowed down beside me, the driver giving me the universal hopeful eyes for "are you leaving?" I nodded and kept walking, the car following us.

Rohan twirled a finger between us. "What would you say this is?"

"It's not anything anymore." I beeped the fob but Rohan planted himself in between me and the door.

"You're–" He clenched his hands into fists, then exhaled and slowly unclenched them. "Go for a different answer."

The driver honked, his expression questioning. I held up a "one minute" finger.

"It's us. Do we have to label it?" I shouldered him aside to open the door.

He huffed a laugh. "Yeah, Nava. Normal people label relationships, not find every excuse in the book to keep denying that they're in one."

"Please. Normal people do that all that time. Not that we're in a relationship. A relationship implies an equal dynamic and that's not how you roll. You don't listen. You barge in when you've been told repeatedly you're not welcome. Violate boundaries left and right–"

Hurt flashed across his face. "You think the kiss was a violation? I gave you every chance to stop it."

I stared at my feet. "You're missing the point."

"No, you're being deliberately obtuse. As usual."

Another honk from the waiting driver. This one long and pointed.

I spun to face him. "Honk again and watch me stand here all freaking day."

He glowered at me and drove off, leaving me with Rohan, stony-faced, his arms crossed.

"I'm hardly the obtuse one. Also?" I beckoned Rohan close with the crook of my index finger. "Little secret. We're not normal. We hunt demons and wield magic. Pretty freaking abnormal. And that's without all the rest of the baggage you Brotherhood boys come with."

"What's that supposed to mean?"

I tossed my purse into the car. "You're broken. All of you. Even as you're all so committed to your fantasy that you're these chill dudes with your shit together."

He actually rolled his eyes at me.

"Don't hold it in, Snowflake. You'll get cancer."

"Then enlighten me." His voice was clipped. "About these many issues."

Another car slowed down next to us.

I shooed it off with a sharp jab, then commenced Rohan's enlightenment. "How about for starters you'd rather die than admit you're still messed up over whatever happened to your cousin?"

His expression went ice cold. "Don't talk about Asha."

"How could I?" I slammed my hand down on the top of the door. "You won't tell me anything about her. You're still punishing yourself for what happened even though you say you've moved on. You're so scared of revealing yourself that every single thing with you is a calculated decision designed to let you stay in control and make sure you have the upper hand. God forbid you give anything away."

"Like you're some open book."

"Compared to you, I am. Plus, I may have trust issues and control issues but at least I've never pretended otherwise."

"No, you revel in it." The flatness in his gold gaze, his body vibrating with barely suppressed violence, that had been him controlling his reaction. With these words, he tipped into an all-consuming black storm. A supernova of fury. His eyes sparked as he stepped toward me. "You revel in this deep 'self-awareness' of yours that's nothing more than an excuse to let yourself off the hook and do exactly what you want."

Fatigue drained the very marrow in my bones. I sank into the driver's seat and jammed my key in the ignition. "If that's how you feel, then why are you here? Did Kane find the ingredients?"

"Not yet. I fingerprinted the spine," he said. "Got a partial match with a Rasha. A deceased Rasha. We have a connection. Not to whether the spine was used to bind the gogota but the Brotherhood did modify them."

I looked at Rohan, trying to find the right words to say thank you. To say something.

The silence stretched out between us, growing tauter and thinner until Rohan pivoted sharply, and in that motion I swore I heard a loud crack as any connection we'd ever had broke with an irrefutable finality.

21

Ari didn't answer his phone so by the time I'd driven back to the chapter house with no contact from him, I'd worked myself into a frantic state, unable to see anything other than my brother's broken bloodied body from when Asmodeus had tortured him.

I ran inside. "Ari?"

I checked every floor with no sign of him, then hit the basement, running into the Vault almost blind with panic.

A dark-haired guy was making out with someone. All I could see was the back of Dude #1. His arms were braced against the wall as he kissed his partner. My red haze only cleared when I noticed the size of the hands that grabbed Dude #1's ass, pulling him closer. Two guys and therefore not Rohan.

Dude #1 groaned, arching his hips into Dude #2, who fisted his hair in Dude #1's hair, tilted his head and sucked hard on his neck.

I was so stuck on the "whoa" of the scene, I'd failed to consider the "who."

Kane and Ari.

"Aaack!" I screeched.

Ari jumped away from Kane, blond hair messed, lips swollen.

"Did you go after Malik at all?" I asked my brother.

Kane went uncharacteristically still. "Malik?"

"Our marid serial killer," I said.

Kane's face and arms turned iridescent purple, his salt-based poison coating his skin, making him deadly to the touch. "Letting off some steam, were we?"

My eyes burned from the salt in the air.

"Since when is that an issue?" Ari said.

Kane shook his head at Ari, contempt on his face.

Ari stepped toward him. "K–"

Kane's hands flew up, keeping Ari at bay, and he stalked out of the room. Ari punched the wall, bloodying his knuckles on the concrete.

"Good job," I said.

"You're one to talk. I told you not to talk to the demon." Had I not just seen the same contemptuous look on Kane, I might not have identified it on my brother because I'd never been the recipient of that expression from him.

"Malik was right," I said. "You've drunk the Kool-Aid your whole life about how you're doing good and how this big noble cause excuses everything to the point where you can't see all the actual damage in your wake."

"By 'damage,' I'm guessing you mean you? Not knowing when to stay out of something?" he fired back, walking off.

I grabbed his arm and spun him around. "You're the one who blew our shot at getting him. Fuck you and your hypocrisy and double standards. All of you, but especially you, Ari. Do you know why Rohan showed up? I was right. There was a Rasha print on the spine. The Brotherhood is up to its neck in dirty dealings and you, darling brother, better figure out where you stand on the matter."

I'd always known that if I gave people a chance to come into my life and be a significant part of it, I was simultaneously giving them the power to hurt me. I just hadn't believed that applied to the person I'd shared a womb with. The one whose presence I'd instinctively sought out through the good and the bad like he had with me.

"Being Wonder Twins was only ever good in theory," Ari said. "The reality? Two Katzes in the same sphere is one too many." Jaw tight enough to shatter, Ari pushed past me, knocking into my shoulder as he left the room.

"You're such a brat," I yelled after him.

I drove over to Leo's apartment building with the window rolled down, holding all the jagged bits of myself together, and willing the frigid night air to seep inside me and make me numb.

"Open up, baby," I said into her intercom. "Mama wants cuddles."

"Sleep-stealing bitch." She buzzed me in.

I got into the elevator, my butt braced against the rail, my head bowed.

I should have forced a different resolution with Ari, kept looking for Malik, done something to further this investigation, but after the shit show that had just gone down, I needed a night to get my head back in the game. When my life had flipped upside down and I'd become Rasha, my greatest wish had been to put Ari back on his rightful path. And I had, except somewhere along the way, I'd also decided that I could be good at this and more importantly, that I could be happy being Rasha. I'd been lost for a long time.

Even after the kiss of regret, I'd been forging ahead, secure in the knowledge that there were certain things I could count on: nothing came between Ari and me, Rohan had my back, and other than demons, people from the Brotherhood were the only ones I had to watch out for.

In the past few weeks, all those certainties had been blown sky high. I felt like I was balancing on a landmine where not knowing who to trust or what to believe was about to have dire consequences, and boo hoo, I still had to find my way out without being blown to smithereens.

Leo greeted me dressed in baggy men's pjs and a scowl. "Why didn't you tell me you made out with Drio in Prague?"

"Huh? Because it was coming off the disaster of the wrap party and barely qualified." I stalked into her apartment. "And how do you know the specifics?"

She padded into her living room, throwing herself down on her couch and pulling a chunky knit blanket with fringe over her legs. "I asked him."

I did a double take. "You what? How? *Why?*"

Leo jutted her chin out.

"Are you seeing him?" I crashed my ass down onto a chair, my jacket falling from my hands onto the floor. "The fuck is going on here?"

"I'm not seeing him. I ran into him before he left. Things happened."

I stared at the giant poster of Andy Warhol's flowers above her head, sorting and rejecting a dozen responses before I settled on, "Things you didn't bother to tell me about."

It wasn't particularly gratifying that in the ensuing stare down, Leo blinked first.

"It's not all about you," she said.

True, but we'd always shared that stuff. I'd have understood, sort of, if she'd known about me and Drio and hadn't wanted to say anything, but that had been news to her and she'd kept silent anyway. I picked up my jacket, ready to bolt in a cloud of self-righteous anger… and went nowhere. First Rohan, then Ari. I wasn't ready to have Leo be the next casualty in my disaster of a personal life.

I gnawed on the inside of my cheek. "Is this because I kept bitching at you about the danger of getting involved with him?"

"Kind of." She plucked at one of the tasseled fringes on the blanket. "And kind of that line between our worlds thing."

I blew out my cheeks, draping my coat on the back of the chair. "Does he know about you?"

"No." Her eyes snapped to mine. "Unlike some."

I crossed the room and crawled onto the sofa beside her. "I'm sorry about the club. I never meant for you to be outed." Leo had left the club before I had that night, and even though I'd left her a gazillion messages apologizing, we'd been playing telephone tag, and this was the first time we'd actually spoken.

She glared at me a bit longer before deflating. "That's on me, as well. What's Ari going to do?"

"Nothing." I had to believe that no matter how angry Ari was or how badly he wanted to side with the Brotherhood that I still knew him well enough to be certain that when it came to Leo, he wouldn't hurt her.

I crossed my fingers and toes for a second anyway.

Leo gnawed on a cuticle.

I grabbed her hand. Sure enough, she'd bitten herself ragged. I smacked her. "Stop self-cannibalizing."

Leo growled but scooted over enough for me to lay on my side facing her. "Enough about all the Rasha. What else is new and exciting?" she asked.

"I want to hear about you and Drio."

"I haven't decided if I'm going to tell you yet, seeing as you didn't tell me first."

"It was a non-starter. There wasn't much to tell." I fluttered my eyelashes at her. "Can I interest you in a marid serial killer?"

Yeah, that got her eyes lighting up with a feverish gleam. "Perhaps. Tell me more."

"He's on the loose and I have no clue how to kill him."

She frowned. "You sure it's a marid?"

"Yup. Why?"

"Fire demons have fiery personalities. Sure, they kill but if they go after someone, it would be more personal, if that makes sense."

"Maybe cold calculation is from his water side," I suggested.

She shook her head. "Water is a secondary power. It doesn't rule their natures."

"Okay, well, he drew the Arabic word for love on his victims and he'd been in a relationship with one. At least from her perspective. Love gone wrong? Crime of passion?"

"How many victims?"

"Seven." I snagged a couch cushion that had fallen on the floor and stuffed it under my head. "In just over two weeks."

"Seven crimes of passion in two weeks? It's plausible. If he's a fourteen-year-old girl. Marids are ancient beings. This isn't a case of too many crushes."

"We may never know why he killed them. It may just come down to *how* we kill him." I sniffed the air. "Are you making curry?"

"Neighbor." Too bad. It smelled really good.

"You need to find the marid's weakness," Leo said.

"We know his weak spot. He keeps bursting into flame before we can hit it."

"Weakness, Nee. Not weak spot. There's a difference."

"Is an ancient demon going to have a weakness?"

"Something that powerful that's survived thousands of years? Their ego is unchecked. For sure, he has a weakness."

I sighed, stuck on the many weaknesses in my own life these days.

"You don't want to expand on your feelings surrounding that sigh, do you?" she asked.

"Nope. Noooo. Naw."

She nodded in relief.

I tugged some of the blanket onto me. "You knit this one? It's gorgeous." Deep reds and blues and soft as a cloud. I snuggled into it.

"Yeah. While I was binge watching *Santa Clarita Diet*."

"Rohan is a giant jerk."

She pulled the pillow out from under my head and swatted me in the face. "You're pathetic. You had your chance to share and you missed it."

"That was on topic."

"Really? Rohan is a risk-averse, middle-aged woman with a new zest for life thanks to turning zombie?"

I scrunched up my face. "Rohan's from L.A. The show takes place in L.A. Ish."

She swatted me again. "If I'm going to be subjected to a Mitra monologue, at least tell me something juicy."

"So only I'm supposed to share?"

She grinned. "Naw. I'm gonna foist all the dirty details on you. But you first so I can judge."

I shot her the finger. She smothered me with the pillow.

"All right!" I said in a muted voice, fighting not to be asphyxiated. I tossed the cushion across the room. "I took Rohan on a date after Cole showed up at the club asking for a second chance."

Leo stuffed her freezing cold feet between my legs. "Whatcha doing there, girl?"

"Driving Rohan out of town and auditioning my transitional?"

"Your delusions are strong, grasshopper."

"No. I'm pretty sure I've driven him out of town now."

"You don't sound too chipper about that."

I mimed shooting myself in the head, then flung my arm over my eyes. "Do you ever miss being sixteen?"

"Don't romanticize it. You couldn't wait to grow up and start your life."

"I want a do-over. Appreciate how good I had it then." A tenor outside on the street sang a beautiful aria, his voice growing fainter and fainter. "Can I stay here tonight?"

Leo rubbed her nose against mine. "Yes."

"Can I borrow something to sleep in?"

"Of course." She hopped up off the couch, returning shortly with a pair of sweats and a T-shirt that she tossed at me.

It was a Fugue State Five concert tee. "You're a cow."

Leo beamed at me.

"For that, we have to watch *Grease*."

Leo planted her hands on her hips. "Is this a happy singalong viewing, a maudlin belting out of 'Hopelessly Devoted' viewing, or a fierce declaration with 'There Are Worse Things I Could Do?'"

I pulled the blanket over my head. It really was soft.

Leo patted my back. "Okay, pumpkin. Put on the movie. I'll make the popcorn." She snickered. "And then get ready to hear everything."

I smiled with the blithe happiness of an idiot who had no clue how much danger she'd be in tomorrow, and reached for the remote.

The light of a new day plus having hung out with my best friend—with only the tiniest twinge of regret for the sexytimes I'd missed out on with Drio—made a world of difference. Okay, a small city block of difference but at least I woke up on Friday ready to jump back in to the investigation.

I hadn't tried to dissuade Leo from seeing Drio if and when he returned, but I had let her know that I had her back. If shit went seriously south with him, I was gonna be there to help with the fallout. Like I would if Ari tried anything stupid.

I headed over to Daniel's place, since at the moment, he was the strongest connection to Malik that we had, pulling up to the curb right as my brother showed up. There was no conversation beyond a chilly "Good morning." We marched up the front stairs and simultaneously knocked on the door.

No answer.

Ari leaned sideways off the balcony to peer in through the slit in the curtains. "Oh shit." He yanked a small lock pick set from his inside coat pocket and, removing a tool, had the door open in seconds.

The place was trashed: broken furniture strewn about the living room and a huge black scorch mark on the wooden floor.

"Daniel!" I ran through every room on the main floor, Ari's footsteps pounding up the stairs.

"Nothing," he called out.

"There's a basement." I flung open the door in the kitchen, fumbled for the light switch, and booted it downstairs, terrified I'd find Daniel's lifeless corpse.

All I found was a gurgling water tank in a half-finished basement, next to a washer and dryer, its door open. Half of the clean laundry had been dumped in a hamper, the rest still inside the machine.

Rust edged the bottom of the tank and a small yogurt container had been placed under the spout to catch the drips, except it had fallen over. I crouched down to straighten it and a flash of white under the tank caught my eye.

I pulled out a fat black felt pen.

"He's not here," Ari said from the staircase.

I held up the marker.

"Fuck." Ari smacked the wall. "Malik's got him."

"You think he's still alive?" We ran upstairs.

"I have no idea. Malik didn't take the others. He just killed them."

"What makes Daniel different? Assuming he didn't escape?"

"Let's see if we can find out," Ari said. "At the very least, find something with his full name on it so we can call and see if he's on duty."

We found a bill laying half under the sofa, next to the wreckage of the coffee table. "Daniel Walsh. Ace, did we do this? Because we had a stupid fight and didn't warn him? Didn't check on him?"

"I did check on him. I swung by last night. He was fine. Even had a couple of friends over." He squatted down and touched the burned wood. "It's still warm."

"Malik can keep his fire from burning anything when he wants to," I said. "So did he not want to or did he lose control?" I shivered, covered in goosebumps. Not merely like someone walking over my gravesite, like someone was walking over *me* and pushing their way inside.

Ari nodded that he'd felt it too, then cocked his head listening, but all was silent.

I called up my magic, a ball of current curved in my palm.

The air grew heavy as Ari reached into the shadows. Darkness coiled around his arm like a whip, he motioned for us to split up.

If Malik was here we found no sign of him. Though I did find a metal box in Daniel's tiny office upstairs containing photos of him over the years, ranging from a toddler grinning and hoisted on the shoulders of his police officer dad, through awkward childhood poses, and good times with friends. There was also a birth certificate listing Daniel's place of birth as Malaysia. That must have been his mother's heritage since in the photos, Daniel's dad was Caucasian.

Ari entered the room and I showed him what I'd found. "I hope we don't have to inform his parents of his death," I said.

"Not today we won't. I called the VPD. He's on-duty."

"Seriously?" I sat down, exhaling heavily. "Did you talk to him?"

"No. I left a message asking him to call me. Stressed it was urgent. If Daniel was here when Malik destroyed the place then he's seen the marid for what he really is. Hopefully he's smart enough to stay away."

"And if Daniel left for work before Malik arrived? If Malik was furious that he missed him?"

Ari placed his hand on my shoulder and guided me out of the room. "Then let's hope we get to Daniel before Malik does."

Our ride back to Demon Club was conducted in silence but not the angry kind. As soon as we got inside, Ari called out for Kane to meet us in the library.

"What?" Kane joined us, but he refused to look at my brother.

Ari looked like he wanted to say something, then nudged my foot under the table.

"Can you find the marid for us with your mad computer skills?" I asked. We'd already confirmed that Malik wasn't at his studio and the person manning the phone at the artists' collective either didn't have or wasn't willing to give out Malik's personal contact information. "At least find his iPhone or something."

Ari smothered a laugh.

"That is so insulting," Kane huffed. "Should the demon have even a hovel to call his own, I will find its exact GPS coordinates."

"You're the best."

"Stating the obvious. Here." Kane slapped a folded piece of paper into my hand.

"Are these the ingredients for the magic-testing spell?"

"That can wait," Ari said. "We need to pin Malik down."

"Thanks for explaining the priority. My feeble girl brain couldn't sort that out." I smoothed out the paper. "I'll deal with this later."

"Whatever," Ari said.

"Far be it for me to ever choose vag over a giant dick," Kane said, "but I agree with Nava. The questions surrounding the spine need to be dealt with."

I scanned the list. "Where do I get Snowdonia Hawkweed?"

"It's extremely rare," Kane said. "I was able to find one sketchy supplier in Rio with a very limited supply. One plant limited."

"Then time is of the essence."

"Good luck," Kane said.

"Kane."

Kane ignored my brother and left the room.

"He's still mad about Malik?" I said. Sure, Ari shouldn't have kissed him to work off his attraction to a demon but on the other hand, Kane knew how shit could happen when dealing with evil spawn. "Kane seems to have a lot of lines thou shalt not cross."

Ari laughed bitterly. "It's more of a spiderweb."

I clutched the ingredient list. "Ari, my most wonderful brother—"

"So much for 'later.'"

"In and out. We can do this in like half an hour."

"No."

"Please. Kane needs time to find Malik anyway. And you said you wouldn't interfere."

"Book a flight to Rio. I won't say a word. But I'm not going to actively help you in this insane quest." He dropped his voice. "It's bad enough you're keeping that demon here. What will they do if they find out you're casting spells?"

I just needed him for this one quick trip, then I'd prove what the Brotherhood was up to and watch Rome burn. "I invoke 'Thistleton.'"

Mrs. Thistleton had been a neighbor of ours who'd constantly asked us to help her out and had perfected the art of the guilt trip. We'd made her name into a joke password between us, where the other person would have to agree to do something, no questions asked, or endure torturous amounts of guilt.

"And I'm invoking 'not gonna help you,'" Ari said.

"You can't. It's Thistleton."

"Can and did."

I crossed my arms. "Then I invoke 'you owe me because I made you Rasha.'"

Ari smiled thinly. "You held out way longer than I expected on lording that over me."

"Are you going to help me or not?"

"Not." He brushed past me.

"If you don't do this for me, I swear I'll never speak to you again."

He turned to face me. "You don't mean that."

"Try me."

His eyes were cool.

What was happening to the two of us? Bad enough my constant fears about our twinness these days, now I found myself doubting our past. My entire life I'd been so certain of our unassailable sibling connection, but with every new conversation we had I was plagued with doubt.

I suppressed a shiver. Was his silence him calling my bluff or *not* wanting to call it? I didn't actually want to know. "Then do this for Leo."

"Why should I help a PD?"

"Because it's Leo and you're not an asshole. The spine is already connected to the Brotherhood and if it's the means of binding demons? Greedy humans being able to harness demon power? That puts Leo at risk of being used. Please."

"Give me the damn address," he snarled.

I exhaled. It was the hollowest victory ever. I mean, yay, he cared about Leo, I just wasn't certain he cared about me.

Without warning, Ari grabbed my wrist. The air heated and the cool light of a drizzly Vancouver day was replaced by an all-pervasive green as we stepped out under a familiar steel tower with a round viewing platform way up top.

The throng of people readjusted themselves around us without a second glance.

I swallowed the metallic bile in my throat. "Holy shit, we're in Seattle."

Intellectually aware that we were invisible to the tourists, business people, moms pushing strollers, and hipsters with lattes flowing around us like we were rocks in a stream didn't keep me from scanning the area.

Ari didn't answer me, didn't comment on our surroundings at all, his expression made of granite.

We jumped again, stepping out under a cloudless sky, redwood trees towering over our heads. I admired their majesty though I could have done without the nausea. A flash of movement caught my eye; a man on a zip line silently whipped past high above. A group of people stood on a platform in a nearby tree awaiting their turn.

Ari's face was covered in a faint sheen of sweat and he was paler than normal.

"Are you all right?" I asked.

"Now you care?"

I bit the inside of my cheek.

Our third stop landed us in a massive plaza flanked by a cathedral and stately buildings that I guessed might be for government use. We stood in the shadow of an enormous flag flying proudly in three colors that all looked like varying shades of green in this light, with a coat of arms on it.

Ari gazed up at it. "Mexico City. One more jump and we should be there."

I took a couple of deep breaths, glad that while my stomach still lurched in "après one too many spinny rides" fashion, I didn't need to hurl. I wished I could hear the music that the buskers in Aztec costume danced to or the rapid-fire Spanish of the fashionistas sashaying through on high heels. A hub of human activity, this plaza was life cranked to eleven but stuck on mute.

As opposed to the sub-arctic glower emanating off of Ari.

"Why can't you support me in this?" I asked.

"Because you have so many issues with the Brotherhood that it's clouding your judgment. Where's your loyalty?"

I dabbed my brow. "Where's yours? I'm your sister. Have you even noticed how I've been treated by this wonderful organization of yours? For the heinous crime of having a vagina?"

"How should they treat you? Sure, you've taken out some demons, helped on a mission, but the rest of us spent twenty years being tested. Proving ourselves. Earning their respect. You want it easy."

"I didn't get the—"

"Chance because they didn't check for a girl. Yeah, we know. But if you were capable of seeing anyone else's viewpoint, maybe you'd realize that soothing your hurt feelings aren't exactly a priority given the ongoing fight against evil."

"Especially if they're busy playing both sides."

Ari growled, curling his fingers and shaking his hands like he wanted to throttle me.

"Forget it. Jump us."

We clasped hands, our hearts separated by the Grand Canyon.

I tumbled out of the darkness into the Emerald City POV of this new location, sprawling on my ass on a carpet of rotting leaves. They were rotting and leaves only by sight. The air was odor-free and the ground under my hands was a textureless smoothness, much like a Barbie doll's va-jay-jay. "Ari?"

And then there was one.

22

My brother may not have been there, but I wasn't alone. The log next to me slithered deeper into the jungle. Squeaking, I leapt to my feet, a burst of magic shooting from my palms at the anaconda.

My power dissipated, unable to pierce the veil between the Emerald City version of the dense rainforest that I was in, and the actual rainforest. Once my adrenaline rush shaking had subsided, I set off looking for Ari.

I have no idea how long I wandered under the canopy of trees, doing my best to keep any suspicions that he'd deliberately abandoned me at bay. The utter silence didn't add to my mental state. My warbled singing was a slight improvement but at least trying to recall actual lyrics instead of the phonetic gibberish I usually butchered songs with kept me occupied as I searched.

Even in my contained panic, my neck had a crick in it from gawking at the macaws, tiny frogs, and monkeys that I passed, but nothing was as impressive as the jaguar that slunk past me, tail swishing, its spots close enough to touch. Being in an actual jungle, even in EC mode, was way more impressive than the illusion that the cù-sith had spun.

Night fell. Not that it got dark here in EC, but the all-pervasive green light deepened. I collapsed on a stump, now stripped down to my bra and boy shorts. I wasn't sure if the normal heat of the jungle was amping up the already high temperatures of Ari's magic, but damn, it was blistering. I was roasting, my skin hot to the touch, but unable to produce sweat. My mouth was dry and sticky and my head throbbed.

I blinked slowly at the welcome sight in front of me. "Oh. There you are." I stumbled forward, reaching for the red Solo Cup that I'd left at the frat party and tipped it back. Empty.

Sports bottles I couldn't open, empty soda cans, and a river that flowed just out of tiptoe reach, I couldn't get hold of anything to quench my desperate thirst.

I sat back down on my director's chair and snapped my fingers. "Craft services!"

No cool bottle of water was delivered. I made a note to fire that department, surveying the film set before me. The lighting wasn't bad, but what was with all the animals? My extras casting director sucked balls.

A massive beetle scuttled out of the bottom of my director's chair. I drew my feet up to my chest. "Speak English?" It continued to ignore me. "Parlez-vous français?"

Nothing.

I gave an understanding nod. These poor animals weren't making any noise. They were deaf mutes. Not a problem. I knew a couple words of ASL. I signed out my name. The beetle didn't sign back. I signed the horns and flicking hand for bullshit.

"Yo! Give me fifty percent less beast and a hundred percent more male. Where are my half-dressed, fully ripped men?"

No one jumped to obey.

I swear, this was the worst crew in the history of mankind. "Music." That always got me going so maybe it would bring out my deadbeat workers. Since apparently I had to do everything around here, I started singing the movie's soundtrack myself. I'd gotten through Aretha's "Respect," Destiny Child's "Independent Woman," and was swaying on my feet, halfway into my phonetic interpretation of Janet Jackson's

"Control," before the parade of loincloth bedecked man candy deigned to arrive.

Had I hired clones? Each one had dark hair, dark skin, gold eyes, and an identical unrepentant smirk.

I shooed them away.

The bastards multiplied, marching around me like the brooms in the *Sorcerer's Apprentice*, their faces set in challenge. I stomped my feet. "This is not what I called for!" It wasn't until I invoked the higher power of "I Will Survive" ordering them to walk out that door that I drove them off, using my last bit of energy.

I collapsed onto my knees. Since my eyes didn't throb when I shut them, I did that, too.

Ari caught me before I fell over, sweeping me into his arms.

I giggled, poking him in the chest. "Why are you wearing a Superman outfit?" My laughter ended on a croak. "Oww. I hurt, Ace."

"Hang on." His voice was shaky.

I smoothed out his eyebrows with my finger. "All is well. Don't panic." Then the world gave a weird twist. My stomach lurched and I swallowed hard.

"We're home," Ari said.

The reassuring scent of pine needles blew over me before a door clicked shut cutting off the stream of cool night air.

"Water," I mumbled through thick lips.

I opened my eyes as far as they would go. Kane was ripping open a small square package. I repeated the word, touching my mouth with my finger in case he didn't understand.

"Stay still," he said. "I have to get this isotonic saline in and rehydrate you."

Hands held me down as a needle pierced my flesh. I cried out, my skin strung so tight, I'd swear jagged cracks splintered out from the needle's point of entry.

"It's in. I'll put you to bed now," Ari said.

"Bed good."

I woke up with a scratchy throat on sheets possessing a thread count that didn't exist in my department store shopping reality. An IV drip was in my arm, the almost-empty bag hanging off a pole.

A small lamp was draped with a scarf to diffuse the light, bathing everything in a mellow rose glow. Rohan, earbuds half fallen out of his ears and his fist closed tight around something, was asleep on a chair next to the bed.

His bed.

Apparently my idiot brother required specific possessive pronouns because when I'd said "bed good" I'd meant my bed.

I pulled the drip from my hand. Between the IV and my own accelerated Rasha healing, I felt fine. The rip of tape sounded way too loud, but the music spilling out from the earbuds tempered it somewhat.

Rohan didn't stir.

I eased the blankets off, swinging my feet onto the floor, fully intending to sneak out, except curiosity got the better of me. Step-by-step, I inched toward Rohan, watching for any change to his posture or breathing. When I got within arm's range, I carefully slid a finger under the earbud wire, easing it toward me, and screwed the earbuds in.

A haunting violin and strings piece swirled around me. Albinoni's "Adagio." The music swelled, taking root in my ribcage. I took wing on the song, a dark knot of ugliness inside me unraveling with each note. Achingly beautiful, the music filled me with life as much as each lungful of oxygen did.

My heart fluttered, breaking open. Having spent so much time in the EC, I was unsure about the solidity of this world. If cracks appeared, what would slip through? Had cracks appeared in me?

I placed a hand on my chest, my eyes darting to Rohan for some kind of confirmation that I was real and solid, but he slept on.

Pressure crushed my temples like a vice, snaking down through my jaw and neck. My teeth throbbed. There was so much beauty in this music and so much darkness in me.

My nails gouged my skin.

Everything I kept so carefully contained was seeping out, the over-stuffed box locked tight in my psyche vibrating harder and harder. The more the melody soared, the more my ribcage started trying to strangle me.

The adagio crested to the climax.

The box inside me expanded, straining at the seams, the lid about to blow right off. I ripped the earbuds out and raced for the door. I reached for the knob...

...and was swung up into Rohan's arms.

I fought him, but he was too strong for me to break his hold. "Let go of me."

He muttered something that sounded like "I wish I could." But that couldn't be right because he deposited me carefully back on the bed, folding the covers over my legs.

"Rest. I have the hawkweed for the spell." He still clutched something in his fist, squeezing it in small pulses.

"How?"

Tighter and tighter he squeezed. The bones in his hands tensed. "I bought it and had it couriered."

"In the hour or two I was gone?"

"Try fifteen."

I blinked. "Still not possible. Couriers require overnight delivery."

"I arranged it privately." This was the first time it hit me that Rohan probably had a lot of money from his rock star days and if anyone could have arranged this, it was him.

Blood trickled out from between his fingers.

I grabbed his hand, forcing it open. "Ro. Stop. You're hurting yourself."

He'd been holding the piece of yaksas horn tight enough that its broken edges had sliced his skin.

I grabbed some tissues off his bedside table and dabbed at the blood.

"It'll heal."

"That's not the point." I glared at him. "Have you spoken to anyone about what you went through?"

Rohan pulled his hand away. "You."

"Do any of you actually use our very fine medical benefits?"

Rohan blinked, the picture of dumb caveman with his uncomprehending look and half-open mouth. "Me kill. No undergo psychoanalysis," he grunted.

I wadded the tissue up and put them on the bedside table since there was no trash can in sight. "Why do I bother?"

Rohan settled himself next to me on the mattress, sitting back against the headboard. "Tell you what. Pass on the name of the shrink you spoke to when you couldn't dance anymore and I'll call them right now."

His arm brushed my belly as he stretched across me to reach his phone. His shirt rode up to expose a strip of ab muscle rippling under his brown skin.

I slid a pillow in front of me. "Oooo, you got me."

"Shocking."

"I didn't want to bare my soul to someone who was being paid to listen, all right?" I snapped. "And there's only so much I'd subject Ari and Leo to. Other people's misery is boring and if you keep it up, you end up still miserable but then you're alone, too."

"What about this ex of yours?"

"Cole dumped me when it all happened," I mumbled. That particular shame hadn't been something I'd wanted to share with Rohan.

"He's an idiot."

"He said I shut him out." I blurted the words out.

"You probably did."

"O-kay." I smoothed down a pulled thread in the blanket.

"When I lost Asha?" He shrugged, bending a knee, and bracing his elbow on it. "I couldn't talk to anyone either."

"Because you felt like if you opened your mouth the only thing that would come out would be a piercing howl and you'd bleed out from the inside?" I snapped my mouth shut.

"Aw, Sparky." Rohan put his arm around me.

"Don't you dare pity me, Mitra."

"I don't. I understand you."

"You do understand me. God." I laughed, shaking my head.

"And if I'd been there," he brushed a lock of hair out of my eyes, "you could have talked all day or been silent for a week. I wouldn't have left."

As if. When my world had come crashing down, Rohan had been on top of his and indulging in all his worst excesses.

But the idea that someone I loved would have understood that I was terrified? That I hadn't been shutting Cole out so much as holding myself in check every single second because if I didn't I was convinced that I'd shatter? That there could exist a reality in which I could have that one person who'd have my back in every way that mattered like I could have his and he wouldn't cause grievous emotional harm?

That's what I'd sacrifice everything for.

I jumped to my feet. "Let's do the spell."

While Rohan gathered the ingredients, I made us coffee. A dull dawn light cracked the clouds open enough for the mist to shimmer silver against the silhouetted trees out back.

The coffee pot stopped burbling. I turned from the window and poured myself a cup.

Which led to me wondering after I'd downed half of it if I should perhaps take one to Rohan. He liked his caffeine as much as I did. I took a second mug out of the cupboard.

Yikes. Did this telegraph "girlfriend?"

I put the mug back.

Except… We were friends and fellow Rasha. I'd get Kane one if he needed it.

I pulled the mug back out. Set it on the counter. Poured coffee into it.

Eyed it like it was a cobra about to strike.

Rohan loped into the kitchen, freshly showered, in a pair of sweatpants that molded to every inch of him, and that white T-shirt of his that was so soft and worn, patches of his skin were exposed. Humming, he opened the fridge, his back to me.

He'd shaved. His gorgeous face was a good thing, but I really liked his stubbled, unpolished edge. Bah. I shot his back the finger. His presence was doing squat to help me deconstruct all the possible meanings, permutations, and ramifications of me giving him a cup of coffee.

Dummy got out the milk.

I glared at him, shoved the mug into his hand, said, "Enjoy your damn coffee," and stomped downstairs to the Vault.

I sat cross-legged on the padded blue mat flooring and read over the spell. It was super straight-forward and I was positive I could do it, but my sum total of spell casting was limited to creating and un-doing wards, and only under supervision. It was better that I didn't attempt this on my own.

Rohan entered carrying a mason jar of purified water mixed with a variety of different tiny rock salts and the shredded deep golden-yellow petals of the hawkweed. He also had a thin paintbrush hooked between two fingers.

"We good to go?" I asked.

"Hit it," he said.

I slapped my palm against the scanner on the interior wall. The iron door to the room imprisoning the gogota slid open.

A rotten meat stench whacked me in the face. I threw my arm over my nose.

The demon could barely lift his head, whispering "Gel. Man." in a slow, broken chant, as he lay curled in a piteous ball next to the iron chair. He'd been leeched of all color and was shriveled to two-thirds of his normal height.

Rohan sat down beside him, placing the mason jar of water and paintbrush out of the demon's reach. "Okay, buddy. This will all be over soon. Nava. Do you remember what to do first?"

"Control experiment." I sat down next to the jar and snapped a hair elastic off my wrist. Setting it on the ground, I zapped a bit of electric magic into it, wrinkling my nose against the charred odor. I picked up the paint brush, dipped it twice in the water mixture, then painted the precise vine pattern detailed in the spell on it. "Galah."

The elastic cycled through a rainbow of colors before gently pulsing pink.

"No way," I said. "If I have gender-stereotyped magic, heads are gonna roll."

I handed Rohan a dried fig which he stabbed with his blades. Once more I did the spell and once more rainbow colors appeared before settling into the pulsing pink.

"Equal opportunity," I said. "Better."

"I rock pink," Rohan said. He lined up the two objects. "That's the winner then. Indicative of Rasha magic."

We tested my hamsa ring that Rabbi Abrams had glamoured up when I'd gone to Prague, to see if rabbi magic manifested the same way as Rasha magic. Rasha magic was inherent to us, whereas rabbis had a limited number of spells they cast, mostly around the rituals involved in testing and inducting hunters.

"Seems we're on the Barbie Dreamhouse end of the pink color spectrum with rabbis being more Barely There lip gloss."

"Like the Sephora Ultra Shine," Rohan said.

"Is this knowledge from wearing or kissing?"

Rohan grinned at me.

"Gel. Man." the demon rasped.

My stomach heaved. I looked longingly out toward the Vault and fresh air. The sooner we got this done, the better. "Hold him."

Rohan pinned the demon down, frowning. "He's not even fighting it."

I repeated the paint job and spell on the metal spine and watched the colors cycle. "Be honest with me. If we learn the Brotherhood is behind it? What then?"

"I don't know."

The colors abruptly disappeared leaving the spine in its original state.

"No. It's not possible." I shook it. There had to be magic on it. I reapplied the vine pattern. "Galah," I said more forcefully.

The same cycling. The same lack of a result. I smacked the floor.

"No magic." I couldn't tell if Rohan sounded relieved or disappointed.

"This demon didn't just sit there and let the Brotherhood mount a two-foot spine on it, then happily bound off to do their bidding. If the spine wasn't the binding agent, then something else was." I painted the pattern on the gogota's head. "Galah."

This time when the rainbow cycling stopped, the gogota was purple.

So was one of Rohan's hands. But the magic traces didn't come from having touched the gogota, because his other hand didn't show any magic. It was only visible on the hand he'd injured on the yaksas horn.

Rohan pulled the piece out. He traced the curve of the horn before closing his fingers around it for a second, then dropped it into my outstretched palm.

I submitted the fragment to the same spell. Same result.

"Purple is demon magic." Rohan studied his hand. "When I cut myself on the horn, I must have gotten a residual trace."

Unconvinced, I sprinted out of the room, not stopping until I got to my bedroom on the top floor. I tore through my closet, flinging hangers out until I found what I was looking for, then I raced back down to the iron room.

One more spell.

I clutched the coat that Gelman had magicked clean when we'd been in Prague. It still smelled faintly of rose petals, even all these weeks later.

The spell finished cycling colors and the coat glowed red.

"Witch magic is red," I said, exhaling. Ari being right would have sucked in so many ways.

"Thus the simplest hypothesis is most likely the correct one. Demon magic is purple," Rohan said.

I couldn't shake the feeling that this was *too* simple. That there was no way the most underhanded agenda going on here was merely the Brotherhood's modifications. I grabbed the gogota's lone remaining hand and shocked it, hard. It tensed against me, too weak for its fingers to even close around my wrist. I pulled my hand away revealing the demon's sticky, silver secretion and, with my free hand, picked up the paintbrush. "My hand should turn purple, then."

Dipping the paint in the hawkweed solution, I painted the vine pattern on my skin and said the magic word.

Blue. Demon magic was blue.

The gogota yelped, a feeble pained cry. Rohan had sliced the metal spine off of the demon. The gogota's fur rippled in tiny convulsions, blood tingeing it in patchy drops.

"Rohan!"

He flipped over the spine, and brandishing the paintbrush like a weapon, snarled the spell. A moment later, the wide swathe of the demon's secretions that had dried to a hard resin on the underside pulsed blue.

Rohan shook the spine but it didn't make the results morph from blue to purple.

"One demon in Prague and another in Askuchar with the same purple magic on them. Why? How are they connected? Whose magic is it?" Rohan thudded his head back against the wall. "If that attack in Askuchar was deliberate and my fucking *Brotherhood* had us bury it to hide something?" Pain etched his features. Rohan whipped the spine against the wall.

I flinched at the loud clatter, then lay my hand on Rohan's shoulder. "We'll figure it out."

The gogota raised its moist eye to mine.

Leaving the demon alive was a cruelty that I wasn't capable of. Or maybe killing it was the cruelty I needed to enact. I sliced the tip of one finger off as purple proof before I killed it.

I barely needed any magic to finish it off.

23

Daniel finally checked in.

Ari and I met him at an out-of-the-way diner. Despite his police uniform being neatly pressed, the cop himself looked rumpled. Bags under his eyes, his hair somewhat greasy, and the hand picking up his coffee cup jittery. "You never worked with Mara, did you?"

"No," I said. "I'm sorry. I didn't."

The chipped white mug rattled against the ceramic plate when he set the cup down.

I blotted the coffee that sloshed onto the table. "Do you maybe want some decaf?"

"I can't sleep."

"Have you been home?" Ari and I were crowded into the tiny booth across from him. The red leather seats were a dull sheen, especially worn in the butt area.

"No. I'm staying with a friend." Daniel fiddled with his unopened creamer.

"Good." Ari dumped cream in his own coffee. "You need to keep away from Malik."

"Yeah, keep away from the handsome, funny, smart guy." Daniel rubbed his temples. "Not a guy though, huh? We spent hours at the museum and he taught me about all kinds of art. I watched him paint. Watched him create such beautiful pieces. How could someone with so much passion and vitality be a monster?"

Ari and I exchanged concerned glances. "There are a lot of monsters out there, Daniel," Ari said. "Some are human, some... aren't. Unfortunately, we can't judge their insides by their outsides."

"That's for damn sure." Daniel pushed his coffee away. "I thought he loved me."

"He might have, in as much as something like him is capable of it," I said.

Daniel's eyes flashed. His fingers twitched down toward the gun holstered at his hip.

"No." I waved my hands. "Do not go after him. I know you hate him but you're not trained to take him down."

"Top of my academy," Daniel said. "I've trained plenty."

"Not for this," Ari said. "Trust that he'll be dealt with and stay with friends or close to other cops until you get the all-clear from me, okay?"

Daniel didn't look happy about it, but he agreed, then saying he needed to get to work, left.

"Poor guy," I said.

"We need to kill Malik." Ari tossed some change down to cover our coffees. "I don't trust Daniel to stay away from him."

We walked back to the car hunched in our coats against the cold wet wind. While Ari drove, I called Kane, explaining that finding Malik had reached a new urgency, and we were on our way back.

Kane made us wait another forty-five minutes before exiting his room, yawning. "Chill out, taskmasters, I have succeeded." He handed me a piece of paper. "Address and phone number. It took a bit to untangle the shell company that owns it."

I whistled. Malik had some swank real estate in Vancouver's Coal Harbour.

"I also took the liberty of looking for any security systems on the place." Kane jogged downstairs, calling for Rohan to meet us in the kitchen because he was convening the "War Room."

Ari stopped on the bottom step. "Did he just take my mission away from me?"

"Naw, I'm sure you're equal partners." Smirking, I skipped off to join Kane and Rohan.

The two more experienced Rasha went over everything they knew about marids, scrutinizing our plan of attack down to the last detail. Had they not been able to give us a secret weapon to take down Malik, they would have insisted on accompanying us. Even so, it was clearly killing them to respect the mission and let Ari and me deal with it.

Kane was still frosty with Ari, mostly directing his comments to me.

Once the men were satisfied with our plan, Ari and I tore the weapons room apart, looking for the small, flat, iron disc called an amplifier that they'd instructed us to find.

"Got it." I backed out of a cupboard, brushing dust off my knees. I twisted the two-inch disc between my fingers. "It doesn't look like much."

"It'll do the trick." Ari held out his hand for it. "Make Malik solid so we can kill him."

I stuffed the disc in my bra.

He dropped his hand. "That's not gonna stop me."

It was totally going to stop him and we both knew it. "If you have the best opportunity to kill Malik, I'll give you the disc. Emet Hatorah." Truth of the Torah and the phrase that our grandparents swore would bring God's wrath down on us if we dared swear an oath on and weren't truthful. I didn't believe it but I didn't not believe it and I'd never broken it.

"You don't trust me to do the same?" he asked.

I patted the amplifier. "Not for a second."

We waited until night to breach the penthouse, all curved glass with sweeping views of the water and city. Real estate in Vancouver was so crazy that I was convinced we were all suffering from Stockholm Syndrome, nodding our heads about what a good deal a shoebox ground floor suite with no view running upwards of half a million dollars was nowadays.

The tower was outfitted with a state of the art security system involving audio, video, a manned desk in the lobby, and regular sweeps by guards. Which begged the question: who else lived here? Former dictators? Satan?

Though security wasn't an issue since Ari was going to shadow-port us directly into Malik's apartment. The issue was the wards spanning across Malik's floor-to-ceiling windows that we bounced off of. And by "bounced," I meant ran into like a car hitting a cement wall. While being twenty-three floors up.

"You're forgiven for abandoning me last time in the EC," I panted, laying safe in a tumbled heap on the roof of the tower, thanks to Ari's quick reflexes. "I wouldn't make a good smear on the sidewalk."

Rain misted down on me. Misting rain was the worst. Rain or don't rain but commit, you asshole drizzle clouds.

"I didn't abandon you. Oof." Ari shoved my leg off of him and rolled himself free. "The strain was too much and I lost control of my magic. I got to the final location and you were gone."

"I'm telling Mom." I wrapped my arms around myself, shivering violently as I checked out the roof. A lot of pigeon droppings. "There's no way off. No door."

"Give me a minute," Ari said. "I'll take us down."

The world lit up with a blinding reddish orange fire, accompanied by a familiar acrid burning. By the time dots had stopped dancing in front of my eyes, Ari was gone.

I ran to the edge of the building and leaned over to see if there was a balcony I could jump down to. It was a sheer drop. Malik's apartment was underneath me but without rappelling equipment and an open window, there was no way to get inside.

I had to get there. Malik had my brother.

I sprinted to the other side of the building and peered down. "Ah, man." I clutched the ledge. I really, really hated heights.

I pulled out my phone and called Kane. "How long would it take you to arrange a helicopter to get me off this roof?"

"If one could even land there? It would take some time."

"Damn it!"

"Uh, babyslay?"

"Ari's not going to be tortured again. Forget it."

"What?!"

"I'll get him." I hung up and stepped up onto the ledge. My heart pounded, icy claws squeezing my chest. Since I didn't like jumping off anything higher than the low diving board, I was rooted to the spot, sweat pooling under my arms and trickling down my back. I dug my nails into my palms. "Move."

Inch by inch, I talked myself off the ledge, my foot edging off further and further until momentum took over and I fell. My high-pitched scream cut off as I hit the outdoor pool two floors down. I smacked my feet on the bottom, but didn't appear to break anything.

I swam to the surface, coughing at all the chlorine that was now up my nose, but glad I'd chosen lightweight pants and a turtleneck for this outing and not jeans and a heavy coat. I might die of hypothermia but at least I wouldn't drown.

I sloshed over to the heavy glass doors and tugged. Locked tight. My magic made quick work of the cheap lock, then I exited the indoor lounge area, closed at this time of night, into the hallway. No doors were harmed in the process.

The elevator required a biometric scan to access the penthouse, so that was out, but the stairwell only needed a quick short circuiting of the scanner. Kane's teachings had been bang-on. People spent a fortune guarding the bottom of a building and only a cursory amount on the top and inside access points.

Lucky for me.

Malik's apartment was the only one up here. There was no camera that I could see and no point in worrying about it. I crossed my fingers that there was no demon ward on this door, and blew it off its hinges.

The city was a glittering jewel set against a midnight blue sky, laid out for my viewing pleasure through two walls of windows in the open-concept floor plan. The floors were burgundy concrete and the fireplace was inset in a single black glass column that supported a bottom corner of what I assumed was the loft bedroom. Being a demon was a lucrative gig, because if Malik made the kind of bank needed to afford this place solely off his art, he'd be all kinds of famous.

There was no sign of my brother or Malik, not on the low leather sofa custom-made to follow the curve of the windows, or in the high-end kitchen, where an open bottle of wine and two glasses sat on the counter.

I raced past the six-foot-by-six-foot glass cube holding wine bottles in wood racks, taking petty delight in the trail of water I left. Around the other side of it was a small hallway.

Malik had my brother pressed up against a hanging black tapestry woven with abstract curves of flame colors. The marid trailed his finger along Ari's chest.

My brother drew in a stuttery breath.

"Nava?" Before I could process why Leo was standing behind me with Daniel, Ari inhaled on a cut-off gasp, clutched his chest, doubled over, and collapsed.

Malik knelt down beside Ari and cradled his head.

"Don't touch him." I slammed my palm against Ari's chest, shocking him, while concentrating a burst of electricity at the marid.

Malik burst into flame before it hit. Leo yelped at the transformation, but while the demon released Ari, he did so with an aggrieved sigh. "This is getting tiresome."

"Then let's shake things up." I braved the heat pouring off Malik to press the amplifier to the flames in his shoulder region, attempting to defibrillate Ari with my other hand.

Malik's flame nostrils flared.

I shocked Ari again, frantic.

The amplifier was working, forcing Malik back into flesh so we could kill him, albeit a billion times slower than I wanted. The marid's right leg had become corporeal. The flames swirling around at his core flickered angrily but the disc prevented him from moving.

I should have been thrilled but all I cared about was the fact that Ari wasn't responding to my defibrillation. I placed my hand on his chest.

He wasn't breathing.

Malik's neck solidified from flame to flesh.

I dug the disc deeper into Malik's shoulder, his body now corporeal all the way up his left side. "Fix him!"

Malik's fingers dug into the tapestry, white-knuckled and shaking, despite his level voice. "I can't."

"Then prepare to die."

He closed his eyes, and fire cascaded down his right arm in a sheath. "You are such a bother."

The disc flew out of my hand. I grabbed for it, then jumped back as flame spurted out of Malik's palm and melted the amplifier into a useless iron puddle on the floor.

Smirking, the demon disappeared. Daniel and Leo were gone as well.

I placed both hands flat on Ari's chest. "Don't you dare die on me, you asshole!"

One more shock.

After the longest moment in history, Ari wheezed in a breath.

I slumped against the wall in a puddle of pool water, keeping a close eye on him.

"Where's Daniel?" Ari's voice was gravely. He waved off my offer of help, and using the wall, sat up.

"Why?"

"Because he's the one who attacked me."

"No. It was Malik."

Ari shook his head. "Trust me. It was Daniel, not Malik. That wasn't marid magic. My guess is Daniel's a hantu." Malaysian possession demon.

"But he's a cop." Silly me. Malik destroying the amplifier wasn't us being fucked. No, our fuckification was reserved for a demon infiltrating those supposed to serve and protect.

"He's also a PD." Ari rubbed his chest, spearing me with a pointed look. "They all turn in the end."

"This has nothing to do with him being a PD and everything to do with him being messed in the head."

Ari grabbed my arm to lever himself onto his feet. We were silent for a moment, Ari recuperating, me feeling my brain explode into tiny splatting pieces.

"Daniel's dad was a cop and with his training, he knows how to commit a crime and get away with it," Ari said as we made our way out of the hallway into Malik's main room, the lights impossibly bright.

I squinted against the glare, wishing I wasn't going into a final showdown with a wet ass.

"That's why he isolated his victims first." My brother stopped to catch his breath. "His human side was organizing the kills, even if his demon side was exacerbating his emotions and his need to get rid of the competition. So who's the next victim?"

"Leo!" Daniel had brought her here and in the chaos, I'd forgotten about her.

"She's fine," Malik stepped into view, his arm draped around Leo's shoulder. There was no sign of Daniel. "Aren't you?"

"I'm fine," she repeated. Her voice was breathy, her eyes wide as she gazed upon him and only him. "Are *you* hurt?"

"Not even a scratch." He smiled at her but his eyes promised me payback.

"What did you do to her?" I demanded.

"The barest kiss to get her in the mood. It wasn't her choice but desperate times. Who wants wine?" He led Leo to the seating area, then left her there like she was a statue for our viewing pleasure.

I made a sound halfway between strangled disbelief and impressed awe at the power of that kiss. "What happened to not hurting humans?"

Oh, his feline smile wasn't smug at all. "She doesn't really count, does she? Being a PD and all."

Ari sank onto the couch, his head buried in shaking hands.

Leo didn't react to the derogatory term. She just stood there paused until Malik directed her otherwise.

"I could have a lot of fun with her. Oh, don't worry, petal," he said, "I'd snap her out of her daze to give me her full consent." He tilted his head, raking a slow gaze over her. "Goblin women." He whistled. "Feisty."

I stood protectively in front of my friend. "You knew that Daniel was killing them."

"The Arabic word for love," Ari said. "He wrote it for you."

I glanced at Leo but there was no change. "Did you send him the victims yourself or just get off on knowing what that fucker was doing to impress you?"

Malik poured the blood-red wine into one glass. "I didn't know. At first."

"Once you did?" Ari prompted.

Malik looked off toward the window before meeting our gaze. "I chose what mattered more." He downed the wine.

Daniel was Malik's weakness. Ari and Leo were mine.

I willed my best friend to snap out of it. To clench her fist at me for being the world's biggest douchebag for having brought this on her. Do something resembling anything, but all she did was stand there with a vacant adoring beam.

"I promise you she'll enjoy every second," Malik said. "She'll die with a smile on her face."

He didn't have to take it that far, but I had no doubt that he would. "What do you want?"

He gave Leo one last look before adopting a more business-like tone. "Daniel for Leonie. I leave the choice up to you two."

"Why do we get a choice?" I said. "Compel us into letting Daniel go free."

"As I've already told you, I don't have that ability. Trust me, if I did, you two would know. I'm surprised you even have to think about it, Ari," Malik said. "What with your clearly defined morality and all. I'd have thought Leonie was acceptable collateral damage."

"The only acceptable collateral damage is you," Ari said.

"That's adorable." Two Rasha in the room with him making death threats and all he did was lick a drop of wine off his finger, giving zero fucks. "Your choice is Daniel or Leonie. Tick tock." Malik shook the bottle, then set it on the counter. He headed for wine cube. "Cabernet this time."

I scoped out the room. Too high to jump, not that the windows opened or there was a sliding door. No way to get to the front door before Malik stopped us. No way to kill him. No shadows here for Ari to jump us into the EC since Malik had doctored the lights to full wattage.

I wanted to scream in frustration. Daniel was going to get away. As was Malik.

Malik returned carrying a new bottle.

Ari flicked his eyes to the window.

I looked but didn't see anything. It was night. It was dark.

Malik screwed in the corkscrew and popped the cork free. "What have you decided?"

"No deal," Ari said.

When the marid's attention was on the glass of wine he was pouring for himself, Ari narrowed his eyes and motioned subtly outside.

I frowned.

He kicked me, pointing at Leo and jerking his chin at the window, mouthing the words "twin war."

Ow. And oh.

I punched him in the arm about five times. "We. Are. Not. Leaving. Leo."

Ari glared at me, my body blocking him from Malik's view. "Overdoing it," he muttered.

"So glad I was an only child," Malik said, coming over to us with his glass. "Hurry up and reach consensus."

I backed off, putting a protective arm around my friend. "Snap her out of it. You win. Leo for Daniel."

Ari growled in frustration, then nodded.

Malik snapped his fingers.

"Nava?" Leo blinked dopily. "What's going on?"

I tightened my hold on her. "Can we go now?"

"No. Daniel needs time to leave town." Malik pulled out his phone, texting Daniel, his head bent over the screen.

Ari touched three fingers to his thigh. Two.

I gathered my magic, fired it at the window...

...and watched my strike go wild as Malik grabbed my wrist and broke it.

"Fuuuuuuuuck!" Magic exploded out of my skin, wine staining my skin like blood.

Glass exploded behind me with a thunderous crash.

A red haze filled my vision. Electricity pounded out of me like bullets from an Uzi, peppering Malik.

He gasped.

His flames swirled tighter and denser, the voltage racking through him. My magic slid through his fire like...

"Charged particles. I read about this." Ari pushed to his feet. "Hold him, Nee. You're putting him out."

The very shape of the demon's flames morphed. Every other time he'd gone fiery, he'd been in control, keeping the outline of a human form. This time there was no shape, merely a jagged blazing starburst; the only identifying features his eyes, now open wide.

"Keep the current oscillating," Ari made a back and forth motion with his hands. "But go hard."

Acting on pure impulse, I made a scooping motion with my good hand as if turning up the dial, the broken one cradled against my chest.

Malik shrunk into himself, getting smaller and smaller. An enraged roar poured out from deep in the center of the flames, bouncing off the walls.

"Holy shitsticks," Leo said, clapping her hands over her ears.

The reds and blues of the marid's flame grew weaker, his cries of rage quieting.

"No!"

There was a second of stunned surprise as Ari and I locked eyes with Daniel, who'd appeared, still in uniform. His features were twisted in fury.

Ari drew in shadow through the broken window from the night sky, coiled it around his arm, and snapped it like a whip at Daniel's wrist.

Daniel placed his hand on the shadow, a ripple rolling out from his flesh up to Ari's shoulder. My brother shivered violently, all the color draining from his face. Even though to witness Ari's magic was to swear it had depth and weight, it was still shadows. Still intangible, but Daniel grabbed onto the magic, snapping its hold.

He pulled his gun, grabbed Leo, and jammed the barrel to her head.

Thanks to the glaring bright lights, I could see exactly how unhinged Daniel was: bloodshot eyes, wrinkled uniform, his hair sticking up every which way like he'd run his hands through it one too many times. "Let Malik go," he said.

Malik had almost sputtered out. I could end him, but could we take Daniel down faster than he could kill Leo?

If I released Malik, I'd have to tell Mandelbaum that it was my fault that the demon got away. Even though he wasn't the serial killer, he was an ancient being of unimaginable power. It would be career suicide. Or my death warrant. Either by the Brotherhood or the marid himself.

Daniel cocked the trigger. "Decide."

I shut down my magic.

Corporeal once more, Malik dragged in a deep breath, collapsing back against the wall with a hard thud.

"Go," Daniel urged.

Malik hesitated and Daniel stared him down, not removing the gun from Leo. Pale, she was a wall of tense muscle, but her chin was jutted up in defiance.

"You foolish boy." Malik lay his hand on Daniel's cheek. He tilted his head at Ari and me. "Until next time, Rasha." Then he disappeared.

"Saving himself. Big surprise." Ari parked himself at my left shoulder.

I appreciated the solidarity but I wasn't taking my eyes off Daniel's weapon. Sweat ran in a thin line between my shoulder blades. "A gun? That's cheating. Have you no sense of demon pride?"

"I'm not a monster!" Daniel's hand shook. The one holding the lethal weapon.

My heart stuttered, stopped, then tried to crawl up my throat. "No one said you were." Please. He was totally a monster. He'd killed seven people. What did he think that made him? A Nobel Peace Prize winner?

"Why don't you put the gun down and talk to us?" Ari said. "Tell us what's going on."

"I just wanted him to love me." His hand tightened on the grip.

"Easy." I held up a hand. The good one since the broken one still dangled uselessly. Though it was highly efficient in producing copious amounts of pain.

"By killing seven people?" Ari said.

Leo sucked in a breath. "Whoa."

Pain twisted Daniel's features. "I couldn't help it. This darkness just took over."

"Bullshit. We've all got darkness in us and yeah, it's harder when it's literal evil, but that makes the humanity that much more precious. And as a cop? You of all people should have understood that."

"Leo," I snapped. "Shut up."

"Let her go, Daniel." Ari spoke quietly, his hand outstretched for the gun.

Daniel turned pleading eyes on me. "You have no idea what it was like to love him and know that he didn't return it. It didn't matter how much I proved I was the only one for him, I was just one of many."

The kicker? I felt bad for the guy. Part of him was still human and that part of him was in a lot of pain. I wasn't excusing his actions, there were no excuses, but I could empathize with at least part of his situation.

"You didn't prove your worth." Ari sneered. "You destroyed any chance of the one thing, the one person you wanted. You killed his lovers, Daniel. Even Malik didn't want you after that. Jakayla, Davide, Max, Reuben, Ellen." With each name Ari stepped closer to Daniel.

"That poor Jane Doe," I added. "Did you even know her name?

Daniel whimpered.

"Tell me. Give her family some closure."

"Anna. Rodriguez." He whispered her name. I wish we could have prevented Anna's death, but if learning her identity meant her family could give her a proper burial, instead of always wondering what had happened to her, I'd take it as a win.

"You killed your own friend, Mara," Ari said.

Daniel's face pulled tight with grief.

"They had lives. Families. You couldn't fully possess them like a pure hantu so you took them over just enough to drain their life force." Ari veered off to Daniel's left, so I went right, forcing Daniel to pick a target.

He chose Ari. Was it wrong of me to feel relieved? Didn't care. Gun barrels were fucking terrifying things to be on the wrong end of.

With Daniel's attention focused on my brother, I sidled in until I was close enough to knock Leo away, pushing her behind me.

Daniel groaned, a low sound of raw anguish. "What I have become? I just loved him so much."

"Let him stand trial," I said.

"Are you kidding?" Leo asked.

"Yes," Daniel said. "Make me face *human* justice."

"Nava." Ari shook his head.

I'd never had a problem killing a PD when they deserved it, and if anyone deserved it, it was Daniel. But his humanity was radiating out at me from behind his hope-filled eyes and I couldn't do it.

"I guess we're not equals after all, Ace."

"You are. You have to be."

"You mean I have to save my own skin."

"That too." Ari nodded sadly and tapped his left temple.

"What do you mean?" Daniel looked between us, confused. "Arrest me."

I took a deep breath. "I'm so, so sorry," I said, and zapped his kill spot.

Daniel's eyes widened in surprise and he disappeared in a cloud of gold dust. Right as a big bang like a firework echoed through the apartment.

My shoulder splintered and I stumbled backward.

Out the window.

24

Fall thirty stories backward into the night and tell me you wouldn't scream.

Wind and my life rushed past. Blood streamed out of the bullet wound torn into my shoulder, hot drops flicking against my face. Being shot was exactly as horrible as seen on TV. Gripping my shoulder using my blood-slicked, non-busted wrist, my nerves locked in full-tilt agony, kept me busy for the first ten or so floors but thirty stories was a really long way to fall.

I had to take a break from my screaming because my throat was getting raw.

Closer and closer the ground came. I fired my magic, but lighting is not a handy spiderweb and gravity continued winning. To make matters worse, using my power had twisted me around so that I now fell face down.

Time to scream again.

Fifty feet... thirty... twenty... This was not going to be pretty.

I closed my eyes.

A hand hooked around my leg. The world snapped into EC, the night sky replaced with a deep green light. We crashed onto the grass, landing hard and rolling apart. Light morphed from green back to midnight blue, thin clouds drifting slowly overhead.

Ari whooped. "I wasn't sure that would work."

His cheek had a smear of gold on it and when I lifted my head, the bloodstains on my shirt were suspiciously sparkly. Damn PD death dust parting gift.

I lay sprawled on my back, breathing through the burn, tears streaming down my face and my hand cradling my shoulder.

"Are you two okay?" Leo's voice reached us before she did. She skidded to a stop, having run out the front door of the building.

"If you're being flexible with the definition." I started panting.

Leo whipped off her sweater, pressing it against my shoulder. "Nee, hang in there. Ari, do something."

"I don't have the energy to jump us," Ari said. "We have to drive. Can you stand?"

Perhaps if I hadn't been dehydrated, failed to kill a marid, and blasted a window open to fall out a penthouse window, I might have managed. As it was, I laughed long and hard with a tinge of hysteria. Leo prodded my shoulder.

I screamed and smacked her hand away. "Don't touch it!"

"I don't think our healing covers expelling bullets," Ari said. "I'm calling Kane."

"Nooo," I wailed. "He'll bring Rohan."

Ari sat down beside me. "Then you have to let me pick you up and get you to the doctor."

"Nope," I said through gritted teeth. "I'm just going to lay here indefinitely until you get me some freaking drugs."

Between the two of them, they managed to prop me in the front seat, Leo's sweater packed between my shoulder and the seat belt, my broken wrist cradled to my chest.

We took Leo home first. She'd snapped out of any remnants of her demon-inspired daze, but she was furious, sitting in the back seat vowing all kinds of painful retributions on the marid. Swearing she was going to call in every single favor from every demon client ever. She ran out of steam midway through a visceral description of how she'd start his disembowelment. Between one word and the next, all her energy left her and she sagged forward in a limp heap.

"Leo?" I mumbled.

"I'm fine."

Ari pulled up in front of her place.

"You want me to come back and stay with you tonight?" I may have only managed every other word of that sentence, but she got it.

"No, thanks. I'll call Madison."

"I see."

She gave me a cute pout. "Don't be mad. She cheers me up with orgasms."

"Eh. I'd take that, too."

She flashed me a wavery grin. "Schmugs, Nee."

"Schmugs."

"Keep the sweater." She opened the passenger door, half twisting back to Ari. "Thanks for deciding I was worth saving, asshole."

Ari flung his door open, limping to catch up to her. I couldn't hear what he said to her but she rolled her eyes at him and he gave her a giant hug.

Then I blacked out a bit until my brother slapped my cheek gently. "Nee, stay with me."

The blur of lights as we drove past storefronts made me nauseous. I pressed my cheek against the cold window. "Do people die of shoulder wounds?"

"No."

"I'm gonna be the first, okay? I was born second but sometimes I'm first. First in my tap competitions. First girl Rasha. First at blowing up my life in spectacular fashion." That wasn't as cool an accomplishment.

"You're not going to die," Ari said.

I shivered, which combined with a bullet wound was totally indicative of impending death. "Why didn't you ever say anything about your sleep terrors continuing? Be honest. Since I'm dying."

"Fucking hell," he muttered. "I didn't want to be seen as weak, all right? I was going to be the best hunter ever."

My hands went clammy. "Ohmigod, I AM dying!"

"What?"

"You never share your feelings." I thunked my head back against the seat, glad of the seatbelt locking me in place. Otherwise, between my swimming vision and mild sensation of vertigo, I'd have slid onto the floor by now. My Rasha healing had numbed my pain but it was fogging my brain up. Everything took on a dreamy cast. "Tell Mom and Dad, well, I can't think of anything, but you're good at that stuff so make something up. I've written the eulogy for you and there's a playlist on my phone called 'Nava, You Irreplaceable You' for everyone to mourn to."

Ari removed his hand from the steering wheel to clasp mine. "Any last words for Rohan?"

I let out a croaky eep.

"Breathe." Ari slapped my cheek again. "I was kidding. You're not dying."

I pressed my palm against the wound hoping it would diffuse the pain. It didn't. "Well then I don't need to apologize for the position I put you in because I know how much being part of the Brotherhood means to you and I'm going to figure out what they're up to. But I hope we're always on the same side anyway because the alternative is unbearable."

To me, the speech sounded highly eloquent, like one step removed from Evita on her balcony singing to the common people. Ari, however, leaned over me, his face scrunched up. "I think I got most of that slurfest."

He pulled up the parking brake and tugged on his earlobe. Our twin code for "I have your back." A code that had been noticeably absent on this mission.

Ari carried me up the front walk, kicking on the doctor's door to get him to hurry up.

The doctor took in the full glory of my shoulder. "I just saw you the other day."

"I lead a busy life," I mumbled.

"Evidently."

I lolled in and out of consciousness for a while after that, though I did come to with him standing over me, holding up forceps. "This is going to hurt."

I blacked out again.

By the time I came to for good, laying on the back seat of our car, my shoulder was bandaged.

I watched dawn break through the back window. It wasn't even one of the better ones, bathing the sky in pinks and soft blues. Nope, this one was the color and attractiveness of dryer lint. Strangely fitting.

Ari sat in the front seat on the phone. "Yes. He's dead." There was a pause. "Thank you. Nava was instrumental–" He tapped the side of his fist against the window twice. "No, it was actually Nava who–" He shot the phone the finger. "Yes, sir. Thank you, again." He tossed the phone in the cup holder. "Fucking Mandelbaum," he said.

I smiled. After all I'd been through, getting the rabbi's approval no longer mattered. I played possum so Ari wouldn't have to apologize for the phone call and then at some point, I actually fell asleep because when Ari woke me, we were back at the chapter house.

He helped me inside.

Kane sat on the bottom step in the foyer waiting. He raked a cold calculating glance over the two of us. "Everyone hale and hearty? Excellent."

"Stop being such an asshole," Ari said. "You've pulled shit in our friendship, too."

Kane stood up. "Which begs the question of why, exactly, we're friends?"

"Whatever, man." The two of them turned away from each other at the same time, Kane to go upstairs and my brother into the kitchen.

Gong. Show.

I headed up as well, going directly into my bedroom, and sitting down by my window. Physically, I was feeling a million times better. I stared out into the night, cocooned in silence, thinking about Daniel.

Thinking about me. I didn't want to be a destructive force. Not with the people I loved.

Or had loved once.

I pulled out my phone.

"Hey, Cole. Did I wake you?" A good bet, given the time, but if I didn't do this now, I was worried I never would.

"Nothing good ever happened in a 6AM phone call." His voice was scratchy with sleep.

"I'm sorry that I shut you out."

"Me too."

This wasn't a jettison, it was a mercy. Cole really was my past. He belonged to a Nava who didn't exist anymore and trying to resurrect that relationship would end up as well as reanimating the dead.

My throat grew tight. It didn't matter how I tried to convince myself otherwise. This was still a sacrifice. "Cole…"

"I know."

"I'm glad I saw you again." I drew a heart in the condensation on the window, then smudged it out. "I got closure."

"Then I'm glad." He yawned again.

"Go back to sleep. Be well."

"Wait. Do you want your Twenty-One Pilots T-shirt back?"

I looked at the Fugue State Five shirt that I'd stolen from Leo, now folded on my pillow. "I'm good."

And the biggest surprise as I hung up? I really was.

There was one more loose end to tie up.

As I stepped down onto the first stair, the skin between my shoulder blades prickled. Stair two: a sickening dread uncoiled in my gut. Stair three: my chest tightened.

Run.

I clutched the bannister, rubbing my palm over the polished wood like I could make a genie appear. A genie who could grant me three wishes, all of them ensuring that if I descended the staircase, and went down the hallway that I'd be safe.

There was a lot about my behavior that I refused to apologize for, but maybe I hadn't been entirely fair to Rohan. Did he have control issues? Emotional issues? No kidding. But he also had my back. That part was good, but what about when he had my heart?

Run.

I sank down on the stair, my head buried in my hands. There was no way I could be in a relationship with him and not fall in love. And love was when things got twisted. Look at Daniel. Or, less demony, Cole. I'd loved him and I'd assumed he would stand by me but he hadn't. Maybe teen love didn't exactly set a high bar, but the principle was sound. The harder you loved, the more at someone's mercy you were, and I wasn't sure I could open myself up given the power I'd be handing over to Rohan.

Maybe I shouldn't make these decisions until after I'd slept for ten hours.

Run!

I pulled myself up and was struck with a vision of myself at eighty having lived a safe, comfortable life, free of a certain infuriating alpha who made me laugh and gave me the greatest sex of my life and who, for all he pushed my buttons, also pushed me to be so much more. Or worse, not even having made it to eighty because I was too scared or too proud.

Ari was right. Humans were greedy. I'd been so committed to getting more and more fortifications to my emotional shields, so committed to living life on my precise terms, that I hadn't clued in to how lonely that existence could be.

I ran down the stairs, skidding to a stop beside Rohan's bed.

He was snoring softly. That made me feel better because without it, he would have just been this too-beautiful mortal, artfully asleep in his tousled sheets, his dark sooty lashes falling across his cheeks and that one single lock of hair drooping across his eyes.

I ran a hand over his naked back and the tattoo across his shoulder blades of the word Kshatriya, the warrior caste, scripted in Hindi in midnight black ink. "Ro?"

He flung an arm over his head.

"Rohan."

"Mmmm?" He snuggled into his pillow. Damn, he was adorable.

I shook his shoulder. "Wake up."

He cracked his eyes open. "What?" His voice was thick and rumbly. He glanced at my bandaged shoulder and wreckage of a shirt. "Busy night?"

"I was shot."

"Of course you were. Anything else?"

I shrugged.

"Bet you kicked ass."

"I may have." I dug my phone out of my pocket. "I want you to listen to something."

"Nava." He lifted his head to squint at the time on my phone. "It's some ungodly hour." He dropped his head back down onto his pillow. "Can we do this later?"

"No." I scrolled through my music until I found the right song and hit play. The opening strains of "You're the One that I Want" came on. I didn't let myself watch him as he listened to it, but when the song faded away, I looked at him expectantly.

His expression gave away nothing. "Why did you play that?" He yanked on the sheet, forcing me to move.

I fluttered my hands, flustered. "Because the lyrics."

"Yeah. I know what the lyrics say."

"That's why."

"I hate to break it to you, Nava, but you're not Sandy. You're Rizzo."

No one else had ever instinctively understood that about me.

I brushed my lips against his. A feather of a caress, my nerves stacked like crates at Costco.

He waited two heartbeats to speak. "You sure?"

"Yeah, Ro. I am." I tugged on his hand. "Upstairs," I said, hitting the bottom of the slippery slope and letting Rohan in to my life in every way possible.

His slow easy smile undid me. "Let's go."

25

I flipped on my bedside lamp and took his hands, tugging him to face me. Stretching up on tiptoe, I kissed his eyelashes. His nose. Pressed my lips to the underside of his jaw and scattered a million soft little caresses over his cheeks, splaying my palms against his chest to capture the warmth of his skin.

His eyes fell shut, his face tilting down to mine.

When I didn't immediately kiss him again, he tensed and cracked open his eyes.

"Sit," I instructed, walking him backward to the mattress. I kicked off my shoes and straddled him, sitting ramrod straight, my eyes drifting to his full, lush lips, trying to figure out the best angle to come at him. Like there was any approach that would keep my shields intact.

I grabbed a scarf from a drawer. "Can I blindfold you?"

His gaze licked across my skin. "Yes."

Amazed that I only fumbled the knot once, I sat back on my calves. He was glorious, sitting back against my headboard, his chest bare, his hair sticking up every which way above the slash of pink and black fabric wrapped around his eyes.

Hands braced on the mattress, I leaned forward and ghosted my lips over his.

Rohan's lips parted tentatively. His fingers dragged along my spine, down to the mattress, finding my hand. He stroked the pad of his thumb over my knuckles, upping the kiss, pressing his mouth more firmly to mine.

I stiffened, a wave of self-preservation rearing its head. Rohan released me and I attempted to get my panicky breathing under control. Hating my cowardice. Given everything else the two of us had done with each other, this kiss should have been easy. "I want to tie your hands up."

His chest rose in a ragged breath and I'd swear his eyes were trained on mine, even through the blindfold. It took him so long to answer that I was convinced he'd refuse. "Do it."

"Incredible. Even your agreement to submission is issued like the most imperious command."

I expected a cocky smirk.

"When your life fell apart, you kept it together by shutting people out." He skipped his fingers across the blanket, one, two, three. "I did it by thinking every decision three moves ahead. If I could bend everything, everyone to my will, nothing bad could happen. After Askuchar, I needed that more than ever. And you were a wild card."

I'd gotten a confession.

I lay my palm on his cheek. "Aw, Snowflake."

"Don't you dare pity me."

"I don't. I understand you."

"I know. God, I know." Still blindfolded, Rohan nuzzled into my hand.

This jumble of emotions blew through me, knocking the breath from my lungs. "Lie down." I didn't have any other scarves or actual bondage ties so I used two thigh-high cotton socks. "This okay?" I asked, tugging on the bow tie connecting his wrists to the bed post.

"Yeah." He stilled, head tilted with an expectant air.

Rohan was one of the most alpha males I knew and yet he had no problem giving up control. To me. Not just in sex. He'd let me take the lead in fights and in finding the spine. If we were going to move

forward, we'd be doing so as equals. Of that I had no doubt. A hum-
mingbird flutter of nervous excitement licked through me.

Taking a slow, deep breath, I cocked my head to the side, and
pressed my mouth to his. My stomach did a backflip. Movies and
books were filled with people losing themselves in kisses. I didn't. I
couldn't. I was too hyperaware of who I was with. The erratic thump
of his heart under my palm. The tension in his corded biceps. His low
rumble when my tongue tangled with his.

I draped myself over him, my weight sinking into his. Threading
my fingers into his hair, I deepened the kiss. We were on the same
wavelength, taking our time, savoring this new taste of each other. His
was equal parts wildness, stubbornness, and gentleness.

I rested my hand on his jaw, my thumb caressing his cheek.

Rohan licked into the corner of my mouth. Every slow, insistent
kiss burned my skin, laying more and more bare between us.

The world fell away.

If this kiss was my white flag, then I intended to draw out every
second of my surrender.

I existed in pieces. The fall of his hair like silk through my fingers.
The fit of our hips, our bodies aligned like puzzle pieces, all hard edges
and rounded corners. The faint hint of bourbon I tasted on him.

I melted closer into him, my heart beating so hard the tremors
rolled along my skin. Our kiss snaked through my veins, tingling the
spaces between my toes, warming the jut of my elbows, and making
the tips of my ears pulse.

"You're beautiful," he said, his lips trailing down my throat. A
heightened prickling that pulled my already taut skin tighter.

"You're blindfolded." I arched up under his touch.

"It doesn't matter. I see you. Bella. Jamila. Sundari." He kissed his
way across my collarbone. Kissed me like he was charting my land-
scape. "Guzal. Mei li in. Linda."

Rohan sucked my breast into his mouth through the fabric of my top. "Nava," he sighed, flicking his tongue over my hardened nipple. My breath caught. So he did it again, his mouth lazily exploring me. "Krasivaya. Areumdaun. Yafa."

His lips descended lower, nipping at me to position me where he wanted me since he was still tied up. His mouth skipped along my abdomen, making me shiver in delight.

"Schoen. Vakker. Utsukushi. So very beautiful." A kiss with each compliment. He worshiped me with his lips and his words.

My insides dissolved into jelly. "How do you know all these terms?"

"I asked the roadies. It totally scored me chicks on tour."

I smacked him.

"Kidding." He paused. "I didn't need help."

I smacked him again. "Bastard," I said, laughing. "I'm gonna molest you now."

"It'll cost ya." He turned his puckered lips up to mine.

A price I'd happily pay.

This kiss wasn't merely hunger. It was ineffable. Inevitable. Blood rushed from my brain in a dizzying surge, my insides stuck in that combustible moment when spark snapped into flame. I was a dancer. I had great balance. You'd never know it to look at me now, clutching at him. Eroded. Vertiginous.

I broke the kiss, dragging in a breath, my breasts hot and aching for his touch. I snapped open the buttons on the jeans that he'd fallen asleep in, expecting to hit boxers. "Fuck me," I said. "You went commando?"

He laughed and the depraved sound jolted straight into Cuntessa.

"Huh." I trailed my fingers down his chest. "So did I."

"It's probably good I didn't know that before," he said in a strangled voice. He strained against his bonds. "Untie me." I gave a sultry laugh and he groaned. "Tease," he said.

I slid down his torso tasting the salt from the sweat on his skin. His erection strained and jerked under my arm. Grinning, I tugged his jeans down to free it, Rohan's growled "touch me," making me wetter than I already was.

I called up my magic, the barest of hums tingling my lips, then I wrapped my mouth around his cock. Nowhere near enough to shock, just enough to blow his mind.

"Holy fuck," Rohan groaned, bucking off the mattress. His low steady stream of filthy commands drove me to the same crazed edge as my electric BJ drove him. I took a heapload of smug satisfaction at his desperate thrashing.

"Bet the other Rasha don't have as fun a party trick," I smirked.

"You're not showing that to anyone else."

"No?"

The blades at Rohan's wrists shot out to slice through his ties, my socks falling in shredded heaps onto the mattress. He ripped the blindfold off, reaching for me. "No."

"Okay," I sighed, not caring he'd broken free.

We fell to the sheets in a tangle of limbs. He pressed me deeper into the mattress, gripping my hips as his mouth slammed on mine with an urgency I matched, kiss for kiss.

Desire shimmered like heat between us.

He wrestled me out of my shirt, so careful of my still-bandaged shoulder. Angling his body closer toward mine, he pinned me down, his leg jutting between my knees, sliding me against his hard thighs. His fingers flexed against the small of my back drawing me closer against him and I moaned, every cell in my body flaring.

"Why did you regret it?" The words tumbled from my mouth.

"What?"

"When you kissed me the first time. Right afterwards, you looked like you wished you could take it back."

Rohan looked mind-wacked, naked, his hair completely wrecked, and his eyes a gold haze. "You want to do this now?"

It wasn't so much want as need. I nodded and braced myself.

"It wasn't regret."

I shifted to move out from under the liar, but he held me fast by the hips.

"It wasn't," he insisted. "I'd wanted you so much when everything was still a game between us. Then I kissed you and I wasn't playing anymore, but you still were."

"Why do you want me?"

He nipped at my mouth. "Fishing for compliments?"

"No," I said. "I know I'm a catch, but you?" I pressed my palms into my thighs and shrugged, my heart in my throat. I forced myself not to squirm under the weight of his direct, unflinching stare.

"I've experienced a lot," he said.

To put it mildly. "The rock star thing."

"Rock god," he corrected, rubbing my nose with his, "but that's not what I meant by experienced. I don't need saving, Nava. But yeah, there's darkness. Surrounded by what we see, what we do to keep this world safe, day in, day out? I only want bright spots around me. And you?" He caught my hands, which I'd laced together so he couldn't see them tremble. "You're a supernova."

"Vague bastard."

Rohan barked a laugh but his eyes practically sparked at me. Talk about supernova. The fires of the universe burned in them and I was caught in their gravitational pull.

I kissed him again, craving this connection. With him. Only him.

His fingers glided up my neck, his thumb resting over my fluttering pulse. I swayed in toward him suckling the hollow of his throat and he hissed, tangling my hair in his hands and ghosting his lips along my jaw before claiming my mouth, a frantic edge to our embrace.

He demanded complete and utter acquiescence, running his hands feverishly over my body. Both of us tearing at my clothing, until we were skin on heated skin.

Rohan rolled away from me for a second to reach under the bed. My moaned complaint tempered when he held Snake Clitspin up.

"You put Snake back and didn't tell me?"

"You anthropomorphized him?" He placed his hands on his hips, his words parroting my earlier ones. "Do I need to rethink this?"

"Try it and die."

He flicked the switch on and pressed Snake into my hands. "Use it on yourself."

I shivered at his words, his voice barely more than a rumble, and slid Snake inside me. "Oh," I gasped.

Rohan put my hand on his cock. "Magic please."

"Happy to oblige." My entire body buzzed, from Snake lighting me up to the current humming through my fingers.

Rohan cupped my jaw, ravaging my mouth. He stroked Cuntessa as I plied my feel-good magic on him. Every atom in the room charged with a palpable build-up of explosive energy. We rode it fast and hard to the precipice and then Rohan pulled Snake away. He grabbed a condom from the drawer I directed him to, sheathed himself, and plunged into me.

I flashed him a dreamy smile, loving that first instance of him filling me so completely.

Rohan rocked into me with slow rolls of his hips, our kisses just as drugged out. He gripped my ass, an almost sharp bite of pain that tightened my nipples.

I lost myself in him and in the tornado of heat building inside me.

Rohan smiled down at me.

This is what it feels like to make love.

I tensed.

Rohan met my eyes and said, "No take-backs." He caught my mouth once more. Not possessive. Not ruthless. Undoing me with gentle and sweet until my pulse roared in my ears and it was getting harder to remember that slow was a valid option. I wrapped my legs around his waist, trying to set a faster tempo.

He stilled my hips.

"It's too much," I said. "I can't contain it."

"Then don't. Look at me."

I wanted nothing more than to close my eyes, but I was trapped. Hypnotized by the volcanic fire in his eyes, like Mowgli under the spell of Kaa.

He kissed me in a way that left no room for walls between us, and I came hard, seconds before he did. We didn't move, Rohan still inside me. My hands flew to my cheeks; I'd never felt so naked.

"I like the way you smell. Coconut," he said. "You remind me of summer." He nuzzled my shoulder.

Stomach churning, I clenched the covers, waiting for the inevitable smirk at how he'd gotten me to lose control, and confused about the serene expression on his face. Not looking away, not *running* away required the most will power I'd ever summoned. I cleared my throat. "So, that was...?"

Rohan mimed shooting himself in the head, then grinned.

That so perfectly summed up my feelings, the knot of tension binding my ribcage unraveled.

He got out of bed to dispose of the condom.

I rolled onto my back. "I think I'm fuck drunk."

"What's that?" He slid back in next to me, curling me possessively into his side. I stuck to him, both of us covered in a faint sheen of sweat.

"Like punch drunk. Light-headed, lack of balance, loss of fine motor skills," I said. Rohan lifted my arm to check and yes, it flopped back down like jelly. "But with orgasms," I continued. "So, better. Hey. What would a breathalyzer for fuck drunk look like?"

"Weirdo." He kissed the top of my head.

I'd missed Rohan this past month and not just because of the sex. I leaned in to kiss him again, certain I would never tire of that activity.

He pressed his hands against my shoulders to stop me. "Wait."

"Wait?" I sat up.

"In or out?"

"Huh?"

"In or out? Of this relationship. Are we dropping the 'not' with the hot boyfriend?"

I smacked his arm. "I kissed you. Extrapolate."

He caught my wrists, hauling me half on top of him. "Nope. That's dangerous where you're concerned. As are most things."

I wriggled to get free, but his low rumble as I rocked against him changed my mind. Maybe one more wriggle. Some boob-brushing against his chest. "You want safe? Date a lifejacket."

"In or out, Sparky?" he asked in a soft voice, his gold eyes boring into mine.

"I don't like that nickname."

"Tough." He wrapped an arm around me.

"Liberty-taking fucker. I haven't given you my answer yet." I rocked against him once more, pleased to find him ready to go again.

"You're going to be the death of me," he groaned.

"You sweet talker."

"Nava." Had it just been desire etched across his features, I would have toyed with him some more but his jaw was tucked low and the corners of his eyes were pulled tight.

This actually mattered to him.

I let out a deep breath. "Totally in."

That won me a slow grin.

I smiled back, light and warmth seeping into every part of me.

"Sparky?" he said.

I wrinkled my nose at him. "Yes, Snowflake?"

He brought his mouth close to my ear. "Can I kiss my girlfriend now?"

I grinned like an idiot, my toes curling under. Holy shit. I was Rohan Mitra's girlfriend. Squeeeeee! "That can be arranged."

And oh, baby, it was.

END OF BOOK THREE

Acknowledgments

Mallory Gibson, funny lady, I owe you for the "C Game" joke. The first time I heard it, I laughed out loud and I still do with each re-read. Thanks for letting me use it.

I cannot praise my editor Alex Yuschik enough. Alex, I am so grateful that you've been on this entire ride with me and I can't wait to do the next three (thirty?) together!

Much love to my husband Loreto, who makes me laugh harder than anyone and still gets me giddy and dizzy for him after all these years.

Last, but never least, this one is for my Wilde Ones. You people keep me stocked in great reads, make delightfully snarky comments on a wealth of topics, and stoke my poor fragile writer's ego with your love of this series. My words, my characters, my heart–I happily give them all to you.

Nava explains awesome Yiddish and Hebrew words used in this series.

- Bar Mitzvah (Hebrew) - A boy's coming of age ceremony when he's thirteen. Moving, ritualistically important and, should the right guests be invited, an excellent way to build the foundation of one's university fund.
- Beseder (Hebrew) – Okay.
- Boker tov (Hebrew) – Good morning.
- Bubelah (Yiddish) – adding "elah" to something gives it that cute diminutive. Literally it means "little grandma" but is used as "sweetie" – generally with children. Yeah, I don't see the logic on that one either.
- Kvetching (Yiddish) – Complaining. But like seriously and chronically getting your whine on. Hand wringing optional.
- L'chaim (Hebrew) - Literally "to life." This is the Jewish "cheers" and really easy to slur after you've had a couple.
- Maspik (Hebrew) – Enough. Sounds way better growled at someone than the English equivalent.
- Mazel tov (Hebrew) – Congratulations. Can be shortened to "mazel mazel" which sounds super snarky and may leave the recipient in doubt as to how to take it.
- Mensch (Yiddish) – a person of integrity and honor. Technically it's gender neutral, though I see it applied way more often to men. Go figure.
- Mishegoss (Yiddish) - Craziness. Senseless behavior or activity. I thought this was my grandmother's nickname for me when I was little.
- Mitzvah (Hebrew) – A good deed. As in "Not punching Drio in the head was my mitzvah for the day."